North of the Ten Commandments

for billie, and luke sam ella and holly kate

North of the Ten Commandments

A collection of Northern Territory literature

edited by David Headon

HODDER & STOUGHTON
Sydney Auckland London Toronto

First published in 1991 by
Hodder and Stoughton (Australia) Pty Limited
10–16 South Street, Rydalmere, NSW 2116

Compilation © David Headon, 1991

This book is copyright. Apart from any fair dealing for
the purposes of private study, research, criticism or review,
as permitted under the Copyright Act, no part may be reproduced
by any process without written permission. Inquiries should
be addressed to the publisher.

National Library of Australia Cataloguing-in-Publication entry
North of the ten commandments.
  Includes index.
  ISBN 0 340 52665 3 (hdbk).
  ISBN 0 340 52666 1 (pbk).
  1. Australian literature. 2. Northern Territory.
  3. Northern Territory – Literary collections. I. Headon,
  David John, 1950–
994.29

Typeset and assembled by Netan Pty Limited
Printed in Hong Kong

North of the Ten Commandments,
North of the Barkly Plains,
Into the forest and jungle,
Drenched by tropic rains.
Tis there my thoughts oft wander,
Tis there I long to be –
But I'm doomed to end in this city –
Ora pro nobis, Domine.

— William Linklater & Lynda Tapp, *Gather No Moss*, 1968

Contents

Preface	xiii
Introduction	xvii

1 Origins — 1

Yiwarrakurlu/Milky Way — *Paddy Japaljarri Sims*	3
Ngapakurlu/Rain — *Paddy Japaljarri Sims*	4
The Milky Way — *Marlindi story of Arnhem Land, told by Narritjan Maymuru*	5
The rainbow serpent — *Djauan legend*	7
Dinosaur Dreamtime — *Mark O'Connor*	10
The seasons of fire — *Billy Marshall-Stoneking*	11
The moon bone — *Wonguri-Manjikai song cycle of north-eastern Arnhem Land*	13
He's singing at Dhadutjmana — *Milingimbi song*	18
Form of taking possession of Port Essington and Melville and Bathurst Islands, 1824 — *Captain J.J. Gordon Bremer*	18
Harbingers of an approaching revolution — *John Lort Stokes*	19
The dawn of liberty, civilisation, and Christianity — *John McDouall Stuart*	20
Captain Cook — *Hobbles Daniyarri*	21
Too many Captain Cooks — *Paddy Wainburranga & Joli Laiwonga*	24

2 'Bare-headed to the sun': Early white voyages and exploration — 27

Bamboo creek — *Mark O'Connor*	29
The coming of the dingoes — *Xavier Herbert*	29
North coast, Blue-Mud Bay — *Matthew Flinders*	33
Our theodolite stand and Mr Cunningham's insect-net — *Captain Phillip Parker King*	35
Geographical memoir of Melville Island, 1826–28 — *Major John Campbell*	37
Any act of cruelty or outrage against the natives — *Alexander Macleay*	40
Character and manners of the Aborigines of New Holland — *Thomas Braidwood Wilson*	41
Speared and pursued at Point Pearce — *John Lort Stokes*	43
The natives were remarkably kind and attentive — *Dr Ludwig Leichhardt*	46
Reconnaissance — *William Hart-Smith*	47

3 'Bone-piled spots': The whites dig in — 49

Camp at Barrow Creek — *F.J. Gillen*	51
Our Adelaide letter — *Northern Territory Times, 1874*	53
Outrages by the blacks — *Northern Territory Times, 1884*	53
Aborigines in the Northern Territory — *Northern Territory Times, 1885*	54
The Daly River murders of 1884 and their aftermath — *Ernestine Hill*	56
Bringing in a new wild gin — *Emily Caroline Creaghe*	57
Martini-Henry carbines talking English — *W.H. Willshire*	58
Out-beyond country — *Alfred Searcy*	61
The Coniston 'massacres' of August 1928 — *Sidney Downer*	62
Coniston — *Commonwealth Board of Enquiry*	64
The tragedy of the Centre — *Northern Territory Times, 1928*	66

On women and wives — *Matt Savage* 67
The combo's anthem — *W.E. (Bill) Harney* 69

4 'Nobody knows what it means': White depiction of Aborigines 71
One big, big fellow feed — *William J. Sowden* 73
Puzzles — *Jerome K. Murif* 73
Narpulda Bola — *Northern Territory Times, 1884* 74
Tranter's shot — *Ernest Favenc* 76
Aborigines and wit — *Rev. J.S. Needham* 80
Moondeen — *William Hart-Smith* 81
goanna — *Lee Cataldi* 82
the honey tree — *Lee Cataldi* 83
In the bed of the River Todd — *G. Oxford* 84
Girls in a park — *Jan Owen* 86
Rain at Gunn Point — *Tony Scanlon* 86
Aborigines passing — *Roland Robinson* 87
Wash day — *Billy Marshall-Stoneking* 87
in th desert you remember — *Eric Beach* 88
A remote area — *Graeme Parsons* 89

5 'Too much blackfeller': The black view 93
My father very much hurt — *Duncan* 95
Wanderer's lament — *W.E. (Bill) Harney & A.P. Elkin* 95
The Malak Malak people lived here — *Bill Parry* 96
An arrangement — *Tim Japangardi Langdon* 97
Coniston story — *Tim Japangardi Langdon* 98
They shot your old father? — *Martin Jampijinpa* 100
Wild ones, mate — *Fred Booth Minmienadgie* 101
All children — *Djawa* 101
All ashes — *Little Mick Inginma* 104
Quiet country — *Amy Laurie* 105
Living black — *Vi Stanton* 106
This is our river, hill, trees, grass — *Pincher Numiari* 108
In Darwin they call me Bobby Wilson — *Robert Tudawali* 110
What's a whitefella? — *Post-primary boys' class, Papunya* 114
First people come to us — *Big Bill Neidjie* 115
Yirrkala Bark Petition — *Petition from the Aboriginal people of Yirrkala to Parliament* 116

6 Pilgrims 119
I had no human speech — *Roland Robinson* 121
Flash Poll — *Alfred Searcy* 121
Dug his own grave — *Alfred Searcy* 122
The old coast track — *William Linklater & Lynda Tapp* 123
Down on the Daly River oh! — *Jim Burgoyne* 126
Goodbye old friend — *David MacKay* 127
Mail oh! — *Mrs Aeneas Gunn* 128
In the land of sweat and sandflies — *Patrick (Paddy) Flynn* 130
Nina Hall, bushwoman of bushwomen — *F.E. Baume* 132
Talking history — *Daisy Nawala Cusack* 133

	The Afghans — *Rex Ingamells*	137
	Wallaby — *Lionel Gee*	137
	Story from Lajamanu — *Abie Jangala*	139
	Shark — *Patrick McCauley*	142
	The pub owner's wife — *Thomas Keneally*	143
	Talking history — *Paddy Fordham Wainburranga*	145
7	**'My spirit, my country'**	**149**
	The land is the art — *James Galarrawuy Yunupingu*	151
	This earth — *Big Bill Neidjie*	151
	Where I was born — *Jack Mirritji*	154
	Yinungkwura/West wind — *Groote Eylandt song*	155
	A trip to the Victoria River, 1887 — *Rev. J.E. Tenison-Woods*	156
	By the Grey Gulf-water — *A.B. (Banjo) Paterson*	159
	Chugga-Kurri — *Michael Terry*	160
	High water — *Frederick T. Macartney*	161
	Black cockatoos — *Roland Robinson*	162
	White cockatoos — *Tony Scanlon*	163
	Flood plains on the coast facing Asia — *Les A. Murray*	163
	rain — *Lee Cataldi*	166
	Instructions for honey ants — *Billy Marshall-Stoneking*	167
8	**A bastard of a place**	**169**
	Death and the desert — *Ivan Archer Rosenblum*	171
	Death of Voss — *Patrick White*	173
	An ideal of the future — *Ernest Favenc*	177
	The hunt — *Aeneas E. Gunn*	178
	The settler. Wet season, N.T. — *Jessie Litchfield*	179
	Jock Driver's funeral — *Xavier Herbert*	180
	The paw paw tree — *Margo Towie*	182
9	**Sites and sightings**	**185**
	Five legends of Uluru — *Paddy Uluru, Albie Uluru, Pompy Douglas & Pompy Wanampi*	187
	S.O.S., Ayers Rock, October 1930 — *Errol Coote*	189
	An apostrophe to Ayers Rock — *Rex Ingamells*	190
	Erecting forked sticks and rafters — *Goulburn Island song cycle*	192
	Yinuma/River — *Groote Eylandt song*	195
	Rowdyism in Borroloola — *Mrs Dominic D. Daly*	196
	Borroloola, capital of the Gulf country — *F.J. Gillen*	196
	Morning in the Macdonnells — *Robert Henderson Croll*	199
	The Roper River's flowing — *W.E. (Bill) Harney*	201
	Deep Well — *Roland Robinson*	202
	Alice — *Thomas Keneally*	202
	Snapshots of Kakadu — *Beverley Farmer*	205
10	**Darwin, mad capital of the north**	**207**
	Port Darwin harbour, 1870 — *Mrs Dominic D. Daly*	209

Mrs Brown on Northern Territory matters — *Northern Territory Times, 1874* — 210
The cycloon, Paddy Cahill and the G.R. — *A.B. (Banjo) Paterson* — 212
The Palmerstonians — *Jerome J. Murif* — 215
Darwin — *Ernestine Hill* — 217
Bloody, bloody Darwin — *Anonymous* — 218
Mango juice — *Graham Calley* — 219
Louvres — *Les A. Murray* — 223
Jacques Tati at the Darwin Hotel — *Fay Zwicky* — 225

11 Adventures, incongruities, incredibilities — 227
Tjukurrpa: Puli kulpi kutjarra/The two little round stones — *Obed Raggett* — 229
A haunt of the jinkarras: A story of Central Australia — *Ernest Favenc* — 230
Victoria Theatre, 1839 — *John Lort Stokes* — 234
Camp life, Port Darwin, 1870 — *Mrs Dominic D. Daly* — 235
Christmas Day, 1873 — *Ernest Giles* — 237
Christmas, 1901 — *F.J. Gillen* — 238
Christmas, 1930 — *W.E. (Bill) Harney* — 240
Playing cricket, 1908 — *Fred Blakeley* — 242
Eating with cannibals — *Herbert Basedow* — 244
The story of Kurnki — *Tutama Tjapangarti* — 246
On the value of blankets — *Neil Murray* — 249
Tales not from the Dreamtime: Pukara (perishing) — *Mark de Graaf* — 249

12 Nature's stage — 255
Drowning the cockroaches, Port Essington — *John Sweatman* — 257
Mrs Englishwoman on the Daly River — *Jessie Litchfield* — 258
White ants in Darwin — *Ernestine Hill* — 260
Crocodile haiku — *Mark O'Connor* — 263
Frogday — *Connie Gregory* — 263
The gecko — *Frederick T. Macartney* — 265
There were rats, rats — *James White* — 265
Auntie Annie and Monty — *Graham Calley* — 266

13 Sprees, drunks, and race meetings — 271
Honey intoxication — *John Sweatman* — 273
Port Darwin Camp races and athletic sports — *Northern Territory Times, 1882* — 273
Drinking saloons and grog shanties, 1872 — *Mrs Dominic D. Daly* — 275
Vile liquor, 1880s — *Alfred Searcy* — 276
McCarthy's brew: A gulf country yarn — *George Essex Evans* — 277
Borroloola races, 1891 — *William Linklater & Lynda Tapp* — 278
A 16th-century view of 'Territory man'? — *Don Campbell* — 281
White dog, the boozing hound — *Keith Willey* — 282
Alice Springs pub — *Robyn Davidson* — 283

14 Opening up the country: Drovers, buffalo hunters, and miners — 285
Working in the stock camp — *Amy Laurie* — 287
The drover's boy — *Ted Egan* — 289
Black stockman — *W. Hart-Smith* — 291

Bush cooks — *Matt Savage*	291
Buffalo shooting in Australia, 1890s — *A.B. (Banjo) Paterson*	296
Don't miss or you'll be a dead fella — *Alex Jupurrurla Wilson*	302
Elegy on the reefs — *Northern Territory Times, 1875*	305
The world's loneliest field — *F.E. Baume*	307
Daily work in the tin mine — *Spider Brennan*	311

15 Rock belong Jesus dreaming — 315

Bring the heathen the true faith — *F.X. Gsell*	317
We're going to take this little girl away — *Topsy Naparrula Nelson*	318
Mary — *W. Hart-Smith*	320
Daly River poem — *George Lavater*	321
God in the silver sea — *Xavier Herbert*	322
The night departs — *W.E. (Bill) Harney*	326
Interview in a desert — *Mark O'Connor*	327

16 'Hang on like I done' — 329

Everywhere there is change — *W.E. (Bill) Harney*	331
We gotta be black and white in this country — *Amy Laurie*	333
if you stay too long in the third world — *Lee Cataldi*	334
My people ... all dead — *Big Bill Neidjie*	336
Trying to hold this place — *Riley Young Winpilin*	336
Speech at Daguragu (Wattie Creek) — *Vincent Lingiari*	337

Acknowledgments	341
Index of authors and storytellers	347

Preface

In 1984 I was invited to co-ordinate the Northern Territory's contribution to the *Oxford Literary Guide to Australia* (1987). As I was living in Darwin at the time, it seemed to be a straightforward task. The literature appeared to be both manageable and well-defined: Mrs Gunn's *We of the Never-Never* (1908), Xavier Herbert's monumental tomes *Capricornia* (1938) and *Poor Fellow My Country* (1975), some Bill Harney, Doug Lockwood and Keith Willey, a few of the more accessible Aboriginal song cycles in translation along with a smattering of the oral testimony material beginning to emerge at the time, and, lastly, the poetry of Roland Robinson and his mates in the 1940s and '50s. And that was about it. Simple. Or so I thought.

I only required a week or two on the job to realise how naive (and culpably white east-coast urban) I had been at the outset, and how complex yet enormously rewarding the job in front of me promised to be. What I didn't anticipate, and only gradually began to comprehend, was how the literature of the North — the Territory itself — would take me firmly in its grasp. As I read, so I began to travel. Learn. And marvel. Aeneas Gunn, the Maluka, said in *We of the Never-Never* that 'It's wonderful how quietly the Territory does its work.' He called it the 'wizard of the Never-Never'. I was caught in its spell like so many before me. Aboriginal mythology testifies to the perennial power of the land to enchant and to inspire.

Even as I scratched the surface of the literature in the early stages of my work on the *Literary Guide*, I realised that the cultural, social and political importance of the material — its inherent quality — demanded the exposure of a more suitable project. It needed to be made more accessible to the public. So *North of the Ten Commandments* was born.

But why 'North of the Ten Commandments'? As the first epigraph at the beginning of this book indicates, I took the phrase from a poem in William Linklater's *Gather No Moss* (1968). Linklater, a goldminer, pearler and stockman better known in his heyday as Billy Miller, left Adelaide and went bush in the 1880s. In the following decades he trekked a vast amount of the Northern Territory, getting to know the terrain that many white Australians then dismissed as wasteland, 'Never-Never' country. With the phrase 'North of the Ten Commandments', Billy Miller no doubt wanted to conjure up images of freedom (from the constraints of organised religion), uniqueness, perhaps lawlessness. A tough, no beg-pardons, white, male world.

In removing the phrase from its original, nostalgic context, I do want to retain Linklater's provocative Australian Legend associations. Yet they relate to only one of many parts of the Territory story. The title 'North of the Ten Commandments' perfectly suits my purposes because, considered out of context, it alludes to that other much, much older story. Not just the European narrative, the one told by white writers for a white readership for the best part of one hundred and fifty years, but the Aboriginal story, the non-Christian one, tens of thousands of years old and therefore adding particular significance and poignancy to the many tragic developments of the last two hundred years.

The writers and story-tellers included in this collection relate an important, even epic tale. They tell a story which in 1988 (white Australia's bicentennial year) rarely received attention because, while it tells of courage and love, it also focusses on killing and conquest, eccentricity and madness, and a land as hostile and murderous as it could be gentle and caring.

It is a true and at times tall story, detailing the way two peoples have had to learn to live with each other in a capricious environment. In the early years of white invasion, the land was usually a catalyst for combat. I would like this collection to move us a little closer to an understanding of that elusive term 'Australianness', as a diverse number of writers and speakers, past and present, testify to the mean, even barbaric behaviour of this country's white and black inhabitants. Yet they also describe men and women imbued with fortitude, audacity, skill and graciousness. They sometimes talk of triumph.

When Rolf Boldrewood in 1893 introduced a volume of stories by the white explorer and writer Ernest Favenc, entitled *The Last of Six*, he commented on the engaging verisimilitude of the contents, and the fact that Favenc was a notable exception to the rule of 'literary manufacture' in Australia, where 'Those who know seldom write, and those who write don't know.' Boldrewood depicted his adventurer-cum-author as 'a leading actor upon Dame Nature's stage [who] has turned scene-painter for the nonce, and limned with lifelike effect the drama of the Waste'. In *North of the Ten Commandments*, I have chosen authors and story-tellers who, like Favenc, are exceptions to Boldrewood's rule. They are at once participants, thespians on a grand stage, and passionate recorders of an exacting reality.

This project would not have been possible without the help of the Northern Territory Council of the Australian Bicentennial Authority and the Northern Territory Government. Research money was essential, especially in the early stages, and both the ABA and Territory Government responded with generous support. I thank them.

Of course, a book of this size and range could only materialise with the assistance of many individuals. In Darwin, Elizabeth Estburgs, librarian in 1982–83 at the Winnellie campus of the Darwin Community College, ably directed my first reading. I would also like to acknowledge Top End help from Lesley Mearns, Baiba Berzins, Alan Powell and Chips Mackinolty. In Alice, Ted Egan, Nerys Evans and Dick Kimber gave me the right kind of guidance. Special mention, however, must be made of three people: Connie Gregory, now Publicity Officer with the Northern Territory University, who was always wholehearted and enthusiastic; Mark de Graaf, who gave me the chance to see the Great Sandy Desert up close and was a fine teacher; and David Carment, who led a bunch of us on trips 'down the track'. These journeys provided the spark. After camping at Jasper Gorge, there was no going back. *North of the Ten Commandments* had begun.

In Canberra, I would like to thank Francesca Baas Becking, David Horton and Robyn Lincoln of the Australian Institute of Aboriginal and Torres Strait Islander Studies, as well as the Institute's library staff, who put up with my ceaseless requests. Peter Read and Debbie Rose encouraged me in the best possible way by sharing their invaluable resources and conclusions. Billy Marshall-Stoneking, in Sydney, did the same.

I can't praise sufficiently the quality and integrity of my workplace: the Department of English at the Australian Defence Force Academy. Professor Harry Heseltine, Joy Hooton and Trish Middleton have been there whenever and wherever needed. Again, two people deserve to be singled out: my research assistant Loes Baker, for her patience, talent, and sense of humour; and the indefatigable Margaret McNally, who never says no (to any messy pencil draft I turn up with) and who has been wonderfully supportive throughout these last few years. She is a typist of the highest order — but, more importantly, always cheery and a delight to be around.

Thanks also go to one of the most enjoyable postgraduate groups I have ever instructed. In the first six months of 1990, I taught a Master of Arts course at ADFA on 'Aboriginal Literature and Themes', and was fortunate enough to be writing my Introduction for this book at the same time. The class helped me to organise my thoughts. Thanks thus go to Peter Burns, Jim Connolly, Caren Florance, Donna Goodacre, Jenny Jenkins, Viv Jolley, Andy McEntee, Carol McKenny, Kevin Percival, Richard Stead and Sandy Stoddart.

Finally, I am indebted to my whole family. My mother and father will never know the many ways they have helped me. My children provide so much joy. My wife, Billie, is my best friend. Always.

Australian history is almost always picturesque; indeed, it is so curious and strange, that it is itself the chiefest novelty the country has to offer, and so it pushes the other novelties into second and third place. It does not read like history, but like the most beautiful lies. And all of a fresh new sort, no mouldy old stale ones. It is full of surprises, and adventures, and incongruities, and contradictions, and incredibilities; but they are all true, they all happened.
— Mark Twain, *Following the Equator*, 1897

>I give you this story.
>This proper, true story.
>People can listen.
>I'm telling this while you've got time . . .
>time for you to make something,
>you know . . .
>history . . .
>book
>I was thinking . . .
>no history written for us when white European start here,
>only few words written.
>Should be more than that.

— Big Bill Neidjie, *Kakadu Man*, 1985

'Look, Doctor. You are in the free land of Australia. A land where nothing is so closely guarded as liberty. You just try to put over a "swiftie" on Australian workers — Unionists — and see what happens!' The trooper laughed. 'And yet, in the Territory there are roughly the same number of aboriginal workers as there are Europeans. Every native worker is a non-unionist! Rum situation. Paradox. Gilbert and Sullivan. That's what I like about the Territory. Burlesque in its most exquisite form.'
— Victor C. Hall, *Bad Medicine*, 1947

The North is cruel to the loafer and to the man who makes alcohol his master, but the North is a fine country for those who can keep its commandments.
— Fred Blakeley, *Hard Liberty*, 1938

>We belong to the ground
>It is our power and we must stay
>Close to it or maybe
>We will get lost.

— Narritjan Maymuru, in J. Isaacs (ed.), *Australian Dreaming*, 1981

Introduction

In September 1824 a small fleet of three ships under the command of Captain J.J. Gordon Bremer arrived at Port Essington, on the Coburg Peninsula of the Northern Territory, and then, three days later, landed on Melville Island. There, Bremer took 'possession of Port Essington' and 'possession of Melville and Bathurst Islands' in the name of 'His Most excellent Majesty, George the IV, King of the United Kingdoms of Great Britain, and Ireland',[1] and erected the Fort Dundas stockade. With a few strokes of an English quill and the arrival of a relatively small number of troops from the colonial garrison, the white invasion of Australia's North had begun.

Now it is certain that Bremer and his party would have rejected the term 'invasion'. Their mission, as they would have understood it, was to respond to the vaguely perceived threats from Holland and France; they had arrived to 'civilise' the North, make it a peaceful and prosperous settlement for English traders and naval vessels. Some of those involved in the project fairly brimmed with enthusiasm. In London, John Barrow, Second Secretary to the Admiralty and a man determined to see Britannia rule on sea and land, jubilantly declared that 'there never was so promising a spot . . . it will become another Singapore'.[2] Barrow's comment was one of the first, but by no means the last judgment by a European about the Northern Territory formulated in complete ignorance. His optimism was not sufficient to inspire his distant troops, however, as Indonesian pirates quickly made their presence felt. Worse still, the local population resented and resisted the English presence. Bremer might have anticipated this response, for weren't these the same 'Indians' who had speared one of Matthew Flinders' men when his expedition was 'discovering' the country aboard the *Investigator* in early 1803? And weren't these the same people who greeted Captain Phillip Parker King's surveying party of 1818 by taking the theodolite stand and insect-net, and then burying their spears in the sand or carrying them between their toes in order to appear unarmed?[3] The local in habitants, it seemed, were still not prepared to eat of the fruits of British 'civilisation'.

Relations went from bad to worse. Major John Campbell, Second Commandant of Fort Dundas (1826–28), labelled the Melville Islanders as 'savages', people who continued 'distrustful, if not even determinedly hostile' until 'the last day'.[4] The Fort Dundas settlement was abandoned in 1829, less than five years after Barrow's lofty proclamations.

In the following one hundred and fifty years of troubled white attempts to occupy the Northern Territory, little changed. Haste, excitement, ignorance, hatred and sometimes sheer stupidity continued to affect the judgment of visitor and resident alike. Inevitably, evaluations varied according to the status and commitment of the observer, but virtually all white commentators displayed a propensity for the pithy Territory tag. The list of labels created in the century following the establishment of Palmerston (Darwin), in 1870, is a long and colourful one. Those strongly supporting Territory growth and willing to ignore the tragic black predicament (and the uninterrupted shooting of Aborigines up until at least the 1930s), favoured phrases such as 'Land of Perpetual Summers', 'Land of Smiles and Wealth', 'Land of Opportunity', 'the Land Poets Sing About', 'Land of Fable', 'Australia's Front Door' or, simply, Australia's 'wonderland'. Sceptics used expressions such as 'the White Elephant of South Australia', 'the hopeless, unwanted door', 'a Land Half-Made', 'the Land of Heat, Rain, Mosquitoes and Sandflies', the 'No Hoper', and, in Xavier Herbert's memorable phrase, a 'Land of Ratbags'.

The literature of the Northern Territory constantly confronts the reader with paradox and contradiction, idiosyncrasy and absurdity, as some of the writers cited in the preliminary epigraphs suggest. Indeed, any book on the subject purporting to be representative and historically accurate is virtually bound to use juxtaposition as its main principle of organisation: black/white, paradise/purgatory, Christian/coloniser, Church/Dreaming, spirit/flesh, civiliser/savage, Wet/Dry, oasis/desert, north/south — to mention only the most prominent. Through a rationale built on binary opposites, *North of the Ten Commandments* attempts to do justice to the extraordinary diversity and grandeur of the region, and its myriad scribes. One thing is certain: the Northern Territory supplies more of Mark Twain's 'incredibilities' of Australian history than any other area in the entire country.

* * * * *

This book represents several years of editorial endeavour. Inevitably, problems arose. The main one involved sifting through and categorising the work of an abundance of diverse writers, almost all of them white up to the 1970s (for obvious reasons), with a steadily increasing number of black writers and storytellers since then. In 1985 I gave the annual Heritage Week lecture in Darwin ('Land of the Dawning or Fag-End of Creation: Will the real Northern Territory please stand up?'), an enjoyable task, which in addition provided me with my initial thematic headings for the project ahead: 'land', 'people', 'black/white relations' and 'eccentricities'. In the fashion of a genealogical tree, these broad groupings soon gave way to an assemblage of tighter, more selective classifications. Eventually, these were pared back to a workable (and, ultimately, final) sixteen. Consistent with the provocative title of the whole collection, I was determined to avoid simple generic sectional titles; hence, I looked to the material itself to supply a suitable rubric. In most cases I found just the right word or phrase to suit my editorial scheme. The reader will also note that all sections except the last, 'Hang on like I done', begin with one or more epigraphs. I decided on this method as the most convenient and effective way to set the scene, to suggest possible ways of approaching the material that follows, and to enable me to parade just a little more of the quality, vigour and provocative character of Territory literature. The preliminary epigraphs serve the same functions for the book as a whole.

Before I introduce each section, let me leave the reader in no doubt concerning my organisational role and priorities as editor and sole compiler. Six considerations determined the book's content:

(i) In his important and influential 1968 Boyer Lectures *After the Dreaming* (1969), Professor W.E.H. Stanner reflected on the inadequacy of so much of his earlier writing. He had been totally overwhelmed by the 'dominance of European interests' and thus, like his colleagues, reduced the historical realities of black–white relations to a 'melancholy footnote'. In arguably the turning point for Australian scholarship on this issue, Stanner said:

> . . . inattention on such a scale cannot possibly be explained by absent-mindedness. It is a structural matter, a view from a window which has been carefully placed to exclude a whole quadrant of the landscape. What may well have begun as a simple forgetting of other possible views turned under habit and over time into something like a cult of forgetfulness practised on a national scale.[5]

The magnificent work of Charles Rowley and Henry Reynolds later motivated a new generation of Australian historians (and readers) to start analysing the real pioneering history of this country — the '*other* side of the frontier', as Reynolds termed it.[6] Sally Morgan's grandmother, Daisy Corunna, states the Aboriginal case with passion and simplicity in *My Place*: 'Could be it's time to tell. Time to tell what it's been like in this country'.[7] *North of the Ten Commandments* has been shaped in part to enable as many writers and speakers as possible to do their bit of truth-telling. The aim is not to prompt feelings of guilt in a white readership — guilt gets nowhere — but to enable us all to know more about what happened, and perhaps act on it.

(ii) There is a wide variety of literary forms here on display — among them, myth, yarn, newspaper editorial, article, song, novel excerpt, joke, letter, interview, poem, short story, diary (or journal) entry and memoir. Obviously, I interpret the term 'literature' broadly. The American literary critic and social commentator Vernon Louis Parrington pointed out in his landmark study, *Main Currents in American Thought* (1927), that American literary historians for centuries held 'an exaggerated regard for aesthetic values'.[8] They were too heavily steeped in the 'genteel tradition' and thus ignored the literature of 'material struggles' and 'vigorous polemics'. In Australia, also, the aesthetic tradition of belles lettres was regarded by literary critics for far too long as the only acceptable domain of the true creative writer. They summarily dismissed Parrington's 'old fashioned beef and puddings' literature of the 'vigorous creative thinkers'. Led by William H. Wilde, Joy Hooton and Barry Andrews, the three authors of *The Oxford Companion to Australian Literature* (1985), a direct challenge to the conservative critical orthodoxy in this country has emerged in recent years to consolidate the achievement of H.M. Green in *A History of Australian Literature* (1961). *North of the Ten Commandments* should be seen as a volume firmly within the more egalitarian, eclectic and lower-brow tradition of Green's *History* and the *Companion*. Within this tradition lies most of the energy and quality, indeed lasting value, of Australian literature.

(iii) Having committed myself to such an inclusive definition of literature, I could hardly use as my yardstick for final selection the usual white criteria of literary value. Leavisite — or any white critical school's — judgments would be absurdly irrelevant. Nancy Keesing, when reviewing Paddy Roe's *Gularabulu* (1983), rebuked the book's use of Aboriginal English: 'As a general reader I unrepentantly *prefer* the older mode, just as I prefer the King James version of the Bible to all later translations . . . '[9] This is distressingly dated criticism of an earlier era. When choosing the items for *North of the Ten Commandments*, alternative criteria had to be sought and utilised, especially for the large component of Aboriginal material. I often made judgments based on political, social, historical and moral grounds — rather than aesthetic quality. When the heart and mind clashed, heart on numerous occasions won out.

(iv) The Literature Board of the Australia Council, since its inception during the Whitlam Labor Government years (1972–75), has played a major role in the encouragement of cultural diversification. One important by-product has been the renewed interest in 'regional' literature. *Wide Domain: Western Australian Themes and Images* (1979), selected by Bruce Bennett and William Grono, and Patrick Morgan's *Shadow and Shine: An Anthology of Gippsland Literature* (1988) are two individual volumes which reinforce the useful (state-by-state) methodology of Peter Pierce's *Oxford Literary Guide to Australia*.[10] *North of the Ten Commandments* continues and extends this fruitful cultural direction. Let me risk a further claim: Northern Territory writing is *the* most exciting expression of regional literature in the country for an assortment of cultural, geographical, environmental and social reasons. These will become clear as the reader works through the collection.

(v) In selecting specific Aboriginal items for inclusion, I found it no simple task to establish geographical demarcation lines. Aboriginal storytellers have scant respect for arbitrary (white) state and territory borders. Material such as the testimony of that incredible bushwoman Amy Laurie, of Kununurra (in Western Australia), has been included because her reminiscences regularly take her into the Territory. She drove the north-west according to the ways of water, rather than complying with a set of geographical fictions established according to the whim of government policy-makers in the south. Selections from the literature of distinguished white visitors to the Northern Territory — among them, Banjo Paterson, Tom Keneally, Fay Zwicky, Beverly Farmer and Les Murray — have also been included. 'Blow-ins' can on occasion provide objectivity and insight not possible from the 'true Territorian'.

(vi) The central aim of *North of the Ten Commandments* is to juxtapose, and on occasion to integrate, the rich traditions of both white and black Australia. White Australians have for far too long directed their imaginative endeavours towards the Old World of Europe. Usually, and not surprisingly, the literature of Great Britain served as the model. The udders of the Mother Country, however, sucked on continuously for the best part of two centuries, are now dry as a bone. We are all fortunate to be living in an era of cultural reappraisal and reorientation. White Australian artists are at last beginning to appreciate the subtleties that mark the relationship between our country as both New World (post-1788) and Old World (pre-1788). Black artists, too, are using white techniques and structures which suit their purposes, with astonishing results — as books such as Jennifer Isaacs's *Aboriginality* (1989) demonstrate.[11] Like the painter Alasdair McGregor (see cover illustration), I look ahead to an Australian culture totally liberated from the parochialism of the past. In the future, the convergences of the cultures of black and white Australia are destined to play a large part. The distinctive features of both groups will remain. Common ground will be tilled; the crop, harvested.

* * * * *

Each item in *North of the Ten Commandments* has been selected and placed carefully, with one editorial eye on the content, the other on the possibilities of that content within a larger, more integrated scheme. While the reader who delves into this book at any point should be pleased with the result, the real rewards await those motivated to work through methodically, from start to finish. The early sections are crucial, providing information necessary to a greater understanding and enjoyment of subsequent material: Sections 1 and 2 establish a framework for Sections 3 to 5 (on Aboriginals and Aboriginality); the first five sections, in turn, lay the foundation for the eleven sections that follow, as they raise most of the important thematic (and theoretical) issues. For this reason, I will introduce the first five sections in some detail.

Section 1, 'Origins', dramatises both the clash and the curious development of variant mythologies and ideologies. White myths of conquest, possession and property — evident in the bureaucratic language of Bremer and the exuberant utterances of Stokes and Stuart — starkly contrast Aboriginal myths of the land, sea and sky, such as those told by Paddy Japaljarri Sims and Narritjan Maymuru. For J.J. Gordon Bremer, the imprimatur of George IV confirms possession based on might; for Japaljarri Sims, countless generations of custodianship stretching back to Dreamtime origins attest to a relationship with the land based on reciprocity and consolidated through reverence and spiritual ties.

Radically different attitudes to the land, the book's primary theme, recur throughout the sixteen sections. Virtually all the Aboriginal material used — including the more contemporary mythologising of Captain Cook as symbolic white invader, and the testimony material on massacre — exudes a feeling of oneness, of comfort with the land, the country as home and provider. White literature, by contrast, is far more ambivalent. Dishonesty, confusion and at times real loathing have historically prevailed. When Second Secretary John Barrow appraised the Northern Territory in 1825, he confirmed the first popular tendency of white writers: to impose a false and, more serious, a wildly impractical image of the writer's own making upon the landscape. The rhetoric of politicians and those in public office, in particular, could not be trusted.

Nineteenth-century government documents are instructive. They say little, but imply much, especially those using the language of 'peaceful' settlement. Alfred Searcy, Sub-collector of Customs in the Northern Territory from 1882 to 1896 (and later to become

Acting Clerk in the South Australian House of Assembly), depicted the North as 'The Land of the Dawning'.[12] By implication, Searcy felt his white contemporaries were starting a colony of significance. This was the beginning; for Searcy, there had been no past in the Territory, or no past worthy of mention. He merely reinforced Captain James Cook's earlier declaration of white possession of the Australian continent — the land was deemed *terra nullius*, wasteland and unoccupied.

Subsequent white commentators enlarged on this 'historical fiction' (as Aboriginal poet and activist Kevin Gilbert has rightly termed it[13]) with a more pervasive scheme. The Reverend Dr Cairns, for example, in his 1862 speech in Melbourne honouring William Landsborough's party (which went in search of the ill-fated Burke and Wills expedition), waxed as lyrical as the occasion demanded:

> One of the characteristic signs of the present age was the very great progress of discovery in opening up regions of the earth which had hitherto been hermetically sealed even to the eye of intelligence... until now [Central Africa and the great Australian Continent] had been unknown lands to the civilized world; and not until the latter half of the nineteenth century had the honour been conferred on the enterprising sons of that wonderful little island far away in the north sea — peopled by Christian Britons — of penetrating the mystery, and finding out that, instead of stony deserts and inhospitable wilds, those countries contained luxuriant fields, abundant water, and balmy woods — inviting homes for millions and millions of human beings... A benignant Providence had lifted the cloud of their ignorance, and they heard a kindly voice calling upon them to arise, to go forth, to possess, to subdue, to people this goodly land.[14]

For Cairns, there simply were no indigenous inhabitants; the land, viewed with English eyes as a rich source of economic growth and prosperity, needed to have order imposed upon it. His conception of the country, at best ill-informed, at worst immoral, typified white thinking on the interior and the North until well into this century.

When Tom Bridges, Governor of South Australia, wrote a Foreword to Philippa Bridges's *A Walk-About in Australia* in July 1925, as he partook of the delicacies of French wine and culture in Paris, he characterised Australia as 'a White Man's Home and the only great inhabitable country still unoccupied in an overpopulated world'.[15] For Bridges, the 'Australian hinterland' had 'boundless' possibilities; the Aborigines were no cipher to European history, they were simply non-existent. Cosily situated a hemisphere away, Bridges could afford careless hyperbole. Throughout the nineteenth century, numerous government policy-makers displayed a similar fondness for flamboyant, usually inaccurate speculation. For those who had to try and match deed with the dream, however, it was a totally different story. Reality could be infinitely cruel. Major John Campbell's grim catalogue of the diseases experienced by those on Melville Island captures the mood of the early colonial outposts. It was all very well for John Lort Stokes, explorer aboard the *H.M.S. Beagle* (1837–43) to pass through the region and conceive of it as 'the centre of a vast system of commerce, the emporium'[16] of the South. He didn't have to live there. Those Europeans who did found their very sanity threatened at times.

Succeeding generations of white writers provided imaginative variations on Campbell's despair, and in doing so confirmed the other popular tendency of the new arrivals: to view the land as hostile and alien. The enemy. Some were appalled by the pestilence and the dark comedy of life in a place where the dead were irreverently referred to as 'worm banquets'.[17] Others recorded their fear, real or imagined, of desert experience. The wide open spaces haunted. Explorer Ernest Favenc's description of the eerie silence makes it seem almost tangible:

> If there is such a thing as darkness which can be felt, then the Australian desert possesses a silence which can be heard, so much does it oppress the intruder into these solitudes... A land such as this, with its great loneliness, its dearth of life, and its enshrouding atmosphere of awe and mystery, has a voice of its own, distinctly different from that of the ordinary Australian bush.[18]

Favenc's response echoes that of Marcus Clarke who, in his influential preface to Adam Lindsay Gordon's *Sea Spray and Smoke Drift* (1876), wrote about the 'Weird Melancholy' and 'the shelterless and silent plains'[19] of the Australian landscape.

When searching for a title for Section 2, on early white voyages and exploration, I settled on 'Bare-headed to the sun', Matthew Flinders's brief but potent description of the death by sunstroke of Thomas Morgan, a marine aboard Flinders's *Investigator* on its 'Voyage to Terra Australis' (1801–03). Contemporary Australian poet Les Murray has referred to the central creative problem of our colonial poets as being their failure or refusal to let ample sunlight in on the page. In a new environment, under a strangely crystal sky, Thomas Morgan literally let in too much sun too quickly. Section 2 reinforces Morgan's fate as metaphor for the first fifty years of European incursions into the Northern Territory (from Flinders to Leichhardt) as expedition after expedition, outpost after outpost, experienced at first-hand how unforgiving the land could be to the transient and the profiteer. If the Territory wasn't home, it could be hell.

Several generations later, Frederick T. Macartney's 'Territory' poems, written in the 1920s, reflect a muse still uneasy in the tropical environment. An influential figure in Australian literary circles in the 1940s and 1950s, Macartney spent about twelve years in Darwin (1921–33) in the Public Service, filling a number of positions from Sheriff to Registrar in Bankruptcy. He seems intuitively aware that he lacks both the imaginative capacity and the relevant vocabulary for the region. Six lines in the poem 'Siesta' sum up not only Macartney's dilemma, but that of a legion of white writers who vainly tried to appreciate the subtleties of Australia's tropics:

> . . . when I rise and stumbling go
> Outside, the sunlight deals me a sudden blow
> Full in the face.
> All trace
> Of dreaming vanishes . . . [20]

Many Northern Hemisphere dreams perished under a pitiless foreign sun below the equator. Only in the work of Roland Robinson, Xavier Herbert and Bill Harney, and a new generation headed by Lee Cataldi, do we have white Territorian writers capable of absorbing and imaginatively depicting the landscape with understanding and love. By contrast, Aboriginal writers and speakers merely have to render their background and their culture, dating back many millenia. Paddy Wainburranga, Amy Laurie, Big Bill Neidjie, Daisy Nawala Cusack, Jack Mirritji, Abie Jangala, Topsy Napurrula Nelson, Riley Young Winpilin, Tutama Tjapangarti — all the Aborigines who contribute to this collection display intimate knowledge of their environment. As Riley Young Winpilin says in the first epigraph to Section 7, Aboriginal leases don't alter — 'you can't wash him out'. It is almost impossible to remain unaffected by the calm assurance of the Aboriginal speakers I have been privileged to include in this volume, an assurance bred in the certainties of land and lore. They are truly at home.

If Sections 1 and 2 reveal the philosophical differences between Aboriginal and European interpretations of the land, then Sections 3 to 5 explore the historical consequences of these differences. Europeans wanted the land and so, according to the era's unwritten laws of Imperialist *real-politik*, they began a stringent military campaign to establish possession. Robert Caldwell, a member of the Pastoral Lands Royal Commission party to central Australia in 1891, went beyond his parliamentary duties to write a long poem entitled *In Our Great North-West, or Incidents and Impressions in Central Australia* (1894). He suffered no illusions about pastoral expansion:

> And the white-skinn'd race, like the rising
>   Of ocean tides on the shore,

>Are drifting still northward, and northward,
>   And seeking for more and more.[21]

But Caldwell was an exception, a man out of step with his era. More typically, when mass murder of Aborigines in the Northern Territory was deemed necessary by government (and its vanguard of colonists) to teach a salutary lesson — at Barrow Creek (1874), Daly River (1884), Jasper Gorge (1895) and Coniston (1928), for example[22] — authors and journalists alike could be counted on to do their part for the cause of expanding Empire.

Newspaper propaganda played a critical role in this process. For massacre to be accepted by the white Territorian community, the Aboriginal 'enemy' had to be stereotyped as less than human, as an animal. Just as one killed pestilence, one killed Aborigines — or so the reasoning went. There was nothing new in this. Pastoral expansion in the eastern states of Australia had taken place in precisely the same way. As W. Pridden wrote in *Australia, Its History and Present Condition* (1843): 'Men, more or less busily engaged in killing and taking possession, are not likely to make a very favourable report about those poor creatures into whose inheritance they have come . . . '[23] Even as he registers his understanding of the ways of the conqueror's propaganda, Pridden himself reflects the power of that process. The indigenous inhabitants are 'poor creatures', barely human, if at all.

Throughout the 1880s and 1890s the *Northern Territory Times*'s editorial staff repeatedly used language in a calculating way. The leader-article written on 4 October 1884, in response to the Daly River murders of four white miners by Aborigines, entitled 'Outrages by the blacks' (and reprinted in Section 3), is typical. When Arthur Phillip brought his cargo of convicts to eastern Australia in 1788 he had orders to establish constructive dialogue with the native inhabitants. The doctrine of the 'Noble Savage' determined government policy at that time. One hundred years later it was a completely different story. A column published in the *Northern Territory Times* of 6 September 1884, just before the Daly River details were known, registers an angry Darwin citizen's objection to 'the maniacal shouts of a howling mob of half-naked savages'. For the column's writer, 'the noble savage looks extremely well in a carefully executed drawing on stone' but (according to that writer) the reality is quite different:

> The blacks should not be permitted to walk the streets half clothed . . . Primitive simplicity must give way to the mighty strides of civilization, and the sooner this fact is impressed upon our native neighbors the better for the self-respect and social tone of the community.

This pervasive myth of European 'civilisation' versus Aboriginal 'savagery' proliferated in the journalism of the period. For this reason, the Daly River massacre had a certain brooding inevitability about it. 'Civilised' people could apparently react to 'savages' in whatever way they saw fit, especially if motivated by vengeance. Killing would beget far more killing. For the indigenous population of the time — men, women and children — this was ominous logic indeed.

When Police Corporal Montagu submitted a report on the constabulary's tactical response to the murder of the Daly River miners, the *Northern Territory Times* made the document the subject of its editorial on 26 December 1885. Montagu concluded, in part:

> What the other parties have done I do not know, but I believe the natives have received such a lesson this time as will exercise a salutary effect over the survivors in the time to come. One result of this expedition has been to convince me of the superiority of the Martini-Henry rifle, both for accuracy of aim and quickness of action.

Martini-Henry carbines would be put to extremely good use by the 'civiliser'. W.H. Willshire, constable in charge of the native police in the Victoria River region in the 1880s, was certainly a keen advocate of its use. Willshire, in fact, has distinct claims to being one of the most murderous, sadistic and paranoid men ever to live in the North, much less to work for the cause of law and order. Police and the press corps, at this time, formed an unholy alliance which effectively advanced the white pastoral cause.

I have arranged the literature of Sections 3 to 5 to enable the reader to obtain a grasp of the historical, political and cultural processes affecting black–white relations, past and present: Section 3, ' "Bone-piled spots": The whites dig in', highlights the language of the coloniser, along with those in the white community concerned enough, and brave enough, to defend the rights of all humankind; Section 4, ' "Nobody knows what it means": White depiction of Aborigines', presents a cross-section of both inept and imaginative attempts by whites to understand Aborigines, beginning with a couple of standard early caricatures in prose, and progressing to a series of perceptive poems by contemporary writers (and concluding with Graeme Parsons's haunting short story, 'A remote area', where the protagonist grapples with black ghosts, past and present); and Section 5, ' "Too much blackfeller": The black view', makes its own eloquent statement about tragedy and triumph.

Section 6, 'Pilgrims', works as a counterpoint to the devastating testimony material which precedes it, as legend, historical fact and rumour co-mingle in a number of enlightening ways. The white myths of Ian Mudie's poem, 'They'll tell you about me' (provided as the first epigraph to Section 6), have been reworked to give Aborigines their rightful place in the narrative of the continent. The Territory is full of so many stirring stories, both European and Aboriginal: Flash Poll the survivor, Alfred Searcy's 'poor old fellow' digging his own grave and destined to drop dead in it, the wrenching simplicity of David MacKay's note written just before he perished in the scrub, Daisy Nawala Cusack's refusal to submit to a life planned for her by others. 'Pilgrims', like several other sections, could easily have been of book length itself. I certainly had the material. When making final selections, quality was the first criterion for inclusion but I also attempted to be as representative as possible. A section almost as good as this one was left on the floor of my study.

Sections 7 and 8, 'My spirit, my country' and 'A bastard of a place', supply the most informative extensions of the first five sections. We get a feel for what the land really means to the black and white population alike, to different generations of men and women. The Aboriginal response is intuitive, knowing; the white response, as we might anticipate, varies profoundly. Puzzlement, anger, and even malevolence, voiced by the white writers in Section 8 contrast with the range of positive responses in Section 7 — from Frederick Macartney's deliberately literary and earnest appreciation of the tropical environment, viewed from the interior of his dwelling, to the affectionate appreciation of 'Instructions for honey ants', by Billy Marshall-Stoneking, and Lee Cataldi's almost transcendental poem, 'rain'.

We go overland in Section 9, 'Sites and sightings', as writers respond to specific geographical (and mythic) locations. Dick Kimber admonished me in Alice a couple of years ago to make sure *North of the Ten Commandments* didn't end up as a 'north of Katherine' collection, a Top-End tour. I trust he'll approve. 'Sites and sightings' was another potentially sizeable section and thus had to be pruned extensively. Any number of geographically aligned clusters of material was possible. Ultimately I chose Uluru as representative and symbolic location, hence the first three entries of the section, and followed these with a selection of other landmarks, regions and towns.

Darwin simply insisted on having a section to itself: Section 10, 'Darwin, mad capital of the north'. What riches I pored over on the tropical capital of white Australia. I settled on Douglas Lockwood's phrase as my title, principally because of my belief that most Darwinians neither regard the description as pejorative nor as an insult. Rather, they rejoice in its relevance. In a country rapidly losing its individual character and becoming more standardised, more homogeneous every year, Darwin's uniqueness and eccentricity grow in significance. Banjo Paterson celebrated that difference at the turn of the century; contemporary writers have consolidated the tradition. Successive Chief Ministers and government officials have more recently attempted to impose a veil of sophistication and economic progressiveness on Darwin and the Territory in general. Frankly, I hope they fail. I'm with the Banjo on this one. As he put it, way back in 1898: 'Some day it will be civilised and spoilt; but up to the present it has triumphantly overthrown all who have attempted to improve it. It is still "the Territory". Long may it wave!'[24]

In celebration of Territory originality, the next three sections — Section 11 'Adventures, incongruities, incredibilities', Section 12 'Nature's stage' and Section 13 'Sprees, drunks, and race meetings' — gather together a range of the more extreme and amusing of Mark Twain's 'incredibilities': among them John Lort Stokes's account of a play at Port Essington in 1839, Mrs Daly's enthusiastic description of the Darwin camp's 'great love for music' in the early 1870s, three perspectives on Christmas Day, Territory-style (1873, 1901 and 1930), a white opinion of black cannibalism, a black opinion of white cannibalism, and a cross-section of the most graphic and imaginative pestilence and alcohol stories to emerge in the literature of the last hundred years and more. I include Section 13 with some misgivings. Alcohol has had an integral social role in the history of the Northern Territory since the establishment of Fort Dundas in 1824. While this has led to a wealth of anecdotes, the comedy and light relief come hard-earned. The toll of human lives and misery continues to grow. In the Territory of 1990, alcoholism represents a serious problem for the white community; for the black community, it is arguably an even greater threat to social cohesion. If alcohol has on occasion been balm for the wounded Territorian spirit, far more often it has actually caused the suffering.

Section 14, 'Opening up the country', began as four separate groupings: drovers, buffalo hunters, miners, and police. In the final stages of selection I was satisfied that the role of the Northern Territory police force, qualitatively different from the rest, was dealt with adequately, indeed more effectively, within other sections. The amalgamation of the other three groups gave me a fine combination of larrikins and adventurers, both Aboriginal and European. From the 1870s onwards, they set forth on a 'fantastic pilgrimage', as William Linklater's epigraph from *Gather No Moss* suggests, one which would reshape the social and political history of the Northern Territory for decades to come. The missions, too, put their particular stamp on the times, one that I have tried to represent fairly by reproducing a broad spectrum of views. From the founding of the Hermannsburg settlement in 1877, missionaries assumed an ambivalent role. Aboriginal men tended to resent the intrusion into their traditional ways; some white pastoralists and police resented the intrusion into their murderous ways. Missionaries copped it from both sides. Today their role is even more controversial, as a growing number of commentators question the extent of the Church's role in cultural conquest.

Paul Foelsche, Inspector of Northern Territory Police from 1870 to 1904, was a man caught between the dictates of his position as a standard-bearer of white 'civilisation' and the whisperings of his own heart. After his retirement he wrote a letter to an old German friend, which read in part:

> This is the end of the road for me. I have done my best; I have tried to understand. It has not always been easy, but it has given me many rewards.
> Much remains. This is an Old Country with an Old People. The New People must remember the claims of the Old People. They were here first, and they have their established customs and institutions. So far as those customs and institutions can be related to our standards, they must be respected...
> The future of the Northern Territory lies with the New People — but only with imagination, sympathy, and above all, energy, will they accomplish it.[25]

It was a vision astonishingly ahead of its time, especially for someone in Foelsche's position. He imagined a more humane and christian community, a community of New People committed to recognising the claims of the Old People.

In Section 16, 'Hang on like I done', Amy Laurie counsels the value of cultural convergence: 'Some people don't like colour, but better to be mixed like the birds and the flowers mixed.' Riley Young Winpilin states that the land is 'mother for everybody'. How to give substance to these inclusive dreams for the future? When Prime Minister Gough Whitlam returned a lease of 1250 square miles (part of Wave Hill Station) to the Gurindji people in August 1975, Vincent Lingiari celebrated: 'We will be mates, White and Black.' It was a historic moment for all Territorians. A time to treasure. The process of reversing a century of dispossession and killing in the Northern Territory had begun.

Many decades after Foelsche, and years and years after the first Land Rights claims were granted, the way ahead is still unclear. Much still remains to be done, but the first steps towards justice, cultural maturity and spiritual accord have been taken. I am confident that *North of the Ten Commandments* will delight the lover of literature; I also want the book to encourage more Australians around this huge and beautiful country to take a few additional strides into a future of integrity and fair-dealing.

Note: When using older sources, I have retained archaic spellings, and I have retained original capitalisation and punctuation throughout the collection. Only quotation marks have been standardised. In order to maximise the amount of material used in this collection, some entries had to be condensed, and this I have indicated by ellipses.

1 See Captain J.J. Gordon Bremer, 'Form of taking possession of Port Essington and Melville and Bathurst Islands, 1824', in Section 1.

2 John Barrow to Horton, 30 April 1825, in *Historical Records of Australia*, series 111, vol. 5, Library Committee of Commonwealth Parliament, Sydney, 1922, p. 793, quoted in Alan Powell, *Far Country: A Short History of the Northern Territory*, Melbourne University Press, Melbourne, 1982, p. 49. I would like to acknowledge my debt to Dr Powell's pioneering historical research.

3 See Matthew Flinders, 'North coast, Blue-Mud Bay', and Phillip Parker King, 'Our theodolite stand and Mr Cunningham's insect-net', in Section 2.

4 See Major John Campbell, 'Geographical memoir of Melville Island, 1826–28', in Section 2.

5 W.E.H. Stanner, *After the Dreaming: The 1968 Boyer Lectures*, Australian Broadcasting Commission, Sydney, 1969, pp.12, 24–5.

6 Henry Reynolds, *The Other Side of the Frontier: Aboriginal Resistance to the European Invasion of Australia*, Penguin, Ringwood, Vic., 1982.

7 Sally Morgan, *My Place*, Fremantle Arts Centre Press, Fremantle, 1987, p. 349.

8 Vernon Louis Parrington, *Main Currents in American Thought*, Harcourt, Brace, New York, 1927, Introduction, pp.vi–vii.

9 Nancy Keesing, 'Language and dignity', *Australian Book Review*, November, 1983, p.17.

10 Bruce Bennett & William Grono (comps), *Wide Domain: Western Australian Themes and Images*, Angus & Robertson, Sydney, 1979; Patrick Morgan (comp), *Shadow and Shine: An Anthology of Gippsland Literature*, Gippsland Institute of Advanced Education, Churchill, Victoria, 1988; Peter Pierce (ed), *The Oxford Literary Guide to Australia*, Oxford University Press, Melbourne, 1987.

11 Jennifer Isaacs, *Aboriginality: Contemporary Aboriginal Paintings and Prints*, University of Queensland Press, St Lucia, 1989.

12 Alfred Searcy, *In Northern Seas*, W.K. Thomas & Co, Adelaide, 1905, p.13. Marcus Clarke, in his Preface to Adam Lindsay Gordon's *Sea Spray and Smoke Drift*, 1876, uses the same phrase to describe Australia.

13 Kevin Gilbert (ed), *Inside Black Australia: An Anthology of Aboriginal Poetry*, Penguin, Ringwood, Vic., 1988, Introduction, p.xx.

14 Cairns quoted in William Landsborough, *Journal of Landsborough's Expedition from Carpentaria in Search of Burke and Wills*, Wilson & Mackinnon, Melbourne, 1862, pp.121–2.

15 Tom, Bridges, Foreword to Philippa Bridges, *A Walk-About in Australia*, Hodder & Stoughton, London, ?1925, pp.vii–viii.

16 John Lort Stokes, *Discoveries in Australia, with an Account of the Coasts and Rivers Explored During the Voyage of the HMS Beagle in the Years 1837–43*, vol.II, T. & W. Boone, London, 1846, p.360.

17 William J. Sowden, *The Northern Territory As It Is*, W.K. Thomas & Co, Adelaide, 1882, p.35.

18 Ernest Favenc, *Voices of the Desert*, Elliot Stock, London, 1905, Preface, pp.xii–xiii.

19 Marcus Clarke, Preface to Adam Lindsay Gordon, *Sea Spray and Smoke Drift*, 1876; repr. in Michael Wilding, *Marcus Clarke* (Portable Australian Authors), University of Queensland Press, St Lucia, 1976, pp.645–6.

20 Frederick T. Macartney, *Preferences*, Angus & Robertson, Sydney, 1941, p.103.

21 Robert Caldwell, *In Our Great North-West, or Incidents and Impressions in Central Australia*, Bonython, Adelaide, 1894, p.53.

22 For more information, see Jay Arthur & Peter Read (comps & eds), A View of the Past: Aboriginal Accounts of Northern Territory History, unpublished, MS held in Australian Institute of Aboriginal and Torres Strait Islander Studies Library, Canberra. I am indebted to Peter Read's important work in this area.

23 W. Pridden, *Australia, Its History and Present Condition*, Burns, London, 1843, p.75.

24 A.B. (Banjo) Paterson, 'The cycloon, Paddy Cahill and the G.R.', in Section 10.

25 Sidney Downer, *Patrol Indefinite: The Northern Territory Police Force*, Rigby, Adelaide, 1963, p.206.

1 Origins

Stories, stories are here.
— Bill Harney, *North of 23°*, 1945

Previous page: Paddy Wainburranga's 'Too many Captain Cooks', painted at Baidjildir billabong, central Arnhem Land, in 1987.

Yiwarrakurlu / Milky Way

Paddy Japaljarri Sims

This Dreaming painting is about the Milky Way, those stars which shine up in the sky at night when we sleep. This story that I am telling is about my fathers in the Dreamtime who made the stars travel across the sky. They were of the Japaljarri-Jungarrayi section. They came from their country in the north and lived in one place. Unchanging, these stars created by the Dreaming did not turn into other sections. They were not made randomly, but by the Japaljarri-Jungarrayi Dreaming who created the Milky Way and carried stars and witi poles as he travelled.

The Dreamtime people travelled and made camp in one place for some time. They conducted male initiation ceremonies. They took leafy branches from trees and bound them together into witi poles, using vines and creepers. These they used when they initiated young men, as we do today.

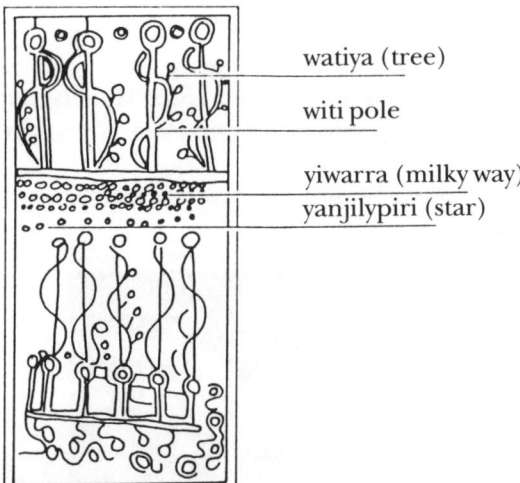 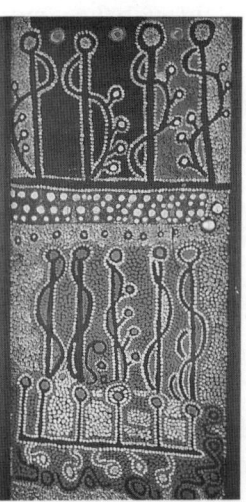

'Yiwarrakurlu/Milky Way', painted by Paddy Japaljarri Sims on a door at Yuendumu School, north-west of Alice Springs. Yuendumu is a community of mostly Warlpiri people. Paddy Japaljarri Stewart, with Sims one of five men (and many children) who painted a number of the school doors, summed up the project this way: 'We painted these Dreamings ... because the children should learn about our Law. The children do not know them and they might become like white people, which we don't want to happen. We are relating these true stories of the Dreamtime.'

I am only telling of that part of the Dreaming story which came from the north. This same Dreaming belongs to others. We all join up — Yarripilangu and Yarrungkanyi. It is a big Dreamtime story about the millions of stars which shine above us as we sleep. It is also about the land which is sacred because it was created by the Dreaming. Special places were made by the Dreaming, which fell down as a shooting star to earth. Thus the Dreaming came to be for people. It is our father which stretches across the sky above us as the Milky Way. This Dreaming stands there from the north. The Japaljarris and Jungarrayis in the Dreamtime travelled a long way from the north side and landed at Purrparlarla. The Dreamtime men, armed with their weapons, travelled through the sky and came down and landed at Purrparlarla. There was a big company travelling together and no one approached them. Some of the Japaljarris disappeared there, while the others kept going straight through by Purrparlarla.

We were taught about these Dreamings by our grandfathers, fathers and elder brothers. They instructed us in the Warlpiri law and told us not to forget what we had been taught; told us to hold on to our law and follow it the right way. I am now telling the Dreaming of the Milky Way, of all those millions of stars up above us, as I was told it by our old men.

Source: Paddy Japaljarri Sims, 'Yiwarrakurlu/Milky Way', in Warlukurlangu Artists, *Kuruwarri/Yuendumu Doors*, Australian Institute of Aboriginal Studies, Canberra, 1987, Door 29, p.127.

Ngapakurlu/Rain

Paddy Japaljarri Sims

These paintings are about a Rain Dreaming which travelled through the country from the south, from Karlipirnpa.

There was another Rain Dreaming belonging to the Jakamarra-Jupurrurla section; coming through the same country as the rain from Karlipirnpa.

'I don't know that Rain,' this Dreaming from the south said to himself. As he travelled north he would stop and camp overnight, then get up in the morning and continue on his way. He camped at a place called Jurntiparnta which belongs to Jampijinpa. He sent out great flashes of lightning which struck the country all around Jurntiparnta, a soakage which belongs to my mother's father.

The Dreaming came through the sky above. It was a person. But I cannot tell the story about the Dreaming person, just about the Rain.

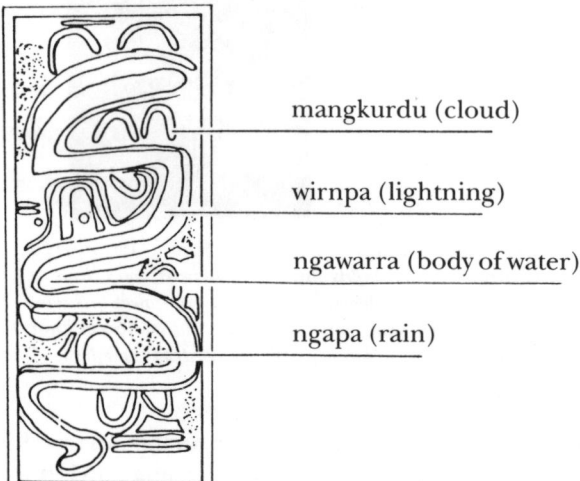

mangkurdu (cloud)

wirnpa (lightning)

ngawarra (body of water)

ngapa (rain)

'Ngapakurlu/Rain', painted by Paddy Japaljarri Sims. The Rain Dreaming came from the south, from Karlipirnpa.

The Dreaming created people out of the small clouds we call 'children'. The Water Dreaming brought its children along and people were created thus. The Rain Dreaming continued north, camping on the way. He was very tired from his long travels. He fell down and then rose up into the sky as vapour to form clouds. He went north and came near the other Rain Dreaming passing to the west. He did not recognise that other Dreaming. He made his camp in the sky. He was very tired and he slept the night there. In the morning he woke up and set off again.

I am the kurdungurlu for this Dreaming and I have correctly told the story of the Rain Dreaming which came from Karlipirnpa.

The other Rain came. It was huge. When the Rain from Karlipirnpa drew close, he saw it there in the north. The Rain from Karlipirnpa was a stranger. The northern country Rain made straight for the stranger who had come from Karlipirnpa. It rose up and formed large rain clouds which covered the other Rain. It fell down to the earth in torrents and disappeared from the sky. It kept on going. It was made to go west. It went under the ground in the form of a stream of water.

I only tell the story of that Rain Dreaming until it becomes a stream. I take the story no further. The water continued flowing and got much bigger. The Rain Dreaming went a long way north and finished there. He just lay there, exhausted and ill and unable to straighten up. 'What will I do to myself?' he kept asking. He killed himself there, unable to cover himself.

I am the real kurdungurlu for this big important story. I bring it from the south and put it away in my mother's father's country. I tell and paint only that part of that big Dreaming.

Source: Paddy Japaljarri Sims, 'Ngapakurlu Rain', in Warlukurlangu Artists, *Kuruwarri/Yuendumu Doors*, Australian Institute of Aboriginal Studies, Canberra, 1987, Door 27, p.119.

The Milky Way

Marlindi story of Arnhem Land, told by Narritjan Maymuru

Olden time, Dreamtime, we gottim nothing star la[1] sky. And no people la this country, nothing. Only bird, animal. Nothing people. Properly dark place night-time. No star la sky.

That old spirit man, Barama, him bin talk la twofeller night bird, two curlew. 'I might change him you feller from bird. Make you man.' That the way that old Barama bin talk. Him bin say, 'You twofeller can camp there la Milmooya, river place. You can catchim 'bout fish, animal, everything for you tucker. Eatim. But no more forget. Everything, bird, animal, everything you friend. No matter I make him you man. No matter you eatim allabout tucker. They still friend la you.'

Barama him bin change that twofeller bird, make him man. Him bin givit new name. Moonaminya, one feller, nother one Yikawanga. Orright, that twofeller new one man bin sit down camp there la Milmooya. River camp. Proper Number One.

All that nother one bird, animal him bin like change la man and womans altogether. Allabout bin talk la Barama. 'Hey, old man, old Barama, we, allabout, what about you change him wefeller, make we people? Same la that twofeller Moonaminya and Yikawanga. We must camp there la Milmooya, catchim 'bout fish, animal, everything we tucker. Allasame.'

'Orright' Barama bin talk. 'I can change him youfeller. I can make him you man and woman, and you mob can camp there la Moonaminya and Yikawanga. You can be hunter allasame. But no more forget. You hunter orright but you gotta be friend for bird, animal, fish, everything. No matter you eatim, you still friend. Savvy?'

So allabout people bin go sitdown there la river Milmooya. Allabout properly happy and allabout proper good hunter for tucker because before they bin bird and animal they self, and they understand.

Moonaminya and Yikawanga bin go look round fish there la Milmooya. They bin make him canoe, paddle and fish spear. They bin catchim big mob fish but only daytime. They can't catchim fish night time because no light, no star, moon, anything there la sky.

Moonaminya and Yikawanga bin talk la allabout. 'We twofeller gotta go travel la canoe look around new one camp there la sky. We twofeller gonna make weself star let you know which way we sit down. We gotta make new camp la youfeller. You can come this new one camp behind, when you feller finish, when you pass away.'

That twofeller bin paddle away, paddle away la canoe, first time la river, then long way more further, right up there on top la sky. That two feller man bin change himself la star. Two properly shiny one star there la sky.

Moonaminya and Yikawanga bin look down la allabout people. Allabout bin still there, hunting la Milmooya. So every time they bin catchim 'bout fish, animal, bird, everything, Moonaminya and Yikawanga bin makim one star there la sky. When any that earth mob bin die finish they relation puttim dead body la bone post, and they spirit bin go straight up there la sky. Boom! Like a that! Star! Straight away new one star there la sky. By and by Moonaminya and Yikawanga gottim big mob star there la sky right on top that river Milmooya. So that what they bin makim that twofeller. River of star. Proper shiny one. Earth

'The legend of the Milky Way', painted by Narritjan Maymuru. The Milky Way is a river of stars created from the spirits of dead people and dominated by Yingalpia the crocodile, who is the Southern Cross.

mob bin look up there la sky, lookim that river of star. Some feller bin callim Milky Way, big mob star look like milk there la sky, but Moonaminya and Yikawanga mob callim that new one Milmooya allasame.

One properly big crocodile there la river Milmooya. Him name Yingalpia. Dreaming crocodile. Yingalpia him bin good friend for Moonaminya and Yikawanga when they bin hunting man. So that twofeller star man bin sing out: 'Hey, Yingalpia, what about you come live la wefeller, la sky?'

So Yingalpia him bin go straight up there la sky. Wheee! Like a that! Him bin swim round, swim round that one starry river. Him head and him leg bin change make him proper shiny one star every one. Five altogether. Moonaminya and Yikawanga bin stop there close up la Yingalpia, because allabout bin good friend that first time when they bin night bird. True story.

Orright, spose you look there la sky night time, you see him Milmooya, that Milky Way. That like river, full up star. Can't finish him! Before, all that star bin people, animal, bird, fish everything. When him die finish allabout go there la sky change la star.

There, underneath la Milky Way, Milmooya, you look, you seeim Southern Cross. That one Yingalpia first time, old crocodile, friendly one, dreaming crocodile. Close up there la Southern Cross you lookim two properly shiny one star. That two feller bright one allabout callim Pointer. That the Moonaminya and Yikawanga. That twofeller Pointer him always stop close up la they friend Yingalpia the crocodile, and they make mark for Milky Way where you look him.

Some time wet season, rain time, you seeim big lightning, and you hearim Bang! Altogether big one thunder. No more fright. That only that twofeller Moonaminya and Yikawanga where him sing song and havim big dance there la sky, every time they makim new one star. That thunder that only didgeridoo where they pullim la sky. And that lightning that only clap stick where they hit him that two feller.

Allabout, everybody there la sky very happy because Moonaminya and Yikawanga bin change him la star altogether. Big mob star.

1 One particular factor which needs to be understood is the use of 'la' throughout. It equals 'longa', which can in turn mean 'belonging to' or 'along' or 'to', e.g.,
That one billycan la me = That's my billycan
Him bin go la school = He went to school
Me twofeller bin go la road = We (two of us) went along the road. — T.E.

Source: Narritjan Maymuru, 'The Milky Way', a Marlindi story of Arnhem Land, as told to Ted Egan.

The rainbow serpent

Djauan legend

The legend and the dreamings of the black rock-snake Kurrichalpongo who changes into Bolong the rainbow serpent, the legend sung by the Djauan in the corroboree called Kunabibbi.

In the Dreamtime the old man Nagacork made a long and deep water hole, called Tala-wung, in the Flying-fox River.

And Nagacork went on a long walkabout and, returning to the billabong, saw the smoke of many camp-fires rising through the pandanus palms and paper-bark trees. He heard the talking and laughter of the many tribes camped among the deep shady trees. And as he came along the river bank he saw the blackfellows swimming and spearing for fish in the river. And he saw the lubras and piccaninnies wading among the lilies and feeling with their hands and feet in the deep mud for the lily-bulbs and mussels. And the lubras were singing and calling as they pushed the boat-like coolamons over the water to one another to hold the food they were gathering.

And when the blackfellows saw the old man Nagacork they called out to him, 'Come on, old man, there's plenty of fish here, plenty of barramundi.' But the old man Nagacork was quiet and said little to them. And Nagacork went on through the trees along the river-bank, and parties of blackfellows and lubras going about from camp to camp passed him as he went.

Nagacork was looking for Jammutt, his water-shooting fish, and he had not seen them in any part of the river. And he turned back again, and as the blackfellows saw him coming they called out to him and pointed to various fish in the river. Other blackfellows ran along the bank, pointing and calling, 'Here, old man, are these the fish you are looking for?' 'No,' said Nagacork, 'they are not my fish.' And other blackfellows waded into the water to drive up other kinds of fish towards Nagacork. But, 'No,' he said, 'those are not my fish. It does not matter. I'll go to my camp.'

And as Nagacork went slowly along he saw a stream of ants passing and repassing and leading over the ground to a big coolibah tree. The stream of ants went up the bark of the tree and, high up on the trunk, disappeared into a large hole. And Nagacork climbed up the tree and looked down into the hole. And soon, in the darkness, he saw the bones of Jammutt, his lost water-shooting fish, that the blackfellows had killed and eaten and had then hidden the bones there.

And the old man Nagacork climbed down the tree and went on and made his camp under a clump of pandanus palms. And he sat with his head on his arms across his knees. He was thinking about his lost fish. And as he sat there he began to sing to himself: 'I wait, wait, wait, wait, wait.'

Suddenly it seemed to him that he was singing up Kurrichalpongo, the black rock-snake. And in a high paper-bark tree above him, Dat-dat, the green parrot, began to call out that he could see Kurrichalpongo, the great rock-snake, coming out of the mountains in the north from a place called Algulcorring, which is on the Wilton River.

And then, far in the sky, above the tops of trees, the old man Nagacork saw the wide curve of a rainbow appearing.

And Kurrichalpongo went under the ground and came and bored a hole in the bank of the billabong and let out a rush a water to drown all the tribes. And as the blackfellows were swimming and wading in the billabong, they saw the water rising. Once the water was up to the thighs of those who were wading, now it was about their chests. And the water rose and covered the reeds and the lilies. It rose and spread over the banks and covered the camps of the many tribes and drowned blackfellows as it rose.

And it was then that many of the blackfellows changed themselves into birds and flew up and away over the water, screaming harshly as they went. And some, to escape from drowning changed into Kooroopir the tortoise and Wooreyong the long-necked tortoise.

And at Talawung, Kurrichalpongo laid many eggs and brought out young rainbow-snakes, and some of these eggs were turned into stone and are there to this day. And the young rainbow-snakes started off to travel in different directions. But Kurrichalpongo went on to Yooloo, which is on the Wilton River. And as Kurrichalpongo travelled along she looked back and saw that the winding track she was making was turning into a deep river with trees and reeds and lilies, and, far behind her in the distance, she saw billabongs gleaming in the sun. And again she looked back and saw all the bush and the mountains springing up behind her as she went along. 'What is happening?' said Kurrichalpongo. 'How am I doing this?'

Now at Warrook-narlook, which is a plain in the Mainoru country, Kurrichalpongo met and fought and Kandagun the dingo. After fighting off Kandagun the dingo, Kurrichalpongo lay down to rest and, on rising, she found she had made the bitter yams that grow there.

And Kurrichalpongo came to Kundiyarung, which is a big swamp, and she went on and came to Munaringi, which is where the Roper River flows into the sea. And she travelled on and came to Luralingi, which is at the Hodgson River.

And at Luralingi two lubras of the Maranbella tribe had run away from their husbands and had found two young men who were sons of Nagacork. Now these two young men had found a lot of little rainbow-snakes in a tree and also in a cave nearby. And the two men cut down the tree and killed the snakes that were in it. And they went into the cave and killed the young snakes there. And they took all these snakes along to their father Nagacork to show him what they had killed for food. But when Nagacork saw the snakes he frowned and said: 'You should not have done this. Those are rainbow-snakes you have killed. You must die for doing this.'

And when Kurrichalpongo came to Luralingi she turned into Bolong the rainbow-snake. And as she did so, a many-tongued lightning forked out into the sky and thunder came with the noise of mountains being split apart with their huge rocks crashing down and the sound of their falling ever following and echoing away. And the rain and the wind came snapping off and uprooting the trees. And the mountains fell down on the tribes and the waters came swirling trees and blackfellows together as it rushed along.

And of the tribes who were drowned there were the Wallipooroo, the Mara, the Yookul, the Karkaringi, the Yarnyoola, the Binbinga, the Narnga and the Karawa.

And Bolong the rainbow-snake turned back into Kurrichalpongo and went down into the ground.

And Kurrichalpongo came to Gurroo-wal-walli, which is near Nutwood, and she came to Arnalyaroo, which is Dunmara, and at Woodoo, which is near Daly Waters, she made the plains and billabongs, and at Waleera she made a big swamp.

And at Moorinjairee, which is Newcastle Waters, Kurrichalpongo met the old man Nagacork and four other rainbow-snakes. And there they held a big meeting and made corroborees.

And at this place called Moorinjairee, where there are hundreds of water-holes, the Dreamtime ended and all the animals there turned into blackfellows. And Kurrichalpongo and the rainbow-snakes went down into the ground.

Source: 'The rainbow serpent', a Djauan legend, in Roland Robinson (comp.), *Legend and Dreaming*, Edwards & Shaw, Sydney, 1952, pp. 19–21.

Dinosaur Dreamtime

Mark O'Connor

(a fantasy for Mt Stegosaurus and the Centre)

The Dreamtime was true. These rocks all lived.
The land was alive and convulsing when the seas were hot mists.
The rocks bubbled and frothed.
Now they lie flat, yet sluggishly steep
with the long barrel-bodies of crested reptiles
and the stumpy side-legs of salamanders.
Bumping the clouds along their spines,
breaking the hail with a mindless brow,
— the first brood of Earth
before she invented cooler blood
and flesh that grew in its own water.

They climbed out unknowing.
The mild air, the sliding rivers
turned the great worms to ice as they slept:
that dreamtime ended their day.
Pygmy brontosaurids grazed on their sleeping flanks,
the long necks moving.

Again the fire-worms crawled out
on a snowy raft that drifted round the Pole;
they moved with boiling lakes on their heads.
Now they hold these valleys between their paws
grimly relenting; or butt the sea-swell,
flicking its spume from rigid tail bones.

The monsters count moons by the million
and the pale watery suns by day.
They are not fooled by summers
or the flickering warmth of forest fires.
The cold ocean of air has invaded them surely
cracking their blood into crystals;
and that subtle and terrible fluid, the water ...

One day they will rise to destroy us
and the forest boil off their sides like mist.

They will wait till the ocean floor sizzles,
the glaciers fly up like sparks,
like fiery chaff
as the sun explodes. When the Warm has begun
they will shiver
ridging their scale-backs against the horizon,
resuming their sinuous travels and wars across the Dreamtime,
their once and now come-alive time.

Source: Mark O'Connor, *Firestick Farming: Selected Poems 1972–1990*, Hale & Iremonger, Sydney, 1990, p.163.

The seasons of fire

Billy Marshall-Stoneking

There is Law for Fire,
singing for Fire,
dancing for Fire —
Fire Dreaming.
You have been there; you have seen it.
You know all the names of Fire:
signal fires, hunting fires,
sleeping fires, fires for light,
fires for cooking, for ceremonies,
healing fires of eucalyptus leaves —
Fire is medicine, magic.
   Fire gave Crow a voice,
flying away in pain.
Fire brings old quarrels to an end.
On top of Uluru, do not drink
at the rockhole of Warnampi
unless you take Fire
or the Snake will bite your spirit
and drought will follow.
Fire can protect you from the Dead Ones.

You have been there, you have seen them.
You know all this Fire.
The penis is Fire.
The vagina is Fire.
Fire is inside the bodies of animals.
The woman hands a fire-stick to the boy
and he becomes a man.
There is a time for every fire.
The fires of January are different
to the fires of June.
In the cold time, a small nudge before sleep
will keep the flame alive all night.
The right ash, the right heat,

the right position of wind, dune and saltbush:
a technology of Fire. The knowledge.

You have been there; you have watched.
You know all the seasons of Fire.
   Hawk stopped Bush Turkey
throwing Fire into the sea.
Fire cannot be stolen now; it lives
everywhere — inside the spinifex and dry wood.
All this is Law.
'The smoking days' — Buyuguyunya — come every year.
The air is full of smoke.
The smoke comes first, then the fire,
and then the smoke …
All this is Law.
Hot is more than two sticks rubbed together; and
no chopping — take only what you can drag:
green wood for shelter;
dead pieces for waru.
The wind from the mouth works kindling.
Fire makes grass seed.
It finds the kangaroo and chases him
to the hunters.
All this is Law.
The burning off and the gathering together are one.

You have been there; you have seen it.
You know all the seasons of Fire.

Source: Billy Marshall-Stoneking, 'The seasons of fire', published originally in *Northern Perspective,* vol.1, no.2, 1989; and then in Marshall-Stoneking, *Singing the Snake: Poems from the Western Desert, 1979–88,* Angus & Robertson, Sydney, 1990.

The moon bone

Wonguri-Manjikai song cycle of north-eastern Arnhem Land

Song 1

The people are making a camp of branches in that country at Arnhem Bay:
With the forked stick, the rail for the whole camp, the *'Mandʒikai* people are making it.
Branches and leaves are about the mouth of the hut: the middle is clear within.
They are thinking of rain, and of storing their clubs in case of a quarrel,
In the country of the Dugong, towards the wide clay pans made by the Moonlight.
Thinking of rain, and of storing the fighting sticks.
They put up the rafters of arm-band-tree wood, put the branches on to the camp,
    at Arnhem Bay, in that place of Dugong …
And they block up the back of the hut with branches.
Carefully place the branches, for this is the camp of the Morning-Pigeon man,
And of the Middle-of-the-Camp man; of the Mangrove-Fish man; of two other head-men,
And of the Clay-pan man; of the *'Baijini*-Anchor man, and of the Arnhem Bay country man;
Of the Whale man and of another head-man; of the Arnhem Bay Creek man;
Of the Scales-of-the-Rock-Cod man; of the Rock Cod man, and of the Place-of-the-
    Water man.

Song 2

They are sitting about in the camp, among the branches, along the back of the camp:
Sitting along in lines in the camp, there in the shade of the paperbark trees:
Sitting along in a line, like the new white spreading clouds:
In the shade of the paperbarks, they are sitting resting like clouds.
People of the clouds, living there like the mist; like the mist sitting resting with arms on
    knees,
In here towards the shade, in this Place, in the shadow of paperbarks.
Sitting there in rows, those *'Wonguri-'Mandʒikai* people, paperbarks along like a cloud.
Living on cycad-nut bread; sitting there with white-stained fingers,
Sitting in there resting, those people of the Sandfly clan …
Sitting there like mist, at that place of the Dugong … and of the Dugong's Entrails …
Sitting resting there in the place of the Dugong …
In that place of the Moonlight Clay Pans, and at the place of the Dugong …
There at that Dugong place they are sitting all along.

Song 3

Wake up from sleeping! Come, we go to see the clay pan, at the place of the Dugong …
Walking along, stepping along, straightening up after resting:
Walking along, looking as we go down on to the clay pan.
Looking for lily plants as we go … and looking for lily foliage …
Circling around, searching towards the middle of the lily leaves to reach the rounded roots.
At that place of the Dugong …
At that place of the Dugong's Tail …
At that place of the Dugong; looking for food with stalks,
For lily foliage, and for the round-nut roots of the lily plant.

Song 4

The birds saw the people walking along.
Crying, the white cockatoos flew over the clay pan of the Moonlight;
From the place of the Dugong they flew, looking for lily-root food; pushing the
    foliage down and eating the soft roots.
Crying, the birds flew down and along the clay pan, at that place of the Dugong …
Crying, flying down there along the clay pan…
At the place of the Dugong, of the Tree-Limbs-Rubbing-Together, and of the Evening Star.
Where the lily-root clay pan is …
Where the cockatoos play, at that place of the Dugong …
Flapping their wings they flew down, crying, 'We saw the people!'
There they are always living, those clans of the white cockatoo …
And there is the Shag woman, and there her clan:
Birds, trampling the lily foliage, eating the soft round roots!

Song 5

An animal track is running along: it is the track of the rat …
Of the male rat, and the female rat, and the young that hang to her teats as she runs,
The male rat hopping along, and the female rat, leaving paw-marks as a sign …
On the clay pans of the Dugong, and in the shade of the trees,
At the Dugong's place, and at the place of her Tail …
Thus, they spread paw-mark messages all along their tracks,
In that place of the Evening Star, in the place of the Dugong …
Among the lily plants and into the mist, into the Dugong place, and into the place of
    her Entrails.
Backwards and forwards the rats run, always hopping along …
Carrying swamp-grass for nesting, over the little tracks, leaving their signs.
Backwards and forwards they run on the clay pan, around the place of the Dugong.
Men saw their tracks at the Dugong's place, in the shade of the trees, on the white clay;
Roads of the rats, paw-marks everywhere, running into the mist.
All around are their signs; and there men saw them down on the clay pan, at the place
    of the Dugong.

Song 6

A duck comes swooping down to the Moonlight clay pan, there at the place of
    the Dugong …
From far away. 'I saw her flying over, in here at the clay pan …'
Floating along, pushing the pool into ripples and preening her feathers.
'I carried these eggs from a long way off, from inland to Arnhem Bay …'
Eggs, eggs, eggs; eggs she is carrying, swimming along.
She preens her feathers, and pulls at the lily foliage,
Drags at the lily leaves with her claws for food.
Swimming along, rippling the water among the lotus plants …
Backwards and forwards: she pulls at the foliage, swimming along, floating and eating.
This bird is taking her food, the lotus food in the clay pan,
At the place of the Dugong there, at the place of the Dugong's Tail …
Swimming along for food, floating, and rippling the water, there at the place of the Lilies.
Taking the lotus, the rounded roots and stalks of the lily; searching and eating there as she
    ripples the water.
'Because I have eggs, I give to my young the sound of the water.'

Splashing and preening herself, she ripples the water, among the lotus ...
Backwards and forwards, swimming along, rippling the water,
Floating along on the clay pan, at the place of the Dugong.

Song 7

People were diving here at the place of the Dugong ...
Here they were digging all around, following up the lily stalks,
Digging into the mud for the rounded roots of the lily,
Digging them out at that place of the Dugong, and of the Evening Star,
Pushing aside the water while digging, and smearing themselves with mud ...
Piling up the mud as they dug, and washing the roots clean.
They saw arm after arm there digging: people thick like the mist ...
The Shag woman too was there, following up the lily stalks.
There they saw arm after arm of the *'Mandʒikai* Sandfly clan,
Following the stalks along, searching and digging for food:
Always there together, those *'Mandʒikai* Sandfly people.
They follow the stalks of the lotus and lily, looking for food.
The lilies that always grow there at the place of the Dugong ...
At that clay pan, at the place of the Dugong, at the place of the lilies.

Song 8

Now the leech is swimming along ... It always lives there in the water ...
It takes hold of the leaves of the lily and pods of the lotus, and climbs up on to their stalks.
Swimming along and grasping hold of the leaves with its head ...
It always lives there in the water, and climbs up on to the people.
Always there, that leech, together with all its clan ...
Swimming along towards the trees, it climbs up and waits for people.
Hear it swimming along through the water, its head out ready to grasp us ...
Always living here and swimming along.
Because that leech is always there, for us, however it came there:
The leech that catches hold of those *'Mandʒikai* Sandfly people ...

Song 9

The prawn is there, at the place of the Dugong, digging out mud with its claws ...
The hard-shelled prawn living there in the water, making soft little noises.
It burrows into the mud and casts it aside, among the lilies ...
Throwing aside the mud, with soft little noises ...
Digging out mud with its claws at the place of the Dugong, the place of the Dugong's Tail ...
Calling the bone *'bukəlili*, the catfish *'bukəlili*, the frog *'bukəlili*, the sacred tree *'bukəlili* ...
The prawn is burrowing, coming up, throwing aside the mud, and digging ...
Climbing up on to the lotus plants and on to their pods ...

Song 10

Swimming along under the water, as bubbles rise to the surface, the tortoise moves in the
     swamp grass.
Swimming among the lily leaves and the grasses, catching them as she moves ...
Pushing them with her short arms. Her shell is marked with designs,
This tortoise carrying her young, in the clay pan, at the place of the Dugong ...

The short-armed *'Mararlpa* tortoise, with special arm-bands, here at the place of the
    Dugong ...
Backwards and forwards she swims, the short-armed one of the *'Mararlpa*, and
    the *'Dalwɔŋu*.
Carrying eggs about, in the clay pan, at the place of the Dugong ...
Her entrails twisting with eggs ...
Swimming along through the grass, and moving her patterned shell.
The tortoise with her young, and her special arm-bands,
Swimming along, moving her shell, with bubbles rising;
Throwing out her arms towards the place of the Dugong ...
This creature with the short arms, swimming and moving her shell;
This tortoise, swimming along with the drift of the water ...
Swimming with her short arms, at the place of the Dugong ...

Song 11

Wild-grape vines are floating there in the billabong:
Their branches, joint by joint, spreading over the water.
Their branches move as they lie, backwards and forwards,
In the wind and the waves, at the Moonlight clay pan, at the place of the Dugong ...
Men see them lying there on the clay pan pool, in the shade of the paperbarks:
Their spreading limbs shift with the wind and the water:
Grape vines with their berries ...
Blown backwards and forwards as they lie, there at the place of the Dugong.
Always there, with their hanging grapes, in the clay pan of the Moonlight ...
Vine plants and roots and jointed limbs, with berry food, spreading over the water.

Song 12

Now the New Moon is hanging, having cast away his bone:
Gradually he grows larger, taking on new bone and flesh.
Over there, far away, he has shed his bone: he shines on the place of the Lotus Root, and the
    place of the Dugong,
On the place of the Evening Star, of the Dugong's Tail, of the Moonlight clay pan ...
His old bone gone, now the New Moon grows larger;
Gradually growing, his new bone growing as well.
Over there, the horns of the old receding Moon bent down, sank into the place
    of the Dugong:
His horns were pointing towards the place of the Dugong.
Now the New Moon swells to fullness, his bone grown larger.
He looks on the water, hanging above it, at the place of the Lotus.
There he comes into sight, hanging above the sea, growing larger and older ...
There far away he has come back, hanging over the clans near Milingimbi ...
Hanging there in the sky, above those clans ...
'Now I'm becoming a big moon, slowly regaining my roundness ...'
In the far distance the horns of the Moon bend down, above Milingimbi,
Hanging a long way off, above Milingimbi Creek ...
Slowly the Moon Bone is growing, hanging there far away.
The bone is shining, the horns of the Moon bend down.
First the sickle Moon on the old Moon's shadow; slowly he grows,
And shining he hangs there at the place of the Evening Star ...
Then far away he goes sinking down, to lose his bone in the sea;

Diving towards the water, he sinks down out of sight.
The old Moon dies to grow new again, to rise up out of the sea.

Song 13

Up and up soars the evening Star, hanging there in the sky.
Men watch it, at the place of the Dugong and of the Clouds, and of the Evening Star,
A long way off, at the place of Mist, of Lilies and of the Dugong.
The Lotus, the Evening Star, hangs there on its long stalk, held by the Spirits.
It shines on that place of the Shade, on the Dugong place, and on to the Moonlight
    clay pan ...
The Evening Star is shining, back towards Milingimbi, and over the *'Wu:lamba* people ...
Hanging there in the distance, towards the place of the Dugong,
The place of the Eggs, of the Tree-Limbs-Rubbing-Together, and of the Moonlight
    clay pan ...
Shining on its short stalk, the Evening Star, always there at the clay pan, at the place of the
    Dugong.
There, far away, the long string hangs at the place of the Evening Star, the place of Lilies.
Away there at Milingimbi ... at the place of the Full Moon,
Hanging above the head of that *'Wɔnguri* tribesman:
The Evening Star goes down across the camp, among the white gum trees ...
Far away, in those places near Milingimbi ...
Goes down among the *'Ŋurulwulu* people, towards the camp and the gum trees,
At the place of the Crocodiles, and of the Evening Star, away towards Milingimbi ...
The Evening Star is going down, the Lotus Flower on its stalk ...
Going down among all those western clans ...
It brushes the heads of the uncircumcised people ...
Sinking down in the sky, that Evening Star, the Lotus ...
Shining on to the foreheads of all those headmen ...
On to the heads of all those Sandfly people ...
It sinks there into the place of the white gum trees, at Milingimbi.

Source: 'The moon bone', a Wonguri–Manjikai song cycle of north-eastern Arnhem Land, trans. Ronald M. Berndt, in *Oceania*, vol.XIX, no.1, 1948, songs 1–13, pp.22–50.

He's singing at Dhadutjmana

Milingimbi song

He's singing at Dhadutjmana
Of the evening sky at Dhurruru
Where trees and rocks are turning red
Where the sun has set.

Red light appearing
Above the hill at Wuypala
Streaming through the stringybark trees
Where the sun has set.

Kangaroo at Gulanydjarrtjarr
Swiftly he kills it
Fresh blood is flowing
Where the sun has set.

At Guthiliya, Guthiliya,
Blood runs into the evening sky
Raw flesh he's eating
Where the sun has set.

Source: Recording (cat. no.AM39A: VII–VIII) obtained by Alice Moyle at Milingimbi in 1963. Free translation by Alice Moyle based on a transcription and literal translation of the song by Beulah Lowe.

Form of taking possession of Port Essington and Melville and Bathurst Islands, 1824

Captain J.J. Gordon Bremer

Form of taking possession of Port Essington

The North Coast of New Holland or Australia, contained between the Meridian of 129° and 135° East of Greenwich, with all the Bays, Rivers, Harbours, Creeks, etc., in, and all the Islands laying off, were taken possession of, in the Name, and in the right of His Most excellent Majesty, George the IV, King of the United Kingdoms of Great Britain, and Ireland, and His Majesty's Colours hoisted at Port Essington, on the 20th September, 1824, by James John Gordon Bremer, Companion of the most honorable, Military Order of the Bath, Captain of His Majesty's Ship the Tamar, and Commanding Officer of His Majesty's Forces, employed on the said Coasts.

His Majesty's Colonial Brig Lady Nelson, and the British Ship Countess of Harcourt in Company.

Form of taking possession of Melville and Bathurst Islands

The North Coast of New Holland or Australia, contained between the Meridian of 129° and 135° East of Greenwich, with all the Bays, Rivers, Harbours, Creeks, etc., in and all the Islands laying off, were taken possession of, in the name and in the right of His Most Excellent Majesty George the IV, King of the United Kingdoms of Great Britain and Ireland, and His Majesty's Colours hoisted at Port Essington, on the 20th September, 1824, and at Melville and Bathurst Islands on the 26th September, 1824, by James John Gordon Bremer, Companion of the most honorable Military Order of the Bath, Captain of His Majesty's Ship the Tamar, and Commanding Officer of His Majesty's Forces, employed on the said Coasts.

His Majesty's Colonial Brig Lady Nelson, and the British Ship Countess of Harcourt in Company.

Source: Form of taking possession of Port Essington and Melville and Bathurst Islands, 20 & 26 September 1824, enclosures to letter from J. J. Gordon Bremer to Earl Bathurst, 11 November 1824, in *Historical Records of Australia*, series III, vol.5, Library Committee of Commonwealth Parliament, Sydney, 1922, pp.780–81.

Harbingers of an approaching revolution

John Lort Stokes

November 14 [1839]. — The morning broke, and we found ourselves apparently alone in the solitudes of the forest: no sound or sign indicated the presence of its more rightful proprietors. Did the savage so soon prepare to yield to the advancing movement of that hitherto fatal civilization before which his name, his race, nay, all traces of his rude existence may ere long pass into oblivion? or did the gathering of the night, and the apparent peaceful aspect of the morn, denote that one gallant struggle would be made ere a strange shout of triumph woke the silent echoes with the glorious name with which we had dignified our new discovery, and which throughout the world sounds as the appropriate title of the fair sovereign of its mightiest people?

A rapid walk brought us to our old bivouac by ten o'clock, without any thing of particular interest having occurred upon the route. We found only one boat at Reach Hopeless, Captain Wickham having gone down the river with the others in order to hasten the watering party …

We learnt from the party at the boat that a large body of the natives had been down watching their movements, and apparently intending if possible to surprise them. Though they had approached very near, they would not have been seen but for a shooting party, which got a view of them from an overlooking height, crawling along the ground with evident caution. They were probably the same party we had encountered higher up, and had traced our trail backwards, in order to see whence, and in what force we had entered their territory. Little did they imagine, as they gazed upon our small party and its solitary boat, that they had seen the harbingers of an approaching revolution in the fortunes of their country!

Source: John Lort Stokes, *Discoveries in Australia, with an Account of the Coasts and Rivers Explored During the Voyage of the HMS Beagle in the Years 1837–43*, vol.II, T. & W. Boone, London, 1846, pp.88–89.

The dawn of liberty, civilisation, and Christianity

John McDouall Stuart

Monday, 23rd April [1860], Centre. — Took Kekwick and the flag, and went to the top of the mount, but found it to be much higher and more difficult of ascent than I anticipated. After a deal of labour, slips, and knocks, we at last arrived on the top. It is quite as high as Mount Serle, if not higher. The view to the north is over a large plain of gums, mulga, and spinifex, with watercourses running through it. The large gum creek that we crossed winds round this hill in a north-east direction; at about ten miles it is joined by another. After joining they take a course more north, and I lost sight of them in the far-distant plain. To the north-north-east is the termination of the hills; to the north-east, east and south-east are broken ranges, and to the north-north-west the ranges on the west side of the plain termi-

Illustration of Central Mount Stuart, from Stuart's Journals *(1865). The British flag is just visible at the top of the mountain (centre background).*

nate. To the north-west are broken ranges; and to the west is a very high peak, between which and this place to the south-west are a number of isolated hills. Built a large cone of stones, in the centre of which I placed a pole with the British flag nailed to it. Near the top of the cone I placed a small bottle, in which there is a slip of paper, with our signatures to it, stating by whom it was raised. We then gave three hearty cheers for the flag, the emblem of civil and religious liberty, and may it be a sign to the natives that the dawn of liberty, civilization, and Christianity is about to break upon them. We can see no water from the top. Descended, but did not reach the camp till after dark. This water still continues, which makes me think there must certainly be more higher up. I have named the range 'John Range', after my friend and well-wisher, John Chambers, Esq., brother to James Chambers, Esq., one of the promoters of this expedition.

Source: William Hardman (ed.), *Explorations in Australia: The Journals of John McDouall Stuart, During the Years 1858–62*, 2nd edn, Saunders, Otley & Co., London, 1865, pp.165-6.

Captain Cook

Hobbles Daniyarri

Right /
Well, I'm speaking today /
I'm named — Hobbles Danayari
and I got a bit of troubling. /
Long way back beginning, I think
right back beginning.
I don't know but
this the biggest troubling /
Ah
when that Captain Cook been come from big England
and come through
down to Sydney Harbour …

Now Captain Cook didn't — givem fair go people
all over Australia today /
That before
he should have give him a fair go
askem people, Aboriginal people.
They own the Northern Territory.
Because Captain Cook should give them fair go whether he say 'good day'
whether he say 'hello'
that's be all right.
But my people
my people Aboriginal people they been fright for Captain Cook, he's a whitefellow /
He's a whitefellow and they been frighten, you know.
They been frighten and really
he should have been give him time
makem him — you know
quiet and askem him quiet time when him
want to try and askem him
whether he can
ask him for the — country
or — cross to see another people
Aboriginal people.
You know, he should have give it him a fair go.

Now when he been start to
knock [kill] my people up in the Sydney
that means he been start to clean [eradicate] my people.
Because Captain Cook
him been come very cheeky
you know.
He don't — he don't askem, make sure
or quieten him
You know
make it right.
And when that
Captain Cook been start and shootem from Sydney
right up,
right up to Darwin Harbour,
all over Australia,
see?
That's wrong.
That Captain Cook been do wrong.
He should tell them
to ask them fair go
whether — whether that Captain Cook listen to my people.
You know?

When him been start up come in
put him boat
into the Mindil beach pocket
and been get off.
And have a look around
see a couple of men there, Aboriginal people, old people.
And it start.
Two my people been look, 'Oh, that's whitefellow.'
They been frighten really
you know.
But if him been come, Captain Cook /
'hello' him
'good day' him
you know
and calm him down
till him — till him been want to get quiet
you know
my people, and he should have askem them.
Because
you can't hunt him like a dog.
No.
Because
that's the land for the Aboriginal people.
Because people on the Northern Territory
Aboriginal people.
Because I know
Captain Cook didn't give them a fair go for them my people.

Now I'm talking again, over.
Right
now — till we can have a friend
friend together now.
I'm speaking on now.
We're friends together —
because we own Australia
every one of them
no matter who
white and black.
We come together join in
whether we can
you know — take it mijelb [ourselves]
love mijelb [each other] one another
and cross-ways marriage
no matter what kind of marriage we can have them
because we own Australia
today
every one of them.
That be all right.
Make it more better
out of the,
out of that big trouble.
You know before
Captain Cook been making lot of cruel
you know.
Now
these days
these days we'll be friendly
we'll be love mijelb
we'll be mates
that be better
better for make that trouble.
Now we'll be come — join in
no matter who white and black or yellow
as far as there.

Source: Hobbles Daniyarri, 'Captain Cook', in Deborah Bird Rose, 'Remembrance', *Aboriginal History*, vol.13, nos 1–2, 1989, pp.138–43.

Too many Captain Cooks

Paddy Wainburranga & Joli Laiwonga

Captain Cook. This is his song. The whole story. This painting. Blankets ... materials ... they were all his things. That's the way we know from Rembarrnga side. We didn't know the new people. But everybody knew: too many Captain Cooks.

But from this painting old people used to sing for him. Nobody here was born then. It was the early days. From a long time ago. My grandfather hadn't been born. My grandfather's grandfather hadn't lived.

The first men knew him, because we've got the song (from them). We call the song *barrambarra*. It tells about everything that has come from Captain Cook.

Captain Cook. Nobody has seen the place of that sort of man. No. Olden days were his times. So we sing his song (like) olden days people.

Not from the days when my father died, or my uncle. But a long time ago when humans first came.

This is a new world now. No-one has seen Captain Cook, but everyone has seen his culture.

Who knows Captain Cook? Nobody has seen him. Captain Cook was around during the time of Satan. Everybody knows Captain Cook. Old people, not young people. You've got to have a lot of learning to know Captain Cook. More culture. Because I know from this song. I can sing it now for this bark painting. This is the way his song goes.

Nobody has seen this from my group before. No. Not from the Rembarrnga group.

Captain Cook and his wives — he only had two wives — he was born many years ago. That was from a long long time ago. Like a million years ago. More than that.

He was like Adam — Adam and Eve. But Adam and Eve were only 'half way' — Captain Cook was there first, before Adam and Eve.

The birds, the trees, developed at the same time. Captain Cook was a yirritja man, from the yirritja group.

Captain Cook was really a business man (involved with law and ceremony). All these people from the Rembarrnga side, from Warramirri side, Gupapyngu, Galpu, Dhalwangu, Balamumu, Gumatj, Nunggubuyu, all the yirritja people have a corroborree for him. From the earliest days. Captain Cook didn't do any wrong. Because people can't have a ceremony for him for nothing. Captain Cook didn't do any bad things.

When Captain Cook died yirritja people took it over. My mob (dhuwa) took over his song too. They call it *barrambarra* ... material stuff, blankets, calico. All the sort of stuff we have — it's got a song. We have a song for it in Rembarrnga for the yirritja group. Not dhuwa men. Not dhuwa people. We call it mother.

Captain Cook was never a bad man. Since he died we have had business (ceremony) for him. There's business for him at Groote Eylandt. I've gone into ceremony for him. It is only for men at Groote.

He was a very serious (important) man.

He was very kind to Aboriginal people in the early, early days, because Captain Cook went all over the world. He didn't interfere. He knew not to interfere when he left Mosquito Island.

Captain Cook wasn't a bad man. Rembarrnga people know that. I don't know about other places. We know his song from our brains.

So we know how Captain Cook used paddles in his boat. We didn't have paddles. Captain Cook made them. People know he had white man's power, white man's things. Blackfellas never had those things, never had any of those things. Axes, steel knives; all came from Captain Cook.

They knew this for a long time when the world was new. He covered up all the bad things. He came to the good law. But when the new Captain Cooks came over — bad things happened.

That's the way it is in Rembarrnga law, but I don't know about other places. It should be the same with everybody because they've all got a song.

This Captain Cook painting shows that all the material stuff: blankets, calico, shirt and trousers; all these things are in the Captain Cook song. According to the Rembarrnga group it is true. It's a yirritja song, and I call it mother.

Joli (Laiwonga) mob knows. Everybody has gone and seen Captain Cook's grave there, where he built that boat. They've got his story.

He always helped Aboriginal people. There were many millions of people in Australia and Captain Cook didn't interfere. He didn't interfere and make a war.

Captain Cook came from Mosquito Island, which is east of New Guinea. He came with with his two wives, a donkey and a nanny goat.

He came from Mosquito Island, that was where his family was: nobody knows how much family he had. We don't know. But we know him. We've got his song. We dance for him; we dance culture for him. Captain Cook he was really a mardayin man. We sings songs belonging to him; now we're taking over. Not just anyone is taking over, only Aboriginal people from Arnhem Land. East Arnhem Land and central Arnhem Land. We've taken over that business from Captain Cook.

Source: Paddy Wainburranga & Joli Laiwonga, 'Too Many Captain Cooks', trans. from Rembarrnga and Kriol by Paddy Wainburranga, Miliwanga Cameron, Penny McDonald & Chips Mackinolty, June 1987.

2 'Bare-headed to the sun': Early white voyages and exploration

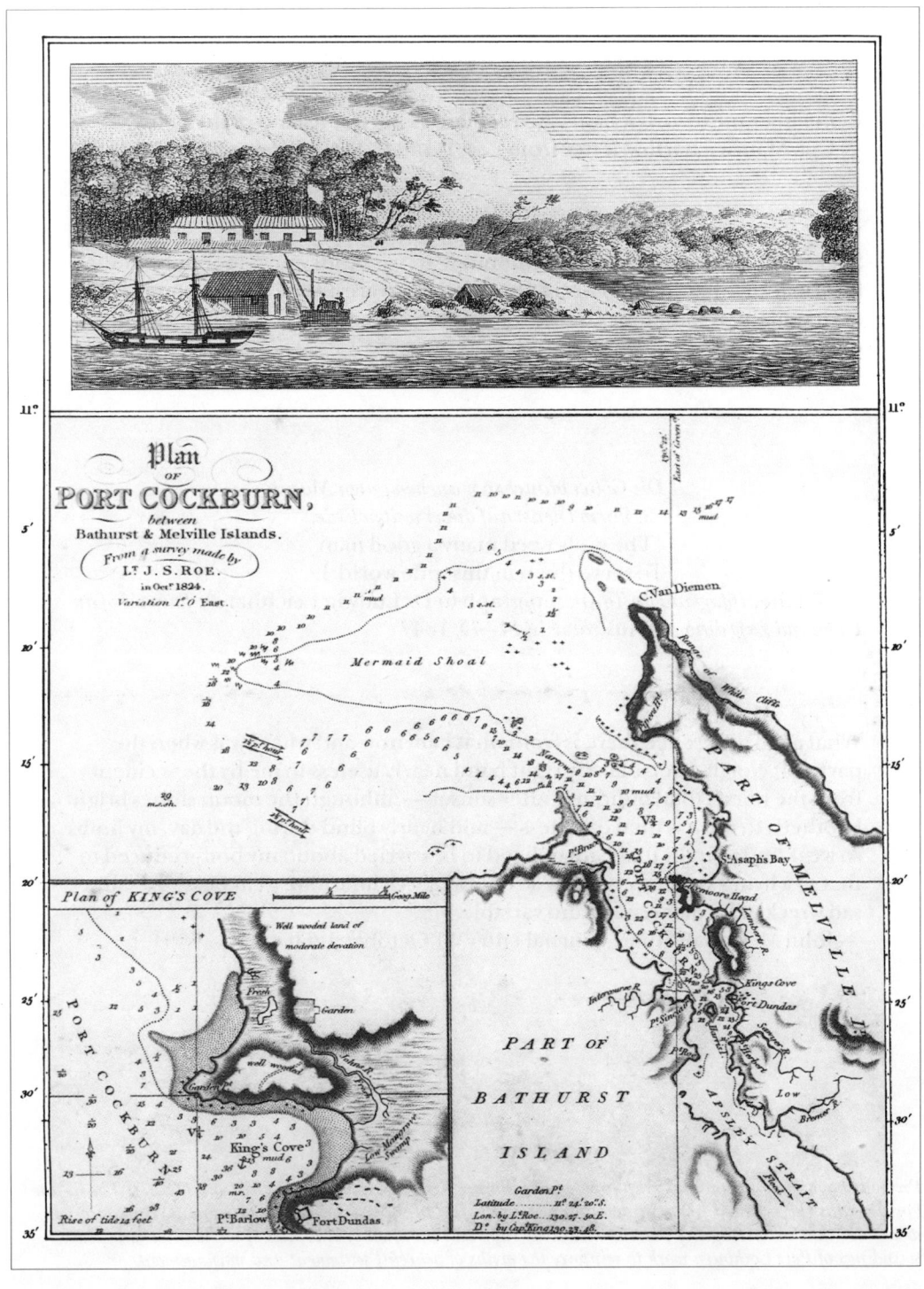

Thomas Morgan, a marine, having been for some time exposed bare-headed to the sun, was struck with a *coup-de-soleil* [sun stroke]; he was brought on board with Mr Whitewood, and died in a state of frenzy, the same night.
— Matthew Flinders, *A Voyage to Terra Australis, 1801, 1802 and 1803,* 1814

Remember me to any person who recollects I am in the land of the being.
— Cpt. Maurice Barlow, letter from Fort Dundas, Melville Island, 19 May 1825

Speaking of natives appearing without spears, reminds me to mention for the information of future explorers, that their arms are always near at hand. They even trail them sometimes between their toes, a fact which travellers should ever bear in mind.
— John Lort Stokes, *Discoveries in Australia 1837–43,* 1846

Die Götter brauchen manchen guten Mann
Zu ihrem Dienst auf dieser weiten Erde.
[The gods need many a good man
To serve them in this wide world.]
— Goethe, *Iphigenia on Tauris,* epigraph in Dr Ludwig Leichhardt, *Journal of an Overland Expedition in Australia 1844–45,* 1847

What a sad difference there is from what I am now and what I was when the party left North Adelaide! My right hand nearly useless to me by the accident from the horse; total blindness after sunset — although the moon shines bright to others, to me it is total darkness — and nearly blind during the day; my limbs so weak and painful that I am obliged to be carried about; my body reduced to that of a living skeleton, and my strength that of infantine weakness — a sad, sad wreck of former days. Wind variable.
— John McDouall Stuart, journal entry, 31 October 1860

Previous page: Illustration and map from Phillip Parker King's Narrative of a Survey *(1827). The ill-fated Fort Dundas (here viewed from Garden Point, Melville Island) appears deceptively tranquil. British society demanded that such images of order immediately supersede the often brutal facts of white invasion. The soundings of Port Cockburn work to reinforce the myths of peaceful settlement and management.*

Bamboo creek

Mark O'Connor

Hardly Australia, this creek lined with 50 foot sticks
of glistering organ-pipe. Sly Macassans brought
this first golden age! — all the rest were gilded frauds.
This plant put an end to shattered stone, offered instead
the flexible timber that could curve
to whatever end: from inch-an-hour tortures
to pagoda screens, and hovels; arch-bridges, cups,
flour-holders, twisted rope. (The shoots edible too.)
And spears. Then bows. And arrows.
A wood-ware supermarket to tempt the tribes
into the age of having.

— In those gold columns was the news
that no stone age could last, a hint
of Europe's and Asia's insistence.
Did some instinct make the black men root up
all offered fruits but the sour tamarind?
— in that pale hand full of seed was the death
of the Dreamtime, crash
of the mountain-ash forests,
stripping of the Bass Strait seals.
It struck. And Father Time
hoisting the slender cane across his shoulders
carried the past off bobbing.

Source: Mark O'Connor, 'Bamboo creek', *Northern Perspective*, vol.12, no.1, 1989, p.8.

The coming of the dingoes

Xavier Herbert

Although that northern part of the Continent of Australia which is called Capricornia was pioneered long after the southern parts, its unofficial early history was even more bloody than that of the others. One probable reason for this is that the pioneers had already had experience in subduing Aborigines in the South and hence were impatient of wasting time with people who they knew were determined to take no immigrants. Another reason is that the Aborigines were there more numerous than in the South and more hostile because used to resisting casual invaders from the near East Indies. A third reason is that the pioneers had difficulty in establishing permanent settlements, having several times to abandon ground they had won with slaughter and go slaughtering again to secure more. This abandoning of ground was due not to the hostility of the natives, hostile enough though they were, but to the violence of the climate, which was not to be withstood even by men so well equipped with lethal weapons and belief in the decency of their purpose as Anglo-Saxon builders of Empire.

The first white settlement in Capricornia was that of Treachery Bay — afterwards called New Westminster — which was set up on what was perhaps the most fertile and pleasant part of the coast and on the bones of half the Karrapillua Tribe. It was the resentment of the Karrapilluas to what probably seemed to them an inexcusable intrusion that was responsible for the choice of the name of Treachery Bay. After having been driven off several times with firearms, the tribe came up smiling, to all appearances unarmed and intending to surrender, but dragging their spears along the ground with their toes. The result of this strategy was havoc. The Karrapilluas were practically exterminated by uncomprehending neighbours into whose domains they were driven. The tribes lived in strict isolation that was rarely broken except in the cause of war. Primitive people that they were, they regarded their territorial rights as sacred.

When New Westminster was for the third time swept into the Silver Sea by the floods of the generous Wet Season, the pioneers abandoned the site to the crocodiles and jabiroos [sic] and devil-crabs, and went in search of a better. Next they founded the settlement of Princetown, on the mouth of what came to be called the Caroline River. In Wet Season the river drove them into barren hills in which it was impossible to live during the harsh Dry Season through lack of water. Later the settlements of Britannia and Port Leroy were founded. All were eventually swept into the Silver Sea. During Wet Season, which normally lasted for five months, beginning in November and slowly developing till the Summer Solstice, from which it raged till the Equinox, a good eighty inches of rain fell in such fertile places on the coast as had been chosen, and did so at the rate of from two to eight inches at a fall. As all these fertile places were low-lying, it was obviously impossible to settle on them permanently. In fact, as the first settlers saw it, the whole vast territory seemed never to be anything for long but either a swamp during Wet Season or a hard-baked desert during the Dry. During the seven months of a normal Dry Season never did a drop of rain fall and rarely did a cloud appear. Fierce suns and harsh hot winds soon dried up the lavished moisture.

It was beginning to look as though the land itself was hostile to anyone but the carefree nomads to whom the Lord gave it, when a man named Brittins Willnot found the site of what came to be the town of Port Zodiac, the only settlement of any size that ever stood permanently on all the long coastline, indeed the only one worthy of the name of Town ever to be set up in the whole vast territory. Capricornia covered an area of about half a million square miles. This site of Willnot's was elevated, and situated in a pleasantly unfertile region where the annual rainfall was only about forty inches. Moreover, it had the advantages of standing as a promontory on a fair-sized navigable harbour and of being directly connected with what came to be called Willnot Plateau, a wide strip of highland that ran right back to the Interior. When gold was found on the Plateau, Port Zodiac became a town.

The site of Port Zodiac was a Corroboree Ground of the Larrapuna Tribe, who left the bones of most of their number to manure it. They called it Mailunga, or the Birth Place, believing it to be a sort of Garden of Eden and apparently revering it. The war they waged to retain possession of this barren spot was perhaps the most desperate that whitemen ever had to engage in with an Australian tribe. Although utterly routed in the first encounter, they continued to harass the pioneers for months, exercising cunning that increased with their desperation. Then someone, discovering that they were hard-put for food since the warring had scared the game from their domains, conceived the idea of making friends with them and giving them several bags of flour spiced with arsenic. Nature is cruel. When dingoes come to a waterhole, the ancient kangaroos, not having teeth or ferocity sharp enough to defend their heritage, must relinquish it or die.

Thus Civilisation was at last planted permanently. However, it spread slowly, and did not take permanent root elsewhere than on the safe ground of the Plateau. Even the low-lying mangrove-cluttered farther shores of Zodiac Harbour remained untrodden by the feet of whitemen for many a year. And this was so with the whole maritime region, most of which, although surveyed from the sea and in parts penetrated and occupied for a while by explorers, remained in much the same state as always. Some of the inhabitants were perhaps amazed and demoralised, but still went on living in the way of old, quite unaware of the presumably enormous fact that they had become subjects of the British Crown.

That part of the coast called Yurracumbunga by the Aborigines, which lay about one hundred and fifty miles to the east of Port Zodiac, was first visited by a whiteman in the year 1885. By that time the inhabitants, having only heard tell of the invaders from survivors of the neighbouring tribe of Karrapillua, were come to regard whitemen rather as creatures of legend, or perhaps more rightly as monsters of legend, since they had heard enough about them to fear them greatly. When one of the monsters, in the shape of Captain Edward Krater, a trepang-fisher, suddenly materialised for them, they thought he was a devil come from the sun, because they first saw him in the ruddy light of dawn and he was carroty. Krater was a man of fine physique, and not quietly carroty as a man might be in these days of clean-shaved faces and close-clipped heads, but blazingly, that being a period when manliness was expressed with hair. When the Yurracumbungas discovered that he was mortal, they dubbed him Munichillu, or the Man of Fire.

Ned Krater wished to establish a base for his trepang-fishing on a certain little island belonging to the Yurracumbungas and called by them Arrikitarriyah, or the Gift of the Sea. This island lay within rifle-shot of the mainland and was well watered and wooded and stocked with game and sheltered from the roll of the ocean by the Tikkalalla Islands, which lay in an extensive group along the northern horizon. The tribe used the island at certain times as a Corroboree Ground. Krater had already visited it before he came into contact with the owners. They first saw him when, waking one morning from heavy sleep following a wild night of corroboree, they found his lugger drifting up the salt-water creek on which they were camped. He was standing on the deck in all his golden glory. They snatched up their arms and flew to cover. One of Krater's crew, who were natives of the Tikkalalla Islands and old enemies of the Yurracumbungas, told the ambuscade at the top of his voice who Krater was and what would happen if it was with hostile intent that they hid, then took up a rifle and with a volley of shots set the echoes ringing and the cockatoos yelling and the hearts of the Yurracumbungas quaking. Krater then went ashore. After spending some hours sneaking about and peeping and listening to and occasionally answering the assurances shouted from time to time by Krater's men, the tribe came back shyly to their gunyahs, among which the Man of Fire had pitched a tent.

Thenceforth till a misunderstanding arose, the Yurracumbungas stayed in the camp, staring at Krater and his strange possessions, and learning from his men all they could tell about whitemen, who were, it seemed, not mere raiders like the brownmen who used sometimes to come to them from the North, but supermen who had come to stay and rule. And they learnt a little about shooting with rifles and catching fish with nets and dynamite and making fires by magic, and came to understand why witnessing such things had disorganised and demoralised and vanquished tribes of whom the islanders spoke. As the islanders said — How could one ever boast again of prowess with spear and kylie after having seen what could be done with rifle and dynamite? Far from hating the invader, the Yurracumbungas welcomed him, thinking that he would become one of them and teach them his magic arts.

The tribes of the locality were divided into family sections, or hordes. When a man or men of one horde visited another, it was the custom to allow them temporary use of such of the womenfolk as they were entitled to call wife by their system of marriage. Because they regarded Krater as a guest and a qualified person, the Yurracumbungas did not mind his asking for the comeliest of their lubras, though they did not offer him one, perhaps because they thought him above wanting one. But they objected strongly when his black crew asked for the same privilege. The islanders were definitely unqualified according to the laws. The granting of such a privilege to them would mean violation of the traditions, the weakening of their system, the demoralisation of their youth. Thus the Yurracumbungas argued. The islanders said that the old order had passed, and to prove it, one of them seized a lubra and ravaged her. The violent quarrel that resulted was settled by Krater, who hurled himself into the mob, bellowing and firing his revolver. Then Krater ordered the Yurracumbungas to give his men what they wanted.

The Yurracumbungas were struck dumb, appalled by their impotence. Night fell. They sat by their fires, staring at Krater and his men. They stared long after Krater had retired to his tent, long after they had relaxed to their own mattresses of bark. Hours passed. All of Krater's men, except two who dozed over rifles before the tent, fell asleep, gorged on a great meal of fish.

The headman of the horde was Kurrinua. He had argued fiercely against violation of the laws. He was a man as big and hairy as Krater. In the middle of the night he nudged the man next to him and whispered. His neighbour passed the whisper on. Before long the whole camp knew of his intention. No one stirred till the tip of the old moon appeared above the bush and splashed the inky creek with silver. Then the man next to Kurrinua crawled without a sound across the clearing of the scrub.

A tiny casuarina nut, shot out of the scrub, struck one of the dozing guards and roused him. He looked about. The camp was silent but for snores and the sigh of the wind in the trees. Then a slight sound in the scrub drew the guard's attention. He listened intently. Again he heard it. Tiny crackling as of a foot treading stealthily on leaves. He rose, and with the movement roused his mate, who whispered. Both listened, heard a peculiar pattering sound, and went, rifle in hand, with backs turned to the camp, to investigate. Louder crackling. Kurrinua and young Impalui rose with stones in hands and sped towards the guards like shadows. The guards were knocked senseless without a sound. The horde rose to knees, women and children and ancients ready to fly, warriors in arms. Kurrinua and Impalui snatched up the rifles, crept to the tent. Kurrinua was crouching at the flap of the tent with rifle raised when — BANG! — a bullet tore through his body, through the tent, crashed into the fire. Impalui had fired accidentally. Kurrinua fell into the tent.

Uproar! Spears whizzed. Rifles crashed. Men roared and howled. The horde rushed, fought fiercely for a moment, wavered, turned and fled. A few of the islanders rushed to the tent, which was collapsed and sprawling about like a landed devil-fish. They pounced on it and dragged it clear of the men beneath, dragged Kurrinua free of Krater's grip.

Kurrinua rolled over and over like a sea-urchin in a gale, got free of clutching hands and kicking feet, rose, and with blood spurting from his back and belly, plunged into the scrub, followed by a hail of bullets. His pursuers lost him. They spread, passed within a yard of where he lay with thigh-bone snapped by a bullet. He crawled towards the isthmus that lay between the creek and sea, bent on reaching the canoes. He heard cries and shots as other fugitives were found. He was in sandy hillocks out of the shelter of the scrub when the hunters, now carrying torches, rushed on to the beach. He rolled into a hollow and buried himself to the neck.

The night passed, slowly for the hunters, all too swiftly for the hunted. No hope now of escaping by canoe. The hunters had dragged the vessels high. But Kurrinua might swim if he could not walk, swim by way of the sea to the passage and the mainland. Surely he had less to fear from crocodiles than from Munichillu and his men. Still he dared not leave the hollow while the hunters prowled the beach, because they would find the wide track of his crawling before he could reach the creek. They splashed along the water's edge, crashed through the scrub, crept among the hillocks, never went far away.

The dark creek silvered. The hunters' torches paled. Birds stirred in the bush. A jabiroo flew in from the sea on great creaking wings, swerved with a swish and a croak at sight of the hunters. Jabiroos were gathering at the Ya-impitulli Billabong for the nesting.

The Nesting of the Storks. It was the time of the great Corroboree of the Circumcision, for which the men of Yurracumbunga were gathering.

Swiftly the sky lost its stars and the scrub found individuality. Footsteps. A shout when they found the blood and the track of crawling. Footsteps pattering. Kurrinua looked his last at the gilded skyline. Another shout. They danced around him, pointing, kicking sand in his eyes. Soon Munichillu came, and with him the light of day, as though that too belonged to the like of him. At his appearance the east flamed suddenly, so that the sand was gilded and fire flashed in his beard. He looked at the face in the sand, grunted, raised his revolver.

Kurrinua's heart beat painfully. His eyes grew hot. The pain of his wounds, which he had kept in check for hours by the power he was bred to use, began to throb. But he did not move a hair. He had been trained to look upon death fearlessly. To do so was to prove oneself a warrior worthy of having lived. His mind sang the Death Corroboree — Ee-yah, ee-yah, ee-tullyai — O mungallinni wurrigai— ee-tukkawunni —

BANG! Kurrinua gasped, heaved out of the sand, writhed, shuddered, died. Ned Krater spat. In his opinion he had done no wrong. He did not know why the savages had attacked him. He thought only of their treachery, which to such as he was intolerable as it was natural to such as they.

Source: Xavier Herbert, *Capricornia*, Publicist Press, Sydney, 1938, ch.1.

North coast, Blue-Mud Bay

Matthew Flinders

Friday, 21 January 1803. — A party of men was sent to cut wood on the following morning, and another to haul the seine; the botanists also landed, and I went to observe the latitude and take bearings from the west end of the island; every person was armed, for marks of feet had been perceived, so newly imprinted on the sand, that we expected to meet with Indians. After accomplishing my objects, I walked with a small party round the north-west end of the island; and then returned over the high land, through a most fatiguing brush wood, towards the wooders and the boat. On clearing the wood, four or five Indians were seen on a hill, half a mile to the left, and some of the wooding party advancing towards them. The sight of us seemed to give the natives an apprehension of being surrounded, for they immediately ran; but our proceeding quietly down to the boat, which I did in the hope that our people might bring on an interview, appeared to satisfy them. The scientific gentlemen accompanied me on board to dinner; and I learned from Mr. Westall, that whilst he was taking a sketch at the east end of the island, a canoe, with six men in it, came over from Woodah. He took little notice of them until, finding they saw him and landed not far off, he thought it prudent to retreat with his servant to the wooding party. The natives followed pretty smartly after him; and when they appeared on the brow of the hill, Mr. Whitewood, the master's mate, and some of his wooders went to meet them in a friendly manner. This was at the time that the appearance of my party caused them to run; but when we left the shore they had stopped, and our people were walking gently up the hill.

The natives had spears, but from the smallness of their number, and our men being armed, I did not apprehend any danger; we had, however, scarcely reached the ship, when the report of muskets was heard; and the people were making signals and carrying some one down to the boat, as if wounded or killed. I immediately despatched two armed boats to their assistance, under the direction of the master; with orders, if he met with the natives, to be friendly and give them presents, and by no means to pursue them into the wood. I suspected, indeed, that our people must have been the aggressors; but told the master, if the Indians had made a wanton attack, to bring off their canoe by way of punishment; intending myself to take such steps on the following day, as might be found expedient.

At five o'clock Mr. Whitewood was brought on board, with four spear wounds in his body. It appeared that the natives, in waiting to receive our men, kept their spears ready, as ours had their muskets. Mr. Whitewood, who was foremost, put out his hand to receive a spear which he supposed was offered; but the Indian, thinking perhaps that an attempt was made to take his arms, ran the spear into the breast of his supposed enemy. The officer snapped his firelock, but it missed, and he retreated to his men; and the Indians, encouraged by this, threw several spears after him, three of which took effect. Our people attempted to fire, and after some time two muskets went off, and the Indians fled; but not without taking away a hat which had been dropped. Thomas Morgan, a marine, having been some time exposed bare-headed to the sun, was struck with a *coup-de-soleil*; he was brought on board with Mr. Whitewood, and died in a state of frenzy, the same night.

So soon as the master had learned what had happened, he went round in the whale boat to the east end of the island, to secure the canoe; and forgetting the orders I had given him, sent Mr. Lacy with the wooders overland, to intercept the natives on that side. Their searches were for some time fruitless; but in the dusk of the evening three Indians were seen by the wooders, and before they could be intercepted had pushed off in the canoe. A sharp fire was commenced after them; and before they got out of reach, one fell and the others leaped out and dived away. A seaman who gave himself the credit of having shot the native, swam off to the canoe, and found him lying dead at the bottom, with a straw hat on his head which he recognised to be his own. Whilst displaying this in triumph, he upset the ticklish vessel, and the body sunk; but the canoe was towed to the shore, and the master returned with it at nine o'clock.

Saturday, 22 January 1803. — I was much concerned at what had happened, and greatly displeased with the master for having acted so contrary to my orders; but the mischief being unfortunately done, a boat was sent in the morning to search for the dead body, the painter being desirous of it to make a drawing, and the naturalist and surgeon for anatomical purposes. The corpse was found lying at the water's edge, not lengthwise, as a body washed up, but with the head on shore and the feet touching the surf. The arms were crossed under the head, with the face downward, in the posture of a man who was just able to crawl out of the water and die; and I very much apprehend this to have been one of the two natives who had leaped out of the canoe, and were thought to have escaped. He was of the middle size, rather slender, had a prominent chest, small legs, and similar features to the inhabitants of other parts of this country; and he appeared to have been circumcised! A musket ball had passed through the shoulder blade, from behind; and penetrating upwards, had lodged in the neck.

The canoe was of bark, but not of one piece, as at Port Jackson; it consisted of two pieces, sewed together lengthwise, with the seam on one side; the two ends were also sewed up, and made tight with gum. Along each gunwale was lashed a small pole; and these were spanned together in five places, with creeping vine, to preserve the shape, and to strengthen the canoe. Its length was thirteen and a half, and the breadth two and a half feet; and it seemed capable of carrying six people, being larger than those generally used at Port Jackson.

It does not accord with the usually timid character of the natives of Terra Australis, to suppose the Indians came over from Isle Woodah for the purpose of making an attack; yet the circumstance of their being without women or children, — their following so briskly after Mr. Westall, — and advancing armed to the wooders, all imply that they rather sought than avoided a quarrel. I can account for this unusual conduct only by supposing, that they might have had differences with, and entertained no respectful opinion of the Asiatic visitors, of whom we had found so many traces, some almost in sight of this place.

The body of Thomas Morgan who died so unfortunately, was this day committed to the deep with the usual ceremony; and the island was named after him, *Morgan's Island*.

Source: Matthew Flinders, *A Voyage to Terra Australis; Undertaken for the Purpose of Completing the Discovery of that Vast Country, and Prosecuted in the Years 1801, 1802, and 1803, in His Majesty's Ship the Investigator*, vol.II, G. & W. Nicol, London, 1814, pp.195–8.

Our theodolite stand and Mr Cunningham's insect-net

Captain Phillip Parker King

16–17 May 1818. — The next morning we passed round Cape Van Diemen; and in the evening anchored off a tabular-shaped hill that formed the south end of a sandy bay. It was dark when we anchored: the next morning we found that we had anchored in the mouth of a very considerable river-like opening, the size of which inspired us with the flattering hope of having made an important discovery, for as yet we had no idea of the insularity of Melville Island.

The table-shaped hill, near our anchorage, was named Luxmore Head, and the bay to the north was called St. Asaph's, in compliment to the Right Reverend the Lord Bishop of that diocese.

The day being Sunday our intention was, after taking bearings from the summit of Luxmore Head, to delay our further proceeding until the next morning, but the circumstances that occurred kept us so much on the alert, that it was any thing but a day of rest. Having landed at the foot of the hill we ascended its summit, but found it so thickly wooded as to deprive us of the view we had anticipated; but, as there were some openings in the trees through which a few distant objects could be distinguished, we made preparations to take their bearings, and while the boat's crew were landing the theodolite, our party were amusing themselves on the top of the hill.

Suddenly however, but fortunately before we had dispersed, we were surprised by natives, who, coming forward armed with spears, obliged us very speedily to retreat to the boat; and in the *sauve qui peut* [each person for themselves, a stampede] sort of way in which we ran down the hill, at which we have frequently since laughed very heartily, our theodolite stand and Mr. Cunningham's insect-net were left behind, which they instantly seized upon. I had fired my fowling-piece at an iguana just before the appearance of the natives, so that we were without any means of defence; but, having reached the boat without accident, where we had our musquets ready, a parley was commenced for the purpose of recovering our losses. After exchanging a silk-handkerchief for a dead bird, which they threw into the water for us to pick up, we made signs that we wanted fresh water, upon which they directed us to go round the point, and upon our pulling in that direction, they followed us, skipping from rock to rock with surprising dexterity and speed. As soon as we reached the sandy beach, on the north side of Luxmore Head, they stopped and invited us to land, which we should have done, had it not been that the noises they made soon collected a large body of natives, who came running from all directions to their assistance; and, in a short time, there were twenty-eight or thirty natives assembled. After a short parley with them, in which they repeatedly asked for axes by imitating the action of chopping, we went on board, intimating to them our intention of returning with some, which we would give to them upon the

'Interview with the natives of St Asaph's Bay, Melville Island', Phillip Parker King's own sketch in his Narrative *(1827). The 'interview' site has obviously been carefully chosen to ensure the option of escape.*

restoration of the stand, which they immediately understood and assented to. The natives had three dogs with them.

On our return to the beach, the natives had again assembled, and shouted loudly as we approached. Besides the whale boat, in which Mr. Bedwell was stationed with an armed party ready to fire if any hostility commenced, we had our jolly-boat, in which I led the way with two men, and carried with me two tomahawks and some chisels. On pulling near the beach the whole party came down and waded into the water towards us; and, in exchange for a few chisels and files, gave us two baskets, one containing fresh water and the other was full of the fruit of the sago-palm, which grows here in great abundance. The basket containing the water was conveyed to us by letting it float on the sea, for their timidity would not let them approach us near enough to place it in our hands; but that containing the fruit, not being buoyant enough to swim, did not permit of this method, so that, after much difficulty, an old man was persuaded to deliver it. This was done in the most cautious manner, and as soon as he was sufficiently near the boat he dropped, or rather threw the basket into my hand and immediately retreated to his companions, who applauded his feat by a loud shout of approbation. In exchange for this I offered him a tomahawk, but his fears would not allow him to come near the boat to receive it. Finding nothing could induce the old man to approach us a second time, I threw it towards him, and upon his catching it the whole tribe began to shout and laugh in the most extravagant way. As soon as they were quiet we made signs for the theodolite stand, which, for a long while, they would not understand; at one time they pretended to think by our pointing towards it, that we meant some spears that were lying near a tree, which they immediately removed: the stand was then taken up by one of their women, and upon our pointing to her, they feigned to think that she was the object of our wishes, and immediately left a female standing up to her middle in the water and retired to some distance to await our proceedings. On pulling towards the woman, who, by the way, could not have been selected by them either for her youth or beauty, she frequently repeated the words 'Ven aca, Ven aca', accompanied with an invitation to land; but, as we approached, she retired towards the shore; when suddenly two natives, who had slowly walked towards us, sprang into the water and made towards the boat with surprising celerity, jumping at each step entirely out of the sea, although it was so deep as to reach their thighs. Their intention was evidently to seize the remaining tomahawk which I had been endeavouring to exchange for the stand, and the foremost had reached within two or three yards of the boat, when I found it necessary, in order to prevent his approach, to threaten to strike him with a wooden club, which had the desired effect. At this moment one of the natives took up the stand, and upon our pointing at him, they appeared to comprehend our object; a consultation was held over the stand which was minutely examined; but, as it was mounted with brass and, perhaps on that account, appeared to them more valuable than a tomahawk, they declined giving it up, and gradually dispersed; or, rather, pretended so to do, for a party of armed natives was observed to conceal themselves under some mangrove bushes near the beach, whilst two canoes were plying about near at hand to entice our approach; the stratagem, however, did not succeed, and we lay off upon our oars for some time without making any movement. Soon afterwards the natives, finding that we had no intention of following them, left their canoes, and performed a dance in the water, which very conspicuously displayed their great muscular power: the dance consisted chiefly of the performers leaping two or three times successively out of the sea, and then violently moving their legs so as to agitate the water into a foam for some distance around them, all the time shouting loudly and laughing immoderately; then they would run through the water for eight or ten yards and perform again; and this was repeated over and over as long as the dance lasted. We were all thoroughly disgusted with them, and felt a degree of distrust that could not be conquered. The men were more muscular and better formed than any we had before seen; they were daubed over with a yellow pigment, which was the colour of the neighbouring cliff, their hair was long and curly, and appeared to be clotted with a whitish paint. During the time of our parley the natives had their spears close at hand, for those who were in the water had them floating near them, and those who were on the beach had them either buried in the sand, or carried them between their toes, in order to deceive us and to appear unarmed; and in this they succeeded, until one of them was detected, when we were pulling towards the woman, by his stooping down and picking up his spear.

Finding that we had no chance of recovering our loss, we returned on board, when the natives also withdrew from the beach, and did not afterwards shew themselves.

Source: Phillip Parker King, *Narrative of a Survey of the Intertropical and Western Coasts of Australia, Performed Between the Years 1818 and 1822*, vol.1, John Murray, London, 1827, pp.109–15.

Geographical memoir of Melville Island, 1826–28

Major John Campbell

At the beginning of August, 1826, His Excellency Lieutenant-General Darling, then Governor of New South Wales, was pleased to appoint me Commandant of Melville Island and directed me to embark on board the Colonial schooner Isabella, with a detachment of troops, some convicts, and various stores, as well as live stock, and to proceed with all despatch through Torres Straits to relieve Captain Barlow and his detachment. On the 19th August we left Port Jackson, and reached Melville Island on the 19th September. The officers and men who had formed the settlement, and had been there about two years, were rejoiced to find that a relief had arrived for them; they gave us a discouraging account of the oppressiveness of the climate, the scarcity of vegetables, the deficiency of fresh meat, the almost impossibility of procuring fish, the dreariness of the situation — (never having been visited by any other than the two small colonial vessels already mentioned as sent from Sydney with supplies, by a man-of-war's boat, which came in for a few hours, whilst the man-of-war, the Slaney, remained outside the reefs, about eighteen miles off; and I believe also that H.M. ship Larne had touched there) — the hostility of the natives, and many other mortifications which conveyed but a gloomy picture of the settlement. I was, however, fortunately not of a temperament to be cast down by these accounts; but on the contrary rejoiced that I had been placed in so novel and interesting a situation, and looked forward with a pleasing anticipation that patience, exertion, and industry would soon bring the settlement to answer the intentions of Government in having formed it ...

Diseases. — During the period I was on Melville Island, we kept a regular hospital register-book, in which every case admitted into the hospital was entered daily, and the disease, treatment, and duration of the patient's illness carefully inserted. I had an opportunity of daily examining this register, and had it copied every morning into the register kept in my own office, for the purpose of transmitting to the colonial secretary at Sydney; therefore, although I cannot exactly carry in my memory the number of deaths, I perfectly recollect the prevailing diseases, most of which I find noted in my journal, as well as many of the deaths. The prevailing diseases were — intermittent, acute, and typhus fevers, constipation of the bowels, vertigo (frequent), dysentery, diarrhoea, rheumatism, scurvy, and nectalopia; the latter disease was very common. The cases of typhus and acute fever appeared at the beginning of the wet season; and when the winds were variable during that period, many were suddenly seized with sickness, violent griping, and delirium. We could not account for the prevalence of nectalopia, or, as it is sometimes called, moon-blindness. Salt meat was certainly generally issued to every person, but they had, besides, a wholesome proportion of flour, rice, or bread, with vinegar, tea, sugar, and a small quantity of vegetables; nor were the settlers exposed to any extraordinary glare from sand or water, and many who had this complaint used very little of their salt meat. Even when fresh meat was issued, this disease prevailed to a considerable extent.

With respect to the scurvy, it appeared to me to be an endemic disease arising from some particular local cause; with new comers, it might be occasioned by a removal from a cool climate to a heated and damp one. This disease only appeared generally at the settlement of Fort Dundas, shortly after its establishment in 1824. The constant use of salt provisions, without vegetables, hard labour during the wet season, and the excessive heat of that season, may have engendered it; and notwithstanding the attention and endeavours of an intelligent and experienced surgeon (Dr. Turner) to prevent and afterwards arrest it, the disease made great progress until the end of 1825, or beginning of 1826. When lime juice was obtained, and vegetables became more plentiful, the disease then subsided. There were, however, several cases of scurvy during 1826, 1827, and 1828, although the utmost caution was taken to guard against it by great attention to cleanliness, use of vegetables, and frequent issues of fresh and preserved meats, pickles, and vinegar. When the first detachment of troops were relieved in 1826, those who replaced them had spirits mixed into grog issued to them every day (the former detachment had no spirits issued); and amongst these very few cases of scurvy appeared, although they lived generally upon salt provisions for the first year, with a very small occasional addition of vegetables, probably once a week.

When the settlement was established in Raffles Bay in 1827, on the north coast of New Holland, and in the same parallel with Fort Dundas, at which place no spirits or wine was issued either to the military or convicts, the scurvy broke out and spread in a rapid and alarming degree, both amongst the soldiers and prisoners.

The site of the settlement and its neighbourhood was dry; the disease occurred during the dry season. The establishment consisted of young healthy men, direct from Sydney, and many of them only a few months from England. The complaint made its appearance among the settlers in six or seven weeks after landing: their diet consisted of a small quantity of salt meat, and occasionally fish (which was caught close to the settlement), with flour, sugar, and tea or coffee. When the malady had attacked and rendered incapable of exertion two-thirds of the settlement, spirits, lime juice and sugar made into punch, was issued to all the worst cases, and grog or wine issued to the military. It immediately remitted in virulence, and ultimately nearly or entirely disappeared. I saw all the sufferers myself, having had occasion to go to Raffles Bay; and from my observations and inquiries, I certainly thought that the scurvy there, as well as on Melville Island, was endemic, and more dependent on climate and local causes than diet.

Considering the consequences of the climate of Melville Island, during my residence there and that of my predecessor, and knowing the unremitting attention that was paid, and measures adopted, in order to preserve health throughout the settlement during my command, I must pronounce it to partake more of the character of an unhealthy than a healthy climate. I should not recommend invalids to go there during any period of the year to be restored to health, from any part of the world; although from May to September, healthy people may continue in the enjoyment of health with rational care; but from the end of September to May, few can escape some attack or other illness. The climate, after a year's residence, is extremely debilitating to Europeans; but on the whole, with proper precautions, it does not often engender any fatal complaint ...

In disposition they [the native inhabitants of Melville Island] are revengeful, prone to stealing, and in their attempts to commit depredations show excessive cunning, dexterity, arrangement, enterprise, and courage. They are affectionate towards their children, and display strong feelings of tenderness when separated from their families; they are also very sensitive to any thing like ridicule. They are good mimics, have a facility in catching up words, and are gifted with considerable observation. When they express joy, they jump about and clap their hands violently upon their posteriors; and in showing contempt, they turn their back, look over the shoulder, and give a smack upon the same part with their hand. In the construction of their canoes, spears, and waddies, they evince much ingenuity, although the workmanship is rough from the want of tools; they are expert swimmers, and dive like ducks. They show no desire whatever for strange ornaments or trinkets; they are polite enough to accept of them without any expression of astonishment or curiosity, but very soon afterwards take an opportunity of slyly dropping them, or throwing them away. The only articles they seemed to covet were hatchets and other cutting tools; but still, when they could steal, they carried off every thing they could lay hold of. As long as we occupied the island, the natives were extremely shy and cautious in all their communications with us; they never intrusted themselves in our power; and notwithstanding my utmost efforts by acts of kindness and forbearance to gain their confidence, and convince them that we desired to be on friendly terms, I found it utterly impossible to accomplish this desirable object. Previous to my arrival they had committed murder, various depredations, and daring acts of violence. They had at length been fired upon whilst committing acts of outrage; and from all my inquiries I believe they had been the first aggressors, by throwing spears. When I assumed the command, I was extremely anxious to court their friendship, as without it, with our limited numbers and means, we never could become acquainted with all the resources of the island, or make them of available use to us: I therefore prevented any of the military or prisoners from putting themselves in contact with the natives without my presence or orders; I allowed no arms to be taken out except by those on whom I could depend, and strictly enjoined that they should only be used against the natives in self-defence, and when by the laws of England it would be justifiable. I feel confident, also, that those orders were strictly attended to; but notwithstanding they continued until the last day distrustful, if not even determinedly hostile. They put two gentlemen of the settlement, one soldier and one of the prisoners, to death, and wantonly wounded several others. During my time we were obliged to fire at them several times; we never knew of any having been killed, although in one or two instances they were wounded; they might have died, and the spirit of revenge might have excited them to other acts of violence. There was a curious inconsistency in their conduct: on one day they would appear good-humoured and friendly, and allow individuals of our settlement to pass unmolested through extended lines of them, and probably on the following day would throw their spears at any individual they could surprise by stealing upon him.

Source: Major John Campbell, 'Geographical memoir of Melville Island and Port Essington, 1826–28', *Journal of the Royal Geographical Society of London,* May 1834, pp.133, 149–51, 153–4.

Any act of cruelty or outrage against the natives

Colonial Secretary Alexander Macleay, letter to Captain Collett Barker

Colonial Secretary's Office,
Sydney,
14 August, 1828.

Sir,

The accompanying is a copy of a Letter, addressed to the late Commandant of the Settlement at Fort Wellington, on the subject of certain proceedings which took place there in the Month of December, 1827.

Captain Smyth deeming it advisable that, if possible, one of the Aboriginal Natives should be taken alive, and brought into the Camp, with double view of conciliating him by kind treatment, and keeping him as a hostage for the good behaviour of the others, offered a Reward of £5, Five Pounds, for the Capture of one, and permitted three Soldiers and two Convicts to go out, armed, for this express purpose. It appears that they fell in with a considerable number of Natives, fired in among them with Slugs, and wounded, at least, one Man and a Woman, with two Children in her Arms, so severely as to prevent their escape. The Man they afterwards put to death, conceiving themselves unable to remove him to the Camp in the feeble state in which he then was. The Woman they endeavoured to take Prisoner, and in resisting this, herself and one of her Children were killed. The other Child, the Soldiers took home.

On receiving the Report of these transactions, the Governor commanded the accompanying Letter to be addressed to Captain Smyth, and a Copy of it is now transmitted to you, that you may be aware of His Excellency's sentiments on the subject, in whose opinion, although every one is undoubtedly warranted in opposing any hostility on the part of the Natives by force, nothing can justify the conduct of the party on the occasion in question.

His Excellency has deemed it unadvisable to take any public Notice of the matter at the present moment; but He directs that you will use every means and opportunity of inculcating on the People at the Settlement generally, the danger they will incur by the Commission of any act of Cruelty or Outrage against the Natives. Nor can he express the surprise He has felt at the circumstances of Slugs having been used by the Soldiers, which he desires you will immediately put a stop to. I have, &C.,

ALEXR. MACLEAY.

Source: Letter from Alexander Macleay, Colonial Secretary of New South Wales, to Captain Collett Barker of the 39th Regiment [and last commandant (1827–29) of Raffles Bay], 14 August 1828, in *Historical Records of Australia*, series III, vol.6, Library Committee of Commonwealth Parliament, Sydney, 1923, p.183.

Character and manners of the Aborigines of New Holland

Thomas Braidwood Wilson

Although it may seem rather paradoxical, yet I do not hesitate to say, that the natives, far from being such untameable savages as originally represented, are, in reality, a mild and merciful race of people. They appeared to be fond of their wives and children; at least, they talked of them with much apparent affection. They have frequently interposed their good offices in preventing the soldiers' children from being chastised: I have seen them run between the mother and child, and beg the former to desist from her (as it appeared to them) unnatural conduct, in punishing her own offspring.

They are, like all uncivilized people, very irascible, but easily pacified; in short, they require to be managed just like children. They were easily taught to distinguish conventional right from wrong, and many instances occurred, which proved their aptitude in this respect.

'Dance of the Aborigines of Raffles Bay', *illustration in Thomas Braidwood Wilson's* Narrative of a Voyage Around the World *(1835). Wilson envisaged an integrated, harmonious community; his graphics were selected accordingly.*

Miago, after having become honest himself, once detected one of his companions endeavouring to secrete a spoon, while they were about to partake of some rice prepared for them[1]; — provoked by this ungrateful behaviour, he instantly took it from the delinquent, and sent him away, without permitting him to have any share of the food.

On first visiting the settlement, a native would invariably pilfer anything that came in his way that he could secrete, but the article was always brought back by those who knew that such conduct was not tolerated by their civilized visitors.

They also soon learned to place confidence in a person whose word was to be depended on. Some of our people acted, perhaps, in rather a reprehensible manner, by promising the natives a *mambrual* (or some other present), merely to get rid of their importunities, without any intention of performing their promise, thinking the natives would forget the circumstance; but, in this supposition, they were completely deceived, being invariably and pertinaciously reminded of their promise, and the natives looked on them as not to be trusted in future; — on the contrary, they placed implicit reliance in those who, having given a promise, performed it punctually.

The chief objects of their desire were tomahawks, large nails, and iron hoops; but, in the progress of time, they took a fancy to various articles of dress. To obtain a shirt, was a great object with them; and they soon became so particular, that if a button were wanting in the collar or sleeves, they was not satisfied till the deficiency was remedied. A coloured handkerchief, which they used to roll neatly round the head, was also much prized.

After they became somewhat polished in their manner, if they saw anything that struck their fancy, they asked for it; if given them, they shewed no visible marks of thankfulness; and, if refused them with firmness, they laid it down quietly.

Some time before we left the coast, they could be trusted implicitly, even with those articles they most highly prized.

It may be justly presumed, that living, as they do, more agreeably to nature, they are subject to fewer diseases than man in a civilized state. But, that they are not altogether exempt from the ills attending animal existence, was very obvious.

'During the inclement and wet weather at the commencement of this year,' observes Dr. Davis, 'a party of the Aborigines was discovered, labouring under acute *bronchitis,* on a low neck of land, near the western boundary of Raffles Bay. During the continuance of the disease (which, in many instances, was severe,) they were very abstemious. The only remedies which we saw them employ, during the acute stage, were cords tied very tightly round their heads, over which they poured cold water.

'On one occasion, the chief (Wellington) lay down on the sand, and caused one of his tribe to stand on his head, — most probably for the purpose of deadening the acute pain he was suffering.

'Several of these people have deep circular impressions, — on their faces in particular, — as if caused by the small-pox. From the inability of making myself understood, the nature of the disease which produced these marks is not yet ascertained.'

The natives described, in language, or, rather, by signs sufficiently significant, the history of this malady, which they call *oie-boie,* and which appears to be very prevalent among them. It evidently bears a resemblance, both in its symptoms and consequences, to small-pox, — being an eruptive disease, attended with fever, and leaving depressions. It frequently destroys the eyes, and I observed more than one native who had thus suffered. Mimaloo's left eye was destroyed by this disease; hence, his English name, *One-eye,* to which he appeared particularly partial. We could not learn whether they used any remedy, except abstinence.

They are also frequently affected with ophthalmia.

It is a singular circumstance, that the Aboriginal tribes of New Holland should possess so very little affinity of language, while in personal figure, manners, mode of life, and implements of war, there is so striking a resemblance.

The dialect of the natives of Raffles Bay is by no means inharmonious, but it was extremely difficult to obtain the true sound of their words, as it frequently happened, that the words (the correct sound of which not being caught at first) were repeated by us as near as we could guess, when they, either through indifference or complaisance, adopted our mode of pronunciation; and it required some pains, on our part, to obviate the effects of their apathy or inconvenient politeness.

Whether they have any idea of a Superior Being, or of a future state of existence, it was impossible for us to ascertain. It was easy enough to reciprocate communication, as far as regarded objects evident to the external senses; but, as may be imagined by those conversant on the subject, any attempt to talk of abstract principles must have proved altogether fruitless.

When it is called to mind that they were just beginning to lay aside suspicion, and to visit the settlement without fear, not long before it was abandoned, it will not seem strange that these particulars, relating to them, are so scanty and imperfect. A little longer intercourse would have enabled a person (inclined to observe their manners, and learn their language) to obtain more correct and extensive information respecting the various Aboriginal tribes on this part of the coast, who, to say the least of it, were treated so cavalierly, in the first instance, by the civilized intruders on their native land.

1 Captain Barker made it an invariable rule to give the natives a mess of boiled rice, *at his own expense*, whenever they visited the settlement. He strictly prohibited their receiving any spirits; and, as that article was very precious, his orders were the more readily complied with. — T.B.W.

Source: Thomas Braidwood Wilson, *Narrative of a Voyage Round the World*, Sherwood, Gilbert & Piper, London, 1835, pp.167–72.

Speared and pursued at Point Pearce

John Lort Stokes

December 7 [1839]. — I left the ship in the morning to make some observations at Point Pearce for the errors of the chronometers. I was accompanied to the shore by Mr. Bynoe, who was going on a shooting excursion. It being high water, I was obliged to select a spot near the cliffs forming the point, for carrying out my intention. That selected was about 60 yards from the wood-crowned cliff which rose behind; thinking such an intervening distance would secure me from the spear of the treacherous native. This caution rather resulted from what had before occurred at Escape Cliffs, where Messrs. Fitzmaurice and Keys so narrowly escaped, than from any idea that natives might be lurking about. Indeed, Mr. Bynoe had been shooting all over the ground yesterday, and had neither seen nor heard anything to indicate their existence in this neighbourhood; though doubtless, from what followed, they had been very busily watching him all the time, and were probably only deterred from making an attack, by the alarm with which his destructive gun, dealing death to the birds, must have filled them. Requiring equal altitudes, I was compelled to revisit the spot in the afternoon for the corresponding observations. The boat in which Mr. Bynoe returned to the ship, was to carry me on shore. We met at the gangway, and in answer to my inquiry, he informed me that he had seen no traces of the natives. He had shot a new and very beautiful bird of the finch tribe, in which the brilliant colours of verdegris green, lilac purple, and bright yellow, were admirably blended.[1] The time was short; half an hour would have sufficed for the observations, and we should have left the coast. As it was now low water, and I had to traverse a coral reef half a mile in width, I resolved to lighten myself of my gun, which I had taken with me in the morning, that I might with greater safety carry the chronometer. On landing I directed Mr. Tarrant and one of the boat's crew to follow with the rest of the instruments. The walking was very bad, the reef being strewed with coral fragments, and interspersed with large pools. With my mind fully occupied by all we had seen of late, I hurried on without waiting, and reached the observation spot, just glancing towards the cliff, which presented nothing to the view except the silvery stems of the never-failing gum-trees.

Captain John Lort Stokes speared at Point Pearce. This illustration, by Conrad Martens, appeared in Stokes's Discoveries in Australia *(1846).*

I had just turned my head round to look after my followers when I was suddenly staggered by a violent and piercing blow about the left shoulder: and ere the dart had ceased to quiver in its destined mark, a loud long yell, such as the savage only can produce, told me by whom I had been speared. One glance sufficed to shew me the cliffs, so lately the abode of silence and solitude, swarming with the dusky forms of the natives, now indulging in all the exuberant action with which the Australian testifies his delight. One tall bushy-headed fellow led the group, and was evidently my successful assailant. I drew out the spear, which had entered the cavity of the chest, and retreated, with all the swiftness I could command, in the hope of reaching those who were coming up from the boat, and were then about half way. I fully expected another spear while my back was turned; but fortunately the savages seemed only to think of getting down to the beach to complete their work. Onward I hurried, carrying the spear, which I had drawn from the wound, and determined if, as I expected, overtaken, to sell my life dearly. Each step, less steady than the former one, reminded me that I was fast losing blood: but I hurried on, still retaining the chronometer, and grasping my only weapon of defence. The savage cry behind soon told me that my pursuers had found their way to the beach: while at every respiration, the air escaping through the orifice of the wound, warned me that the strength by which I was still enabled to struggle through the deep pools and various other impediments in my path, must fail me soon. I had fallen twice: each disaster being announced by a shout of vindictive triumph, from the blood-hounds behind. To add to my distress, I now saw, with utter dismay, that Mr. Tarrant, and the man with the instruments, unconscious of the fact that I had been speared, and therefore believing that I could make good my escape, were moving off towards the boat. I gave up all hope, and with that rapid glance at the past, which in such an hour crowds the whole history of life upon the mind, and one brief mental act of supplication or rather submission to Him in whose hands are the issues of life and death, I prepared for the last dread struggle. At that moment the attention of the retreating party was aroused by a boat approaching hastily from the ship; the first long, loud, wild shriek of the natives having most providentially apprised those on board of our danger. They turned and perceived that I was completely exhausted. I spent the last struggling energy I possessed to join them. Supported on each side I had just strength to direct them to turn towards our savage enemies: who were hurrying on in a long file, shouting and waving their clubs, and were now only about thirty yards off. Our turning, momentarily checked their advance, whilst their force increased. During these very few and awfully anxious moments, a party, headed by Lieut. Emery, hastened over the reef to our support. Another moment, and ours would have been the fate of so many other explorers; — the hand of the savage almost grasped our throats — we should have fallen a sacrifice in the cause of discovery, and our bones left to moulder on this distant shore, would have been trodden heedlessly under foot by the wandering native.

At the sight of Lieut. Emery's party, the natives flew with the utmost rapidity, covering their flight, either from chance or skill, by my party; in a moment the air, so lately echoing with their ferocious yells, was silent, and the scene of their intended massacre, as lonely and deserted as before!

I was soon got down to the boat, lifted over the ship's side, and stretched on the poop cabin table, under the care of Mr. Bynoe, who on probing the wound gave me a cheering hope of its not proving fatal. The anxiety with which I watched his countenance, and listened to the words of life or death, the reader may imagine, but I cannot attempt to describe. The natives never throw a spear when the eye of the person they aim at is turned towards them, supposing that every one, like themselves, can avoid it. This was most fortunate, as, my side being towards them, the spear had to pass through the thick muscles of the breast before reaching my lungs. Another circumstance in my favour was that I had been very much reduced by my late exertions.

The sufferings of that night I will not fatigue my readers by describing; but I can never forget the anxiety with which Mr. Bynoe watched over me during the whole of it. Neither can I forget my feelings of gratitude to the Almighty when my sunken eyes the next morning once more caught the first rays of the sun. It seemed as though I could discover in these an assurance that my hour was not yet come, and that it would be my lot for some time longer to gaze with grateful pleasure on their splendour.

1 Figured by Mr. Gould from this specimen as *Amadina Gouldiæ*. —J.L.S.

Source: John Lort Stokes, *Discoveries in Australia, with an Account of the Coasts and Rivers Explored During the Voyage of the HMS Beagle in the Years 1837–43*, vol.II, T. & W. Boone, London, 1846, pp.106–11.

The natives were remarkably kind and attentive

Dr Ludwig Leichhardt

December 2 [1845]. — Whilst we were waiting for our bullock, which had returned to the running brook, a fine native stepped out of the forest with the ease and grace of an Apollo, with a smiling countenance, and with the confidence of a man to whom the white face was perfectly familiar. He was unarmed, but a great number of his companions were keeping back to watch the reception he should meet with. We received him, of course, most cordially; and upon being joined by another good-looking little man, we heard him utter distinctly the words, *'Commandant!' 'come here!!' 'very good!!!' 'what's your name?!!!!'* If my readers have at all identified themselves with my feelings throughout this trying journey; if they have only imagined a tithe of the difficulties we have encountered, they will readily imagine the startling effect which these, as it were, magic words produced — we were electrified — our joy knew no limits, and I was ready to embrace the fellows, who, seeing the happiness with which they inspired us, joined, with a most merry grin, in the loud expression of our feelings. We gave them various presents, particularly leather belts, and received in return a great number of bunches of goose feathers, which the natives use to brush away the flies. They knew the white people of Victoria,[1] and called them Balanda, which is nothing more than 'Hollanders'; a name used by the Malays, from whom they received it. We had most fortunately a small collection of words, made by Mr. Gilbert when at Port Essington; so that we were enabled to ask for water (ōbert); for the road (állun); for Limbo cardja, which was the name of the Harbour. I wished very much to induce them to become our guides; and the two principal men, Eooanberry and Minorelli, promised to accompany us, but they afterwards changed they minds ...

The natives were remarkably kind and attentive, and offered us the rind of the rose-coloured Eugenia apple, the cabbage of the Seaforthia palm, a fruit which I did not know, and the nut-like swelling of the rhizoma of either a grass or a sedge. The last had a sweet taste, was very mealy and nourishing, and the best article of the food of the natives we had yet tasted. They called it 'Allamurr' (the natives of Port Essington, 'Murnatt'), and were extremely fond of it. The plant grew in depressions of the plains, where the boys and young men were occupied the whole day in digging for it. The women went in search of other food; either to the sea-coast to collect shell-fish, — and many were the broad paths which led across the plains from the forest land to the salt-water — or to the brushes to gather the fruits of the season, and the cabbage of the palms. The men armed with a wommala, and with a bundle of goose spears, made of a strong reed or bamboo(?), gave up their time to hunting. It seemed that they speared the geese only when flying; and would crouch down whenever they saw a flight of them approaching: the geese, however, knew their enemies so well, that they immediately turned upon seeing a native rise to put his spear into the throwing stick. Some of my companions asserted that they had seen them hit their object at the almost incredible distance of 200 yards: but, making all due allowance for the guess, I could not help thinking how formidable they would have been had they been enemies instead of friends. They remained with us the whole afternoon; all the tribe and many visitors, in all about seventy persons, squatting down with crossed legs in the narrow shades of the trunks of trees, and shifting their position as the sun advanced. Their wives were out in search of food; but many of their children were with them, which they duly introduced to us. They were fine, stout, well made men, with pleasing and intelligent countenances. One or two attempts were made to rob us of some trifles; but I was careful; and we avoided the unpleasant necessity of shewing any discontent on that head. As it grew late, and they became hungry, they rose, and explained that they were under the necessity of leaving us, to go and satisfy their hunger; but that they would shortly return, and admire, and talk again. They went to the digging ground, about half a mile in the plain, where the boys were collecting Allamurr, and brought us a good supply of it; in return for which various presents were made to them. We became very fond of this little tuber: and I dare say the feast of Allamurr with Eooanberry's and Minorelli's tribe will long remain in the recollection of my companions. They brought us also a thin grey snake, about four feet long, which they put on the coals and roasted. It was poisonous, and was called 'Yullo'. At nightfall, after filling their koolimans with water, there being none at their camp, they took their leave, and retired to their camping place on the opposite hill where a plentiful dinner awaited them. They were very urgent in inviting us to accompany them, and by way of inducement, most unequivocally offered us their sable partners. We had to take great care of our bullock, as the beast invariably charged the natives whenever he obtained a sight of them, and he would alone have prevented their attacking us; for the whole tribe were so much afraid of him, that, upon our calling out 'the bullock', they were immediately ready to bolt; with the exception of Eooanberry and Minorelli, who looked to us for protection. I had not, however, the slightest fear and apprehension of any treachery on the part of the natives; for my frequent intercourse with the natives of Australia had taught me to distinguish easily between the smooth tongue of deceit, with which they try to ensnare their victim, and the open expression of kind and friendly feelings, or those of confidence and respect. I remember several instances of the most cold-blooded smooth-tongued treachery, and of the most extraordinary gullibility of the natives; but I am sure that a careful observer is more than a match for these simple children of nature, and that he can easily read the bad intention in their unsteady, greedy, glistening eyes.

1 Settlement of Victoria, Port Essington, named by Captain J.J.G. Bremer on 3 November 1838.

Source: Ludwig Leichhardt, *Journal of an Overland Expedition in Australia, from Moreton Bay to Port Essington, 1844–45*, T. & W. Boone, London, 1847, pp.502–7.

Reconnaissance

William Hart-Smith

Watch how the wilderness absorbs a party
making for the summit of a hill:

Grass first, waves of golden water
lapping at their knees. They are soon lost.

The trees flow back silently
across the hole that was made;

Men have gone into it armed
and become as nothing;

Of their purposefulness and commotion
nothing remains.

Source: William Hart-Smith, *Harvest*, Georgian House, Melbourne, 1945, p.21.

Facing page: 'Native prisoners in chains', published in The Lone Hand *(1 March 1911). Such pictures abound in the literature of the North: whip-thin, bemused Aboriginal captives; menacing black-trackers; white overseer(s) in pervasive, aristocratic pose.*

3 'Bone-piled spots': The whites dig in

All over the land were bone-piled spots where lazy Aborigines were taught not to steal a whiteman's bullocks. For natives who were unable to work there was the fourpenny Compound. But for some reason or other that institution was not popular. Most Aborigines who had been born in freedom preferred to do their starving in the bush. And all the while the Nation was boasting to the world of its Freedom and Manliness and Honesty. Australia Felix!
— Xavier Herbert, *Capricornia*, 1938

From Noltenius Lagoon I travelled a few miles through the bush to the old open-cut diggings where the miners were attacked. There I found a grave and a mis-spelled epitaph, 'T. Schollert. MURED BY BLACKS. Sept. 24 – '84'.
—Keith Willey, *Ghosts of the Big Country*, 1975

On the Lower Victoria, at Auvergne, Sullivan Creek, and the Fitzmaurice, places situated within the influence of tidal waters, there dwells a bloodthirsty tribe known for their atrocious deeds. They wait for the boss and stockmen to leave the station, and then come in and murder the cook and steal the rations, and the oily, soapy hypocrites in towns, who know nothing about it, will tell you 'It is done because white men take their lubras.' I only wish some of those canting snufflers were placed in some of the predicaments I have been in with the wild cannibals. Religion won't aid you then; nothing but a good Winchester or Martini carbine, in conjunction with a Colt's revolver.
— W. H. Willshire, *The Land of the Dawning: Being Facts Gleaned from Cannibals in the Australian Stone Age*, 1896

Fully nine out of every ten murders in the North have been due, directly or in part, to unauthorized interference with gins. Not all the true facts ever get into print, of course, but those who have been privileged to peep behind the scenes know more than the general public can ever know, or will ever want to know.
— Jessie Litchfield, *Far-North Memories*, 1930

As the festive season is drawing near and all civilised communities are looking forward to happy reunions and reassurance of goodwill among all nations it is again my privilege as president of the Aborinese [sic] Protection League to extend our good wishes to the native inhabitants of Australia who may not have the advantages of participating in the Christmas celebrations being arranged in all towns and settled districts and to express our sincere wishes that the coming year may be the dawn of a new era of greater happiness and contentment among all aboriginal subjects of His Majesty the King.
— Dr Herbert Basedow, 'A message to Aboriginals', *Northern Territory Times*, 21 December 1928

> This, the land of the ancient folk,
> The empty plains;
> A few thin bones in the sand-dunes,
> The silent rains.

— R. A. Swan, 'Epitaph to the vanished tribes', 1950

Camp at Barrow Creek

F.J. Gillen

June, 7th [1901]. — Camp No. 33. Barrow Creek. Bar. 28.165. Aneroid 1725. A.T. 66. S.T. 61. Up in time for 8 o'clock breakfast we are having our meals at the Station but sleeping at our own camp. Busy all day unpacking stores etc. Collected from natives 4 spears 3 clubs 17 pitchies 9 shields 13 boomerangs 8 churinga 7 stone knives 6 magic knouts Atilika 3 hair girdles 2 curved adzes some fur necklets and string in return for which we served out flour tomahawks butchers knives pocket knives beads looking glasses. Native women and children brought in a number of lizards and animals 1 legless lizard being of very recently known and rare variety. On the 23rd of February 1874 this Station was attacked by blacks and the Station Master and Cook were killed their graves are close to the Station in a neatly fenced stone enclosure with a headstone bearing the following inscription:

> In Memoriam
> John L. Stapleton Station Master
> and John Frank Lineman
> Killed by Natives at Barrow Creek
> 23rd February, 1874.

the graves are still tended with care by the local officials. Close by, today, a number of natives were camped one of whom is said to have been implicated in the attack he was one of those pursued by the Avenging party of whites and only escaped being shot by hiding himself in a hole the mouth of which he closed with a tussock of porcupine. In the annals of Native treachery there is no crueller or more unprovoked attack than that in which poor Stapleton and Frank lost their lives. Stapleton had been kind to the point of weakness to the natives giving them almost everything they asked for until their demands became wholly

Barrow Creek Telegraph Station, viewed from the rear (June 1901). The Station Master, John Stapleton, and lineman, John Frank, were killed by Aborigines who attacked the Station in February 1874. A punitive expedition — the first official white massacre party in the Northern Territory — under Trooper Samuel Gason, spent some two months in the area shooting Kaititja and Warramunga people. The Adelaide Advertiser *wanted retribution to be 'sharp, swift, and severe'. It was, thus establishing a pattern which would continue in the Territory for more than half a century.*

unreasonable and he was unable to comply with them. Then without warning of any kind the natives assembled on the evening of the 23rd of February 74 and attacked the staff who were, having had tea, sitting out at the north western corner of the building which was originally built in the form of a stockade. The staff seeing the natives approaching fully armed along the northern side of the building ran around in the opposite direction hoping to reach the gateway which they found guarded by armed blacks there was no alternative but to make a rush for the gate and this they did while the cruel spears were thrust at them from a distance of a few feet. Frank reached the kitchen door only to fall pierced through the heart by a spear Stapleton received a spear in the groin and lived a few brief hours knowing that he was mortally wounded; he had a wife and bairns in Adelaide and to me as an operator in the Adelaide office fell the painful duty of conducting a telegraphic conversation between the dying man at the Barrow and his heartbroken wife in Adelaide. Flint the Assistant received a severe spear wound in the thigh while other members of the staff escaped with only trifling scratches. The following verses signed 'Geoffrey Crabthorn' and published in the Adelaide Register of March 3rd 1874 are surely worth recording here.

'The Last Message'

There is a threadlike creek in a stony bed
With dull brown tufts of a stunted shrub
An open plain where the grass is dead
And sombre forest and tangled scrub
There's a long low range stretching far away
And readily fashioned of rough hewn stone
In the mellowing light of the fading day
Stand the high white walls of a station lone
In a darkened room of the building drear
There's a deep red stain where the life stream ran
The poisoned point of a broken spear
And the pain pinched face of a dying man
There's a faithful friend who has faintly heard
A whispered wish from the trembling mouth
There's a throbbing needle that sends the word
Twelve hundred miles to the peaceful South
There's a woman who sits in a lofty hall
And waits with a wan and bloodless face
While the terrible moments seem to crawl
For a word one word from the far off place.
There's a message that comes on its path of fire
The whispered wish of the Station lone
And an answer that flies on the mystic wire
From the woman that sits with the face of stone
Husband and wife but how far apart
With never a clasp of the dear ones hand
Yet mighty science how great thou art
They speak o'er forest and scrub and land
And the pain pinched features no longer wince
And a tear of joy from the dim eye slips
At the fond last words that a moment since
Came fresh and warm from the Wifes sweet lips.

Source: *Gillen's Diary: Camp Jottings of F. J. Gillen on the Spencer and Gillen Expedition Across Australia 1901-1902*, Libraries Board of South Australia, Adelaide, 1968, pp.107-9.

Our Adelaide letter

Northern Territory Times, 1874

From our own Correspondent
Adelaide, 26 February

Adelaide has been thrown into a state of great excitement by the intelligence of the murderous attack of the natives on the Barrow Creek Telegraph Station. When the news first reached Adelaide the public were staggered with astonishment, for not a warning word had been given about any anticipated danger, and it is evident, from the defenceless position in which the staff of Barrow Creek were surprised, that they had placed too much confidence in the treacherous natives — a confidence which has been dearly paid for by the loss of two valuable lives. Great anxiety was felt to ascertain what action the Government would take in this emergency, for it was felt that an anxious responsibility was cast upon them, which they must bravely face. Speedy retribution was demanded, it being felt that only by striking terror into the hearts of the natives, can the lives of the white men along the whole line be rendered safe. The Government, no doubt, were in constant communication with officials along the line as to the possibility of sending help to the distressed camp at Barrow Creek; but when two days elapsed without the Government making a sign as to their intended policy, great impatience was manifested, for it was felt that the retribution to be effective must be speedy and severe. It is understood that Trooper Gason — in whose discretion much confidence is placed — has been instructed to take steps, which it is hoped will inspire in the minds of the natives a wholesome terror, and prevent the recurrence of such reprisals as the one which is so greatly deplored. The necessity of stern measures is shown by the news to hand this morning, that the natives have besieged the Barrow Creek Station, and that the whites are appealing anxiously for reinforcement. The emergency is a serious one. It is to be hoped that it will be met in a manner which, while not erring on the side of undue harshness towards the untutored blacks, will impress the native mind with the fact that the whites are not to be molested and murderously assaulted with impunity. I need hardly add that the deepest sympathy is felt for Mrs. Stapleton and her family in the crushing sorrow which has fallen upon them.

Source: 'Our Adelaide letter', from the *Northern Territory Times*, 10 April 1874.

Outrages by the blacks

Editorial, Northern Territory Times, 1884

It is to be earnestly hoped that the sad experiences of the last few weeks will not be allowed to fade from the memories of our readers, without some action being taken to guard against the repetition of such horrible outrages. Something more will be required than merely sending out to capture the offenders; the whole question of the position of the aborigines in the Territory will require careful and patient consideration in its various bearings. There can be little doubt that the attack upon poor Noltenius, Houschildt, and party, was a premeditated and carefully organised scheme; the object of which was plunder. No one who knew the murdered men, and their honest, large-hearted natures, can, for one minute, imagine, that any reasonable cause was given to the natives for the attack, visitors to the copper camp have borne witness to the kind manner in which the natives were treated, the only fault with which the poor murdered fellows can be charged, is that they were too kind and had far too much confidence in the harmless nature of the blacks; for this fault they suffered the most horrible of deaths, at the hands of a race of creatures resembling men in form, but with no more trace of human feeling in their natures, than the Siberian wolves. Sickly sentiment and Exeter Hall humanitarianism should be valued at their true worth, our European settlers must be allowed to till the soil and extract the wealth from the land which they have made their home, free from the murdering raids of these savages. Backward the natives must move before the tide of civilization, or, if they will not give place peaceably, and show that their natures are as dangerous as the venomous serpent, even as every man will crush a snake under his heel, so must the hand of every man be raised against a tribe of inhuman monsters, whose cowardly and murderous nature renders them unfit to live.

If, in the annals of the Territory, any record could be produced, which would show that the natives had been harshly treated, or shot down indiscriminately, by the Europeans, there might be some cause to plead that these murders were only what the blacks considered just revenge; but there are no such records. The Territory has been singularly free from the class of men who would shoot a native without great provocation; and as a rule those among the native tribes, who have come into the townships, have been treated with kindness, and well paid for any little work done. The simple truth is — that they are murderers and robbers by nature, and nothing but the most severe punishment will have any lasting effect upon them, it should follow the offence promptly, legal technicalities should be utterly dispensed with, and a sharp lesson administered, while their hands are yet red with the blood of our plucky fellow-colonists, will do more to ensure the future safety of the Europeans, than all the circuitous and slow processes of punishment which would be meted out in accordance with the provisions of the Law. Queenslanders have been roundly abused for the manner in which their aborigines have been *dispersed,* but if we consider the hundreds of murders similar to last month's tragedy which have brought upon the natives, in Queensland, a just and speedy punishment for their crimes what we have before thought cruelty and revenge, now assumes the appearance of a practical and sensible method of dealing with a horde of bloodthirsty wretches, who are utterly out of the reach of any other mode of punishment or retribution. We believe some of the right class of men are now on the tracks of the Daly River natives, but we do not expect to hear many particulars of their chase; the less the better, in such cases as the present, it is far more sensible to avoid complications by the exercise of a judicious reticence.

Source: 'Outrages by the blacks', editorial, *Northern Territory Times,* 4 October 1884.

Aborigines in the Northern Territory

Letter to the editor, Northern Territory Times, 1885

Sir, — As Parliament meets in a day or two, I trust that you will allow me to call attention to the new policy towards the aborigines introduced by the present Government. I have always understood that the South Australians pride themselves on treating the original possessors of the soil in a humane manner — to use the cant term, 'as men and as brothers'. If not, what is the meaning of the rather ugly flag we have adopted? Britannia is represented offering a Bible to a naked blackfellow. As a flag it is not effective, but the sentiment it expresses is admirable. Our present Government has at its head the Hon. J. Colton, who is known not only as a wise statesman, but as a pious Christian; he was lately Chairman of the Wesleyan Conference; he frequently presides over the meetings of the Y.M.C.A.; and he is a member of the Aborigines' Protection Society. Surely during his administration the 'man and brother' policy should be carried out to its fullest extent. Now let us look at the true state of affairs.

Last year five settlers on the Daly River, Northern Territory, were attacked by the natives; four of them were killed, and one escaped badly wounded, although I am glad to say he is now amongst us in good health. The attack was most treacherous and unprovoked; the natives had been kindly treated, and, as the murderers have since confessed, their only motive was to obtain the stores which the settlers had. The majority of the unfortunate men were old pioneers, well known and highly respected in the Territory, where the greatest regret was felt at their fate. For this crime the proper punishment would have been the arrest and execution of the murderers, either after the proper legal formalities, or, what would have been more successful as a deterrent, after a fair but summary trial. In Mr. Tolmer's book on the early days of South Australia he gives an account of how the Murray-mouth blacks were punished for the murder of a ship-wrecked crew; this might have formed a precedent for what I suggest. That the arrest and conviction of the murderers was quite possible is proved by the fact that four of the murderers have actually been arrested, found guilty after a fair trial, and are now waiting the carrying out of their sentence. But the Government were not content with the slow steps of justice. While Inspector Foelsche and a police party were out securing the actual murderers, another party, consisting of non-official persons, but armed and provisioned by the Government, were let loose to act as they thought best. This was called the 'Houschildt Rescue' party, from a fiction that they went to rescue Mr. Houschildt, about whose fate there had been some uncertainty, but as Corporal Montagu came in and reported the finding of Houschildt's body a few days before the rescue party started, the name is misleading. The men who formed this party insisted that they should be allowed to go unaccompanied by a single policeman. The Minister of Justice and Education is reported to have hesitated about giving his consent to their going, but finally he yielded to the urgency of the Government Resident, who strongly pressed it. As a salve to his conscience, or to save appearances, he gave, however, instructions that they were on no account to fire on the natives unless in self-defence.

What this party did has never been made public, but the officers on board the S.S. 'Palmerston', which was lying in the Daly River when the rescue party arrived there, say that all one night they heard a constant discharge of firearms. There was good moonlight at the time. These may have been used in self-defence, but as none of the party were wounded this seems improbable. The general belief in the Territory was that they simply shot down every native they saw, women and children included. While this was going on, and before the Inspector of Police had returned from the Daly River, three teamsters reported that they had been attacked by the natives at Argument Flat, about twenty miles from Southport. According to their account the natives flourished their spears and demanded tucker; the teamsters resisted, and shot five or six of them. There were three weak points about this tale. None of the teamsters were wounded; it is unusual for natives to attack in the bold way described; and, lastly, it was admitted that there were women with the natives (one of the killed was a lubra, I think). Now it is well known that the natives when they mean mischief always keep their woman out of the way. The proper course would have been to have held an inquest on the bodies of the natives, and a Jury should have decided whether they came by death through wilful murder or justifiable homicide. This could easily have been done. But no; the Government Resident, as soon as he heard of the affair, arranged that another non-official party should be armed and sent out to follow up the natives. They were sent, and returned in due time reporting that they did not fall in with any natives. This answer quite satisfied the Government Resident, who seems to be of the most unsuspicious nature. Of course the party were not asked to account for the Government ammunition they took away; and a few days after some of the men were boasting over their cups that they had shot forty-seven, including women and children; in fact, that they had stuck up a camp and killed every one in it. This may have been a lie, but every one fully believed them. I stated that the Inspector of Police was absent when this second party was sent out, or it might have been thought that the Government Resident acted on his advice, as he is an officer of long experience. As matters stand all the credit is due to the Government Resident himself.

It is difficult to say how many natives have been killed altogether for the Daly River outrage: but from all I have learned from different sources, I should say not less than 150, a great part of these women and children; and then the men who have been proved guilty have still to be hung. Some may call this justice; others may say that it is not exactly right, but then how is the country to be stocked unless something of the sort is done? I do not express an opinion, I only wish to let the public of South Australia know what is actually being done.

Source: 'Aborigines in the Northern Territory', letter to the editor, *Northern Territory Times*, 11 July 1885.

The Daly River murders of 1884 and their aftermath

Ernestine Hill

The Daly River murders and their aftermath were notorious in the north for fifty years, held up as an example of the traitorous nature of all Australian blacks. If there was reason for the crime, the one white man left alive, in loyalty to his dead mates, did not tell. The Wilwonga people of Pine Creek were practically wiped out. To quote records: 'The horrible crime aroused the wrath of all residents and fellow-miners, who set out in several parties and severely punished the natives, who tried to escape by seeking shelter in the waters of the billabongs.'

The affair took two years of 'bush riding' to clear up, until there was a storm of protest in the south at 'cold-blooded mass murder of the blacks', with formation of native protection societies shouted down in the north with vehemence and vituperation. There was talk in the Territory of importing that horror of Queensland, the Black Police. 'Here noble pioneers,' wrote one of the noble pioneers,

> 'are hurled into eternity by blood-thirsty savages without bell, book or candle. We don't want the Native Women's Protection Society to preach to us who live in the bush about the modesty, purity and chastity of degraded creatures known to us as black gins but who the city association greets as 'black sisters'. Well, I do not envy them the relationship they covet, but when they tell us that nearly all the murders of white men in the Territory may be traced to abuses of the women, they lie.'

Unfortunately the missions and associations, in sweeping indictments and thunder-and-lightning damnation, repudiated the brotherly love they counselled — as they sometimes do today. Anger and resentment rankled in the north where the lonely white man far out in the bush was never sure that he would wake up in the morning. Slanders levelled at him from the safe and well-fed south, whether he was guilty or not, intensified racial hatred, sometimes with tragic sequel for the ignorant, mostly innocent, blacks.

When Lenehan, head stockman on Macarthur River, was killed while hunting down cattle-killers — when 'Kid Gloves', a man who manicured his nails with a pocket-knife, was speared while fishing on a creek of Victoria River — when Koop was maimed for life near Calvert Downs, Marstin in the cutter *Spey* murdered in the mangroves near Borroloola, Captain Thoms waddied to death on his lugger at Carrington's Landing of the Macarthur, there were ruthless and terrible ridings. The Mbiah tribe of Macarthur River was annihilated, leaving one little girl and boy hiding in the trees. They grew up to be Kitty Karlo Pon of Darwin, and Jupiter, a stockman of Macarthur River Station, both loved and respected by their white friends through life. Many a cave of blackfellows' bones all over the north harks back to the old punitive raids.

Outside the zone of the law the hunt of human game was free for all where nobody knew about it. Depraved and vicious white men shot women. 'Go for the breeders!' — that grim phrase is still remembered in the north. Pot-shot murderers were few and far out, very seldom the pioneers or bushmen to whom the blacks were help and companionship, wife, home and human fibre — the only comradeship of life. They were rotten driftwood, morons with a 'cowboys and Indians' complex, or blind, bitter self-righteous men who looked upon the natives as wild beasts.

With one of these a true bushman, Billy Miller Linklater, author of *The Magic Snake*, was riding one day in the [eighteen-]eighties, out north of the Roper. They heard a faint chipping, and saw a very young mother, with a baby, chopping out a 'sugar-bag'. At sight of the white men she dropped the tomahawk in fright and climbed a tall gum-tree, her piccaninny on her back. Outlined in gold sunlight, they were gentle and pretty as a koala bear and her baby.

'Give us a cartridge, Billy,' said the riding-mate. 'I'm goin' to drop her.'

'You'll drop me first,' said Billy, 'or, by God, I'll tell the world.'

'Nits is lice,' said the riding-mate. 'Them brutes cleaned me out o' my station in Queensland, and I get 'em whenever I see 'em.'

'The only cartridge you'll get from me,' said Billy, 'comes quick out o' this gun. For God's sake come on, and let the poor little blighter alone.'

Source: Ernestine Hill, *The Territory*, Angus & Robertson, Sydney, 1951, pp.197-8.

Bringing in a new wild gin

Emily Caroline Creaghe

31 January 1883. — Left Copper mine at ¼ to 7 a.m. and camped at 'L' Tree in the middle of the day. Travelled on again at 4 and came across the mountains during a severe thunderstorm, and arrived at Carl Creek (the Shadforths station) at half past 7, heartily glad to get to the end of my journey. Did about 25 miles in all today.

1 February 1883. — They are all early risers here, so we were up soon after daylight, and breakfasted before 7. The household consists of Mr. and Mrs. Shadforth and ten children, only six of whom are at home just now. The house is a log one partitioned off into four rooms with no ceilings, so that the slightest whisper can be heard all over it. Very hot but no flies or mosquitoes. There are two gins as servants, but most of the work falls on Mrs. Shadforth and the girls.

2 February 1883. — Mr. Bob Shadforth came home today, and brought Mr. Willie Taylor with him. Gentlemen seem to call in pretty constantly on their way out to their stations. Very hot and we had a thunderstorm in the afternoon. The principal amusement is bathing, as the river runs a few yards from the house, so the two girls and I go in two or three times during the day, and were not deterred by the sight of crocodiles watching us on the bank nearby as this particular species are not supposed to be man eaters.

3 February 1883. — In the afternoon Mr. Doyle who has a station about a mile or so from here brought three horses and took us for a ride, and Mr. Lamond (Miss Shadforth's fiancé) the Inspector of the Native Police, camped about two miles from here came also, returning here for the evening ...

20 February 1883. — The rainy season seems to have set in properly. Mr. Shadforth and Ernest [Favenc] came home but had to leave the dray at Gregory Downs as the roads were too heavy and the rivers too high. They brought a new black gin with them who can't speak a word of English. The usual method here of bringing in a new wild gin is to put a rope round her neck and drag her along from horseback, the gin on foot.

21 February 1883. — The new gin whom they call 'Bella' is chained up to a tree a few yards from the house, and is not to be loosed until they think she is tamed.

23 February 1883. — Still raining heavily. The new gin 'Bella' made Topsy (an old one) jealous and the latter threw a firestick at her and said she would kill her. The stick flew past Mrs. Shadforth's face, so Madame Topsy got a thrashing.

24 February 1883. — 'Bella', the new gin, decamped in the night, whether it was because of Topsy's threat to kill her, or discontent at this life we don't know. They tracked her as far as the O'Shanassy but that river is a 'banker' so they could not go after her any further. There is no mail expected for two months owing to the floods.

Source: Diary of Emily Caroline Creaghe (née Robinson, later Barrett), member of the exploration party partnered by Ernest Favenc and Harry A. Creaghe and accompanied by Lindsay Crawford, in possession of Mitchell Library, Sydney (ML MSS 2982).

Martini-Henry carbines talking English

W. H. Willshire

In the month of June, 1894, we came across some tracks of natives that had been recently killing cattle on the Victoria Run. We followed them along to where they ascended a sandstone range. We also went up with our horses, and in a few miles of very rough travelling saw a rock waterhole, where the natives had camped and left evidence of their late depredations, viz., lumps of fat and fresh meatbones. We still kept on their tracks, and were travelling on high stony tablelands. Just before sunset we came to the brink of a frowning precipice. Down below was a motionless sea of gums, with the Wickham River meandering on its course. After a great deal of trouble we got to the bottom by a precipitous descent, and camped on the bank of the river. In the night we heard restless alligators thrashing and disturbing the water. Next morning we picked up the tracks and crossed the river, and in two hours we came upon the cattle killers camped close to the river. They commenced running, and many of them escaped in the tropical growth, whilst others were protected by an impenetrable phalanx of reeds. We returned to their camp and destroyed a quantity of spears and other native weapons, shot several of their dogs, and captured a boy of fifteen, who was very precocious and parted with information in reference to his brethren and their wanton mischief in a voluntary manner.

We came back and crossed the river at the same place, and again camped for the night. Next morning we went on, picked up another set of tracks on Black Gin Creek, followed them up, and at 3 p.m. came upon a large mob of natives camped amongst rocks of enormous magnitude and long dry grass, growing like a thick crop of wheat on the side of a mountain. They scattered in all directions, setting fire to the grass on each side of us, throwing occasional spears, and yelling at us. It's no use mincing matters — the Martini-Henry carbines at this critical moment were talking English in the silent majesty of those great eternal rocks. The mountain was swathed in a regal robe of fiery grandeur, and its ominous roar was close upon us. The weird, awful beauty of the scene held us spellbound for a few seconds. Out from between the rocks came a strapping young girl, with the agility of a mountain creature. She jumped from rock to rock, straight to the grey horse that I was sitting upon, took hold of my stirrup-iron, and ran alongside until we were out of danger. She was arrayed in her native modesty, and I may state this was the prettiest black girl I ever saw. She would not leave us, but when we camped sat down on our swags and smiled at the horses, all the time trying to tell us something, while a couple of imprisoned sun-beams seemed to be basking around her dimpled cheeks, and the grass beneath her feet shed tears of newly fallen dew. She was remarkably handsome, and every lineament of her face indicated a good disposition. One of my boys informed me that she wished to come in with us to the station. When I said she could if she liked a thrill of delight went to her heart and hope once more dawned.

In the morning my boss tracker formed himself into a deputation of one, and with that fawning servility so characteristic of his race asked me if I would allow him to have this pretty girl for his wife. I replied yes, but if you ever lay your hand upon her to ill-treat or abuse her in any way whatever I shall take her from you and send her back to the bush. You deserve her for faithfulness and endurance. The other boys and yourself have been most useful allies to me, and nearly all my success has been due to your own impetuous bravery. He was now in the seventh heaven of happiness, and, without further ceremony, took this flower of the wild waste away from my camp to stroll round for a few hours, with the intention of looking out for an iguana. I suppose he struck a solid basis for the commencement of a honeymoon. He soon returned with the now frowning beauty, who looked as if she had been the recipient of some unwelcome overtures. Her aristocratic spouse put on his uniform, went out on horseback, and returned in an hour with a wreath of wild orange blossom, which he twined round the head of his beautiful bride. With smiles of sweet confusion her gentle and affectionate disposition was exhibited at the kind and hospitable way in which the native police showered their favours upon her. We ascertained from her that her name was Pun-garra, which, in the native language, means a kiss. Untutored, innocent, and uncivilized, yet loving for the first time, in the green valley of her birth and the valley of her love, correctly called the 'Valley of Humiliation,' this fresh original daughter of nature conducted us with natural dignity from place to place in her own country, and possessing a prettiness which some white people would give much to possess. Every line in the contour of her person was the perfection of feminine beauty. She moved with a grace beyond all power of reproduction. She had the bust of a Juno, and hands which would delight a sculptor. I'll write no more about this enthralling daughter of the sunny south, but tell you what we saw at a little spring in the sandstone ranges. We suddenly surprised a small band of natives that were camped there. On observing our horses they all ran away with the exception of one woman who was *enceinte* [pregnant]. On going through their assets we discovered the cooked portions of a girl they had been eating when we turned up. I picked up one leg, including thigh and foot, and asked the woman in her own language if it was good. It would do when they could get no other food she said. We gave her a good big feed of bread and beef, and whilst she was eating that we buried the remains of the cannibal feast. In the meantime some of the others came back to have a look at us, and Pun-garra had a long conversation with them. We elicited from them that the blackfellows on Wave Hill, an adjacent station, were killing the squatter's cattle. It is surprising what a lot of cattle and what a lot of damage these bad natives do in the course of a year. The pioneer settlers in these wild parts have a lot to put up with. Cattle are so much afraid of these black demons on foot that they run and worry themselves to such an extent that they become poor, and are afraid to go in to water.

'The author and a boy native', from W.H. Willshire's The Land of the Dawning: Being Facts Gleaned from Cannibals in the Australian Stone Age *(1896). Willshire was Officer-in-Charge of the feared Interior Patrol of the Northern Territory throughout the 1880s. F.J. Gillen referred to Willshire's methods as 'sheer bloody murder' and, indeed, he succeeded in having Willshire actually charged with murder in 1891. Defended by one of South Australia's leading barristers, Sir John Downer, Willshire was acquitted.*

If those people who live in towns and take the part of the wild natives were the owners of cattle stations here they would not be so quick at trying to get a man hanged for shooting them as they are now. Let them consider the station books, when items like the following appear on the margin of every year's return: — 'Four hundred destroyed by blacks.' On going into their camps you can see bones, heads, horns, skin, and feet of many cattle they have killed in the past. When will the Government wake up to the necessity of providing adequate native police to those settlers who pay them big rentals for the country they occupy? As I have written so often on this subject, I will not recapitulate, but let me state that there is not a living man in Australia that could tell you more about the wilful and wanton destruction of property, and how good prime beef has rotted away in the sun through the action of the black scoundrels, than the author of this little book. Surely with all the experience he has had amongst the native cattle-killers, some member of the existing Government might condescend to ask him to make a suggestion as to the means of putting a stop to it altogether. It is within the bounds of possibility, and will not be very expensive either. There is no shooting or wounding or cruelty in the suggestion.

Whilst tracking some natives who had been killing cattle on the Victoria Run in August, 1894, we came upon them camped in a gorge off the north bank of the River Wickham. The war cry sounded through the tribe, and they picked up their spears and commenced climbing the precipitous sides. As there was no getting away the females and children crawled into rocky embrasures, and there they remained. When we had finished with the male portion we brought the black gins and their offspring out from their rocky alcoves.

Source: W. H. Willshire, *The Land of the Dawning: Being Facts Gleaned from Cannibals in the Australian Stone Age*, W. K. Thomas & Co., Adelaide, 1896, pp.40-43.

Out-beyond country

Alfred Searcy

There were many murders by the niggers which the police had to look into, and which necessitated much travelling, sometimes with great hardships. There can be no doubt that many of the murders were caused by the white men taking away the black women from their tribes. Nearly all the drovers, cattlemen, and station hands had their 'black boys' (gins). No objection was raised by the black men to interference with their women so long as they were not abducted. It is the taking away of the women that has been the cause of so many white men having been rubbed out by the niggers. These women are invaluable to the white cattlemen, for, besides the companionship, they become splendid horsewomen, and good with cattle. They are useful to find water, settle the camp, boil the billy, and track and bring in the horses in the mornings. In fact, it is impossible to enumerate the advantages of having a good gin 'out-back'. The black women are, as a rule, well treated by those who take them. In the great out-beyond half-caste children never live. There can be no doubt that at times many of the blacks have been put away by some brutes just for the fun of killing, by others for revenge, but mostly the niggers brought the trouble on themselves by interfering with the cattle. In many of these cases no report ever reached the police. In one instance, so a man told me who was concerned in it, a whole nigger camp was wiped out. Some years ago I got a letter from a man who was attacked by the niggers in the Gulf country, and received some eleven spear wounds. He recovered. In his letter he said, 'I now shoot at sight; killed to date thirty-seven.' Thus it will ever be in developing a new country where the aborigines are at all hostile, and where there is no recognised authority to deal with them. A man who goes into the out-beyond country in a measure carries his life in his own hands. He may throw it away, as many do, or he may take measures to protect his life and property, which — to those who live where the law and police can always be applied to — may appear cruel and harsh. Not for a moment would I defend those who wantonly shoot down the blacks, but it must always be remembered that at times stern measures, and even shooting, are necessary.

One man, I remember well, boasted to me that he never carried a revolver. He said he did all the punishment he wanted with a stock-whip and a wire-cracker. 'When I want to be particularly severe,' he remarked, 'I cut the top off a sapling and sharpen the remaining stump, bend it down, and drive it through the palms of both hands of the nigger.' That seemed awfully brutal to me, but that man assured me on his oath that he did it. I wonder whether the cruelty he practised ever came back to him in his struggle for life in the river — he was drowned in the Katherine.

Source: Alfred Searcy, *In Australian Tropics,* 2nd edn, George Robertson, London & Sydney, 1909, pp.173–5.

The Coniston 'massacres' of August 1928

Sidney Downer

Within a year of [Major George Vernon] Dudley's retirement [as Commissioner of the Northern Territory Mounted Police] in 1927, a drama was enacted with a mortality rate which, by comparison, made *Titus Andronicus* appear like one of J.M. Barrie's soppier works. It provoked an explosion of self-righteousness from the south equalled in violence only by the outcry arising from the Daly River Copper Landing murders forty-two years before.

The event was the so-called Coniston 'massacres' of August 1928, and the principal protagonist was Mounted Constable William George Murray, of the Northern Territory Mounted Police.

To understand the circumstances of a tragedy in which thirty-one aborigines lost their lives, one must turn back, principally with the assistance of an article by explorer Michael Terry, in the magazine *People,* to the terms and conditions of life for both white and black races in the Centre many years earlier.

Mr Terry, perhaps over-emphatically, describes the circumstances from which the Coniston 'Massacres' stemmed, as 'the last war of the aborigines against the intruding whites.' (A number of battles still remained to be fought in the north.) It was waged, he says, over a diffuse 'front' of about one hundred and fifty miles, the central point of which was roughly two hundred miles north-west of Alice Springs on the Lander River. Napperby and Coniston stations were prominent in the story. There, or thereabouts, for half a century or so, white men had been trying to establish cattle-runs on the trackless lands west of the Lander River.

Those lands and the desert still further west were the home of the warlike, nomadic tribe of the Warramullas, and it was they who, incited by outlaw blacks and, according to Mr Terry, 'some free-lance white missionaries,' decided, in the words of one of them, 'This no more longa white fella; longa black fella. White fella can't sit down longa black fella. White fella shift.'

For forty years there had been sporadic violence, with settlers, miners, trappers, and prospectors under attack, many times with fatal consequences. By 1926, affairs were marching towards their climax as more and more cattlemen abandoned their holdings because of the unequal contest against over-powering weight of numbers.

In May 1928 an expedition, of which Mr Terry was the leader, set out from Port Hedland in the north-west of Western Australia. Their objective was gold, and their general plan was to head for country east of the border between Western Australia and the Northern Territory, and thence cross two hundred and sixty miles of waterless desert south-easterly to the fringe of white settlement along the Lander.

At Tanami, about three hundred miles due west of Tennant Creek and at that time the most isolated settlement in Australia, the party met Mounted Constable Don Hood, of the Northern Territory Mounted Police. Hood and Constable Dan Toohey had been ordered to Tanami to establish a police post, both as a delicate hint to the Warramullas, and to supply information to white settlers.

Hood warned the expedition of danger ahead. He told them that one of the Warramullas had raided his camp one night and speared his best horse. Hood and Toohey had followed the marauder's tracks and shot him.

After a description of the alarms and excursions of that hazardous journey, including an attempt by native warriors to burn out the police camp by lighting dry spinifex, Mr Terry turns to the crime which started the trail of events leading to the Coniston 'Massacres.'

> Early in August a party of Warramullas went on a marauding expedition along the Lander River, intending to go first to Randall Stafford's station, Coniston, and then attack all other whites they could find.
>
> Just after sun-up on August 7th, they came to the camp of an old dingo-poisoner named Fred Brooks at a soak in a creek about fourteen miles west of Stafford's place. When the Warramullas found Brooks at the soak they realised that he could spread word that they were on the warpath, so they decided to kill him.

This would appear to have been an acceptable motive for the crime which ensued, but not to the muddle-heads of the south, who alleged that Brooks had been interfering with the lubras and that his murder was a justifiable act of vengeance. As Brooks was over seventy at the time of his death, such conduct on his part seems highly improbable.

Brooks was placing new greenhide laces into pack-bags when the Warramullas rushed him. His arms and legs were held while his head was battered with axes and waddies. His body was then thrown into a grave, so shallow that his feet stuck out. The scene is known to this day as Brooks's Soak.

The attackers then set out for Coniston to attack Stafford, but he was ready for them and drove them off. Stafford's life was saved by Brooks's faithful black boy, who had run, in the great heat, across fourteen miles of treeless plain to Coniston to warn the men of the pending attack.

The bush-telegraph works fast in the Territory, and news of Brooks's murder soon reached Mounted Constable W.G. Murray at his police-post at Barrow Creek, one hundred and sixty miles north of Alice Springs, the site of a hideous massacre of Overland Telegraph linesmen half a century earlier.

Murray had been nine years in the Northern Territory Mounted Police. A well-set-up man, six foot two in height, quiet and methodical, and a notable horseman and first-rate shot, with a reputation for firmness in handling both black and white miscreants, he had joined the force in 1919 after four years' service with the 4th Light Horse on Gallipoli and in France. He had been wounded four times in action.

It was this resolute man to whom was entrusted the task of bringing in Brooks's murderers. On 16 August, nine days after Brooks's death, orders from Alice Springs sent Murray, together with Stafford and three black-trackers, to a native camp fourteen miles from Coniston.

Source: Sidney Downer, *Patrol Indefinite: The Northern Territory Police Force*, Rigby, Adelaide, 1963, pp.117–19.

Coniston

Commonwealth Board of Enquiry

Commonwealth of Australia (Central Australia), Office of the Government Resident, Alice Springs, 18 January 1929.
  Finding of Board of Enquiry concerning the killing of natives in Central Australia by Police Parties and others and concerning other matters.

The members of the Board arrived at Alice Springs on 29 December 1928 at 9 p.m. and the Enquiry was opened the following day and adjourned from place to place. The Board travelled by motor car approximately 2,500 miles principally over country never previously traversed by car and evidence was taken very often under most difficult conditions.

Thirty witnesses were examined in all and the Enquiry was formally closed on the 18 January 1929 at Alice Springs.

It was found impracticable to examine the witness Alick Wilson. He was ill in the Hospital at Darwin when the Enquiry opened and it was ascertained one week before the conclusion of same that it would be six weeks before he could arrive at Alice Springs. Constable Murray intimated that he did not desire his presence so the Board dispensed with his evidence. In any case, he was, on most occasions, in charge of the packhorses back from the shooting.

The evidence of Tracker Major could not be taken — his services had been dispensed with and he had gone 'bush'.

The Aboriginal boy Dodger was not called as he witnessed none of the shooting — he being with the packhorses.

The matters enquired into are dealt with in ceriatum hereunder:

a. In respect to the shooting of seventeen natives in pursuing the murderers of Brooks the evidence of the following reputable settlers, i.e. William Briscoe, Randal Beresford Stafford, and John Saxby corroborated the account given by Mounted Constable Murray which shortly is to the effect that, on each of four separate occasions, the pursued natives who had been identified by Tracker Major as being implicated in the murder of Brooks, after being repeatedly warned to lay down their weapons, were the aggressors and attacked Mounted Constable Murray who, on each such occasion, was endeavouring to effect the arrest of the guilty natives and for that purpose was on foot and his horse had galloped back to where the packhorses were camped.

Each of the witnesses was subjected to a rigorous cross examination and each of them emphatically stated that the shooting was absolutely necessary to save their own lives. After the first shooting, the Police Party followed up those implicated in the murder — hence the four separate occasions when shooting occurred. Constable Murray also shot one Aboriginal who had attacked him at Coniston Station.

Tracker Paddy corroborates Constable Murray's account, and here again it was essential to shoot to protect himself. Constable Murray cannot say who shot the lubras but those two lubras, with others, were amongst his attackers on the first occasion and as all the Aboriginals, male and female, were mixed up, the shooting of two lubras could easily have been quite unintentional and accidental. There is no evidence to the contrary. Briscoe and Stafford state they shot no natives. Saxby says he fired eight or nine shots with a rifle and heard two other firearms discharged and we are of the opinion that he was afraid to admit that he killed some of the blacks. The Board is prepared to believe the evidence of all witnesses.

b. Respecting the shooting of fourteen natives implicated in the attack on W. Morton, the evidence of Mounted Constable Murray is corroborated in every detail by Mr Morton.

Morton can speak the 'lingo' of that particular tribe (the Walmallas). This tribe was also implicated in the murder of Brooks. Morton swears he warned the natives repeatedly, on each occasion, to sit down and put their weapons down on the ground; that they refused; and that on each occasion when Constable Murray dismounted to endeavour to effect an arrest, the natives attacked with boomerangs, spears, nulla nullas and a tomahawk and it was necessary, in order to save their own lives, that the blacks should be shot.

Morton knew each of the blacks who attacked him as they had at times worked for him and he identified them on each occasion and in some instances blacks were allowed to go free as they were not implicated in the attack on him.

The Board sees no reason to doubt the evidence in this case.

Morton also shot one of the Aboriginals dead when he was attacked at his camp and the Board is of the opinion he was fully justified in so doing.

c. Respecting the shooting of an Aboriginal by settler H. Tilmouth, the Board examined Tilmouth and an intelligent Aboriginal in his employ who corroborated Tilmouth's story, and has no hesitation in finding that the shooting was justified in this case.

Dealing generally with the suggestion that the shooting of the blacks by the Police Party was in the nature of a reprisal or a punitive expedition on which there is not a scintilla of evidence, the Board, in addition, would like to emphasize the following points which appear to discount such a suggestion.

1. If a massacre of the blacks was contemplated, would they not have shot every one at Coniston where the first encounter took place and not have allowed 23 of them to go free?
2. Would not the Police Party, in Morton's case, have shot the six adult male natives who were allowed to go free when Morton said they were not identified with those who attacked him?
3. If a massacre was intended, is it likely that Constable Murray would have dismounted from his horse on each occasion and alone gone amongst the natives at the risk of being killed, to effect arrests when all the party could have remained mounted and, from a distance of safety, wiped out all the blacks?
4. If a massacre was intended, why tend to the wounded as the evidence shows was done in several cases?

Constable Murray was called throughout the Enquiry. Had he desired to disguise the number of natives killed, he could have done so in his official reports and evidence. Furthermore, if a massacre was intended, the Police Party could, as the evidence shows, have killed a hundred natives.

The Board unanimously answers the first three questions as follows:
(a) The shooting was justified;
(b) The shooting was justified;
(c) The shooting was justified.

d. Regarding question (d), the Board unanimously finds:
1. No provocation has been given which could reasonably account for the depredations by the Aboriginals and their attacks on white men in Central Australia.
2. In the opinion of the Board, the following are the reasons for the Aboriginals' action:
(a) the advance of the Walmalla tribe on a marauding expedition from the border of Western Australia into the Coniston country — the tribe had intentioned to wipe out the settlers and working boys, as the evidence shows;
(b) unattached Missionaries wandering from place to place, having no previous knowl-

edge of blacks and their customs and preaching a doctrine of equality;
(c) inexperienced white settlers making free with the natives and treating them as equals;
(d) semi-civilized natives migrating and getting in touch with myalls;
(e) semi-civilized natives losing their skills for hunting wild game through lack of practice, preying on the working boys at stations.
(f) a woman Missionary living amongst naked blacks thus lowering their respect for the whites;
(g) crimes and minor offences by natives going unpunished owing to insufficient Police;
(h) insufficient Police patrols;
(i) imprisonment not being a deterrent to native offenders;
(j) escaped prisoners from Darwin not being rearrested — wandering about in their native country and causing unrest and preaching revolt against the whites.

In conclusion, the Board wishes to state that there is no evidence of any starvation of blacks in Central Australia. On the contrary, there is evidence of ample native food and water.

Chairman: A.H. O'Kelly
Members: J.C. Cawood, Government Resident
P.A. Giles, Police Inspector

Source: Finding of Commonwealth Board of Enquiry, Office of the Government Resident, Alice Springs, 18 January 1929.

The tragedy of the Centre

Northern Territory Times, 1928

During a sermon at the Methodist Church on Sunday, Rev. Stanley Jarvis, said the recent murder wherein Frederick Brooks was alleged to have been killed by certain natives near Alice Springs was remarkable for amazing admissions made by the Police. It would not be right for him as a missionary of the Methodist Church to keep silent when such extraordinary revelations have been made as revealed during the hearing of the case in the Supreme Court. Constable Murray admits that he and his party shot down 17 natives at odd times during the 20 days' hunt for alleged murderers. It has shocked the community. First a native was shot over the left eye and lingered in agony for 14 days and then died. Again according to published evidence, they met a number of blacks one of whom was armed. The constable threw the man down, the other natives ran for their spears and to use Murray's own words 'I could see they intended to fight, so drastic action was taken resulting in a number of aboriginals being shot'. They intended and were ruthlessly shot down. In the camp close by were women and children who in terror, armed themselves with sticks and it is alleged made an attack on the police party and two were killed. A few days later some men, women and children were met. Six men came to the front and threw a couple of boomerangs apiece and for their offence and defence were also shot. The constable said that he shot to kill. The tragedy of it all! In one instance a bullet from a high powered rifle passed through one native and killed another. Other natives were met and some shot. And so the horrors continued and the sands became bloodstained. Seventeen lives were taken, two natives captured and taken to Darwin, a thousand miles away, and the Court acquitted them. Who will take them back to their country? Will they ever get back? Mr Justice Mallam is reported to have remarked during the recital of these tragic events 'Mowed them down wholesale!' People want to know if any others were killed. It appears impossible for all those bands of natives to be associated with the murder of Brooks and it looks as if they were shot down at different places just to teach them and others a lesson. The Federal Government is being asked to appoint a Commission of Inquiry. These tragedies and horrors make the natives bitter towards white men and they wait their time to retaliate, yes, the police party shot to kill and seventeen were slain, and all for what?

Source: 'The tragedy of the Centre', sermon by the Reverend Stanley Jarvis reported in the *Northern Territory Times*, 13 November 1928.

On women and wives

Matt Savage

The Aborigines certainly did have their good points — and particularly the women. It is no good saying one thing and meaning another: the outback would still have been in its wild state if it had not been for the lubras.

None of us would have come up here and lived like a hermit. Even the married blokes liked a bit of variety in their lives. So you might say the lubras were the real pioneers because without them there would have been no settlement — or at least it would have come much more slowly.

The Aboriginal standards of beauty are quite different from our own. But in every mob of blacks you would find one or two who kept themselves cleaner than the rest and looked a bit outstanding. Of course these were the ones the whites went for first.

I remember one who was a coppery colour. This was up near the northern coast; so maybe she had some Malay blood. Anyway, she was always available for a date. She would come down to your camp with maybe only a towel wrapped around her waist, and she would whip this off and crawl into your swag. A thoroughly good naughty, too! She had a husband but he didn't mind, so long as you gave her a present to take back to him.

Many a man who brought his wife to the Far North lived to regret his marriage — especially if he had been accustomed to gay times with the blacks. In my experience every one of these blokes went back to the lubras. And the wives hated them for it.

Usually the white women were the better lookers. But though there might not have been many oil paintings among the blacks, they certainly did have something, because after a week or a month or a year of marriage, the husbands would go sneaking back to them.

I never liked the white women on the stations. They always had their noses in the air. I could not understand why they were so all-fired proud about what they'd got. The old cow has the same thing and uses it for the same purpose.

The station wives hated the lubras. I suppose they were jealous. They treated the blacks like animals. You might read about the hardships these women endured in the bush. That's all bunkum. Those who came to the Kimberleys had never had it so good in their lives before.

I never heard of any well-educated women in good positions throwing that away to come north. The ones I met were just ordinary. Probably they had been slaveys in the city, working in pubs or as waitresses in restaurants.

Then they would arrive in the Kimberleys where they had nothing to do but to queen it

Matt Savage, the 'Boss Drover', in his camp several miles from Alice Springs. At rear are his wife Ivy and second daughter Patsy. In front are eldest daughter Sheilagh (left) and youngest daughter Noreen.

over an army of black servants. The lubras took care of all the household chores; the washing, the cleaning, the cooking, the nursing of the kids. Half the time they even suckled the babies.

Some wives took an interest in the garden and made a great name for themselves because of their flowers or their vegetables; but even here they just gave the orders — the blacks did the actual work.

The attitude of some whites — men and women — towards the Aborigines was rather like that of a mediaeval baron towards his slaves and serfs. Often this applied to the white and part-Aboriginal stockmen as well.

The most conceited station managers were those who were married to a white woman. Often they would put the staff in the kitchen while the family ate alone in the dining room with an Aboriginal to pull the punkah fan and keep a breeze about their heads. The managers who were bachelors varied but some were as bad as the married blokes.

Source: Keith Willey, *Boss Drover: Stories Related to the Author by Matt Savage*, Rigby, Adelaide, 1971.

The combo's[1] anthem

W. E. (Bill) Harney

When stock-panels slam on the last gnarled beast,
And the smoke signals rise, we will ride to the feast
Where the pandanus fairies are singing their songs,
And the wild ducks are mating by quiet billabongs.

'Neath black velvet banners we'll carve our way through
As we march to the drone of a didgeredu.
We love and we laugh as pale introverts sigh,
We sneer at protectors, his laws we defy.
                      whose (?)

We know each 'girl's' name by her track on the sand,
The Belles of the rivers, the 'Girls from inland',
The Maids of the mountains, and lor' I forgot
The Sirens from sea-shores, the best of the lot.

They are comely and dark, and the glint of their eyes
Are as dew-drops that gleam on a wintry sun-rise.
And the firm rounded breasts that seductively tease
Are like seed-pods that sway from squat baobab trees.

So hail Borroloola, the Ord, V.R.D.
The 'Nash' and the 'Hill' for a cracker old spree.
We are riding with cheques and we sing as we come
For a gut-full of wooing, a gut-full of rum.

Let gin-shepherds watch when the rain clouds appear,
And the ring of horse-bells tell his 'girls' when we're near.
He will lock up his 'Studs' but we'll steal them away
To our paper-bark fires till breaking of day.

For green is the grass where the early rains fall,
Our pack-bags are full, so we'll answer the call
To ride down bush tracks and old friendships renew
To the beat of a tap-stick and didgeredu,
To the beat of a tap-stick and didgeredu.

1. 'Combo' is a colloquial Northern Australian term meaning a white man who lives with an Aboriginal woman.

Source: W.E. (Bill) Harney, *Life Among the Aborigines*, Robert Hale, London, 1957.

4 'Nobody knows what it means': White depiction of Aborigines

We then gave 3 hearty cheers for the flag, the emblem of civil & religious liberty, and may it be a sign to the natives that the dawn of liberty, civilisation, and Christianity is about to break upon them.
— John McDouall Stuart, journal entry, 23 April 1860

The black man in the north of Australia has exactly the same instincts as his brethren in the south. The race is identical, and the experience of years has only tended to prove that the aboriginals are not amenable to civilisation, and are barely capable of receiving and retaining the truths of Christianity.
— Mrs Dominic D. Daly, *Digging, Squatting, and Pioneering Life*, 1887

It is a pity that this dark race is doomed to extinction. But when one reflects on the fate of high civilisations in the past ages, which succumbed mainly because of a growing disregard of ethics and social and economic basic facts, it surely behoves us seriously to think of our unique and responsible position as guardians of Australia. This is now the only continent under the hegemony of one people; and with the best British pioneering traditions to live up to, it should, in such favourable and unprecedented opportunities, lead the van of Christian civilisation.
— Gordon Buchanan, *Packhorse and Waterhole*, 1934

Civilised people are still too raw and greedy to be true Christians.
— Peter Differ, in Xavier Herbert, *Capricornia*, 1938

Two hundred years ago
dark figures leaned a forked tree on this cliff,
and rigged a cradle for the artist.
And nobody knows why they did it
Nobody knows what it means.
— Mark O'Connor, 'Rock paintings, Katherine Gorge', n.d.

Previous page: W. Baldwin Spencer: 'Two Aranda women with a baby, Alice Springs'. This is a special photograph indeed, since Spencer was able to avoid the stiff and uncomfortable nature of virtually all the early posed photographs of Aborigines taken by whites. Spontaneity and warmth here triumph over scientific design.

One big, big fellow feed

William J. Sowden

I should have recorded before an interesting event — the distribution by the visitors of largesse to the blacks, in public half-circle assembled in front of the hotel [in Darwin]. The gift was in the shape of flour — next to tobacco the best-esteemed native luxury — doled out in a grocer's scoop in anything but grocer fashion by Mr. Knight. The sight was certainly the most interesting seen on this trip. Oh, such degraded specimens of humanity! — less manlike some than a grinning and chattering monkey looking at them from the hotel door. I question whether, on the whole, any beings bearing the semblance of humanity could be found more low-sunk than these. Physically the men were well-made, though disproportionately light of tibia; but the women were lank and puffy and distorted, and, for the most part, ugly as the Father of Mischief. Some few, however — the young ones — were well-looking comparatively. 'Twas pitiful, though still amusing, to see these people as they came for flour — came with old tins, and bits of dirty paper, and rags, and leaves. First an old lubra (unanimously voted a living skeleton — thin and wizened and dried beyond belief), holding a chubby child on her shoulder; then an obese woman — the only stout one I had seen here yet; then a matron with twin children, the one cross-legged upon her shoulder, the other affectionately supported by the neck under her arm; then an 'angular parallelogram' in the shape of a man 6ft. 4in. high; then some of these sneaking back again for more; and at the end an ugly woman with a pretty child, who grabbed a handful of the flour and made its face a perfect piebald, and rubbing it into its eyes and crying with the pain caused little milky rivulets to flow adown its nose. And then, quarrelling over the food as pigs quarrel over a bone, and quite as thankless to the donor, with a profuse spitting (not to have seen a tobacco-chewing native salivate is something to be thankful for!) and a screeching and jabbering and a discordant whir like the alarm-note of a quail, but more discordant — the dusky crowd moved off to their camp to put their different lots of flour together and to have for once, at least, 'one big, big fellow feed,' the while their benefactors went upon their journey.

Source: William J. Sowden, *The Northern Territory As It Is*, W. K. Thomas & Co., Adelaide, 1882, p.28.

Puzzles

Jerome K. Murif

The first beholding of adult blackfellows and blackfellowesses naked, may be slightly shocking to sensitive nerves. An uncomfortable, uneasy feeling will probably be induced. But this creepiness soon passes, and one comes to either look upon or pass unnoticed the ungarbed blackfellow (and later on the average lubra), as he might the apes and monkeys in a zoological gardens.

Some of the habits of those animals are theirs, too; when collected and watched awhile it will for evermore 'go without saying' to the observer that they are natural-born hunters.

They have no thought for the things of the morrow, but they consider the birds of the air and how they shall catch them. The youths are adept in the art of stone throwing; lubras, though, are by far the better hands. They ask not for money as wages — only 'tucka', 'toombacca' or 'bacca', and 'ole clo'.

One of them in a quiet confidential chat gave it as his opinion — 'White fella big one fool; him *work* all the time!'

I explained how it might be: the whitefellow worked to save up money with which to purchase leisure in his old age — 'all the same sleep all day *then*,' I explained.

After ruminating — 'Why not him sleep all day along-a *now?*' he asked puzzled. And so puzzled me.

Sometimes there is a charm in the simplicity of their 'English'.

'That one big fool hoss,' remarked a blackboy, referring to an animal which, instead of remaining near and feeding, had a tiresome habit of travelling afar off when hobbled out of an evening — 'every day him walk about all night.'

This boy had seen a kangaroo close by the camp, and made an observation to that effect to his employer, — thinking probably the latter would like to have a shot at it.

'What sort of kangaroo; Big fellow?'

'N-o,' came the answer slowly, 'not big pella.'

'Little fellow, then?' by way of suggestion.

'N-o,' still the reply, 'not little pella.'

'Well what size was it?' impatiently.

'Lee-tle bit big pella.'

It is fellow, fella, pfellow, pfeller, pfella, pella according to the pliancy of the talker's tongue.

Source: Jerome K. Murif, *From Ocean to Ocean: Across a Continent on a Bicycle,* George Robertson, Melbourne, 1897, pp.135-6.

Narpulda Bola

Northern Territory Times, 1884

Our readers will remember Mr. D. Lindsay's description of a picturesque waterfall seen by him on his trip to Bynoe Harbour. The following is the aboriginal legend attached to it, versified by Mr W. E. Adcock.—

>Stand here on the verge and look down in the pool,
>Canst thou see the two rocks in its eddy so cool?
>Go down on thy knees, and gaze long in the water,
>For there are Nargêtho and King Umbilla's daughter.
>
>The black man has bound to this precipice hoary,
>A tale of affection, a true lover's story,
>How, the water descending, the cataracts pour
>Cleaves the face of the rock with a deafening roar;
>And as springs from the ledges the hurrying streams —
>How they flash to the sun in absorbing his beams —
>Sheer rises the precipice; mortal in vain
>Might essay its ascent, none its summit could gain;
>Hence came the event in the far away time
>That the primœval man has embodied in rhyme.

Ages agone, the Woolna tribe — the native bards declare —
Chose Umbilla to be their King, and he had a daughter fair
Taller than most of womankind, straight as the bilion tree,
Swifter than Atalanta was, a peerless maiden she!
The promised bride of Nargêtho, the boldest of the race,
And tallest of the Molineaux, the hero of the chase;
His the proud boast to win and wear the snowy triple plume,
And after death on lofty branch to have suspended tomb.

Such were the happy lovers who together roamed the glade
And hunted for the bowers that the satin bird had made,
Or trapped the nimble kangaroo and fished upon the lake,
Or stood upon the shelving strand to watch the rollers break.

Once Nargêtho and his betrothed were passing the ravine
When on the brink of yonder cliff they stood to view the scene;
On further verge Nargêtho saw the rare and valued flower
That Woolna maidens prize so much to deck their bridal bower;
To gain it for his cherished one the warrior essayed
And o'er the brink he leant to grasp the guerdon for his maid.

Alas! that it should happen so, that scribe should have to tell
But from the rock to gorge beneath the hapless lover fell,
And crushed and bleeding unto death, his face towards the sky,
Mulga could see his cherished form and hear his feeble cry.
Pity the shrieks, the agony of that despairing maid,
Her loved one stricken unto death, far, far from mortal aid.

'I come, my Nargêtho, I come!' the frantic maiden cried,
And bounded from the dizzy height to reach her lover's side;
Thus those affection bound in life together met their death,
In contact drew their latest sighs and last expiring breath.

The natives say that from the spot the maiden took her leap
This noble cataract shot forth into the canyon deep,
And in the pool below they see, now petrified to stone,
The forms of the two loving souls who perished there alone.
'Narpulda Bola' is the stream that boundeth from above,
Which rendered into English is 'sweet descending love.'

Source: *Northern Territory Times,* 11 October 1884.

Tranter's shot

Ernest Favenc

'I shot him like a dog!' said Tranter, as he got off his horse and proceeded to unsaddle.

'Whom did you shoot?' asked the new superintendent, who was standing by.

'Never mind,' returned Tranter. 'I'm not going to give myself away, but I shot him like a dog.'

There was bad blood between Tranter and the new super., and, as Tranter was about to leave, he was far from respectful in his manner.

The new super. was a young man from the South, and Tranter was an old Gulf hand. The new super. was a black-protector and temperance-advocate, and objected to swearing. Tranter, to sustain his character as an old Gulf hand, swore the most blood-curdling oaths in his presence, and told the most awful lies he could invent about black atrocities. Consequently, they fell out, and Tranter was leaving the station.

'Now, look here,' said the super., 'I'll get to the bottom of this — I'll just follow your tracks and find out what you have been up to.'

'You'll find him safe enough,' said Tranter, '*he* won't get away.'

The wrathful superintendent had his horse brought up, and started back on Tranter's track, taking another man with him. The trail was not hard to follow, as Tranter had been after horses and they had come home along a cattle-track.

The two had gone about five miles when a loud, wailing cry suddenly startled them. They were in scrubby country at the foot of a low conglomerate rise, with many boulders strewn about.

Following the direction of the cry, they came to an old gin seated on the ground cutting herself, or endeavouring to do so, with a piece of broken glass, and occasionally uttering the wail that had first attracted their notice. Green, the super., knew that this was a sign of mourning, and guessed that he was on the right track.

'There's been murder here,' he said, dismounting and approaching the gin. She took no notice of them, but kept on moaning and scraping at her breast.

'Let's look about,' said the man, 'they always go on like this, and we can't stop her.'

They searched awhile without result, the gin still maintaining her lamentation. Then Green, having made up his mind that a vile outrage had been committed, remounted, and they cantered back to the station.

'I will get F——,' he said, naming the native-police inspector, 'to bring a trooper and search.'

The 'barracks' were only some three miles from the station, and F—— was soon up there with his smartest tracker.

Meantime, Green had been trying to extract from Tranter what he had done with the body of his victim.

'I shot him like a dog, and I buried him like a dog,' was all he could obtain in answer. 'Go and find him, *he* won't run away.'

Green was infuriated, but he knew he could do nothing until evidence of the murder was established.

With one delay and another it was late in the afternoon ere Green, F——, and the black trooper arrived at the scene of the tragedy. The old gin was still sitting there raising her requiem song, but the black boy could obtain no information from her.

'Some fellow bin go bung,' was all he was assured of.

They searched without avail until dusk, and then had to depart unsatisfied, the most astonishing thing being that they could find no tracks of blacks other than those of the gin.

Green took counsel with F——, but the latter could say nothing, except that the fact of the presence of the gin sounding the death-wail and Tranter's boasting were not sufficient evidence to obtain a warrant on. For himself he thought, from what he had seen, that Tranter had shot a blackfellow there, but his mere belief would go for nothing. However, he slept at the station and promised to renew the search as early as possible.

Green passed a sleepless night. Here was a chance right into his hands of vindicating his opinions as to the murderous treatment of the natives, and he seemed most unaccountably baffled. He vowed that he would leave no stone unturned on the morrow, and at daylight fell asleep and slept so long that it was late when they got away.

Arrived at the fatal spot they at once set to work and began to examine the ground. The old gin had gone back to camp, and they were undisturbed by her outcries. Green had brought two men with him, so they were a strong party.

Suddenly the black trooper stopped and stamped his foot, 'What for me —— fool?' he exclaimed. 'Me know what that fellow shoot!'

'What?' cried the others, crowding round.

'You know, can't find em track — only old gin's track.'

'Yes.'

'Of course, that one shoot 'em piccaniny. Gin bin carry it.'

This probable solution, so much more horrible than they had expected, struck them all as the true one, and they hastened to the spot where the old native woman had been squatting. The trooper set to work and rolled away the boulder she had been leaning against, then he threw out some of the smaller stones, and, putting down his hand, drew forth by one leg the ghastly object of their search — the corpse of a fine fat dog, evidently the late property of the lamenting lubra.

Tranter was even with the super., who never got over the chaff, but returned south.

Source: Ernest Favenc, *The Last of Six: Tales of the Australian Tropics* (the Bulletin series, no.3), Bulletin Newspaper Co., Sydney, 1893.

A photograph from the extraordinary collection of W. Baldwin Spencer, evolutionary biologist and anthropologist: 'One of the oldest Aranda men, aged between seventy and eighty years. He is an Oknirabata, *a very wise old man.' The Museum of Victoria has some 1800 of Spencer's negatives, produced between 1894 and 1926.*

Photograph by W. Baldwin Spencer: 'Elderly Tiwi men seated on the ground. Melville Island, 1912'.

A selection of the wonderful sketches of F.J. Gillen, drawn in his diary (for his wife) during the 1901–1902 expedition through central Australia to study the Aranda people.
(i) Ilpalyurkna, a totem headman or Inkwartinja, of the Unmatjira: 'a much valued member of our staff and quite a walking encyclopaedia of the lore of his tribe'. (ii) Imbarkwa, headman of the Rain totem and perhaps the most influential man in his tribe. Gillen deemed him a Kaitish [sic] celebrity: 'He prefers the whiteman's mutton to the blackman's jew lizard and on more than one occasion he has gratified his appetite by robbing the local sheep yard. From our point of view he is a pure savage and therefore a fine fellow ...'
(iii) Ungwangna, a Kaitish girl: '[She] has a keen appreciation of our lolly tin which is now in a depleted condition'. (iv) Kaitish girl: '[also] a constant worshipper at the Shrine of our lolly tin'. (v) Thuritkarrie, a Warramunga man: 'perhaps one of the most expert stone tomahawk makers in his tribe'. (vi) Warramunga man 'whose Alcheringa ancestor was a Curlew'. (vii) Warramunga boy 'wearing his hair in the manner peculiar to lads of his age'. (viii) Miang-un-tupu: 'at certain seasons of the year she sings native chants which bring about a large increase in the number of lizards'. (ix) Bartunga, the oldest woman in the Warramunga tribe: 'probably the only woman in the whole wide world, who in full possession of her faculties has voluntarily refrained from speaking for between thirty and forty years. Her silence began with the death of her first husband's brother'.

Aborigines and wit

Rev. J. S. Needham

Some people say they [the Aborigines] have no wit. I had to go across to Cairns to take a service. I left a blackfellow behind to take the service for me. When we got across there we did not have too many at 11 o'clock service, but we had a good crowd at 7.30 and one of the blacks said to me: You say these people Church of England, I think they belong Flying Fox religion, they only come out in the night. One fellow coming out saw one of those little Baby Austins. Just as he came out he said: I nearly trod on it. There was a church meeting in Sydney, and an aboriginal who is doing anthropological research work was giving a lecture on the beliefs and customs of his own people and at the end he left his lecture open to question. One man in the hall thought he was going to take the blackfellow down, and he said: Mr Unaipon I understand the men of your race have a habit of eating the meat and throwing the bones over their shoulder to their wives; is that true? Quite true, said the lecturer, and very deplorable, but not unique; I know a race some of whose men spend all their money in the public houses and take nothing home to their wives at all. There was another occasion, we had a black with us at a missionary exhibition, and he did not want to get a particular train and the Secretary I had running this was very determined he should catch that particular train; he rushed him out to the car and got him to the station five minutes before the train was due. Just as they were going to get into the train David said: I left my false teeth at home. He did not intend to catch that train, and he was too good for them. There was another well known case; one doctor asked him on one occasion: You have no friends, will you sign this paper saying that when you die I can have your body [and] I will give you £5? He thought that was a good idea, so he signed quite a number of papers for different doctors, he thought it a good source of income, and when he died there was competition as to who would get his body. The same boy was up before the Magistrate on one occasion, and the Magistrate said: I have seen too much of you, this time I give you three months jail. He said: Not this time boss, give me another chance. He was persistent, and he got the chance; and the Judge said: Very well I suspend the sentence until 4 o'clock this afternoon, and if you are in Adelaide at 4 o'clock this afternoon you get three months jail. He said: Thank you boss; and went to sleep it off. About 4.30 half an hour after his time was up, he was perfectly well drunk, he could hardly stand straight, and went to a house to beg for some clothes. But the Magistrate was at the house where he knocked, having afternoon tea, and he came out to tell him he should have been out of the city and would have to go to jail, but the blackfellow said: It's alright boss. I only came to say goodbye.

Source: The Reverend J. S. Needham, 'Aborigines of Australia', *Northern Territory Times*, 5 June 1928.

Moondeen

William Hart-Smith

Moondeen, the oldest man of the river tribe,
Too old for the council of elders,
Thin as the meanest desert myall,
Felt something happening within him.

As he chipped at the throwing-stick
Fixed between his old knees,
He watched the little rock-lizards that gleamed and shone
Going over his feet sometimes,
Quick and cold as a drop of rain.
And he thought a long time about that.

As he worked the euro fat into the wood,
Rubbing fiercely till it came smooth
Like the black stones in the river,
Then pushed it into the hot ashes again
And rubbed, and went on rubbing,
He remembered that the wood had once been a tree;
He thought about the trees,
And made one name of them all,
One name which would be for one tree
Yet all of them together,
And he muttered it over and over to himself.
He thought about the throwing-stick he was making
And who would hunt with it, and lose it, and where,
And where it would lie one day lost forever,
And how long was forever;
And he dreamed adventures about it whilst he was still awake.

He thought about the river,
Where it started, right down to where it ended,
Pouring into the great water that stretches away forever;
He thought about it all day long,
Until the men came back from their hunting
And the dogs and women went out to meet them
With a dust and a hullalooing,
Which made him forget the word he had almost made for the river

And a rage took fire within him over nothing at all.
Nobody knew why Moondeen was always angry and short-tempered,
Spat like a lizard when disturbed.

Source: William Hart-Smith, *Harvest*, Georgian House, Melbourne, 1945, pp.14-15.

goanna

Lee Cataldi

the women run swiftly through the grass
the large women
the dry grass
the goanna runs swiftly the yellow goanna with long legs
how do they know which way it runs
chanting they prevent it running back
they run swiftly to a clump of grass
one among a thousand bushes
and hit it firmly across the back

the dry grass rustles like a forgotten sea
they put the dead goanna in a tin
a goanna that tastes like chicken with a backbone like a big fish

no matter how old the woman when the goanna
breaks for freedom from his disturbed nest she runs

more swiftly than he

Source: Lee Cataldi, *Women Who Live on the Ground: Poems 1978–1988,* Penguin, Ringwood, Vic., 1990, p.42.

the honey tree

Lee Cataldi

      1

we will never get to the honey tree each day
brings more sad news each day
another spear breaks
      meanwhile
rats gnaw at the roots of the ancient tree
the green shoots wither

hunter who could bring down the wild cat running
      never again
will we sit by a fire on the plain south of Parnta at midday
in the shade of a bean tree
      never again
lie quietly at midnight under familiar stars

the Japanangkas remove the possessions of their brother
a blanket a billy-can a rifle
and no-one now can visit the camp

so neatly constructed
deserted it lies

      2

so much water
so many bridges looking back
it is the progress of our history
the muddy ebb
the debris in the swamp the bad air
and now like a hippy without a passport
on the beach in Goa

I am here we lie out on the sands
between the fires a mother
tells a story of the moon
her words float outwards into the night

the night that swallows everything
languages history

3

the women have danced all night
all night their feet have shaped and reshaped the dust
the men have been singing
the songs that reconnect night and dawn   and right on time
the sun comes up
in the right place
our efforts are not misplaced   and the two boys
for whom this sun rises on this morning are brought forward
into the light
the mothers surround them and pick off the tufts of white kapok
which they put in their hair   with this gesture
they free them from childhood

the place has been burnt
blackened sticks under a blistering sun
the mourners hastily
climb down from the truck and scatter
all around women cry softly   their shaved heads
covered in clay and dust
they suffer from thirst yet from the red earth
new grass springs   by nightfall
everything is soaked in rain

4

Japanangka my friend you have gone
you have been released from the claims of the living
and from the wires and nets of the white man's heaven
you have left
grass and trees an empty hut
the wind whose message is unchanged
the law whose passage is unbroken

Source: Lee Cataldi, *Women Who Live on the Ground: Poems 1978–1988,* Penguin, Ringwood, Vic., 1990, pp.51-3.

In the bed of the River Todd

G. Oxford

'Mechanised', they push a stroller through the trees,
Two women and a child move across the river bed.
They live in the river's path,
The whole family,
Ready to move when
The water comes down.

Large fat wet drops fall lazily a little while,
A circle of black legs and arms disrupts and
Spreads to the wide edges, sheltering.
All one family —
'He's my sort of brother,
King of the River.'

Old men and young together for company,
Poor old men cheerily, with blind eyes, blind tongues,
Struggle to see, fight to express thoughts
In words wholly foreign.
Still unintelligible —
What, what do they say?

Trigger Morgan tells tall stories and reads;
Haltingly reads, proudly, like a six-year-old.
Still a wonder he can cope with a strange tongue,
With small schooling and
Little dreamtime, but
'Plenty good time' — he's travelled.

Ross Davis sports a hat, riding boots, Indian belt.
He wears a silk shirt, and talks readily.
Caterpillar totem, but ashamed is he,
To be in the river
With the boozed and the bottle
Drinking uncaringly.

'King of the River Bed', Les Turner sits sideways and silent.
Take his photo, just a dollar (I decline), 'It's better.'
A man with talent in watercolour, with Aboriginal name alone,
Sits painting on board brought
To the sandy river by Thomas, wrapped
In blue tissue paper.

Cheerfully friendly they tell stories to amuse us white children
So much younger in folklore.
Do they know they can teach us? Slowly in their eyes,
Knowledge of our ignorance gleams
Reflected from our
Eager listening faces.

Source: G. Oxford, *'In the bed of the River Todd'*, in *Aboriginal Voices* (a unit of the Social Education Materials Project), Curriculum Development Centre, Woden, ACT, 1978, pp.10-11.

Girls in a park

Jan Owen

Thin-legged, solid-bodied, they
swing by, easy of elbow and knee.
One leaps up for a twig — a heavy grace
that like their skin is dark;
their clothes, a rejoicing of colours,
are alien to them still
as the trim ways of this park.
Five of them, all talking —
a bubble of vowels that rise and tumble in flight
above the magnolias perched on naked bark.
This is the secret language of birds,
the palatal twitter of light:
each word lifts off with a whoosh
of feathers, flutters and dips and glides,
then plumps down on a bough which sways and sways —
tantalizing wrens just out of reach.
Stranger to this softness in the air,
I hold my breath to hear: sidelong they watch,
and Deereeree the wagtail, rainbow-lover,
skitters behind their eyes.
Then, Lesson One repeated five times over —
smile, Pitjantjatjara for *recognize*.

Source: Jan Owen, 'Girls in a park', *Northern Perspective*, vol.8, no.2, 1985, p.90.

Rain at Gunn Point

Tony Scanlon

It is raining at Gunn Point: from Arnhem Land
the monsoon clouds have come wallowing to the west —
and now they hang weeping on this decaying peninsula.
It is raining steadily deep into the night,
raining on the shabby dormitories where the prisoners
lie on beds of peeling iron, sagging wires;
lie on their backs with their hands behind their heads —
men from Milingimbi, from Oenpelli, Alyangula;
from the dying moieties of the Pellew islands;
men from the empty lands around Papunya and Mount Wedge.
And Black Elvis, and Jacky Gallipoli, Beachball and Turkey,
and men of the Tiwi and the Aranda whose names
sound like water running in the Stone Country
lie awake and listen to the clouds crying.

Tomorrow they will rise with the siren and go about
the futile exercises which pass for work; but tonight
they lie awake and stare with dark, glistening eyes
at the ceiling, seeing only the thunderheads
gathering over Maningrida, over Borroloola.

Source: Tony Scanlon, 'Rain at Gunn Point', *Maryland Poetry Review*, Fall/Winter 1989, p.11.

Aborigines passing

Roland Robinson

I hear laughter coming from frangipanni darkness
across the road, rapid, rippling laughter answered
by deeper throated, still liquid laughter from under
bauhinia boughs. It's the Aborigines going past,
carrying bundles of pandanus palm fronds, talking,
calling in laughter-calling voices. I've heard
laughter in someone's chatter as though the silver-
eye's lisping song came searching through sickle
shaped leaves of the eucalypt. I hear laughter
passing into bauhinia, poinciana, hibiscus darkness.

Source: Roland Robinson, 'Aborigines passing', *Northern Perspective*, vol.7, no.1, 1984, p.32.

Wash day

Billy Marshall-Stoneking

Monica and Victor come over to my place
to do their laundry
because there's nothing at their place.
They show up on Sunday
with faded dresses, frayed shirts
and dusty blankets,
placing them with great care
into the squat, barrel-chested wringer
(the whites unsorted from the coloureds).
I put a country n western record on
while the clothes and blankets squish —
S'fump S'fump S'fump —
turning the water a dull red.

In the lounge room
Monica and Victor sit on green cane chairs
sipping tea and reading comics.
We speak very little to each other.
I don't want to scare them away —
We are trying very hard.
Our relationship has grown, so slowly —

From nothing to laundry.

Source: Billy Marshall-Stoneking, 'Wash day', published originally in *Off the Record*, Penguin, Ringwood, Vic., 1985; and then in Marshall-Stoneking, *Singing the Snake: Poems from the Western Desert, 1979–88*, Angus & Robertson, Sydney, 1990.

in th desert you remember

Eric Beach

that th world's round, so that th whirl of ants
in th ring road of honey ants dreaming
is perfectly sensible, & th wheel we walk
doesn't bump along a rut of happiness
towards an absurd fence in a fine cemetery
nor are we left with a notion of prayer
dumped every sunday with th garbage
so good to see someone arriving
knowing they come from a long line of footprints
& laughing at mirages of mountain ranges —
'it goes west, a long way, that one'
but th man who believes in th book
lives in a world too crowded for this kind of humour
preaching to th red earth from his green quarter acre
from behind barbed wire with his guard dog & flowers
walking straight ahead, not seeing th sand painting
that boots & hooves destroy, th man unmaking
in uncomfortable clothes in a church made awkward
by stiff corners, collars, & clean thoughts
that won't last out of sight of water
still, a spiritual people must sing
groping in a new dark, & hearing sticks clicking
in th dry places where th old religion
hums to itself, & may be overheard

Source: Eric Beach, 'in th desert you remember', published originally in *Overland*, no. 100, September 1985, p.82.

A remote area

Graeme Parsons

There is a map of the world on the desk top. The desk is new, like the cupboard and the bed. With nothing else to do, I have an impulse to sit and pore over the map. There is a chair outside on the verandah. I drag it in and am about to sit down when I see that there is a rip on the seat. The vinyl has been slashed and yellow foam rubber is dribbling out. Also, between the rip and the back-rest, someone has written a name in thick black texta.

David Giliwingi. It is underlined jaggedly and asterisked all round.

Someone called David Giliwingi stayed in this room too. Slept in this bed. Turned on the shower and waited too long for the hot. Was that his discarded chip packet I found in the bottom of the cupboard, sheltering the crisp cadaver of a cockroach?

David Giliwingi. Perhaps he didn't stay here at all. Perhaps he lives right outside in the town, the settlement — call it what you will — and just came to the verandah one afternoon to rest and get out of the wind. He might have noticed the chair, leaning on its back legs and holding the flyscreen door shut. He could have marked it then and there, casual but decisive, a statement.

Why did he have the texta with him? How would I know? I've come to check the council's accounts. Nobody told me there was a ceremony today and that I'd have to wait alone in this hostel for visiting strangers, government balanda. Tomorrow I can do what I came for and get out.

It might not have been him at all. It might have been his brother. Maybe it was his ghost.

Ghosts. Who ever thinks of them these days? Why think of them here? It's no place for ghosts. It's too young, too new, all bolted steel frame and cladding. The ghosts of the old people are well and truly gone. They've no reason to hang around here. Things are changing. The people are settled. They gouge roads up to the coast, drive Toyotas six hours to the whitefeller town for beer. They cheer at basketball games and they have this hostel for visiting balanda.

David Giliwingi could be working in Darwin, or coming back now on the plane with whitefeller documents and blackfeller plans. I think someone else wrote his name on the seat. I'll ask about him. He's a man on the move, for sure. I should know him.

The wind finally snaps open the flyscreen door, slamming it back against the green metal cladding. My head jerks up and I see a motorbike roar past, churning up a wave of filmy orange dust to be whipped away by the wind. The rider is wearing dark glasses, a young man. It might be David Giliwingi, headed for the ceremony.

The bike engine cuts out and the wind, shedding dust, brings the ceremony sounds to my door: sticks beating out a steady rhythm on wood, didgeridoo persistent as heartbeat thrumming and throbbing in the background, the leader's wailing voice. The song reaches its climax and there is a chorus of shouts, sharp and final. Silence, punctuated by the guttural cries of crows. I do not know what it means. The plane will take me out tomorrow.

Perhaps that was David Giliwingi I saw yesterday at the airport. The policeman had a heavy arm across his shoulder and for a moment — until I saw the shove and the stumble — I thought the scene touching. He was about fifteen, five foot nothing with legs like grass stalks. Later, somebody told me he'd been stealing from the store and sniffing petrol. Would that boy have written on this chair, one demented and meaningless night? Would he have written anywhere at all? Would he ever? The court and the prison are in Darwin. I saw his small expressionless face in the window behind the pilot, till it disappeared behind the propeller blur. It came to me then: this is another country.

It's not true of course. I look at the map of the world on the desk top. There is Australia, pink Australia, hanging from its neck at Asia's tail, surrounded by flecks and specks as it floats humpbacked in the great blue bowl of the Indian and Pacific. And I can put my finger down on the hump and cover ten thousand square miles of wilderness, with this place in the middle. I tell myself I am not in another country.

I spread my thumb and middle finger to measure the distance between Melbourne and here. Along the same line, north north-west, I measure the distance again. My finger lands on Manila. I try the same thing with Sydney and finish up in Negros. Then I try it from Perth and finish up in the ocean among the specks of the Marshall Islands. I save Brisbane for later.

One thing is clear. Australia is in the wrong place. If I had a stanley knife, I'd cut it out. Delicately, precisely, taking Bass Strait so as not to lose Tasmania, I'd excise it from its southern limbo. A real nice tradesman's job; Australia on the move. I'd float her east across the Pacific and berth her, snug and appropriate, between Hawaii and California.

No good. The east coast'd be too Latin.

Move her up and turn her on her side so Melbourne faces Seattle. The Yanks'd help with the manoeuvring: a few blasts in the right places to settle her in. David Giliwingi would love it, all those black faces walking down city streets. He could sing the blues and live in Harlem.

But I haven't got a stanley knife.

Who the hell was Stanley anyway, and how did he get a knife named after him? Is he floating in some limbo now, drifting through a disembodied gallery of hardware stores and studio drawers, contemplating neat blue handles and screw-in blades among jumbles of tools and pencils, thinking it was all worthwhile? Stanley. A name immortalised. It might have been a place in England for all I know, or a factory. But somewhere, there was a person. Did he have mustard on his sausages? Did he grind his teeth in his sleep? Did he dream? Did he ever sit in an empty room and wonder, or was he too damn busy?

I'm sitting on David Giliwingi. I stand up and look at his name again. It hasn't gone away; it's just the same. Did he make that gash on the vinyl? Did he do it with a stanley knife?

The wind blows the door open again and slams it against the cladding. I look up to see a child watching me from the road. His hair is matted with dust and he is smiling, his teeth as white as honesty. I stand up and wave to him. He calls 'Hello' and waves back. I want to ask him his name, to draw him into conversation, but he mounts his bike and cycles erratically away. I even step out onto the verandah and open my mouth to call after him.

I descend the steps and reach the road. My thongs are submerged in fine dust. There are trees around the corner. I meet an old man.

'Who is David Giliwingi?' I ask.

He coughs and smiles and asks me for a cigarette. I give him one, hoping it will help.

'Who is David Giliwingi?' I ask again.

His smile deepens. It is a smile which seems to have alighted on his face from beyond. It seems to be forcing its way back into his features, into their darkest recesses. I light the cigarette for him. He holds my hand steady. His face is darker than soil and creased like dry mountains. He exhales and disappears in smoke.

A middle-aged woman is sitting on the ground, further back in the tree-shade. She is wearing a cotton dress, its material patterned with yellow and blue flowers.

'Have you heard of David Giliwingi?' I ask her.

She draws a circle in the dirt, two dots for eyes and a line for a mouth. She points at it.

I go back to my hostel room and try to sleep. I am haunted by geography. Everything is adrift. I should have kept the lid on my fantasies. Stanley knives and floating Australias, ghosts and David Giliwingi. Whoever he is, or was, I curse him. My sleep suffers because of him and the afternoon drags with only the promise of an empty night before columns of figures in the morning and, afterwards, a return to my civilisation.

It is twilight and noises from outside are multiplying suddenly. Four-wheel drives and trucks clashing gears as they growl around the bend, the didgeridoo droning again, country and western on a ghetto blaster, children shrieking, dogs yelping, a group of people talking loudly on the verandah in a language as foreign to me as Egyptian. So much happening. My room seems like the centre of the human universe. Whose round empty face did that woman draw?

I fall asleep.

He is in my dream. He could be anywhere but he had to turn up here.

'I see you're staying in my room,' he says. I can't make out his face.

'It's anybody's room,' I say. 'It's a hostel, a visitor's place. All you have to do is pay the rent.'

'I never paid any rent,' he says.

'Then it's not your room,' I tell him. 'How can it be?'

I don't hear anything but I think he might be laughing.

Now he is coming at me out of smoke, wearing the old man's face.

'Did you cut that vinyl?' I ask him.

He doesn't answer.

'You shouldn't do that. It's not your property.'

The old man's gaze is steady and comes from inside. His teeth are rotten but his chest is hairless and smooth like a boy's. He speaks, but the words are unintelligible. He puts out his hand, not begging but demanding. I reach for my pocket but the cigarettes aren't there. He waits, and he is expecting something. I am afraid. I do not want to know about David Giliwingi.

The old man stabs his finger at my heart. I am afraid of what he wants from me. I wish he was the old man on the road, the smiling man who held my hand to cup the flame. He holds his finger steady and I can feel it reaching inside to where my blood trickles and gushes, where it pulses in my arteries to the rhythm of stamping on dry earth.

I am a bag of blood, a trembling bag of blood. If that pointing finger burns a hole, my life will gush, a crimson gout to spread and turn black in the sun with empty parchment skin for starving dogs to gnaw.

Still the finger does not move. I try hard to think of other things, pink Australias plunging across the oceans in search of comfortable moorings, stanley knives ripping from the sky like summer lightning. But the dream keeps pulling me away. Even when I wake myself, it catches me in the act of trying to get my fingers into that vinyl crack in the seat cover, just to hold on to the cool material of day-world life. It's no good though.

Outside it's dark, and the old man hasn't left me. He is speaking now, and it's the same thing over and over again. There is no choice. I have to listen. I have to feel that finger pointing.

'...wingi, Giliwingi, Giliwingi.'

Source: Published originally under the title, 'A rural area', in *Northern Perspective,* vol.11, no.1, 1988, pp.11-13.

5 'Too much blackfeller': The black view

Them bloody-whatsa-European come on after that. Banging, banging time now. They [my people] didn't know that, they reckon lightning somewhere. And they reckon, 'Ah that man get out bush.' They reckon that lightning. Another bloke drop. Yeah, bang! Another bloke drop. Bang! 'nother bloke. They bin look at, you know, they bin looking eye. Something wrong? Got a blood come through the nose. 'Oh, might be lightning.' Bang! See? They didn't catch on for a while. They pick up all the women and European takem away, you know? And the Aborigine just follow them up.
— Daly Bulgara, interview with Peter Read, 1977

All our mob been shot. My grandmother Maryanne ... bin die poor bugger. A lot of people bin shot there. Working man, too. All the working man bin shot too. You know, they bin go to corroboree, working people. Stirling [cattle station on the upper Hanson] men, and from Barrow Creek.
— Neddy Jakamarra, interview with Petronella Wafer, 1981

Did the white men ever shoot those women and children then, and piccaninnies?
Yes. Hittem, killem. Yeah, same way they killem killem long stick. Gottem stick, knockem in the head or neck. Them kid, piccaninny, small one, like a goanna, hittem longa tree. Bashem longa stone, chuckem longa stone, or killem. Might be too cruel. Just bashem. You know, too small to shootem, too small. Women bin run-away, they roundem up, shootem.
Why did they do that?
I dunno. Oh, they bin like to killem, finishem up tribe. Take all of their country. Might be they want to takem big place, you know, this country.
— Chicken Gonagun & Sandy Mambookyi, interview with Peter Read, 1977

They shot anybody, they told me. One old woman they caught right out in the plain. She was digging for nuts and she tried to explain what she was getting, you know, something to eat. One white man shot her there.
— Dinah Kurratji, interview with Peter Read, 1977

And they bin turnem round, and shootem all. All people all, like bullock. Old people bin here, this country. Old people, like bullock. Big mob, woman, kid, man. Too much woman. Too much ... too much man. Too much blackfeller. All Warlpiri you know, all Warlpiri. Poor bugger.
— Jimmy Jungarrayi, interview with Peter Read, 1977

When the old Captain Cook died, other people started thinking they could make Captain Cook another way. New people. Maybe all his sons.

Too many Captain Cooks.

They started shooting people then. New Captain Cook people. That was new. New people did that. Those are the people that made war when Captain Cook died; because they didn't care, they didn't know, all those young people.

They are the ones who have been stealing all the women and killing people. They have made war. War makers, those New Captain Cooks.
— Paddy Wainburranga, ?1987

Previous page: Striking Gurindji stockmen after they had walked off in protest at the appalling working conditions at Wave Hill Station in 1966. The era of assertiveness and determination to achieve a semblance of equality had begun.

My father very much hurt

Duncan

Mister — My father go up tree 'long my country to get 'em stick. Him fall down; very much hurt; foot very bad. Me, Duncan, him son, carry him long camp; put stick on leg; but no get better.

You say now, Mister, that big corroboree Parliament give blackfellow plenty physic, plenty good things; so now you make Doctor come long camp and see my father; then him get better, and me, Duncan, sit long printing paper, be what whitefellow call printer's berrowa.

Very good,
                    DUNCAN.

Source: Letter from Duncan to the editor, *Northern Territory Times*, 2 January 1874.

Wanderer's lament

W. E. Harney & A. P. Elkin

(Walaka rhythm)

Poor fellow me,
Poor fellow me,
My country
It gave me,
All that I see,
Gifts that I see,
All that I see,
Poor fellow me.

Once I was gay,
Once I was gay,
Once I was gay,
Poor fellow me,
Then came the day,
I went away,
Now I am grey,
Poor fellow me.

Now I'm alone,
Now I'm alone,
Now I'm alone,
Poor fellow me.
Nothing I own,
Spirit has flown,
Poor fellow me.

So let me die,
Peaceful I lie,
Let my shade fly,
Poor fellow me.
Poor fellow me.

Source: W. E. Harney & A. P. Elkin, *Songs of the Songmen: Aboriginal Myths Retold*, F. W. Cheshire, Melbourne, 1949, p.110.

The Malak Malak people lived here

Bill Parry

The Malak Malak people ... lived here before white men come here ... after a while when Dr Cook [sic] went back some people came into this country and started mining and one thing and another — a copper mine down Daly River, and the Malak Malak people seen the white human beings, on the track, bush roads — no motorcars them days; they carried their swag on their back [and] billycan; they came to the copper mine and found some copper. So Aboriginal people seen some different human being ... They were white and the Aboriginal people say, 'We black, how this come?' So, they said to one another, 'We'll have to watch this bloke, he might upset the world.'

So watch him, watch him ... it took a while, and they got closer and closer to the white European. They didn't know what was going on; they seen a white man striking a match, they said, 'Hello, that's a quick light, we use the fire-sticks' — rub a coupla sticks to make our fire. The white man ... puts the billy on, and the billy starts to boil so he puts tea in the water and the Aboriginal people watching him: 'This is new, what's he doing to this water putting colour in it?' White man got sugar, put it in the tea and the Aboriginal said, 'What's that?' — talking with their hands to the white man. They couldn't talk English, and the white man couldn't talk back — too deaf — so they give em a taste of this tea — 'Oo, this is good, good tucker' ... thinking, 'The damper we make we gotta soak it in the water, we gotta wait for the wheat, make our own, but this is better ...'

And the white man said, 'Any woman round here?' and they said, 'Yeah, they our wives.' And the white man said to the Aboriginal people, 'Can we take some?' But they didn't want to part with their wives. So the Chinaman and white men got hungry for wives, so they took the women from the Aboriginal people and kept them in their shelters. They just took 'em. And the Aboriginal people said, 'They got something that can kill us, we [only] got spear.' So they won the woman.

Source: From the interview of Bill Parry by Ann Magrath, in Magrath, *Born in the Cattle*, Allen & Unwin, Sydney, 1987, pp.2-3.

An arrangement

Tim Japangardi Langdon

In the old days [1928] there used to be a group of Aboriginals working for [dingo-poisoner, Fred] Brooks. They were digging a dam and dragging the dirt out with camels. There was an old man who had about three or four wives. Brooks started sleeping with an Aboriginal wife. Then he took one called Martha for three days and threatened the man he would shoot them if they didn't leave him alone. The old men made an arrangement so they could kill Brooks.

The old men asked Martha to shout out so all the men ran to where Brooks was sleeping. They threw boomerangs at Brooks then old Japananka the wronged husband cut Brooks with an axe round the throat. Then the old man dragged Brooks who was dead and took him to a rabbit hole. There they pushed him inside.

After that they went to another place. One white bloke was going to visit Brooks so as he got to the camp there was no one around, he looked around, he saw the blood everywhere. Then he saw marks of a body which was dragged. He followed it and ended up in a rabbit hole. He saw two feet sticking up. He saw the blood. He quickly went and got the police to tracking the killers.

All the white men rounded up a mob. They started out to Brooks place. They saw nothing. They buried Brooks body then started looking for killers. The white men saw some Aboriginals in a camp. They surrounded them in a circle so that no one could escape. They shot every one of them. They let two old blokes free. One was Jamajinpa because he was blind ...

Source: From the recollection by Tim Japangardi Langdon, trans. from Walpiri by Otto Jungarrayi Sims, and collected by Mary Laughren, 1975, in Peter Read (ed.), *Social History of the Northern Territory*, vol.7, AGPS, Canberra, 1978, p.16.

Coniston story

Tim Japangardi Langdon

Yurrkuru is our name for the place where the fighting between Aboriginals and whites started. The white owner of Coniston Station was a man called Randall Stafford. At that time [1928] a man with camels was digging out soakages and making a dam at Yurrkuru on the west side of Coniston Station. His name was Frederick Brooks. The camels were used to dig out the earth. Brooks' tent stood on the west side of the soakage. Where he was digging women used to come regularly for water. Thus it was that the white man got to talk to them as they came up to get water.

This white fellow used to go with his rifle towards the camp situated to the south where our people were living. Those living there were Pukirdiwara, Walypalipakarnu, Yukunypungu and Nyalinypa. The white man used to go into the camp and drag off women in front of the men whom he threatened with his rifle.

One day he took off north with Jangari Japangardi's mother, Napurrula, and slept with her. He kept her for a long time in his tent as his woman. Back at the camp at Yurrkuru they looked for her but when night came she still wasn't to be found. He kept her for two nights and didn't send her back home. He continued sleeping with her the next day and although they went north looking for her, the men didn't find her. The white man kept her for three days. After that he sent her back home.

The old men met her and told Napurrula: 'If you go back again, you can hold him for us and yell out.' They then returned to the camp. The old men said: 'He might take away our woman from us, so we will have to kill that white man.' (Do you know where those people were from? Those old men were from Lurnpakurlangu.) Then they said that they would have to send her in the morning. And so they sent her there the following morning.

The old men followed the creek back. Japangardi himself had a club and so did Japaljarri (Napurrula's uncle). They each carried two boomerangs. Japanangka (Napurrula's husband) went with an axe. They went along the eastern side of the creek. Then they hid close by where the white man was digging the dam unaware of what was going on.

He went into his tent and Napurrula went on after him. Meanwhile those old men were standing by listening. Napurrula yelled out. The old men ran straight up to the tent with their boomerangs. Japaljarri was the first one to strike the white man and he struck him a blow on the back of the jaw. The white man staggered and caught hold of the tent posts. Then another man, Japanangka, broke a club over the back of his neck.

The white man was now staggering around and falling down all over the place. Japanangka took his axe and struck the white man on the neck and killed him outright.

Then they dragged the body west towards the creek and shoved it into a rabbit burrow near a black-berry bush and a white-wood tree. Having thus disposed of the body they went back home.

At that same time Alec Wilson Jupurrula came with some men to that creek which is north of Yuendumu on the other side of Wakurlpu (Rock Hill) where the two rock-holes lie. The killing of the white man had taken place just before they arrived there. They were carrying a white man (Jo Brown) who was very sick. They brought him to the other side of Wakurlpu. There they looked after him and tried to treat him. This white man thought to himself that he was very ill indeed and he said to Jupurrula: 'I am probably dying.' So he sent Jupurrula to Yimampi (Coniston Station) where there were other whites. Jupurrula set off with one camel. He headed towards that same place where the people had killed the white man. Jupurrula didn't find anyone in the tent but came across the body in the creek bed to the east. He headed straight for Yimampi further east. There he told the white people what he had seen. From Yimampi the whites set out by truck for Alice Springs to get more whites including policemen. They all came with lots of horses to attack the Aboriginal people. They returned to where the dead man lay in the rabbit hole and buried him in a proper grave.

They then split up into two parties; one went south and the other west. There was a camp to the south where the ones responsible for killing the white man had been camping. The whites coming from the north were then ready to attack towards the south. They shot all the people they found. They attacked in the late evening. Many people ran away to hide during the fighting. The whites sent away two old men, one of whom was a blind man called Rdakamuru and another called Wantapurrupurru from Yarrungkanyi in the west. The whites told them: 'Go away and take the women with you.'

Meanwhile the ones who had killed the white man were still alive and making their way through the rocky hills. They came to Yalkarajirri where they joined another camp. Japaljarri left the other two and went east to a place called Yurnturrpurlu.

Some people were camped near a soakage called Yarlalinji near Yajampiyi (Mount Denison). A lot of old men walking around south of there were all shot. Many others travelled at night and some were shot as they arrived exhausted at the watering place. These were drinking when they were shot.

There were a lot of people camped at Ngarntampi, all of whom were shot by the whites. However, there was a Jangala man who arrived there from the west and who was very thirsty. As he approached he was on the lookout for signs of people who might be living near there. He only came across whites there. He said to himself: 'All my family must have been killed by these whites. I might as well get shot too.' He went back to his camp at Lampalypa.

The whites then came further west to Yipirri (Mission Creek) and shot people camped there. As the whites turned back from there to return east they came across another lot of people and shot them all.

An old blind man Japanangka was wandering around calling out for any people who might be still around when he was bitten by a dingo. That was on the Juka-juka hills at Yarltiri (near Mission Creek).

The whites went back keeping to the south. One Jungarrayi was coming from the west and he caught sight of the whites and so he went into the water to hide. The whites came and shot him there. His name was Yakirrki. The whites dragged his body northwards and threw it away in a creek bed.

Other whites returned to Alice Springs to get more bullets. They then came back in search of other Warlpiris. They shot people they found around their camp fires.

Some Warlpiris had made a bush fire to the north and when the whites saw it they headed that way to attack whoever might be there. A lot of Warlpiris were camped by a waterhole. The whites came there and shot them all. There were really a lot of people living in that camp. They didn't even know about the trouble and the killing of the white man.

After that the whites headed further north to Ngunurlurru to shoot more people before returning to Yimampi (Coniston). They looked around for more Warlpiris but didn't find any.

Then there was a Jampijinpa man coming towards them but he didn't know there were whites around. Only one white caught sight of him and raced to attack him as he was on a horse. Jampijinpa ran ahead and the white chased after him. Jampijinpa climbed into a hollow tree trunk and hid there. At first just one white man was looking for him but later he shouted out to the others and they all came to look for Jampijinpa. They lit a fire in order to flush out the Warlpiri man but he stayed inside the hollow tree. He covered himself over with spinifex so that he would not be seen. The whites kept the fire going till night fell. Then the man climbed out of the hollow tree and ran away. He returned to the camp and related his story to the others.

Then there were two Japaljarris who were unaware of what was happening. They came from the west. They just came to drink some water. They drank and then set off from the watering place. They struck camp and were putting up a wind-break when they saw many whites coming to attack them with rifles. The two Japaljarris only had shields to protect themselves so they started singing themselves for protection. The whites started shooting at them. The two Japaljarris stood one in front of the other. The whites shot and shot at them. The two men kept blocking the bullets. The whites eventually ran out of bullets. They spoke to the two men: 'Well you two are the winners.' They gave them shirts, trousers and tobacco.

These two Japaljarris then went west to Yuendumu and stayed there for a long time. Later they went back north and that's where they died. Before they died they went to Lirrakilpirri (on the western side of Lake Surprise) where many of us were living. Later we people came back south to Lurnpakurlangu (Mount Doreen) where we worked. Many others later came here to Yuendumu.

Source: Tim Japangardi Langdon, 'Coniston story', transcribed by George Jampijinpa and translated from Walpiri by Mary Laughren, in *Yurrkuru-Kurlu*, Yuendumu School, 1978, pp.18-20.

They shot your old father?

Martin Jampijinpa

They shot your old father?
    Yeah.
What place?
    Down at Tippinba.
Were you there when they shot your father?
    Yeah, little boy, when I was a little boy ... I seen him. [Mounted Constable W.G.] Murray grabbed me then and he's hold me on the shoulder. There was a big camp there. They [the tribespeople] was getting in all the bush tucker. But he shot about ten o'clock in the morning, eight o'clock in the morning. Shot at seven, eight, that way.
What happened then?
    They yardem round, bringem to one mob ... and they shot it two or three shot guns going, people was going. [Alec] Wilson was there, Nugget Morton, what's his name was there too, Jack [Cusack] and Murray ... they all sit round here, all the old people was sleeping here. Round 'em up, just like cattle ... and bringem to one mob this way just suddenly. And shot it there.
Did some feller try and run away through those horses?
    No, they couldn't run away.
Did they shoot men, women and weehis [boys]?
    Oh no, man. Women, they just lettem go free.
But if all the people were there, and they'd got shot guns they couldn't tell if they were hitting men or what.
    No, they just draftem out, like cattle. We draftem out cow and calf. They bin just pushem out.
Push the men out?
    Yeah weehis and girls, and roundem up the men. Shootem all the men.

Source: From the interview by Peter Read in August 1977 of Martin Jampijinpa (Aboriginal survivor of the Coniston massacre of 1928), in John Cribbin, *The Killing Times*, Fontana/Collins, Sydney, 1984, p.161.

Wild ones, mate

Fred Booth Minmienadgie

Mr Booth's extraordinary actions and opinions need not necessarily be taken as typical of Aboriginal people working for whites. His story does show, though, the possible consequences of police and pastoral expeditions against the bush people. It is uncertain whether Fred Booth Minmienadgie was acting under orders from the policeman, or whether he did as he pleased.

The wild blackfeller. Oh, shot him, half a hundred. Just about night-time, one bastard run away. I shot him on the leg, fall arse over head.
  'Where's some blackfeller?' old sargeant said.
  'I shot one feller over here, crawl about on his knee. I must have broken his knee.'
  'Oh, good. Where's 'nother fellers?'
  'I shot him in the bloody head. Oh, he's in the creek, I think.'
  Old sargeant looked round, 'Oh, here's one bastard shot.'
  He's crawling [fast] around to get up, you know. Old sargeant put a gun on him. Look round, he wasn't there in the creek. Look round, oh, he's dead, that feller. I shot him in the neck. Here, right here you see.
  You were a police tracker?
  No, we drovers.
  When you shot those fellers, what do you do then? Fire, or what?
  Burnem, make a big fire, burnem. 'Set the fire on him,' policeman said, sargeant, 'Set the fire on him. To burn. They no good.'
  How many fellers in the fire?
  Oh, about fifteen. Fifteen blackfellers.
  Proper wild ones?
  Yeah, wild ones, mate. No good, they kill you quick.
  If you saw some wild fellow, like, he might be walking along, he didn't see you, would you still shoot him or wait till he threw a spear at you?
  Yeah, we can see the bastard a long way 'way. Yeah, coming along this is blackfeller going spinifex. Oh, there he is, jumping over the horses. Soon as he jump out, and bang! Finish him.

Source: From the interview of Fred Booth Minmienadgie in 1977, in Jay Arthur & Peter Read (comps & eds), A view of the past: Aboriginal accounts of Northern Territory history (unpub.), MS pp.32-3.

All children

Djawa

What will we do? We'll have to stay here at Mirki. We won't be able to get away, but the jungle will hide us.'
  Then, 'What will we do?'
  'I don't know. What will we do? Maybe we can all climb up into the trees, up in a tree we can all sleep, we'll stay up in a tree all the time.'
  'And all the children?'
  'All the children will be put up into a tree too. We can all stay.'

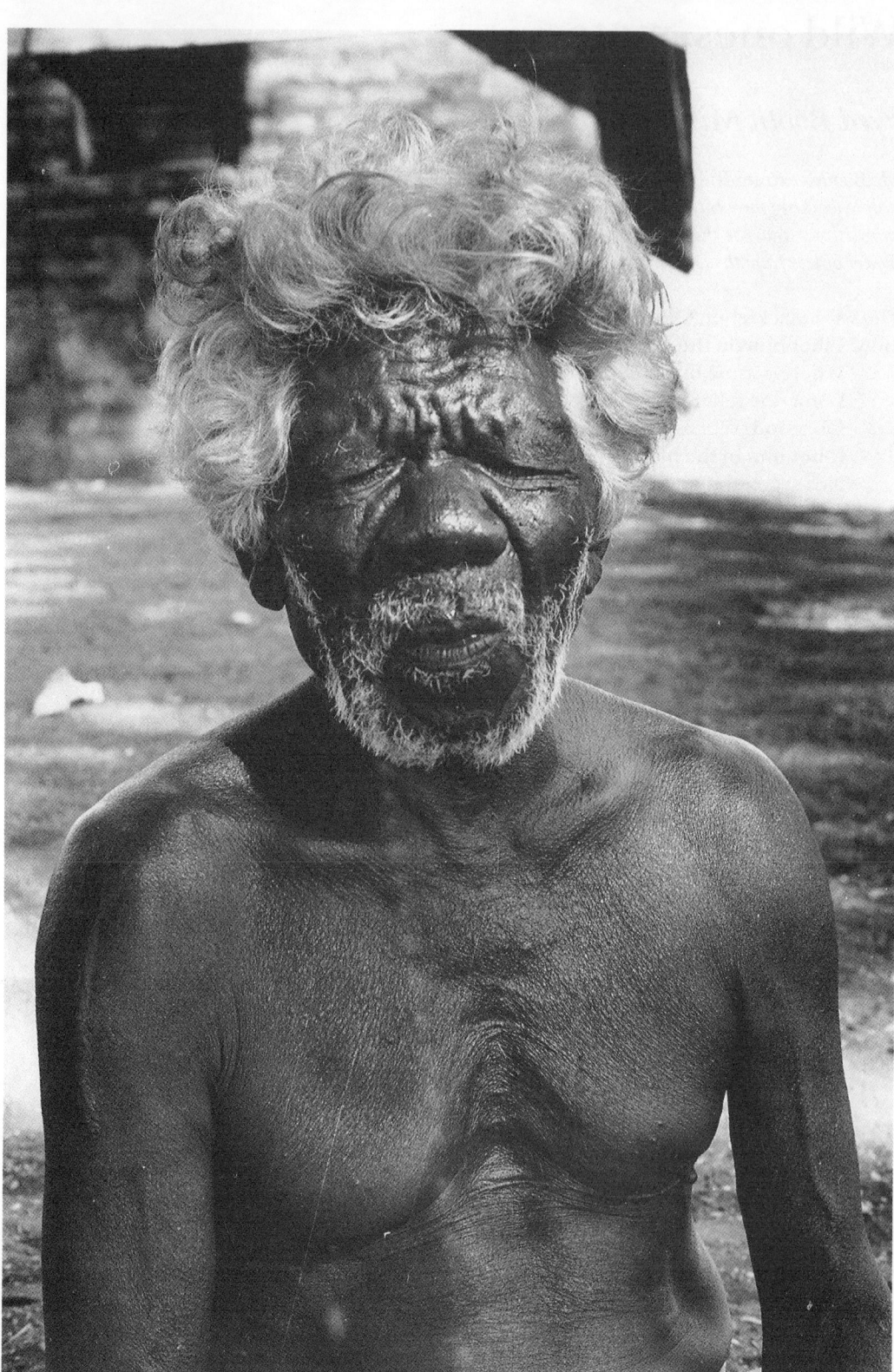

Djawa, Milingimbi, November 1977.

So they all lay up in the trees. They climbed up, all of them, into a tree. Into a tree they climbed, all of them. They sat there, they didn't say anything, nothing. They were very careful for each other. The white men arrived, and went into the thick jungle area. They entered, and stood there.

'This is their place, where did they go?'

'Ah, there they are!'

'Ah, yes!'

And the rest of them arrived, and more as well. A lot of them, enemies, arrived, yes, enemies. Yes, and they all stood around, where the pond is.

'Where are they?'

'Here they are. They've all climbed up into these trees.'

Then they said, 'We'll shoot at them. Straight up into the trees.'

One stood here, one stood there, one stood there. Think about the noise that those guns made, shooting up into the trees. Shooting, shooting, shooting, up into the trees. They all fell down onto the ground, and just lay there all over the ground, every one of them, until they were all dead. But one of them was still alive. The horses had passed him on the way there. He saw them, and he hid in the cycad palms, underneath them. It might have been cycads or pandanus, something like that.

'These bushes are thick. I will lie down here so that while they are shooting at them, I will stay alive,' he said. His name, the child who was hiding, was Ditjarama ... And he hid all by himself.

So they shot at them until they were all dead, and in the morning they came back again, and found nothing. They were all lying dead. They left them there, all adults, and off they went. They talked about it with their boss.

'Serves them right. How many did you kill?'

'There must have been a hundred of them. Hiding up in the trees. We shot at them into the trees, and they all came falling down. Lots and lots of them.'

Well, they slept, there at Murwangi.

'I think I'll go and see them.'

Maybe he was feeling sorry, but then again, maybe he wasn't. But anyway, off he went, he wanted to go by himself, just the boss. Off he went, and there he saw a lot of children, just like the ones we've got at Milingimbi school, boys and girls, just like that he saw them all, they were playing. Up he rode. He tied up his horse, and went over and met them.

'Hey, it's me!' Like that. The children were all very happy. Then, 'Come on, come on, come on. Gather round me here. I'm a nice man. I'm just like you are,' he said, 'Good, I won't do anything to you.'

And the children stood there.

'Hey children. Wait! Just a minute! How many of you are there?' Like that. So the children lined up, and stood in two straight lines. How many? Two, two lines. Just like soldiers do. One line here, one line there, two of them. And the white man stood in front of them.

'Now you watch me,' he said, 'Watch me carefully, and look at this, it's my spear.'

You see he had a repeater rifle, one which fires a lot of bullets. That's what he had, that white man.

'You watch me carefully! Just watch me. Don't look anywhere, keep your eyes on me.'

And he pulled the trigger, I think. And they all just went falling down onto the ground. Every one of them, just lying there, and not only a few, lots of them. Children, just like we have here at school, girls and boys. All those children just like our ones here at Milingimbi.

Source: From the interview of Djawa in Milingimbi, 1977, by Michael J. Christie, published originally in *Gupapuyngu*; translated in Jay Arthur & Peter Read (comps & eds), A view of the past: Aboriginal accounts of Northern Territory history (unpub.), MS pp.56-9.

All ashes

Little Mick Inginma

When the Bilignara [people] arrived at the station, they were ordered to sit down. The Aboriginal trackers chained them up. Then the policeman, whom Little Mick Inginma identified elsewhere as O'Keefe, directed that a meal be given to the prisoners.

They come around that gully there, you know that creek, little creek. They bin come around that corner now, countem all the way. Countem. He right, right enough for that chain, see, because they have long chain.

'Come up, straight up here,' that policeman said, 'come on, nothing hurt.' Telembat [told them], 'Righto, altogether go there, sit down, sit down there, near a tree.'

Well [the policeman] bin sing out [to] all the tracker, you know. They come in from creek. Come out, and puttem chain now longa all this mob. That chain there, only hanging up, and other chain bin round, I think, where that lump. Tree bin coverem up, you know. Him bin like that again, but chain bin round, big one. Well they bin puttem chain now longa neck. Linem up.

'Righto. Gottem plenty tea, plenty tucker. Givem a feed.'

He bin givem feed for last [time].

Well, this two, this Aboriginal [one of the prisoners], this blackfeller bin askembat [asked] this two-feller [woman], gottem language, 'You two-feller mightem be pullem me-feller leg. For nothing. We might be get killed.'

Gottem language. He tellem, 'No, no. Him mightem be puttem that chain longa you-feller [to] quieten him. Just makem you-feller, makem little bit quiet. Like a dog. We alda [always] tiem up, ain't it? Makem quiet?'

This two-feller woman talk, keep going, see? Righto.

All right, this policeman bin tellem, 'You altogether run that way now. Line up.'

After tucker, like, afternoon. That way sun. Four o'clock or three o'clock. Sing out, all this tracker mob, bin there longa creek.

'Come on, all you trackers.'

Makem ready. [Then the policeman said to the prisoners,] 'Now, go on!'

Kickem in the rib, one of them.

'All start. Right! Line up!'

Tu! Tu! Tu! Tu! Tu! Tu! Tu! Finish.

The prisoners dead, Little Mick Inginma now describes how the bodies were heaped up and burned.

They bin gatherem up all that now. Gottem chain. Puttem on mob. Takem down to that creek where you and me bin crossem. Puttem heap there. Chuckem big mob of wood. All that dead one now he bin gatherem up, takem there longa that creek, little one. Cartem, we two-feller [we] crossem today.

All right, chuckem all that there now heap, everything, dog and all. They burnem now. They puttem big mob of wood, there, type of thing. And chuckem kerosene, strike some matches, and burnem. Lot. No anything left, eh? All ashes. Burnem finish. Lot.

There are no bones or other signs of the massacre on the site. Little Mick Inginma explained that the whites, after massacres, burned the bodies in a creek bed wherever possible. The waters of the next Wet Season would thus destroy any incriminating evidence.

Source: From the interview of Little Mick Inginma in 1977, in Jay Arthur & Peter Read (comps & eds), A view of the past: Aboriginal accounts of Northern Territory history (unpub.), MS pp.125-8.

Quiet country

Amy Laurie

I've never been in school. My experience was on the bullock. That's why I sit down and think all the time that I'm getting old now, that nobody knows my home, my friends. We had many years of travelling; they're all gone. Since I left the grog, over two years ago, I started thinking then, and now all my memories have come back to me. That's why I like to tell the story and everything like that of what I knew when I was a kid. All my memory came back to me of what my great-grandfather, great-grandmother told me. That's how I came to think about old time stories.

My grandmother was Gurindji, a dark girl. My mother was Djaru from Ord River. She married to colour — a black-feller, Aranda from Hermannsburg — and he was a good black-feller too, with his own horses and things like that. He came from Darwin my [other] old grandfather. And this white bloke, a Scotsman — old Jim McDonald — that's the grandfather who grew me up. My grannie fell in love with old man McDonald and that's why he had six sons [she had six children] — one in Queensland, Alec ['Sandy'] McDonald, Duncan McDonald. My mother and my uncle, they're black, but the others were half-castes.

We all came to that quiet country you know [the area now 'pacified', when the first violence was over], but before that the black people didn't know the white man, didn't know horses. My great-great-grandmother and grandfather didn't know anything [about white things (ways)]. When they saw the [first] white man coming with the wagons through Inverway Station down to Sturt Creek, they reckoned, 'That's the Mamu — devil-devil.' ... My great-grandmother told me when I was a good size girl — not real tall ... The first horses they saw they killed them for meat; they cut them on the front — brisket part — and left the rest ... My great-grandfather and mother used to tell me about that first white man ... They tried to run away, running around in a little bit of bush and scrub and singing with the boomerang. 'That's the white devil-devil riding 'nother devil-devil,' they used to say. 'Yes, that's the devil coming. Look out!' And the white man kept riding closer. Then they started singing the devil. They were killing with the boomerang, singing 'k-i-l-l-i-n-g the boomerang' like that, and these two came right up. The black-fellers got up and ran away. That was Leichhardt [possibly Lake Hall, as there is no evidence that Leichhardt reached the Kimberleys] travelling with the wagon team to Inverway and down to Ord River. He started shooting them ...

The old native people used to have a camp there, at a lily pond straight down from the junction of the Ord River and the big Ord River. They were fishing all along the river, [using a technique of] rolling up the spinifex grass to get the fish. They never did anything to the bloke; just fishing. The white man was coming up — all in white, and the first Aborigine who looked at him was afraid and ran away ... and you know what they [the white men] did next? Shot the lot! But two young boys got away. They were underneath the grass that they rolled the fish in, and they put those lily roots on top of their heads ... Two old fellers who were sitting up making the big fire for fish on top of the bank ... thought the noise was the stones cracking in the fire ... The two boys went up to Turner to tell the other mob there was some sort of a people in this country who kills you. 'They had something long on one finger [hand], and when it points and coughs, people die. A big mob are dead in the water like fish,' they were telling this mob. 'Don't wait when you see them. There's some sort of an animal they ride bigger than kangaroo'... that's the horse. After that they didn't start to fight because they had nothing to fight with — only boomerangs and a few spears. They went over to the other side of the hill then, near Turkey Creek, and went up in the hills and stayed around there, never coming down to the river.

Later that bloke [probably (celebrated white doctor Nat) Buchanan] came up with the wagon and started mustering all the black-fellers, and quietening them all down. This is how they started Ord River Station. My grannie was a young girl then camping at the creek where the Racecourse is now ... The white man came there and made the camp. They had tents everywhere, and were quietening down all the bush black-fellers. They'd get all the young girls and young boys for the work ... and they didn't want to fight. The mob from Dunham River down to Wyndham and over at Gordon Downs were cheeky. They used to spear the whites, but not around this way ... They thought he was a devil all the time until my father came. He had a bit of a language and he'd say, 'This a different mob of people. They're black and we're white; that's gotta be our company in this world.'

Before that, people would come into the station for their kids, because they took all the women and some young boys, and taught them to talk English and kept them on the stations ... Men about twenty-one or thirty, they shot them down. One thing, they never killed all the kids — only the big men who might be strong, some married men and single boys, but not all the young teenage boys ... They quietened them down like the horses. The white blokes told them, 'We don't want to kill you.' My father knew the language, and talked — 'Not kill, because we wanta be mate longa white man. Muster the horses, the bullock and everything, and learn you English and all that.'

My father, Mulga Jim, went right to Kalumburu quietening all the people, you know. He used to tell them not to run away but stand up. They had nothing on, and didn't know who the stockmen were. There was not a station or anything, just tents, donkey wagons, bullock wagons. That bloke Leichhardt [or Lake Hall] from Queensland, he came right up to the Ord River, and that's where he finished up. The blokes who quietened down the people started on young girls — pretty dark ladies — and that's where the half-castes come from. All the young white men chased the dark woman and the half-castes were bred from this. The dark girls used to be frightened of the white man, but later they were getting married to them all around ... The old men told the white bloke, 'All right, you wantim this young girl, you can havim, you can live with him.' They'd say, 'Yes, I'm too old now, you can take him.' ['Him' here means 'her'.] They used to grow them up. The blokes gave them everything — blankets, clothes, things like that; they didn't know how to use them. The white men taught them how to make a bed and cover himself up, and flour ... they started making paint to paint themselves for the corroboree. They were wasting the flour! ... All the time people like my great-grandfather and mother used to tell us, 'We didn't know horses. We didn't know white man. We didn't know everything! From Ord River right up to Mistake Creek, right up to Flora Valley, down to here — they didn't know anything. Poor feller, I reckon. What they want to shoot him like that for?

Source: From the interview of Amy Laurie by Ann Magrath, in Isobel White, Diane Barwick & Betty Meehan (eds), *Fighters and Singers: The Lives of Some Australian Aboriginal Women*, Allen & Unwin, Sydney, 1985, pp.80-82.

Living black

Vi Stanton

My father was always involved in people issues, you know, grassroots issues, and my mother was dead set against institutions because of what happened to her. She went to all the Aboriginal camps as midwife for a lot of the women and to this day people say to me 'Look that one there, that one been born from your mother's finger' (laughs). They talk like that. It's incredible the people I've met since that said they were born from my mother.

You know, when we were young, nobody worried that you were part-Aboriginal; we didn't realise that we were different. All those years I'd been quite, well, self-assured, you know? Then I discovered that I wasn't quite the person I'd thought I was all those years. I lost all my sense of knowing who I was in the 1950s. I was so shocked that I burnt the damned exemption that my husband got for me.

It wasn't that people wouldn't identify as Aboriginals. It was that ordinance. A lot of our people, when they'd been known as part-Aboriginals had a horror of being called Aboriginals again because it meant the same as second-grade citizens ... they had no citizenship. And many of them didn't want to be known as Aboriginals because they were completely institutionalised and the fact that you were half-white meant that you weren't completely on the bottom. It was drummed into them in the institutions that they'd been given this opportunity ... (angrily and sarcastically) they must be a little bit cleverer because they were half-white, after all. Because the tribal people, look at them, they're so dirty and illiterate, stupid and nasty, smelly ... all this indoctrination. The divisions form unconsciously within the institutionalised person. That is why I think it's incredible that my mother could be taken away at six and yet she learnt enough of her background to be able to impart it to me and even the language.

This is a very important point. You hear a lot of stories about the tribal people rejecting their children, the half-castes. It's not true. It's incredible what my mother learnt about herself when the tribal people weren't even supposed to come near her. My mother was in the compound, huge wire fence, concentration camp fence and the tribal people, old tribal women would come up to the fence and call the little children over. When the children came over they would hold their little hands through the wire and tell them who they were, who their mothers were, where they'd come from, what their skin was, what their totem and dreaming was. They were caught, belted by the authorities and told not to mix with the dirty blacks, told that they should drive the black people away. There was this constant battle for the children's minds.

The tribal people had no freedom at all, they had no choice. They were under that ordinance. Part-Aboriginals had to get this exemption. You had to be 'deemed worthy' of it. If some native affairs official thought you shouldn't be exempted, he jolly well had the final say. Citizens' rights! Every little concession we gained we had to fight for and a lot of people don't understand what it was like. We never had press. We had no expertise and knowledge but we were fighting. Members of my family were in the services. My cousin went right through the war; New Guinea, Malaya and with the British occupation forces in Japan. All that time he was accepted; a mate, a soldier, a man. When he came back to his home town he couldn't go into a pub to have a drink with his mates!

These institutions ... It was quite simple, really, what the authorities were going to do. The girls were going to be domestics, the men were going to be labourers for the officials in Darwin. Great! The girls were placed in homes. My mother went to a good family and she grew very attached to them, but not everybody was so lucky. But by the same token my mother was deeply affected by being institutionalised and she did try, desperately, to find all of her people. It obsessed her. They all had different names. Her brother was called Jack Brumby — completely different. How would you find your brothers and sisters, eh? She only knew the skin totems, where she came from and who her people were. She methodically went through the families, somehow or other, I don't know. We weren't well off, but every bit of money she could afford, she made trips back to her tribal country to find out who she was ... her people. She was an incredible person. She found her mother, her sisters and her brothers.

My uncle's Jack Brumby and he used to tell of the Aboriginal women darkening the kids' skin with charcoal so that they wouldn't be taken. The kids kept absolutely dirty and grimy so that their fair skins wouldn't be picked because you couldn't have fair skins on these pastoral properties, eh? The embarrassment. In time the women used to take off into the bush when it was time for a little yeller-feller to be born and Jack Brumby wasn't caught until he was quite a big lad. He was so wild and ungovernable and always racing away. They called him Jack because he was black and Brumby because when they caught him he was squealing and fighting, as wild as a brumby. There were some white people up there called Brumby. We sometimes thought it might have been one of the Brumbys that fathered him, but I heard the other story that they called him Brumby Jack because he was very hard to catch. Of course there could be lots of stories but that's the one I heard about my uncle.

But I know exactly who I am and what I am in the kinship line because of my mother. I think it's beautiful to understand a bit of the old laws, who I am allowed to speak to and why our people survived without all this inbreeding that has plagued Aborigines in other places. I've been to conferences down south and some of the southern Aboriginals have said that it seemed odd that I didn't speak to tribal people seeing as we both came from the Northern Territory. They didn't realise, it's just not allowed.

My husband had to take a skin grouping, before he could marry me. My mother said that, you know, even if I didn't understand it fully at the time. He just had to be the right skin and they asked him would he take it and he said yes. He didn't take it as a joke or for kicks. He tried to respect my situation. I don't have any complex about being half-white, myself. My grandfather on my father's side really tried to understand my grandmother and her people and why they did things in a particular way. He tried to learn the language and it was atrocious because he was Irish and he couldn't, his accent was no good and he couldn't ... it was shocking. To this day they've got little stories they tell about him. No, I don't have any complex about being half-white and yet I've heard people, like Bobbi Sykes, who are very anti and very bitter about it. I can appreciate why a lot of our people are anti-white but I can't do that because I had a grandfather who really was very, very good.

Source: From the interview of Vi Stanton by Kevin Gilbert, in Gilbert, *Living Black: Blacks Talk to Kevin Gilbert*, Penguin, Ringwood, Vic., 1978, pp.10-13.

This is our river, hill, trees, grass

Pincher Numiari

Before the White European came to Sydney Harbour and started shooting we from Sydney, through Queensland and up to Darwin, back to Wave Hill. When they first came they had a bullock wagon. All this area around here. On the Victoria River at Wave Hill, he stayed there and put up paper bark houses. After that, when he got that place going, he went to find Aborigine all over and shot the whole lot. He found a big mob of black fellows knob here, he shot the lot — I don't know how many hundred he shot. Wave Hill Victoria River, Black Fellow Creek to No. 4 bore, at the airstrip just over Wattie Creek in the scrub. Aborigine all over been getting shot — I don't know how many hundreds. My old grandfather told me that before he passed on. People here did nothing to white European when he came. White European always been treating we like a dog, used to put the tucker for we behind the wood heap. Aborigine been good enough to work hard for these white European. They used to come looking for men. They took them to near Dry Gully and shot him like a dog. Aborigine used to do hard job and we worked for them because we been frightened because those Whites had rifles. Aborigines couldn't do nothing or they shoot we. He forced us. Sometime Aborigine want to run away, but they follow him up and shoot him. He walked over to the married man's camp and took his missus, sometimes for night, sometimes for good. You see half-caste all over Australia. He used to steal him lady and our ground, our land. He steal 'im. When they first come, they shot 'im like a dog, straight. Them Aborigines didn't know what to do, poor buggers. They had idea, they been look after themselves before the White European came. They got their own tools. They been look after theyselves. Spear for kangaroo, emu bone for spearing fish — lots of ideas. No bullock yet, no horses, they know bush medicine. How many thousands of people were here before the White European came? They look theirself. We didn't have sisters, welfare — we look after ourself.

When I been born, we working on stations all over Australia. I been born in Inverway. I work for Vesteys[1] when I was a boy, I worked for Vesteys all my life until I got married. They used to give us floggings if we slept too long. Inverway — everyone work there for 3 brothers. Then we work for Vesteys. We work pretty hard then — we only got one stick of tobacco and one matches, that's all. Station manager gave one pair of trousers and shirt. When they finish work they give 2 pairs of trousers and shirt, but you gotta give him back for next year. They put your name in a book and next year you get same trouser and shirt. Right up to now it's hard. At Wave Hill, they treat Aborigine like dog. Them welfare used to come over, talk big — we do this, we'll do this. How long we been there working for Vesteys all over Australia? Welfare done nothing for Aborigine. They talk BIG. Now, they still do nothing. I've seen it happen too much.

We are still fighting for land. Government hard too. He should give us land so we can work these cattle and horses. He just make it hard, right up to now. Them Canberra mob, they do nothing for we, we get help from no-one. We walk off from station, no proper wages, no good conditions. Vesteys no good. Tommy Vincent led us to walk off — all of them men, women and piccaninnies we walk to Victoria River. People came in by plane from Sydney and Melbourne with T.V. and old fella was talking, Tommy Vincent. He was pretty strong old fella. That Tom Fisher wanted us to go to Wave Hill again. We been camping there for a while. The Vesteys bought beef down to the river to get us back to Wave Hill. We been starving but old fella he strong, so we shifted to near the Wave Hill settlement. Bill Jeffries from settlement asked me and Tommy Vincent to go by plane to Darwin, talk about fighting for our block. They asked us about going back with Tom Fisher. Then welfare mob put all our talk on paper and say 'We'll help you'. Welfare — nothing been done through them see, they big talk and push around Aboriginal people. I never been to school, but I can use my brain to see how they been working. I am going to make it hard for the welfare, me. After Darwin, back at settlement I been working there and then I picked up all my things and I picked this place here at Wattie Creek. That's where we are now, Daguragu. We sit around, whose going to help Aborigine? Oh, no-one going to help we. We got bush tucker. We can look after ourself anyway, don't you worry about that. Welfare, them Government mob, they say they are going to do so much. They don't do anything though.

We have this land, we going to live here forever. We got the law, we got our own law. White European got their law. This land belong to we, no matter where, all over Australia. All Aborigine, we got the same blood, no matter half-caste. European just want to walk over, take this land. We walk off station so we can help piccaninny. We got to be strong — one way. We gotta stick together. We don't have to listen to boss in Canberra. We sitting on our own land. We can put up fence and put the cattle and horses in — this is our land. We don't go over to White European houses in Sydney or Melbourne. This mob should listen to we. I'm talking proper way to people all over Australia.

We tell them we want lot of land. The welfare say 'Hang on little while — wait till I see the big boss in Canberra'. You can't get answer. Only our friends in Melbourne give us some money. No big groups help we. We must take this place, we can't listen to anybody, we must live here forever.

Dexter [Daniels] came here from Canberra, he say all cattle belong to Vestey. He say we gotta wait. We reckon those cattle and horse been born now with Aborigine. They for Aborigine people. They born in we fella land. We work hard for Vestey, them cattle not his, like Dexter says. We want them clean-skins.

This is our river, hill, trees, grass belong to Aborigine — not White European. Not good talking. We know he want to clean all our land out — no cattle, no nothing left for we. Government and the Vestey mob. They don't think for poor bugger Aborigine all over Australia, they gonna leave us nothing. Aborigine got no cheque. Some land got mineral, white European bring out grader for minerals, he never pay money to Aboriginal — just leave him like a dog. He don't know ceremony place for Aborigine — he's a NEW man, we don't know him. He don't know our law.

We'll keep fighting. We can't give away the land. Cattle, we fight hard for that. Clinic, school, Aboriginal way. We want Aboriginal people to help we. All those ladies and men get paid through we, that welfare. That settlement no good. We can't let things go like this, we must stick together. I am only one man. Only we stick together so we can beat them. We can look after ourself. That's all. I'm finished now talking ...

1 Vestey Brothers. In 1914 the Vestey organisation bought Wave Hill station and began to build the Darwin meatworks. They would become the largest landholders and meatworks operators in Australia. — D.H.

Source: From the interview of Pincher Numiari by Cheryl Buchanan, at Wattie Creek, from *Black News Service*, vol.1, no.2, 1975.

In Darwin they call me Bobby Wilson

Robert Tudawali

My name is Robert Tudawali. In Darwin they call me Bobby Wilson. Tudawali is my real tribal name. I am a member of the Tiwi tribe. I was brought up in Melville Island. When I was young I lived there, and hunted and fought and sang like all my people. No clothes. No worries. The country I ran in was my own — every rock and tree meant something to me. Then I came into Darwin to live with the Wilson family; that's why my name is Wilson. Years ago, Charles Chauvel came to Darwin and gave me the part of Marbuk in the film *Jedda*. I acted in that film and in the *Whiplash* series on television. When you're down South acting, everything is pretty good, people are friendly. But when you come back to Darwin it's different. You're just another black fella. Only low wage jobs. You can have a drink down South but not in Darwin. You can in Darwin now, but in those days you couldn't unless you were a citizen. I was made a citizen and all my friends and relations were wards of the State, had their names in the Stud Book — so if I drank with them it was a criminal offence. First time I got arrested was for that.

In Darwin, plenty of white people wanted to drink with me after *Jedda* and some policemen didn't like this, I reckon. One day a policeman said to me: 'You're under arrest.' I said: 'Come again?' He said: 'You're under arrest for supplying alcohol to a ward of the State.' Anyway, if I drank with Aborigines who were wards of the State I got arrested. I've been arrested a lot of times since then a'course — for drink.

After *Whiplash* there was no Australian films made — anyway, I didn't get any parts in the South again. I drank too much and my wife went away.

They sent me back to Melville Island, sent away just like any other black fella. But I was no good in the bush any more. Later on, they let me come back to Darwin but I was no good there either. Used to leave jobs, go walkabout — couldn't get a job with decent wages, anyway. Got on the grog and was put in jail. I got myself fit again and took up boxing in the tents. I had a lot of fights against all-comers and made a bit of money, but that game is no good so I gave it up. I felt sick and went to the doctor. He gave me a check-up and said I had

TB, so I was in hospital for a long time.

When I was better I lived in Bagot Reserve. I got a few quid there. My job was painter. I drank a lot of plonk. I got into Fannie Bay plenty of times, but it didn't worry me.

One day, I was drinking in Vic Hotel in Darwin and I met Frank Hardy there. I knew about him in the South. He writes books. We had a drink and a bit of a yarn. He told me about a meeting of Aborigines at Rapid Creek to start the Council for Aboriginal Rights. So I thought about this, and I said to myself: 'Maybe he's right. I could do something to help my people,' but I told him: 'I can't even help myself.'

Anyway, I went to Rapid Creek that Sunday and someone called out my name for vice-president and I was elected. I felt very good to do my bit for the Rights Council. I didn't really know much about it. Dexter Daniels talked to me next day and he told me he was going to start more strikes. And he did start one at Wave Hill.

Robert Tudawali being interviewed on the dry bed of the Victoria River by Frank Bennett (for A.B.C. television). In his last years, as he fought alcoholism, Tudawali played a prominent role in the advancement of the Aboriginal cause in the Northern Territory.

The Rights Council asked me to go to Wave Hill to take rations down. I went there with Dexter and Brian Manning. They were pleased to see us at Wave Hill. We told them we had supplies and more would come from Elliott later on. We told them they would get help from the South and about the wages they were fighting for — that it wouldn't be long.

I didn't have no grog on the trip except a bottle of plonk going down. I felt a bit dry but I reckon I got that grog beat. I still have a drink mind you, but I got it beat.

When I came back to Darwin a Welfare Officer in Bagot said: 'Are you on strike, Bobby?' and I said: 'No, not exactly. I'm helping my people. A bit too busy to work in Bagot for a while.'

I went back to Wave Hill again with Dexter, Stan Davey and George Gibbs. And on the

Poster advertising Charles Chauvel's film 'Jedda'. Robert Tudawali had the leading male role.

way we went to VRD [Victoria River Downs station] but we couldn't see the stockmen. They were away in the stock camp. When we drove past Mount Sanford we saw some aboriginal stockmen and we talked to them about wages, and they said they had no pay for several months. Dexter said: 'You better go on strike, too,' and they said: 'All right.'

At Wave Hill, second time, I sat down and spoke to the Aborigines, those youngsters especially. Dexter took one group and I took another, according to skin colour, and we explained: Equal pay on all cattle stations. They told us their fathers worked at Wave Hill, died out, and the youngsters took their jobs. They didn't seem to care about money, except a few quid walkabout time. We had to explain. What do you work for? You should get money, proper wages. If you have childrens you got to support them. And buy them school books and buy your own clothes and build a house. Better to be independent that way than have Welfare on your back. Not only men, I told them, but wife can earn good money and help keep children.

They told us that every night the white ringers and jackeroos from Wave Hill station came in Land Rovers. Only one woman went with them and she didn't even bother to take her little baby. But when those ringers knew we were there they didn't come near the place.

Frank Hardy came down there in an aeroplane and me and Dexter went with him to Wave Hill station to get back some property that was there. When I saw those humpies I couldn't believe it. My people used to live like that, I thought, back when I was a child. And said to myself: This shouldn't be happening now. Those houses should be pulled down.

Well, Frank said I could do a good job South for my people. He spoke to Hal Alexander of Actors Equity and Hal wrote me a letter. I was used to cameras and microphones and could memorise words to say. Would come in handy. I didn't feel too good so I went to the hospital for a check-up and they said I had TB again. It turned out I was too ill to go. I was sorry to miss out on that. I could have done a good job speaking at meetings. I wanted to explain the main thing: 'My people need to be independent. It's a bit hard. They are not used to handling money but they got to start some time. Every native should handle his own money. It is better for them to look after their own children and old people, not Welfare.' I want to tell them that down South. Maybe I get a chance to go down later on. I feel a hundred per cent again now.

And while I'm down South I might get a chance to go back with films now that I feel fit again. If any company asks me to do a film I'll be glad to do a part. I hear there are some Australian films being made again now.

Anyway, I feel kind of happy because I did a little bit of a job for my people, when a lot of people reckoned I couldn't do it.

Source: From the passage by Robert Tudawali in Frank Hardy, *The Unlucky Australians*, Thomas Nelson, Melbourne, 1968, pp.145-8.

What's a whitefella?

Post-primary boys' class, Papunya

Whitefellas are rich
Whitefellas have new cars
Whitefellas wear clean clothes
Tourists come out
look 'round my country
find gold or something
go back
spread em word
Whitefellas run   properly
run settlement properly
do it proper way
Whitefellas say: we're going to
Alice Springs   but
talk talk talk talk
waste time   maybe one hour
Whitefellas talk too much
sometime lie
sometime true
Whitefellas talk mean
Whitefellas cheat
say: this *good* car
Whitefellas got strange eyes
Tourists don't care
they look funny
women wear shorts too tight
Whitefella got no shame
Whitefellas don't turn back
because they're millionaire
Whitefellas complain too much
about everything — even whitefellas
Whitefellas don't help each other
Whitefellas take photo without asking
Whitefellas stare
Whitefellas don't feel
anything.

Source: 'What's a whitefella?', by the post-primary boys' class at Papunya School, 1981. Poem collected by Billy Marshall-Stoneking.

First people come to us

Big Bill Neidjie

First people come to us,
they started and run our life ... quick.
They bring drink.
First they should ask about fish, cave, dreaming, but ...
they rush in.
They make school ... teach.
Now Aborigine losing it,
losing everything.
Nearly all dead my people,
my old people gone.

Those first people was too quick,
wasn't Aborigine fault.
Still Aborigine all around 1929 ...
1952, 1953 few left but ...
1970 to 1979 ... gone.
Only me, Robin Gaden and Felix Holmes.

Each man he stay ...
stay on his own country.
He can't move his country ...
so he stay there,
stay with his language.
Language is different ...
like skin.
Skin can be different,
but blood same.
Blood and bone ...
all same.
Man can't split himself.

White European can't say
'Oh, that Aborigine no good.'
Might be that Aborigine alright.
Man can't growl at Aborigine,
Aborigine can't growl at white European ...
Because both ways.
Might be both good men,
might be both no good ...
you never know.

So you should get understand yourself.
No matter Aborigine or white European.
I was keeping this story myself.
It was secret in my mind,
but I see what other people doing,
and I was feeling sad.

Source: Big Bill Neidjie, 'First people come to us', in Big Bill Neidjie, Stephen Davis & Allan Fox, *Kakadu Man*, Resource Managers, Darwin, 1987, pp.37-8.

Yirrkala Bark Petition

Petition from the Aboriginal people of Yirrkala to Parliament

To the Honourable Speaker and Members of the House of Representatives in Parliament Assembled

The Humble Petition of the Undersigned aboriginal people of Yirrkala, being members of the Balamumu, Narrkala, Gapiny, and Miliwurrwurr people and Djapu, Mangalili, Madarrpa, Magarrwanalinirri, Gumaitj, Djambarrpuynu, Marrakulu, Galpu, Dhalnayu, Wangurri, Warramirri, Maymil, Rirritjinu, tribes, respectfully sheweth —

1. That nearly 500 people of the above tribes are residents of the land excised from the Aboriginal Reserve in Arnhem Land.
2. That the procedures of the excision of this land and the fate of the people on it were never explained to them beforehand, and were kept secret from them.
3. That when Welfare Officers and Government officials came to inform them of decisions taken without them and against them, they did not undertake to convey to the Government in Canberra the views and feelings of the Yirrkala aboriginal people.
4. That the land in question has been hunting and food gathering land for the Yirrkala tribes from time immemorial; we were all born here.
5. That places sacred to the Yirrkala people, as well as vital to their livelihood are in the excised land, especially Melville Bay.
6. That the people of this area fear that their needs and interests will be completely ignored as they have been ignored in the past, and they fear that the fate which has overtaken the Larrakeah tribe will overtake them.
7. And they humbly pray that the Honourable the House of Representatives will appoint a Committee, accompanied by competent interpreters, to hear the views of the Yirrkala people before permitting the excision of this land.
8. They humbly pray that no arrangements be entered into with any company which will destroy the livelihood and independence of the Yirrkala people.
And your petitioners as in duty bound will ever pray God to help you and us.

(English translation)

Certified as a correct translation. Kim E. Beazley

Bukudjulni gonga'yurru napurrunha Yirrkalalili Yulnunha malanha Balamumu, Narrkala, Gapiny, Miliwurrwurr nanapurru dhuwala mala, ga Djapu, Mangalili, Madarrpa, Magarrwanalinirri, Djambarrpuynu, Gumaitj, Marrakula, Galpu, Dhabunyu, Wangurri, Warramirri, Maymil, Riritjinu malamanapamirri djal dhunapa.

1. Dhuwala yulnu mala galki 500 nhina ga dhiyala wananura. Dhuwala wanga Arnhem Land yurru djaw'yunna naburrungala.

2. Dhuwala wanga djaw'yunna ga nhaltjana yurru yulnungunydja dhiyala wanga nura nhaltjanna dhu dharrpanna yulnu walandja yakana lakarama madayangumuna.

3. Dhuwala nunhi Welfare Officers ga Government bungawa lakarama yulnuwa malanuwa nhaltjarra nhuma gana wanganaminha yaka nula napurrungu lakarama wlala yaka lakarama Governmentgala nunhala Canberra nhaltjanna napurruga guyana yulnuyu Yirrkala.

4. Dhuwala wänga napurrungyu balanu larrunarawu napurrungu näthawa, guyawu, miyspunuwu, maypalwu nunhi napurru gana nhinana bitjarrayi näthilimirri, napurru dhawalguyanana dhiyala wänganura.

5. Dhuwala wänga yurru dharpalnha yurru yulnuwalandja malawala, ga dharrpalnha dhuwala bala yulnuwuyndja nhinanharawu Melville Bathurru wänga balandayu djaw'yun nyumukunin.

6. Dhuwala yulnundja mala yurru nhämana balandawunu nha mulkurru nhämä yurru moma ga darangan yalalanumirrinha nhaltjanna dhu napurru bitjarra nhakuna Larrakeahyu momara wlalanguwuy wänga.

7. Nuli dhu bungawayu House of Representatives djaw'yn yulnuwala näthili yurru nha dhu lakarama interpreteruy bungawalala yulnu matha, yurru nha dhu djaw'yun dhuwala wängandja.

8. Nunhiyina dhu märrlayun marrama'-ndja nhinanharawu yulnuwu marrnamathinyarawu.

Dhuwala napuru yulnu mala yurru liyamirriyama bitjan bili marr yurru napurru hha gonga' yunna wangarr'yu.

(Australian matha)

(Here follow the signatures)

Source: Yirrkala Bark Petition of 1963, reproduced in Edgar Wells, *Reward and Punishment in Arnhem Land 1962-1963*, Australian Institute of Aboriginal Studies, Canberra, 1982, app.2, pp.127-8. Petition drawn up 16 July 1963, completed and carried by aeroplane to Canberra 24 July 1963.

6 Pilgrims

There were people everywhere, and motor cars and dogs ... too many dogs, barking and barking and barking. Proper cheeky buggers too. Poor me. It was too noisy. My eagle — the one that had followed me in the bush, that had protected me, that had warned when danger was near — that eagle couldn't stay. It was frightened by the white men's motor cars and by all the cheeky dogs that might bite it. It flew away, poor thing. I lost power when it left me, you know ... and it never came back.
— Tutama Tjapangarti, talking to Billy Marshall-Stoneking, 1980

Many a strange tale could be told of the life and doings on the back blocks, and the extraordinary characters met with at a place like Roper, which was looked upon as a sanctuary for the rest of the States. Many had faces that would take the edge off a razor, smash a mirror, or burst a camera. There were no police within many hundreds of miles, no telegraph nearer than the overland line, and no mail service.
— Alfred Searcy, *In Australian Tropics,* 1909

... all madmen travel north, and once there cannot get away from the place.
— Bill Harney, *North of 23°,* 1945

        Me, yesterday I was rumour,
        today I am legend,
        tomorrow, history.
        If you'd like to know more of me
        inquire at the pub at Tennant Creek
        or at any drover's camp
        or shearing-shed
        or shout any bloke in any bar a drink,
        or yarn to any bloke asleep on any beach;
        they'll tell you about me,
        they'll tell you more than I know myself.
— Ian Mudie, 'They'll tell you about me', 1952

Previous page: Paul Foelsche arrived in Darwin in 1870 to become Inspector of Northern Territory Police, a position he held for thirty-four years. Like Gillen and Spencer, Foelsche found time to indulge his great passion, photography, and left as his legacy a collection of great historical and cultural importance. This one is titled 'Native camp, Port Essington, November 1877'. The formidable 'Flash Poll' is the centre figure.

I had no human speech

Roland Robinson

I had no human speech. I heard
the quail-thrush cry out of the stones
and cry again its crystal word
out of the mountains' crumbling bones.

I had no human word, beyond
all words I knew the rush of ash-
grey wings that gloomed in one respond
storm-grey, to swerve, a crimson flash.

The speech that silence shapes, but keeps:
a ruin and the writhe of thin
ghost-gums against their rain-blue deeps
of night and ranges I drank in.

I lived where mountains moved and stood
round me. I saw their natures change,
deepen and fire from mood to mood,
and found the kingfisher blue range;

and found, where huge dark heliotrope
shadows pied a range's power,
mauve-purple at the foothill's slope,
the parakelia, the desert-flower.

Yet, human, with unresting thought
tormented, turned away from these
presences, from converse sought
with deserts, flowers, stones, and trees.

Source: Roland Robinson, *The Language of Sand*, Lyre Bird Writers, Sydney, 1949, p.1; reproduced in Gloria Rawlinson & W. Hart-Smith (eds), *Jindyworobak Anthology*, Jindyworobak, Melbourne, 1951, pp.64–5.

Flash Poll

Alfred Searcy

At Port Essington I always had a great friend to meet me in 'Flash Poll' — an ancient black dame, who was a young woman when the soldiers were stationed there [1838-49], and a fine woman she must have been, judging from her appearance even when I saw her. Many a good yarn I had with her about the old days, and some funny stories she told. The old woman remembered the officers well, particularly the chaplain. Poll could still repeat like a parrot a prayer and sing a psalm; but I am bound to say that singing was not her strong forte. She had a great command of a certain sort of language, which she did not hesitate to use when her liver, for instance, was out of order. As sure as she said the prayer and sang the Psalm, she wound up with 'Give it tobacco, give it nobbler,' both of which she got at times. Whenever I said goodbye, Poll always rattled off a list of things she wanted. They would have fitted out a decent bush shanty. Once a year I did send her turkey red, tobacco, pipes, and a bottle of medicine. Flash Poll thought a lot of me, in fact, she promised me her skull, but I am afraid that interesting relic will never come my way. Her pet way of showing her grief at my departure was to ask for a knife to cut her head. Poll was a great hand at making hats out of leaves of a palm tree. The amount of work in one was enormous, and generally occupied about six months. I have to this day one of the hats that Poll made.

Source: Alfred Searcy, *In Northern Seas: Being Mr Alfred Searcy's Experiences on the North Coast of Australia*, W. K. Thomas & Co., Adelaide, 1905, p.46.

Dug his own grave

Alfred Searcy

Soon after leaving one of our mid-day halting places we came across a poor old fellow, nearly naked, crawling round a hole like a grave, and moaning the while. He was literally a bag of bones. We spoke to him several times, but beyond a vacant stare he took no notice, and continued his crawling and moaning. We boiled the billy and fed him with damper, soaked in tea, after which we laid him on a blanket under a shady tree, and he fell asleep.

The little property lying about indicated that he was a prospector — alone, without food and beyond hope or fear. Was the hole his last miner's test, or had something prompted him to dig his grave? There was no telling. Suddenly the poor fellow started out of sleep, waved his hand, and cried, 'Good-bye, mates,' fell back and died.

After searching his body, from which we removed a heavy belt with many pockets, we rolled him in a blanket, and buried him in the grave which his own hands had prepared.

The few things strewn about gave no clue to the poor fellow's identity. The belt contained a number of nuggets of gold, and some small pieces of quartz, thickly studded with the precious metal. [Constable] O'Donohue thought he had been a 'hatter', prospecting up towards Blue Mud Bay, where it was generally supposed gold existed, and that he had struck it rich. The belt of gold we eventually handed to the police trooper at the Roper; but up to the time of our leaving the Gulf country, no evidence was forthcoming as to his identity.

O'Donohue suggested that we should put up a rough fence around the unknown one. As we sat down for a rest after the completion of this task, O'Donohue made the trite remark that history often repeated itself, and went on, while I filled my pipe, to give an instance from his experience.

I was stationed at Brock's Creek, began my mate, when one day up came a big fellow named Jim Sinclair on one of his team horses. He had ridden thirty miles for my services, which meant that I had to accompany him to an outlying station camp, and satisfy myself that the neck of a horsebreaker named Paddy Hyde had been broken through a visitation of God, while in the discharge of his duty — at any rate that was the way Jim put it.

This statement was corroborated — that is to say, Paddy had been thrown, and it was found, when picked up, that his neck was broken; so I gave the order for burial asked for. As there was nothing better for a coffin than a sheet of galvanised iron which helped to make the roof of the one hut at the camp, this was bent over, Paddy was laid within and made secure by a rope passed around it several times. A grave was then dug, and the late plucky rider laid to rest. We farewelled each other and took our respective ways.

It was about a year after this that I chanced to pass the camp in question, when who should I encounter but Jim and his mates, putting up just such a fence as we have completed. I said:

'Hallo, Jim, what are you up to?'

'O, putting a few sticks round Paddy,' replied Jim.

'Paddy isn't buried there,' I said.

'Well, I ought to know — You remember I dug his grave,' was Jim's reply.

'All the same, old man, he sleeps a half-dozen yards this side of that sapling,' said I, pointing to the spot.

Jim straightened himself, flicked the sweat from his eyebrows with his index finger, told the men in a casual way to knock off, and opened up a conversation on other matters.

Some time after this I again chanced on my worthy, when I asked him if he had completed his fence or had taken my tip.

'Took your tip,' said Jim, 'We did no more that day. Next morning I was up in good time, ran a shaft down at the spot you mentioned, and struck the lode all right. You'll see the fence when you pass that way.'

'Jim was a hard case,' added O'Donohue as he lit his pipe.

Source: Alfred Searcy, *By Flood and Field: Adventures Ashore and Afloat in North Australia,* George Robertson, Melbourne, 1911, pp.267-9.

The old coast track

William Linklater & Lynda Tapp

Some quaint characters travelled the [Gulf] track, and some significant personalities, too. I came to know many of them. There was German Charlie, of a gentle gaiety, who had cheerfully wheeled his barrow over a thousand and a half miles from disappointment at Croydon. There was Mother O'Neill, who had also followed gold rushes in North Queensland, and had been on the Palmer gold-fields in the seventies. She would have a shack of bark and hessian put up, and the diggers would build her an oven for baking bread. Then she would open a place where they could get a feed and, if they were lucky, a bottle of rum and whisky.

Hearing that Esau, an Afghan, was going to the Kimberleys, she asked him for a lift. He warned her that she would have to ride a camel and, undaunted, Mother O'Neill said she would learn. Tall, plump and handsome, and full of dignity and humour, Esau was a very grand gentleman indeed. A good Mohammedan, he obeyed all the teachings of the Koran, especially the law that says: If a man is hungry, feed him.

Before coming to Australia, he had fought in the Kabul massacres against the British, but had later gone over to his erstwhile enemies and fought with Roberts' army at Kandahar. He was a rare hand at dealing with sickness, and many diggers and drovers had cause to bless his memory. I have good cause to remember him myself.

Leaving Winton, which is 1450 miles from Halls Creek, Esau rode the leading camel and Mother O'Neill the last; if one of the nose strings broke, she would then be able to tell him. They arrived at the Katherine in 1886, then pushed on to Victoria River Downs, formed only three years previously. On the next lap of the journey, Mother O'Neill went for a walk as a change from camel riding and got lost. Esau and some diggers found her on a little hill between Poison and Black Gin Creeks, so the name on the official Territory maps reads Mother O'Neill's Hill. Safely at Halls Creek, Mother O'Neill was soon installed in a café and sly grog shop; but she also nursed the sick, laid out the dead, and was kind. Many years afterwards, Mother O'Neill retired to the spot which was named after her. Here, ten miles from Halls Creek, she sold milk and mutton from the goats she reared, and died at a ripe old age.

There was a reserved and silent woman known as Red Jack. Rumour had it that her husband had died, and her babies had been burned to death. At all events, she dressed as a man and made for the Gulf of Carpentaria. She was a superb horsewoman, and used to wander the country, taking work at times as cook on the stations where she was written on the books simply as Red Jack.

Among the characters who frequented the track was Malachi Ryan who lived mostly in the blacks' camps. Trailing a blanket, his conversation gibberish, his antics were so strange that he was generally supposed to be silly. At all events, the blacks frequently showed marked benevolence to the mentally afflicted, and while other white men might be speared, they gave Malachi all the help in their power, touching their heads significantly by way of explanation. He lived without working.

William Linklater (also known as Billy Miller) and two friends from Mrs Aeneas Gunn's We of the Never-Never *(1908): Jack McLeod, the 'Quiet Stockman' (right) and Tom Pearce, 'Mine Host' (left).*

Another habitué of the Track made himself a permanent camp — after Diogenes — in an empty tank. A wealthy brother in one of the eastern capitals had him transferred to an expensive nursing home, but he disappeared, and was later discovered walking back to the Northern Territory in his pyjamas. Percy of Chevy Chase as he was known, or alternatively, Dirty Percy, was really an English nobleman. When asked, 'Why are you so dirty, Percy?' he would say, 'Because I had my face washed so much for me when I was young.'

Every third man in the bush made rhymes in those days, but Percy's were too Rabelaisian to quote, though the metrical quality was high. On inheriting a very large fortune, he returned to England.

There was Pretty Peter, too, with his involved horsetrading; and Billy the Whistler, who had played for his living in Sydney and could make his whistle sound exactly like bagpipes. Then there was Alligator Jack, who came from the Cumberland Lake District, and spoke in a high squeaky voice. Coming out with the Wave Hill cattle in 1883, he quarrelled with a man on the Calvert River. He had knocked the fellow down and was biting him when Nat Buchanan rode up and said in his gentle way, 'Jack, you are just as bad as an alligator'. Alligator Jack resented his new name, but he bore it from Burketown to Wyndham, and there was nothing he could do about it.

Travelling out to the fields, a hard-case woman came to a flat near Wyndham where 500 New Zealanders were waiting for the end of the wet season so they could get to the mines at Halls Creek. There were many boab trees about, and because the men had cut their names in the soft wood, it came to be known as New Zealanders' Camp. It was too good a chance to miss. The lady of doubtful fame pulled up and began trading, and because her shanty was on Deadhorse Creek, she became Mother Deadhorse. Her sole claim to my remembrance is that when I met her some years later she sold very bad grog.

Among those who sought the rainbow's end in the East Kimberleys was a company known as the Ragged Thirteen whose members were to become famous or notorious according to the point of view. There has been much controversy about the composition of the group.

Early in 1886, on their way to the Halls Creek fields, seven of them travelled along the Overland Telegraph Line: Wonaka Jack and his brother, George Brown, both of Moonta; Sandy Myrtle, who got his nickname because he had been manager of Myrtle Station; Jack Daley, a young farmer from Terowie; Jimmy Woodforde, a prospector from the MacDonnell Ranges; Scotty Campbell who had deserted his ship at Port Augusta; and that debonair spirit, Tommy the Rag, surname unknown, for whom many people would have had another epithet.

From North Queensland via the Coast Track came Tom Holmes and Jim Fitzgerald, stockmen of the Gulf country; Larrikin Bill Smith, also a stockman; Jim Carney, brother-in-law of Maori Reid, the owner of that redoubtable little vessel *The Good Intent;* Bob Andison, a young man from the Isle of Skye; and Jack Woods of New England, New South Wales. These six arrived at Newcastle Waters while the other seven were camped there, and decided to travel to the Katherine together. While they were at Johnston's Water-hole, along came Old Bluey Buchanan and his son, Gordon, and after supper they strolled over for a chat round the camp fire. All the Queensland men would know or know of Nat Buchanan. During the exchange of news, Nat counted them and said, 'You number thirteen, the devil's number.'

Source: William Linklater & Lynda Tapp, *Gather No Moss,* Macmillan, Melbourne, 1968, pp.64-7.

Down on the Daly River oh!

Jim Burgoyne

Now come all ye sports that want a bit of fun,
Roll up your swags and pack up a gun;
Get a bit of flour, sugar and tea,
And don't forget a gallon of Gordon's O.P.
Crank up your Lizzie, and come along with me,
And I'll show you such sights as you never did see,
Down on the Daly River Oh!

[*Chorus:*]
There was Wallaby George and Charlie Dargie,
Old Skinny Davis and Jimmy Panquee,
Big-mouthed Charlie and old Paree,
The Tipperary Pong and Jim Wilkie;
And where'er you may roam
You will find yourself at home,
They are noted for their hospitality.
You are awoke in the morn, and your heart's filled with glee
By a little dark maid with a pannikin of tea,
And she'll give you such a welcome, you won't wish to go
Away from the Daly River Oh!

I saw a buffalo and a fat Chinee
Run a dead-heat to the foot of a tree;
The Chinaman flew, he didn't feel the ruts,
But the buffalo stopped with a bullet in the guts.
As the wild birds rose at the sound of the gun
The water dropped a foot in the silver billabong;
With geese, ducks and feathers, you couldn't see the sun
Down by the Daly River Oh!

[*Repeat Chorus*]

While the buffalo kicked, we poured in the lead;
We killed him ten times to make sure he was dead;
We drew out our knives and we all hopped in —
Three whites, two Chows, four bucks and a gin.
We tore off his hide and ripped him up the guts,
Took his little tit-bits, his fancy funny cuts,
Then we cranked up the Lizzie and shouted 'Right oh!
All aboard for the Daly River Oh!'

[*Chorus*]

Now I saw a nigger sitting in an old gum tree,
The crows had picked his eyes out, so he couldn't see.
Never and never a word spoke he,
For he was as dead as dead could be.
He was just about ripe and the smell was high,
Like a billabong of fish when the water goes dry.
When Dargie threw a gibber, that hit him in the mush,
And the dead went 'Poof' and we all went bush
Down by the Daly River Oh!

Source: Jim Burgoyne, 'Down on the Daly River oh!', collected by W. E. (Bill) Harney, in Harney, *North of 23°*, Australasian Publishing Co., Sydney, 1946, pp.218-20.

Goodbye old friend

David MacKay

Bluebush
2.1. [18]93

My dear Hutton,

I am dying here for want of water. Horses also dying. If any recover please sell them, and send the proceeds to my mother with my love. Pay Jerry Connolly £5 out of them. Horses all done. No escape from perishing. Write to my sister, Mrs. Higgins. Give her my love for all.

Goodbye old friend. I am off.

David MacKay

Source: Last letter of David MacKay, 2 January 1893, in William Linklater & Lynda Tapp, *Gather No Moss*, Macmillan, Melbourne, 1968, p.94.

Mail oh!

Mrs Aeneas Gunn

Every available day of the Dry was needed for the work; but there is one thing in the Never-Never that refuses to take a secondary place — the mailman; and at the end of a week we all found, once again, that we had business at the homestead: for six weeks had slipped away since our last mail-day, and the Fizzer was due once more.

The Fizzer was due at sun-down, and for the Fizzer to be due meant that the Fizzer would arrive; and by six o'clock we had all got cricks in our necks with trying to go about as usual, and yet keep an expectant eye on the north track.

The Fizzer is unlike every type of man excepting a bush mail-man. Hard, sinewy, dauntless, and enduring, he travels day after day and month after month, practically alone — 'on me Pat Malone', he calls it — with or without a black boy, according to circumstances, and five trips out of his yearly eight throwing dice with death along his dry stages, and yet at all times as merry as a grig, and as chirrupy as a young grass-hopper.

With a light-hearted 'So long, chaps,' he sets out from the Katherine on his thousand-mile ride, and with a cheery 'What ho, chaps! Here we are again!' rides in again within five weeks with that journey behind him.

A thousand miles on horseback 'on me Pat Malone', into the Australian interior and out again, travelling twice over three long dry stages and several shorter ones, and keeping strictly within the Government time-limit, would be a life-experience to the men who set that limit — if it wasn't a death-experience. 'Like to see one of 'em doing it 'emselves,' says the Fizzer. Yet never a day late, and rarely an hour, he does it eight times a year, with a 'So long, chaps', and a 'Here we are again.'

The Fizzer was due at sun-down, and at sun-down a puff of dust rose on the track, and as a cry of 'Mail oh!' went up all round the homestead, the Fizzer rode out of the dust.

'Hullo! What ho, boys!' he shouted in welcome, and the next moment we were in the midst of his clattering team of pack-horses.

For five minutes everything was in confusion; horse bells and hobbles jingling and clanging, harness rattling, as horses shook themselves free, and pack-bags, swags, and saddles came to the ground with loud, creaking flops. Everyone was lending a hand, and the Fizzer, moving in and out among the horses, shouted a medley of news and instructions and welcome.

'News? Stacks of it!' he shouted. The Fizzer always shouted. 'The gay time we had at the Katherine! Here, steady with that pack-bag. It's breakables! How's the raisin market? Eh, lads!' with many chuckles. 'Sore back here, fetch along the balsam. What ho, Cheon!' as Cheon appeared and greeted him as an old friend. 'Heard you were here. You're the boy for my money. You *bally* ass! Keep 'em back from the water there.' This last was for the black boy. It took discrimination to fit the Fizzer's remarks on to the right person. Then as a pack-bag dropped at the Maluka's feet, he added: 'That's the station lot, boss. Full bags, missus! Two on 'em. You'll be doing the disappearing trick in half a mo'.'

In 'half a mo' ' the seals were broken, and the mail-matter shaken out on the ground. A cascade of papers, magazines, and books, with a fat, firm little packet of letters among them: forty letters in all — thirty of them falling to my lot — thirty fat, bursting envelopes, and in another 'half mo' ' we had all slipped away in different directions — each with our precious mail matter — doing the 'disappearing trick' even to the Fizzer's satisfaction.

The Fizzer smiled amiably after the retreating figures, and then went to be entertained by Cheon. He expected nothing else. He provided feasts all along his route, and was prepared to stand aside while the bush-folk feasted. Perhaps in the silence that fell over the bush homes, after his mail-bags were opened, his own heart slipped away to dear ones, who were waiting somewhere for news of our Fizzer.

Eight mails *only* in a year is not all disadvantage. Townsfolk who have eight hundred tiny doses of mail-matter doled out to them, like men on sick diet, can form little idea of the pleasure of that feast of 'full bags and two on 'em', for like thirsty camels we drank it all in — every drop of it — in long, deep satisfying draughts. It may have been a disadvantage, perhaps, to have been so thirsty; but then only the thirsty soul knows the sweetness of slaking that thirst.

After a full hour's silence the last written sheet was laid down, and I found the Maluka watching and smiling.

'Enjoyed your trip South, little 'un?' he said, and I came back to the bush with a start, to find the supper dead cold. But then supper came every night and the Fizzer once in forty-two.

At the first sound of voices, Cheon bustled in. 'New-fellow tea, I think,' he said, and bustled out again with the teapot (Cheon had had many years' experience of bush mail-days), and in a few minutes the unpalatable supper was taken away, and cold roast beef and tomatoes stood in its place.

After supper, as we went for our evening stroll, we stayed for a little while where the men were lounging, and after a general interchange of news the Fizzer's turn came.

News! He had said he had stacks of it, and he now bubbled over with it. The horse teams were 'just behind', and the 'Macs' almost at the front gate. The Sanguine Scot? Of course he was all right; always was, but reckoned bullock-punching wasn't all it was cracked up to be; thought his troubles were over when he got out of the sandy country, but hadn't reckoned on the black soil flats. 'Wouldn't be surprised if he took to punching something else besides bullocks before he's through with it,' the Fizzer shouted, roaring with delight at the recollection of the Sanguine Scot in a tight place. On and on he went with his news, and for two hours afterwards, as we sat chewing the cud of our mail-matter, we could hear him laughing and shouting and 'chiacking'.

At daybreak he was at it again, shouting among his horses, as he culled his team of 'done-ups', and soon after breakfast was at the head of the south track with all aboard.

'So long, chaps,' he called. 'See you again half past eleven four weeks'; and by 'half past eleven four weeks' he would have carried his precious freight of letters to the yearning, waiting men and women hidden away in the heart of Australia, and be out again, laden with Inside letters for the Outside world.

At all seasons of the year he calls the first two hundred miles of his trip a 'kid's game'. 'Water somewhere nearly every day, and a decent camp most nights.' And although he speaks of the next hundred and fifty as being a 'bit off during the Dry', he faces its seventy-five-mile dry stage, sitting loosely in the saddle, with the same cheery 'So long, chaps.'

Five miles to 'get a pace up' — a drink and then that seventy-five miles of Dry, with any 'temperature they can spare from other parts', and not one drop of water in all its length for the horses. Straight on top of that, with the same horses and the same temperature, a run of twenty miles, mails dropped at Newcastle Waters, and another run of fifty into Powell's Creek, dry or otherwise according to circumstances.

'Takes a bit of fizzing to get into the Powell before the fourth sun-down,' the Fizzer says — for, forgetting that there can be no change of horses, and leaving no time for a 'spell' after the 'seventy-five-mile dry', the time limit for that one hundred and fifty miles, in a country where four miles an hour is good travelling on good roads, has been fixed at three and a half days. 'Four, they call it,' said the Fizzer, 'forgetting I can't leave the water till midday. Takes a bit of fizzing all right'; and yet at Powell's Creek no one has yet discovered whether the Fizzer comes at sun-down, or the sun goes down when the Fizzer comes.

'A bit off,' he calls that stage, with a school-boy shrug of his shoulders; but at Renner's Springs, twenty miles farther on, the shoulders set square, and the man comes to the surface. The dice-throwing begins there, and the stakes are high — a man's life against a man's judgment...

It is men like the Fizzer who, 'keeping the roads open', lay the foundation-stones of great cities; and yet when cities creep into the Never-Never along the Fizzer's mail route, in all probability they will be called after Members of Parliament and the Prime Ministers of that day, grandsons, perhaps, of the men who forgot to keep the old well in repair, while our Fizzer and the mail-man who perished will be forgotten; for townsfolk are apt to forget the beginnings of things.

Source: Mrs Aeneas Gunn, *We of the Never-Never*, Hutchinson & Co, London, 1908, pp.145-50.

In the land of sweat and sandflies

Patrick (Paddy) Flynn

In the land of sweat and sandflies
Where the Mary River flows —
And rum and hard-tack whisky —
Where there's blacks and buffaloes;
In a big bend o' the river
There's a shack o' brush and tin
Where dwells an Irish huntin' man
Be the name o' Patrick Flynn.
And Patrick had a birthday
As he did quite frequently,
And so it was we found him
Beneath a banyan tree.
'Come in and welcome', Paddy boomed.
To a lubra (with a wink): 'An Millie, bring the combo rum, for me friends will have a drink.'

Well, pannikins filled, we toasted Pat;
Bullfrogs joined the chorus.
Blackfellows belted tapsticks
And danced corroboree for us;
And all the bush things took to heel
At the rattatan and din,
As we wingdinged on the Mary
In honour o' Paddy Flynn.
The presents were the usual,
Tobacco and things like that.

Some fish hooks and a pocket knife —
We thought a lot of Pat.
Well, day dawned on the Mary,
There were empties all lying by.
Dragonflies buzzed the river,
Magpie geese honked in the sky.
'Be up,' Paddy yelled and we wakened,
As he belted a kerosene tin.
(No fancy chiming alarm clocks for OUR mate, Paddy Flynn).

We had fresh barramundi for breakfast
And mangoes that melt in your mouth;
And, especially for the occasion,
Some wines that came from down south.
' 'Tis glad me heart is to do it,
Though, bedad, it's pearls before swine,'
Grinned Pat as he opened a bottle
Of Orlando Rare Vintage Wine.

Well, the pannikins barely were emptied
When we spotted a bull buffalo
Drinking, down be the mangroves,
Where the old Mary waters flow.
So we all fired wide in the hurry;
We missed the old coot be a mile.
Then Paddy took off cross the sandhills
In true Tipperary style.
He yelled and let fly — bang! On the dot —
The buffalo dropped with a snort,
While we cursed and picked up the pieces
Of a bottle of Old Tawny Port.

But we all cheered the conquering hero
And gave speeches, as well as we could —
While blackfellows carved up the carcass —
Enough for the whole neighbourhood.
So we've signed, with respect, this wine label,
In tribute, where headaches begin,
To a marksman of Gold Medal vintage —
Patrick T. Michael Flynn.

Source: Patrick (Paddy) Flynn, 'In the land of sweat and sandflies', in Keith Willey, *Ghosts of the Big Country*, Rigby, Adelaide, 1975, pp.221-2.

Nina Hall, bushwoman of bushwomen

F. E. Baume

When gold was in the air parties surged through Alice Springs on an unreceding tide. But no party ever given in Australia could reach the heights of that which farewelled a bushwoman of bushwomen when she passed through the Alice from the 'top end' on her way to Adelaide.

Nina Hall is known wherever a miner scratches or a stockman swears. Hers has been no life near a silken divan nor path through an easy glade. As the wife and the widow of Arthur Pearce, who put in the first well at Tanami, she has roamed the North from Broome to Birdum and Wyndham to Ryan's Well. She is a magnificent woman of the bush.

When the stockmen are in and the prospectors have the showings in the little bags and they call for a drink, they call for Mrs. Hall. She goes to the little parlor in Kilgariff's Stuart Arms Hotel. At the piano she sits and the men crowd in, in shirts and flannels, sandshoes and gigglers (which are elastic-sided boots), and she sings to them. Then does her voice lose its hardness, the hardness of a sun-scorched life, and she brings tears to the eyes of the worst of them. 'Worst,' did I say? Probably the word should have been 'best,' for the harder they are north of the Territory, the better they are, and the oilier ones are the bad.

So Alice Springs went to Nina Hall's party the night before she left for Adelaide, just on 1,000 miles to the south. She had nearly perished to the North. Her feet were still blistered from her ordeal: the sick man whom she had walked 15 miles over the desert to succour was still ill at a station far off. But it was her party night, and the men were in.

At the piano, set vividly against the dirty plaster wall, Frank Ashwood, a giant miner, who years ago had been at Broken Hill, played a fox-trot. It was a good fox-trot and Mona, the barmaid, who had lived in Adelaide, was enjoying it. But Nina Hall thought otherwise. 'Get off that seat, sonny,' she called. 'Give us some of the old stuff, Paddy.'

Paddy Ryan, six feet and bending, with a moustache a film company would have bought, stood by the piano. In a voice quavering with many kinds of emotion he began, 'Where the River Shannon's Flowing.'

'Good horseman!' called Ned Larkin, 70-odd and still droving from Camooweal to the South. 'Good horseman!'

Paddy stopped. 'Who's singing this song, Ned?' he quavered, and suddenly sat down quietly, and was soon asleep. They forgot all about him at once.

Mrs. Hall sat on the piano stool and sang 'Mother Machree.' The round that followed cost 27/-. Then she sang 'Until' and 'An Emblem.' Ned Larkin was too tearful after it to say anything but 'Good horseman!' The next round cost 27/-.

Before Mrs. Hall could start her next song, Jack Atherton, the veteran, white-bearded prospector, who found the now famous Burdekin Duck claim at The Granites, rose to his full height. 'Gentlemen and drovers,' he began.

There was a roar of laughter. Old Ned Larkin rose valiantly, sat down and murmured, 'Good horseman, but it's an insult all the same.' Then someone walked over and patted his bald head, much to the horror of a young and whiskered drover, who regarded Ned much as a schoolboy regards the Governor-General.

There was an interruption at this stage, and another round was the only solution. An extra two cattlemen made the round 30/-.

Then Jack Atherton wiped his beard and began. 'We of the North' — they call Atherton the philosopher up here — 'we of the North have a code.' Paddy Ryan took a sudden interest. 'Lode, Jack, lode,' he said, and slept again. 'Never talk, Jack,' said Ned Larkin, completely recovered from the head-patting. 'Never talk,' and Atherton went on: 'That code is the bush code. I have half a damper, then you have half my half a damper; you have a pound, I have a pound. Twenty-four years ago Arthur Pearce, this girlie's husband (the girlie is 53 and proud of it!) was my mate at old Tanami. We knew him when he was at Wyndham and we knew him at the goldfields. He was a bushman and a man, and to-night we drink with one whom he loved, and the years roll on.'

It was a long speech for old Jack. It was too much for old Ned. 'Good horseman!' he said, and his old eyes filled with tears. But it woke up Paddy Ryan and Paddy O'Neill, and it moved a bank man, who had just arrived, to fixing the next round. Mrs. Hall did the rounds of the men and shook their hands, looked hard at them and cried a little. But they got her back to the piano and they sang 'Auld Lang Syne' for Arthur Pearce, who was there in spirit, and then they led Frank Ashwood back to the piano and he gave them a barn dance. Jim Escreet, the lucky prospector, who was leaving for the South in the morning, danced with Dick Atherton.

Paddy O'Neill did an Irish jig on his own and took off his shoes to do it, and midnight came before they knew it. There was never a word of swearing and never a ribald joke, for there was a bushwoman present, and that is the law of the bush. When the dawn was breaking I mentioned this to old Ned Larkin. He smiled a very tired smile and he said, 'Never talk,' and then, 'She's a grand old horsewoman.'

Source: F. E. Baume, *Tragedy Track: The Story of the Granites*, Frank C. Johnson, Sydney, 1933, pp. 158-61.

Talking history

Daisy Nawala Cusack

Daisy Nawala Cusack was born on Limbunyah Station. Her mother was a Gurindji and her father was the station overseer. At the age of six, while her mother was in a Darwin hospital and her father was at another station, she was taken from her home by police and, after a long journey on horseback and lugger, she arrived at the Kahlin home in Darwin.

At the age of thirteen, she was taken out of the home to work for the family of Mr Asche, the Solicitor-General. At a very young age, she became Nanny to Austen Asche, [later] Chief Justice of the Northern Territory Supreme Court. She stayed with the Asches until she was 16 and travelled with them to Melbourne, where one of her childhood memories is riding on the back of Phar Lap.

Returning to Darwin, she worked as a cleaner at the hospital until she was trained as a nurse's aide by Dr Cook, the then Protector of Aborigines. She worked at the Katherine Hospital with Dr Fenton, an early flying doctor. After her marriage, she lived in Darwin in a house she had bought with savings from her wages. During the war, she was evacuated to Mildura after her house was machine-gunned by a lone Japanese plane.

She returned to Darwin after the war and resumed working as a cleaner at the Darwin Hospital after she and her husband separated. She now [1987] lives a peaceful and happy retirement, with her three daughters and numerous grandchildren regular visitors.

What I first remember at Limbunyah Station was, I used to ride horses. Bareback. You couldn't get the saddles cos my father would kill you. I'd steal the bridles from the stables. I was the one that done the most stealing because I was the boss's daughter and they thought I wouldn't get belted.

I used to get more hidings and always used to get into mischief, you know. We used to go down, down to the flats near the gardens. We'd ride horses and we'd come back and there was another girl there with us, she's a cousin of mine and she was really a pig. She always used to tell, tell the boss's wife — my father's wife. If he was away mustering, tell the cook ... Old Ah Bin.

I can remember my father ... big tall bloke with a big moustache — biggest man I guarantee, he just about had to bend down coming through the door. They used to call him something that meant humpy back.

He was a wonderful stockman, taught me how to ride a horse and even bought me a little Shetland pony. And he taught this little pony never to let any other kids get on, only me. The other kids they just used to get on. This little horse liked that and pretended to roll over on the kid.

It was a fringe camp ... nothing, it wasn't a big camp, about a dozen people, my mother and her husband. Just a station camp, you know, that had little sheds. I always wanted to go out under the bough sheds, you know, like they even have nowadays, you know, under the trees.

My mum was married to a full-blooded Aboriginal. What a wonderful old man he was, my stepfather, loveliest man. I think I loved him more than my own father, I think. You know, he was really gentle, like he was my real father, like he was to my two brothers.

We had plenty to eat, we never worried about what we ate. We never starved. It wasn't as if it was hundreds of Aboriginal people there. We always had our own cow and we've always had butter, you know. We used to make our own butter, which I never liked, butter, until I came to Darwin.

They used to teach us how to go and find [bush tucker], not that we wanted it, but it was always handy for us, that if we did get out into the bush we would know what to pick. I remember things like peanuts and there was another thing, it was like a big round potato growing out in the plain. It was black, it was more like a carrot, but it had a black sort of rim.

They used to bring that home and they used to have to put it in water for a day or so. Then they used to hit it against two stones until it became, like, rubbery. They used to have little white specks in them. We couldn't eat them because of that little white speck. We just had to hit that, you know, on the stone until that disappeared. It was just lovely and yellow then, that was the time to eat it. But they used to soak it in water for a couple of days because it was poison. You just couldn't get them out of the ground and eat them.

Yeah, a cheeky thing, that's what I can remember ... these wild oranges ... these other little black berries that used to grow during the wet season. Hundreds of different types of food. Lily roots, of course, you know. We used to dig that out of the ground, a lot of things, different types of plants. I never see them now, you know. This part has got different plums ... they've got different types of wild food than inland.

We had this bloke, this Chinese cook, used to bake bread. When I came to Darwin I just couldn't get over the food we had to eat [at Kahlin]. I think I starved for two days and then I had to eat because there was nothing else.

Then we had a bloke called Mr Carpenter. He was a white person. He used to do the saddles and check for any repairs. He was like a jack of all trades, he fixed the houses. I remember he fell off and broke his leg and his leg was out like that. We had to go down to the creek or the billabong and put the ... stand up like that so we could get the leeches and put them into this thing — that was to bring the leeches home — and there they were sticking out of the leaves. Oh, the thought of it now. [We] took it off and put it in a bucket of water, in with his leg and they sucked the bad blood out.

I was about six, I think, because I can remember, yes, we got taken away on horseback. We rode from Limbunyah station to Timber Creek all the way. Because we got taken by the police. And these same wild Aborigines that live up on some range or other — this is only from what I have been told — they knew we were coming from the time we left. They followed us all the way through and I remember asking my brother: Why did they follow us? And he said, because they knew they were taking you away and they wanted to see that you were safe and nothing happened to you on the way. They were more or less our guide all the way, but you could never see them. But the police tracker knew they were around, watching us all through day and night till we got to Timber Creek.

Long trip. The bloke who took us, his name was Constable Tom Turner. Very well known in the Darwin area, he worked around here. Lovely fellow, he was very good to us. He took us and we sat at the police station till a lugger [came]. I think we must have stayed there for about a week or so till the boat came in and then we went down to the Victoria Depot, which is down from Timber Creek. We got on the boat there and I was seasick and when we got into the open after we left Victoria River, out in the wild open, you know, I've never seen anything like it, you know, this wide, the sea. I remember the old fella that was the skipper of the boat. That was Mr Damaso. Family up here [Darwin] now. As a matter of fact, Esther's [youngest daughter] ex-husband was a Damaso and Des's mother was the daughter of this old man Damaso.

Daisy Nawala Cusack meets her brothers, Peter and Spider Julama, for the first time in sixty years.

Never, never a day passed when I didn't think about country. I think about it all the time. I think the biggest thrill of my life was when a girlfriend of mine, she works for the Social Security, she said to me, 'Aunty, do you want to come with me to Hooker Creek?' I said yeh, I would love to come. I've never been there. I've heard about it. Wave Hill, I'd never been to Wave Hill when I was a child. And when I went past a great big tank it said: Wave Hill this way. I said Wave Hill! I couldn't be too far from Limbunyah. I said to Cathy: That way, that's my people. She said: don't worry love, we're going to pull into Wave Hill now.

When we got to Wave Hill it was in the afternoon and she turned around and I seen all these big hefty looking ladies there, lovely coloured people working in the office ... she turned around and said: Hey you mob, this girl belong to your country. And they said: Yeah? Where you come from? And I said Nawala from Limbunyah. Well, the roars and screaming going on all over the place. From nowhere I remembered the language: Girl here from Limbunyah, and they were yelling at me, and they came and surrounded me. And I said: You know, you mob, I'm looking for my brother. They said: Who your brother?

And I said: My brother name Peter and Spider. And I was only talking to his wife! Well, she got that excited.

I hadn't seen my two brothers for 60 years. As we pulled in near the canteen at Hooker Creek, Connie Bush and I sitting in the front of the car, and my brother came up to me and touched me like this and said: Hello, my sister. Now can you beat that? I said: Who are you? He said: I'm Peter, your big brother. He could see me just about, but he is completely blind now, I believe.

When we went up and met ... in our custom, there's not ... as much as they love you, they don't, they can't, they just get you and shake you by the hand. And they don't call you by your name. They call you sister and brother, you see. And I knew I can't, I felt like loving them, but I just held his hand. And he said to me — and poor old fella, he just held me by the hand and he was crying; he was blind and I just sat down with him on the bed. I remember I had to call him brother and his biggest smile and I said: You all right, brother? And he said: You remember all the same, everything sister we taught you. And I said: Little bit, you know.

So the next time I went down I just got about two hundred dollars worth of groceries and things because he's getting old. See, they get their killer, like the meat, they get a lot of meat supplied to them down there so they're not short of meat down there. But he said to me: We can't get too many bush food at Wave Hill, not like Limbunyah. I don't know why but he said: I want to go back there, and he wants to die there.

But this last time Esther took us and Josie [second daughter] went down there and the kids and he wanted to see all the kids. And he could just see all the kids playing there and each of these kids, he tells the dreaming time. How it all happened, you know. My dreaming time is the Big Snake, supposed to travel around all over the Territory and kill people and live in a great rockhole which is at Limbunyah Station.

I can always remember why I was allowed to swim there. They used to get a stone, throw it to the rockhole and that was for the snake, so it was OK to swim. But me, I could swim in the rockhole and it wasn't till I went back that my brother told me the whole story behind it. They never even seen Chelsea [grand-daughter] when he gave Chelsea dreamingtime name. It means blue water and when he saw Chelsea with that white skin and blue eyes, you know, what a coincidence. Never ever saw the kid when he gave them their name, each of these kids have got, you know, you can sit down and listen to it for hours. They are really proud of it, those children of mine, you know,

I was asking him more than anything else whether I was dreaming different things, I left it when I was so young. Different things, he corrected me on different things. But he just couldn't get over it, the things that I remembered when I was a little girl. He said: You remember everything well. [I said] I wanted to ask you whether I was dreaming or imagining it. Was it a thing that never happened? He said: No, it happened all right, everything happened.

I remember initiation time, you know, when they have these kids taken into the scrub and make them into what they call young men. And I remember popping up to see if I could see what they were doing. I was coloured kid. If I was a fullblood, they would have killed me on the spot. It was only for men, you see, but, you know, when you are young, you want to look into everything. That's what they told me, but I wouldn't dare ask them, because you are not supposed to talk about them. That's sacred to them.

That's why I reckon they are such marvellous people. What they remember. They can tell you stories, you can sit down and listen to them and never get tired. And my little grandson Travis, he never sits still, when he gets there with his mouth open he can listen to his old uncle talking: Oh Nanna, I can listen to that old man. Well you listen to him because he is a very, very clever old man. Whatever he tells you is true, you know.

Source: Daisy Nawala Cusack, 'Talking history', *Land Rights News*, vol.2, no.5, December 1987, pp.30-31.

The Afghans

Rex Ingamells

Four Afghans sit in evening light,
With features dusked by turbans white,

But eyes like sun-glow I've seen smoulder
On a lonely desert boulder.

In circle, cross-legged, they converse,
With accents guttural and terse.

Unknowable are nomad faces
Till you haunt all desert places:

The same pent dreams glint there unknown
As on the eve-lit boulder-stone.

Earth brother, I must stranger be
To such fierce taciturnity.

Source: Rex Ingamells, *Gumtops*, F. W. Preece, Adelaide, 1935, p.6.

Wallaby

Lionel Gee

Of course there were many black camp followers on the Tanami Gold Field, and they were not altogether myalls (wild natives). Most of them drifted down from the Sturt Creek country, where there are a few outback cattle stations, and therefore they knew a little of the white man and his ways, and could speak a few words of pidgin English.

As hewers of wood and drawers of water and in helping with the camels and horses, they were very useful. A happy-go-luck lot with laughter always hung on a hair trigger, they received much rough kindness from the diggers, liberal food supplies, and also discarded garments, which they proudly wore all the time, day and night. Every blackfellow has a name bestowed upon him, to which he sticks tenaciously, and doesn't like to be called out of it.

This fellow got the name of *Wallaby*. He was an ordinary fuzzy-headed be-whiskered black, clad in an old pair of dungaree pants, and the remains of shirt. He used to 'hump' wood and water for Paddy Finnigan, and after he had done his chores he sat contentedly around the rest of the time with the other blacks. But one night Wallaby slept too close to the fire, with the result that one of his legs from the inside of the knee to the heel was badly burned — burnt almost away, and even the bone was charred. Paddy was much distressed over his henchman's condition.

'Burnt all the poor feller's calf right away, leastways blackfellows don't have no calfs, but it all burnt off there.'

Paddy dressed the leg as well as he could and wrapped it up. Then he went to the store, gave three shillings for a tin of condensed milk, mixed an old jam tin full of it, filled Wallaby's pipe, and put the two things alongside him.

'Now you just buck up, Wallaby,' he said, 'and you'll be all right.'

The other blacks were very unsympathetic. Their attitude, indeed, was that of callous indifference, and they one and all expressed the decided opinion that Wallaby must die.

'Wallaby bin die all right — him die.'

But Wallaby seemed in no pain, and was supremely indifferent to everything. His time was passed in a state between daze and doze, with an occasional little sip of the milk, and a puff or two of the pipe. Sergeant, a big black who came from somewhere near Wallaby's country, and could speak his lingo, informed me that Nemesis had overtaken Wallaby — that a spell or a curse, a sort of ju-ju had been laid upon him in consequence of his own misdeeds, and that the burning was no accident, but the working of this fate.

'Wallaby him run away 'nother blackfeller gin, other blackfeller him make mud and sing longa star; Wallaby bin die all right.'

These Jeremiads annoyed Paddy very much.

'Shut up or I bin knock some of yer ugly heads off. No more you go dead Wallaby. Buck up, Big feller, buck up Wallaby, you bin savee.'

But Wallaby declined to buck up. Like the first Mrs. Dombey he could not 'make an effort.' Days passed by; he became thinner and thinner, and finally quietly flickered out — died.

Among these blacks my boy Jack was as a Triton amongst minnows. He came from far off Pine Creek, had been associated with white men all his life, had ridden in a railway train, and had seen the big steamers at Port Darwin. He had also served a short time in Fanny Bay Gaol, of which he was proudly reminiscent. He knew things, was full of yabber and corroboree songs, and moreover discoursed most hideous music from a long wooden drone pipe, a fearful and wonderful novelty to these denizens of the spinifex country. He was regarded as (so to speak) a Bostonian of the highest culture, and with (to quote Mr. Boffin) 'feelings of hadmiration approaching haw' by these simple savages, and their little stocks of information were open to him.

So, being rather curious, I instructed Jack to find out all about this matter. I knew, of course, that aborigines never regard death as proceeding from natural causes, but I wanted to ascertain what particular variety of 'bone' had been pointed at Wallaby. Jack investigated, and one evening came to me and with rolling eyeballs and abundant gesticulation gave me information, which I jotted down in my notebook.

'Suppose blackfeller bin take away gin belong ole man or any man and then him go away long way, nother place altogether. Ole man very sorry, very cross that gin go away; so him tell other boss blackfeller him mates. Him yabber long them. Then they go longa bush and get um mud, wet mud longa bush. Sometime white mud, sometime black mud, him work him up like him make um damper, then him make um thing all same a froaig (frog) all same white fellow dough. Make um head, make um two arms, make um benjy (stomach), make um two legs; then him put it long a sun. All blackfellow sing all the time. Before him make um mud him bin make big fire all same bake um damper, then spread out fire, then him take um mud thing put him longa middle fire and cover him up — then go away. All the time they bin sing to twofeller little star that away (south), to watch after blackfeller that take um gin.'

'This blackfeller, him away; him play about him all right, bye an bye him go cranky longa head. That fire, that mud, that star catch him. Next morning him feel all right. By an bye him say "Me too much cold, want um big feller fire"; him lay down there — too hot. Him go way longa bush, lay down; and then came back again longa fire. Then him get too hot again, and say "shift um fire back little bit," and then him go fast asleep. Star ready catch um now, and fire come along and burn him leg big. Him wake up and sing out. Other blackfeller sorry, but him say other blackfeller long way off bin make um mud, and him die. Then by and bye him get bad; no more eat um tucker and him die.'

So far Jack; and, after all, it is not so many years ago since some of our ancestors and ancestresses used to make waxen images of their enemies and stick pins into them with intent to do grievous bodily harm. It seems to me that the deserted husband calls in his spiritual advisers — say the Archdeacon and rural dean of the district, and the local rector with his church wardens — and that all the time they are doing their business they chant an invocation and appeal to the two small stars in the south; and then these stars search out the co-respondent and punish him.

According to the novels, plays and magazines of the day, modern society is drifting into a dreadful state, of which the increasing breach of the seventh commandment is one of the most alarming signs. What a change would be made could we only adopt the simple and efficacious procedure of our coloured brother — the Australian aboriginal.

Source: Lionel Gee, *Bush Tracks and Gold Fields*, F. W. Preece, Adelaide, 1926, pp.34-6.

Story from Lajamanu

Abie Jangala

I was born in the bush, maybe 20 km from Thompsons Rockhole, about 200 km south of Lajamanu. I grew up with my parents and when I was old enough to walk, my father took me around and showed me the tracks of the animals we hunted, like kangaroos, wallabies and goannas. I was too young to go with the men to hunt kangaroos, because they would have to walk too far for that, but I tried to catch *warrana*, a kind of blue-tongue, pink in colour with a red nose, that lives in the desert. They are very hard to catch. During the day they hide themselves in holes in the ground, that have many tunnels between them, but at night they go out to hunt for ants. We could only catch them in the wet season, because then they come out of their holes in the early morning and late afternoon. In the winter we couldn't catch them at all, because they sleep in their holes during that time.

My father showed me how to catch red bandicoots too. They can run very fast and we could only catch them in their nests, that they make in hollow logs. We moved around in that area, our country, the men hunted and the women gathered different kinds of bush-tucker: *yarla* (yams), *wayiti* (little white carrots), *yawaki* (bushplums), *kararrpa* (yellow berries) and grubs, goanna and so on. I helped the women to find those too.

When my time had come to be initiated, my father and the other men took me and they made me a young man there. After that I stayed in that same area, hunting with my friends. According to our law I couldn't come near women anymore, not even my own mother. I had to learn all that and also I had to learn the dreamtime stories of that place, and my father explained those to me. There are big boulders there, and one of those looks like someone bending down. That boulder is a man, called Jangala, who in the dreamtime had taken some sacred objects away from his people. This was a terrible thing he had done and the people speared him for that. He was stabbed many times, went down on his knees and was then killed with spears, boomerangs, nulla nullas and *warlanypa*, a kind of battle axe. From that time on he stands there, as a rock. This place is sacred to Jangala and Jampijinpa and my father told me:

'This is your dreaming country, and mine. When I die, you will take my place and be in charge of that dreaming. You will have your own corroborree that you can show to your children when they are going to be initiated or you can teach this to your younger brothers, who will in turn teach it to their children. So you don't have to dance somebody else's corroborree, you have your own.'

We had heard that in Granites, to the west, a strange kind of people, with white skins were staying. One day my father decided to have a look at those people, so we walked to Granites, where we saw them working in the coppermine there. To me those white people looked strange and I couldn't understand the way they were talking. We stayed there for a few days and then went back to the bush again. There was a road that went from Granites to Thompsons Rockhole and on to Alice Springs, but we didn't go there, we stayed in our own country, east of Thompsons Rockhole and lived there off the land.

When I was about 16 years old, my father took me back to Thompsons Rockhole and showed me more dances of the dreamtime. There were of course other men present, but only my father could dance these corroborrees, as they were his. We call it *parnpa* and *puwarripa*. My father thought I should learn more, because I was a bit older now, already a young man, but I still didn't know very much and my father was worried about that. He showed me all the different ceremonies and then said to me:

'I have shown you everything now and I think you are now old enough to go on your own. I don't think I can teach you any more. But if you still need me to teach you, you can always come back.'

I left him and went to Granites, to have a look again at those white people and what they were doing. Some of my people were working in the mine and they were given food for that. One of the Europeans there asked me if I wanted to have a job, and I accepted. He treated me well and taught me how to work properly. I even learned how to drive a truck! The whites spoke in Pidgin English to us and I learned that quickly so that I could speak to the Europeans. I spoke for others, who didn't know English, too.

For about $1\frac{1}{2}$ years I worked in the mine in Granites, and then I went east, to the bush again, to see my father. I stayed in my country for about two years, occasionally visiting my father, going off on my own, coming back again. I learned more about our business and then I was a real man, around 21 years old.

Again I went to Granites to work in the mines and I had a look in Tanami too. But I didn't like Tanami; after a few days I was back in Granites again where I worked for another few weeks before returning to the bush.

I visited my father there again for a couple of weeks and learned still more about our rituals. I had to learn all that, because I would be in charge of our dreaming country and its sacred places when my father would have passed away. According to our law other people could not come to my dreaming country, just as I could not come to theirs. That is why I always went back to the same place. My father taught me the Water-dreaming, that belongs to Jangala and Jampijinpa. One of the Dreamtime heroes, from whom Jangala and Jampijinpa are descended, travelled through that country from Thompsons Rockhole to Kurlupurlurnu, a lake south of Lajamanu. This is the country of the Water-, Rain-, Clouds- and Thunder-dreaming and is therefore sacred to us.

I went back to Granites to work. When I was there for a few weeks, an Army truck came from Alice Springs and collected me and other young men. The war had broken out, Japan had taken Indonesia and Darwin had been bombed. Everybody from about 16 to 30 years old had to go in the army. We were taken to Alice Springs and we built army barracks, the picture theatre, airstrips and the bitumen road from Alice Springs to Daly Waters. There were about 4000 Aborigines and 4000 Europeans working in the army there. It was a good life, a bit rough, we had to work hard and were pushed around, but still I liked it. During this time I went to Tennant Creek for a holiday and stayed there for a while.

When the war was over, we were released, and I went to Yuendumu, where my family had gone to stay, with other people from that area. An Aboriginal Reserve was established there and I worked there in Yuendumu for five years, making roads, cutting trees, building the airstrip and cutting timber for boughshelters and sheds.

The Government wanted to make a road to Catfish, more than 600 km north of Yuendumu, where they planned to make an Aboriginal settlement. The man, who was driving the grader, didn't know the way and asked it someone would come with him. I thought about it and then offered to go and I asked Roger Jangala if he would come too. There was an old wagon trail and we showed him which direction to go, until we came to Supplejack, 450 km from Yuendumu.

We camped in Supplejack, but I didn't like it there. It was country I didn't know and it made me sad to be away from my own place. I wanted to go back to my country. Roger and I talked it over and then we decided to walk back to Yuendumu again.

We told the driver of the grader how he had to go from there on and we set out for the long walk back to the south. In those days we were strong and we could walk the whole day, from sunrise to sundown, hunting our food, finding bush-tucker everywhere and we knew where to look for water. But we followed the road as we were still in country we didn't know.

After a week or so we arrived in Granites, where I met some of my people and I decided to have a rest there. For about a week I worked in the mine again and then walked back to Yuendumu, where I stayed with my people for about three years.

When the road to Catfish was completed, the Government, through Social Welfare, decided to move 20 of our people to Catfish, to make a settlement. Two Government officials, Ted Evans and Mr Ryan, collected twenty of us, including myself, by truck. We were not asked, we were simply told to go.

On the back of the truck we went, to a place we didn't know, away from our country where we had grown up, away from our dreaming places. We went via Granites, Tanami, Black Hills, Supplejack and from there on it was in country I had never been myself.

We arrived in Hooker Creek and we camped there. There was one bore there, near the creek and the place didn't look too bad. The Government officials asked us if we would stay in Hooker Creek, instead of going on to Catfish, and we agreed to that.

There was nothing in Hooker Creek, apart from that one bore. There was no windmill for pumping water, it had to be done by hand. We had to get some bushes and build humpies for ourselves and then we had to start building a shed, that could be used as a garage, to repair the trucks. First this shed only had a roof, no walls, as we were short of building material. We built a house on the place where the mechanic Pat Johnson's house stands now, and when that was finished, the Government people stayed there. We also built a store, on the place where the school library is now.

I stayed in Hooker Creek for about $1\frac{1}{2}$ years, and then I wanted to go back to Yuendumu again to see my family there. I asked the Government official if I could have a holiday and he agreed, I could get a lift on a truck to Yuendumu.

My father was getting old now and I saw him in Yuendumu for the last time. He said to me:

'I am old and sick now and I will die soon. You can take care of yourself, you don't need anybody to look after you anymore, or to teach you. You can go now and don't have to come back.'

After about a year in Yuendumu the Government decided to take the first group of people they wanted to move, to Hooker Creek. About 200 people were collected by truck and again, nobody was asked if they wanted to go, they were just told. I went with them back to Hooker Creek, where they had to start a new life.

But after two months some people started to drift back. This was not our country, this was Gurinji country, we didn't have our dreaming sites here, and especially the old people were not happy. So they simply walked back, all the way, to Yuendumu, Mt Doreen, and Granites. Others stayed for about ten months and then walked back. But I stayed, with others, and we built an airstrip, on the place where the transmitter station and the rubbish dump is now. It was hard work, we had to cut and clear away all the bushes and trees and the European overseers were rough to us, always shouting at us and pushing us around. We were never paid any wages, just given rations of food, like everywhere.

The airstrip was no good when it was completed. During the wet season the planes got bogged in the mud. Once we had to push a plane about 1 km to the office. It tried to take off, but it didn't get enough speed and it crashed down again. The people who were in it were alright, but we decided to build another airstrip, a longer one, and that is the airstrip we have today.

Since I came here for the first time, Hooker Creek or Lajamanu, as it is called now, has changed a lot. Many houses have been built, bore-holes have been dug and many people live here now. Children have been born here and that means their dreaming place is here, so we have started to think of Lajamanu as our country now. The Europeans who live here are also better than those we had before; we are not pushed around anymore as we used to, we can speak to them now.

When I look at my people now and think of how it was when I was a boy, I can see many changes. We are wearing clothes now, we buy food in the shop, drive cars and when we go hunting, we use rifles instead of spears and boomerangs. But all that is not important. Our own law and our own ceremonies are still important to us and if I go to dance my corroborees, I leave my clothes, car and rifle behind and go to the ceremonies as my forefathers have done for thousands of years. *Yapakurlangu* or Aboriginal law still is our law. It is the law of the *Walyajarra*, the people who lived and died a thousand years ago, and we cannot change that. We are Warlpiri Aborigines. *Kardiyakurlangu* or white man's law alone is no good to us and you can see that when you look at those Aborigines who live in towns like Darwin, Alice Springs or Katherine. They cannot live properly like Aborigines, they are away from their dreaming sites and cannot go to their rituals. There are Aborigines and part-Aborigines who live in cities and want to speak for us, on our behalf. We don't want to have anything to do with them. We are Warlpiri and we can speak for ourselves. We have our own ways, our own traditions and our own law, and with it we want to decide our own future.

Source: Abie Jangala, 'Story from Lajamanu', in A. Jangala, J. Jangala, M. Jupurrula Luther, P. Jakamarra, S. Japangardi, P. P. Jangala, and R. Jakamarra, *Stories from Lajamanu*, Northern Territory Department of Education, Darwin, 1977, pp.3-7.

Shark

Patrick McCauley

I am living alone in an isolated community. I start working on the day, drawing the spaces together. There are sick times, mostly in the hot afternoons, and in the night. I fill them with drawn out well planned dinners. I diminish the great pile of unread books from one shelf in the bedroom, to another shelf in the lounge room. I begin to walk the beach which goes for about two miles one way and three the other.

Descending the cliff in front of my house early Saturday morning, I turn left along the sand. A packet of tobacco, a fishing line, and a pair of shorts is all I need for the entire weekend. I walk past the barge landing, where once a month the big red old barge, which was a landing craft in the second world war, brings in heavy equipment and booze, and a party goes all night on the beach. I swim the first small creek, and walk inland for a way, to work my way around the rocks at the point. About a mile further on, I come to a very wide creek; it looks deep, and the water is flowing out quickly. The salt water crocodile is now a protected animal, and has bred into plague proportions on Melville Island. I look at the creek; I can see crocodiles everywhere, I can hear them roaring. I decide this is far enough, and take out my fishing line. There are sand flies beneath the hot hot shade of the dogwood trees; I must not scratch the bites, otherwise the sores will turn into tropical ulcers; the sand flies will bite, there are millions of them; they are biting my legs; they itch in the sticky heat. I clear my mind of their presence, and try to think of nothing, or something else, anything! I decide to go for a swim; sitting carefully in the water, looking everywhere for sharks, and jellyfish and crocodiles, and any other monster (which there must surely be!) I splash myself quietly, feeling the cool water drain down my back; feel the sand fly itches stop for a second; then the salt dry tight on my back in the unbearable sun; feel my mind in hot void alone; I hear a splash.

There is my old hand-line, running down the beach, being pulled by some mad fish into the sea. I rush out of the water; (oh the beautiful beautiful fish, who takes away the sand fly salt sun) grab the red reel as it jerks its way down the sand, and hold on to the weight pulling at the other end. The line slices the water like a cheese knife, and we carve figures of eight in the flat river mouth; fish pulls hard, I give him more of my share of the line, fish goes slack, coming straight at the shore, I take back my share of the line: more line, I reel him in, then he turns hard heading for the mouth of the creek again, I give him back my share, then pull with him, he comes slow, with a few slips here and there, until I can see the dorsal fin of a small school shark rise angrily to the shallows of the beach.

That night I eat shark on the beach. Beautiful shark which the black people will not eat because of its vicious flesh, and which the white people will not eat because of its mercury content. Shark, great fish who slices up the water with me on the end of its death line; (oh shark do you catch me, or do I catch you?) big fish with curved triangular body, pointed at both ends for speed, small fast fins (which are not the fastest in the sea); a million years old shark! A sandpaper back and a soft, so soft, white belly; are you all bad? (designed like hunger, moving in the wind, you survive) No, shark, I do not hate you as we play together; I eat you and wonder who has caught who.

I sit by the fire on the beach in the night. I smoke tobacco and burp shark smells.

Source: Patrick McCauley, Hunt, written in 1975 at Snake Bay, Melville Island (unpub.).

The pub owner's wife

Thomas Keneally

The pub owner's wife was in her mid-forties, her husband a little older. Together they ran a pub on one of the roads in the Top End, southeast of Darwin. Among clumps of pandanus and palms, it sat under a vast sky and catered to a thirsty clientele. Their customers were truck drivers, Aboriginal and white stockmen, miners passing to and from Darwin, illicit tropical bird smugglers, bull catchers, buffalo shooters, aerial musterers. Since it was a noisy pub, the pub owner and his wife lived in a house some distance off, and the wife would walk down to the pub from the house every evening to help out in the bar. It was a dark walk through a sparsely populated landscape, and her husband considered it a dangerous one. He could not say specifically who it was he feared would attack her, but he was aware of the violence and madness which always seemed close to realisation in the humidity and endemic drunkenness of the Top End. He therefore pressed her to carry a .25 Biretta with her whenever she walked down to the pub at night. 'I'm not worried about the blackfellers,' he told her, 'it's the mad white bastards that worry me.'

His fears had reasonable statistical grounds. The annual average for murders in the Territory is fourteen times the Australian national mean; the prevalence of fire-arms, geographic remoteness, grievances germinating richly beneath the humid sun and fed on liquor, the high rate of individual eccentricity, the mysterious business of Aboriginal retribution — all that helped the figures along and made it wise for a woman walking at night through a concentration of drinkers to go armed.

It became a habitual matter for the publican's wife to carry the small revolver, though the pub owner himself may well have forgotten that he had pressed the weapon on her.

Lately she approached the pub in the evenings with a certain sense of grievance. Among the regulars were a number of hard-drinking women. She was aware that intimate signals passed across the bar between some of them and her husband. She hoped it was all just a bit of social byplay. She had never seen anything more than that.

As well as her minor sexual suspicions, she hated the rowdiness of the pub, the aggravation that prevailed there, the racial insults, the struggle to get the aggressor and the drunk out of the door at closing time, the turning from an eventually closed and locked front door to see the swill, the vomit, the sometimes overturned furniture.

One night in 1980, carrying her bag, the Biretta half-remembered inside it, she strolled down as usual from the house to the pub. She passed through the screen of battered four-wheel-drives in front of the place, familiar vehicles, each of them matched to the face of some regular boozer already inside and settled down to an evening of hectic drinking. She went to the back of the pub and came into the bar through the office. From the office door she could not see her husband serving the customers. She presumed he was in the storeroom. She went out into the night again and saw the heavy door of the storeroom ajar, a little light spilling through it. Opening the door further, she saw her husband in there with one of the women customers.

The pub owner was of course astounded. He dragged his trousers up, belted them and walked towards her, beginning to speak. He discovered, before she did, that the Biretta was in her hand. As he reached the door she shot him through the wrist. The bullet passed through and hit his buckle. 'Bloody surprised he had his buckle done up,' some of the local people would say later.

Bleeding, he turned away from her and ran away into the open night. She shot him twice in the buttocks. It did not occur to her to take any vengeance on the woman. The pub owner travelled in a wide circle, then stumbled into the pub and collapsed. The pub owner's wife went into the office and wept, while the barmaid called the local police station.

The pub owner was rushed to Darwin by ambulance. The pub owner's wife was put in the caged back of a police van and also driven to Darwin. She was appalled by her murderous impulse, yet at the same time too angry to be repentant. When the Darwin magistrate released her on bail, she went to visit her husband in hospital.

It is the sort of crime which in the Old Testament atmosphere of the Northern Territory attracted a light sentence, a mere fifteen months, to be served in the new Fannie Bay prison. Fannie Bay has been historically, a foul and tragic place, though the new wing is air-conditioned and the regimen more humane that it has previously been. But to go to prison was, she found, still a shocking business. 'If I'd killed him and got twenty years,' she said, 'I'd be better off dead.' But reading got her through — 'She's a great reader,' her husband used to boast to people before the shooting.

The pub owner himself might have suffered the worst punishment. As soon as his wounds began to heal, he found that they were considered undignified injuries. According to the contradictory morality of a frontier town, a man is permitted to liaise with strange women, but he is not permitted to be caught by his wife nor to be shot in the buttocks. The first night he hobbled back behind the bar of his pub, the locals were merciless. 'Here's Ray again,' one of them yelled. 'Half-shot as always.' He proved very paranoid about shooting jokes, and about the possibility of further attacks. He bought new weapons — Magnum revolvers, shot guns. The jokes continued for a time, but there was a limit to them.

The pub owner's wife was paroled after nine months. She met her husband again. They were old-fashioned people, it was unlikely that, having both survived the shoot-out, they would separate and seek a divorce. The passionate shooting probably added something — a spice, a brio — to the middle reaches of their marriage.

They decided that the pub was not good for their marriage, and put it on the market, selling it easily. For, although it was what Australians call 'a blood house', a rough boozer, it was a gold mine. The former pub owner and his wife bought the local store, and can be found there behind that more prosaic counter today. When people come in and ask the wife to witness documents for them, she tells them with the pride appropriate to a survivor, 'No use asking me, I've got a criminal record.'

Source: Thomas Keneally, *Outback,* Hodder & Stoughton, Sydney, 1983, pp.79-80.

Talking history

Paddy Fordham Wainburranga

Paddy Fordham Wainburranga was born at Bamdibu in central Arnhem Land in the early 1930s. After the war, he and his family moved to Maranboy and later Dandangle, a government settlement.

In his late teens Wainburranga started work as a stockman, travelling from station to station in the VRD and Murranji areas of the Northern Territory. At Gorrie he was given the name Fordham by the station owners at the time.

Paddy lived at Maningrida on the coast of Arnhem Land in the 60s and 70s. During this period, he was active in the outstation movement. With other Rembarrnga people, Paddy helped establish Guyun, one of the first outstations in the Maningrida area. Paddy has lived the last ten years at Beswick, an Aboriginal cattle station 30 kilometres from Barunga (formerly Bamyili).

Wainburranga is a painter and storyteller, and active in the teaching of dance to younger people. In 1987, he revisited his country in Arnhem Land while making the film Too Many Captain Cooks, *which is about the Rembarrnga account of Captain Cook.*

I'm here telling you this story in this place called Bulara — that's the big country name for this area.

Old people used to live here a long time ago under this shady tree. The tree is called muban. Every Christmas time we eat the muban fruit when it is ripe. It's like a plum.

All the old people — even my father and my great-grandfather — used to camp here for maybe one to three days and used to hunt emus here and gather bush tucker.

This place is called Baijildir billabong. This country is dhuwa country belonging to the Mirraitja, Kabudubud and Kanjirra clans.

We are not far from Bamdibu, where I was born. Everybody knew Bamdibu, no matter what tribe they were from. It is dhuwa country there, too — my grandfather's place.

Not just myself, but all the brothers and sisters, every one of our family belongs to that place. It's Rembarrnga country, in the centre of Arnhem Land. It is for the Mirraitja, Balngara and Kabudubud clans.

I was born in this part of Arnhem Land. There was no white man's tucker then. I was brought up on breastmilk, my mother raised me on her breast. This was before I saw a white man.

My mother took me three times by foot all the way from Arnhem Land to the Northern Territory. She took me over there, brought me back again, took me over there and brought me back again to Arnhem Land where I grew up.

I didn't know what was going on. I didn't know my mother and father had seen the white man over there, I didn't know.

They had a bit of a town at Katherine then. Only a peanut farm and a few houses. Not all built up like the big city it is today.

So my mother brought me back here and I grew up. When the war time came, when the war was being fought and the bombs were coming down, my mother and father told me: 'Hey! All your uncles, all the family have been gone a long time. To Maranboy. What about us going?' Well, I didn't know.

Anyway, all the family, my father and his four wives, all my brothers and sisters walked down. It took us three or four weeks to get there. To the Territory. Maranboy. The war was going on; it was before I was a young man.

I became a young man after the war and then I learnt about the white man. How the white man treated me. How he gave me clothes. Native Affairs government. They sent our people out of Arnhem Land.

And before the Native Affairs government — they went before the war, all over Arnhem Land, right up in the centre of Arnhem Land. Rembarrnga people, Ngalkbun people. They all cleared out. All went to Katherine, or to Bamyili, or to Bewsick Station. Some were in Darwin, some in Borroloola, some in Roper River.

Now what I'm thinking is the families want to come back. We have our own culture, our own family clans. No good we live like that in settlements. We can't live another way just because Native Affairs gave the people too many other ways, too many different ways of thinking. Too many problems.

My father was left-handed. He had five children; two girls and three boys. We survived but the old man was dead by the Second World War — or just after the war came to Arnhem Land. My father was left-handed and he used to kill kangaroos. He was better than me!

No flour or sugar in those days. We used to live like that.

He hunted for emu, goanna, birds. Different kinds of birds — jabiru, brolga, all those kinds of things we ate. That's how I grew up. That's how I was taught.

My father was a left-handed man — full Rembarrnga tribe, from the Mirraitja clan.

His Aboriginal name was bularn.ngu — meaning 'left hand man'. His real name was Kinyiyn Kinyiyn. That was my father's name when he was living in this country, way before citizenship times.

He used to live and work in this country before the Second World War. And after that we went away. We followed those people into the Territory.

That's the way we got stuck up there, and our father died there. He never came back to this land. He tried to come back but all his young brothers — he had three young brothers — stopped him.

And the government gave him the name Tony Farrell — Kinyiyn Kinyiyn! That first Native Welfare mob gave him a name. Mr Bruce Allen, old Billy Harney mob. My father died in the Territory. That's my father's story.

We'd always travel with a lot of kids. We would travel with no water from the morning, though sometimes we'd get water from hollow logs. You know there's lots of water lying in hollow logs from storm rains.

We used to make our camp sometimes with no water. Then early in the morning we'd get up and sing out and look at the country carefully, so we could find water and go hunting.

That's what this part of Arnhem Land is like. Other places are all right but here in the middle you've got to sing out. You've got to talk to the country. You can't just travel quiet, no! Otherwise you might get lost, or have to travel much further. That's law for the centre of Arnhem Land. For Rembarrnga people.

My father used to do it. We used to get up early in the morning and he'd sing out and talk. Sometimes he didn't talk early in the morning, only when travelling and we used to stop and he'd talk then in language.

It would make you look carefully at the country, so you could see the signs, so you could see which way to go.

It's different altogether here in Arnhem Land, in the middle of Arnhem Land. That's been the law from the beginning.

The law about singing out was made like that to make you notice that all the trees here are your countrymen, your relations. All the trees and the birds are your relations.

There are different kinds of birds here. They can't talk to you straight up. You've got to

Paddy Fordham Wainburranga, drawn by Chips Mackinolty at Baidjildir billabong, central Arnhem Land, in July 1987.

sing out to them so they can know you.

This is especially the case with the one called Baidjadjabobok, the male, the female is called Kankarkalawidjutub. This bird doesn't live anywhere else in the Northern Territory, or East Arnhem Land or on the Oenpelli side. It's just in the middle of Arnhem Land.

When it sings out: 'baidjadjabobok, baidjadjabobok, baidjadjabobok, baidjadjabobok', he's calling right out into the country, like a shanghai, into Arnhem Land.

He can make you get lost, too. You can't find your way. You can walk out a couple of miles and you'll get lost there.

This bird is very powerful. Everyone knows that. He can make you get lost. He can make you do anything, even if you don't want to.

This is especially the way if you've missed the land for a long time.

That's why I've come here: chasing my grandfather's and mother's land, here in the centre of Arnhem Land.

It's not every one's understanding now, about country. But me, I've got respect. From my grandfather's way because it's my ceremony ground. Near my birthplace Bamdibu.

It's called Bawurrung. It's only half a mile from Bamdibu, a ceremony ground from the earliest days. My father had that ceremony there. My grandfather had it too, but no one alive knows him. He died a long time ago.

So here I am. I started this morning from yirritja country, where I camped at a big billabong called Kalarrdayin. I am at Baijildir now.

Oh! Good living! A quiet life. A long way from here to Bawurupanta. A long way off to Maningrida or Milingimbi. All the ideas are different here.

I think that's because, when I think back, my father didn't speak any other language than Rembarrnga. He didn't talk Ngalkbon. He didn't talk Maiali. He didn't talk Djinang.

That's the way I learnt, and came back to the story of this land. You've got to think about it — that's what I do. I come back to this way of thinking here, to have a good look at this land.

That's why I talked to the birds this morning, and all the birds were happy. All the birds were really happy and sang out: 'Oh! That's a relation of ours. That's a relation we didn't know about.' That's the way they spoke, and they were happy then to sing out.

Now, in the morning and afternoon time they will speak. When I first came here it was silent — only trees! But the birds were there all the time.

Source: Paddy Fordham Wainburranga, 'Talking history', *Land Rights News*, vol.2, no.9, July 1988, p.46

7 'My spirit, my country'

My lease can't wash out. No rain will wash him out him, no anything will take it away. That's mine lease. White man lease, you read him out on the paper, you change him next year, nother lease. That's what they call special lease, you know, whitefellow law. Mine lease you can't wash him out. He stand up there, no matter rain can be hit him, you can't wash him out. He'll be there for years and years, till I die, till another man will take over that lease. Same lease. That lease forever. We call him, that lease, blackfellow law.
— Riley Young Winpilin, interview with Debbie Rose, 1984

If you looked long enough you'd see a lot of things. That what this country's like where it hasn't been defaced by our pale-faced brethren. I mean both real things and those that are unreal to the unknowing. This is a land of spirits. Don't forget that it was divined as such even before found by the unbelievers. The mariners who dreamt of its existence called it *Terra Australis del Espiritu Santo*, South Land of the Holy Spirit, from which at last the lovely name Australia, South Land, came.
— Jeremy Delacy, in Xavier Herbert, *Poor Fellow My Country*, 1975

Sometimes people say that Aborigines are deprived, because they have to stay in humpies while Europeans live in houses, but we don't feel this way. We have been having humpies all the time. People don't understand. We are just like that. We don't go to places like Katherine where we would live in a good house. We don't like it — we would prefer to have fire and a windbreak and stay there, because a house is just like a big jail or something like that. It's true! People who are sitting in it cannot see far.
— Paddy Patrick Jingala, *Stories from Lajamanu*, 1977

> Rock stays,
> earth stays.
> I die and put my bones in cave or earth.
> Soon my bones become earth ...
> all the same.
> My spirit has gone back to my country ...
> my mother.

— Big Bill Neidjie, conclusion to *Kakadu Man*, 1987

Previous page: Collage in Frederick T. Macartney's Proof Against Failure *(1967). Macartney spent twelve years in the Northern Territory (1921–33) in a range of government posts such as Public Trustee, Sheriff, Registrar in Bankruptcy and Registrar General of Births, Deaths and Marriages. Deeply conservative by nature, Macartney did produce some haunting linocuts to accompany the lyric verse written during his Top End stay.*

The land is the art

James Galarrawuy Yunupingu

The land is my back-bone. I can only stand straight, happy, proud and not ashamed about my colour because I still have land. The land is the art. I can paint, dance, create and sing as my ancestors did before me. My people recorded these things about our land this way, so that I and all others like me may do the same.

I think of land as the history of my nation. It tells us how we came into being and what system we must live. My great ancestor who lived in the times of history planned everything that we practise now. The law of history says that we must not take land, fight over land, steal land, give land and so on. My land is mine only because I came in spirit from that land, and so did my ancestors of the same land. We may have come in dreams to the living member of the family, to notify them that the spirit has come from that part of our land and that he will be conceiving in this particular mother.

My land is my foundation. I stand, live and perform as long as I have something firm and hard to stand on. If there is a flood on my land I will have to swim and all Gumatj clan will have to swim, but not for long, we will surely perish, then we will be just like thousands of other people whose lands have been stolen away from them. We will be the lowest people in the world, because you have broken down my back-bone, taken away my arts, history and the foundation. You have left me with nothing.

Without my land I am nothing. Only a black feller who doesn't care about anything in the world. My people don't want to be like you.

Source: Passage by James Galarrawuy Yunupingu, in Keith Cole, *The Aborigines of Arnhem Land,* Rigby, Adelaide, 1979, p.149.

This earth

Big Bill Neidjie

This earth …
I never damage,
I look after.
Fire is nothing,
just clean up.
When you burn,
New grass coming up,
That mean good animal soon …
might be goose, long-neck turtle, goanna, possum.
Burn him off …
new grass coming up,
new life all over.

I don't know about white European way.
We, Aborigine, burn ...
Make things grow.
Tree grow,
every night he grow.
Daylight ...
he stop.
Just about dark ...
he start again.
Just about morning I look.
I say,
'Oh, nice tree this.'

      ...

When you sleep,
tree growing like other trees ...
they got lots of blood ...

We must get rain.
Law says we get rain.
He come along wet season and go dry season.
Rain come down and give us new fresh water.
Plants coming up new ...
yam, creeper all plants new.
Then we get fruit, honey and things to live.

Tree, he change with rain.
He get new leaf,
he got to come because rain.
Yam he getting big too.

Old people say
'You dig yam?
Well you digging your granny or mother ...
through the belly.
You must cover it up,
cover again.
When you get yam you cover over,
then no hole through there.
Yam can grow again.'

'You hang onto this story' they say.
So I hang on.
I tell kids.
When they get yam, leave hole,
I say
'Who leave that hole?
Cover him up.'
They say
'We forget.'
I tell them
'You leaving hole ...
you killing yam.
You killing yourself.
You hang onto your country.
That one I fight for ...
I got him.
Now he's yours.
I'll be dead,
I'll be coming to earth.'

All these places for us ...
all belong Gagadju.
We use them all the time.
Old people used to move around,
camp different place.
Wet season, dry season ...
always camp different place.

Wet season ...
we camp high place,
get plenty goose egg.
No trouble for fresh water.

Dry season ...
move along floodplain,
billabong got plenty food.
Even food there when everything dry out.

All Gagudju used to visit ...
used to come here to billabong ...
dry season camp.
Plenty file snake, long-neck turtle.
Early dry season ...
good lily.
Just about middle dry season ...
file snake, long-neck turtle,
lily flowering.

Everybody camp,
like holiday.
Plenty food this place.
Good time for ceremony,
stay maybe one or two weeks.

Pelican, Jabiru, White Cockatoo ...
all got to come back,
make him like before.

Fish ...
he listen.
He say
'Oh, somebody there.'
Him frightened,
too many Toyota.
Make me worry too.

I look after my country,
now lily coming back.
Lily, nuts, birds, fish ...
whole lot coming back.

We got to look after,
can't waste anything.
We always used what we got ...
old people and me.

Source: Big Bill Neidjie, extracts from 'I give you this story', in Big Bill Neidjie, Stephen Davis & Allan Fox, *Kakadu Man*, Resource Managers, Darwin, 1987, pp.35, 40-42.

Where I was born

Jack Mirritji

My name is Mirritji. I was born at Warngibimirri.

One day I asked my stepfather [my father's brother — uncle] to explain to me where I was born. He told me this story.

It happened on one of my parents' fishing trips that he killed a bog water goanna. That night, back at the camp, he had a dream of me. I came to him and said: 'Father, you killed my spirit when you caught that water goanna. That water goanna was me.'

When he had that dream he woke suddenly and ran to my mother, telling her that she was going to have a baby soon. She didn't believe him at first, until he told her about the dream. Afterwards she became very sick, and about nine months later I was born.

My grandmother cut my cord when I was born, and carried me in her dilly bag for about two months. Later she gave me to another related tribe, Ganalbingu, for my birth ceremony. Then my father took me to a paperbark tree and cut a wooden cradle with a white man's axe for me to sleep in.

My grandmother looked after me while my mother was out hunting — gathering yams, lily roots, bandicoots, and many other things to eat.

I did not know where I was born until my second father [father's brother] had explained it to me. Wrngimirri is about ten miles south of the Arafura homestead [Murwangi]. The homestead has been gone many years.

In the beginning I lived in a small place called Japirdijapinmi near a creek, surrounded by mountains.

Our camp had belonged to all my ancestors before me, and it was situated about eight miles south of the old Arafura homestead, in the eastern part of the area we called Djumurru [Arnhem Land]. All round there are cliffs, jungle, swamp, billabongs, springs, waterholes and rivers running into the sea.

This was the time of my life in the bush country, when I lived on my tribesmen's land, and in the village of my countrymen. We were moving round all the time, visiting relatives in different parts of the scrub, and in different bush shelters. I moved with my parents and friends, making camp in places where we met other groups of people — sometimes two or three.

My name is Mirritji; my skin is Balang; my tribe is Jinang; my moiety is Dhuwa; my group is Manharrngu — this means I am of the sugar bag [honey] people Yarrpany. For all of the time when I lived in the bush, we lived by the law of the Mardayin [the old time Aboriginal law] and the rules made by custom and tradition [juburr].

Source: Jack Mirritji, *My People's Life: An Aboriginal's Own Life,* Milingimbi Learning Centre, Milingimbi, 1976, pp.2-3.

Yinungkwura / West wind

Groote Eylandt song

Ningerrikba arakba
Ekbilyuwalyu-wa,
Ekburriyalku-wa.
Ningerrikba arakba
Ekbilyuwalyu-wa,
Ekburriyalku-wa,
Ekbulmadangku-wa.
Yinikumalaba.
Mamamuruku-wa
Marrkalarruwa-wa,
Mabilyuwenda-wa,
Marrkirrkawuru-wa.
Ningikbuldarrmanga
Nganyangu-manja.
Ngamanga Ekilyangba?
Nganyangu-manja.
Ngamanga Ekilyangba?
Ningakuma alika.

I've tossed it now, wind and song,
To the flat land,
Bare, treeless flat land.
I've tossed it now, wind and song,
To the flat land,
Bare, treeless flat land,
To the sandy flats.
The wind is testing its strength,
Blowing down to the ants' path
With its tiny pebbles,
Down to tiny heaps of gravel,
Down to all the heaps of gravel.
I followed the flat land
In my country.
Where is Ekilyangba?
It's in my country.
Where is Ekilyangba?
I've set my foot there.

Ningumangalyilyaka	I've trodden
Mamuruku-manja,	On the path,
Mulukwarrjamiyama,	The narrow path,
Yuwebu-langumanja,	Ant' path.
Wurralukwurruma.	Red ants,
Wurrurukuweba,	Meat ants,
Wurrurukwaluwa.	Tiny ants.
Nayengba wurruweba,	Parrots screeched,
Nenukwirrumaja.	Flying low over their ant friends.
Yinumamurukwa,	Ant paths,
Yinumalika.	Ant tracks.
Nalbajena amarda,	Wind striking grass,
Nalkuwayijina,	Parting grass,
Nakubakarrdanga.	Rustling.
Yinungkwarrki-langwa,	My grandfather's wind,
Yirukwaluwu-langwa,	Tiny ants' wind,
Yimurndajamiyamu-langwa.	Thin ants' wind.
Nalyangkarrnga yinungkwura.	The west wind has veered away.

Source: From a recording (cat. no. AM41B: I [in Australian Institute of Aboriginal Studies, Canberra]) obtained on Groote Eylandt in 1963 by Alice Moyle. Words transcribed and translated by Judith Stokes.

A trip to the Victoria River, 1887

Rev. J. E. Tenison-Woods

Anyone who has read the works of Captain [John Lort] Stokes, who discovered this river, will remember the romantic enthusiasm with which he made his boat expedition along its waters. He and many others thought that it was a kind of Australian River Nile, and that its sources would be found in the very centre of the continent. It was owing to this idea that A. C. Gregory made his celebrated expedition to the watershed in 1854, when the now great Baron Von Müeller won his spurs as botanist to the party. But the rule in Australia seems to be that the importance of rivers is inversely proportionate to the promise at the mouth. The Victoria was not found navigable for 150 miles, and the watershed at the source is not 1500 feet above the sea. Nevertheless its opening is the outlet of many waters, and it forms, apart from its associations with the history of exploration, one of the most interesting geographical features on the north coast. For this reason I was very anxious to visit it especially as the geology promised to throw much light on what I had seen elsewhere in Australia ...

We had when morning dawned a fine day and smooth water, with a gentle swell. After passing the inconspicuous red headland of Point Charles, at the entrance of Port Darwin, there was nothing to look at but the sea and the sky, and the sky and the sea, for the shores of North Australia are low. Now and then one would discern a faint black line or a few trees on the horizon, but generally we were out of sight of land. To go any nearer would be unsafe even for such a little boat as ours, for the water is so very shallow. With the glass one could discern on one or two points or headlands, some red rocks, or low cliffs 20 to 30 feet high, certainly no higher. This is the appearance of the whole of the coast between Port Darwin and the mouth of the Victoria. A little way inland there is a dark fringe of forest vegetation, showing slightly elevated land, but of mountains or even hills there are none. Sometimes a very small hummock or a ridge becomes conspicuous from the absence of competitors, but such exceptions are scarce. So this, in brief, was all we saw for the first day, except the reef on which the Brisbane was wrecked, and this was only a discoloured patch on which the sea broke angrily.

At night we anchored in a little bay just inside Cape Ford, a low point as usual. There was a line of dark rocks in front, then sand, and then red cliffs the size of a small house. Behind was a thin level line of dark forest. It was impossible to make up a landscape with fewer materials. All day long the air was murky with smoke from many large bush fires. The sky was brown and curtained with streaks of smoke, and the sun went down red and flaming, but for two hours before it was quite hidden. If one did not know the cause one would certainly say that the heavens were lowering and threatening, and full of evil portent. Our anchorage was not far from the mouth of the Daly River, which drains such an immense area of country, very nearly as great as the Victoria and yet with such a narrow opening into Anson's Bay that it was never seen or its existence suspected by any of the marine surveyors. Mr. Stevens had never anchored here before, so we went in feeling our way. The night was beautiful and mild, and, in fact, a little chilly. I was glad of the shelter of our fore-cabin, nay, our only cabin, which was doing temporary duty as a fore-hold for special parcels. It was not a bad little cabin, and by duly adjusting the tea-chests, saddlery, stationery, bacon, wire, surveying instruments, and fire-bricks, there was a fair amount of sleep to be got out of it.

The change of tide roused us before dawn, and made us heave up anchor and away. It was a beautiful morning, bright and silvery, before dawn, by the light of the waning moon and the planet Venus. As the morning broke, the red sunrise beneath, the blueish grey of the sky above, and the silver moon and stars made a glorious combination of colour and brightness. The coast soon showed up in the cold, grey mist, and then our previous day's experience was repeated — green, bright water, with a foamy ripple upon it and a low coastline, from which columns and clouds of smoke were everywhere rising. In the middle of the day we stood in close to Cape Hay to clear many outside reefs and banks. This is a passage discovered by our indefatigable skipper. At 2.30 p.m. we passed Point Pearce, and then in a moment the whole aspect of the sea was changed. It became turbid and muddy. The tide was flowing one way, and the stream another, so the tide rips and ripple were such as to make one imagine that breakers were on all sides of us. The little steamer jumped and skipped about in a most lively manner; indeed, it required a strong arm, and much care to keep her head to the stream. It was such a change that for a moment or two the effect was quite startling, and made one think that the size of the Victoria was really greater than it is ...

We got over all the flats about midday, and then came to a point where there was but one deep channel. This emerged from the ranges to the southward which appeared looming on the horizon at sunset of last evening. As soon as we passed the point, the character of the river was completely altered. Enclosed between high banks into a stream sometimes not quarter of a mile wide, it rushed and roared with impetuosity which looked really threatening. There were eddies and whirlpools, tide rips, and boiling, tumbling narrows, which took the helmsman all he knew to make the Victoria keep her way. It was a regular wrestle. Though our speed was so good, yet the stream would almost have its will at times. It required most careful steering. If the least little helm were given at the turns, the whirlpools would twist her half-way round ere she would be brought up. Then there would be a pause, and the launch would quiver and heel over in the frothy turmoil all around us, until the river would yield the point, and wheel away on its mad, rushing, bubbling race. Woe to anyone who should fall overboard in such a place. I don't know what small boats could do. It reminded me of an exciting journey up the rapids of the Katsura River in Japan.

With a change in the river the character of the banks had changed. Instead of the long stretches of mangrove flats we had hills about 400 feet high close to the water's edge. They were lightly timbered with what most colonists would call scrubby vegetation, while the soil looked poor and light. But the rocks were remarkable features. At first the surface was broken up into boulders, rugged cliffs, and rocky outliers, such as one usually sees in a granite country. But the stones wanted the rounded outlines of granite. Before long the outcrop assumed the most fantastic shapes. There were masses of rough-hewn blocks piled into mimic masonry of every form. One hill was protected by a long low wall of red and white square stones; another was a mass of fragments of quite a monumental character, like a cemetery or a stone cutter's yard, only a good deal more jumbled. Then one would see a fair representation of ruins — a castle or a tower, one would say — but, as the windings of the river gave rise to different points of view, it changed into as many forms as faces in the fire. The colour of most of these rock masses is red, but not a uniform red. There are brown-reds and fiery-reds, light and dark reds, bright and deep reds, in every variety. There is no monotony, but rather such an endless vareigation that it is bewildering. After all, what wonders can be done with varying tints of one colour. But the general aspect is lurid, and it gives the impression of a true land of Edom ...

It is difficult to convey the impression which this large, lonely river makes upon a stranger. I am used to the lonely wilds of Australia, and have been familiar with them for more than half my lifetime, yet this great solitude of a river strangely impressed me. However, it had a beauty of its own. As the sun set the colours of the hills changed into surprising hues of purple, out of which the red cliffs stood in lurid patches. This was set off by an orange sky and a blue haze, while the calm and stillness made the columns of smoke rolling upwards throw a mysterious gloom over all. There were bright specks of flame visible when twilight set in, and the stars were reflected on the turbid murmuring river. There were natives about at no great distance — not likely to come near us, however. They are treacherous tribes on all the river, and not to be trusted for a moment. The night set in with a heavy dew and a brilliant canopy of stars. I took the first watch, and part of the second, and while my four shipmates slept on the deck the stillness of the scene was inconceivable to those who have never strayed far from the busy haunts of men. Not a sound on any side but the rippling of the tide and the slow measured breathing of the crew. I have never had an experience like it and could scarcely tear myself away to go below when the night was far advanced.

Source: The Reverend J. E. Tenison-Woods, 'A trip to the Victoria River', *Sydney Morning Herald*, 21 May 1887.

By the Grey Gulf-water

A. B. (Banjo) Paterson

Far to the northward there lies a land,
   A wonderful land that the winds blow over,
And none may fathom nor understand
   The charm it holds for the restless rover;
A great grey chaos — a land half made,
   Where endless space is and no life stirreth;
And the soul of a man will recoil afraid
   From the sphinx-like visage that Nature weareth.
But old Dame Nature, though scornful, craves
   Her dole of death and her share of slaughter;
Many indeed are the nameless graves
   Where her victims sleep by the Grey Gulf-water.

Slowly and slowly those grey streams glide,
   Drifting along with a languid motion,
Lapping the reed beds on either side,
   Wending their way to the Northern Ocean.
Grey are the plains where the emus pass
   Silent and slow, with their staid demeanour;
Over the dead men's graves the grass
   Maybe is waving a trifle greener.
Down in the world where men toil and spin
   Dame Nature smiles as man's hand has taught her;
Only the dead men her smiles can win
   In the great lone land by the Grey Gulf-water.

For the strength of man is an insect's strength,
   In the face of that mighty plain and river,
And the life of a man is a moment's length
   To the life of the stream that will run for ever.
And so it cometh they take no part
   In small-world worries; each hardy rover
Rideth abroad and is light of heart,
   With the plains around and the blue sky over.
And up in the heavens the brown lark sings
   The songs that the strange wild land has taught her;
Full of thanksgiving her sweet song rings —
   And I wish I were back by the Grey Gulf-water.

Source: A. B. (Banjo) Paterson, *Singer of the Bush: Complete Works 1885-1900*, Angus & Robertson, Sydney, 1983; published originally in the *Bulletin*, 11 December 1897.

Chugga-Kurri

Michael Terry

For several days [in 1933] we had not seen any Aborigines but well knew they were about for suddenly a tall column of smoke went up about three miles distant; slender at first, then more dense, to ascend slender again. Obviously 'smoke talk' was going on and doubtless about us. We could hear their high-pitched calls 'Wipella pou ... wipella pou ...' ('Wipella' was the nearest they could reproduce 'White fellow' and 'pou ...' that long-carrying trailing sound with which the desert Aborigines customarily end their call.)

We moved north-west until we reached Carnegie Bluff, the eastern-most point reached by the Carnegie Expedition from the west in 1897. The average altitude of the desert in that area is about 500 metres above sea level. Yet in a day or two I noticed some kind of general depression in the mirage. The far-away scene was, as ever, vague within blue immensity. Distant points danced in the mirage, shrouded by heat haze — yet there was a definite sinking in the earth-level.

About noon the following day I rode on quickly and when my camel reached the top of a sandhill I just gaped in astonishment at what I saw lying ahead of me. To the east lay a line of sandstone cliffs, hundreds of feet in height. The ground sloped gently down towards them and at the foot of the cliffs arose scattered clumps of tall gum trees. As I sat gaping, motionless on my camel, a flock of white-winged corellas flew over me. A sure sign of water. Then through the heat haze I could perceive threads of shining lines near the cliffs like green snakes in the desert. And I knew what they were: creeks. In that moment of anticipation and tingling with excitement I urged Dick, my riding camel, down the long gentle slope towards the cliffs. He responded eagerly, moving with that silky shuffle of a willing camel which smells water. Soon I came upon the abandoned campsite of a party of about fifteen Aborigines. Their tracks showed they were moving north and were not far ahead of me for the ashes of their fire were still warm. This made me wary for I knew through the disturbing silence I was being watched. So I loosened my revolver in its holster ready for emergency. Thus I rode for about two miles, my camel maintaining a fast shuffle whilst all around the signs of water and fertility increased. Ti-tree appeared. There was golden wattle in full bloom. A sandy creek. A pool of water. Then a patch of thick scrub and low bush, tropical in its luxuriance, barred the way. Dismounting, I pushed my way through — to emerge with glorious suddenness on the edge of a lake some 110 m long and about 8 m wide. I gazed at it, entranced. Water, the sheen of cool, cool water and in such quantities as to be almost unbelievable in that type of desert country. All around the edge was greenness and except for great numbers of birds I seemed to be utterly alone. It was like a dream of beauty and coolness suddenly come true.

Different men react differently to the same set of circumstances. My reaction was to tear off my clothes and leap joyously into the water and into the undreamed pleasure of a swim in the desert. I had forgotten all about the possibility of hostile Aborigines. My revolver lay unheeded in its holster on the sandy margin of the lake.

After I had bathed I scrambled out and still dripping with that wonderful water my first job was to light a signal to Nicker and O'Grady. But so profuse was the herbage around about, so new, so green, that kindling for a smoke was almost difficult to find — an incredible circumstance, a complete reversal of the desert conditions we had known. After scratching around I was able to light a signal. As soon as they came up, Nicker was so excited when he saw the water that he jumped in fully clothed ...

Later we three, Stan O'Grady, Ben Nicker and myself, stood on the rim above that rich and fertile valley and just looked and looked at what lay before our eyes. It seemed that at last, quite accidently, a legendary place known to the blacks — 'Good country; mob tucker;

mob water ...' had been found.

We were gazing upon the fabled CHUGGA-KURRI.

We spent several days exploring Hidden Basin as I called it (for, true to its name, it is completely hidden) and the surrounding country but as we were not scientists but gold prospectors and had people backing us we could only spend a certain amount of time in the valley. Nevertheless, from the superficial study I was able to make, it was pretty clear what had happened. My aneroid showed that the floor of the Basin lay at 200 m above sea level — that is, about 200-300 m lower than the surrounding country. We estimated that the red sandstone cliffs were 100 m high with an upward slope at the summit. A considerable downward movement of the sandstone strata must have occurred ages ago with the result that the horizontally bedded sandstone had been shorn off to form the cliffs on the eastern margin while elsewhere the beds had been sharply buckled into anticlines and synclines.

I have often been asked whether the water in Hidden Basin is permanent. I believe with some evidence that it is. The Basin is full of wild life, mainly marsupials and birds. Significantly, we found the tracks of several ibis in the moist sand. Now, the ibis is an inhabitant of large open pools and marshy ground and does not, like the ducks, migrate over long distances to get to water. Where, however, the water in Hidden Basin comes from I do not know. As it lies so much lower than the surrounding country and is so extensive, it is maybe in the nature of a huge soak. All I know is that the wattle still blooms in that hidden valley and the half legend that I heard tell of so long ago turned out to be true.

Source: Michael Terry, 'Chugga-Kurri' [1933], in Charlotte Barnard (comp.), *The Last Explorer*, ANU Press and North Australia Research Unit (Darwin), ANU, Canberra, 1987, pp.73-5.

High water

Frederick T. Macartney

Palm-fronds give my shutter-sashes
The grace of eyes with long eyelashes,
And they look out at break of day
On mangroves paddling in a bay
Like wading girls, who, when the waves rise,
Hold gathered skirts about their thighs.

What still is left of love in me
Is for the earth and sky and sea —
The shapes they have, their strife and play
And colours, even the flats of gray
Cadaverous ebb-drained mud — the bare
Dead body of noon, with death's harsh stare.

A new moon drops down sunset-dazed
Or an old moon comes up amazed.
The tide returns; to hear it stir
Brings happiness, as if it were
A child asleep where now I go
To listen at my door tiptoe.

Source: Frederick T. Macartney, *Preferences: Poems*, Angus & Robertson, Sydney, 1941, p.71.

Black cockatoos

Roland Robinson

Rise then, you screaming mob of black cockatoos,
and spread your red barred tail feathers out and scream
over the spears of the reeds and the purple lilies,
over the red rock walls of this sun-gashed gorge,
and gather in broken and screaming flight and turn
heading far up this jade green river's reaches.
So shall I find me harsh and blendless words
of barbarous beauty enough to sing this land.

Source: Roland Robinson, 'Black cockatoos', in Rex Ingamells (ed.), *Jindyworobak Anthology*, Jindyworobak, Melbourne, 1947, p.26.

W. Baldwin Spencer: 'Kakadu men and boys hunting with spears in a dug-out canoe on the Oenpelli Lagoon. East Alligator River, June–August 1912'.

White cockatoos

Tony Scanlon

With the infallible timing shared by infants
the white cockatoos select the time
of deepest sleep to erupt into dawn.
Racketing and clattering twenty feet
above my room, they go to breakfast
calling to each other and the world,
good natured, garrulous, companionable.
But there is always one — it must be the same —
the late-riser whose wings flog urgently,
a minute behind the last stragglers
of the ragged formation: bleary eyed,
hung-over on last night's fermented berries,
abusing those clean-living buggers up ahead.

Source: Tony Scanlon, 'White cockatoos', *Northern Perspective*, vol.10, no.2, 1987, p.24.

Flood plains on the coast facing Asia

Les A. Murray

Hitching blur to a caged propeller
with its motor racket swelling
barroom to barrage, our aluminium
airboat has crossed the black coffee
lagoon and swum out onto
one enormous crinkling green.
Now like a rocket loudening
to liftoff, it erects the earsplitting
wigwam we must travel in
everywhere here, and starts skimming
at speed on the never-never
meadows of the monsoon wetland.

Birds lift, scattering before us
over the primeval irrigation,
leaf-running jacanas, twin-boomed
with supplicant bare feet for tails;
knob-headed magpie geese
row into the air ahead of us;
waterlilies lean away, to go
under as we overrun them
and resurrect behind us.
We leave at most a darker green
trace on the universal glittering
and, waterproof in cream and blue,
waterlilies on their stems, circling.

Our shattering car
crossing exposed and seeping spaces
brings us to finely stinking places,
yet whatever riceless paddies
we reach, of whatever grass
there is always sheeting spray
underhull for our passage;
and the Intermediate Egret leaps
aloft out of stagnant colours
and many a double-barrelled crossbow
shoots vegetable breath emphatically
from the haunts of flaking buffalo;
water glinting everywhere, like ice,
we traverse speeds humans once reached
in such surroundings mainly
as soldiers, in the tropic wars.

At times, we fold our windtunnel
away, in its blackened steel sail
and sit, for talk and contemplation.
For instance, off the deadly islet,
a swamp-surrounded sandstone knoll
split, cabled, commissured
with fig trees' python roots.
Watched by distant plateau cliffs
stitched millennially in every crevice
with the bark-entubed dead
we do not go ashore.
Those hills are ancient stone gods
just beginning to be literature.

We release again the warring sound
of our peaceful tour, and go sledding
headlong through mounded paperbark
copses, on reaches of maroon
grit, our wake unravelling
over green curd where logs lie digesting
and over the breast-lifting deeps
of the file snake, whom the women here
tread on, scoop up, clamp head-first in their teeth
and jerk to death, then carry home as meat.

Loudest without speech, we shear
for miles on the paddock of nymphaeas
still hoisting up the paired pied geese,
their black goslings toddling below them.
We, a family with baby and two friends
one swift metal skin above the food-chains,
the extensible wet life-chains of which
our civility and wake are one stretch,
the pelicans circling over us another
and the cat-napping peace of the secure,
of eagles, lions and two-year-old George
asleep beneath his pink linen hat as
we enter domains of flowering lotus.

In our propeller's stiffened silence
we stand up among scalloped leaves
that are flickering for hundreds of acres
on their deeper water. The lotus
prove a breezy nonhuman gathering
of this planet, with their olive-studded
rubbery cocktail glasses, loose carmine roses,
salmon buds like the five-fingertips-joined
gesture of summation, of *ecco!*
waist-high around us in all their greenery
on yeasty frog water. We receive this
sidelong, speaking our wiry language
in which so many others ghost and flicker.

We discuss Leichhardt's party and their qualities
when, hauling the year 1845
through here, with spearheads embedded in it,
their bullock drays reached and began skirting
this bar of literal water
after the desert months which had been
themselves a kind of swimming,
a salt undersea plodding, monster-haunted
with odd very pure surfacings.
We also receive, in drifts of calm
hushing, which fret the baby boy,
how the fuzzed gold innumerable cables
by which this garden hangs skyward
branch beneath the surface, like dreams.

The powerful dreams of being harmless,
the many chains snapped and stretched hard for that:
both shimmer behind our run back
toward the escarpments where stallion-eyed
Lightning lives, who'd shiver all heights
down and make of the earth,
one oozing, feeding peneplain.
Unprotected Lightning: there are his wild horses
and brolgas, and far heron not rising.
Suddenly we run over a crocodile.
On an unlilied deep, bare even
of minute water fern, it leaped out,
surged man-swift straight under us. We ran over it.
We circle back. Unhurt, it floats, peering
from each small eye turret, then annulls
buoyancy and merges subtly under,
swollen leathers becoming gargoyle stone,
chains of contour, with pineapple abdomen.

Source: Les A. Murray, *The Daylight Moon*, Angus & Robertson, Sydney, 1987, pp.1-3.

rain

Lee Cataldi

in the desert
rain
falls on the dust on the ground
baked and rebaked dry as old tiles
everything runs and alters
rivers make new passages   mud
flows into new openings

bushes explode their smells into the soft air
promising
that in the morning we will wake to a different universe
the dry creek bed now a wide lake
uninterrupted water frontages
the sky open like a tap

mud might swirl up between our toes
water run out of our hair
the view become invisible just a smear
if we could step into the rain's embrace

and disappear

Source: Lee Cataldi, *The Women Who Live on the Ground: Poems 1978–1988*, Penguin, Ringwood, Vic., 1990, p.25.

Instructions for honey ants

Billy Marshall-Stoneking

Work with the end of your dress
tucked up between your legs.
Speak in whispers; laugh silently;
do not whistle. Whistling, especially,
brings bad luck. Do not be afraid
to feel where you cannot see.
Disappear into the earth
with crowbar and billy can;
go down, maybe ten feet.
If you find them there, it is better
when children are waiting.
This is marangkatja: a gift.
Love what you are after.

Source: Billy Marshall-Stoneking, 'Instructions for honey ants', published originally in *Instructions for Honey Ants* (Mattara Prize Anthology), University of Newcastle, 1983; and then in Marshall-Stoneking, *Singing the Snake: Poems from the Western Desert, 1979–88*, Angus & Robertson, Sydney, 1990.

8 A bastard of a place

It's a wide silent land … a brooding land … and full of spirit things, even if you don't believe in them. Unless you can come to love it, you come to hate it …
—Jeremy Delacy, in Xavier Herbert, *Poor Fellow My Country*, 1975

> To the northward, the southward, or westward,
>   No matter which way we turned;
> For sixty or seventy miles or more,
>   The whole of the country is burned.

— D. Landale Beetson, *Central Australian Exploring Rhymes and Camel-Back Jingles*, 1893

The hands of the fettlers shot up to wave, their mouths opened wide to shout — then mad Joe Ballest shrieked, leapt out of hands and on to the road, and rushed at the engine with fists raised. Hands and mouths were paralysed. Eyes — nothing but eyes — eyes — bulging and horrified!
— Xavier Herbert, *Capricornia*, 1938

For the best part of a hundred years or so, the Northern Territory of Australia has defied all efforts to develop it. Nature has said to man, 'You can come here, but you will come with very little and you will go away with less.' Drought and distance: floods, fires and famine: these were the weapons of the Territory and so far no one has been able to prevail against them.
— A.B. (Banjo) Paterson, from 'The Northern Territory', a wireless talk, 1930s.

This is the greatest bastard of a place on earth.
— Gig, in Sumner Locke Elliott, *Rusty Bugles*, 1948

Previous page: The very dapper Alfred Searcy, Sub-collector of Customs in the Territory from 1882 to 1896, took great delight in depicting the inability of Europeans to cope with an unforgiving environment in his three entertaining books on the tropics: In Northern Seas *(1905),* In Australian Tropics *(1909) and* By Flood and Field *(1911).*

Death and the desert

Ivan Archer Rosenblum

The sun set threateningly — a ball of red-hot copper, full and round, amidst the misty purple of the horizon. In the upper sky, bands of green and greenish-yellow, through which the stars peeped, looked down on the desert and its tragedy. And all around and above — silence, the ominous, fateful silence that more often precedes a storm than follows one, the grim silence that hints of approaching doom, that seems a prelude of death.

Only a fortnight had passed since Henry Weston and his party had set out to pioneer the way through the desert to the newly discovered goldfield at Natami, in the desolate North-west of Australia; only a fortnight, and yet disaster had already overtaken them. They had prospered until a tornado had hurtled down, killing the camels and scattering and

Frontispiece from Ivan Archer Rosenblum's Stella Sothern *(1911). Pot-boiler novels of this kind, penned by writers who had never been to the Northern Territory, were extremely popular in southern cities in the early decades of this century. In this sketch, it is difficult to ascertain who is the more uncomfortable when confronted by a desert setting: artist Harry Julius or Rosenblum's sartorially resplendent though overheated protagonist.*

burying the stores, and, worst mishap of all, ruining their instruments. The track was obliterated.

For three days Weston had struggled on alone, hoping against hope, fighting a forlorn battle against the inexorable elements. He had seen his two mates perish of thirst in that cruel desert which has claimed numberless victims, hiding with sand and silence all traces of its tragedies. The first died cursing God for keeping 'the clouds just out of reach'; the second, laughing heartily as he pointed at the desert, saying — 'We could do with a shower; a little rain would improve the going; anyhow, I'll have a pound on the favourite and chance it.' And so he had a win, for Death was favourite, and Death always wins. And now Henry Weston, surveyor and explorer, lay down to die in the desert alone. He had fought on until he could stand up no longer. He was out-lasted by opposing circumstance; he had taken his beating like a man. All that was left was to die.

Pale and emaciated he had struggled onwards until he fell, and, when he fell, he lay too utterly weary even to despair, too absolutely beaten to heed what further evil fate might send ... Already in the upper sky the stars were showing vaguely through the haze. He was conscious of the constellation of the Cross glowing dimly and with ever diminishing lustre as he, himself, became weaker and weaker. The Southern Cross! What memories it awakened even in that grim hour of dire extremity. He thought of home, of Warrawee township, and of beautiful, fragrant, peaceful Golden Gully where Stella Sothern lived. How nebulous it all seemed; how impalpable, intangible, unreal, as he lay there whilst the shadows surely deepened and his power of concentration became less and less. Yet, amidst the clouded realm of phantoms and unrealities, there still was dominant the distinct form of the sweet woman who would wait in vain for his return. As he passed, slowly, surely drifting, drifting, into the gloom, he still could see his loved and lost Stella — his star — smiling on him with ineffable charm.

Only a fortnight ago he had ridden from Golden Gully with a light heart; without any presentiment of evil. He was to blaze a trail to the new goldfields, and then return to claim his wife. Weston was one of the popular men of his district; somewhat reserved, as the bushman mostly is, no talker, but a doer. He was a notable horseman, a fine shot, and an experienced explorer. He had won many a steeplechase as a gentleman rider, and had gone with the Bush Contingent to South Africa, when the Empire had called on her sons. Stella had persuaded him, but resultlessly, to abandon the attempt to cross the desert. He had compromised by definitely agreeing that this expedition should be his last. He, and his party, fully equipped, had started for the interior on a glorious morning of January. Everything had seemed propitious. But the unexpected had happened, and they had stumbled on to tragedy.

Suddenly Weston, with a supreme effort, raised himself on his elbows. He seemed to be listening. They say that men in their awful extremity hear weird mysterious voices coming to them from the unknown; that the dying musician hears far sweeter melodies, harmonies more pregnant with vital meaning and potent suggestion, than ever had come to him in his hours of health and so-called sanity. Who shall say?

For a moment the stricken man seemed to be listening, the next he fell back. And just then the scene darkened, and night descended on the desert.

Source: Ivan Archer Rosenblum, Prologue to *Stella Sothern: A Story of Bohemia and the Bush*, NSW Bookstall, Sydney, 1911, pp.1-3.

Death of Voss

Patrick White

Voss attempted to count the days, but the simplest sums would swell into a calculation of universal time, so vast that it filled his mouth with one whole mealy potato, cold certainly, but of unmanageable proportions.

Once he asked:

'Harry? *Wie lang sind wir schon hier?* How many days? We must catch the horses, or we will rot as we lie in this one place.'

As if to rot were avoidable. By moving. But it was not.

'We rot by living,' he sighed.

Grace lay only in the varying speeds at which the process of decomposition took place, and the lovely colours of putrescence that some souls were allowed to wear. For, in the end, everything was of flesh, the soul elliptical in shape.

During those days many people entered the hut. They would step across the form of the white boy, and stand, and observe the man.

Once, in the presence of a congregation, the old blackfellow, the guardian, or familiar, put into the white man's mouth a whole wichetty grub.

The solemnity of his act was immense.

The white man was conscious of that pinch of soft, white flesh, but rather more of its flavour, not unlike that of the almond, which also is elliptical. He mumbled it on his tongue for a while before attempting to swallow it, and at once the soft thing became the struggling wafer of his boyhood, that absorbed the unworthiness in his hot mouth, and would not go down. As then, his fear was that his sinful wafer might be discovered, lying before him, half-digested, upon the floor.

He did, however, swallow the grub in time.

The grave blackfellows became used to the presence of the white man. He who had appeared with the snake was perhaps also of supernatural origin, and must be respected, even loved. Safety is bought with love, for a little. So they even fetched their children to look at the white man, who lay with his eyes closed, and whose eyelids were a pale golden like the belly skin of the heavenly snake.

In the sweet, Gothic gloom in which the man himself walked at times, by effort, over cold tiles, beneath gold-leaf, and grey-blue mould of the sky, the scents were ascending, of thick incense, probably, and lilies doing obeisance. It would also be the bones of the saints, he reasoned, that were exuding a perfume of sanctity. One, however, was a stinking lily, or suspect saint.

It began to overpower.

One burning afternoon the blacks dragged away the profane body of the white boy, which was rising where it lay. They let out yells, and kicked the offending corpse rather a lot. It was swelling. It had become a green woman, that they took and threw into the gully with the body of the other white man, who had let his own spirit out.

The plump body and the dried one lay together in the gully.

There let them breed maggots together, white maggots, cried one blackfellow, who was a poet.

Everybody laughed.

Then they were singing, though in soft, reverential voices, for it was still the season of the snake that could devour them; they were singing:

> 'White maggots are drying up,
> White maggots are drying up...'

Voss, who heard them, saw that the palm of his otherwise yellow hand was still astonishingly white.

'Harry,' he called out in his loneliness, 'come and read to me.'

And then:

'Ein guter Junge.'

And again, still fascinated by his own surprising hand:

'*Ach,* Harry is, naturally, dead.'

Only he was left, only he could endure it, and that because at last he was truly humbled.

So saints acquire sanctity who are only bones.

He laughed.

It was both easy and difficult. For he was still a man, bound by the threads of his fate. A whole knot of it.

At night he lay and looked through the thin twigs, at the stars, but more especially at the Comet, which appeared to have glided almost the length of its appointed course. It was fading, or else his eyes were.

'That, Harry,' he said, 'is the Southern Cross, I believe, to the south of the mainmast. That is where, doubtless, their snake will burrow in and we shall not see him again.'

'Are you frightened?' he asked.

He himself, he realised, had always been most abominably frightened, even at the height of his divine power, a frail god upon a rickety throne, afraid of opening letters, of making decisions, afraid of the instinctive knowledge in the eyes of mules, of the innocent eyes of good men, of the elastic nature of the passions, even of the devotion he had received from some men, and one woman, and dogs.

Now, at least, reduced to the bones of manhood, he could admit to all this and listen to his teeth rattling in the darkness.

'*O Jesus,*' he cried, *'rette mich nur! Du lieber!'* [Save me! Dear one!]

Of this too, mortally frightened, of the arms, or sticks, reaching down from the eternal tree, and tears of blood, and candlewax. Of the great legend becoming truth.

Towards evening the old man who sat with the explorer cut into the latter's forearm, experimentally, cautiously, to see whether the blood would flow. It did, if feebly. The old man rubbed a finger in the dark, poor blood. He smelled it, too. Then he spat upon his finger, to wash off the stain.

The following day, which could also prove to be the last, was a burning one. The blacks, who had watched the sky most of the night in anticipation of the Great Snake's disappearance, were particularly sullen. They had suffered a fraud, it seemed. Only the women were indifferent. Having risen from the dust and the demands of their husbands, they were engaged in their usual pursuit of digging for yams. All except one young woman, who was exhausted by celestial visions. Almost inverted, she had dreamt dizzily of yellow stars falling, and of the suave, golden flesh, full of kindness for her, that she had touched with her own hand.

Consequently, this young person, to whom a mystery had been revealed, as if she were an old man, increased in importance in the eyes of the others. Her companions were diffident of sharing their chatter. They talked round, rather than to the young initiate, who had been, until recently, the little girl they had given to Jackie, the boy from a tribe to the eastward.

That day the men returned earlier than usual from the hunt, and were questioning the unfortunate Jackie, who suffered the miseries of language. They could not hew the answers out of his silence. He remained an unhappy, lumpish youth.

Then the old fellow who had let the blood of the white man came into their midst showing his finger. This member was examined by everyone of responsible age, although there was no longer any trace of blood. By sundown, all were angry and sullen.

So the explorer waited. He did not fear tortures of the body, for little enough of that remained. It was some final torment of the spirit that he might not have the strength to endure. For a long time that night he did not dare raise his eyes towards the sky. When he did, at last, there were the nails of the Cross still eating into it, but the Comet, he saw, was gone.

There was almost continuous tramping and stamping on earth. It had become obvious to the blacks that they were saved, which should have been the signal to express simple joy, if, during all those days, they had not been deceived, both by the Snake and by the white man. So the blacks were very angry indeed, if also glad that one of the agents responsible for their deception still remained to them.

Voss listened.

Their feet were thumping the ground. The men had painted their bodies with the warm colours of the earth they knew totem by totem, and which had prevailed at last over the cold, nebulous country of the stars. The homely spirits were dancing, who had vanquished the dreadful ones of darkness. The animals had come out again, in soft, musky fur and feather. They were dancing their contribution to life. And the dust was hot beneath their feet.

Voss could hear them. As it was no longer possible for him to turn his neck more than an inch or two, he did not see, but could smell the stench of their armpits. The black bodies were sweating at every pore.

Then he heard the first scream; he heard the rattle of chains, and knew.

In the night the blackfellows were killing the horses and mules of the white men, as it was now their right. The emaciated animals could not rear up, but made an attempt with their hobbled forelegs. Some, ridiculously, fell over sideways. Their eyes were glittering with fear in the firelight. Their nostrils were stiff. Blood ran. Those animals that smelled the blood, and were not yet touched, screamed more frightfully than those which were already dying. Tongues were lolling out. If the mules were silenter, they were also perhaps more desperate, like big, caught fish leaping and squirming upon the bank of a river. But their eyes glazed finally.

None of this was seen by Voss, but at one stage the spear seemed to enter his own hide, and he screamed through his thin throat with his little, leathery strip of remaining tongue. For all suffering he screamed.

Ah, Lord, let him bear it.

Soon the bowels of the dying animals were filling the night. The glistening, greenish caverns of their bellies were open. Drunk with the foetid smells, the blacks were running amongst the carcasses, tearing out the varnished livers, and hacking off the rough tongues.

Almost before the blood was dry on their hands, they had fallen to gorging themselves, and in a very short time, or so it seemed, were sucking the charred bones, and some were coughing for a final square of singed hide that had stuck in going down. It was, on the whole, a poor feast, but the bellies of all had swelled out. If they were beyond pardon, it was their lean lives that had damned them.

Voss heard the sucking of fingers beside the fires, as the blacks drowsed off into silence, deeper, closer, their own skins almost singed upon the coals.

As for himself, a cool wind of dreaming began about this time to blow upon his face, and it seemed as if he might even escape from that pocket of purgatory in which he had been caught. His cheeks, above his exhausted beard, were supple and unfamiliar. The sleek, kind gelding stood, and was rubbing its muzzle against its foreleg, to gentle music of metal, which persisted after he had mounted. Once he had ridden away, he did not look back at the past, so great was his confidence in the future.

Thus hopeful, it was obvious she must be at his side, and, in fact, he heard a second horse blowing out its nostrils, the sound so pitched he would have known it to be morning without the other infallible sign of a prevailing pearliness. As they rode, the valleys became startling in their sonorous reds, their crenellations broken by tenuous Rhenish turrets of great subtlety and beauty. Once, upon the banks of a transparent river, the waters of which were not needed to quench thirst, so persuasive was the air which flowed into and over their bodies, they dismounted to pick the lilies that were growing there. They were the prayers, she said, which she had let fall during the outward journey to his coronation, and which, on the cancellation of that ceremony, had sprung up as food to tide them over the long journey back in search of human status. She advised him to sample these nourishing blooms. So they stood there munching awhile. The lilies tasted floury, but wholesome. Moreover, he suspected that the juices present in the stalks would enable them to be rendered down easily into a gelatinous, sustaining soup. But of greater importance were his own words of love that he was able at last to put into her mouth. So great was her faith, she received these white wafers without surprise.

After lingering some time with their discoveries, the two figures, unaffected by the interminable nature of the journey, and by their own smallness in the immense landscape, remounted their stout horses and rode on. They were for ever examining objects of wonder: the wounds in the side of a brigalow palm, that they remembered having seen somewhere before; stones that sweated a wild honey; and upon one memorable occasion, a species of soul, elliptical in shape, of a substance similar to human flesh, from which fresh knives were continually growing in place of those that were wrenched out.

All these objects of scientific interest the husband was constantly explaining to his wife, and it was quite touching to observe the interest the latter professed even when most bored.

From this luminous state Voss returned for a moment in the early morning. His faculties promised support, and he felt that he was ready to meet the supreme emergency with strength and resignation.

All that night, the blacks, although stupefied by gorging, had been turning in their sleep beside the fires, as if they were full but not yet fulfilled. About the grey hour several old men and warriors arose. Almost at once their bodies became purposeful, and they were joined by the guardian of the white man, who went and roused the boy Jackie.

Now, Jackie, whether sleeping or not, immediately went through all the appearance of waking, and himself gave an imitation of purposefulness, while shuddering like black water. He was still terribly supple and young. His left cheek bore the imprint of a bone-handled clasp-knife given him by Mr Voss, and upon which he had been lying. It was perhaps this sad possession, certainly his most precious, which had begun to fill him with sullenness. He was ready, however, to expiate his innocence.

All moved quickly towards the twig shelter, an ominous humpy in that light. Jackie went in, crowded upon by several members of his adoptive tribe still doubtful of his honesty. But the spirits of the place were kind to Jackie: they held him up by the armpits as he knelt at the side of Mr Voss.

He could just see that the pale eyes of the white man were looking, whether at him or through him, he did not attempt to discover, but quickly stabbed with his knife and his breath between the windpipe and the muscular part of the throat.

His audience was hissing.

The boy was stabbing, and sawing, and cutting, and breaking, with all of his increasing, but confused manhood, above all, breaking. He must break the terrible magic that bound him remorselessly, endlessly, to the white men.

When Jackie had got the head off, he ran outside followed by the witnesses, and flung the thing at the feet of the elders, who had been clever enough to see to it that they should not do the deed themselves.

The boy stood for a moment beneath the morning star. The whole air was trembling on his skin. As for the head-thing, it knocked against a few stones, and lay like any melon. How much was left of the man it no longer represented? His dreams fled into the air, his blood ran out upon the dry earth, which drank it up immediately. Whether dreams breed, or the earth responds to a pint of blood, the instant of death does not tell.

Source: Patrick White, *Voss*, Penguin, Harmondsworth, 1957, pp.388-94.

An ideal of the future

Ernest Favenc

Shunned and dreaded; untrodden, drear;
A realm of hunger, of thirst, of fear,
The desert heart of Australia lies —
An iron land — beneath brazen skies:
Where a dewless morn greets the summer days,
And the wide plains loom through a trembling haze;
Where with calm, still lakelets, 'neath shadowy rocks,
The delusive mirage the wanderer mocks:
Where the pools of rain, that fell fresh and sweet,
Turn salt ere they dry in the blistering heat;
Where the hot winds roam over scrub and sand,
And the sun shines down on a lifeless land.
There, the passionless stars long vigils keep
O'er a silent waste, in a dreamless sleep.
Not even the wild dog's cry is heard,
Nor the wailing hoot of a flitting bird.
At times, gaunt, meagre figures pass
Through the mulga scrub and the prickly grass,
Searching for roots ere the day expire,
Then, huddle close round the flickering fire
Hungry and thirsty, at break of day
Rise, like black shadows, and stalk away.

Desert! You keep your secrets well
Of the gallant hearts who failed and fell;
You hold their bones in a close embrace;
You make no sign, and they left no trace.
Unrelenting, dire, in your sternest mood,
You watched them die in your solitude:
Your burning breast was their lonely bed;
In the unknown land sleep the long-lost dead.

The time draws near when the low, bare hills
Will echo the songs of a thousand rills.
Deep down in the beds of the old-world streams,
They sleep unheeded and dream their dreams;
Till the magic drill bids them wake again,
And they rise to water the thirsty plain.

The whispering stalks of the maize grow higher,
For the scrub has fallen 'neath axe and fire.
Where the spinifex grew, 'midst the sandstone rocks,
Browse the lowing herds and the bleating flocks;
And the sun now shines on the peaceful scene
Of farm, and orchard, and vineyard green.
The iron horse has bridged the space
That only the camel before dared face.
Rippling downward in limpid waves,
The waters well from the sunless caves,
Till the bare lagoons, sun-baked and dried,
Are filled to the brim with the flowing tide.
And children play in the grassy glade
Where the lost explorers' bones are laid.

Source: Ernest Favenc, *Voices of the Desert*, Elliot Stock, London, 1905, pp.20-22.

The hunt

Aeneas E. Gunn

We had not gone very far when we startled a pheasant from its noontide nap in one of the isolated clumps of trees. A vigorous series of 'Poo-hoo-hoos' rang out on the still midday air. The blacks, who are almost preternaturally keen in detecting any abnormality in the natural effect surrounding them, were, doubtless, instantly on the alert, for, although we waited long in the hiding the trees assured us, we had hardly commenced to move from cover when we saw several dusky figures running across the salt marsh into the mangroves. We started in pursuit at a run, but when we reached the camp we found it, as we expected, deserted. The fire was still burning, and the haste in which the blackfellows had left their camp was evidenced by the fact that they had forgotten to take with them what must have been the largest part of their weapons. Boomerangs, spears, throwing sticks, nulahs, shields, and remnants of a half-consumed meal of roasted baobab nuts, were lying about the place. We did not then wait to make a collection of aboriginal curiosities, but, picking up the tracks of the retreating savages, followed them into the mangroves. The successful pursuit of blackfellows in such a tangle of roots and branches was almost as hopeless of achievement as the proverbial search for a needle in a stack of hay; but the chagrin we felt over the defeat of our previous purpose fired our spirits with relentless zeal, and, each selecting a track, we followed the diverging footmarks through the dense, dark, eerie, smelling inferno, with the instinct of sleuth hounds. Nothing will ever obliterate from my memory the impressions that hunt made on my mind. The place seemed to be the very heart of the huge solitude in which we were situated. Overhead there was a dark, closely knitted canopy of leaves. Only here and there a patch of ineffably blue sky, that appeared to be immeasurably distant, gleamed through rifts in the firmament of foliage. Through the apertures the sun shot vertical shafts of golden light that counterfeited gilded pillars, except where their masses were broken by contact with the trunks and limbs of the trees. But the lights that stole through only made the gloom more ghostly and unreal by the contrast. It was like a weird, uncanny underworld, a vast, shapeless vault, whose roof was supported by gnarled and knotted trunks, carved with fantastic devices by the processes of Nature. Slender flying buttresses vaulted away from the trunks in long series of elliptical arches. The whole scheme of design of the jungle might have been that of an unimaginable mediaeval cathedral, conceived in a nightmare and executed in a delirium. It seemed to be peopled by unseen, silent, thinking, feeling beings, capable of action, and the twisted and contorted boughs and branches, stretching out hideous, mud-stained arms, that appeared ever intent on catching and holding one in their loathsome embraces, intensified the impression. The atmosphere was stifling, and permeated with a hot, miasmatic vapour. The silence was intense, and broken only by faint sounds of something moving forward, the gasping of shellfish that lay in the mud or clung to the roots and trunks of the mangroves. So still was it one could almost hear the moisture exuding from the ooze, or the sap coursing in the veins of the trees. But there was a track in the mud, a purpose in my heart, which did not become less insistent as every now and then on ahead I could hear a crack, the sound of a branch pushed aside, and its swishing swing back into place. Nothing was visible. There was no distance, no vista, no perspective, only knotted and twisted trunks, a tangle of boughs and branches and roots, of roots and branches and boughs above, a roof of leaden leaves underfoot, a slushy noisome ooze of decaying leaves, roots, shells, and mud.

Source: Aeneas E. Gunn, passage quoted in Alfred Searcy, *In Northern Seas: Being Mr Alfred Searcy's Experiences on the North Coast of Australia*, W.K. Thomas & Co, Adelaide, 1905, pp.17-18.

The settler. Wet season, N. T.

Jessie Litchfield

My cattle have gone swimming
    With the sharks down Anson Bay —
And my goats have gone to glory,
    And the little fishes play
Round the corpses of my horses,
    And my harrow, plough, and dray.

My selection's under water,
    And I'm up a milkwood tree,
For the house where I resided
    Has gone floating out to sea,
And my milkwood's started shifting,
    So to-morrow I may be
Driving Venus' teams of dolphins
    And with Thetis taking tea.

I'll be growing scales all over,
    I'll have fins instead of hands,
I'll be ploughing up sea-beaches
    At Neptune's stern commands;
And I'll find old Ocean drier
    Than these flooded river-lands.

Far as human eye can wander
   It can sight no spot of ground;
Just the water — swirling — whirling —
   As my brain goes whirling round.
It's a mug's game, this selecting
   On the river-flats, I've found;
And the biggest flat among them
   Is this flat now getting drowned.

Source: Jessie Litchfield, 'The settler. Wet season, N.T.', in Janet Dickinson, *Jessie Litchfield: Grand Old Lady of the Territory,* Janet Dickinson, Blackwater, Qld, 1982, p.92.

Jock Driver's funeral

Xavier Herbert

Jock's funeral was arranged for the morning of the day after his demise. For that reason half the white population wore white coats and black ties at breakfast. But as though the heavens were mourning him, seven inches of rain fell that day, in one long roaring shower. Therefore Jock lay in the mortuary, peeped at by the native orderlies and the lubras that worked in the laundry and yard, and coveted by ants that could not pass the doctored vaseline with which the table-legs were smeared.

   The grief of the heavens was overdone. Next day was worse. During the morning the rain roared down at the rate of an inch an hour. The man at the Post Office who gauged the rain did so with a bucket. But since it was desired that Jock should be buried with respect, as he could not be followed to his grave by flies, delay could go no further. Joe Crowe sent word around that the funeral would start at noon.

   Only a quarter of the white population attended, and that clad in khaki and oil-skins. Cars and covered buggies and Joe Crowe's cab gathered in the hospital grounds. On the veranda, watching not with indecent frankness but from behind the creepered lattice, were the white patients and the staff. Watching from the kitchen, all-seeing but unseen, were the orderlies and the halfcaste maids and the cook, who was a Greek. The hearse had not yet come.

   All eyes were fixed on the mortuary. The mourners all looked mournful …

   Above the roar of rain the mourners heard the sound of wheels, and turned with one accord and stared to right. Soon into view a shaggy horse trudged, hauling a vehicle that was just a box on wheels, a black box shaped like a coffin and little bigger, with large unglazed portholes in the sides. Joe Crowe was perched in the driving-seat, clad in oil-skins and sou'-wester, crouched in the rain, clutching two iron buckets. The hearse rolled past the Lazaret, crashed over a roaring drain, barked a pawpaw tree with the hub of a wheel, stopped when a clothes-line of the laundry hurled Joe flat.

   Joe got down and backed the hearse to the mortuary door, then climbed up and got the buckets. Pall-bearers left their vehicle and came splashing, bringing glass-covered artificial wreaths, and followed Joe into the mortuary, to stand behind him while he drew from his coat a brace and bit and bored eight holes in the coffin-lid. Joe bored with care, so as not to betray the fact that rosewood might produce white shavings and not to bore eight holes in that which lay beneath.

   The cortège set out, wound mournfully through the sheeting rain down the Mailunga Road. The gates of the cemetery were open. The grave was open too, sheltered by a huge

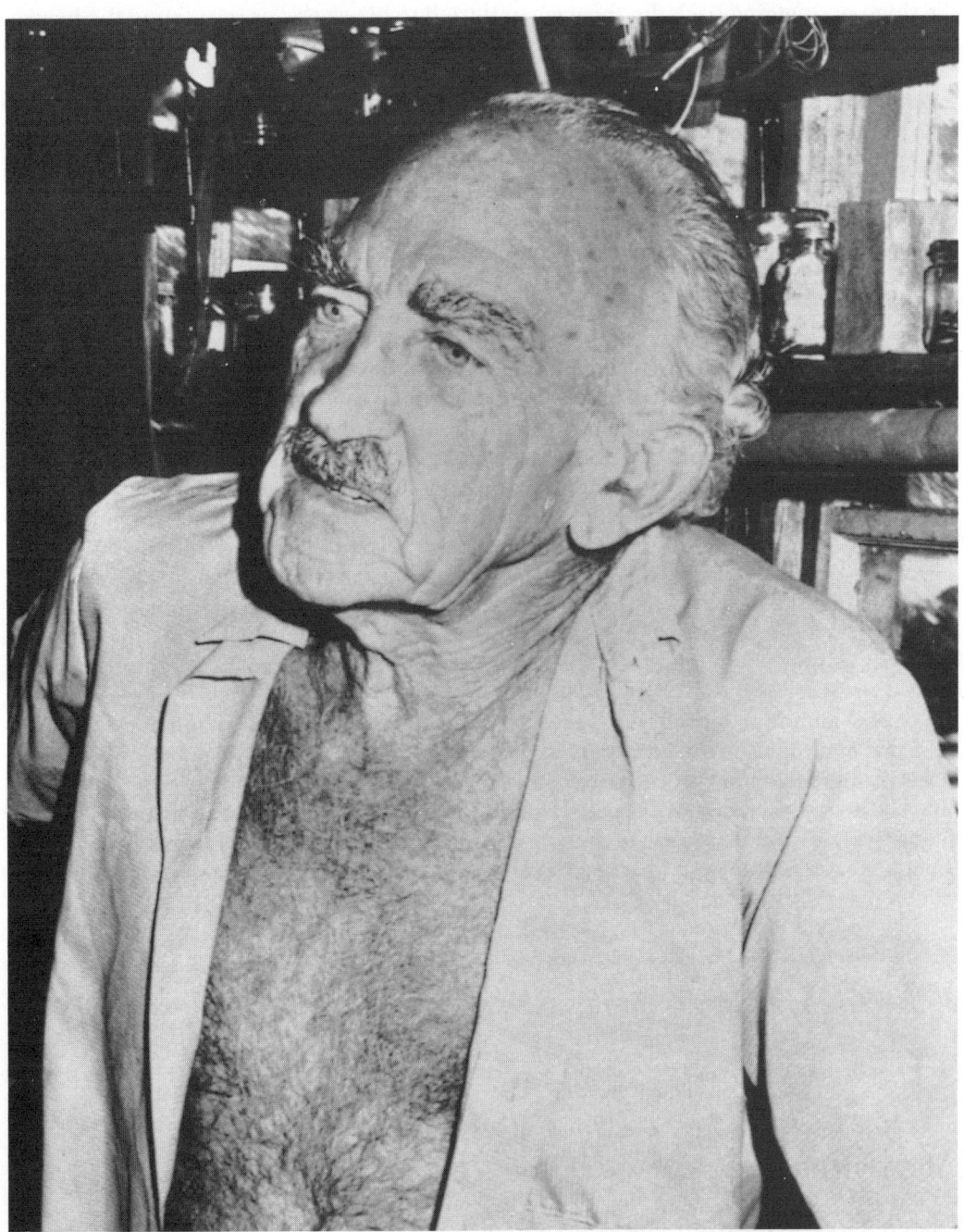

Xavier Herbert in typical combative pose. Herbert's Capricornia *(1938) reads like an elongated last act of a Shakespearian tragedy. His characters succumb, one by one, either to an alien land or to the predatory nature of their human associates. The black comedy of Jock Driver's death and subsequent funeral is typical.*

tarpaulin sheet to which the mourners rushed, stumbling apologetically over other graves, blasphemously over ruts and gutters. A clay ridge built about the grave to stem the flood had given way, so that the grave was brimming. Joe Crowe brought a shovel and a coil of rope from the tool-shed, and under the gaze of solemn eyes set to work to repair the ridge. Then he took up one of the buckets; and one of the mourners took the other; and they set to work to bail the grave. All the male mourners took a hand at either bailing or repairing the ridge or dragging back the sheet when it tried to blow away or restraining the hearse-horse when it tried to wander; all, that is, except the Rev. Gordon Prayter, who, being the officiating clergyman, perhaps could not be called exactly male or mourner; he just watched.

Joe's pipe slipped from his belt and fell into the grave. Work was stopped while he solemnly dipped for it. Still the rain roared down. For every bucketful of water bailed a half poured in. Still the solemn ones worked on, not daring to stop till the water was reduced below the level of the eye, lest the burial should look indecently like a drowning. Joe called a halt when the water was down three feet. When the coffin was lifted from the hearse three blow-flies shot out of the holes in the lid and dashed off guiltily.

Mr. Prayter's work began. With sou'-wester under arm, and oilskin open so that God might see the stole and know that there was no deception, he chanted from a prayer-book in a tone exactly like that of a blackfellow devil-dovvening:

'I knawt my redeem livtan ateel stan ladday pon yearth — tutairk unnerself sawlvar dear brothah heah deported, we tharfore committees bardy tuther groon, earth tearth, ash tash, dusser duss, in shore unsartin hawper razraction tarnal laif awmen.'

He stopped and took up a handful of mullock. The stones clattered on the coffin; the mud remained in his hand. He put away his book, wiped his fingers on his streaming coat, then turned away with most of the other mourners. Only the workers and the indecently curious could stay to see the sinking of the stone-weighted coffin, to hear the hiss and gurgle of the bubbles rushing from the vents. The others went back to the carriages, back to town, to dry clothes and the shelter of bars and houses and liquor in which to drown the sorrows they had never felt, quite at a loss to know which was the worst offence, frank indifference or pretence.

About an hour after the burial of Jock, a cockeye bob roared out of the north and tore the front veranda from the First and Last, blew two Chinese children right across Killarney Street from their father's doorstep to that of a Greek who had lately tried to take their father's life, wrecked one of the mail-boat's derricks, blew a few trees down, and was gone, taking the rain-clouds with it. The sun blazed down as bright and hot as vaporizing silver. As though Heaven's grief were like the grief of Man — an hour or two of weeping, then back to laughter and the workaday.

Source: Xavier Herbert, *Capricornia*, Publicist Press, Sydney, 1938, ch.10.

The paw paw tree

Margo Towie

I found the cat in the bathroom with a bird in its mouth. I'd never have noticed if the taste of twenty four hours of life hadn't made my mouth unbearable at that point. The cat wasn't concerned with my presence, he continued his torturous game. The bird quivered beneath the cat's paw. It was emitting a piercing shriek quite at odds with its usual joyful sound. I lurched toward the cat. 'You bastard' I yelled. My anger bubbled and boiled, blinding me with passion and fury.

I caught him downstairs amongst a multitude of pot plants. The bird clung to my finger in terror, its heart visibly pounding with fear. The cat squirmed angrily under my other arm. I put the bird on the bottom of an upturned milo tin which covers the amputated main trunk of the paw paw tree. I stood on a chair to reach. Then I locked the cat in the bathroom until the bird had flown away.

At night the flying foxes swing chattering and fighting from the few remaining branches of the paw paw tree. They tear gluttonously at the fruit, spilling half chewed paw paws to the ground where they lie like rotting corpses. By day the cats lie in wait for the scavengers to come. Few victims evade the marauding cats. I found a chewed up lizard in the downstairs toilet once.

David came last night. It was the first time he'd visited for a month. I know because I keep an account in my diary. I was down stairs, sitting at my desk trying to write a story when he walked into my room. Really I was waiting for him to come, I'd been waiting all day. I didn't tell him though. I pretended that I was writing a story, I told him I was finding it very hard. He thought that was why I was upset; really it was because I'd been waiting all day for him to come. He began massaging my shoulders to calm me down and I lay on the bed to make it easier for him and better for me. We nearly began to make love but stopped. He told me he didn't want me but we made love anyway. Afterwards we shared a cigarette and then he went home.

At night when I try to sleep the cats moan and wail under my window. They live in the room next door which is piled to the ceiling with junk. It's so full the door won't close. Sometimes when I can't sleep I take a pill which fades me out quickly and quietly. Last night I fell asleep easily. Tonight the bats are shrieking and fighting in the battered paw paw tree. They fly away like silent spectres when I throw an empty beer can at them. Their wings slice viciously through the air. Then the air is very still.

In the wet season the sky is often heavy with clouds, storms roll in across the sky flashing with fury. The trees chatter a warning and gusts of air scatter all that is untethered before the storm. When the maelstrom strikes leaves and branches are often ripped from trees. The world is drowned in the deluge. Afterwards the air hangs like a sodden veil and mosquitoes breed in the puddles. The paw paw tree was beaten by such a storm. The main trunk died; the tree has never really recovered. I missed that storm. That night my consciousness had been numbed by a sleeping pill. The mosquitoes sucked at my body unchallenged and the heart of the paw paw tree died.

Tonight the sky is cloudless. A full moon is sailing through the night like a searchlight. The cats are at it again under my window, wailing and moaning. 'PSSHT' I hiss and hear them bound away through the long grass. I see in last year's diary that it's twelve months today since David and I first made love. Last night was the first time for four months and five days. When I turn off my light the paw paw tree throws its shadow across my bed. The flying foxes, now silent, are returning to swing from the disfigured silhouette.

I lie curled around my pillow waiting for sleep to come. The night is quiet and still. The stillness and silence turn into emptiness and sit like a small ball in the pit of my stomach. I feel it spreading. The emptiness grips with vice-like ferocity. Clouds are gathering in the perimeters of my mind. I sense them joining forces. The chatter of the storm gets louder and louder. I feel the passion rising like bile in my throat. Curled tightly around my pillow I break the stillness to toss myself across the bed. A dull roar fills my mind although the night itself is silent. The fury is pervasive. All resolve is scattered before the storm. I grope blindly on the floor for the insipid jar of calmness.

Source: Margo Towie, 'The paw paw tree', *Northern Perspective*, vol.8, no.2, 1985, pp.53-4.

9 Sites and sightings

The north–south line and Central Australia — that Wonderland! How many Australians know it? If it were owned by Americans you would learn of it on the pages of every newspaper, on the picture screen at night, by sketches from the wireless stations, and we should call it Yankee skite. We keep it dark. We are content to ride on the tail of the world when we might direct that world of pleasure-loving people.

Is the hush-hush policy designed to send Australians travelling abroad? Is it for revenue from the advertisement of foreign tourist places? Why is this country shrouded in darkness and ignorance by the Governments of Australia?

Sleep on, wise Yabber-men! Sleep on!
— Fred Blakeley, *Hard Liberty*, 1938

The drover's mob is a cloud of dust,
The drover's mob is a sacred trust,
Where the Devil says 'Can't!' and God says 'Must!'
Out on the Murran-ji ...
— Frank Flynn, *Northern Gateway*, 1963

When you make the overland journey, you shake hands with Australia; you rub shoulders with it.
— John Binning, *Target Area*, 1943

Papunya is more than it seems. For a while, I used to think of it as Paris, in negative. Here was a community of artists, dancers, actors, shamans and eccentrics, story-tellers and political activists, all part of a place the significance of which stretched back to 'creation times' — to 'the Dreamtime'. This was no dying race, but a gigantic family of individuals whose kinship system is among the most complex of human structures ever conceived.
— Billy Marshall-Stoneking, 'The power of the song', 1988

Previous page: The ageless beauty and grace of the MacDonnells contrast starkly with the pervasive and manufactured surrealism of the eight radomes at the C.I.A.'s Pine Gap facility, Alice Springs.

Five legends of Uluru

Paddy Uluru, Albie Uluru, Pompy Douglas & Pompy Wanampi

The Wiyai Kutjara story: The two boys

Uluru (Ayers Rock itself) was built up during the creation period by the two boys who played in the mud after rain. When they had finished their game they travelled south to Wiputa, on the northern side of the Musgrave Ranges, where they killed and cooked the euro. Then the boys turned north again toward Atila (Mount Connor). A few miles southwest of the Mount, at Anari one boy threw his *tjuni* (wooden club) at a hare wallaby, but the club struck the ground and made a fresh-water spring. This boy refused to reveal where he had found the water and the other boy nearly died of thirst. Fighting together, the two boys made their way to the table-topped Mount Conner, on top of which their bodies are preserved as boulders.

The Mala story: The hare wallabies

The Mala wallabies came from Mawurungu, near Yuendumu, travelling south through the Haasts Bluff area and arriving at Uluru on its northern side at Katjitilkil. Here, they began to dance, the men at one site, the women at another. When the women were not dancing, they gathered food for the whole group. The women's camp was at Taputji, the small isolated dome on the north-east side of Uluru, where one of their *wana* (digging sticks) can be seen transformed into stone.

While the dances were in progress, the Mala received an invitation to go to Kikingkura, near Docker River, to attend the dances of the Wintalka men. The men sent their invitation through Panpanpanala, the Bell-Bird. But the Mala were already committed to their own celebrations, so they refused to leave, and the Bell-Bird returned to the Wintalka in the Petermann Ranges calling 'Pak, Pak' ('They can't come, they can't come'), the call he makes today.

When they heard that their invitation had been rejected, the Wintalka men decided to send a malevolent dingo-like *mamu* (an evil spirit) to punish the Mala. This creature, called Kurrpanngu, ran eastwards until he had picked up the Mala track at Mulyayiti (Mount Currie), then turned south and followed them to Uluru. He crept up to Tjukutjapinya, where the Mala women were dancing. The hair skirts, or *mawulari*, worn by the women were transformed into pendant cones of rock at Tjukutjapi rockshelter. Kurrpanngu peered over a projecting rock spur, but the women drove him off, and he continued around the base of the Rock to Inintitjara, where the Mala men were sleeping. Lunpa, the Kingfisher woman, was with them, and she called out a warning but too late to prevent Kurrpanngu leaping into the camp. At Inintjitjara, Lunpa is transformed into a boulder, looking up at the paw marks Kurrpanngu left in the side of the cliff.

The surviving Mala ran southwards from Uluru, splitting into two lines. One line ran close to the northern spur of the Musgrave Ranges on to Ulkiya, the other fled past Altjinta, near the present site of Mulga Park Homestead.

The Kuniya story: The pythons

The Kuniya converged on Uluru from three directions. One group came westward from Waltanta (the present site of Erldunda homestead), and Paku-paku; another came south through Wilpiya (Wilbia Well); and a third, northwards, from the area of Yunanpa (Mitchell's Knob). One of the Kuniya women carried her eggs on her head, using a *manguri* (grass head-pad) to cushion them. She buried these eggs at the eastern end of Uluru. While they were camped at Uluru, the Kuniya were attacked by a party of Liru (poisonous snake) warriors. The Liru had journeyed along the southern flank of the Petermann Ranges from beyond Wangkari (Gills Pinnacle).

At Alyurungu, on the south-west face of Uluru, are pock marks in the rock, the scars left by the warriors' spears; two black-stained watercourses are the transformed bodies of two Liru. The fight centred on Mutitjulu (Maggie's Spring). Here a Kuniya woman fought using her *wana*; her features are preserved in the eastern face of the gorge. The features of the Liru warrior she attacked can be seen in the western face, where his eye, head wounds (transformed into vertical cracks), and severed nose form part of the cliff.

Above Mutitjulu is Uluru rock hole. This is the home of a Kuniya who releases the water into Mutitjulu. If the flow stops during drought, the snake can be dislodged by standing at Mutitjulu and calling 'Kuka! Kuka! Kuka!' (Meat! Meat! Meat!). The journey to Uluru and the Liru snakes' attack are described in the public song cycle recording the Kuniya story.

Mita and Lunkata story: The blue-tongued lizards

At Wangka Arrkal, on the border of South Australia beyond Mulga Park, two Bell-Bird brothers were stalking an emu. Disturbed, the animal ran northwards toward Uluru, where it was killed by Mita and Lungkata, Blue-Tongue Lizard men. The two Lizards cut up the emu meat with a stone axe at Kurumpa. Large joints of meat survive as a fractured slab of sandstone on the west side of Mutitjulu, but the Lizards buried the thigh at Kalaya Tjunta (Emu Thigh), a spur on the south-east face of the Rock. When the Bell-Bird brothers arrived, the lizards handed them a skinny portion of their quarry, claiming that there was nothing else. In revenge, the hunters set fire to the Lizards' shelter. The two men attempted to escape by climbing the rock face, but they fell back and were burned to death. Lichen on the rock face at Mita Kampantja is the smoke from the fire, and the lizard men survive as two half-buried boulders.

Cave where Tjati, the Red Lizard, died at Kantju.

The Tjati story: The red lizard

Tjati is a small, red lizard who lives on the mulga flats. In the creation period, he travelled to Uluru past Atila. When Tjati threw his *kali*, a curved throwing stick, it embedded itself in the north face of Uluru. Tjati scooped with his hands into the rock face to retrieve the *kali*, leaving a series of bowl-shaped hollows at Walaritja. Unable to recover his weapon, Tjati finally died in a cave at Kantju, where his other implements and bodily remains survive as large boulders on the cave floor. *Tjati* is the Yankuntjatjara name for the lizard the Pitjantjatjara call *lingka*.

Source: Five legends of Uluru, told by Paddy Uluru, Albie Uluru, Pompy Douglas & Pompy Wanampi, to Robert Layton, in *Uluru: An Aboriginal History of Ayers Rock*, Australian Institute of Aboriginal Studies, Canberra, 1986, pp.5-10.

S. O. S., Ayers Rock, October 1930

Errol Coote

I had been told that Ayer's Rock is sacred ground for the natives, and that they resent the presence of white men there. It is where they carry out their rituals associated with the 'making of men.' As a result, I was feeling nervy, and decided to sleep in the cockpit of the 'plane that night, drawing the cockpit cover over myself.

As the stars were coming out I fired three shots from my automatic, hoping that they would be answered by the ground party, if they were approaching.

But no answer came. Just the sighing of the wind and the distant call of the mopoke.

It must have been about half-past eight when I heard a growl like distant thunder. It was coming steadily closer, and I wondered whatever it could be.

I was not left long in doubt. Like a stinging fury the wind had arrived for its nightly sonata at the Rock, playing an accompaniment to the chorus of the ghosts of departed aborigines, which are supposed to dwell in the cavernous heights of the desert monolith.

It howled all night, ripping the sand up in great clouds, and flinging it in blinding barrages against the 'plane.

At crack of dawn I crawled from my cramped position in the cockpit and lit a tiny fire. I did not want to attract the natives. My breakfast was a cup of tea. Eats were reserved for the night meal. For luncheon I would have a nip of wine and a cigarette.

I set off for the Rock immediately I had gulped the tea, determined to circle it on this visit. I took with me a tin of red aeroplane 'dope' to paint signs on the Rock at convenient waterholes, in case anybody came in.

To the accompaniment of the plaintive and very solemn note of the bell-bird, 'Klonk-ker-lonk-ker-lonkylonk,' I made good time for the first half of my journey. Then the heat became terrific, and I had to pull up several times to rest under desert oaks, which are a type of casuarina tree.

The ground was covered with lizards — large and small, and of such variegated colouring that even without suffering from over-indulgence in liquor anyone could be pardoned if he saw green, yellow, and pink reptiles. There were black ones with yellow stripes, speckled grey, and yellow varieties, brown ones, while in the spinifex patches were big terra-cotta lizards, that lifted their tails and ran like dogs through the desert herbage.

As for snakes, it was their happy hunting-ground. The rains that had recently fallen had brought them out. They were everywhere. Mostly they were the green spinifex snake, deadly venomous.

The scene reminded me of Sinbad the Sailor when he found the valley of diamonds and the place was littered with reptiles. The reptiles were here, but no diamonds.

I reached the Rock and painted my first S.O.S. sign on a huge boulder alongside a rock-hole. The legend was:

S.O.S. 'Plane 5 miles S.W. Rock,, Coote, 29/10/30.

As I circled the Rock I repeated this about a dozen times.

I felt very tiny travelling at the base of Ayer's Rock. It was about eight miles around the monolith, which is almost square in shape. Of felspar formation, its sides are scarred with breaks high up near the summit, looking like giant flakes of honey-comb. There are innumerable caves at its foot, in practically all of which I saw aboriginal paintings. In one of them were two piles of brushwood against the far wall. Lifting the brushwood away I saw a pile of *churingas*, both of stone and of wood. Hastily I replaced the covering. They were the sacred totems of some tribe, and interference with them would be dangerous in the extreme. The cave was weird. I could almost feel the spirits of the Alcheringa — that mysterious place away back in the past where the fathers of all the tribes originally came from — staring at me from the walls of the cavern. I breathed more freely when I ran out into the open air again.

Source: Errol Coote, *Hell's Airport and Lasseter's Lost Legacy*, Investigator Press, Adelaide, 1981, pp.208-11.

An apostrophe to Ayers Rock

Rex Ingamells

(Uluru, Katatjuta and Atila are the native names for Ayers Rock, Mt. Olga and Mt. Conner. Ayers Rock is the largest monolith in the world, measuring seven miles around at the base and reaching a height of eleven hundred feet. The three formations stand in a straight line, east to west, the Rock being situated between the other two, at a distance sixty miles west of Mt. Conner and twenty east of Mt. Olga.)

Uluru of the eagles, standing between
Atila, the flat-topped mountain,
and Katatjuta's thirty conglomerate pillars ...

I have known the dawn
one shattering voice of birds to celebrate
the magnificent beauty of the Rock, Uluru;
I have known the Sun
assume her hair-string veil to hide her face
from the evening dazzle of the Rock, Uluru;

I have known the night
one radiance of moon, cicadas chanting
the astounding history of the Rock, Uluru.

Surely I have proved elision of Time,
gone more than distance to drink at the springs of wonder!

• • •

Mulga after mulga, mallee after mallee,
ridge-top after ridge-top, valley after valley ...

The distance-traversing sandhills throng:
the saltbush spinifex
spinifex bluebush
bluebush, saltbush
sandhills throng ...

Lizard and snake,
whisper across the ground,
whisper by gibber and stick, or make
no slightest sound ...

Casuarinas preen on the red sand-plain
through the heat-heavy noon ...

Myriad tufts of silvergrass
are ground-mist to the moon.

       . . .

It would not be enough to walk,
footsore, a thousand miles to you, Uluru,
Rock, Uluru, over the dry and harsh
expanses of sand and gibber, ridge and valley,
saltbush, bluebush, spinifex, mulga,
casuarina,
beneath the unblinking blue.

Arrival is more than physical: it is
the dreaming at the inner shrine,
with sun and star, sun and star,
moon after moon,
message-stick and tjurunga,
rock-hole and dune.

Approach, Uluru, must
be with eyes clear for taking
the great red contours or black buttress of stars,
and mind staunch for making
the incredible journey that still
remains to be made
beyond sight, touch and hearing.

Approach, Uluru, must
be from a Past so distant
that Man is but a perilous dream of Nature,
instinct of Being,
and suns and storms are furiously beating on
a vast, unshatterable stone diprotodon.

Approach must be naked of Knowledge, except
what is relevant.

Here the red euro has lept
the jumble of boulders at the west base;
here the sun smites and the ages go by;
here the moon's
a male hunter, with bright woomera, spear and boomerang,
striding scarps where, in the world's dawn, the winds sang
the same chants as now,
intoning awesome Dreamtime corroborees
here, vast Rock,
through your caves and your crowding trees.

• • •

As I stepped out from one of your Caves of Paintings,
I knew myself forever part of you,
inspirited through ochre, charcoal and pipeclay,
through aeons of ochre, charcoal and pipeclay,
into your colourful darkness of timeless Being —
yesterday, today and ever after
eternal Dreaming in your heart, Uluru.

As I stepped out from one of your Caves of Paintings,
you and the wedge-tailed eagle soared together
high in the battering blue;
and I, in your vibrant shade, Uluru, knew
life-strength that wells alone
from your stupendous quietness of stone.

Source: Rex Ingamells, 'Extracts from ULURU: An apostrophe to Ayers Rock', in Colin Thiele (ed.), *Jindyworobak Anthology*, Jindyworobak Publications, Georgian House, Middle Park, Vic., 1953, pp.31-33.

Erecting forked sticks and rafters

Goulburn Island song cycle

Song 1

Erecting forked sticks and rafters, posts for the floor, making the roof of the hut like a sea-eagle's nest:
They are always there, at the billabong of the goose eggs, at the wide expanse of water.
As they build, they think of the monsoon rains — rain and wind from the west, clouds spreading over the billabong ...
They cover the sides of the hut, placing rails on the forked sticks.
We saw the heaving chests of the builders, calling invocations for the clouds rising in the west ...

With heaving chests, calling the invocations ...
Making the door of the hut, preparing it within ...
They think of the coming rain, and the west wind ... wind bringing the rain, spreading over this country.
Carefully, therefore, prepare the hut, with its roof, and its posts ...
We saw the heaving chests of men of the Maiar'maiar clan, clans from the Woolen River ...
They are always there at that place, that billabong edged with bamboo,
There by the wide expanse of water ... carefully laying the rails.

Song 2

There is the framework, the rafters and door of the hut.
We saw the heaving chests of Goulburn Island men and Burara men, as they made it,
Preparing the stilted hut, like a sea-eagle's nest in a tree.
We saw their heaving chests as they invoked the Yulunggul Snakes, their coiling, and crawling ...
Invoking the coiling Snakes and their entrails ... and building stilted huts all over the billabong,
At the place of the Rising Western Clouds ... at the place of Standing Clouds: spreading all over the sky at the place of Coloured Reflections.
Huts all around, at the Sea-Eagle place, at Milingimbi Point, and over towards the Sandspit near Goulburn Islands ...
My hut is nearing completion,
With forked sticks and roof like a sea-eagle's nest, with rails and door ...
They are always there at that billabong, with the wide expanse of water ...
It is almost ready. We make these huts all around, and north-east of Milingimbi.
Clouds banking along the horizon, passing north-eastward over the Crocodile Islands ...
Thus they were making the huts. We saw their heaving chests and the rising clouds from the west, small clouds rising and spreading,
Saw their heaving chests, as black clouds came bringing a sheet of rain,
Sound of thunder, roaring of wind and rain ...
I am making it for myself, with forked sticks and with rails ...
Thunder leaving its noise for me, sound rolling along the bottom of the clouds,
Echoing on the billabong, across the wide expanse of water ...
I am making my sea-eagle nest to float in the rising waters of the billabong.
I am making it, and later the lightning will play on its roof and on me inside,
For its tongue flickers along the horizon, and thunder rolls along the bottom of the clouds,
Clouds rising from the place of the Wawalag sisters, from where they were swallowed ...
I am preparing for you, clouds massing along the horizon: using my posts, my forked sticks and my rails ...
You, clouds, are banking along for me ...
The wind brings clouds, of the *jiridja* moiety — clouds like penes.
A cool wind blows, easing the heat and bringing the small clouds ...
Thunder rolling along the bottom of the clouds, as the lightning flashes ...
I am making it ready for you, fixing the door and the inside:
Because I invoke the clouds rising from Goulburn Islands ...
I am making it for myself, to float across the billabong,
Across the wide expanse of water, to float like a sea-eagle's nest ...
We saw their heaving chests, as they invoked the clouds rising from Goulburn Islands ...

Song 3

Get the clapping sticks and the didjeridu, for we feel the urge for enjoyment.
Hear the rhythmic beat, and the singing of Goulburn Island people, clans from the Woolen River ...
Chests turned towards the cold west wind, and the sound of the didjeridu ...
Rhythmically beating, within the huts like sea-eagle nests ...
Sound from within the huts, spreading across the country ...
Clapping-sticks at the Sandspit near Goulburn Islands, at the place of Western Clouds, and of Standing Clouds, and at Milingimbi Creek ...
Opposite Milingimbi, at the place of Coloured Reflections ... sticks clapping within the huts,
Sticks clapping, for we feel the urge for enjoyment: invoking the western rain clouds ...
Sound rising like clouds, wafted across the waters to Milingimbi:
Like clouds banking up, the sound hovers over the Island of Clouds ...
Cold wind from the west, striking their chests ...
It is ours! With this singing the wind begins to blow, swaying the branches,
Cold stranger wind from somewhere, from Goulburn Islands!

Song 4

Take clay and coloured ochres, and put them on!
They paint chests and breasts with clay, in water-designs,
Hang round their necks the padded fighting-bags.
They paint themselves, those Goulburn Island people, and clans from the Woolen River ...
They are always there, at the wide expanse of water ...
They take more clay, for painting the fighting-sticks ...
Paint on their chests designs of water-snakes ...
And paint the boomerangs with coloured ochres ...
Painting the small boomerangs ...
Calling the invocations ... all over the country, and at the place of the Wawalag sisters ...
Painting themselves at Milingimbi Point, at the place of Standing Clouds.
At the place of the Western Clouds, at the place of Coloured Reflections ...

Source: 'Goulburn Island song cycle', Songs 1–4 of 27 Songs, in Ronald M. Berndt (comp. and trans.), *Love Songs of Arnhem Land*, Nelson, Melbourne, 1976, pp.49-53.

Yinuma / River

Groote Eylandt song

Yinuma

Ningirnjirrukwa, Wurrakwakwa,
    Laba mabalyingu-manja, Arrindingmanja *yange*
Ningirnjirrukwa, Wurrakwakwa,
    Laba mabalyingu-manja, Arrindingmanja *yange*
Akena yarrijirra-wa yarrka.
    Kwija, nuwabalngdakba, Arrindingmanja *yange*
Akena abulalu-wa.
Arrka eminenu-wa nakwulyadinga.

Akena naminuwadarrka.
    Nuwabalngkaburamukwa, Arrindingmanja *yange*
Akena namanga yambuda
    Arrka nengkingkuwaraka, Arrindingmanja *yange*
Akena nuwekbarrngayina, aba nuwabulalida.

River

Slowly I glided with the rays, Wurrakwakwa,
    Singing by night at Arrindingmanja.
Slowly I glided with the rays, Wurrakwakwa,
    Singing by night at Arrindingmanja,
While the river slipped out to sea.
    Rays feeding here and there at Arrindingmanja,
Moving in to the shallows.
Tide nearing the reef, the rays' reef, shining.

Rays and tide move aside.
    Tide overturning silt at Arrindingmanja.
Strong pulling tide
    Sweeping sand as it flows at Arrindingmanja.
And rays following single file, surfacing.

Source: From a recording (cat. no. AM11A: V) obtained on Groote Eylandt in 1962 by Alice Moyle. Words transcribed and translated by Judith Stokes.

Rowdyism in Borroloola

Mrs Dominic D. Daly

[T]he latest instance of rowdyism is to be found at Booroola [i.e. Borroloola], a township on the MacArthur River in the Carpentaria country. It is impossible to define a reason for the Gulf Settlements attaining this unenviable notoriety, unless it is owing to the remoteness of their locality, and the kind of *Ultima Thule* [utmost limit] that part of Australia seems to be. Anyway, the MacArthur Settlement has gained the character borne by the other districts there.

From what the newspapers say, the state of things at Booroola last year was quite as wild and lawless as California in the days of Judge Lynch and 'vigilance committees.'

According to all accounts, horse and cattle stealing was carried on with impunity. Sometimes the wrathy owner of the missing horses undertook to recover them himself. If he overtook the thief he was glad to rescue the horses without in any way punishing him, unless he was able to give him a thrashing; legal redress was simply unattainable. One correspondent says: 'Horse-stealing may not seem a heinous crime to those living in settled districts, but it is a very different matter to a man travelling through country infested with hostile natives, and where the stages are long between the waters or safe camp. Then it probably means "for want of a horse the rider was lost." '

But horse-stealing was not the worst of the crimes in this 'No man's land.' Occasionally a drunken brawl ended in a free fight. Knives were drawn, shots exchanged, sometimes without much danger, at other times with the loss of a life or two; but there were no police to take the matter up, and it was too far for a private individual to attempt to take a prisoner to justice, even if he could ensure conviction, for it was impossible to take witnesses hundreds of miles out of their way to hang a man, and so crime went unpunished.

This is a new phase in the history of the Northern Territory, which had hitherto been a law-abiding settlement. Steps were, however, taken to remedy this; a Resident [Mr Gilbert R. McMinn] and some police were sent to Booroola, which, in spite of its rowdyism, is a rising place.

Source: Mrs Dominic D. Daly, *Digging, Squatting and Pioneering Life in the Northern Territory of South Australia*, Sampson Low, Marston, Searle & Rivington, London, 1887, pp.306-7.

Borroloola, capital of the Gulf country

F. J. Gillen

2 November 1900. — Camp No. 70. Borroloola. We are in the saddle at 5.45 full of eagerness to see the Capital of the Gulf country, Borroloola, or 'Town' as it is invariably called by the Station hands whom we have met en route. After travelling over 16 miles of uninteresting plain and forest we caught sight of the galvanized iron roofs of the buildings and amongst them we saw a red patch which we took to be a roof of red tiles but which afterwards turned out to be a beautiful flame tree in full flower. A few minutes more landed us in the town which consists of an irregular row of five buildings the first a public house, the second a store, the third the police station, the fourth the Local Court and Magistrates quarters and 5th, lying modestly in the background, a little house occupied by a Chinese Tailor. Truly a drearily cheerless hot looking, sun stricken place, with nothing about its immediate surroundings to indicate that it is in the tropics — Long ago we pictured it a beautiful spot rich in tropic growth, the buildings almost hidden by the richness of the vegetation — For some time we have known that it was not quite all we had pictured it but the ghastly uninteresting reality is worse than anything we anticipated.

The Town was surveyed about 18 years ago and the Government established quarterly steamer communication with Pt. Darwin for the purpose of stimulating the pastoral industry and making it easy for the pastoralists to obtain their supplies of stores. The place was believed to have a great future before it and at first things boomed along merrily two public houses sprung up, also two stores, one of each remains and were it not for other ventures it is doubtful if the publican would make a living. A resident Magistrate who also acted as Sub-Collector of Customs and Warden of Goldfields was appointed and provided with comfortable quarters. The Magistrate has been withdrawn, there was nothing for him to do in any of his capacities and for some years his quarters have been unoccupied but carefully looked after by the Police Officer whose quarters are close by. By the courtesy of this Police Officer Mr. Stott we are now occupying the Magistrates quarters where we shall remain during our stay here. The McArthur River is here a very fine stream of water flowing North and South and less than half a mile from the Town. The River with its splendidly timbered banks is very picturesque but one has to walk down to it to see its beauties. From the township only the tops of the trees can be seen. It is well stocked with fish and abounds in Alligators or rather Crocodiles for there are no Alligators in Australia. There are two species of Crocodile in this river, Crocodilus porosus commonly called an Alligator and Philas Johnstoni a much smaller long snouted beast commonly called Crocodile. The local police officer tells me that he has seen the former grow to a length of 17ft. 10 inches while the latter only grows to

Members of the 1901–02 Central Australian Expedition assembled at Alice Springs, 18 May 1901. Seated: F.J. Gillen (left) and W. Baldwin Spencer. Standing: Erlikiliakirra (left), mounted trooper Chance (middle) and Purula.

a length of 6 or 7 feet and is harmless. The larger variety often kills horses and cattle that happen to stray into the shallower parts of the river stream and the publican here has been a considerable sufferer in that respect. He informs us that he has killed a great number of Crocodiles by means of baits poisoned with Strychnine, these he suspends from the limb of a tree overhanging the water and the Crocodiles readily take them. Sand bars prevent vessels of any considerable tonnage from coming up the River so the trading steamer which arrives quarterly anchors at the mouth where goods and passengers are transhipped into a small Schooner. The mouth of the River is distant 40 miles from the Town.

Rich copper deposits have been found at various places within 120 miles of the Town and some of the mines are being prospected for the purpose of sending down bulk samples of ore for treatment at Sydney. The Borroloola-ites are sanguine that in the near future a great mining industry will be developed and they already talk of asking the Government to erect smelters at the mouth of the River.

In the afternoon we visited the Chinese garden situated 3/4 of a mile from the Town. It is about 2 or 3 acres in extent quite an ideal garden with a stream of spring water running through its entire length. The soil is dark grey almost black and various tropical fruits such as Mangoes, Pineapple, Custard apple and Bananas flourish in it. We are disappointed to find that none of these fruits are ripe. The garden has lately changed hands and is now occupied by a lean gaunt one eyed whiteman named Price to whom gardening is a new experience. Just above the garden there is a fine fresh water spring throwing off a continuous stream of water which runs into a small creek called the Rocky and thence into the McArthur, along this stream there is a fine growth of Pandanus palms which give to the place a tropical appearance and suggest millions of mosquitoes. After visiting the garden we sauntered down to the McArthur River — One never does anything more than saunter in this climate it's far too hot — and called at the Blacks camps where we found a number of men — all curly headed and some very fine physical types — preparing for a Corroboree; they had heard of our coming and the nature of our mission and seemed glad to see us. All the men present were members of the Anewla Tribe whose country extends down to the Coast and includes the Pellew islands. Many of them had pipes fashioned like the Chinese opium pipes and made out of bamboo.

3 November 1900. — Camp No. 70. The morning was spent with some men of the Anewla and Mara tribes but so far we have not anything of importance to record. We have attached to our staff a man named Umbarari who is a member of the Mara tribe whose country is on the Limmen and Roper Rivers. Spencer not very well. His wife's name is Tokalina. I spent most of the afternoon in the camp of the Anewla cultivating friendly relations. They are cheery fine looking fellows, cannibals to a man and one old rascal who admired my portly form looked as if he would, quite in a friendly way, like to breakfast off some of it. They wear on their arms and around their necks ornaments made of plaited bamboo grass — They make and use bark canoes in which they hunt the Dugong which is said to be plentiful about the mouth of the river. We have arranged with them to make us two of these canoes. Some of them talk Malay and two of the young men had been to Macassar with Malay traders. The Malays have been fishing and trading on this coast for over a hundred years and we are rather afraid that the coast blacks will have adopted some of their customs. On the Sir Edward Pellew group of Islands which lie about (?) miles from the mouth of the River there are a great number of blacks who collect tortoise shell and pearl shell for the Malays who in return give them rice tobacco and a sort of rum called Arrack. Some years ago the Islanders were very fierce and treacherous but they are now fairly quiet and many of them come up to Borroloola where they pick up tobacco knives and other articles much coveted by the savage. Some years ago a Chinese gardener here accidentally shot a Lubra and being ignorant of British Law he thought the best thing he could do was to bury the body and thus conceal the death. He did so and the proceedings were watched by some men of the Anewla Tribe who as soon as the Chinaman had completed his task exhumed the body and eat [sic] it. I was a little shocked to find that some of the men whose society I was cultivating this afternoon were active partakers in the feast.

The funny thing about it is that when they had consumed the body they trooped up to the Police Station and gave information to the Police of what had happened taking with them as evidence the breastbone in which some shot were embedded and a number of loose shot which they had extracted from the body. The Chinaman was tried for murder and acquitted and he and the blacks enjoyed their trip to Pt. Darwin immensely...

12 January 1901. — Raining nearly all day 105 points registered. Trying to kill time reading novels. Oh that we could get away from this wretched hole, it seems such an utter waste of life being cooped up here with nothing to do and the uncertainty as to when we shall get away is a source of continuous worry. The wet season appears to have set in. There is weeping and wailing and tugging of pig tails amongst the local sons of the flowery land (China). It is the custom to send the bones of all Chinamen who die outside their motherland back to China and it is believed that unless this is done the deceased cannot enter paradise. The poorest Chinaman dies in peace knowing that sooner or later his generous countrymen will see that his bones are deported to his native land. Some few days ago the local Chinkies disinterred the remains of two of their countrymen who died here some years ago. The bones were placed in calico bags preparatory to being packed in boxes and shipped off to China. The Niggers appropriated the bags and emptied the contents in a heap so that the bones have become mixed and it is now impossible to tell to which individual the different bones belonged. The Chinkies are greatly troubled and they seem to think that Ah Kim will be transported to Paradise with some of Ah Sin's limbs and vice versa. Visions of a lopside Chinese angel are too much for the Mongolian.

Source: *Gillen's Diary: Camp Jottings of F. J. Gillen on the Spencer and Gillen Expedition Across Australia 1901-1902,* Libraries Board of South Australia, Adelaide, 1968, pp.313-17.

Morning in the Macdonnells

Robert Henderson Croll

I fell in love with the Macdonnells. The best season in which to see them is winter. Here is a note written on the spot in that season (May 1934), a note which does all too little justice to their rare charm:

For early morning beauty I am prepared to uphold the claim of the Macdonnell Ranges against the rest of the world. It is true that I have not seen the rest of the world, but I feel in this matter much as the old physician did about the strawberry: 'Doubtless God could have made a better berry, but doubtless He never did.' Looking up from my writing for another view before the splendour fades, my first impression becomes conviction that surely nothing better than this has been created.

We are camped on a flat between the public well and the railway line. Behind us, to the north, lies the township of Alice Springs, capital of Central Australia, about half a mile away. Roosters are crowing there, and a drift of white smoke from the first of the breakfast fires is spreading slowly down the valley of the Todd, scarcely moving, and keeping very low. Fine white-stemmed gums in the middle distance add greatly to the value of the picture.

But it is to the south that we turn with assured expectation, for we have been here now five days, and no morning yet has disappointed us. Some two miles away is the great wall of rock pierced by the gateway known as Heavitree Gap, and ending, from this aspect, with the abrupt peak of Mount Gillen. It is Gillen who first sees the sun. The flat is still in shadow, there is no hint of colour at our level, when Gillen suddenly flushes pink — like the Sultan's turret he has been caught in a 'noose of light.' Rapidly the glow extends. Between looking down and looking up, the crest of the range has reddened from end to end and the pure tone is flowing downwards to the base. Now the whole line of the mountain is rose-pink, shining as if lighted from within.

Not a breath of air is stirring. The trees stand as if asleep. In keeping with the peace of the scene a Jackeroo Bird, the mellowest singer of them all, pipes a few perfect flute calls, and a near-by magpie croons quietly as if for his own private ear.

A crow strikes an unexpected note of humour. Crows are everywhere about the outskirts of the town, white-eyed, well groomed, always hungry. A capable musician should compose the Song of the Crow: it is astonishing the variety of notes the bird has. This one is apparently attempting a rendering of 'Hark, Hark the Lark!' He gets as far as 'Ar-cark-ca-cark,' but wisely stops at that. My sympathy goes out to a bird with such ambitions and such a voice!

One of the taller trees has caught the light and all at once our shadows lie stretched on the ground before us — the sun is here! From far away comes the noisy gossip of a large flock of Galahs. Louder it grows until they are passing right above us, heading, every morning, towards the Gap. When they fly high their wings fairly twinkle and they flutter like pink petals against the blue. Almost invariably a few drop lower to examine us and, as they settle, the dead bough they have chosen seems suddenly to have flowered. With much arching of crests and *sotto voce* remarks they stay for awhile, then, as one bird, they depart. We thought Galahs could not fly without shrieking, but sometimes an alarm call is sounded, the babel is hushed instantly, and the flock swoops low between the trees, travelling fast and silently for some distance.

Bird life is fairly plentiful, though this has been a dry season in the Centre. Black Cockatoos flap heavily along, creaking like rusty gates, a Whistling Eagle calls not unmusically, and sails by on steady wing, the Crested Bell-bird, most ventriloquial of singers, defies you to say whether he is near or far, those handsome creatures the Ulbujas, better known as the Port Lincoln Parrots, display their sleek dark heads and golden collars as they feed in the higher branches, Babblers make strange cat-calls, hopping distractedly about as they do so, trim Soldier-birds come fearlessly for scraps, and Red-eared Finches wheeze in their funny asthmatic way, often alighting within a few feet of us.

A soft tinkling comes from the rear. We turn to see a luminous cloud against the eastern light, the dust raised by the sharp hooves of the town herd of goats. Very picturesque they are — long-horned and long-bearded Billys, sedate matrons, frolicsome kids — of every age and every colour. Marching placidly with them are a few sheep and, moving them on as they would pause to snatch a mouthful here and there, are two aboriginal women, walking with the ease and grace of carriage for which these people are famous. They call to their charges and to their three dogs in rapid, soft Arunta, and the herd passes, in a golden haze, to feed somewhere to the west and return at sundown.

The Alice is awake. Domestic sounds come from the dwellings to remind us of the homes we have left a thousand miles away. To close the eyes for a moment is to forget that the city is no longer with us; to open them is to see a team of camels stalking solemnly past.

But the range — the range is the thing! You turn to find that the warm glory has gone; a new tone has taken its place. The whole long line of hill has come forward a step; every detail of rock and tree is now so plain in the clear air that you doubt the knowledge that they are so far away. Presently the colour will change again and towards the end of what, to Alice Springs, is a typical winter day, bright and sunny, the bold escarpments will take on a faint powdered blue which grows deeper and richer until they are no longer a definite mountain chain, but merely a sombre line at which the stars cease.

Only one thing is more beautiful than the fading light of evening: it is the miracle of the morning.

Source: Robert Henderson Croll, *Wide Horizons: Wanderings in Central Australia*, 2nd edn, Angus & Robertson, Sydney, 1937, pp.10-12.

The Roper River's flowing

W.E. (Bill) Harney

Lilies blue amidst green shadow, where the wattle trees are blooming,
    By the banks of yellow rushes where the finches dart and play —
Make a floating sapphire pathway for the Roper waters coming
    To swirl beside my campfire at the breaking of the day.

From Mataranka's Nedjik spring and Kuran's swirling stream,
    The waters run where, row by row, the emerald green pandanus grow;
And shining bright or flecked with blue, the eddies whirl and gleam
    Or pause to catch, like tall white ghosts, the Leichhardt's as they flow.

And the rapids of Narmurangan, where water-lilies sway,
    Tell a tale of love and beauty to hills red beneath the sun —
And the native children shouting, as beside the reeds they play,
    See Murrawallies's living waters glitter silver as they run.

The tales of this old country are the songs I hear them singing;
    How the 'Mungri' — bulrush people — poled their rafts of bark and vine,
Crouching low amidst the bulrush when they heard the hide thongs ringing,
    As the Urapunji horse-teams creaked towards the O.T. line.

Then the Never-Never people came with drays and wagons creaking,
    Toiling through the distance by the Roper waters gleaming
As they build up yard and homestead, ever moving out and seeking,
    Sleeping ever in the bushlands, they now rest within its 'Dreaming'.

By the waters of Queungun where the tea-tree blooms are drifting,
    By the Elsey station homestead on the dull brown banks nearby,
By the reeds of Narramungun where the lotus stems are lifting
    Rose-pink buds above the surface to a sunlit northern sky.

Now over tribal trading tracks the motor trucks are groaning,
    The wireless strains at evening drown the low corroboree;
And the silvery mail-plane's engine beats a cadence in this droning,
    Keeping rhythm with the Roper tumbling on towards the sea.

Source: W.E. (Bill) Harney, *Content to Lie in the Sun*, Robert Hale, London, 1958, p.142.

Deep Well

Roland Robinson

I am at Deep Well where the spirit-trees
writhe in cool white limbs and budgerigar-
green hair along the watercourse carved out
in deep red earth, a red dry course that goes
past the deep well, past the ruined stone
homestead where the wandering blacks make camp
(their campfire burning like a star at rest
among dark ruins of the fallen stone)
to find the spinifex and ochre-red
sandhills of a land inhabited by those
tall dark tribesmen with long hair and voices
thin and far and, deepening, like a sea.
I am at Deep Well where the fettlers' car
travels towards the cool blue rising wave
that is the Ooraminna Range, and starts
those pure birds screaming from the scrub to swerve,
reveal their pristine blush in wings and breasts,
to scatter, settle and flower the desert-oak.
Here I have chosen to be a fettler, work
to lay the red-gum sleepers, line and spike
the rails with adze and hammer, shovel and bar,
to straighten up and find my mates, myself
lost in the spinifex flowing down in waves
to meet the shadow-sharpened range and know
myself grown lean and hard again with toil.
Here, in the valley camp where hills increase
in dark blue depths, the desert hakea stands
holding the restless finches and a single star.

Source: Roland Robinson, 'Deep Well', published originally in R.G. Howarth (ed.), *Jindyworobak Anthology*, Jindyworobak Publications, Melbourne, 1949, p.10; and then in Robinson, *Tumult of the Swans*, Lyre Bird Writers, Sydney, 1953, p.26.

Alice

Thomas Keneally

The Alice of Alice Springs was named after the wife of the South Australian Postmaster General who had supervised the building of the Overland Telegraph. The *Springs* derives from the spring which rises north of the present town near the Telegraph station itself.

The stone buildings of the Telegraph station with which Alice began are still there, in part a compound, in part a fortress. In the summer of 1872, telegraph station managers travelling north to take over the three plum stations — Barrow Creek, Tennant Creek, Alice Springs — found that the environment would not be easy. One of them died of thirst and two of them survived only by turning back and drinking the blood of their horses.

The town which was founded to the south of the Telegraph station grew very slowly and was for a time called Stuart, in honour of the doughty little Scot who first crossed Australia south to north without any of the grievous drama and death associated with the ill-fated expedition undertaken by Robert O'Hara Burke and William John Wills in 1860. But again it was like Palmerston and Darwin. The title Stuart vanished. The more prosaic name of Alice Springs prevailed. But over what sort of town?

Doris Bradshaw, who first came to Alice in 1899 when her father was appointed manager of the Overland Telegraph station, wrote: 'The villagers at that time were few indeed — perhaps not more than twelve or thirteen. As we passed through the village on our arrival we first saw Mounted Constable Charles Brookes, his wife, and four children at the Police Camp on the southern side of Heavitree Gap. He must have been one of the loneliest policemen in the world, especially as his duties required him to be long distances away from home on horse and camel patrols. Some of my most vivid recollections are of Constable Brooks returning to Alice Springs with lines of Aboriginal prisoners chained by the neck. They never failed to stir in my youthfully democratic breast a deep sense of outrage and revulsion ... Only one white woman lived in the township itself. She was Mrs Charles Meyers, whose husband had established a saddlery business.'

It is hard to jump from such beginnings to the fatal manoeuvrings of the Cold War. But in fact the Alice of frontier madmen, rare white women, of bush panache and eccentricity seems to be involved for good or ill more intimately in modern geopolitics than perhaps any other Australian town or city.

'An Atom Bomb for Alice' says the cover of a mass market thriller in the bookshop in the Alice Springs Casino. And one of the ironies of Australia's most famous frontier town is that many Australians consider it the most prominent nuclear target in the South West Pacific. The reason is a Joint Defence facility twenty-seven kilometres southwest of the Alice at Pine Gap. Its existence is frankly proclaimed. Anyone can see it from a commercial plane on approach or take-off from Alice Springs. Its white domes sit oddly among the eroded and palpably ancient spines of the MacDonnell Range. But those who attempt to photograph its six domes are turned away by Australian Commonwealth policemen who patrol its security fences.

When Gough Whitlam was engaged in the 1972 campaign which led to his election as Prime Minister of Australia, he promised the electorate that he would make known to them the secret functions of Pine Gap. Having visited the site, however, and been briefed by its directors, he announced that the purpose of Pine Gap was too significant to be disclosed to the Australian people. 'I emphasize they [the facilities at Pine Gap] are not part of weapon systems. They cannot be used to make war on any country ... we never had a mandate to break the Joint Defence Agreement.' Elsewhere he said: 'We never told the people at the election that we would disclose other people's secrets.'

On a recent visit to Washington, Australian Prime Minister Robert J. Hawke, after meeting the Director of the C.I.A. and the U.S. Defence Secretary, said that he accepted the risk of U.S. defence facilities such as Pine Gap in view of 'global strategic considerations'. (He simultaneously received from the C.I.A. an assurance that, contrary to Australian legend, the Agency had not been involved in the fall of Gough Whitlam in 1975.)

In the absence of firm news, of any definite statement by the authorities about the function of Pine Gap, rumours abound both among the Australian Press and in Alice itself. One of the more exotic ones, common in Alice Springs pubs and sometimes revamped by the Australian Press, asserts that apart from being a prime nuclear target Pine Gap is a centre for bird smuggling.

Many such fantastic rumours are encouraged in part by the regular arrival at and departure from Alice Springs airport of Globemasters and Galaxies servicing the facility. The Press and the locals have always claimed that the inwards and outwards cargoes of these transports go largely unsupervized by Australian customs officials.

A scenario much favoured by the Australian Press runs like this. We know from the U.S. Senate's enquiry into C.I.A. operations that at the end of the Vietnam war the Southeast Asian division of the Agency was in disarray. In those circumstances, given the genial remoteness of Pine Gap and the complacency of Australian officials, Pine Gap could have provided the Agency with an excellent fall-back position from which some of its unfinished business in Southeast Asia could be finalized.

The Anti-Gap group in Alice, who call themselves 'Concerned Citizens of Alice Springs' are worried both that the base involves a risk of nuclear attack and that it is a stronghold for an Agency which, as the U.S. Senate enquiry into the C.I.A. shows, has not always been under the firm control of the U.S. government or let its masters know the details of its activities.

Defenders of the Pine Gap installation say that it is a Joint Defence facility, that the Australian Armed Forces benefit in terms of intelligence because of its existence. For the Alice itself, it brings a large infusion of wealthy, intelligent Americans. They participate in local affairs. They are visible at the Henley-on-Todd Regatta and on civic and artistic committees throughout town. Alice has the nation's fifth largest art prize — such style would be impossible without the Pine Gap people. The Art Centre being built in Araluen is so large and well equipped that one would associate it with a place many times the size of the Alice. Under the Joint Defence Agreement, cooks, gardeners, mechanics, maids are all recruited from among the local population. They are briefed at a fundamental level on the purpose of the installation and none of them objects, say the defenders, or feels that his national pride has been demeaned. Opponents, of course, say that Australians are involved only on a menial level and that, though Australians make up exactly half of the base's two hundred and fifty employees, in 1981 only sixteen of the Australians were technicians (only eight were scientists). The Gap's defenders further point out that no one knows whether the Russians have a correct or incorrect assessment of what the place is, but that whatever it is, any sensible enemy could knock Pine Gap out with 'a small team of trusted saboteurs with two-inch mortars. That would put it out of action for five years.'

In April 1977, Christopher John Boyce, an employee of an electronics company, TRW Systems Inc., who had C.I.A. clearance, was arrested in Los Angeles and put on trial for selling technical secrets to the Russians. He described some of the information he passed to the Russians in the following terms: 'I agreed to write a statement concerning what I believe to be violations of law against the Australians. I informed them that I worked in a communications room and part of my daily duties was to continue a deception against the Australians. I learned about the way in which we could practise day-to-day deceptions in our transmission to the Australians.'

Boyce never specified during his trial what the day-to-day deceptions against the Australians were, but more recently, on a network current affairs programme in the United States, Boyce mentioned Pine Gap as the key to the deception, and said that the activities of the installation subverted the sovereignty of Australia. The American Senator Daniel Moynihan, however, denied that the Australians were in any way disadvantaged by the existence of Pine Gap. In any case, the Boyce trial, the book he later wrote, and the interviews he gives have all enriched Australian suspicions of the domes at Pine Gap.

According to the Australian press, Pine Gap watches and helps guide satellites which float above the earth at between 30,000 and 40,000 kilometres. This type of high satellite is called the 647. It can pick up by its infra-red telescope the energy emissions of missile exhausts during the early powered stages of flight. It is therefore crucial to America's early warning system, since it can provide pictures of intercontinental ballistic missiles in flight. Pine Gap also helps control the Big Bird and Keyhole spy satellites, which are capable of taking photographs with a resolution of fifteen centimetres from a height of one hundred and fifty kilometres. The Australian press has also claimed that Pine Gap is one of the three keys to the Pyramider communication system of the C.I.A. One satellite is permanently positioned over Pine Gap, another over Redondo Beach in California, a third over C.I.A. headquarters at Langley, Virginia, on the outskirts of Washington. These three satellites enable C.I.A. operatives to plant sensors which monitor nuclear tests throughout the world. In 1978, for example, the C.I.A. placed such a sensor, aimed at China's nuclear installation at Lop Nor in Sinkiang Province, on top of a mountain in the Himalayas. There have been claims that levels of hydrogen fluoride over the MacDonnell Ranges are abnormally high and that this shows that the C.I.A. is illicitly working on chemical laser projects there.

Pravda, in an editorial in 1980, ambiguously warned that the presence of Pine Gap and other American installations endangered the Australian population. Among Australian politicians, the new Australian Prime Minister, Bob Hawke, has taken a different direction in the Pine Gap argument. Yes, he says, it may be a risk, but it is important enough to maintain the base in terms of the U.S. alliance.

Meanwhile, at an Alice level, the American presence seems largely a welcome thing. The American Ambassador graces the shenanigans of Henley-on-Todd with his presence, stands on the fake steamboat called *Pistil Dawn* and goes to the trouble of making a speech to the only partially attentive crowd. The American alliance, which began with MacArthur dropping from the skies onto Batchelor Field and watching a grainy Western in Kilgariff's Cinema in Alice, is consecrated further in the dry bed on the Todd on Regatta day. And, as in 1942, no one really knows, except the discreet men of Pine Gap, whether there will be bombs for Alice.

Source: Thomas Keneally, *Outback,* Hodder & Stoughton, Sydney, 1983, pp.136, 141-4, 146.

Snapshots of Kakadu

Beverley Farmer

(for Jane Moore)

The water has left
these cracked, high-ledged cliffs and fish
drawn up high and dry,
their bones heaved free of ripples,
have sunk themselves in deep stone.

Shapes burn in the cliff,
a flow of beings — colours
of flame, of smoulder.
Butterflies balance. You draw
the tossed hot heads of sand palms.

Spotted butterflies
flap loose at the cave mouth near
the hanging spider.
She steps to unwind a bee.
The spots settle in the rocks.

What's that small white ring
in and out of the water
in the photograph
of the billabong at dusk?
Is it the rising half-moon?

The moon was full. It's
there in the lily puddle,
that torn white shadow.
The ring's an egret skimming
low, mirrored, long wings dipping.

Source: Beverley Farmer, 'Snapshots of Kakadu', *Northern Perspective*, vol.9, no.2, 1986, p.84.

10 Darwin, mad capital of the north

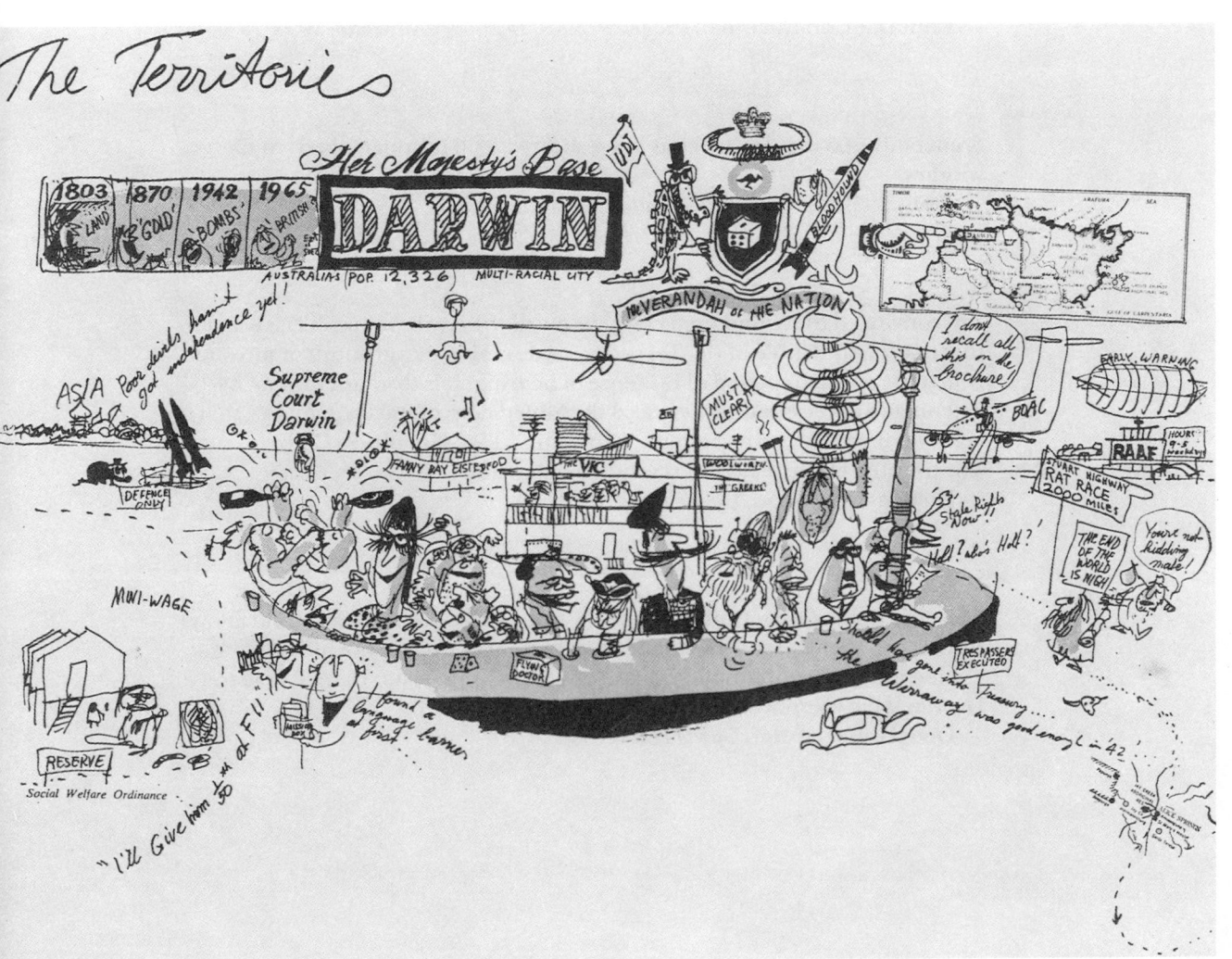

But the European of Palmerston had very often no home, only a house; and the poor bachelors or grass-widowers sat lonely in their houses, or drank at the public houses, deploring the fate that had left them stranded on this barren coast.

And through the grave stillness of the forest night which enveloped the little town you could hear the hoarse chant from the camp of the aborigines and see the red reflection of their fires under the tree-tops.
— Knut Dahl, on Darwin in the mid-1890s, *In Savage Australia*, 1927

Somebody said that Darwin was like a shop with all its soiled goods in the window.
— Philippa Bridges, *A Walk-About in Australia*, ?1925

I'm convinced that blind men could be extraordinarily happy in Darwin. For that matter, the whole of the Territory is a desirable playground for anyone who hasn't been deprived of his sense of hearing. It is through the ear, by listening to endless outbackery and the fabled tales of the Darwinians, that one achieves unconscious happiness. The Mango Tree Happiness Club, contributed in the pleasantest way to my share of that.
— Douglas Lockwood, *Up the Track*, 1964

The civic fathers aren't going to like my saying this, but Darwin is, and always has been, a slightly zany town. They had better get used to the idea. Why not exploit its tourist potential? What more compelling poster than 'Come to Darwin, Mad Capital of the North'?
— Douglas Lockwood, *Up the Track*, 1964

Previous page: This Bruce Petty cartoon — with its echoes of Pieter Brueghel the Elder — reflects contemporary Darwin's curious mixture of eccentricity and charm.

Port Darwin harbour, 1870

Mrs Dominic D. Daly

We got under weigh [sic] very early, an obliging flood tide lifted the *Bengal* off her unwelcome resting-place, and [our] two ships sailed almost side by side into the harbour of Port Darwin.

It is a generally conceded opinion, and agreed to by all those who have visited the Northern Territory, that in point of beauty Port Darwin has few equals; only two other harbours were ever named, when a comparison with this one was sought for — those of Sydney and Rio Janeiro. Having made the entrance of this magnificent haven, we found ourselves sailing into an immense space of perfectly smooth water, where, it has been said of this, as of other large harbours, the whole British fleet might lie at anchor.

The shores were clothed with masses of rich green vegetation down to the water's edge, and the cliffs overspread with thickly growing palms, in all the variety one would expect to see so far north. Ironbark trees, casuarinas and the bright green milkwood tree grew here in great luxuriance. It looked what it was, — a land of perpetual summer. We sailed along, passing smooth white beaches, on to which waterfalls from the overhanging cliffs shed glittering streams of crystal, dancing and shimmering in the sunlight. The air was warm and light, and a fair wind wafted us each moment nearer our future home. Beautiful it certainly was; but oh! so lonely and desolate, not a sign of human habitation could we yet discern; no living creature, not even a solitary blackfellow walked these lovely beaches. It was all just as nature had made it, just as it had remained from the beginning of time — untouched and untrodden by the foot of man; a region known only to the degraded tribes of savages, who had hitherto been the sole occupiers of this magnificent piece of country.

The scene of our exile — for such we deemed it then — though surpassingly beautiful in itself, was, from this very loneliness, hardly inviting to N. and myself, for we were at that time far too strongly attached to the pomps and vanities of this wicked world to appreciate being banished from all we had hitherto enjoyed so keenly.

At last we came in sight of the little settlement; it was situated in a gully on a broad tract of level ground between two steeply rising hills, having the sea on both sides. The 'camp,' to use the name so familiar to every one, and which to this day it has retained, consisted of a number of log and iron houses on either side of the gully. On Fort Hill to our right, a steep hill with a flat summit, one of the most prominent landmarks of the harbour, was a flagstaff, on which the Union Jack was flying. It was delightful to find the familiar flag in this far-away corner of the British Empire. Close to the flagstaff was a lonely grave — the last resting-place of a young surveyor who was treacherously murdered at Fred's Pass by the natives during the surveying expedition a year before. The opposite hill was covered with green shrubs, and at this moment it literally swarmed with black men and women. These unclothed spectators were the 'oldest inhabitants' of this part of the world — members of the Larrakiah tribe. The heads of the clan were amongst this eager and excited crowd. But as far as we could discern, there was nothing to distinguish them from the lesser lights of that barbarous horde of natives.

The men, for the most part, only used one leg in standing, the other one was neatly tucked against its fellow thigh. Any support lacking in this unusual pose was supplied by a tall bundle of spears, firmly grasped in the owner's hand, resting on the ground like a number of alpenstocks.

The women talked and chattered incessantly, while here and there the wondering eyes of a dusky-skinned piccaninny watched proceedings from a coign of vantage over its mother's shoulder. There were numbers of children who ran about hither and thither, pointing to us, sometimes cutting capers, and going off in shrieks of laughter.

I cannot say; on looking back to what my impressions were then, that I viewed the prospect of having so large a tribe of natives for our immediate neighbours as by any means an unmixed joy. I had certainly known something of the Australian blackfellow in other parts of the colony. I had met him not exactly 'black but comely,' but as a tame appendage to some outlying sheep station, a tracker of horses, and a finder of kangaroo. I had also met him on the coast, supplying the wants of the civilised community with fish, ducks, or any wild fowl he could snare or shoot. Here the aboriginal presented himself in an entirely new aspect. We were the smaller number, they the greater, and moreover this crowd of savages was armed to the teeth.

My younger brothers and sisters looked very awestruck at this first glimpse of barbaric life, and I fear many of the theories they had formed about going into the wilds alone, and experiencing some Robinson Crusoe-like adventures, were suddenly 'knocked on the head,' to use a forcible colonial expression, one, however, which rather pointed to their probable fate if they had attempted anything of the kind.

A closer view of the camp did not tend to raise our spirits to any very exalted elevation — a handful of log huts, with crowds of natives looking over our heads; and this tiny settlement literally the only one in the vast tract of Northern Australia. Looking straight through the gully, away over the roofs of the buildings, one beheld a long stretch of water, bounded like the other parts of the harbour by a mass of densely wooded and uninhabited country, which extended as far as the eye could reach. We realised, too, that no hope of regular communication with the outer world could be looked for, as the settlement had not become sufficiently important to induce a line of steamers to call there.

However, this was looking at the question only from our point of view. The arrival of these two ships in one day was a great event in the history of the Northern Territory. Nothing had been done since the survey was finished, and progress was at a standstill. We brought letters to those in camp from friends and relatives far away. And the *Bengal*, whose mails were of a later date than ours, brought the welcome news that an agreement had been concluded between the British Australian Telegraph Company and the Adelaide Government to bring Australia into telegraphic communication with, not only the mother country, but the whole world.

Source: Mrs Dominic D. Daly, *Digging, Squatting and Pioneering Life in the Northern Territory of South Australia*, Sampson Low, Marston, Searle & Rivington, London, 1887, pp.43-8.

Mrs Brown on Northern Territory matters

Northern Territory Times, 1874

Thank goodness! here I am agin sitting on a rail cheer — yes, so it is, a rail cheer. Oh, Mrs. Burt, you can't think how thankful I am to be here agin. Have-ee got a cup of tea in the pot? Don't matter so long as it is hot and strong if the cup is a little one. Well, child, I'm jest now stepped ashore from that nasty steamer the 'Woolner;' and well she's named, for she es as dirty and greasy as her namesics in the bush. Have I sen 'em? I'm sorry to say I h-a-a-ve, Mrs. Burt; both men and wimmin — if you may call 'em sich. Oh, the horrid brutes, specially when they've nothin' on 'em. What! you don't believe it, Mrs. Burt? Well, all I got to say es — go and see for yerself. See em yerself, cheld, in all their 'manchesty of nature,' as the pooet sais; but I don't believe in all pooets, for one on 'em sais, sais he, 'Nature onadorned es the most adorned,' or some sich words. Mrs. Burt, call him pooet or what you will, but I would send sich a onuman retch to sarch for the North Pole without a shirt; yes, that I would, Mrs. Burt. Where did you get this tee? it's very good tee; or, praps, I haven't been used to good tee lately. Yes, I've been to the Northern Territory for the first and the *last* time, you may be ashoored, Mrs. Burt, for what with the fever, and ager, and prickly het; and what with the bully and the tinn'd fish! Oh, I was by the side ov a feller when he opened a tin of fish one day, and I had to run for my very life, my dear; all the ody-coloun was a vapperated from my anchiker, and as luck wud haave et, I run agin the wind, an' was soon out o' the smell ov et, or else I don't think I shud be here to-day, my dear Mrs. Burt, to tell-ee ov et. Well, you know, Mrs. Burt, what I went there for. Yes, you know, I thought my experience was anuff to give me a livin' in sich a place. You know, Mrs. Burt, that several yung wimin went out theer sometime afore I started, and I naturally thought — Well, poor dears, there's nobody can tell what kind o' nusses there is there, an' ef anything should happen to 'em, when a good nuss was wanted, an' she wasn't to hand, why you know, Mrs. Burt, so well as I do, that t'wud be a bad job; so I went, you know, on quite flinantrofic grounds. When I told Brown what I was a going to doo, he sais, sais he, 'You can do what you think best, but I'm of 'pinion that you'll soon be back agen.' An' my dear, I wish I had a tak'd his warning. Was I say-sick? well, warn't I, to tell the truth ov et; and many a time when we was a rolling about, and the say a washing up agin them little round holes they call winders — no, sidelites — I never could tell what they tuk the name from. Well, one nite, when I thought I was getting better like, an' there were another woman in the same caben — poor think, she didn't know to a day, Mrs. Burt — well, as I was a sayin', one nite the nasty steamer was a rollin' an' a pitchin' and a screwinen every way, an' I was jest a thinking, well, that there kreeking can't last long, shee'l go all to pieces, when slap-dash, com'd in, right over my clean nite-gown and cap, that I had a put only that nite, a rigler sowser. Well, I was a goin' to jump up, but I didn't. I lide pashently down where I were, an' was filling myself up for a good scream — lor, Mrs. Burt, ef I cud only have got out that there scream, as I was a making up like, I do think I shud ha' feel'd better; but jest as I was a goin' to open my mouth — I had opened it — when slap dash com'd another sowser, and filled it, an' afore I cud clear out my mouth, com'd another! Well, I thoft, 'tes all over, when all at once com'd that scream I had been stoppt upon afore. Well, my dear, I spose 'twas a good loud one, for I thoft everybody in the ship was a running up over my head, and jest then the steward run into the cabin, and axed, 'What in the world is the matter here?' He, however, soon seed what it wor that had frightened me so, and took and shet up the 'bull's eye,' he called it, but I never seed a bull's nor any other eye that cried sich great big tears — and salt they was too — as that ded. Well, my dear, we got to the great place called Port Darwin at last, and glad enuff I war, you may be sure, to set my feet upon 'terrer firmer' (that's what they called the sea beech there) again you may depend upon it. Well I got lodgings at last after a good deal ov sarchen about; and sich lodgens, my dear, you never see'd, and I hope shall never see again. 'What, do you call this a bedroom?' says I (this was to the woman who show'd me in), 'why the rats will come in between these sticks,' sais I, 'there's room enough for a kangaroo to come in in the nite,' sais I. An', my dear Mrs. Burt, you shud ha see'd the look that that there woman goov'd me as she dropt down a piece of canves where there oft to be a door, you know. Only fancy! a Creschchan woman with only a piece of canves for a door to her sanktitorum, as tes called. Oh, my gracious! Mrs. Burt, you may be able because you are a woman, to fancy what was my feelinks every time I see'd that piece of canves shake like with the wind I spose. And then the woman looked in, and said, 'Es your neam Brown?' 'Yes,' sais I, 'why not?' 'Because,' she said, 'thare's a man with y'r boxes.' So I tore to the door, I mean the pieces of canvas, to keep the man from comin' in. 'Oh, my grashus!' sais I, 'whoever have you got with you?' for jest at that very moment, I seed a great woolly head, with three whitey shinen places in the face. These was the two eyes and the teeth of a blackfeller. Well, jest then the other man moved a one side a bit to put my box down, and there was the black; and you shud a seed him and his toilet; why nuthen but a little bit of a apern, an' a bit ov string tied round one of his rists, jest like what our nibur, Mrs. What's-her-name, do tie on to her girl, when she do want the snuff she is senden for, tied up in two papers, — jest like that my dear, and nuthen else in the world else! An' the apern esn't bigger nor your babby's bib! 'I want ten bob,' says the man with the box. 'Larry Keear!' sais the the nigger. 'What's that,' sais I, 'I don't keep no "larry keerars";' and, my dear Mrs. Burt, you shud a seed that blackey smile. You ca'dn't compare et weth enything but Tim Murphy's sign ov the Bull and Mouth. 'Bacca, plower, tum-tum,' sais the mouth. So I found out thar that the man with my box was called Tom, and though I thoft that his 'ten bob' was a raather high charge, I paid et down in two new half-crowns and five shillin', so that he cud take away the mouth, the bib, and the bit ov string. I was goin' to take up my boxes and carry them into my bedroom, when, 'Larry Keeur, 'bacca, tum-tum,' sais the nigger; and leaving Tom to give him some 'bacca I got out ov site behind the piece ov canves like a shot. Well, I lide down in my close, and I spose as I was very tired, went to sleepe, but, there was the room rolling an' pitchen about, and every now and then the great wooley head, with the three white places in the face, and the bib, and bit ov string round the rist, and Larry Keeur, berry good, baccy, tum-tum, wud be maken me jump in my trubled slepe all through that hot, sweating, miserable nite. Well, my dear Mrs. Burt, what do you think? Just as the grey day was a breaking through the sticks and slabs as the wall ov my room was a made on, the woman that kep' the house com'd in, and sais she, 'Your wanted,' sais she. Well, I jumps up, for I was all dressed, but raather tumbled like, and I sais, sais I, 'What?' 'Your wanted,' sais she, 'dedn't there a woman came in the steamer with you?' 'Yes,' sais I. 'Well, your wanted,' sais she, 'and here's a lubra come to show you the way.' And shure anuff, my dear, there wor a black woman jest like the nigger, only she had a skirt on. Well, I went away with her — but musn't stay to tell you how I got on the whole week, for if I do I shan't sleep to nite. Well, my dear woman, this es the best cup ov tee and toast I've had sence I left home, and to-morrow morning I must start by the early coach for theer agin, and to suffer Brown's gibes for the next week. I will come down agin, and tell you a bit of my experience and mind on N.T. (as they call it) matters, that will open your eyes more nor a bit, I can ashure you. Now, my dear Mrs. Burt, I'm not going to say anythink agin the country, because I do think, from what I've heerd and seed, that it will be a great country; but tes the way tes managed, and the backbitin' and middlin' with every body's business but their own with the people, most ov'em, that makes it bad, very bad, indeed. I can only say that I am thankful I'm out ov et. But, as I was a saying, I'm tired, an' must wish you a good nite for the time — good nite.

Source: 'Mrs Brown on Northern Territory matters', *Northern Territory Times*, 29 May 1874.

The cycloon, Paddy Cahill and the G.R.

A. B. (Banjo) Paterson

Far in the north of Australia lies a little-known land, a vast half-finished sort of region, wherein Nature has been apparently practising how to make better places. This is the Northern Territory of South Australia. Britain, it is said, thinks of establishing an Imperial naval station at Port Darwin. But let Britain beware! The Northern Territory has 'broke' everybody that ever touched it in any shape or form, and it will break Britain if she meddles with it. The decline and fall of the British Empire will date from the day that Britannia starts to monkey with the Northern Territory.

This vast possession, which extends halfway down the continent of Australia, is not, strictly speaking, a part of the S.A. province. It is a Crown possession, handed over to the

Adelaide folk to manage and work for their own loss, and for years they have poured their capital like water into this huge sink. And still, after swallowing two and a half millions of Government money, and Heaven only knows how much private capital, the place is steadily going seventy thousand a year to the bad. Year after year the South Australians have swallowed the same old wheeze about the immense undeveloped resources of 'our magnificent Northern Territory', and have hung on pluckily, in the hope of one day getting some of their money back — and possibly also in the fear of the N.T.'s resumption as a Crown colony, an event which would at once be followed by an influx of cheap Asiatics from Britain's Eastern possessions. And, in fact, the Territory itself is now clamouring for the introduction of the cheap and nasty Chow, notwithstanding that it is breeding its own Chinky fast enough, in all conscience. The Territory people want more Chows, and would gladly cut loose from South Australia to get them. As for the trifle of two and a half millions that they owe, they would attend to that small matter after the wet season. In the Territory everything good is always going to happen after the wet season.

The capital of the Northern Territory is Palmerston on Port Darwin, a harbour little, if at all, inferior to Port Jackson. Palmerston is unique among Australian towns, inasmuch as it is filled with the boilings over of the great cauldron of Oriental humanity. Here comes the vagrant and shifting population of all the Eastern races. Here are gathered together Canton coolies, Japanese pearl divers, Malays, Manilamen, Portuguese from adjacent Timor, Cingalese, Zanzibar niggers looking for billets as stokers, frail (but not fair) damsels from Kobe; all sorts and conditions of men. Kipling tells what befell the man who 'tried to hustle the East', but the man who tried to hustle Palmerston would get a knife in him quick and lively. The Chow and the Jap and the Malay consider themselves quite as good as any alleged white man. In Japtown (the Easterner's quarters) Chinese children by the dozen play about all day long in the dusty streets; gaily dressed cheerful little barbarians, revelling in the heat. The goldfields are all worked by Chinese labour; hundreds of Chinese fossick about the old alluvial claims; fifty pearling luggers go out every tide, carrying seven hands each, practically all coloured men — 350 yellow, brown, and brindled vagrants moving backwards and forwards with the tide. And more boats building and more brindle-coloured Japanese arriving every month. To supply the needs of all these, there are stores of every kind in Japtown, and the storekeepers all deal with the East for their supplies. There is an Eastern flavour over everything; when the Palmerstonians want to gamble at the annual races they do it by Calcutta sweeps, an Eastern form of betting little known or practised elsewhere in Australia.

Palmerston is supported by the pearlers, the gold mines, and the Government officials. The Overland Telegraph ends at Palmerston and employs a large staff known as the O.T. men; and the Singapore cable which there leaves Australia, also employs a large staff of British and Australasian Telegraph ('B.A.T.') officials. These, with a publican or two, the Government Resident (always referred to as 'the G.R.'), a couple of lawyers, a doctor, a few storekeepers, customs and railway officials and Paddy Cahill, the buffalo shooter, pretty well make up the white population of a place upon which the Government has nevertheless squandered money madly. The huge jetty cost £70,000 and ere it was well finished the *teredo* [ship worms] had eaten the piles away, and a gigantic crane, that had just been erected, fell into the water with a mighty splash. It is there still, but they will get it out 'after the wet season'. Also, the little tin-pot railway to Pine Creek cost a million and doesn't pay working expenses; and yet S.A. Parliament talks of spending nine millions in prolonging this useless railway down the centre of the continent.

There's a curse on all N.T. undertakings. Private enterprise, as represented by Fisher and Lyons, Dr Brown, and many other 'big' men of the past, has poured into it hundreds of thousands of pounds in cattle stocking and so on. What is there to show for it all? When not dead, the cattle are unsaleable, because there are no markets. Not a station in the Territory today would fetch at auction half the money it cost; not a mine in the Territory pay steady interest on its capital. Sugar planting and quinine planting have failed; the blacks now hunt for wild goose eggs on the lagoons at Sergison's abandoned sugar plantation and the wild buffaloes wallow in the swamps below Beatrice Hills where the quinine was. Once, though, a ray of hope broke the gloom when ruby-like gems were discovered in the MacDonnell ranges. These stones look exactly like rubies, which at their best are far more valuable than diamonds, and as they lay about in any quantity it was thought for a while that the Territory was Saved. A few three-bushel bags were hastily filled with 'rubies' and sent to England. Alas, the curse of the Territory was on those stones — the English experts on examination pronounced them no more than worthless natural *simulacra* of the ruby. The gold mines were rich down to water level; but there the ore became refractory, and now all the mining is surface. A few market riggers bought a lot of mines from the Chinese for about £17,000 and then subdivided these properties, and watered the capital till it now stands at about £90,000 nominal value. But subdivide and water as they like, they are still the same £17,000 worth of Chinese gold mine and apparently not likely to pay interest on even that modest capital. Out in the ranges are all sorts of prospectus claims — some of them good shows; but no one does any work in the Territory. They put everything off till 'after the wet season'. It is the land of Later On. If a Northern Territory man knew that his mine was full of gold, he would not dig it out. He would sit down and wait for a Chinaman to come along and take it on tribute. If no Chinaman came, he would 'send it Home to float'. Said one miner, 'I'd sooner be in W.A. on one feed a day than be on good gold here. They don't 'elp a man to do nothin' here. If the G.R. would only let us have a Guv'ment battery we might get some stone out and have a crushin'.' And there he sat waiting for a Government battery. Waiting — always waiting, that is the typical Northern Territory attitude. The old brisk days have gone; the pushing men have departed; and those who have stayed have got the white-ant in their systems. There is always a wet season just past or coming. If it is past, they wait 'till the ground dries'; and by the time it *is* dry they think the next wet season might come early, and they — wait!

The Government sent up a buoy to mark a dangerous reef. The buoy was taken out with great ceremony, and anchored over the reef, and immediately sank. They didn't get it up again. It is at the bottom of the sea now, and the reef is unmarked. Another buoy got adrift from a dangerous reef; this buoy was cruising Vernon Straits for some time, but no one fetched it back. When some lepers were discovered at Palmerston once, a leper station was formed at a little island in the harbour, and the lepers were landed there with great precaution, but as soon as the tide went down (it falls 24 feet) the lepers calmly waded ashore and returned to town. Nobody bothered any more about them.

There is only one great landmark in Palmerston history — the cyclone which some years ago blew the town down. A lot of it isn't rebuilt yet. This atmospheric disturbance, locally known as 'the cycloon' is one of the three topics of conversation in Palmerston; the second is the Government Resident (the G.R.). He is an English barrister, and, in his own person, Supreme Court, Head of the Mining Jurisdiction, Protector of Blacks, and Police Magistrate. No wonder they talk about him. Good man for the position too as he doesn't care a damn for anybody, and, starting from that safe basis, discharges his varied duties with a light heart. The third subject of discussion is Paddy Cahill, the buffalo shooter; he is popularly reported to pursue the infuriated buffalo at full gallop, standing on his saddle, and dressed in a towel and a diamond ring, and yelling like a wild Indian. The trinity of the N.T.: the cycloon, the G.R., and Paddy Cahill! The inhabitants sit about the shady verandahs and drink, and talk about one or all of these three. They start drinking square gin immediately after breakfast, and keep it up at intervals till midnight. They don't do anything else to speak of, yet they have a curious delusion that they are a very energetic and reckless set of people. But it's all talk and drink. Palmerston is the city of booze, blow, and blasphemy. There is an Act compelling a publican to refuse drink to an habitual inebriate. This is locally known as the 'Dog Act' and to be brought under the Dog Act is a glorious distinction, a sort of V.C. of Northern Territory life.

To sum up, the Northern Territory is a vast, wild land, full of huge possibilities, but, up to now, a colossal failure. She has leagues and leagues of magnificent country — with no water. Miles and miles of splendidly watered country — where the grass is sour, rank, and worthless. Mines with rich ore — that it doesn't pay to treat. Quantities of precious stones — that have no value. The pastoral industry and the mines are not paying, and the pearling, which does, is getting too much into Jap hands. The hordes of aliens that have accumulated are a menace to the rest of Australia. Nevertheless, the white folk there are hospitable to a fault. The strangers within their gates never have a dull moment — nor a sober one — if the inhabitants can help it. And, after all the hard things I have written about it, I would give 'my weary soul' to be back in Palmerston in that curious lukewarm atmosphere and watch the white-sailed pearling boats beating out; to see the giant form of Barney Flynn, the buffalo shooter, stalking emu-like through the dwarfish crowd of Japs and Manilamen; to be back once more with the B.A.T. and the O.T. and Paddy Cahill and the G.R., while the Cycloon hummed and buzzed on the horizon; or to be in the buffalo-camp with Rees and Martin, shooting big, blue bulls at full gallop, or riding home in the cool moonlight with the packhorses laden with hides.

If you've heard the East a'callin' you don't never heed naught else.

And the man who once goes to the Territory always has a hankering to get back there. Some day it will be civilised and spoilt; but up to the present it has triumphantly overthrown all who have attempted to improve it. It is still 'the Territory'. Long may it wave!

Source: A.B. (Banjo) Paterson, published originally in the *Bulletin*, 31 December 1898; and then in *Singer of the Bush: Complete Works 1885-1900*, Angus & Robertson, Sydney, 1983, pp.303-5.

The Palmerstonians

Jerome J. Murif

These Palmerstonians, who treated me so handsomely, are a laughter-loving and generously hospitable people.

The European residents, being very largely civil servants are as such prohibited from entering the field of politics. This disability hangs heavily on them, and is ruinously enervating and mischievous in its effects. Peacefully, contentedly, unprogressively as the calm and happy dead are they. Earnest consideration and study of the wants and welfare of the land in which they live are neglected and the action to which such grave study ever prompts men is wanting. Their lives are rounds of light gaieties and small pleasures. A picnic, dance, a sports day or a concert is ever an absorbing topic.

These are not right lives for white men, such as they are, to live; but the embargo forces them to live it. Nothing so retards a country's progress, nothing perhaps is so great a hindrance to the development of its resources, as a non-political feeling among the inhabitants. Here politics are taboo. The real business of life, the stirring cry of 'Advance Australia!' is awfully lacking.

Remove the disability, take away the restraint, make an exception in favour of those civil servants who live so far up north in South Australia, unmuzzle those who have it in them to speak, and the people of the Territory — the Territory itself — will soon be heard of. So long as they are not heard from, so long must the Territory continue as a heavy weight.

One of the most popular Foelsche photographs of early European settlement in the North: view of Palmerston, Port Darwin, taken from Fort Hill, March 1887.

Chinese, who are ready and willing to work night or day and seven days a week, have ousted Europeans from many branches of trade. Hairdressing, tailoring and bootmaking are all done by them or Japanese.

Paper kite flying seems to be those people's most favoured form of recreation. Of a breezy evening the main street of Chinatown, running parallel with and distant but a couple of hundred yards from Palmerston's principal street, is indicated by half a dozen or more kites rising up into or stationary in mid-air. The ends of the retaining strings are either fastened to shop verandah posts or proudly held by their yellow owners.

These kites, built on scientific principles, are made very large and of fantastic shapes. Hollow 'musical' reeds are attached; and when kite flying is 'on' the loud monotonous humming of these wind instruments pervades every nook and cranny in Palmerston.

Every visitor gets a crick in his neck from looking skywards.

Many blacks hang about the town. The roads are unmetalled. The loose soil is dark brown, and consists of sand mixed with particles of friable ironstone. The three varieties of tracks which show prominently everywhere are suggestive — a few of booted whites, many of sandalled Chinamen, and over and under all those of unshod natives.

The thermometer does not register very high. But here there is a stuffy, suffocating, sweat-producing latent heat the whole year round, with very few weeks' cool to brace the enervated up.

One misses the heavenly blue of southern climes. The sky has ever in it a hazy dull metallic grey.

The town is on a table-land, and is well laid out. The drainage is good; hence malarial fever, once pretty prevalent, is now less common.

The chefs are invariably Chinamen; this applies to most of the Northern Territory. Hence one hears the word 'chow, chow' used commonly by the whites to denote meals or meal time — 'Chow's ready,' 'come to chow,' 'There goes the Chow bell,' and such like expressions.

A nobbler is disposed of with one indefinite 'Chin, chin.' Freely translated it means something between a *votre sante* and 'another coffin nail.'

And, over and above all, is a splendid, almost prodigal hospitality.

Source: Jerome J. Murif, *From Ocean to Ocean: Across a Continent on a Bicycle*, George Robertson, Melbourne, 1897, pp.183-5.

Darwin

Ernestine Hill

Man Fong Lau and Wing Cheong Sing —
    All the names along the street,
    Sound an Eastern music sweet,
A guitar of single string,
        Ping of lute and tang of 'cello
            Plucked by little nails of jade.
        Scarlet poinciana shade,
    Cassias drooping, lantern-yellow,
Veil a hidden byway where
Eyes oblique and blue-black hair,
        Squats a trousered Mongol maid.

Frangipani, white with flowers,
    Altar-candles in the gloom,
    Lights the dimly purpled bloom
Of the bougainvillea bowers,
        Blows soft-petalled on the wind
            By the shuttered balconies;
            While with tangled traceries
        Of bamboo and tamarind,
    And palms that tropic suns caress,
    Far and bright and shadowless,
        Gleams the blue of dazzled seas.

Where the curve of jetty swings,
    And the pearling-luggers ride
    In the ripple of the tide,
Quietly, with folded wings,
        Comes a snatch of island tongue
            In across the water blown,
            Or the sleepy monotone
        Of a Koepang chantey sung,
Or swift oars, with dip and flash,
Break the silver with a splash,
        Where a black man rows alone.

Latticed windows in the night,
   Slippered footsteps in the day,
   Shuffling down a devious way,
Lead to some unnamed delight,
     And the sun goes down in gold
       Panopling of clouds and sea,
     And the moon's a wizardry,
   Subtly young and slily old,
Where quick Love, with yellow eyes,
Crouches waiting, leopard-wise,
    In the shadow of a tree.

Source: Ernestine Hill, *The Great Australian Loneliness,* Robertson & Mullens, Sydney, 1956, pp.141-2.

Bloody, bloody Darwin

Anonymous

This rhyme, with its heavy-handed use of the Great Australian Adjective, was probably written by an Australian soldier serving in Darwin. It had widespread popularity during World War II.

This bloody town's a bloody cuss,
No bloody tram, no bloody bus,
And no one cares for bloody us,
Oh, bloody bloody bloody!

The bloody roads are bloody bad,
The bloody folks are bloody mad,
They even say — You bloody cad!
Oh, bloody bloody bloody!

All bloody clouds, all bloody rains,
No bloody kerbs, no bloody drains;
The Council has no bloody brains,
Oh, bloody bloody bloody!

And everything so bloody dear:
A bloody bob for bloody beer!
And it is good? — no bloody fear!
Oh, bloody bloody bloody!

The bloody flicks are bloody old,
All bloody seats are bloody sold:
You can't get in for bloody gold,
Oh, bloody bloody bloody!

The bloody dances make me smile;
The bloody bands are bloody vile —
They only cramp your bloody style,
Oh, bloody bloody bloody!

Darwin was rocked, in 1942, by Japanese bombers. This war damage, on McKay Street, was photographed on 19 December 1942. As with Tracy, the war experience failed to realise literature of lasting quality. It may yet.

No bloody sports, no bloody games,
No bloody fun with bloody dames —
Won't even give their bloody names,
Oh, bloody bloody bloody!

Best bloody place is bloody bed
With bloody lice on your bloody head,
And then they think you're bloody dead,
Oh, bloody bloody bloody!

Source: 'Bloody, bloody Darwin', anonymous poem in Bill Wannan (comp.), *Robust, Ribald and Rude Verse in Australia*, Lansdowne, Sydney, 1972, p.94.

Mango juice

Graham Calley

October and November, in Darwin, is the wife beating season. It's a fact. You ask anyone from the Top End. Along with the start of the football season it's the main recreation at that time. It goes on everywhere, no risk. If you don't believe me, you ask the police. They'll tell you, and what they see is only the tip of it.

October and November is when the mangoes come in and it's the mangoes that does it.

Have you ever eaten mangoes? Really got stuck into mobs of them I mean, real ripe and straight off the tree. There's nothin like them. Everybody has them growing in their yard in Darwin and a bloke will eat a dozen in a day.

Well, you know the flavour of the juice. It's like nothin else you ever tasted and it's real powerful stuff. It spreads through you and it gurgles and ferments around inside you and then it does somethin to you. It mixes up with them hormones that grow the hair on your chest and it brings out the ape in a bloke, makes a real man out of him, sort of primitive like.

They don't know how it works, but it works, I tell you. I've seen blokes that was henpecked all year come out swingin, only three weeks into the mango season. I remember one skinny little feller I used to work with. He had a great bony, bloody wife like a Tanami camel. She gave him a hell of a life. 'Do this, do that! Where you been? Where you goin? Where's me money? You been boozin again?' It went on and on. And then come the mango season and he's into them. Two, three weeks and he goes home one night and Whamo, Whamo, Bang! He knocks the old girl out cold as a squid.

There's another bloke I know handles his missus just prime in the mango season; and he's only got one arm. But the real story you want to hear is about Henry. Henry was a classic.

Henry and his wife come up from the south, Adelaide I think it was. Henry Longbottom was his name, which is a hell of a bloody name to carry round with you, especially up here in the Territory where nobody's fussy what they say.

I got to know him because he moved in next door to me at Fanny Bay. Him and me used to yarn over the fence sometimes. His wife would say gooday but she was a bit icy, I thought. Maybe she didn't approve of blokes stayin single like me.

Henry was a tallish sort of bloke, but he was thin and not hung together right. He had a long neck and big feet that turned out when he walked. His knees was big and bony and when he first come up and was all white, he was a horrible sight in shorts. He stooped forward a bit too, and that made his shoulders cave in like a bent coathanger. His face was a failure, no risk. It was long and sort of on a slant, like it was hung crooked off his ears. He had glasses and a sagging moustache, so he always looked sad.

He was a nice enough bloke to talk to but he was no great stick of dynamite. In fact he was about as droopy as he looked.

He worked for the government and he had a pretty top sort of job, I think. I couldn't see it meself, how he could have held down a top job with that flamin name and the droopy way he was. But then them government blokes is a dead mob anyway.

I suppose he must have held his end up in his office but I tell you what, he run a poor second to the doormat at home.

His missus was a real hard case. Judy was her name and whatever made those two get married would have to be a bloody mystery. Can you imagine, for a start, a woman deliberately fixin herself up with a handle like Longbottom. Maybe she never heard it right until after the wedding. Then again, maybe he was all she could get. She was no Mona Lisa and if she carried on before she was married like she did when I saw her, she'd surely cut the field a bit. She was small, with short red hair and a pinched in nose and a chin that was straight and pointed like the stingin end of a wasp. She might have done something with her face if only she would have smiled but she went around all the time like she had a bloody bull ant in her knickers. She had a voice like a black cockatoo and she used to saw away at old Henry until even the cockroaches would clear out.

If ever I saw a case of henpeck, it was that bloke. I didn't know whether to reckon he was a joke or a bloody disgrace. Sometimes she'd yell at him the whole evening and he'd hardly say a word. One time there she threw a book he was reading across the lawn and he just walks over and picks it up and starts putting it together again. I tried pouring some Carlton Draught into him one evening to put a bit of starch in him but the stupid bastard got pissed on the third can and the gorgon came and got him and yelled at him all night.

I realised then that the mango juice was the only thing that would do him any good. It was only just after the mango season that they arrived in Darwin though, so I had to watch the poor bastard bein chased and chewed up for a whole year nearly. You know how these

Darwin houses are built. Not much thicker than cardboard the walls are. I used to hear old Henry gettin the sharp end from morning to night sometimes. It used to get on my wick. I'm not a chauvinist. I reckon I'm a male patriot. I was just hangin out for the mango season. I intended to ram that bloke full of them.

Well, the mango season came around and do you know what happened? Bloody Henry goes off down south on some sort of training course for six weeks. Six bloody weeks! He hardly got a flamin mango into him. He came back just the same bent, goat faced, dumb bastard that he was when he left and Judy was steamin and fumin like an overcharged battery. She chased him about wherever he went, with her needle chin stuck out and her cockatoo voice fair strippin the paint off the walls. It bored through the cardboard into my place and nearly drove me round the twist. With ten months to go to the next mango season, I didn't see how I was goin to stand it.

As things turned out, though, I was saved from going round the bend by Judy herself. She got a lover. Now don't laugh. It's a fact. Wasp chin, cockatoo voice and all, she was gettin laid by this bloke from the Technology Institute.

She had taken a job there part time in the office and it was just no time after that when I saw her one night in Peppis, rubbin and bumpin with this fat, dark haired bloke with sidelevers and tight pants and a way out shirt to make himself look young. Judy was done up like a fruit salad and I wondered where in hell she'd parked Henry for the night.

I slipped out of the place before she saw me, because I was there with another bloke's wife and I didn't want any complications.

Darwin's a small place and it didn't take me too long to find out who the boyfriend was. I found out a lot more too. Judy was in and out of his place like a hornet building a nest. All hours she was there. God knows how she kept Henry in the dark. Probably he never imagined that any bloke would take her on. I was bloody amazed meself but then again its a tropical climate up here and there's no accounting for taste in the sex game.

Whatever it was that got Judy warming this bloke's bed, the effect, as far as I was concerned, was all good. She shined up like a canary with new feathers. She got off Henry's back and her voice moved down a few octaves until she sounded nearly human. Some evenings it was so quiet I thought she was not there, which of course sometimes she wasn't, being on the nest, and Henry thinking she was working overtime. Anyway, this went on for six months or more. Judy was subdued, Henry looked nearly ready to risk a smile sometime and I was able to get to sleep at night. Then Henry found out.

Judy and the bloke had got careless, see, and he came around to her place sometimes when Henry was at work. Well, Henry come home early this day and there they were. Henry walked right in on them. I was at home at the time, in the garden, and I saw Henry walk into the house and just two minutes later walk out again. He never said a word. He was pale and he looked pretty grim and miserable but he never said a word. His duck feet seemed to flap out more than ever as he walked to his car.

Next thing, I heard Judy and the boyfriend having a few words. The old cockatoo voice was back. A few minutes later the bloke comes out and drives off.

Henry come back later and I tell you what, he's a cold fish. He just goes inside and packs a couple of cases and comes out again. Judy was right into him. No doubt she was feelin guilty and tryin to yell her way out of it. Henry never said a word to her. He was there about half an hour, then he come out with his two cases, got in his car and off.

Well, Henry stayed away and after about a week the boyfriend moved in, more or less. I didn't get to know him. As a matter of fact I didn't much take to the look of him and, like I told you, me and Judy had never had much to say to each other, so she never introduced us.

A couple of months went by and we was into the mango season, when I ran into Henry one Saturday at the football. He says to come home for a drink. He looked different, not so bent over and sad like, and I swear his duck feet were straighter. I says 'Yeah I'd like a drink' and we went to his place. It was a unit right in the city, near where he worked.

I followed him into the kitchen to get the beers and when he opened the fridge, it was stacked with bloody mangoes.

I never said nothing then but later on, when we'd had a few beers, I asked him if he'd been gettin into the mangoes. He was a bit pissed and looked at me, sought of thoughtful, for a moment.

'Sam', he says, very slow and careful in his public service voice, 'Sam, I am loading myself with mangoes like ramming powder down the barrel of a cannon.'

He was sitting forward peering at me and he had a wild look about him.

'You want to know why I am charging myself with mangoes. I will tell you. In one week from now, I am going to drive to Fanny Bay and I am going to belt the bloody ears off my wife.' He sat back.

Well! How would you be, ay? What could I say?

'Good on yer, mate,' I gasped 'good on yer!'

Now I don't think I'm any more nosey than the next bloke, but you have to admit this was too much to miss. Every night for the next week I went straight home from work, to be on hand to see what was going to happen. On Thursday I realised that the boyfriend's car hadn't been about for a couple of days and I hadn't seen Judy either although I knew she was home. On Friday I got caught up over a few tubes with the boys and didn't get back until nearly six. Judy was in the garden but she shot inside when she saw me. I lit the barbecue and chucked on a steak.

About half past six, Henry's car pulls up. He sat in it for a few minutes after turning off the motor. I watched him through the clump of bananas near me barbecue. I wondered if the mango juice would work. Henry opened the door and got out. He stood up straight and sort of stuck his chin out. He looked fair dinkum. Even his moustache was straight out and fierce lookin. He marched down the drive and knocked on the front door. Knocked on his own front door mind you. Christ, I thought, he's goin to lay her out right there on the mat.

I slipped across and pretended to look in the letter box so I could see better.

The door opened and I held my breath. Henry seemed to bring his arm back. I'm waitin for it and then Henry says 'Shit' and steps back. Then Judy came into the light and I saw her face.

Henry moved back in again the next day and the boyfriend never came back. Things is very quiet next door and I haven't heard the old cockatoo voice for months. Henry's quite matey and he has a new look about him.

Judy still doesn't have much to say to me. She never spoke to anybody at all for a few weeks there. How could she, really, with that beautiful black eye the boyfriend had given her?

Source: Graham Calley, 'Mango juice', *Northern Perspective*, vol.8, no.2, 1985, pp.49-52.

Louvres

Les A. Murray

In the banana zone, in the poinciana tropics
reality is stacked on handsbreadth shelving,
open and shut, it is ruled across with lines
as in a gleaming gritty exercise book.

The world is seen through a cranked or levered
weatherboarding of explosive glass
angled floor-to-ceiling. Horizons which metre
the dazzling outdoors into green-edged couplets.

In the louvred latitudes
children fly to sleep in triplanes, and
cool nights are eerie with retracting flaps.

Their houses stand aloft among bougainvillea,
covered bridges that lead down a shining hall
from love to mystery to breakfast,
from babyhood to moving-out day

and visitors shimmer up in columnar gauges
to touch lives lived behind gauze
in a lantern of inventory,
slick vector geometries glossing the months of rain.

There, nudity is dizzily cubist, and directions
have to include: stage left, add an inch of breeze
or: enter a glistening tendril.

For drinkers under cyclonic pressure, such
a house can be a bridge of scythes —
groundlings scuffing by stop only for denouements.

But everyone comes out on platforms of command
to survey cloudy flame-trees, the plain of streets, the future:
only then descending to the level of affairs

and if these things are done in the green season
what to do in the crystalline dry? Well
below in the struts of laundry is the four-wheel drive

vehicle in which to make an expedition
to the bush, or as we now say, the Land,
the three quarters of our continent
set aside for mystic poetry.

Source: Les A. Murray, 'Louvres', published originally in the *Sydney Morning Herald*, 10 November 1984; and then in Murray, *The Daylight Moon*, Angus & Robertson, Sydney, 1987, p.20.

It has been difficult for any Northern Territory writer, trying to capture the Cyclone Tracy experience and its scale of devastation, to compete with the photographs taken on Christmas Day 1974.

Jacques Tati at the Darwin Hotel

Fay Zwicky

Bonjour, words! Tell me where I am!

A thousand miles from everywhere,
they say.

Palm-fringed patio,
a buzz of mauve, cerise,
a blaze of pink and gold and green,
cascades of luminous bouganvillea

and frangipanni fretworking
a weightless turquoise sky.

Mangoes drop their headlong smoothness
down the ropy vines, arched mangrove
roots, tangibles
unlimited.

'Minimum dress for this area will be
shirts, shorts, shoes, and long socks'

The trustful waitress leaves me juggling
tiny plastic rectangles of butter
marmalade, honey. I ferret clumsily
around the toast.

And there's the coast!

Improbable tall palms
a still metallic sea
and miles of sky …

People going out and coming in.
A boy is sweeping slowly up the path.

Here's a man with sideburns
short and chunky in his long white socks.
Determined.

He's carrying 2 large cases out.
The path is long, the greenery too frivolous.

And there's his wife. Her back is young and white
but she's not young. She limps to take a frontal shot.
They have to leave.

Her husband makes his second savage trip,
puts down the bags to help her with the light.
The boy is sweeping slowly.

It's hard so far away and she's unsure just where
the meter is. He shows her.
She snaps and snaps again. She's sorry
there's a satyr in the shrubbery
eating toast.

It won't be like the travel posters say
but after all a holiday's
a holiday.

Source: Fay Zwicky, 'Jacques Tati at the Darwin Hotel', *Northern Perspective*, vol.9, no.1, 1986, pp.80-81.

11 Adventures, incongruities, incredibilities

… but they are all true, they all happened.
— Mark Twain, *Following the Equator*, 1897

Previous page: Fred Blakeley, miner and general roustabout, set out in the Dry season of 1908 with two friends (the O'Neill brothers) to ride from White Cliffs, north-east of Broken Hill, to Darwin, a distance of 2200 miles. The party completed the journey in two and a half months, accompanied by Blakeley's dog, Jethro. In true Lawsonian tradition, it was Jethro, and his seemingly indestructible pads, who drew all the praise from awed Territorians. Blakeley depicted the party's adventures in Hard Liberty *(1938).*

Tjukurrpa: Puli kulpi kutjarra/
The two little round stones

Obed Raggett

Ula kutjarra anu, ngurra wanma. Angkula nyangu utuwari ngarrintjala. Punturringu kapitjarra, ngulurringu paluru kutjarra. Kapi puntulingku ngalyanu, mungarrtji.

Paluru kutjarra puli kaputu wiima kutjarra mantjinu, waningu. Waninytjalu puli paluru punturringu kulpitjarralpi ngarangu.

Paluru kutjarra tjarrparra ngarringu. Waru kutjarra kulpi palulu.

Tjintungka palya pakara anu. Anu nyangu, utuwari ngarrinytjala. Punturringu kapi puntulingku ngalyanu. Katirra yurringu puli panyapa.

Palunyangka kutjupa nyakula waningu. Kutjupa palunyalpi mantjinu, kapi ilarringu puntulingku, mungarrtji. Puli palunya putu waningu (uuu), waningu (uuuu), waningu (uuu) wiya kutu.

Watalpi kapingka ngalya pungkukatingu, ula palunya kutjarrata. Kapi kutjurringu mirri pungu palunya kutjarra, ngaatjangka. Puli kaputu kutjarra.

Two boys went out hunting; they went a long way. They saw some clouds coming up in the afternoon. The clouds got bigger and bigger with rain. The two boys were frightened by the clouds and the rain.

Picking up their two little stones, they threw them. When they threw them the stones got bigger and bigger. They got very big, and each stone had a cave in it.

The two boys went into the caves. One boy went into one cave, and the other boy went into the other cave. That night there was a big rain. Each boy built a fire inside his cave. They slept safely in those caves.

The next morning they woke up and they went out hunting. The rain had gone. They hunted and hunted, and then they saw some clouds coming up again. They became frightened because the clouds were so big. But the two boys still had their stones.

Next morning when they woke up, they picked up the two little stones and went on hunting. As they walked along they saw two other stones, two better-looking ones, so they changed stones. They threw away those two little stones they had been using before and they picked up the two new stones.

Then they saw more clouds coming up, and they saw that the rain was coming close. The two boys threw those two new stones so that they would grow bigger, but those two new stones didn't grow bigger. So the boys threw them again and again, waiting for those stones to save them. But those new stones didn't grow any bigger. When the rain came, it killed those two boys.

Source: Obed Raggett, *The Stories of Obed Raggett: English Pintubi Parallel Text*, Billy Marshall-Stoneking (ed.), Alternative Publishing Co-op., Sydney, 1980, pp.48-52.

A haunt of the jinkarras: A story of Central Australia

Ernest Favenc

In May, 1889, the dead body of a man was found on one of the tributaries of the Finke River, in the extreme North of South Australia [the Northern Territory was then part of South Australia]. The body, by all appearances, had been lying there some months and was accidentally discovered by some surveyors making a flying survey with camels. Amongst the few effects was a Lett's Diary containing the following narrative, which, although in many places almost illegible and much weather-stained, has been since, with some trouble, deciphered and transcribed by the surveyor in charge of the party ...

March 10, 1888. — Started out this morning with Jackson, who is the only survivor of a party of three who lost their horses on a dry stage when looking for country; he was found and cared for by the blacks, and finally made his way into the telegraph-line, where I picked him up when out with a repairing-party. Since then I got him a job on the station, and in return he has told me about the ruby-field of which we are now in search; thanks to the late thunder-storms we have as yet met with no obstacles to our progress. I have great faith in him as a bushman, but being a man without any education and naturally taciturn, he is not very lively company, and I find myself thrown on to the resource of a diary for amusement.

March 17. — Seven days since we left Charlotte Waters, and we are now approaching the country familiar to Jackson during his sojourn with the natives two years ago. He is confident that we shall gain the gorge in the M'Donnell Ranges to-morrow, early.

March 18. — Amongst the ranges, plenty of water, and Jackson has recognised several peaks in the near neighbourhood of the gorge, where he saw the rubies.

March 19. — Camped in Ruby Gorge, as I have named this pass, for we have come straight to the place and found the rubies without any hindrance at all. I have about twenty magnificent stones and hundreds of small ones; one of the stones in particular is almost living fire, and must be of great value. Jackson had no idea of the value of the find, except that it may be worth a few pounds, with which he will be quite satisfied. As there is good feed and water, and we have plenty of rations, will camp here for a day or two and spell the horses before returning.

March 20. — Been inspecting some caves in the ranges. One of them seems to penetrate a great distance — will go to-morrow with Jackson and take candles and examine it.

March 25. — Had a terrible experience the last four days. Why on earth did I not go back at once with the rubies? Now I may never get back. Jackson and I started to explore the cave early in the morning. We found nothing extraordinary about it for some time. As usual, there were numbers of bats, and here and there were marks of fire on the rocks, as though the natives had camped in it at times. After some search, Jackson discovered a passage which we followed down a steep incline for a long distance. As we got on we encountered a strong draught of air and had to be very careful of our candles. Suddenly the passage opened and we found ourselves in a low chamber in which we could scarcely stand upright. I looked hastily around, and saw a dark figure like a large monkey suddenly spring from a rock and disappear with what sounded like a splash. 'What on earth was that?' I said to Jackson. 'A jinkarra,' he replied, in his slow, stolid way. 'I heard about them from the blacks, they live underground.' 'What are they?' I asked. 'I couldn't make out,' he replied; 'the blacks talked about jinkarras, and made signs that they were underground, so I suppose that was one.'

We went over to the place where I had seen the figure and, as the air was now comparatively still and fresh, our candles burnt well and we could see plainly. The splash was no illusion, for an underground stream of some size ran through the chamber, and, on looking closer, in the sand on the floor of the cavern we could see tracks like those of human feet.

We sat down and had something to eat. The water was beautifully fresh and icily cold, and I tried to obtain from Jackson all he knew about the jinkarras. It was very little beyond what he had already told me. The natives spoke of them as something, animals or men, he could not make out which, living in the ranges underground. They used to frighten the children by crying out 'jinkarra!' to them at night.

The stream that flowed through the cavern was very sluggish and apparently not deep, as I could see the white sand at a distance under the rays of the candle; it disappeared beneath a rocky arch about two feet above its surface. Strange to say, when near this place I could detect a peculiar smell as of something burning, and this odour appeared to come through the arch. I drew Jackson's attention to it, and proposed wading down the channel of the stream if not too deep, but he suggested going back to camp first and getting more rations, which, being very reasonable, I agreed to.

It took us too long returning to camp to think of starting that day, but next morning we got away early and were soon beside the subterranean stream. The water was bitterly cold but not very deep, and we had provided ourselves with stout saplings as poles and had our revolvers and some rations strapped on our shoulders. It was an awful wade through the chilly water, our heads nearly touching the slimy top of the arch, our candles throwing a faint, flickering gleam on the surface of the stream. Fortunately the bottom was splendid — hard, smooth sand — and, after wading for about twenty minutes, we suddenly emerged into another cavern, but its extent we could not discern at first for our attention was taken up with other matters.

The air was laden with pungent smoke, the place illuminated with a score of smouldering fires, and tenanted by a crowd of the most hideous beings I ever saw. They espied us in an instant, and flew wildly about, jabbering frantically, until we were nearly deafened. Recovering ourselves, we waded out of the water, and tried to approach some of these creatures, but they hid away in the dark corners, and we could not lay hands on any of them. As well as we could make out in the murky light, they were human beings, but savages of the most degraded type, far below that of the common Australian blackfellow. They had long arms, shaggy heads of hair, small twinkling eyes, and were very low of stature. They kept up a confused jabber, half whistling, half chattering, and were utterly without clothes, paint, or any ornaments. I approached one of their fires, and found it to consist of a kind of peat or turf; some small bones of vermin were lying around, and a rude club or two. While gazing at these things I suddenly heard a piercing shriek, and, looking up, found that Jackson, by a sudden spring, had succeeded in capturing one of these creatures, who was struggling and uttering terrible yells. I went to his assistance, and together we succeeded in holding him still while we examined him by the light of our candles. The others, meanwhile, ceased their clamour and watched us curiously.

Never had I seen so repulsive a wretch as our prisoner. Apparently he was a young man about two or three and twenty, hardly five feet high at the outside, lean, with thin legs and long arms. He was trembling all over, and the perspiration dripped from him. He had scarcely any forehead, and a shaggy mass of hair crowned his head, and grew a long way down his spine. His eyes were small, red and bloodshot; I have often experienced the strong odour emitted by aborigines when heated or excited, but never did I meet with anything so offensive as the rank smell emanating from this being. Suddenly Jackson exclaimed: 'Look! look! he's got a tail!' I looked and nearly relaxed my grasp of the brute in surprise. There was no doubt about it, this strange being had about three inches of a monkey-like tail.

'Let's catch another,' I said to Jackson after the first emotion of surprise had passed. We looked around after sticking our candles upright in the sand. 'There's one in the corner,' muttered Jackson to me, and as soon as I saw the one he meant we released our prisoner and made simultaneous rush at the cowering form. We were successful, and when we dragged our captive to the light we found it to be a woman. Our curiosity was soon satisfied — the tail was the badge of the whole tribe, and we let our second captive go.

My first impulse was to go and rinse my hands in the stream, the contact had been so repulsive to me. It was the same with Jackson. I pondered what I should do. I had a great desire to take one of these singular beings back with me, and I thought with pride of the reputation I should gain as their discoverer. Then I reflected that I could always find them again, and it would be better to come back with a larger party after safely disposing of the rubies and securing the ground.

'There's no way out of this place,' I said to Jackson.

'Think not?' he replied.

'No,' I said, 'or these things would have cleared out; they must know every nook and cranny.'

'Umph!' he said, as though satisfied; 'shall we go back now?'

I was on the point of saying 'yes,' and had I done so all would have been well; but, unfortunately, some motive of infernal curiosity prompted me to say — 'No! let us have a look round first.' Lighting another candle each, so that we had plenty of light, we wandered round the cave, which was of considerable extent, the unclean inhabitants flitting before us with beast-like cries. Presently we had made a half-circuit of the cave and were approaching the stream, for we could hear a rushing sound as though it plunged over a fall. This noise grew louder, and now I noticed that all the natives had disappeared, and it struck me that they had retreated through the passage we had penetrated, which was now unguarded. Suddenly Jackson, who was ahead, exclaimed that there was a large opening. As he spoke he turned to enter it; I called out to him to be careful, but my voice was lost in a cry of alarm as he slipped, stumbled, and with a shriek of horror disappeared from my view. So sudden was the shock, and so awful my surroundings, that I sank down utterly unnerved, comprehending but one thing: that I was alone in this gruesome cavern inhabited by strange, unnatural creations.

After a while I braced myself up, and began to look about. Holding my candle aloft I crawled on my stomach to the spot whence my companion had disappeared. My hand touched a slippery decline; peering cautiously ahead I saw that the rocks sloped abruptly downwards, and were covered with slime, as though under water at times. One step on the treacherous surface and a man's doom was sealed — head-long into the unknown abyss he was bound to go, and this had been the fate of the unhappy Jackson. As I lay trembling on the edge of this fatal chasm, listening for the faintest sound from below, it struck me that the noise of the rushing water was both louder and nearer. I lay and listened. There was no doubt about it — the waters were rising. With a thrill of deadly horror it flashed across me that if the stream rose it would prevent my return, as I could not thread the subterranean passage under water. Rising hastily I hurried back to the upper end of the cavern, following the edge of the water. A glance assured me I was a prisoner — the flood was up to the top of the arch, and the stream much broader than when we entered. The rations and candles we had left carelessly on the sand had disappeared, covered by the rising water. I was alone, with nothing but about a candle and a-half between me and darkness and death.

I blew out the candle, threw myself on the sand and thought. I brought all my courage to bear on the prospect before me, so as not to let it daunt me. First, the natives had evidently retreated before the water rose too high, their fires were all out, and a dead silence reigned. I had the cavern to myself, which was better than their horrid company. Next, the rising was periodical, and evidently was the cause of the slimy, slippery rock which had robbed me of my only companion. I remembered instances in the interior where lagoons rose and fell at certain times without any visible cause. Then came the thought — for how long would the overflow continue? I had fresh air and plenty of water, and so I could live for days; probably the flood only lasted twelve or twenty-four hours. But an awful fear seized on me. Could I maintain my reason in this worse than Egyptian darkness — a darkness so thick, definite and overpowering that I cannot describe it, truly a darkness that could be felt? I had heard of men who could not endure twenty-four hours in a dark cell, but had clamoured to be taken out. Supposing my reason deserted me, and during some delirious interlude the stream rose and fell again!

These thoughts were too agonising. I rose and paced a step or two on the sand. I made a resolution during that short walk. I had matches — fortunately, with a bushman's instinct, I had put a box in my pouch when we started to investigate the cavern. I had a candle and a-half, and, thank Heaven! my watch. I would calculate four hours as nearly as possible, and every four hours I would strike a match and enjoy the luxury of a little light. I pursued this plan, and by doing so left that devilish pit with reason. It was sixty hours before the stream fell, and what I suffered during that time no tongue can tell, no brain imagine.

That awful darkness was at times peopled by forms that, for hideousness, no nightmare could surpass. Invisible, but still palpably present, they surrounded and sought to drive me down the chasm wherein my companion had fallen. The loathsome inhabitants of that cavern came back in fancy and gibbered and whistled around me. I could smell them — feel their sickening touch. If I slept I awoke from, perhaps, a pleasant dream to the stern fact that I was alone in darkness in the depth of the earth. When first I found that the water was receding was perhaps the hardest time of all, for my anxiety to leave the chamber tenanted by such phantoms was overpowering. But I resisted. I held to my will until I knew I could safely venture, and then waded slowly and determinedly up the stream; up the sloping passage, through the outer cave, and emerged in the light of day — the blessed, glorious light, with a wild shout of joy.

I must have fainted; when I came to myself I was still at the mouth of the cave, but now it was night, the bright, starlit, lonely, silent night of the Australian desert. I felt no hunger nor fear of the future; one delicious sense of rest and relief thrilled my whole being. I lay there watching the dearly-loved Austral constellations in simple, peaceful ecstasy. And then I slept, slept till the sun aroused me, and I arose and took my way to our deserted camp. A few crows arose and cawed defiantly at me, and the leather straps bore the marks of a dingo's teeth, otherwise the camp was untouched. I lit a fire, cooked a meal, ate, and rested once more. The reaction had set in after the intense strain I had endured, and I felt myself incapable of thinking or purposing anything. This state lasted for four-and-twenty hours — then I awoke to the fact that I had to find the horses, and make my way home alone — for, alas, as I bitterly thought, I was now, through my curiosity, alone, and, worst of all, the cause of my companion's death. Had I come away when he proposed, he would be alive, and I should have escaped the awful experience I have endured.

I have written this down while it is fresh in my memory; to morrow I start to look for the horses. If I reach the telegraph-line safely I will come back and follow up the discovery of this unknown race, the connecting and long-sought-for link; if not, somebody else may find this and follow up the clue. I have plotted out the course from Charlotte Waters here by dead-reckoning.

March 26th. — No sign of the horses. They have evidently made back. I will make up a light pack and follow them. If I do not overtake them I may be able to get on to the line on foot. The stages between the water-holes, on our way out were not very long, and I ought to manage it safely.

END OF THE DIARY

Note. — The surveyor, who is well-known in South Australia, adds the following postscript: —

The unfortunate man was identified as an operator on the overland line. He had been in the service a long time, and was very much liked. The facts about picking up Jackson when out with a repairing party have also been verified. The dead man had obtained six months' leave of absence, and it was supposed he had gone down to Adelaide. The tradition of the jinkarras is common among the natives of the M'Donnell Range. I have often heard it. No rubies or anything of value were found on the body.

Source: Ernest Favenc, *The Last of Six: Tales of the Australian Tropics* (the Bulletin series, no.3), Bulletin Newspaper Co., Sydney, 1893, pp.19-28.

Victoria Theatre, 1839

John Lort Stokes

A breeze springing up late in the morning, we beat along the north side of the Coburg Peninsula, entering Port Essington at dusk. In working round Vashon Head, we found the water shoal very rapidly to 12, 9, and 7 fathoms on approaching it; on the bearing S. 30° W. This head is fronted by a reef of some extent, which similar to the other at the entrance of Port Essington, cannot be distinguished, owing to the muddy colour of the water; it is therefore necessary that the lead should be kept constantly going when in its vicinity. When daylight broke, we found no fresh arrival to greet our anxious gaze, the Britomart being still the only guardian of the port. Her solitary aspect at once destroyed our hopes of supplies, and on reaching the settlement our fears proved to have too much foundation. Hope, however, is the last feeling which leaves the human breast, and in this instance did not desert us; as there was still a chance of a vessel arriving, while we were engaged in watering the ship.

Harden S. Melville's sketch of Port Essington. Melville was the official artist aboard H.M.S. Fly, *one of several ships used by the Royal Navy to chart Australian waters between 1837 and 1850. John Sweatman used the illustration in his* Journal *(1845–47), as did J. Beete Jukes in his* Narrative of the Surveying Voyage of H.M.S. Fly, 1942–1846 *(1847).*

The news of our discovery of the Adelaide was hailed with infinite satisfaction, and the numerous speculations and ideas on the subject which were at once afloat, afforded an agreeable variety to the monotony of existence in the settlement, where however at the moment of our arrival an unusual degree of excitement prevailed through the activity of Captain Stanley. Ever anxious to provide for the amusement of others, he had been for some time engaged in getting up a play, which was now nearly ready to be performed. Its name I regret to have forgotten; it was however nothing very deep, and was selected from a volume that had already performed a voyage to the North Pole. This adventurous play book, which had certainly done its duty, was originally picked up by its owner on Tower-hill. The scenery was painted by Captain Stanley with earths of the country, who also was stage manager and general planner of the whole. The wives of some of the garrison supplied female costumes, while a large workshop was converted into a theatre. At length, after the difficulties usually attendant on private theatricals, every thing was in readiness for the first performance of the drama in Northern Australia. Tickets were issued, of which I have one before me, a small piece of card containing the words — 'Victoria Theatre, Port Essington, August 24th, 1839.' In after years this will be looked upon as a curious relic in connection with the history of this part of the continent. As if to cause the first performance of a play at Victoria, to take place under smiling auspices, such as the occasion properly called for, H.M.S. Pelorus arrived with supplies and letters from Sydney. The previous growing dearth of provisions had rendered it somewhat difficult to secure a very happily disposed audience, an empty stomach being apt to provoke fault finding; but the arrival of a ship on the very play day caused a crowded and delighted attendance. Every thing went off smoothly, and with hearty peals of laughter. All the characters being supported by men, the female personages of the drama presented a most grotesque appearance; moreover the 'act drop' being an old ensign, the ladies could be seen through it, regaling themselves, during these intervals, with a pipe. The whole affair gave infinite satisfaction, while ours was greatly enhanced, and our minds prepared for any duty, by the timely arrival of supplies and letters, of both of which we fortunately received our share.

Source: John Lort Stokes, *Discoveries in Australia, with an Account of the Coasts and Rivers Explored During the Voyage of the HMS Beagle in the Years 1837-43*, vol.1, T. & W. Boone, London, 1846, pp.432-4.

Camp life, Port Darwin, 1870

Mrs Dominic D. Daly

The first thing we turned our attention to after landing was to arrange our small quarters in the most comfortable manner and to make them as homelike as possible. The huts were very rough, and it was only by dint of management that we fitted into them at all. The sleeping apartments were in a large log hut divided by partitions. The spaces between the poles were plugged with 'paper' bark — a species of gum tree whose bark is nearly white, and peels off in loose flakes; our roof was of bark also; indeed this material was called into requisition very freely throughout the settlement. The ironbark trees are 'rung' at a certain height top and bottom, and the bark detached in one sheet; it is then wetted, and laid out flat on the ground, huge stones being placed to keep it from rolling up again. This was laid on the framework of the roof when it was ready for use, and then saplings were laid across and lashed down so as to prevent it blowing off in a sudden squall. The floor of our hut was made of mud, pressed flat, and mixed with gravel, sand and limestone, well rolled till a smooth surface was obtained. Glass windows were unknown — our windows were frames filled with unbleached calico, and they swung on a pivot, propped open by a stick which was fitted for the purpose. The floor was a great trial of patience, for every clean dress we put on became soiled round the edges immediately. We had only one sitting-room, which was joined to the sleeping apartments by a covered way. This was a galvanised iron hut, about twenty feet long, lined with deal and possessing the luxury of a wooden floor; its windows were sheets of iron propped open in the usual way; there was a door at each end, and we habitually sat in a draught for the sake of air. The iron roof was shaded by bark, but it was a very hot room at any time. We arranged our furniture here to the best advantage, but owing to the incongruous medley, the room reminded me of nothing so forcibly as a broker's shop — chests of drawers, sideboards, chiffoniers, tables of every description and shape elbowed each other, seeming as lost as we were at the strange and novel associations in which they found themselves.

After a time we got things into some degree of order, and became so used to living in this cramped space that it seemed wonderful we ever wished for anything larger. We made a verandah, which added greatly to our comfort, by means of saplings fixed in the ground, and covered with a canvas awning. Here we spent the greater part of our time; a table and all the most comfortable chairs were put here; it quite answered the purpose of an extra sitting-room, and was by far the most favoured resort of our small quarters. Here in the evening the gentlemen smoked pipes or cigars, yarns were spun, and discussions on every topic of interest took place in spite of occasional onslaughts from sandflies and mosquitoes.

The camp had a great love for music. Nearly all the men played the concertina, some were flute-players. And surely they all sang! for night after night when work was over they assembled under a shady tree in the middle of the camp, and a regular musical entertainment took place. Each man sang his song, either accompanying himself with his own concertina, or enlisting the services of a chum for this purpose. I could almost give a list of the favourite camp melodies. 'Wait for the Turn of the Tide' was very popular. The fact of 'Rome not being Built in a Day, my Boys' seemed to encourage their efforts in developing the Northern Territory. 'Paddle your own Canoe' was another favourite song, the chorus always taken up lustily by the company; besides the more sentimental ballads of 'When other Lips,' 'Her bright Smile haunts me still,' and 'Ever of Thee.' These were generally sung by a police trooper who owned a fine tenor voice. It sounded quite pretty coming through the stillness of the night; the only other sound to be heard was the washing of the waves over the shingle at our feet, or the wind rustling through the slender leaves of a clump of corkscrew palms. Some of the men spent the evening in walking round Fort Point, the only promenade the camp possessed. A pathway had been made here by cutting down a portion of the hill, and levelling the ground at its base. It was a pretty walk, as one had the sea on one's right all the way round, and a fine view of the south and east arms of the harbour could be gained from here.

The delight of the community knew no bounds when we used our piano for the first time. N. had a lovely clear soprano voice, and when she began some of her favourite songs, such as 'Bid me Discourse,' and 'Oft in the stilly Night,' a crowd collected round the house, which only dispersed when we had gone through our entire repertoire of songs and duets.

I shall never forget the astonishment of the Larrakiahs when they saw the piano for the the first time. They could not understand where the sound came from, and were not satisfied till I had opened the instrument and shown them its internal economy; the little white hammers that touched the strings each time I struck the keys amused them immensely. They liked music, and often asked us to play to them.

Source: Mrs Dominic D. Daly, *Digging, Squatting and Pioneering Life in the Northern Territory of South Australia*, Sampson Low, Marston, Searle & Rivington, London, 1887, pp.50-53.

Christmas Day, 1873

Ernest Giles

And now comes Thursday, 25th December, Christmas Day, 1873. Ah, how the time flies! Years following years, steal something every day; at last they steal us from ourselves away. What Horace says is, Eheu fugaces, anni labuntur postume, postume: —Years glide away, and are lost to me, lost to me.

While Jimmy Andrews was away after the others, upon the horse that was tied up all night, we were startled out of our propriety by the howls and yells of a pack of fiends in human form and aboriginal appearance, who had clambered up the rocks just above our camp. I could only see some ten or a dozen in the front, but scores more were dodging in and out among the rocks. The more prominent throng were led by an ancient individual, who, having fitted a spear, was just in the act of throwing it down amongst us, when Gibson seized a rifle, and presented him with a conical Christmas box, which smote the rocks with such force, and in such near proximity to his hinder parts, that in a great measure it checked his fiery ardour, and induced most of his more timorous following to climb with most perturbed activity over the rocks. The ancient more slowly followed, and then from behind the fastness of his rocky shield, he spoke spears and boomerangs to us, though he used none. He, however, poured out the vials of his wrath upon us, as he probably thought to some purpose. I was not linguist enough to be able to translate all he said; but I am sure my free interpretation of the gist of his remarks is correct, for he undoubtedly stigmatised us as a vile and useless set of lazy, crawling, white-faced wretches, who came sitting on hideous brutes of hippogryphs, being too lazy to walk like black men, and took upon ourselves the right to occupy any country or waters we might chance to find; that we killed and ate any wallabies and other game we happened to see, thereby depriving him and his friends of their natural, lawful food, and that our conduct had so incensed himself and his noble friends, who were now in the shelter of the rocks near him, that he begged us to take warning that it was the unanimous determination of himself and his noble friends to destroy such vermin as he considered us, and our horses to be, and drive us from the face of the earth.

It appeared to me, however, that his harangue required punctuation, so I showed him the rifle again, whereupon he incontinently indulged in a full stop. The natives then retired from those rocks, and commenced their attack by throwing spears through the teatree from the opposite side of the creek. Here we had the back of our gunyah for a shield, and could poke the muzzles of our guns and rifles through the interstices of the boughs. We were compelled to discharge our pieces at them to ensure our peace and safety.

Our last discharge drove away the enemy, and soon after, Jimmy came with all the horses. Gibson shot a wallaby, and we had fried chops for our Christmas dinner. We drew from the medical department a bottle of rum to celebrate Christmas and victory. We had an excellent dinner (for explorers), although we had eaten our Christmas pudding two days before. We perhaps had no occasion to envy any one their Christmas dinner, although perhaps we did. Thermometer 106° in the shade. On this occasion Mr. Tietkens, who was almost a professional, sang us some songs in a fine, deep, clear voice, and Gibson sang two or three love songs, not altogether badly; then it was Jimmy's turn. He said he didn't know no love songs, but he would give us Tommy or Paddy Brennan. This gentleman appears to have started in business as a highwayman in the romantic mountains of Limerick. One verse that Jimmy gave, and which pleased us most, because we couldn't quite understand it, was: —

> 'It was in sweet Limerick (er) citty [sic]
> That he left his mother dear;
> And in the Limerick (er) mountains,
> He commenced his wild caroo-oo.'

Upon our inquiring what a caroo was, Jimmy said he didn't know. No doubt it was something very desperate, and we considered we were perhaps upon a bit of a wild caroo ourselves.

Source: Ernest Giles, *Australia Twice Traversed: The Romance of Exploration, from 1872 to 1876*, Sampson Low, Marston, Searle & Rivington, London, 1889, pp.249-52.

Christmas, 1901

F. J. Gillen

23 December 1901. — We have been up nearly all night. A most anxious time. Chance was bitten on the leg by some poisonous reptile, probably a large centipede, about 9 o'clock yesterday evening when on his way home from the Police Station. We at once rubbed in some sal volatile but it was not strong enough to counteract the poison; in a few minutes the leg began to swell and in an hour after the poor old geezer was in agony and continued suffering horribly all night. We administered laudanum to deaden the pain. His sufferings continued until 10 a.m. when happily he dosed off and had an hour or two of broken rest. By noon the pain had become much modified and in the afternoon he had a refreshing sleep. Chance did not see the reptile and we were not at all sure that he had not been bitten by a snake and for some hours we were very anxious about him. At dawn I lay down and dosing off dreamt that he was dead, that I was writing a note breaking the news to his wife and that Spencer was packing his things in a box, a horrible dream and I awoke in a cold perspiration and was relieved to hear his pitiful groans.

Borroloola has been enjoying its dear little self — two court cases 1 assault the other abusive language all residents but one interested in the cases. These people do enjoy a court case. Hang them I wish they'd hold over their differences till we have gone. I am reading Meredith's 'The Amazing Marriage' a very clever book, high class literature, just a little too high to be thoroughly appreciated or understood by my modest mental capacities.

In the evening the old geezer is able to limp about. We are delighted to see him on the move again. Thunderstorm with 27 points rain during the afternoon. Mail due tomorrow. Tis weary work waiting here for news of the Steamer.

24 December 1901. — A cool night — that is cool for Borroloola and we awake comparatively fresh. I finish 'The Amazing Marriage' and am disgusted with its ending. It appears to me that the best modern writers destroy much of the best work by making their stories end unhappily.

Personally I prefer the old style of story in which the villain either met his deserts or repented in sack cloth and ashes and everybody else married and lived happily ever after. I think the present generation of writers lose sight of the fact that people mostly read novels to be amused or as a pleasant means of passing the time and not, as many of them appear to think, judging by the ending of their stories, merely to be depressed. Bah I'd like to wring Meredith's neck much as I admire his genius. Chance about again but very limpy and looking rather washed out. Thunderstorm with a few 6 points of rain in afternoon. Mail due tonight not arrived. Traveller arrived today reports that in all probability there is now a dry stage of 80 miles between Top Camp and Anthony's Lagoon, if this be true the Lord only knows when we shall get a mail. Cheerful.

25 December 1901. — A Merry Christmas to you my diary and to all the loved ones who may read your pages. The day begins dull overcast and threatening but cool. Nothing more unlike Christmas could well be imagined. We wish each other a Merry Christmas about every half hour just by way of reminder that it is the festive season. Spencer and I think of our kiddies and fervently wish that we could be with them to participate in the enjoyment of their presents. We breakfast off lean, oh! so lean, steak and afterwards watch Chance preparing a leaner chicken (its about 7 years old really but we call it a chicken) for the midday banquet. We admire the development of the breast bone and agree that it is abnormal rather than admit that its prominence is due to the absence of flesh on the bones. A Merry Christmas by my halidom oh my diary! The blacks brought up a poisonous snake a curious looking beast quite new to us its body being covered with short spines.

After dinner — I apologise to the fowl I retract everything and cheerfully admit that it is a chicken a young tender tasty succulent, juicy delicious though not fleshy bird. Washed down with a bottle of cool Walkerville ale it was a feast not to be despised. The pudding well it was a failure the old geezer allowed the water to get into it and when it emerged from the pot it was merely a moist squash and the niggers are now being regaled upon it. We are invited to Christmas dinner at the Police Station this evening. 10 p.m. we have dined sumptuously never was there seen such a spread at far Borroloola the dinner party numbered six there was food enough prepared for 18. It gladdened us to see a white clean tablecloth with serviettes once more. The menu consisted of soup, roast fowls, beef, mutton, three sorts of vegetables, plum duff, blancmange with tinned fruits, cake, watermelon, mangoes, bottled ale, Lager and English wine and whisky followed by coffee and cigars.

The party assembled at the Police Station arrayed in their best. Spencer gorgeous. Too hot to wear coats so at a mild hint from us our host bid us hang up our coats. A pleasant evening was spent spinning yarns. Some of McLeod's stories about the early days of Borroloola are well worth preserving. The gardener whose premises are about 3/4 of a mile outside the town also gave a Christmas dinner to which he invited several travellers, men out of work who happened to be in the Town. Great preparations were made for this dinner and three cases of beer were laid in. The guests numbered 7 or 8. The dinner I understand passed off very well but about 4 o'clock in the afternoon things became a bit mixed and the harmony of the proceedings was abruptly broken up by the host, now comfortably drunk, running amuck at his guests. He fought with one and challenged others and the guests in various stages of intoxication were to be seen wending their ways unsteadily in all directions until mine Host was left alone in his glory.

So endeth the record of my Christmas of 1901.

Source: *Gillen's Diary: Camp Jottings of F.J. Gillen on the Spencer and Gillen Expedition Across Australia 1901-1902*, Libraries Board of South Australia, Adelaide, 1968, pp.348-51.

Christmas, 1930

W. E. (Bill) Harney

[A]s a gesture of goodwill I told my mates that Linda [Harney's wife] and I expected them all for Christmas dinner the next day.

That Christmas dinner was one to remember. Instead of one cook steaming over an open bush fire we all helped with the meal. Charlie sent up some roosters and they, with a wild turkey, we cooked in a ground oven, blackfellow fashion. The vegetables came from the garden of the cattle station and the whopper plum-duff which Linda cooked in a large cast-iron camp oven on the open fire was a real beauty.

Puddin supplied a bottle of beer for all the guests and, as we had no refrigerators in those days, we cooled them down with wet corn sacks hung beneath the shady whitewood trees. The meal was a cracker success as we toasted each other and ate up big.

The day was hot, but we did not mind. Out on the red ridges a mirage had the trees floating in the air upon its mirror-like surface, and materialising out of it as people from another world came some of Linda's relations with their children and dogs to share in the feast.

One elderly black woman called Fanny, who claimed she was a sort of half-grandmother to our children, always hovered around our camp as a sort of protective covering for the kiddies, whom she really loved, and to her went a big helping of the day's cheer. She was a garrulous old soul and repeatedly displayed a grubby-looking bandage tied around her hand.

Puddin unfortunately asked her what was wrong, and immediately she was off talking about her tribal affairs and about a fight she had got into with another old dame a few weeks before. 'We been fight for nothing,' she declared. 'That old woman been breakem my finger so I been tie finger with rag to keep out blow-fly ... too many maggot.'

'A nice Christmas conversation,' said one of our guests.

Puddin foolishly asked her about the finger, so off came the dirty piece of rag for everybody to inspect her finger, which looked like a black hunk of greenhide ready to fall off.

Puddin became all professional as he watched Fanny twiddle the dried finger, and remarked, 'No more long-time it fall off properly way.'

'Him too much humbug,' grumbled Fanny as she pointed to the offending member, 'more better cut off this one bone.' She pointed to a piece of dried bone that protruded from the healed part of the finger. 'Him only rubbish one.'

Puddin became all professional and remarked, 'Only a minor operation ... has anyone got a pair of bolt-cutters?'

Linda mentioned an old pair we had in the tool box, so out they came, and as Fanny nonchalantly looked on, the tinker inserted the dried bone between the cutter's jaws close to the flesh. I heard a snap, and the deed was done.

'Properly good one,' commented Fanny as she buried the discarded piece of bone with her foot and went on with her second serving of plum-duff.

The incident had us all talking about doctors and their cures. I inadvertently mentioned the name of one doctor and was rebuked by a chap called 'Cordwood Joe' that 'he couldn't arse-gut a possum'. To prove his point, Cordwood Joe went on with a long-winded tale of how that doctor could not cure him of a sickness that was fixed up by a Chinese herbalist in a few days.

The possum story had Puddin telling us about a hypochondriacal bush lad that was about to go to the local doctor to be operated for haemorrhoids. 'We could hear him groaning away in the next bedroom of the local pub about his complaints. We got a real gut-full of him ... knowing he'd be listening to what we had to say me mate give him the works.

' "A simple operation," he told me with a wink in his eye and a nod towards the next room. "I had me piles cut out and all the doc did was put a gadget thing like an umbrella inter the grummet. When it takes a hook the doc pulls yer gut out just like yer do when dressing a sheep. When he gets the infected part out he puts a clip thing like a clothes-peg around yer gut to stop it from fallin' inside, then with a pair of scissors ... snip ... snip ... out come the infected part which he tosses away. Then he sews the good part on to the grummet and yer as good as new again.'

'What happened to the sick bloke?' I inquired.

'Off to the scrub next day.'

To many people this sort of conversation at a mixed table would cause surprise, but Linda laughed with the rest and I certainly did not care: we were above prudery and a good yarn well told was always welcome. To me the best stories in the bush are those which cannot be printed. Linda often warned me that if she happened to be in bed and my mates visited our camp, to stress on them that she was fast asleep. By doing that she would be on to the taboo tales from the storytellers, but I never noticed that any of the tales were filthy and nobody swore when they suspected a woman to be in the camp.

So that Christmas we yarned on till the cool of the evening, when we moved away from the tent shade into the open air, and as we did Cordwood Joe — so called because he was a number-one axeman — gave us a display with his 'blades'. He always carried these in his swag and kept them clean and as sharp as a razor. Now shirtless, he stood up and held them as one does a set of clubs. He commenced to whistle a tune and as he did so the blades flashed as he twirled them with perfect rhythm. Linda's face was alight with amazement and I could have cried with happiness and cursed at the same time to think that Cordwood was on the lam. He swung the blades with quiet content and I am sure he was doing that to thank us and his Maker with this sort of prayer. When he had finished Puddin muttered a soft 'Amen' and Linda breathed with relief after considering what might have happened if Cordwood had blundered with those whirling blades of steel.

To me Christmas Day is a time when everybody seems to be content and at peace with the World. Old friends are remembered and deceased ones brought to life again as a sort of re-incarnation. As a gift to Linda, Puddin pulled out of a sack a hand-wrought baby bath made from strong galvanised iron; of all the gifts I have ever known I still think of that simple token of friendship which made Linda so happy.

Then as night fell we sat in the circle of light made by the camp fire and sang old-time tunes. Some newly arrived foot-sore swagmen who were on the lam and seeking work came up to share the remnants of our dinner. Telling us about their adventures and their hungry days, I just could not reconcile those sordid facts with this great day of Christ's birth.

The stars shone bright that night and out of the Aboriginal camps came the chanting and beating of tap-sticks. It was a night of good-will to all men. I looked upon the face of the new arrivals. They were Australians and tough men. They had come a long way to here, but they had one hundred and eighty miles without human habitation for the next leg of their journey. I thought of Lawson's poem 'When time meant tucker and tramp you must where the plains are far and wide'.

One of the footsore men was a returned soldier who had won a D.C.M. His face was hard and bitter as he told us all about Marxism and the workers losing their chains in the future. After bidding us 'Goodnight' I heard them singing a strange song as they moved through the night. It was a parody on a hymn and it told all of how

> 'Long-haired preachers come out every night,
> Try to teach us what's wrong and what's right;
> But when asked about something to eat,
> They will answer in voices ever so sweet.

> You will eat bye and bye,
> In that glorious land above the sky;
> Work and pray, live on hay,
> You'll get pie in the sky when you die.'

    I too had been to the war and I too had seen the servants of the Lord eat and drink with the bosses in the officers' mess.
    Yet the song those swaggies sung that Christmas night was a warning to us all that the depression and the dole was here in the Northern Territory.

Source: 'Christmas, 1930', from W. E. (Bill) Harney, *Grief, Gaiety and Aborigines,* Rigby, Adelaide, 1961, pp.29-32.

Playing cricket, 1908

Fred Blakeley

Dick and I wanted a game of cricket, and as only two other white players were available we made up our elevens with two whites apiece, and a mixed team of young Chinamen and Aboriginals to complete them. We let the Chinamen use bats, but the Abos had to play with round green sticks, for they were mighty hitters, and unless caught they were not to be got out, for they never missed a ball.
    The game would start with Abos complete in shirt and pants, but as the excitement of the game commenced their clothes came off, and you could tell its stages by their approach to nakedness.
    The captains had a difficult job. They required an interpreter for both Chinese and Aboriginal, and had to umpire the game as well as captain their own teams, getting instructions and decisions translated as well as might be. Most of the umpire's work fell on Dick, for if the opposing captain-umpire gave a decision that was not popular both teams would appeal to Dick, and whatever he might say was final. In this way it was gradually established that Dick was umpire for both sides, and as he was the best bat too, and liked to have his innings, the position sometimes grew embarrassing.
    One day he ran the other batsman out. The latter was a Chinaman and our best scorer, like lightning between wickets; so when he topped a ball downfield Dick called, but not before he was himself half-way up the pitch. The Chinaman ran, but before he had got half-way an Abo had gathered up the ball and sent the stumps flying. Then there was a great to-do. Dick would not give him out, but tried to explain it was his fault and not the Chinaman's. This had to be translated for the benefit of Chinese and Aboriginals, and between the yabber of the interpreters and the yabber of the players, black and yellow, we nearly died. After about twenty minutes we got the game going again, and with the strike to Dick, who, as he was still laughing, fell easy victim to the next ball.
    Dick looked rather fine on these occasions, with his crash suit, pith helmet, and cigar almost a foot long always stuck in his mouth. The Chinamen provided a canvas deck-chair for him, and he used to sit under the shade of a tree outside the boundary and give his decisions from there. Sometimes he was obliged to go over to the wicket and take the stick from an Abo who would not accept a judgment and go out. The Abos looked so much alike that it was hard to distinguish, and Dick made no effort to do so, but would simply hand the stick to anybody near, and wasn't there a roar if he happened to give it to a fieldsman from the opposing side! As for the fellow who had refused to go out, he was quite satisfied if Dick

would put him on fielding, for all the Abos hated sitting down waiting their turn to bat.

The only way we could tell who was who was by chalking a number on their backs. Some were marked B. These only bowled, and seldom got a bat if ever. It was of no use to call 'Over,' for they thought we meant them to go and bowl from the other end, so the only way for an umpire to change the bowling was to give the ball to some one else. Then he must take the previous bowler by the arm and lead him to a place on the field.

No white player ever chased a ball. We bowled sometimes, but it was better fun to watch the Abos, and when we were batting we took fine care that none of their half-throws hit us, for often I would not see the ball, and, as pretty well everything was on the wicket, if one got by it generally ended the innings. The Natives would dance with joy whenever they got a player out.

The five or six Chinamen surprised us after a time, for they took to the game and practised every evening, and as there were some good cabinet-makers in Chinatown we were never without a fine supply of bats made from native timbers and fixed, of course, to the old handles.

Every Sunday brought a match, and picking the sides was a pantomime in itself, because the players of the previous week refused to be dropped. If allowed to field, however, they made no objection if they never got the bat, so there was no fixed number on a side. The fielding was great. Even if there were but eleven in the field it was difficult to get runs, but sometimes we had nearly fifty fielding, and then, I can tell you, runs were seldom got.

We had a marvellous wicket-keeper, the smartest thing I ever saw. He seemed to pluck those fast balls from the air as though he took them from a table, and he stood right up to the stumps. His anticipation was remarkable. If one of the white players tried a late cut this Aboriginal would be there before him, and, shooting his long arm out fully two feet, would take the ball before the batsman had a chance of glancing it. If a man snicked a ball he was gone a million, for I don't remember when a catch was missed. This chap was always naked when he played, and I think that even that daring fellow Oldfield might have turned green with envy had he watched that wicket-keeper. He kept wicket for both teams, for it was impossible to make him understand a difference between the sides. He never got a bat. His job was wicket-keeping, and he would not let anybody take that job from him.

There was a good all-rounder Chinaman, the only one, in fact, who ever made fifty runs. He bowled an under-arm spin ball, and I have seen some of his slow ones stop and spin before going forward, but though he tricked the Abos for a time, I do not remember any one of them to get his stumps knocked down. These Abos, with their round green sticks, were severe on cricket balls, and we needed a new one for each match.

These fellows were like lightning in the field, never afraid of the fastest ball, and rarely using both hands for a catch. If an Abo took an exceptionally good catch we would give him a white stripe across the chest with a piece of chalk, and of this he was very proud. I can assure you that if a ball were lofted three feet from the ground some Abo got a stripe. It was funny at times to see them, in their eagerness, crowding the batsman, eager to snatch the ball as it left his bat. Sometimes we had to stop the game and make them all withdraw to their proper places, but the rearrangement did not last long, for in a few overs they were back again. An over consisted of twenty to fifty balls, for it was easier to let them bowl on than to argue with them. We might call them all kinds of names, but they did not mind, perhaps because they did not understand us.

The audience was worth watching.

The whole population of Chinatown would come to see the match, for they were keen cricketers, and the Abo camp would be there in a body. I have already mentioned that the Natives started play with something on them in the shape of clothes, and that these were discarded as excitement grew, but I have not told you that this form of enthusiasm communicated itself to the Native audience outside the boundary, and that the women cast away their garments in a sort of ecstasy of barracking. As the game grew hot their hope of boundary balls grew high, and it was always 'stacks on the mill' when a ball was lifted over the boundary; *lifted* I say, because it was almost impossible to hit one there along the ground.

There were never any dull patches in those games. They were full of exciting incidents. We never succeeded in making the Abos realize that 'over the boundary is six,' and they would run out everything. This feature of the game was made more lively by the fact that at one end of the ground was a large water-hole, and when a ball was knocked into the water the batsmen ran on steadily. Such a ball was considered fair game by all the Abos — players and audience. Sometimes there would be twenty to thirty men and women diving and splashing in a struggle to be the first to get the ball, while the field was deserted by all players except the two batsmen, who ran diligently between the wickets.

If one could reproduce the scene on the cricket ground in Sydney or in Melbourne, what a grand day it would be!

Source: Fred Blakeley, *Hard Liberty*, George G. Harrap & Co., London, 1938, pp.265-9.

Eating with cannibals

Herbert Basedow

I vividly [remember] an occasion when I was traversing Berringin tribal ground, east of the Fitzmaurice River in North Australia, and was one evening by accident thrown into the company of a group of natives who were in possession of a corpse. Whether this man had fallen in a fight or had died from natural causes I never was able to ascertain. The body was lying on a bed of leafy branches in a small cleared quadrangular space surrounded by six or seven crude bark shelters.

Having made camp a few hundred yards away, hobbled my horses and prepared for the night, I ate a humble meal. My curiosity was aroused by the unusual activity of my newly made neighbors at so late an hour; so I walked across to a group of them who were seated around a fire on the near side of the quadrangle. They were a wild-looking lot, and did not seem to take kindly to my presence. I gave to each a few boiled sweets, which they accepted but retained in their hands. I then tried to draw them into conversation, but with rather discouraging results. They could not speak a word of English, and I knew nothing of their dialect; but while I tried to make myself understood they frequently exchanged a sentence or two with other men who were seated on the opposite side of the quadrangle.

In stepping across from my camp to theirs I had noticed a powerful odor of cooking meat; and, not suspecting its gruesome origin, had thought to myself that it was quite appetising. Then I saw that those opposite were eating — or, I might say, heard they were eating, for there was no mistaking the noise of munching.

I realised that my presence was embarrassing to the little group in front of me, and went across to those who were participating in what appeared to be an official banquet. Imagine my horror when I observed that they were consuming human flesh! The smell here was overpowering — beefy, sweet, gamey, sickly; it is difficult to define it.

The corpse had been removed from its leafy bier, and before me, in the centre of the group of some fifteen men, was the unquestionable evidence of crude surgical dissection. Two or three joints of cooked human meat lay on the ground, and from them the party had cut or pulled strips to feast upon. Close by was a partly uncovered oven from which the meat had been taken; from the part still covered with hot sand and ashes little puffs of steam and smoke, shooting upwards, indicated that more pieces were being cooked. No trace of the corpse was visible, and I wondered whether it had all been quartered. This was, of course, hardly likely, but what they had done with the mutilated carcass remained a mystery. It is of course possible that they had carried it away soon after my arrival early in the evening. The atmosphere was reeking with an odor which by then had become nauseating to me. Yet, under conditions somewhat unfriendly and strained, I thought it would not be politic to make known my feelings of disgust.

I repeated my usual peace-offerings, handing them sweets and other little gifts. This benevolence brought about a crisis which was not only tense but fraught with disastrous possibilities; for one of the men in response rose to his feet, grabbed a chunk of the steaming meat and handed it to me!

The fellow looked so savagely at me that, before I knew what had happened, the ghastly gift was in my possession. I dared not throw it away, for that would have amounted to an open declaration of hostilities; nor could I have returned it to the donor, because that would have been regarded as a discourtesy no less significant. I could not run the risk of insulting these people; they had a bad reputation, and I had only two attendants with me, one a half-caste, the other a full-blooded boy from the Port Darwin district.

What was I to do? All eyes were upon me. I knew very well what they were implying. The party expected me to sit and eat with them. As they waited, the old man who had presented me with the morsel delivered a touching oration. The proceedings altogether amounted to a solemn funeral rite. Only able-bodied men were participating in the meal. At a little distance were a few old men, women and children who were cowering about the bark shelters without even venturing to steal a glance at the celebrants. The greater, I realised, was the compliment paid to me, individually, as one worthy to do homage to the spirit of the dead.

One can afford to laugh after nearly thirty years have passed. If I looked anything like I felt, I must have looked queer. But at the time there were no two ways about it; our safety was at stake. We were separated from the outposts of civilisation by some two hundred miles, and against the numbers around us we were powerless. I thought of the old German proverb which obliges the Devil to eat flies! The easiest way out of the difficulty was obviously to partake of the awful repast. In my dilemma I even weighed the wisdom of resorting to this extreme measure. It would be better to eat human flesh under coercion than be eaten myself. If I fell, it was more than likely that I would be eaten, because I had established quite a reputation among the tribes as a fairly accurate marksman, a virtue which might be considered well worthy of acquiring by so simple a method. Again, I thought it might be a unique experience, unpleasant though it seemed, to be in a position to fathom the palate of a cannibal-connoisseur. Thus I meditated, all during the flash of a single moment, and looked at the chunk in my hand. It resembled a piece of undercooked veal, pink, shreddy and grained. I shuddered at the idea of carrying the thought into effect.

An inspiration came to help me. Making respectful gestures, I indicated to the warriors that I would do honor to the departed at my own campfire. I took a chance, for, whether they were agreeable or not, I turned my back on them and walked away.

Source: Herbert Basedow, *Knights of the Boomerang*, Endeavour Press, Sydney, 1935, pp.224-9.

The story of Kurnki

Tutama Tjapangarti

There was this bloke called Kurnki;[1] and a German; and Tjukarnku. There were three of them, all white men. Kurnki was the boss. Kurnki was no good; he used to shoot Aboriginal people and eat them. Poor fellas. Kurnki was a cheeky bugger. He'd cut them up and cook them in a bucket. This was before a lot of whitefellas came here [to Central Australia].

Kurnki, the German and Tjukarnku were travelling with a big mob of camels, maybe 10 in all. That was the first time I saw tracks, camel tracks. I was camped at Purtjanya.[2]

One morning I was out hunting for *kuka*, meat. I was getting a lot of goanna. That's when I saw those tracks the first time. 'Tjurilku!'[3] What's this?' I said.

I climbed up a hill to have a look, then I saw them — that big mob of camels. And those three white men were there, putting chains on the camels, hobbling them. All the camels, big mob: tie 'em up, tie 'em up, tie 'em up…!

Those men cooked my brother-in-law. Kurnki tied him to a tree and hit him and hit him and hit him, everywhere.

Once, those white men came out at a place called Marrpurinya[4] and they found us. They came up to us and were touching us and squeezing our bellies. They were saying, 'Oh, this one's really fat. Oh, fat!' Then Kurnki said, 'Hey you mob, you want to give me a woman? Tjiiki-tjiiki?' We all ran away; we didn't know what they were saying — but we knew they might try to kill us.

Minypurrunya[5] was saying that maybe we shouldn't run away. He said, 'They might give us tucker.' But I remembered something my big brother said. He told me that these men had given him meat to eat once, and it was a dead body — from a man! At first he didn't know it was a man, but when he ate it, it tasted different and the fat ran out at the sides of his mouth and dribbled down his chin. Not like *marlu*.[6] After he tasted it he told those men that he had to go for firewood, but he just ran away. My brother, and the people he was with, ran away. They were afraid they might be killed.

Sandhill, sandhill, sandhill, sandhill they went, and when the sun was low they stopped — on a hill, a high hill — and they made a fire and they slept on top. That night they heard a gun — *parul! parul! parul! parul!* — and when that gun was out of bullets they heard another gun — *parul! parul! parul! parul!* Oh! My big brother sat down and wondered: what are we going to do now? Then everyone sat down, and they began to sing. They sang[7] that gun so it wouldn't work; they sang all those guns. Finished! Those men couldn't work them after that. Kurnki was saying: 'Hey, what's the matter with this gun?' They were nothing; they wouldn't shoot. That whitefella was trying really hard, putting oil in and everything, trying to start it, but no — none of those guns worked …

One day, I was walking and saw some dog tracks. I followed them and after a while I saw that dog. I said to myself: what's that dog smelling? I had a look. Camel tracks! It was that same mob — Kurnki's mob! I climbed to the top of a hill and a long way off I could see smoke; it was their fire burning. I walked to another hill and climbed up for a better look. Now I could see them very close: Kurnki and his two friends. One was cooking and one was putting up tents. Some camels had handcuffs on and some camels didn't. I watched and watched and watched and — oh! Those whitefellas were cheeky buggers! I walked back *pinytju*,[8] back to my camp. I said *'Kurta!*[9] Whitefellas north of here — cheeky buggers; they shoot people!' And I said to another old man, 'You remember? We used to hear about those white men shooting people south of the Petermann Ranges.' He remembered. Then I said, 'Let's grab a fire-stick, spears and spear-throwers, damper, and get away from this place.'

That night we left. We went over one hill and then another, and we camped over the other side of that second hill. We slept in a creek bed.

Morning time. First thing: another old man and I climbed to the top of the hill. From the top of that hill we could still see the fire from that whitefellas' camp. We had a little fire to keep us warm while we watched them. The women and children stayed at the creek. Karlnya and I, we watched the whitefellas load up their camels — putting on saddles, putting on saddles, putting on saddles.

Then they grabbed a really big, fat camel and strapped all their food on him — really tight, no *yurrinytja!*[10] Meat, flour, bread, everything. We were watching and watching, from the top of that hill.

Later, we went back to the creek for something to eat, and after eating we came back to that hill and we could still see those white men and the camels. Now we were all looking — women, children, everyone — looking from the top of that hill. They were all packed now, and we watched them as they went in the direction of Puyutjanunya.[11] Gone! They were gone! We watched until we couldn't see them any more.

Then we started tracking them. We tracked them past Puyutjanunya and Winganytjirrinya and Tjalyitjatanya. Later, we found some steel pickets in the ground where those men had been looking for gold or something. They'd dug a lot of holes everywhere, and maybe taken a lot of gold away in bags.

We went into one of their camps after they had gone. They had left a lot of tucker; we saw tea, bread, flour, but we didn't know what it was; we were really *ngurrpa*.[12] We left it. I thought: if those whitefellas weren't such cheeky buggers we could ask them to show us how to cook this. Then I said, 'Hey you mob! What are we going to do with this?' I said, 'We might take it anyway; we might try it in water.' But then I thought, no, we might get *lanyparrikupangka*.[13] We forgot about it and went for *wangurnu*, bush tucker.

While we were getting bush tucker I started thinking about that whitefella tucker again. I thought maybe we should go back and try it. We went back.

When we got back to that whitefellas' camp we found a big knife. It was a good one; maybe for kuka. Oh! We were really lucky to find that knife. Really good for cutting marlu. After finding that knife we went away; we took the knife and left the tucker.

Next day, we started following their track again and we found another place where they had camped, at a place called Puyurrnganya. We walked back to where they'd left all that tucker.

When we got back we had another look around. Dingos had gotten into their flour. I said to the others, 'Those dingos are eating that tucker and they're still alive; it must be okay!' That's true — that was the first time I knew whitefella tucker was okay.

After that we went for marlu. Lurlitu Tjakamarra and I went together and we speared two marlu. We brought them back to camp and ate them. We also had *yawilyuru*.[14] We cleaned the ground around the tree and hit the branches. When they fell down we could pick them up easily. The *piti*[15] was really full! Oh, big mob of tucker! We put water in the piti to make them cool. We left it for a while until they were cold and soft. Then we ate them.

But I was still thinking about that whitefella tucker …

One day, the whitefellas went to get their camels. They loaded them up, but one camel was too lazy. He wouldn't get up, no way. So those whitefellas shot him and they left that camel there with some of his load. Then the three white men and the other camels went away.

My brother and his mob came down. In the distance they could see those white men were making bush fires as they went. Maybe they were thinking people would see the smoke, and would come to see what was happening.

Later, those whitefellas let those camels go to eat some grass, but they didn't tie them up and the camels ran away. They might have been homesick. Kurnki chased after them, chasing and chasing and chasing, but he only caught one. Now those whitefellas had to walk.

They tracked those other camels and all the time they were making more bush fires. They just kept looking for those camels, but they couldn't find them. Finally, they came to Nyarnypinytjanya.[16] They camped there with one camel.

Next day they loaded up that camel and started off again. They started finding saddles, ropes, chains, canvas; it was spread out everywhere from those camels who got away. Everything that belonged to those whitefellas was everywhere! Those camels were ... gone!

After a while those camels came out in another place, a long way away, and some Aboriginal people saw them. They found them drinking at a waterhole in mulga country. Those people were hiding and watching all those camels coming up for a drink. They were coming and coming, close enough to touch. They were drinking and eating grass. My brother was there. He said, 'Okay, let's spear them.' Another brother said, 'No, leave them; don't kill those camels.' But that other brother said, 'No, we gotta kill them. You remember? That whitefella mob that owns those camels shoots people; they tried to shoot us before.'

Then all those men came and stood around those camels. The camels were all finished drinking; they were resting under the mulga trees. Then my brother gave the word and everyone started throwing their spears. Whole lot. They went in, spear, spear, spear. Some spears broke against the sides of the camels as they twisted and turned trying to get away. Some of those camels ran a long way with those spears in them. People at Nyarnypinytja saw them. They pulled the spears out and let the camels go, somewhere.

One time, my father-in-law went to speak to Kurnki. But my father-in-law didn't speak any English ... and Kurnki only spoke English. They couldn't talk to each other. My father-in-law, Pulutjanu, said, 'Who have you been shooting? Why are you shooting at people?' Those whitefellas didn't say anything. Later, they shot my father-in-law ...

1. *Kurnki:* The name given by Aboriginal people to a white man who roamed between Lake Mackay and the Petermann Ranges sometime in the 1930s. The name is probably derived from the Pintupi verb *kurntinu,* meaning 'to shoot'.
2. *Purtjanya:* A dry creek bed west of Lake Hopkins in Western Australia.
3. *Tjurilku:* An expletive.
4. *Marrpurinya:* A rockhole west of the Kintore Ranges in the Northern Territory.
5. *Minypurrunya:* A man's name.
6. *Marlu:* Kangaroo.
7. *'Sang':* To sing a chant for the manipulation of events. For example, 'They sang him and he died.'
8. *Pinytju:* Walking so as not to leave a track, hopping from one spinifex clump to another.
9. *Kurta:* Older brother (relationship term).
10. *Yurrinytja:* To move or wriggle.
11. *Puyutjanunya:* A rockhole north of Lake Hopkins.
12. *Ngurrpa:* Naive, uninformed.
13. *Lanyparrikupangka:* Sickness; anything which causes disease.
14. *Yawilyuru:* Black, sweet fruit, similar to grapes.
15. *Piti:* A wooden dish.
16. *Nyarnypinytjanya:* Name of a place.

Source: Tutama Tjapangarti, 'The story of Kurnki', trans. by Paul Bruno Tjampitjinpa & Billy Marshall-Stoneking, in Ulli Beir & Colin Johnson (eds), *Longwater: Aboriginal Art and Literature Annual,* Aboriginal Artists Agency Sydney, 1988, pp.37–42.

On the value of blankets

Neil Murray

Once I picked up a drover south of Mataranka,
took him to Daly Waters,
he offered me a new blanket for the ride —
I refused.
He said, 'Don't be a bloody fool'.

Once at sunset
I was asked by a young Aboriginal man
to take him sixty miles out west to some remote camp.
I asked, 'What for?'
He said, 'You gotta take me I got a pulankit there!'

That same bloke
had his blankets pinched one night
by some woman we gave a lift to in Alice Springs.
I heard him say in the morning,
'Some puckin bastard bin stealin my pulankits!
I gotta look for pulankita now'.

Several weeks later
I asked that man if he'd got his blankets back,
he said, 'I bin seen that girl, she gonna gimme
two pulankits when I go to Yuendumu.'

Source: Neil Murray, *Starting Procedure: Poems and Prose (to be read aloud)*, Papunya Literature Production Centre, Papunya, 1980, p.25.

Tales not from the Dreamtime: Pukara (perishing)[1]

Mark de Graaf

The heat of the early morning sun made us move faster. The little blue car accepted the load once more without protest. To save water, the plates and mugs were wiped with toilet paper and then it was back to the faint wheel tracks that led east, forever closer to Rogie's country. Perhaps this winter the drought might break; it could not go on much longer. For six years now the country had made do, and so had the people.

The preoccupation with the withered look of the land made us quiet. Rogie frowned as he shook his head, 'Too much piki',[2] he said. 'We got to sing'm up rain.' It was early April, the Easter break. The teachers at the small government school on the mission had scattered in all directions.

The going had been good this morning, but now the track was becoming hard to see. Among the tufts of grass deep ruts showed where water had flowed, a long time ago. After crossing a deep but small dry creek, the Volkswagen came around the foot of a hill, and out of the range country we had been in up till now. Moving down the long slope towards the open country to the east, we now faced the sun front-on.

The thin stalks of the spinifex were higher here, glistening with the low light behind them. 'Rain been 'ere. Thunderstorm, you know, right 'ere.' The drought had made the sand loose and the small car needed all it had to keep going. Only one sandhill barred the way. A few months before it had taken several hours before we could cross it. But now, with the experience of the last trip, we made it in just one desperate effort. From the top of the dune just a brief glimpse of the hilly country to the east. 'Katanara, that one, Possum's country.'[3] Possum a small, kind and rotund man waved us goodbye, his brown belly bulging over the bright blue bathing trunks, spears in one hand and a billy in the other. I realised now why he had left his camp so early this morning. A reminder that we should go straight past Katanara, past that 'big place', the grave of the ancestral Possum. Both Rogie and I had been to the site, but neither of us had the right to go there without the rightful custodian.

A mulga branch scratched against the side of the car and Rogie put his hand on my arm. 'That's okay. Scratches don't matter!' The grip on my arm tightened. 'Wanti,'[4] he whispered, peering through the windscreen as the car bumped along. 'Wanti. Little mob there.' I followed his gaze, fixed on the crest of a spinifex-clad sanddune ahead of us. Then I saw it too. The car slowed to a stop in the heavy sand, side on to the direction of travel. Something was moving there among the stalks.

Rogie got out and walked up the rise, awkwardly, the stockman's boots losing traction in the sand. He stopped and looked ahead with a puzzled look on his face. Then he walked on and cleared the crest. I walked around the car, checking, and sat down in the thin shade of a scraggly mulga and waited. There were no bird calls, no insects humming, the land was almost dead. The light breeze of the early morning had gone. Now nothing moved. The silence was oppressive, only broken by the ticking sounds of the exhaust as it cooled. Life here seemed confined to ants, and nothing but ants. It was just after eight o'clock but the temperature was already over a hundred degrees.

The rise was quite low but it still blocked my view to the east. When I got to the top, I saw Rogie walking back slowly. He saw me and waved me on, then made the hand sign that meant 'car'. His hands kept talking but I could only understand that there were 'people' there, 'sitting down'.

The car had to clear the rise at some speed to keep traction, but Rogie jumped out of the spinifex on to the track and made me slow down and then stop. 'Leave'm here'. His faced looked grim, his body tense. Then I saw them, two children, lying under a corkwood tree, their eyes closed. Rogie moved under a nearby bush, brushed away some of the sticks and sat down. His eyes met mine, a rare event. 'Big trouble. You want'm blanket,' he whispered, 'bit a-tucker, little bit-a water.' He looked at the children, who were lying motionless, flies crawling around their mouths, their eyelids, around their ears and on their limbs. Their limbs. I suddenly realised how thin they were.

Together we placed the children on the blanket. There was not much shade, but then you need less shade lying down. The boy opened his eyes briefly and looked at me as we moved him first. The little girl did not respond, although her chest was heaving gently. She was alive. I became more conscious of their condition now, the knee joints protruding from their thin legs. Their faces looked old and haggard, the cheeks sunken. 'That mob he belong your school …' his voice trailed off. I looked again and recognised the boy. Beside him was an old cup with some edible corkwood flowers and two billies. One billie contained some edible tree gum, the other a small marble.

I had to ask the question. 'What do we do now? What has happened?' Rogie did not answer. He pointed at the tracks of the small feet, leading like a thin trail east across the open plain, as far as the eye could see. Then, 'Something wrong,' he said. 'No mother.' He moved over to the boy and, kneeling, spoke softly to him, too soft for me to hear. The boy stirred, one side of his mouth moving. I could not hear any sound. The children's tracks were curious. Even with my untrained eyes I could see that they had been stumbling along, especially the girl. In several places, she had fallen down or had sat down. The boy's tracks could be seen to be stopping, sometimes returning, as he urged her on. So that is what Rogie had seen. Two kids stumbling across the spinifex, alone. Back at the car, I got out the cardboard box containing the small portable transmitter and a coil of aerial wire. The craggy skeleton of a burnt desert oak was just in the right place. Rogie agreed. 'Get the mission truck, he gotta come quick.'

Reception was clear. The usual grocery orders, orders for spare parts, messages for other stations. The mission came on briefly and I attempted to cut in so that they would know I was standing by. There was no response. When the session ended, I called the Flying Doctor base and asked them to call the mission. Again, there was no answer. The base operator understood our predicament and would keep trying. Just after he signed off, the mission came on briefly, stating that they would take 'action'. So, they had been listening. I replied by asking them when they would arrive. Silence. Perhaps they were concerned at the publicity. The base operator asked us to remain on standby and I left the set running. Rogie had been listening. 'He coming?' I nodded. 'I hope so.' I looked at the kids, resting in the shrinking shade. 'We've gotta find'm.'[5] Rogie whispered. He pointed east, with his mouth, lips pointed. East. In the mid-distance, Lightning Rocks stood out as an untidy pile of rocks. Ninety years before, John Forrest's party had placed a stone cairn on its summit. He had crossed from west to east in a good season, and in the cool of the year.

The sun was already low in the western sky when the small mission truck came into view. The mission nurse took over with accustomed authority. Rogie spoke briefly with the boy as he adjusted the blankets that separated them from the floorboards of the traytop. The little girl remained asleep, lying uneasily in the back of the truck, her head against the steelside. I lifted her head up gently and placed an empty chaff bag under it. It would be a rough ride back to the mission, several hours of slow grinding work, followed by the dust of the last section.

Rogie did not want to camp. We had to go on, fast now, to find the mother. I did not ask what the boy said. Sooner or later he would tell me. We passed Lightning Rocks and moved on to Pilpiring,[6] a jumbled heap of granite boulders. The soak on the west side had no water in it, but the mud at the bottom was wet. The children's footprints were all around and Rogie showed me where the little hands had scraped up the mud to hold against parched lips. From here the tracks led east, just two sets of footprints.

At Winpul, again the tracks led to the waterhole. But this one was completely dry. Whites call this place 'Winburn Rocks'. Someone had scratched John Forrest's name on the rock face. Not the explorer himself, because it said 'Sir John Forrest'. On another face it said 'Jesus Saves'. I don't thing Rogie could read. It was getting too dark to see now and reluctantly we camped.

Long before daybreak, Rogie had the fire going and the sun did not rise until we had been under way for almost half an hour. It was hard to see the children's tracks with the harsh light against us, but Rogie's hands moved each time he saw them. 'We've got to watch'm Papulangkata,' he said. So that is what the boy had told him. Papulangkata was the name of the abandoned Blackstone Mining Camp, now coming into view.

We had been here before. Rogie had shown me where a shot had been fired at the Aboriginal group by one of the miners. It had been an unhappy relationship, terminated only a few years ago when the miners moved out. Even though Blackstone had been part of the Central Desert Reserve, a portion had been excised so that mining could take place. Mines before people.

The children's camp of nearly a week before was right next to the track. I watched Rogie as he stepped around carefully, noticing every sign in the dirt and everything lying around. A calico bag with women's clothes, a tin of tobacco, a digging dish with a piece of soap and some dark material I could not make out from where I stood. Rogie told me. 'His hair,'[5] he said. He followed the tracks leading to a forty-four gallon drum lying on its side, no bung. He withdrew his finger and smelled it. I followed suit. There was some water in the drum but it had an oily smell. Walking around in a wide circle now, Rogie looked at all the tracks. When he came back he said, 'That way.' He pointed north, away from the track which continued east across the border into South Australia.

Camped that night, Rogie mentioned his fears. 'He is sick, that woman. He might still be alright.' I said I would talk to the Flying Doctor again to tell them where we were going. We had some extra fuel, enough to get to the next supply at Musgrave Park, two hundred kilometres east. Water would be a problem; the nearest was a bore in South Australia. It would be less than a day's run while we were on the track, but we were already half a day off the track now. The children had checked out the rockhole we found after breakfast, but it was dry. Their tracks went east, so we were now parallel to our original track.

The going was quite heavy. The little car got bogged many times and constant wheeling around the mulga sticks made us lose much time. Rogie sat there, brooding eyes under the stockman's hat, each time showing with a nonchalant movement of the hand the way to go. Sometimes he would walk ahead, following the kid's tracks as they had chased a lizard, and, in one case, a rabbit. 'No water, no tucker,' he said grimly. It must have taken them about three or four days to get from here to where we found them. No wonder they had been so weak.

The late afternoon session with the Flying Doctor base brought some news. The mission had given an account of the events obtained from the boy. The mother had been ill and she had told the children to go ahead from waterhole to waterhole and not to wait for her at the mining camp. She had been ill. The Kalgoorlie police had been told and we were asked to keep them informed via the base.

Early the next morning, as Rogie walked ahead while I slowly brought up the car, he suddenly stopped and called me over. I saw it too. There were three sets of tracks here, the two children's tracks and one set of bigger imprints. The children had walked west, the way we had just come, the mother had gone south-west, in a straight line to the Blackstone camp. 'Ngura kutjarra,'[7] he said. I knew what he meant. Somewhere between this place and the camp the mother must be, unless she had changed direction. I swung the wheel around and followed Rogie, who was walking quite fast now, chewing a spinifex stalk as he went along. Our third flat tyre took longer than usual to fix and Rogie came back to talk to me. 'He's sick feller,' he said. He pointed at the tracks. The toemarks were elongated as if the feet were dragging along. Some steps were of different length. She had not walked straight but swayed from side to side. I noticed Rogie now casting long looks ahead as if he expected to see something any minute. He showed me where she had camped. 'Morning time,' he said. The imprint of the body was on the west side of the small tree. The next camp was on the south-side of a tree, a midday camp. The distance between the two camps was less than a mile. Gradually, I began to understand what Rogie was seeing all the time. A woman struggling in the heat, dragging herself along to get to the drum of water at the mining camp. She had sent her kids ahead with most of her belongings via a different route to check out another waterhole and catch some game along the way. We were getting quite near Blackstone camp now; I could see the range clearly above the mulga that we had to force our way through. Another flat tyre delayed us too long and we had to make camp. Rogie walked ahead while I made something to eat. It was almost dark when he got back. 'Nothing,' he said, making the characteristic gesture with the hand. 'Poor bugger, my cousin.' We ate in silence. In fact, the whole trip so far had been a very quiet one. The events of the second day had put a stamp on all our activities.

Early the next day the heat was kept away for a few hours by a cool south-easterly, but about mid-morning it became still. Rogie was walking ahead very slowly now, peering through the scrub before moving on. It did not matter because I had to go slow also, there were just too many stakes. I figured we could only be a few miles from the Blackstone camp. Rogie stopped again to inspect the tracks. He walked back to the car and I stopped. 'We walk,' he said. I left the car and walked behind him. Only a few minutes later he stopped again. 'Kulila,'[8] he motioned me to come nearer. 'Mungu pini,[9] you know flies.' Then I heard it too. A faint buzzing sound. A few more steps and then we saw her.

She had fallen into her fire, one leg awkwardly cocked at an unusual angle. She lay face down. Nearby a crowbar, a plate, nothing else. Rogie turned away. It was then the smell hit me. It was a smell I had experienced before, after the Battle of Arnhem, my hometown, in September, 1944. I walked back to the car and Rogie caught up to me. 'We gotta bury 'm now,' he said. 'Before night-time.' The ground was almost too hard. It took a long time before we had a hole large enough. The burial was undignified. The rope around the ankle came off once and when we dragged the body across to the hole, it became obvious that she must have been dead for about a week. Several times I had to stop. The stench made me retch. It was hot now, midday or later, and the moving of the body had made the flies active. I don't know why I did it, but I made a cross out of two pieces of timber. 'So people can find her,' I said unconvincingly. I took a label off one of the boxes in the car and tied it to the cross. A pencilled name and the date.

The cross erected by Mark de Graaf and his friend Rogie to mark the grave of the Aboriginal woman.

In about a mile and a half we reached the mining camp and then headed east. We drove until late that night. The track was much better now, where it had been used by the miners. Camp was made just inside the South Australian border. Before we settled down to sleep, Rogie said. 'He knew all the time, that woman. That's why he cut 's hair.'

Notes
1 'Pukara' — perishing, perish.
2 'Piki' — dry.
3 'Katanara' — place name.
4 'Wanti' — stop, leave it.
5 In Aboriginal English there is no distinction in pronouns between male and female. 'He' equals 'She'.
6 'Pilpiring' — place name.
7 'Ngura kutjarra' — literally 'camps/two', meaning in between.
8 'Kulila' — listen.
9 'Mungu pini' — many flies.

Source: Mark de Graaf, 'Tales not from the Dreamtime: Pukara ', *Northern Perspective*, vol.7, no.2, 1985, pp.16-20.

12 Nature's stage

What's that? I don't care where you've been, or what you've seen, I say you have never seen mosquitoes till you have been in the Territory. You've got to have a cheesecloth mosquito net because the ordinary net is no good up there. Why isn't it any good? Because when they settle on it, it tears with their weight and once they get inside the net, there's nothing but a skeleton left in the bed by the time your friends get to you.
— A. B. Paterson, from 'Wild horses', a wireless talk, 1930s

One afternoon I was in the baths with a lad about two years younger than myself. We had waded into about four feet of water, when my companion gave a cry of pain and disappeared. I rushed to him, and as I plunged to pick him up, the whole of the upper part of my body seemed as if it were being seared with red-hot irons.
— Alfred Searcy (1880s), *By Flood and Field*, 1911

You are aware, no doubt, that the tropical cockroaches grow to a great size, and are full of business. An immense fellow sailed in to my room at our quarters one night, and on examining it I found a great number of ticks fastened upon the stomach portion of its body. You may have heard that these insects have a great predilection for finger and toe nails. When in the [ship 'Flying'] 'Cloud' asleep I had my toenails nibbled right down to the quick. The rats on board were beastly familiar. They often made one's body the means of reaching the deck as quickly as possible. I woke up one night, and found a great brute seated on my face,
— Alfred Searcy, *In Northern Seas*, 1905

The wise old swaggy moon bespoke
bush-concert for tonight,
and all the frogs together croak
for his and my delight.
— Rex Ingamells, *News of the Sun*, 1942

If there is a Valhalla for flies, then many of them earned their place in it by their actions at the Granites. Never did any aspirant for Paradise in a holy war attack so fiercely.
— F. E. Baume, *Tragedy Track*, 1932

Travellers in northern Australia will agree that, all things being equal, one should show nothing but abject obedience to the invariable command of the green ant — 'Get out!'
— F. X. Gsell, *The Bishop With 150 Wives*, 1956

Previous page: Thomas Baines (1822–75) was a valued member of Augustus Gregory's North Australian Expedition of 1855–56. His sketches, watercolours and oil paintings comprise a permanent record of the epic journey. This watercolour, painted around 1855, is not surprisingly entitled 'Alligator, Victoria River', and from it Baines would later produce his famous oil painting.

Drowning the cockroaches, Port Essington

John Sweatman

I have before made mention of the cockroaches on board, and the various attempts we had made to get rid of them by smoking ship &c. Although these means had at times thinned their numbers considerably, they had still increased again afterwards and had now become a most intolerable nuisance: we could never sleep below for them, for apart from the nuisance of having such disgusting animals crawling over one they used actually to eat away the skin from our extremities while we slept; nay, we could hardly sit in our mess after dark, they flew about like birds, I have even seen the lights put out by them, and as they were an inch and a half long with sharp claws, and with a most disgusting odour which they communicated to everything they touched, it was perfect misery to be among them. Nothing was safe from their ravages, I had to poison all the ship's books and papers with corrosive sublimate to keep them from being devoured, and the damage done to the stores and provisions was beyond everything. The bread in particular, suffered, being only in bags and as I foresaw that I must necessarily have a large deficiency of that article, I obtained Mr. Yule's sanction to a regular experiment to see how much was actually destroyed by the vermin alone. I had a new bag of bread brought from the stores at Victoria [Coburg Peninsula], weighed and tallied in the presence of the signing officers, full 112 lbs. It was then sealed and placed with about a dozen others in the bread room. This was the day before we sailed for Ki; the day after our return, i.e. after 20 days, I had it taken out and without being opened, weighed again in presence of the same officers — it weighed only 65 lbs! having thus lost three-sevenths in that short time by the consumption by the cockroaches alone: the bag was eaten to rags and the biscuits like honeycomb, I took out the first that came to hand and having poisoned it to prevent further decay, sealed it up and sent it home with my accounts, as the best evidence I could give of the real cause of my deficiency which amounted to 712 lbs. beyond my tenths or nearly 3000 lbs. in all. Notwithstanding this, and although I also sent certificates of all the above signed by all the signing officers, they made me answerable for the whole, only allowing it to be carried to my next account.

For some time past, Mr. Yule had given the ship's boys so much a pint, for any cockroaches they might kill and from dark till 8 P.M. there was always a perpetual tapping going on about the lower deck, with shoes &c. in procuring them, and one boy often got 2 or 3 pints in a night: still their numbers did not seem to diminish and the skipper began to find this plan expensive, and as it would never do to have all our provisions & stores destroyed in this way, he resolved to take the most vigorous measures to exterminate them, by sinking the vessel altogether and it was for this purpose she was taken to Point Record. It would not do to land our stores &c. at Victoria as in the first place we should thereby introduce the vermin there, and besides the place was so infested with white ants that we ran a risk of having a good part of them destroyed, only the spirits therefore were left in Lambrick's charge and everything else was landed on Point Record. A huge tent was made of the ship's sails for the people to live in, another was appropriated to our mess, a third held all the provisions, and in it I also took up my abode and converted part of it into an office. Mr. Yule's little tent and a small one for the powder completed our encampment. It was the fourth time the vessel had been entirely cleared out, during as many years, and only those who have experienced clearing out a ship can judge of the nuisance and inconvenience of it; it is worse than changing one's house tenfold; everything gets into confusion, your traps get spoilt, broken, lost, plundered & everything else that's bad, you can get no regular meals, no place to sleep in, no one to attend to you, nothing you want. However there was no help for it had we gone to sea again with the myriads of cockroaches we had on board, we should have been devoured alive.

As we had reason to believe from the bolts being driven up in the 'Castlereagh's' kelson, and from her holding so bad a wind, that her keel was injured, Mr. Yule resolved to heave her down and have a look at her bottom and she was therefore cleared out at the same time as us, her encampment being situated a few hundred yards further up towards the point. On the 14th. the 'Bramble' being completely emptied, was moved round the point on to a mud flat where there would be just her own depth at L[ow] W[ater] the 'legs' were got under her, hatches being nailed at their base to prevent their sinking in the mud, and a scuttle being cut in her side to admit the water, she was sunk on the afternoon of the 15th. of August. At high water she was completely covered, above the tops of the round houses abaft; and the cockroaches came up by millions to take refuge on the rigging, but the people were stationed all about with buckets to wash them down and a regular water frolic took place: the sea was covered with the dead who were washed on shore in heaps where the natives gathered them up in handfuls to eat them! Their old place of refuge inside the bulwarks, availed them nothing now, and by night the vessel was completely cleared of them. It was originally intended that she should only remain under water 24 hours, but unfortunately one of the hatches which supported the legs, gave way, the leg sank into the soft mud and the vessel heeled over on her broadside, whence it was found impossible to right her for 72 hours. At last by anchoring the 'Castlereagh' close to and getting tackles from her to the 'Bramble's' mast heads, we succeeded in getting the latter upright, and at low water when all the water had run out of her to the back of the scuttle, the latter was closed and the vessel pumped dry and at H.W. floated off into deep water. An idea may be formed of the number of cockroaches we had had on board, by the fact (entered in the Log) that no less than 500 gallons of the vermin were measured out of the hold independent of the myriads who were washed away by the sea and which were fully as many. Fancy this in a vessel of only 165 tons, what a nice state she must have been in.

Source: Jim Allen & Peter Corris (eds), *The Journal of John Sweatman* [1845-47], University of Queensland Press, St Lucia, 1977, pp.127-9.

Mrs Englishwoman on the Daly River

Jessie Litchfield

We received an object-lesson on how *not* to live in the north Australian bush when a gentleman, recently arrived from 'Home' [England], took up a selection on the Daly River, and decided to have his wife out there with him. She also was a new arrival, London-born and bred, without the slightest knowledge of bush life. She brought all her furniture with her to Darwin, for transhipment to the Daly. Darwin folk, although admiring her piano, silver cake-baskets, brocade-covered chairs, bevelled-glass mirrors, aluminium cooking-utensils, egg-shell china, and silver cutlery, warned her that such furniture would be a burden to her in the bush, and they advised her to store all her costly goods in Darwin, just to take the plainest and simplest things with her to the Daly. Unfortunately, she did not follow this advice; possibly in imagination she saw herself as a pioneer of civilization in the bush, setting the out-back women an example.

All her elaborate furniture was sent up to the Daly by lugger, much to its skipper's disgust; for the bulkier articles had to be stowed on deck, where they were soon stained with sea-spray and eaten by cockroaches. When they arrived at the Daly, all the furniture had to be temporarily stowed under tarpaulins; for Mrs English-woman discovered that the 'commodious Colonial mansion' she had imagined, was simply a bark humpy, some ten feet by

Like the photographs of Paul Foelsche, those of H.W. Christie provide an invaluable record of early European settlement in northern Australia. Alfred Searcy used this photograph in his In Australian Tropics *(1909) with the caption: 'A little pleasantry in the Tropics — flying ants, Point Charles light-house'. (Thank heavens for wire screens these days!)*

twelve, with an ant-bed floor. Borers ate her elaborate furniture; white-ants destroyed her sideboards; ginger-ants built in her piano, and cockroaches lived in her brocaded chairs. Frogs, centipedes, and spiders made uninvited calls upon her; open fires blackened her aluminium cooking-utensils, soon bumped out of shape by the clumsy fingers of the blacks who stole all her silver cutlery.

When the wet set in, lace curtains, embroidered bedspreads, and toilet covers became mildewed in a single night; her crocodile dressing-case grew hoary whiskers, and the glued portions became unstuck; her elaborate house-gowns, tea-gowns, and rest-gowns became discoloured with wet bark, blackened with mildew, and eaten into holes by cockroaches and crickets. Her husband's evening dress suits made a meal for the white-ants with the camphor-wood chest that housed them.

So a very unhappy English couple abandoned their selection in disgust, and returned to their London flat, leaving the bush-women still unconverted.

Source: Jessie Litchfield, *Far-north Memories: Being the Account of Ten Years Spent on the Diamond-drills, and of Things that Happened in those Days*, Angus & Robertson, Sydney, 1930, pp.157-8.

White ants in Darwin

Ernestine Hill

So the Front Gate of Australia gallantly laughed away its fears of invasion … but there was a more formidable enemy within the gateposts. Besieged by this enemy unseen, unheard, unconquerable, Darwin, like London Bridge, was falling down.

One of the least of God's creatures, blind, defenceless, insensible, was eating away the fruits of all their labours, eating their hopes and their homes to a hollow shell.

White ants …

The discovery of this deep, dark and deadly work was another laurel to the Bard. Occasionally in these years a Dutch ship or a P. and O. mail steamer would call on her way through Torres Straits to Singapore and India, with celebrities aboard. On one memorable night the world-famous Madame Carandini, with a kindly thought of the exiles, gave a concert on shipboard, lifting to those remote stars the voice that princes travelled far to hear. When Morton Tavares, a ham actor of the grand old school, whose wife had eloped with the captain of a ship, found himself down on his luck and marooned in Darwin, the good-hearted little town and its diggers gave him a benefit to raise his fare to Calcutta. He chose the court scene from *The Merchant of Venice,* his utterly villainous Shylock with a B.A.T. Antonio and a portly Portia striding the boards of Barclay's Room, packed to its wide-open galvanized-iron doors.

The Mercy Speech literally rocked the rafters, and in the furore of the final curtain the whole of the front stalls went through the floor!

That was the end of Barclay's Room. The old shack was badly aslant in the morning, and the next Cock-eyed Bob blew it down. Goyder's old storehouse had lightened the meagre lives of the settlers with many a merry night, but Shakespeare was asking too much.

Within five years white ants had reduced the houses of the pioneers to a shell of masticated pulp. They undermined the jetty at Southport — cargoes stored there suddenly fell into the sea. They demolished roots at their foundations — trees and shrubs, while you were looking at them, foolishly fell over. Beds caved in in the night. Tables collapsed during dinner, steps as one ascended, chairs as one sat down. Telegraph poles dangled in the wires, the parties constantly riding to renew them.

These most rapacious of animals, in an ingenious paradox, have no stomach — internal parasites do all their digesting for them.

White ants ate the Residency piano, the mails in the post-office, the pegs of the miner's claims, wagon-wheels while they were standing, blankets of sleepers in the night. They chewed jagged holes in the walls of the court-house and the police station, digested Government records, broke up the jail — a bad Arab named Abdulla, who had given the police no end of trouble to catch him, simply pushed a beam and walked out. A trooper found his trunk filled with sawdust and buttons. A blacksmith reported that they had carried away his anvil, but he found it buried in the rubble that had been the block.

At the Residency it cost £400 a year to keep the Resident indoors — he had a carpenter on the premises renewing walls and floors at regular wages, 13s. a day. One of the Darwin dandies complained that white ants devoured a pair of duelling pistols and his opera hat, then topped up on his iron dumb-bells. At the B.A.T. they regaled themselves on billiard-balls, leaving a hollow globe of paint, then bored through sheets of lead to set the verandah posts aslant. They ate out the strongroom of the bank, and while the bank manager was building another they came up in thousands through the wet cement and twiddled their antennae at him in derision.

A mining director, absent for three months, came back to his home, put his key in the door, and the whole house fell flat. Then the Resident announced that they had invaded his wine-cellar, perforated the metal tops of bottles, polished off the corks. Darwin was on a slant, everything at a stagger, a honeycomb of dry rot.

Of all living creatures, the termite is most destructive to man's handiwork, and of all termites the North Australian *Mastotermes darwiniensis* is most primitive and most ruinous. It virtually owns Australia north of Capricorn, extracting a revenue duty of forty per cent on production. It wreaks more havoc than the earthquakes of New Zealand. Those vast, still, pindan sands of Western Queensland, the Territory and North-west are perpetual motion, millions of mandibles grinding away Nature's eternal building and rebuilding.

Once, in poetic mood out there, I remarked to a bushman the sound within the silence ... a mighty monotone of hush, a bell-like high note scarcely heard yet all pervading, ringing beyond the silence.

'Y'r quite right, missus,' he said. 'It's the white ants chewin'.'

In an empire of two million square miles, here is the greatest social organisation in the world ... of sightless workers born to work till death, of cities built of the stuff of their bodies, the endless dwarf cities of tenements and towers red roan as the sand, or ghastly grey as the clay. Termite social law is merciless and blind as humanity in war. There are workers, soldiers, nymphs, a diminutive king and a monstrous queen, the State, mother of a multitude. There are no strategists where all is strategy, no field-marshals in a robot regimentation, no shift-bosses where all is mechanical slavery — but if you destroy the mother of a race, that race is gone.

Kick an ant-hill. See the soldiers rush out to link legs in vicious resistance to block the opening, blind fighters with an armour-plated unicorn head that they flail from side to side, *Flammen-werfer* throwing an acid spray that encloses and corrodes a small enemy. This saliva cements the ant-hills. It is also the secretion that penetrated the Resident's zinc-sealed wine-bottles and the B.A.T. billiard-balls. It can penetrate sheet iron and it can corrode glass. The termite armies seal themselves with it, and become a living wall of mailed heads. Heroic defenders, they never turn their backs to the enemy, because their abject rear is unprotected, soft and grub-like, like a hermit crab's.

When things are quiet, the soldiers stand aside and the workers seal the walls with the secretion. The eternal breeding, building, harvesting, feeding, goes on. These pulpy, veined creatures, half an inch long, fleshy and grey with a head like a wax match, toil like munition workers till they drop dead, to be immediately devoured by their kind — there is no waste in an ant-hill. The queen, when her procreative functions fail, soon dies and is devoured by her subjects — they fly, they swarm, they mate, they destroy each other and are destroyed and eaten. The survivors establish another state, enthrone another queen. After their brief mating flight in the sunshine, they shed their wings and burrow to build and breed again.

North of the Tropic you travel the endless ant-hill cities, varying in colour with earth, and in form with soil formation, and slant of wind. The west of Queensland and the Centre is one vast wilderness of cones and tombstones, increasing in height to the north till at Cape York they are like kiln chimneys. At Pine Creek, the amazing Gothic cathedrals with fluted buttresses and towers are twenty-five feet high. At Darwin slab monoliths, 'magnetic' or 'meridional' ant-hills, flat-planed north and south, are dreadnoughts in line ahead across the Cemetery Plain; in Kimberley great slag dumps seem to be piled with buckets of wet sand, at Broome are the domes of scarlet clay that Dampier believed to be 'the abode of Hottentots in the savannah'. Ghosts of the drovers who died out there are the ant-hills of the Murran-ji.

Out below the Granites in the Territory west, and on the road through the rugged red ranges to Borroloola on the Gulf are the most remarkable ant-hill cities that I know, 'madman's galleries' surely unique in the world and covering hundreds of square miles ... of glaucous yellow clay, or slaty grey, or terra-cotta, half-finished effigies of a crazed sculptor

Ant hill, near Rum Jungle, 1887.

whose addled dreams in shrouded sand return ever and again to the Old Master theme of Madonna and Child. In half-formed imagery they challenge the piled clouds above ... a coronation group, king, bishop, knight and page; imbecile cherubs; Three Wise Monkeys; a leprous torso of Hercules; a cowled pilgrim with a pack on his back; Rodin's 'The Burghers of Calais' half melted away; pock-marked Shakespeare in a broken ruff — the imagination skips from fantasies to fantods as the car wanders through that chamber of horrors that is built with the stuff of their bodies by the white ants.

Chop off a section of those Gothic towers in miniature, and you disclose a marvel of engineering in architecture as complicated as the city of New York, with highways, subways, ramps, bridges, silos, factories, clinics, spiral staircases, mezzanines, cellars, ventilation shafts, air conditioning — Nature thought of it all first. The granaries are packed with grass sawn with minute exactitude in lengths corresponding within the millionth of an inch. There is a dizzying one-way traffic of entities in endless belts of motion steady as the circulation of the blood through arteries, veins and capillaries.

The queen, three inches long and bloated with fecundity, lies in a domed aortal chamber a foot across and inches high. She spends her whole life in a horrible disgorgement of eggs at the rate of one a second, and she lives thirty years; long files of workers stuff morsels into her mouth that have been predigested by their own bodies — anything from sweet grass to historical records — and carry away her eggs to the heated incubation chambers. Beneath her pallid white obesity lies the little king, with her a life prisoner of communal law.

All is the intelligence of faultless instinct. When a nest is blown down, or chopped open in chunks, the workers swiftly cement the queen in a solid block of clay that resists the axe, and within an hour they are on the job again to build a skyscraper about her in a month. Should a spring burst beneath it, these termites develop a waterproof solution to line the nest and turn that hot spring into account in cooking their edible mould and hatching the rising generation. The big shift of workers goes on at night when birds, ants and other enemies are at home in bed. The honeycomb domes and spires grow in the starlight.

Which reminds me of the tale they tell at Pine Creek, of the stockman who stayed too long at the pub, set out to find his droving camp with a rolling gait and a song, and fell by the wayside. He awoke next morning powerless to move, bound hand and foot in earthy darkness, with a tickling irritation all over like Gulliver on the Lilliputian shore. He thought he was buried alive. In cold sweat of terror he groaned and shouted, trying to remember the holy words he learned at mother's knee.

The cook in the droving camp, packing his pots and pans while the ringers were moving on the cattle, was startled to hear '… an ant-hill carryin' on like anything, and recitin' the Lord's Prayer! I reckoned the place was bewitched by a parson or somethink, an' by golly I was goin' to hop it quick, an' ole Bert woulda been there yet if I hadn'ta happened to see a couple o' swan-neck spurs stickin' out!'

Source: Ernestine Hill, *The Territory,* Angus & Robertson, Sydney, 1951, pp. 143-6.

Crocodile haiku

Mark O'Connor

How the magic of the river
is enhanced by the crocodile in it!
Each ripple a richer meaning.

Source: Mark O'Connor, *Firestick Farming: Selected Poems 1972–1990,* Hale & Iremonger, Sydney, 1990, p.172.

Frogday

Connie Gregory

Tinted glass looks out on palms, balmy, tropical, cool-looking. Deceptive. Inside 19° outside 35° and steamy. It's on the walkway, the end office. People stop to check their hair, nose or hems before entering the building. Some lounge against the windows and have 'interesting' conversations. Those that know about inside looking out don't do it. I've got quite used to observing people; looking straight at their eyes unobserved. It's boring really. I've got a one-way mirror to outside when I remember to look up from my work.

Rush job again today. Deadline 11 am. Take the phone off the hook and then the switchgirl sends a message to please put it back on, lots of urgent calls. Hang it up. Another deadline comes by 'phone.

Surrounded by figures. Juggle. The computer goes down. Stare out the window. See the frog. It's tucked up onto where the glass meets the air conditioner in the bottom pane. Big, pale green and wet looking.

The boss comes in. Move the 11 am deadline to the side. Supply can wait for their estimates he says and do these figures for him by lunchtime. Okay. I sweat on the computer coming back on line. Ring several areas for their input. It's not their deadline but mine. Try to keep the whine out of my voice.

The tea lady comes in — look there's a frog — yep, it's still there hanging on.

A group of Arts students stops outside the window — look there's a frog. They go up and *talk* to it. 'Hello froggie.' Each one gets up close to observe the frog — 'It's turned off ... isn't it cute ... have a nice day frog.' I can't concentrate. Feel prodded. Get up and look closely at the frog. Green and cool, unperturbed. A student pokes it. I quickly throw open the top window startling him.

'Leave him alone,' I yell, 'can't you see it doesn't want to be disturbed.' I am shaking with anger and I don't particularly like frogs. He pokes out his tongue — 'it's not your frog!' — he tries to prise it loose; the frog objects. 'Can't you see he likes it there?' I growl. Student group laughs and moves on. Silly really, should have let them take it and put it in the bushes.

Computer back on, can't concentrate. Dig out the office humour book. It falls open at the page that says that the bitterness of poor quality remains long after the sweetness of meeting the deadline schedule has been forgotten. Yeah, yeah, my life is full of sweetness.

My tea's gone cold. Telephone rings. Interstate. Reminding me of deadline for next week but needed earlier. Please telex tomorrow. Add it to the urgent list. Maybe we'll get a cyclone tonight to blow all the papers away. Just a small one.

'Hello frog.' It's one of the typists talking, stroking the frog. Why do people talk to frogs? All morning people stop and talk at the frog — it's disrupting me. Why can't they leave it alone? My telephone refuses to stop ringing. The list of people to call back mounts.

I finish the boss's figures. Take them around but he's gone to lunch. Oh yes, he needs those for tomorrow afternoon his secretary smiles. I feel sick. Supply rings — where are the estimates? Okay, after lunch, I'll work through.

The frog people are driving me mad with their talk. Decide to remove frog. Go outside and stand there and growl and clap. It won't listen. It ignores me. Clever frog. Somebody walks by and says leave the poor thing alone. Why don't you leave me alone you big toad, I snap. Go inside feeling foolish. Crawl to my seat. Got a headache. The 'phone rings and I let it — it rings for a long time, and stops. I turn down the sound switch. It rings again with a soft buzz. I'm getting smart.

Maybe I should get an answering machine. Spend five minutes thinking of what sort of message I will put on it. My headache eases.

All afternoon the usual range of people come wanting this and that and firing deadlines. The first 'no' escapes my lips, it becomes easier after that. Need a holiday.

I put a sign on my door that says *'Do not disturb. Working on deadline'*, tell the switch no calls however urgent. It works. Study the frog. It's spread flatter but is still exposed to voices and prods.

I go outside into the heat to speak to the smart frog against the cool glass on the humming conditioner. 'You and I frog, we're having a hard day.' Boss walks by on way back from wet lunch, laughs saying to leave the poor fellow alone, but stops and pokes it and says hello. 'Done those figures yet?' I nod. (Yes, you can now leave me alone until your next wolf-cry.) He nods. 'Good; good; come round and have a drink later.' Say sorry, can't come, got too many deadlines to meet. His eyes boggle. Go back inside, write a sign for frog saying *'Do not disturb. Working on deadline.'* Stick it on outside window next to frog. People read sign and smile. Snooze until 6 pm. Everything quiet, everybody gone; except me and frog. On the way out speak to frog — 'Not a bad frogday, eh?' Clean my desk up in the morning. Frog's gone. Fill out application for leave forms.

Source: Connie Gregory, 'Frogday', in Ann Granat (comp.), *Storyteller: Stories by Australian Writers*, Brooks Waterloo, Vic., 1988, pp.19-21.

The gecko

Frederick T. Macartney

That little lizard in the roof
Makes mirth of a small tune.
Perhaps he puts love to its proof
This afternoon;

Or lifts his head, spying at last
His lady's open door,
And chuckles as he scampers past,
Lovesick no more.

Source: Frederick T. Macartney, *Preferences: Poems*, Angus & Robertson, Sydney, 1941, p.74.

There were rats, rats

James White

I had known a couple of rat and mice invasions but nothing to compare with the plague throughout the Territory in 1935. There were countless thousands scuttling around day and night. Not a thing in the stock-camp escaped their notice. It was almost impossible to keep food out of their reach and they even tackled the truck tyres, saddlery and other gear. At night we used to sit round the camp fire with lengths of wire, pieces of bread as bait, and swot them. We scored several hundred each night. At first the Aboriginals thought them great 'tuckout' but, in due course, tired of their rat dinners. Following the rats came a plague of cats — terrible-looking, mangy animals. In time both disappeared and everything returned to normal.

There were rats, rats
Countless bloody rats
At Brunette Downs in Nineteen thirty-five,
They just ate, ate
I'm tellin' you this mate
It's a bloomin' wonder we're a-bloody-live.

They would munch, munch
Tomorrow's bloody lunch
And the plum pud made for afters if they could,
And they'd chew, chew
We never really knew
What made the tyres on lorries taste so good.

They would gnaw, gnaw
Everything they saw
Our saddlery, the packs and other gear,
They would bite, bite
Everything in sight
As Richard slept they nipped bits off his ear.

Well, one bright night
We doused the kero light
And with a six foot hunk of fencing wire,
We just sat, pat
Still as any cat
With foodstuffs used for bait around the fire.

We got one ton
I tell you it was fun
We must have had Dick Whittington on side,
It was swat, swat
And as we got that lot
There were a few we could have tasted fried.

They were boys' joys
Oh what a bloody noise
As they filled their bellies full of rodent fare,
They would toast, roast
That's what they liked most
Yes, toss 'em in the fire and eat 'em rare.

Then came cats, cats
Countless bloody cats
Cringing, mangy buggers from the plain,
Soon our mate's fate
Was just another date
With camp life back to normal once again.

Source: James White, *Cooloolooghini*, Mundigee, Terrigal, 1983.

Auntie Annie and Monty

Graham Calley

Auntie Annie was not a real aunt. Mum and Dad never told us kids who she was. In fact, they were always a bit sort of quiet about her, particularly Mum. I think Dad may have known her before he married Mum. I remember that they got a letter asking if she could come and stay and there was a lot of talk between Mum and Dad and Mum wasn't too pleased, and Dad said 'Aw give her a break Wen. She's had a rough time.' Wen was Mum. Dad called her that. Short for Wendy.

Anyway, Mum must have let Auntie Annie come, because Dad went into Darwin to get her off the Greyhound bus one evening. Mum made me help her clean up the old caravan under the mango tree that nobody had stayed in for a while. I asked her about who it was that was coming, because we kids didn't really know what it was all about, only what we'd heard by listening in like. She still wouldn't say. Told me to wait and see. I think she was still not too happy about it. She was thumping things about in the caravan.

When we heard the car coming back, me and Petey and Trixie all ran out and followed Dad up the drive and round the back to the caravan. We were all standin in a row watchin to see the lady and Trixie was suckin her thumb and was all ready to run off to Mum if the lady was too fearsome.

Anyway, the lady got out and she had red hair and she was pretty and a bit younger than Mum and she came straight over to us and said 'Hello kids. I've heard all about you. I'm Auntie Annie.' I sort of half smiled at her I think, but Petey just had his mouth open like Mum tells him not to and Trixie tried to wrap herself in my skirt, with her thumb stuck right in her mouth. We don't get many visitors here on the block at Humpty Doo, you see!

Mum came out then and Dad introduced her and the lady and then Mum made us all come and shake hands with the lady properly, except little Trixie who wouldn't take her thumb out of her mouth and the lady bent down quickly and kissed her. She laughed a lot. She was nice.

When she unpacked her cases she had some sweets for us and she called us into the caravan and told us to call her Auntie Annie. Petey stopped starin at her with his mouth open and Trixie took her thumb out of her mouth and put the toffee in.

From then on Auntie Annie stayed in the caravan and I think she would have been there about a year with us. She was real fun. She never did nothing slowly and quietly like Mum did. She used to say some things that Mum wouldn't let us say too. She and Dad used to yell things at each other sometime and be laughin and me and Petey and Trixie would laugh but we didn't really know what was funny and Auntie Annie would pick up Trixie and give her a hug and tell her she had no business to be laughin. She was quieter though when Mum was about.

I think Mum didn't quite like Auntie Annie. I saw her looking at her a few times. I think she reckoned that Dad spent too much time talking to her. I heard Mum and Dad arguin sometimes. Mum never raised her voice much and they shut up if any of us kids was about but I heard them. Dad used to get annoyed if Mum went on a bit and he'd go off in the old truck and be away all day. Him and Jacky Wilson, who is an aboriginal bloke, used to shoot buffaloes for pet meat and sometimes they were gone for two or three days.

Then one day Auntie Annie found Monty. She found him by accident when she was hunting rats. Rats used to get real bad sometimes round Humpty Doo and Auntie Annie had a down on rats. When they used to build up a bit and start getting cheeky inside the house and fighting all night in the ceiling she used to go to war on them.

Sockeye, our bluey bitch and her pup, the only one Mum let us keep, used to be right into this and as Auntie Annie poked and prodded at the nests or burned the rats out with paper or flooded them out with the hose, Sockeye and Pup were onto them. They didn't often miss. We kids did the out fielding with sticks and stones.

Auntie Annie's rat wars usually lasted all day and from early morning the place was a riot. There were rats and dogs and kids going every which way and sometimes Dad joined in which pleased us kids no end — especially when he pretended to get a rat up his trouser leg and hopped about and carried on and shouted till we nearly bust ourselves. There'd be smoke and water everywhere and rats squeaking and dogs barking and kids yellin and Auntie Annie with her hair all about screamin 'Do this, do that, get that one, watch out he'll getcha.' Sometimes we would hit one another and then have a fight or the dogs would fight. We got filthy dirty. Gee they were marvellous days.

I don't think Mum took to them all that much though. She used to stay inside or just walk through all the chaos, doin what she was doin as though it wasn't happenin. She used to treat Dad like he was a big kid and she just shook her head watchin Auntie Annie. Only sometimes she'd yell if one of us did something real silly like putting a fire up under the eaves.

The other one that didn't join in was Melissa. She was Mum's big white fluffy cat and I reckon she thought rats was nothing to do with her, which was funny, her bein a cat. She never ever paid no attention to them. Dad said she was dead lazy. In fact, once Dad said she was that lazy she'd need a hand to have a good shit. Mum told him to shut up that filthy language in front of the kids. Anyway she never joined in. She'd just lay on the back step and watch it all and duck inside if we got too close with the hose or whatever.

Anyway, I was tellin you how we found Monty. It was on one of these war days and things was wound up like I've been tellin you. Little Petey yelled out that a couple of rats had run up the drain pipe that comes down from the roof. Auntie Annie got the ladder an climbed up and stuck the hose in the pipe at the top to flush them out and us and the dogs waited at the bottom to get them. Auntie Annie had the hose going in there full bore and we was peerin at the bottom end but no water came out. We looked up then just in time to see the water come spurtin back up the top. The next moment Auntie Annie gives a big scream and nearly falls off the ladder. She comes down like the rungs was red hot and then over the top of the gutter we see the head of a flamin big snake movin about. More and more of him came out and then he slithered up onto the roof and we had to get back to see him. I tell you what, he was a big snake. He was all over the roof.

We yelled to Dad to come and see him and Dad yelled to keep an eye on him 'till he got the gun. This was even better than the rat war with Dad gettin the gun and all. Dad came runnin out with the gun held all ready to fire and this was the real stuff but when he saw that snake he stopped. 'Cripes' he said 'a python. You don't blow out a python. They're good to have about. They're better on rats than anything else. Leave him. Let him have a go.'

I think Auntie Annie was not too sure about this. She hadn't said nothing since she came down that ladder and she was pretty pale still. She looked from Dad to the snake and back again. 'Are you sure Fred? Are you sure it's not poisonous?'

'No, it's not poisonous. Like I told you, it's a python. There's lots of them up here round Darwin. They don't bite, they just squeeze you to death. You want to watch out in bed tonight Annie, he might give you a bit of a cuddle.' We giggled a bit. We reckoned if Mum had been there she would have said something to Dad about talkin like that to Auntie Annie.

As it was, when we told Mum about the snake she wasn't impressed. Dad told her over and over that he was harmless and would keep the rats down, but I don't think she was too happy. Us kids wanted him to stay but Auntie Annie was a bit quiet. She saw Dad's argument but I think she was not keen to be matey with a snake. Mum said she just didn't like the idea of a snake about but she didn't have any really good reason. We had no chooks because the wild cats had got them all and Dad said the snake would live on the rats anyway. Finally Mum said the snake might hurt us kids and Dad patted little Trixie's backside and said the snake would never get its mouth open that far and Mum told him to cut out bein coarse.

Dad made a mistake then though. He looked at Melissa, asleep on a chair as usual and he said she'd make a great dinner for the snake. He said she was so lazy she probably wouldn't notice being swallowed. Mum got really crooked. She said if that snake touched Melissa, she'd blow its head off. Dad said she'd probably blow her own foot off and Mum got real annoyed and yelled at Dad and then Dad did his block and it went on 'till tea time.

Anyway, the snake stayed and we called him Monty and he must have had a great appetite for rats because he certainly thinned them out. We saw him quite often draped about the mango tree or curled up in the damp earth, near the vegetable patch or sort of dust-bathing himself in the sun. We all got used to him about the place. The dogs gave up barking at him and used to just lie with their heads on their paws watching him. We kids used to go up real close and call him Monty and he seemed to like it. Not that he smiled or wagged his tail or nothing, but he seemed happy. Dad told us not to go too close because one of them coils around you could hurt he reckoned. We saw him kill rats a couple of times and its no doubt Dad was right, the quick way those rats stopped kickin.

Mum sort of ignored Monty. She called him 'that snake' and I seen her eyein him off a couple of times when he was close to the fern patch near the back door where Melissa always slept in the daytime. Melissa herself never seemed to take no notice of Monty except once when Monty slipped his wicked looking head out from under the verandah about a foot from where she was sleepin and she shot straight up in the air about three feet with all her hair out and a real twitchy look on her.

After Monty had been with us about a month, the rats were pretty well thinned out and we wondered if he would move on. Then Melissa disappeared. She didn't come in for her tea one night and Mum went to the door and called her. She didn't come. Mum didn't say nothing and we never thought much about it but later when Melissa's dinner was still not touched, Mum said in a flat kind of a way 'Melissa's not come in.' She was lookin at Dad and we all knew what she was thinkin.

We all went outside then and walked all over the block and out on the road callin Melissa, but it was a dark night and there's lots of trees and bushes and a couple of sheds and an old car and some other junk on the block and we never saw no sign of her. It was a bit scary too. We was thinkin of Melissa being inside of Monty. I started thinkin all over again about one of them cold slippery sort of coils round me and I didn't poke into no bushes much. Little Petey and Trixie never went outside the light.

When we came in again, Mum looked pretty upset. She was sure 'that snake' had took Melissa. Dad looked like he wanted to say something funny but he didn't and we were glad 'cause Mum looked like she would fly off if he had of.

All next day we hunted for Melissa on the block and all up and down the road and in the neighbours' blocks but all the time we really thought it was hopeless. The more we looked, the more we were sure that Monty had eaten her. Monty himself was missing but that was nothing new, he often disappeared for days at a time and we never knew where he was. There were plenty of places on our block or round about where he could hole up and be hard to find and Dad said he probably fed up big then rested for a few days. We wondered if he'd fed up big this time on Melissa.

Mum got very edgy and things got sort of anyhow between her and Dad and also between her and Auntie Annie. I think Mum blamed Auntie Annie for the snake although this was unfair, Auntie Annie had never been too strong on letting him stay even though he did her work for her on the rats. She was upset about Melissa too. Anyhow on the second day after Melissa disappeared, Mum and Auntie Annie had a big row and said a lot of nasty things to each other and in the end, Auntie Annie started cryin and said she was going to leave. That upset us kids cause we liked Auntie Annie and we didn't like all this fightin anyway and Trixie started to cry and Mum told her to shut up and smacked her and she cried even more and we all cleared off outside to our cubby house. Trixie and Petey were snivellin and I was pretty much that way myself. It was all a big mess.

The next day Dad took Auntie Annie into town with the same two battered old suitcases she had when she came. Nobody was talkin much and I'm not sure where she was goin. I think she was gettin a bus to go south to Sydney. We all cried again when she left except Mum who said goodbye very polite and then went inside quickly.

The place went sort of dead without Auntie Annie. We lay about waitin for Dad to get back from Darwin, but when he did he was grumpy with us and wasn't talkin to Mum. Finally we all went down to Ginger Johnie's place because Dad had some buffalo calves he was rearin and we helped Ginger cut some grass for them and then Ginger and I had a go at ridin one of them.

Another couple of days we knew that Melissa was gone for good and we were gettin over missin Auntie Annie and things was sort of settlin down again. Then Mrs Spadzig came in and said she had seen Melissa. Mrs Spadzig lives on a block across the road. She is from

Europe somewhere and she is hard to understand. She has a lot of goats and Dad says she smells like a goat and he calls her Mrs Spastic but not to her face. Anyway, she said she had seen a fluffy white cat running down near the bottom of her block, below her goat pens.

We all streamed across the road after Mrs Spadzig, past her little shack and her weedy orchard and ramshackle goat pens. Then we started to search in all the long grass and rubbish and vines and scrub that covered the lower few acres of the block. Mum was calling all the time, 'Melissa, Melissa' and suddenly there, in a little clearing, was Melissa. Her long fur was a bit dirty and knotted but it was her alright.

Mum ran to pick her up but she just turned and slipped through the grass. We followed her easy enough because we could see her white bushy tail sticking up and she wasn't going fast. She ran to an old car body that was rusting away in the long grass. She jumped through a missing front window and over onto the back seat. We peered in through the dirty windows and on the back seat amongst some rags were two kittens, snowy white. Mum reached in through the open window and stroked Melissa but she didn't try to pick up or touch the kittens. Then she called us all to come away and we left Melissa alone.

'Well I'm blowed', says Mum, 'I never knew she was pregnant'.

'You wouldn't,' says Dad 'with all that fur and her being such a lay about anyway.'

Mum looked happier than she had for days and Dad took a chance.

'You was wrong accusin Monty, wasn't yer love?'

Mum stopped and stared ahead of her a moment.

'Yeah I suppose I was. I suppose I was a bit wrong about Annie too.'

Dad had stopped too and was looking at her. We kids was a few yards off watching them both.

'No love! I don't reckon! Time for her to go. Them big knockers of hers was gettin at me.'

We kids held our breath waitin for Mum to explode about that sort of language. Mum never did though. She just looked at Dad a moment then stuck her arm in his and said 'C'mon we'll get a cuppa tea.'

Monty never came back but he's around the blocks, still chasin rats. I hope he comes back to us sometime.

Source: Graham Calley, 'Auntie Annie and Monty', *Northern Perspective*, vol.7, no.2, 1985, pp.12-24.

13 Sprees, drunks, and race meetings

I know of one shooter who shot and sent away over five thousand hides in one year. Such, however, was his improvidence that he had to borrow £50 that year to pay his drink bill.
— W. E. Harney, *North of 23°*, 1945

> Oh, when I'm dead don't bury me at all,
> But pickle my bones in alcohawl;
> Place a bottle of grog each end of me,
> And be assured I'll R.I.P.

— Mooch's song in Xavier Herbert, *Capricornia*, 1938

Previous page: The Commercial, in Mitchell Street, one of Palmerston's first hotels. Paul Foelsche organised the clientele for this verandah shot in February 1874.

Honey intoxication

John Sweatman

Notwithstanding the disappointment we had experienced with regard to our stores, we managed to keep a pretty good mess while we remained at Point Record. We had fresh pork 5 times a week from Victoria but of this, as may be supposed, we soon got heartily tired; nothing is so insupportable as a long continued course of pig. However we could always get plenty of fish by a haul of the seine, and there was very tolerable shooting: one bird in particular, a gigantic species of crane, called from its peculiar habits of frequenting the native camps, 'the native companion' was far from uncommon & one specimen would furnish two days food for our mess, for it stood 5 feet high & was a fleshy bird, eating very like young beef. Ducks & geese were also abundant, if we gave a native a musket & a dozen charges of powder & shot, ordering him to bring in a dozen geese, he would always do it and bag half a dozen for himself into the bargain by sneaking under the mangroves or half under water into a flock and never firing unless sure of his aim and having 2 or 3 birds in a line. On the hills at the back of Barrow bay, we got plenty of small but delicate wallabies by running them down with dogs, and the native women brought in a constant supply of oysters, maroin and honey, so that we wanted for nothing. The oysters were mud, and very large and good, from them the natives get a good many small but often tolerably good pearls: maroin is the name given to the young shoots at the top of the cabbage palm, which when boiled forms a good and nutritious vegetable but to obtain it the tree must be cut down and of course destroyed. The honey is obtained by the natives out of holes in the trees, they are very expert in discovering the nests & cutting out the combs, meeting no difficulty from the bees which are small and stingless: they are excessively fond of the honey and it is amusing, though at the same time not a little disgusting, to see the way they cram comb and all into their mouths with both hands at once. After filling their bellies with honey, they drink copiously of water and this has the effect of making them absolutely intoxicated, as much as if they had been drinking spirits: I have seen a man actually unable to walk, through nothing else but this.

Source: Jim Allen & Peter Corris (eds), *The Journal of John Sweatman* [1845-47], University of Queensland Press, St Lucia, 1977, pp.132-3.

Port Darwin Camp races and athletic sports

Northern Territory Times, 1882

On Wednesday, 24th instant, (Queen's birthday) our usually quiet little neighbourhood was stirred into unwonted activity.

At 9 o'clock horsemen were to be seen coming from all directions and assembling at Host Allwright's hotel, Port Darwin Camp, preparatory to going out to the racecourse where the long-talked-of event was to take place between Mr. H. Roberts' Bellman and Mr. H. Allwright's colt Don Juan, for £200 aside; distance one mile and a half. After a pleasant ride of two miles, the rendezvous was reached, and but a short time elapsed before the horses and jockeys put in an appearance. Both horses were in splendid fettle, and the betting was equal. Mr. W. Lawrie rode Bellman, Mr. Leonard Elvey the colt; Mr. Baye acted as starter and Mr. C.W. Nash as judge. Both horses made a splendid start, but it was quite evident that Bellman was too much for the colt, as he gradually took the lead and came in an easy winner, hard held, by about three lengths. Time, 2 min. 58 sec. The colt's backers were not satisfied that he had done his best, so they matched him to run again next day for £100 aside, the colt being allowed 10 lbs. less weight than what he carried the previous day. Mr. Herring rode the colt on this occasion. This was again an easy victory for the old horse, winning by four lengths.

The next event was a Chinese horse race for £5 aside, between Ah Sup's Ringrail Roarer, and Ah Qui's Bog-trotter. It was the most amusing event of the day, both horses doing a preliminary canter through the bush before their riders could get them up to the starting post. Bog-trotter came in an easy winner by half-a-mile.

There being no booth or refreshment stall on the course, owing to some mismanagement on Mr. Allwright's part in not obtaining a permit in time, and as the spectators were anxiously waiting to moisten the bronchial tubes, it was deemed advisable to return to Port Darwin Camp and hold the sports there.

The sports commenced at 2 p.m., there being about 400 persons on the ground, including white, black, and copper-coloured, some of the spectators having come from Palmerston and Southport. I must not forget to mention that several of the fair sex, both British and Foreign, graced the ground by their presence. It was quite a treat to witness with what ease and grace they sat their prancing grey steeds while watching the sports; they quite astonished the natives. Their costume, I am certain, would not have disgraced either the Flemington or Morphetville course. As I do not, as a rule, peruse the 'Ladies' Column,' I shall not attempt to describe the paraphernalia. Everything passed off very successful, it being one of the most orderly meetings held up country.

There were one or two skirmishes during the day between a few of the slightly elevated members, but owing to the vigilance of Corporal Montague and Trooper Baye, the disturbances were easily quelled.

On account of there being so many events on the list, it was decided to put half of them off until the following day, which was accordingly done. The following is the list of events and the names of the winners:–

1st. — Maiden Race. Four entries for this event, Jacky, an aboriginal, winning easily. Prize £3.

2nd. — Hop, Step, and Jump. Four entered. Spencer won easily, jumping 22ft. Prize £2.

3rd. — Throwing the Hammer. McInnis winning, 33 yards. Prize £1 10s.

4th. — Quoit Match. Eight entered for this event, Winn and Clyma being the winners. Prize £3.

5th. — Running Long Jump. Four entries, Spencer winning with 14ft. Prize £2.

6th. — Standing Long Jump. Four entered, Spencer winning with 9ft. 8in. Prize £1 10s.

7th. — Throwing the Hammer. Three entered, Spencer winning, 32 yards. Prize £2.

8th. — Running High Jump. Three entered for this, which was the closest contest of the day, Baye and Spencer both getting over 5ft.; the stakes were divided. Prize £2.

9th. — Champion Stakes, 100 yards. Spencer won. Prize £10.

10th. — Rifle Match. 15 entries. The shooting was very poor, Kirwan winning. Prize £3.

11th. — Throwing the Cricket Ball. Four entries. Won easily by Baye, 91 yards. Prize £2.

12th. — Handicap, 150 yards. Five entries. Spencer (the Queensland champion) was again to the front. Prize £15.

13th. — Pole-leaping. Five entries, Kirwan winning, 8ft. 6in. Prize £2.

14th. — Revolver Match. Eight entries. The shooting was poor, Kirwan winning. Prize £3.

15th. — Three-legged Race. Eight entries. Kirwan and Jacky winners.

16th. — Consolation Stakes, 100 yards. Five entries. G. H. Cooper, winner.

Source: 'Port Darwin Camp races and athletic sports', *Northern Territory Times*, 3 June 1882.

Drinking saloons and grog shanties, 1872

Mrs Dominic D. Daly

[The] influx of trade and population made great changes in the settlement. Shops were opened, in which, like the general stores so common all over Australia, one could purchase anything, from a bag of flour to a roll of silk. As soon as the principal store was opened, I was asked amongst others to go and inspect the stock. I was amazed at the sight of such a medley of things. The newest shapes in straw hats were lying side by side with camp ovens and frying-pans, while flannel and Oxford shirts, together with wideawake felt hats, vests, collars, and ties, kept company with boxes of tea, bags of flour, and ready-tapped barrels of whiskey, rum, and gin. It was a thirsty time, I fear, and judging from the effects one saw, the liquor supplied could have been none of the best.

Drinking saloons were very soon opened — did ever a settlement start without one? — and their deadly consequences were soon apparent. The hardships undergone by the men, added to excitement, low diet, and not a little from their own faults, alas! brought on sickness. The ground had been newly turned up, all over the settlement, when the building of the rude shanties took place. This in itself was a fertile source of fever, as it is in any newly-opened country in the tropics; and for the first time since I had known Port Darwin, a severe epidemic of fever broke out, nearly every one in the place caught it, and my time was taken up for some considerable time in nursing those of my people who were attacked. The doctor had his hands full, as the air was so impregnated with malaria that men who had only landed some twenty-four hours were laid low with this extraordinarily violent type of fever. Many of the sufferers never left Port Darwin for the [gold] reefs at all; they lay shaking in the miseries of ague in their tents or huts, suffering agonies of heat in the intervals that elapse between the hot and the cold stages. When they were well enough to be moved, the sufferers left by the first ship that sailed away out of the harbour. These were some of the causes that led to people's faith being shaken in the Port Darwin goldfields, as the returning diggers, even without giving the country a fair trial, abused it most violently. It was, however, a wretched time for everyone, and this epidemic took place in the dry season too. There was no hospital, or any accommodation for the sick men. Each mate nursed his fellow, and some strikingly pathetic touches of devotion were shown here and there amongst them. There was no one to cook the necessary food that the invalids required to pick up their strength; no fowls to be bought, to make into the essence that is so generally given to fever patients wherever I have been since. Nothing but the hideous brown tin of canned meat to turn into soup for the pale-faced, sunken-eyed men that met one at every turn — strongly-built and powerfully-made fellows, whose weakness was pitiable in the extreme; all the more so from the fact that they were totally unaccustomed to this new form of sickness which had seized upon them so suddenly, and with so little warning. The grog shanties were always full, I am sorry to say, and, in spite of the depression that reigned on every side, they drove a stirring and paying trade. This is a sample of what was sold to the poor fellows so lately recovering from fever — gin and kerosene mixed with Worcester sauce, and flavoured with ginger and sugar. Such a mixture seems awful to contemplate. Yet this was the poison these unfortunate men had to drink, and to pay a heavy price for it too. This deadly concoction simply maddened those who partook of it, and to this cause as well as the climate must be attributed the severity of the cases that came under treatment.

Source: Mrs Dominic D. Daly, *Digging, Squatting and Pioneering Life in the Northern Territory of South Australia*, Sampson Low, Marson, Searle & Rivington, London, 1887, pp.148-51.

Vile liquor, 1880s

Alfred Searcy

To be a successful shanty-keeper a man must be able to shoot, fight, and ride well. He must also be a good bushman and gambler. It is necessary that he should have a knowledge of the handwriting of the station owners and managers in the district.

As a rule, vile liquor is sold in the shanties. Accounts are rarely kept of the drinks consumed by the customers. There it is, help yourself, as much as you like, and as long as you like, that is, of course, if you have first handed in your cheque, and consequently, 'your breath is sweet.' The cheque having been knocked down, the outfit follows, ending generally in a fit of delirium tremens, from which some recover, but many don't. These shanty-keepers out back were, in my time, a terrible curse, not alone to the poor bushman, but to the squatters on whose country they settled, for they were the means of drawing numbers of cattle and horse thieves about the place. I knew the owner of a station who was thus afflicted. He tried many means of getting rid of the shanty-man and his wife — a bad lot, the pair, regular outlaws — but failed. As a last resource he put a fire-stick into the tent and brush buildings, the whole lot being burned with the stock of spirits and ale. Floating grog-shops, or, as they are called, bum-boats, were another terrible infliction.

Two men, with a van and pair of horses, a rum and whisky cask, and some chemicals, would travel through the country, visiting the stations and cattle camps, and sell the vile compound. They would also gamble and indulge in any little villainy that would rake in the dollars. They were never known to run short of grog, yet they never received any. They manufactured it themselves at great profit, but at the cost of many a life. As can be imagined, great sprees and drunks often eventuated, especially at race-meetings. It would be drink, drink, for days, perhaps weeks, until every drop of intoxicating liquor was consumed. The after effects would be terrible. Recourse would then be had to every imaginable drink, such as Worcester Sauce, Friar's Balsam, Pain Killer, until that supply was exhausted. Some of the poor fellows would finish up in delirium tremens, with others bordering on them. Men in their sane moments would tie themselves up to a tree at night, others would hopple themselves, fearing that they would wander in their mad moments into the bush and be lost.

Source: Alfred Searcy, *In Australian Tropics*, 2nd edn, George Robertson, London & Sydney, 1909, pp.152-4.

McCarthy's brew: A gulf country yarn

George Essex Evans

The teams of Black McCarthy crawled adown the Norman road,
The ground was bare, the bullocks spare, and grievous was the load,
And the brown hawks wheeled above them and the heat-waves throbbed and glowed.

With lolling tongues and blood-shot eyes and sinews all a-strain
McCarthy's bullocks staggered on across the sun-cracked plain,
The wagons lumbering after and the drivers raising Cain …

Three mournful figures sat around the camp-fire's fitful glare —
McKinlay Jim and 'Spotty' and McCarthy's self they were —
But their spirits were so dismal that they couldn't raise a swear!

'Twas not the long, dry stage ahead that made those bold hearts shrink,
The drought-cursed ground, the dying stock, the water thick as ink,
But — the drinking curse was on them, and they had no grog to drink!

Then with a bound up from the ground, McCarthy jumped and cried:
' 'Tis vain! 'Tis vain! I go insane. These pangs in my inside!
Some sort of grog, for love of God, invent, concoct, provide!'

McKinlay Jim straight answered him: 'Those lotions, sauce, and things
Should surely make a brew to slake these thirstful sufferings —
A brew that slakes, a brew that wakes and burns and bucks and stings.'

Down came the cases from the load — they wrenched them wide with force.
They poured and mixed and stirred a brew that would have killed a horse —
Cayenne, pain-killer, pickles, embrocation, Worcester sauce!

O, wild and high and fierce and free the orgy rose that night;
The songs they sang, the deeds they did, no poet could indite;
To see them pass that billy round — it was a fearsome sight.

The dingo heard them and with tail between his legs he fled!
The curlew saw them and he ceased his wailing for the dead!
Each frightened bullock on the plain went straightway off his head!

Alas! and there are those who say that at the dawn of day
Three perforated carriers round a smouldering camp-fire lay:
They did not think McCarthy's brew would take them in that way!

McCarthy's teams at Normanton no more the Gulf men see.
McCarthy's bullocks roam the wilds exuberant and free;
McCarthy lies — an instance of preserved anatomee!

Go. Take the moral of this song, which in deep grief I write:
Don't ever drink McCarthy's brew. Be warned in case you might —
Gulf whisky kills at twenty yards, but this stuff kills at sight!

Source: George Essex Evans, 'McCarthy's brew: A gulf country yarn', n.d., in Douglas Stewart & Nancy Keesing (eds), *Australian Bush Ballads*, Angus & Robertson, Sydney, 1955, pp.223-4.

Borroloola races, 1891

William Linklater & Lynda Tapp

At Borroloola I was commissioned to train the race horses belonging to a publican, and one of the perquisites was a daily ration of liquor. This meant I had plenty of help with the early morning exercising, for my apprentices were more than willing to be paid in whisky.

Soon the stockmen from hundreds of miles round began converging on the township. Borroloola consisted of two hotels, three stores, two Government buildings and a few small shacks, but during the period of the races the population of between forty and fifty, including Chinese, would grow by about a hundred, and a hilarious time would be had by all.

The country round about — now considered one of the furthest outback spots in Australia — is undulating and fairly well wooded, but very boggy in the wet season. In the

The old delicensed pub at Borroloola. Territory drinking holes have a character all their own.

February of the wet of 1891, sixteen inches of rain fell in five days. As the town was situated about forty miles from the mouth of the McArthur River, supplies usually came by sea, but the arrival dates of vessels were uncertain. Universal sympathy was extended to the character who left his horses on a patch of high ground, waded twenty miles with a steadily growing thirst, and arrived with £300 spending money in a town with no grog.

Originally formed as a depot for the Overland Telegraph construction, Borroloola had been of considerable importance during the cattle migration and exodus from the Queensland mines. There were generally eight or nine teams waiting for the small mail and supply ships. Often a man would ride in a hundred miles to collect the mail for his district, leaving his station at the mercy of the blacks.

Many travellers celebrated rowdily at Borroloola before plunging into the wilderness that lay between the town and the next carousal. Some residents complained strenuously about all this riotous living and at length arranged to have two constables stationed there. Stung to action by this, one cheerful group confiscated the police horses and, after driving them a long way into wild country, lit fires to cover the trail. However, one of the black trackers was so skilful that he was able to lead the troopers straight over the burnt-out country to their horses.

In fact, liquor, learning and lawlessness were the chief interests of early Borroloola. Sly-grog selling was particularly prevalent in the McArthur River district, and on the Tablelands. It came by packhorse, with the teamsters, with the hawkers, and by the normal sea route. Whatever else was lacking, there was usually plenty of grog. Men worn down by bad food and monotony were not only ready for a spree, but willing to pay for it handsomely. So, wherever men were at work, the racketeers found them.

Inevitably, there was gambling, too, and soon a peaceful camp would be alive with drunks fighting and cursing, and easy victims for the grog-sellers' hangers-on. Men got into debt, and health suffered. About this time a group who had been tank-sinking on Brunette Downs started in with good cheques for a rest and a change of diet. (The Chinese had fine gardens at Borroloola, and there were plenty of vegetables for all, as well as carrots for race horses.) But these men fell to the grog sellers, wrecked their finances, and had to abandon all ideas of a rest and amenities.

Sporadic efforts were made to put the traffic down, but there was not much sting in them. One man operating on the Tablelands was caught and fined twenty-five pounds. When it was found that he was nine pounds short, the names of the J.P. who had tried him and the constable who had arrested him figured prominently on the subscription list to save him from three months' gaol.

Borroloola was famous for its library all over the north. A sympathetic vice-regal visitor was instrumental in arranging a Carnegie grant for the town, so Borroloola had a splendid collection of books. They were a grand boon to the settlers within a radius of 200 miles. When the importance of the town waned, the books were left to solitary confinement in the goal and the ravages of white ants.

Tom Williams and his jockey, Mick Kinnaird, came to the races all the way from Alice Springs with two horses. Above all else in the world, Tom loved race horses and racing, and although he drank very little, anyone could buy a fight with him very cheaply.

Paddie Lennie, a young Irishman who did yard building and fencing on the Barkly Tablelands, hoped to foster the carnival spirit. He had some good mares and a stallion running on the Ranken River on a block of 400 square miles, leased but not used by Austral Downs. Paddy had permission to run his mares on it, and soon bred up a small mob of good horses.

Now Paddy had picked out one of the best of his colts and brought it to Borroloola to be entered in the Lady's Bracelet in the name of his black concubine, Ranken Mary Anne, the belle of the Ranken River. When nominations were called for the Lady's Bracelet, Paddy handed in his written nomination:

Name of horse	*Daniel O'Connor*
Age	*Four years*
Colour	*Bay*
Name of lady	*Ranken Mary Anne of the Ranken River*

Of course the secretary refused to accept the nomination, and Paddy punched him. The secretary sailed into Paddy, and the fight ended in a draw, with black eyes all round. Then the secretary said that he would put it to the committee, and if the members accepted the nomination, it would be all right with him.

Paddy agreed to this and started to canvass the individual members before the meeting took place. He would ask a committee man if he intended to vote for the acceptance of his nomination. If the man said no, Paddy fought him. If Paddy lost, he would provoke another fight an hour later, and bruised and black-eyed would come up for a third and fourth encounter if necessary. Realizing that he would have to fight every time he and Paddy met, the committee man would finally surrender. When Paddy had worked his way through the whole committee they agreed, unanimously, to accept the nomination in the name of his black concubine. These daily fights were among the best of the pre-race attractions.

The great day came and a good crowd of stockmen, drovers, yard builders, fencers, station managers and others turned up. Of course there was a bar close to the bough shed grandstand, and horses, carts, and even a few buggies, and the general excitement helped to make it a gala scene. About £250 had been collected for prize money.

There was another rousing fight when Alick Wilson approached the jockeys to ride his horse, The Iguana, in the Maiden Plate. When they said they had come to ride horses, not reptiles, they had to deal with a deeply affronted man.

It was time for the Lady's Bracelet and Paddy Lennie, wearing green jacket and cap, led Daniel O'Connor to the clerk of the scales to weigh out. He had a grin all over his battered face when he did his preliminary in front of the grandstand, announcing in a loud voice, 'For Ranken Mary Anne'. The rest is anticlimax, for Paddy came in last, and after the race got blind drunk as a fitting finale.

Paddy is a legend now, for he became a hatter, one of those who, as they say, married his horses. His mob went on breeding, but Paddy refused to sell or dispose of any in any way. Increasing rapidly, they went wild and became a great nuisance over a vast area of country. Paddy was cursed from there to nowhere, and turned into the perfect example of the never welcome guest. He was a landless man, but someone so close to the earth that he insisted on his right to run his multitude of horses anywhere. It was said that he never saw an empty bottle but he filled it with water and planted it in some tree to serve some possible future need; and he left caches of food inside the remains of animals dead on the plains. The sky was his roof, and he shared the larder of the primitive blacks though they grudged him the goannas and grubs he took.

Today, we hear that the brumbies are bad in the north, and there is a suggestion that a bonus should be paid for every pair of ears brought in. I wonder if Paddy turns in his shallow grave.

Source: William Linklater & Lynda Tapp, *Gather No Moss*, Macmillan, Melbourne, 1968, pp.83-7.

A 16th-century view of 'Territory man'?

Don Campbell

(With apologies to Spencer's 'Faery Queene')

In greene vine leaves he was right fitly clad;
   For other clothes he could not weare for heat,
   And on his head an yvie girland had,
   From under which fast trickled downe the sweat:
   Still as he rode, he somewhat still did eat,
   And in his hand did beare a bouzing can,
   Of which he supt so oft, that on his seat
   His dronken corse he scarse upholden can,
In shape and life more like an monster, than a man.

Source: Don Campbell, 'A 16th-century view of "Territory man"?', *Northern Perspective*, vol.2, no.2, 1979, p.23.

Charismatic Katherine bookmaker Fred Miners lays the odds at a Victoria River Downs race meeting in the early 1960s — with what looks like the prototype for the renowned 'Darwin Stubby' in his left hand.

White Dog, the boozing hound

Keith Willey

[On] the subject of liquor, I would like to repeat an obituary I wrote for the Northern Territory Times *several years ago [c. 1960] on White Dog, boon companion of many a late-night session at the Victoria Hotel:*

Darwin pubs have lost their best-known customer. White Dog, the boozing hound, passed away in his sleep the other night.

White Dog is all they ever called him. But he was known not only to every resident, but to the tens of thousands of visitors who have passed through Darwin over the last decade. Local people would point to him with pride as he lay grunting on the footpath, as a real tourist attraction. His age is unknown, but he is believed to have been around eight or nine years.

White Dog used to be a fox terrier once. But years of happy guzzling gradually turned him into a four-stone monster with a gut like a five-gallon keg and meaty jowls stretching six or eight inches from ear to ear. He was a cheerful drinker, widely known as the only dog in Darwin which could smile.

Each morning and afternoon he would waddle down to the hotel. There was nothing snobbish about White Dog. He preferred the public bar, where the beer was cheaper. There he would while away three-quarters of his waking time.

White Dog never touched whisky or rum. But he dearly liked his beer. Sometimes he would drink it from a cup or jug. But what he really loved was to lap beer up from the concrete floor where fellow-drinkers had thoughtfully poured it for him. In his heyday White Dog seldom left the bar until ejected at 10.10 p.m. When not grogging on he was generally to be found near either the Bank of New South Wales or the Commonwealth Bank. He adopted the Wales as his home. There he would lurch to sleep off his nightly sessions. He liked the Commonwealth Bank, too, and often staggered over to scrounge a meal.

When his hangovers were particularly acute — and White Dog must have had some whoppers — customers would often find him snoozing beneath the palm trees or snoring, with a happy grin on his face, right in the middle of a bank's main entrance.

White Dog was a regular drinker, but there was nothing offensive about him. He could hold his liquor better than many of his two-legged pot companions. Sometimes, deep in his cups, he would stagger slightly as he left the pub. But no one ever had to carry him home. He had no kennel, as few would have been broad enough to hold him. He slept where he fell.

A thorough gentleman, he never chased cats or female dogs and was never known to bite the hand that fed him. No snarl ever escaped his lips; only happy snorts and gurgles.

Seven or eight months ago tragedy entered White Dog's cheerful world of booze and bones. He fell ill. The bank boys took him to a vet. and the verdict was ... dropsy! Poor White Dog was ordered onto the water wagon. He lived his last few months quietly, without his beer. Most of the time he spent sleeping, or eating. Occasionally he would peep wistfully through the swinging doors, but he could not be coaxed to touch a drop. White Dog died in his sleep, without pain. For him the bung is out of the barrel; the last bottle drained. Here's to you, White Dog. Darwin won't seem the same place without you.

Source: Keith Willey, *Eaters of the Lotus*, Jacaranda Press, Brisbane, 1964, pp.115-16.

Alice Springs pub

Robyn Davidson

The pub had four major divisions. The Saloon Bar, where I worked, catered for many of the regulars — truckies, station hands, some of them part-Aboriginal, and the occasional black ringer (station hand) who had just been paid a two-hundred-dollar cheque to be cashed at the pub, of which little would be left by the next morning. However, blacks, despite the easy pickings, were tacitly frowned upon here and didn't often come in. The Lounge Bar catered for tourists and some of the regulars of a slightly higher social standing although there was general flow between the two areas. The Pool Room allowed blacks in but grudgingly, and the Inner Bar, a cosy, tastelessly decorated room, was where the police, lawyers and upper-class whites drank. Here blacks were forbidden. This was not legal or stated but it was enforced none the less under the guise of, 'Patrons are requested to wear neat attire etc.' It was known by the hard cases in the saloon as the Poofters' Bar. At least this pub didn't have a dog window, as most of the others in the Northern Territory had. These were small windows around the back where booze was sold to the blacks.

I lived in a draughty cement pigeon-hole out the back, furnished with an aluminium bed covered by a stained shocking pink chenille bedspread. I wrote cheery letters home, telling everyone how I was practising animal training on giant cockroaches, how I bullwhipped them into submission but was afraid they might one day turn against me, which was why I had refrained from putting my head in their mouths. But the jokes hid a growing depression...

One does not have to delve too deeply to discover why some of the world's angriest feminists breathed crisp blue Australian air during their formative years, before packing their kangaroo-skin bags and scurrying over to London or New York or any place where the antipodean machismo would fade gently from their battle-scarred consciousnesses like some grisly nightmare at dawn. Anyone who has worked in a men-only bar in Alice Springs will know what I mean.

Some of the men would be hanging around the doors at opening time and, after a full twelve hours of saturation, leave reluctantly, and often on all fours, at closing time. Others had their set hours and set places and set friends and swapped yarns for a while, always the same stories, always the same reactions. Others sat on their own in a corner dreaming of god knows what. Some were crazy, some were mean, and some, oh those few rare gems, were amiable, helpful and humorous. By nine p.m. some would be in tears over lost opportunities, lost women, or lost hope. And while they wept, and while I held their hands across the counter saying there there, they pissed silently and unselfconsciously up against the bar.

To really come to grips with the Australian cult of misogyny, one has to plod back through all two hundred years of white Australia's history, and land on the shore of the 'wide brown land' with a bunch of hard-done-by whingeing convicts. Actually, the place where they landed was relatively green and inviting, the wide brown stuff was to come later. One imagines life was none too easy in the colony, but the boys learnt to stick together and when they'd done their stretch, if they were still sound of limb, they ventured into the forbidding country beyond to try and scratch a pitiful living. They were tough and they had absolutely nothing to lose. And they had alcohol to soften the blow. By the 1840s it began to dawn on the residents that something was missing — sheep and women. The former they imported from Spain, a stroke of genius that was to set Australia on the economic map; the latter they brought over in boats from the poor-houses and orphanages of England. Since there were never enough to go round (women, that is) one can visualize only too clearly the frenzied rush on the Sydney wharves when the girls came bravely sailing in. Such a traumatic racial memory is hard to blot out in a mere century, and the cult is sustained and revitalized in every pub in the country, especially in the outback where the stereotyped image of the Aussie male is still so sentimentally clung to. The modern-day manifestation is almost totally devoid of charm. He is biased, bigoted, boring and, above all, brutal. His enjoyments in life are limited to fighting, shooting and drinking. To him a mate includes anyone who is not a wop, wog, pom, coon, boong, nigger, rice-eye, kyke, chink, Iti, nip, frog, kraut, commie, poofter, slope, wanker, and yes, shiela, chick or bird.

One night in the pub one of the kinder regulars whispered to me, 'You ought to be more careful, girl, you know you've been nominated by some of these blokes as the next town rape case. You shouldn't be so friendly.'

I was devastated. What had I done but patted the odd shoulder or helped out the occasional paralytic or listened in silence to some heart-breaking hard luck story. I felt really frightened for the first time.

On another occasion I had taken over from someone in the Inner Bar. There were maybe half a dozen men drinking in there quietly, including two or three policemen. Suddenly an old dishevelled drunken Aboriginal woman came in and started yelling abuse and obscenities at the cops. A big burly policeman went over to her and started banging her head against the wall. 'Shuttup and get out, you old gin,' he shouted back. I was about to deparalyse my limbs, leap over the bar and stop him, when he dragged her out to the door and shoved her into the street. Not a person moved off their stools and presently everyone went back to their drinks with a few cracks about the stupidity of coons. I shed some tears behind the bar that night when no one was looking, not of self-pity but of helpless anger and disgust.

Source: Robyn Davidson, *Tracks*, Granada, London, 1980, pp.32-5.

14 Opening up the country: Drovers, buffalo hunters, and miners

For among the diggers and drovers, saints, poets and poddy-dodgers, who rode and plodded in the wake of the first handful, there was no-one to record this fantastic pilgrimage. It will never be known how many died of thirst, drink and disease; how many were murdered, speared, or committed suicide. But it is certain that had the tale been chronicled, the total of adventure and steadfast endurance would have established the migration as one of the greatest mass exploits of all time.
— William Linklater & Lynda Tapp, *Gather No Moss*, 1968

What had been done to the country they had passed through, by pigs and cattle, was nothing compared with what the gold miners of forty or fifty years before had done to the region they now entered. It was hereabouts that Civilization of the land had begun in force where the process known as Opening Up The Country had really begun. Quite literally had this country been Opened Up.
— Xavier Herbert, *Poor Fellow My Country*, 1975

Previous page: Spider Brennan with a mining bucket, at Maranboy Siding, near Katherine.

Working in the stock camp

Amy Laurie

When I was a little baby, when I was born, I was at Kirkimbie Station, Northern Territory. We had a bit of a cattle station there, but they left it after all the stockmen had a row ... I was reared up in Western Australia because my father moved away from the Territory to find another job. He used to get paid, but he was the most sensible out of that big mob who worked on the station mustering bullocks and things like that when I was a little one. He came to Salt Pan with old man McDonald, Duncan, Sandy and somewhere about three or four hundred horses. I can just remember shifting from Kirkimbie Station to Salt Pan. We used to work on that salt — it grows really big — and there was a spring running through it, and lots of stone heaps. You wash it with the water and next morning you just get something like a big spoon to scoop up all the salt. Very good place. We used to cart the salt by donkey wagon to Ord River Station. That was around 1922. It flooded then — Ord River Station, Turner, Flora Valley, Mistake Creek. They were all flooded, and we nearly got drowned except that we were on a little island.

That's why my grandfather shifted from there and we went to Palm Springs, near Halls Creek. This place had a big garden and grew bananas, dates and vegetables. We couldn't stop there long, and they didn't make a living because the kids ate all the fruit. Jack Skeehan, David Skeehan's father, had that place. That's where grandfather [Jim McDonald] died. Duncan was a teenage boy, Sandy was a good size boy, and I was a middle aged 'boy'. Skeehan sold all the horses to my father; they could pick out whichever horse they wanted ... 'I want that horse.' 'All right you can take this one now' — like that. But my two uncles said, 'No, we don't want any horses.' My father took six, seven, maybe eight horses with saddles and everything, just for the family. Timor ponies — a good lot of horses. He sold all of them. That's why we came down this way then. My father came down to Spring Creek [a Vestey's Station in northern Western Australia], and we started work. I was only a girl then — somewhere about nineteen — riding horses. From when I was young, I worked the bullocks the same as the boys ... Women used to like it you know, like to be alone, droving all the time. Some friends and I, we all liked it. Riding horses and working in the stock camp — that was my experience ... I first started when I was about ten.

When I was a little one, you know what those stockmen used to do? Chuck me over! Pick me up from my bed. They'd say, 'You wanta sleep all the time?' Bang! — and down in the water. There was a big mob of girls and boys; they did it to all of them ... We'd be coming back wet, cold ... sometimes about six o'clock in the morning, before sunrise, we had to go on the horses. 'No go out!' 'Oh, really?' When I got up to twenty-one I was married — tribal law you know — and left the place with my husband, and that year he died, droving. He was a boy from Queensland named Alec Smith. He had taught me to ride when I was younger. He used to make me get on the horses and when I fell down from the horse he gotta belt me — give me a whipping. 'You gotta stick to the saddle', he'd say ... I liked riding, but it's a long job. You get tired riding such a long, long way. A hard life but I used to like it.

I was working with a bloke called Nugget Quinlan, who also came from Queensland. He had a droving station, and we stopped and worked for him there at Nine Mile Station [near Wyndham]. My father, my mother and some others were with me. They've all died now, but each would work ... walking the cattle to No. 3 Bore, Gordon Downs and Sturt Creek, then go to No. 4, call in at No. 7, and more. We used to meet them cattle. And I on a horse. We'd go to Wyndham, to the dock there, to the aerodrome which they cut all the trees down to make. That's where the road was for the bullock; it was a clear tunnel which met up with the river at the base of Coolibah Pocket. We'd go to Colorado boundary, from there to Maxwell Plain at Carlton Reach — the Racecourse now. We used to call it Lily Creek when we were droving. Sometimes we'd camp up at a place called Four Mile. That bloke Terry [Brahn] has a place that used to be our camping area for the bullocks, and a stockyard belonging to Ivanhoe Station was right where the PWD [Public Works Department] yard is now. This country had no houses of any sort. It was just a wild country — a big jungle. They just cut all the trees down.

    Those droving days were good. I used to do cooking and horsetailing. I'd pack up all those packs on the horses, on all the roads, make the camp-places where the bullock can lay and cook by myself. We'd camp all the way from Waterloo right to here, the Kununurra racecourse. Some boys came up from Wyndham and I had a holiday. We were short-handed man — only five of us — three men and two women. All those other mates have now died ... I reckon I had my best days because of cattle work. Droving is the best. These young people, when they say 'I can't ride a horse', they can't. Day and night I watched the bullocks. Might be horsetailing from eight in the night up to ten at night, then another man or woman would come in and watch when you're asleep ... all the way like that, we'd watch the bullocks. Sometimes there'd be a big rush — you've got to be on a horse. They used to be really wild bullocks. We had one rush down there at Four Mile on that road to Cockatoo. You know where Bubba Darey lives at Golden Gate? We came through that way with all Victoria River bullocks — really big ones that carry trees and all. They had another rush with lots of bullocks. We were camping up near here and another mob was at the racecourse. That night the two of us — that mob and this mob — got mixed up. We didn't know what bullocks belonged to who but for earmarks. The Rosewood mob went back to Rosewood, the Victoria mob back to Victoria River Downs. Oh, we had a lot of rough times. You can't put that cattle through the gorge. You've got to jump off your horses, leave your horses sitting down. Some of the mob has got to be in front and another mob cuts the other mob off; and, half-'n'-half, you've got to put them through the gorge. When that big rain came one time we were at No. 3 Bore. No trees there, just a plain. They càll it Munga Plain — this side of Dirrindudu. Oh, you can't hold the cattle there. They go this way and that way, and make the ground very dry. You've got to move them all along. Big work there. I could've been a millionaire if I'd known — if they would have paid me! I keep thinking about that. I left droving because I had a kid, though for a while I carried the kid in the saddle. When I was about twenty-two, I started having a baby. I wasn't like these young girls today: I didn't play with the young boys like these girls. The first baby I had was to a Chinese half-cast, George Ah Kim, who I was living with before Darkie Green picked me up. He was born in Australia to a black mother, and his father had a garden at Muggs Lagoon. He was well-educated — come back from China. I only had him for one year, and soon as the baby was born, he had an accident on Rosewood Station. A horse fell on top of him and he died. Might be wild horse, quiet horse, the drovers they were always changing horses — fresh horse every day. I remember the last time I went down droving through Cockatoo Lagoon up to Coolibah, right down to Wyndham and back. That took a long time. After that I thought well I can't ride horses, can't put kids on them, so I told my boss, 'I can't ride a horse anymore 'cause I got a family now, coming.' When I was young I never had none.

    In those days we never got nothing — no wages. You know that day [in those days] coloured people can't get paid or something like that. Some blokes, the white man, got paid. But I never got no money out of it. Old Quinlan started thinking about the pay like the Queensland award, and one time he said like, 'All right, you are a very good woman. I'll give you six horses.' He gave me saddles, bridles, packs and things, and I started selling those horses. He gave me clothes, and we used to eat tucker all right, but all the rest of the time we were working for him we were never paid anything but tucker and clothes, and anything we wanted from the store. Anything you wanted you got because we didn't know money. Some people came in from working on Ord River and Mistake Creek Stations. They said, 'What's the matter this one don't pay you?' 'You know money?' 'No ...' After that Quinlan was telling us, 'Now, I'm gonna pay you next year like ...' Oh, we were there for nearly two years droving with him ... and this New Year of another year came and I started getting forty dollar a month like that, and I recognised the money. It was £2 or a £3 note — pounds before, not the dollar.

I used to give the money to my husband. I had this Darkie Green then, and he'd buy all the things, because he had his schooling and his friends and things like that, not me. He was a coloured man. You know a long time ago, Afghans were in this country, with camel wagons, donkey wagons, travelling on the road. His mother was running around with the Afghan, so he had a bit of colour in him. Oh, they're all different — different nations you know — some Chinaman, some Afghan; there's got to be some Japanese at Halls Creek. They're coming on these young girls.

When I was a younger woman with kids I saw everybody chasing after white men for husbands, but I didn't think about all that. A lot of blokes asked me and I said, 'I don't know, not right thing. Might be for some people ... I got too many of my own relations, and my parents.' A *lot* of blokes asked me you know. I said 'I can't' and how I felt. If I was on my own, with no family to think about, like my uncle, and all the others, my parents' relations, then maybe. But I was afraid they'd say 'Oh, we don't want to go to that woman now — she married to the [white] bloke ...'

When they bombed Wyndham [March 1942], in that Second War — Japanese war — I was with Darkie Green, and I had two daughters, Phyllis and Pearly — one four and one a baby. We were camping near Wyndham and that night the bomb fell. We walked away that night — all night with the two kids ... We broke all the green grass and put it all over the truck to cover it up. We had a big truck with a load, and we were frightened. We travelled right back to Rosewood and worked there then. On our way we went camping and all the black-fellers were everywhere. They didn't know about the bombs. All the 'sensible' boys and girls talked to them. They were still myalls. We travelled all night telling the folk to look out for bombs, but those other people couldn't understand, and today you can't put any sense into them yet.

Source: From the interview of Amy Laurie by Ann Magrath, in Isobel White, Diane Barwick & Betty Meehan (eds), *Fighters and Singers: The Lives of Some Australian Aboriginal Women*, Allen & Unwin, Sydney, 1985, pp.83-6.

The drover's boy

Ted Egan

They couldn't understand why the drover cried
As they buried the drover's boy
For the drover had always seemed so hard
To the men in his employ.
A bolting horse, a stirrup lost
And the drover's boy was dead.
The shovelled dirt, a mumbled word
And it's back to the road ahead
And forget about, the drover's boy.

They couldn't understand why the drover cut
A lock of the dead boy's hair.
He put it in the band of his battered old hat.
As they watched him standing there,
He told them: 'Take the cattle on,
I'll sit with the boy a while',
A silent thought, a pipe to smoke,
And it's ride another mile,
And forget about the drover's boy.

They couldn't understand why the drover and the boy
Always camped so far away,
For the tall white man and the slim black boy
Had never had much to say .
And the boy would be gone at break of dawn,
Tail the horses, carry on,
While the drover roused the sleeping men,
'Daylight, hit the road again,
And follow the drover's boy.'
Follow the drover's boy.

In the Camooweal Pub they talked about
The death of the drover's boy,
They drank their rum with a stranger who'd come
From a Kimberley run, FitzRoy,
And he told of the massacre in the west
Barest details, guess the rest,
Shoot the bucks, grab a gin,
Cut her hair, break her in,
Call her a boy, the drover's boy
Call her a boy, the drover's boy.

So when they build that Stockman's Hall of Fame
And they talk about the droving game,
Remember the girl who was bedmate and guide,
Rode with the drover side by side,
Watched the bullocks, flayed the hide,
Faithful wife, never a bride,
Bred his sons for the cattle runs.
Don't weep ... for the drover's boy
Don't mourn ... for the drover's boy
But don't forget ... the drover's boy.

Source: Ted Egan, words to the song 'The drover's boy', in Egan & Peter Forrest, *The Overlanders Songbook*, Greenhouse Publications, Richmond, Vic., 1984, p.49.

Black stockman

W. Hart-Smith

We talked about tobacco and the difficulties of getting it,
Quilp smoking an old black pipe,
Sucking at the ashes of ashes.
I gave him two cigarettes and his well-being broke into blossom
Just like a wrinkled old gum putting a white head
High into a singing cloud of bees.
'This is good tobacco,' he said.

The horse's head drooped lower and lower,
Flies pitched on the lids of his closed eyes and walked
Bravely round the inside of the bit-ring and off
On to the white-flecked lips. His tail hung thin,
Listless as a branch of leaves,
Paper-bark leaves above a billabong.

And we talked about cattle; we talked … But I
Lived in a long hiatus filled with a dreaming, seeing,
As eyes wandered, cows
Ankle-deep in black mud, reaching out
Long necks towards the soupy water, saw
The last limp leaves of dying lilies,
And a rotting blossom,

Talking to Quilp,
Talking to Quilp at the tail of a sleepy herd.

Source: W. Hart-Smith, *The Unceasing Ground: Poems*, Angus & Robertson, Sydney, 1946, p.5.

Bush cooks

Matt Savage

The cook was a very important man on a cattle station. If he knew his job, you would have a contented camp. If he was no good — and most of them were lousy — you would have fellows calling for their cheques and preparing to move on.

All the cooks I ever knew were eccentric in one way or another, and they all had nicknames: Blue Bob and Red Bob, Snorter Miller, Cuckoo Jack, Short-Stop Turner and Weary Willie Smith.

There was little Jacky Allan. Five-Day Jacky, we called him, because he would never stay more than five days in the one job. Another chap, Fleming, had a very fair skin and he was covered in great brown freckles and patches of red. Some blokes called him the Flamingo while others called him the Spotted Dog.

When I was running Montejinnie station the first cook I had was Weary Willie Smith.

He was with me for four or five months and he just about poisoned me.

We had delivered some bullocks at Victoria River Downs and were camped on the creek, waiting for the annual race meeting to begin, when Willie heard for the first time of cochineal — the stuff you use in puddings and sweets. He insisted I buy him a bottle and that evening he mixed up a brownie. He must have poured the cochineal on afterwards because when we cut into the brownie we found a lot of big red blotches. I asked a fellow to join us in a pannikin of tea. 'Have a piece of brownie!' I said.

He cut some off. 'Crikey,' he said, 'what's this?'

'I don't know,' I said. 'It looks like spotted dog to me.' We ate it anyway and it was not so bad. I had tasted much worse while Willie was cooking for me out in the mustering camp.

Soon after that race meeting he left Montejinnie, intending to go to Katherine. The wet season was on and though Willie had followed stock work all his life he was a hopeless bushman. He must have taken a wrong turning somewhere on the Dry River track beyond Nellie's Hole.

Nobody ever found him or his packs and saddles, though his horses did wander in to the out-station at Nellie's Hole a couple of months afterwards. I felt sorry for Weary Willie but he was not the man to worry about anything. I reckon that once he knew the position was hopeless he would have just laid back on the grass, with maybe a saddle under his head, and died easy.

Another cook who disappeared was Jack Hennessy. He was on Montejinnie at the same time as a quarrelsome little ex-boxer named Micky Gray. Hennessy liked to help with the mustering but he was very short-sighted. He would see what he reckoned was some cattle only to gallop across and discover he was herding a mob of ant-hills.

Micky Gray would laugh at him and shove him about, and presently Jack had had enough. He went into the cookhouse, took an old automatic pistol from a drawer and strapped it to his belt. Micky saw it all right because he said to me: 'Look at that bloke. He's got a revolver on his belt.'

I have noticed that fellows who are handy with their fists are often very frightened of firearms. Anyway Micky left him strictly alone from then on.

Not long afterwards Hennessy left Montejinnie and I said to Micky: 'Remember that pistol of Jack's?'

'My word I do,' he said. 'And he'd have used it too.'

'Not likely,' I said. 'There was a bullet jammed in the barrel. He couldn't have fired it if he'd tried.'

'What?' said Mickey. 'I wish I'd known that. I was all set to give him a thrashing!'

Meanwhile Hennessy had gone off in search of a dream. Once, long before, we had been mustering on Crown land just beyond the station boundary. This was a fine stretch of country, with plenty of water and plenty of cleanskin cattle, and Jack reckoned he was going to take it up as his own property.

'But you can hardly see,' I said. 'You'll never find it again.'

Nonetheless, after he left Montejinnie he went to see the authorities at Katherine and they gave him title to the land. He assembled a horse plant and rode out to look his new place over — and that was the last anybody saw of him.

He might have been injured in a fall. He might have missed the block altogether and wandered off into the desert. We were surprised that none of his horses came back; they also had disappeared without trace. The only thing we knew for certain was that poor old Jack Hennessy was no longer with us.

I was on Wave Hill station, Vestey's place in the Northern Territory, when a fellow named Ted Lang arrived carrying his swag and asking for a job as cook. I felt sorry for him, so I hired him. He told me he was English and had been a sailor.

He had knocked about the New Guinea coast for years in a lugger, mudlarking and trading and, I suppose, chasing the girls. Anyway he was a queer bird and a bloody awful cook — even worse than the average.

Ted Lang amused the blacks immensely. They would follow him about and watch him, laughing at everything he did. He had almost no clothes when he arrived. If he wanted a shirt he would simply scrounge a piece of old calico, cut a hole for his head and put a few stitches under the armpits.

He had never learned to ride. We would give him the quietest old horse in the camp and he would poke along behind the packhorses. Ted was bald and for some reason his hat would not stay on. So he would carry it while his old head would be shining in the sun.

He had a rolling gait — a real sailor's walk. Even the way he made a damper or used a shovel was all wrong and the blacks had endless fun imitating him in their corroborees. Just about everything he did amused them.

Packing up the camp was the cook's job while the stockmen went ahead with the cattle. One morning the boy driving the pack-train pointed out to Ted that he had left behind half a dozen pannikins.

'Oh, I'll fix those,' Ted said. Rather than unpack everything, he just strung the handles of the pannikins through his belt. When he rode in to camp that night he was clanking like a lot of cow-bells and fellows were looking around everywhere to see what was wrong with the cattle.

We all believed Ted was broke but we found out later he had more than a thousand dollars in a bank in the south. He was with me for a few months; then he bought some camels and headed off towards Hall's Creek. I heard he had plenty of trouble on the way, constantly losing his camels and then finding them again. I reckoned it would not be long before he went back to foot-walking.

Short-Stop Turner cooked, at one time or another, for nearly every station in the Kimberleys and the Northern Territory. He never stayed long anywhere — as you might guess from the nickname. I had him for a week, working in the mustering camp out of Montejinnie. Then he quit.

I said: 'What about your week's pay? I'll send a boy into the homestead to notify them if you like.'

'Oh no,' Short-Stop said. 'I'll be going that way myself.'

He rode off to Montejinnie which at the time was an out-station of Victoria River Downs. I had thought he would go on to the V.R.D. homestead and ask the manager there, Alf Martin, for his money. Instead he sat down at Montejinnie and he was still camped there when Alf came along three weeks later.

Short-Stop demanded his pay plus the waiting-time. They argued points of law and the upshot was that Alf had to give him four weeks wages for one week's work.

Martin was furious. 'Next time a bloke quits in the mustering camp,' he said, 'don't take his word for anything. Send a boy in with him to make sure he collects his money straightaway.'

Jack Beasley was another old-time cook who worked on various stations around the East Kimberleys just before the first World War. One day he and some other blokes bought supplies in Turkey Creek, then rode to their camp a few miles away to make dinner. When the meal was ready they could not find the pepper.

It was in a tin, exactly the size of some tins of curry powder, and they could not tell which was which. None of them could read or write, but they knew a few letters and brands and they were puzzling over the labels.

One chap took up a tin of curry powder. 'This is the pepper,' he said.

'No it isn't,' said Beasley.

'How do you know?'

'Well,' Jack said, 'I know the word "pepper" has a lot of "Ps" in it. I can't see very many "Ps" on that label.'

The other chap insisted so they opened the tin anyway and, sure enough, it was curry powder. Jack was like that. He could not read nor write, but he knew some of the answers just the same.

Once I watched him going through a picture book with a little boy. They were flipping the pages and taking turns to say the names of the animals: 'Horse' ... 'Camel' ... 'Donkey' ... 'Pig' ...

Beasley turned up a picture of a tiger. He gazed at it in amazement. 'Pussy-cat!' he said. 'And a big bastard, too!'

Apart from the cooking, Jack was a first-class stockman. He formed Soudan station and later took up a property in the East Kimberleys. He made plenty of money but he never did learn to write his name. Instead he would sign cheques with his brand, which was the initials 'JB' conjoined.

The chaps in Kimberley knew cattle and the bush, but some were mighty ignorant of everything else. A travelling salesman came through selling bile beans — those little pills which are said to cure constipation.

One stockman was so delighted with the results, he said: 'Show me them things again. They look like beans.'

'They're bile beans,' the traveller said. 'They cost twenty cents a box.'

'Crikey,' the stockman said, 'I'll plant a few. This garden here will grow anything. At twenty cents a box I ought to make a fortune.'

Some cooks took on the job either because they liked it or because they were no use for anything else. Others were men who had to give up stockwork because of injury or ill-health.

One of the very best bush cooks was Possum Dillon. Fellows would talk about how good his brownies and johnny cakes and dampers were; and he could do some amazing things with a lump of salt beef. I often wondered about his nickname.

'He got it,' Jack Butler told me, 'because he has two bloody great tufts of hair sticking up out of his shoulders. I saw them one day while he was swimming.'

I watched Possum for months after hearing that, but he never let me see him with his shirt off. He was so very sensitive about it that I reckon the yarn was true.

One of those who came to cooking late in life was Billy Miller [William Linklater]. He died a few years ago in Sydney where he had made something of a name with his poems and tales about the bush. Billy was small and wiry, and as a young chap he had been a fine horseman. He was not nearly so good a hand at cooking but the fellows liked him so much that they seldom complained.

He worked for a while on Bedford Downs south-west of Turkey Creek in the East Kimberleys. When the mustering camp was away Billy would have the homestead to himself, apart from a few of the house lubras.

The owner, Bob Sexton, had instructed him that if any bush blacks came in he was to fire a few shots and frighten them off. Billy was a notoriously bad marksman so we reckoned there was no danger of him hitting anybody.

The previous cook on Bedford had run a few fowls but all the hens had died and the only survivor was an old rooster who slept in a bloodwood tree between the black's camp and the kitchen.

One night Billy heard strange voices in the camp. He fired a random shot and to his astonishment and horror he heard the thud of a body falling to the ground. He rushed to the camp in case someone was wounded; but the place was deserted.

Next morning he found the old rooster lying dead below his favourite perch on the bloodwood tree. If he had really been trying to hit that bird the shot would not have gone within fifty feet of it. Anyway, Bob Sexton took the rifle off Billy after that.

'The blacks would be safe enough if you were aiming at them,' he said. 'But when you're shooting to miss, they're in grave danger.'

Poddy Murray was more than a good bush cook — he was a friend to nearly everybody who knew him. He was a short, plump fellow — hence the nickname — and he had a wonderful gift of sizing up a man's character within a few minutes of meeting him.

Poddy was not very fond of Government servants, policemen or missionaries. Once he said to me: 'Matt, I could make all the missionaries shut up shop simply by bringing in one order — that they can't have a lubra on the place under forty years of age.'

He told a policeman, Sheridan: 'Look, Sherry, you take all these unwanted, half-caste kids into the Government compounds and just ruin them. You train the boys to be layabouts and the girls to be slaveys and harlots, and then you turn the poor devils loose. I blame you because the troopers are responsible for a lot more half-castes than the bushmen are.

'I reckon the best way for the blacks to help themselves would be to sail in and knock over a few policemen. I don't mean to kill them, but just to give them a good bashing and then go bush. It would be even better if they'd take on the missionaries; and maybe get to a few of the officials in Darwin. After a bit of this, I reckon the blacks would have the public on their side.'

Poddy Murray was not quarrelsome but if anybody provoked him he would show fight. Out on the Barkly Tableland a fellow known as Thomson the Dane marched into the camp, full of rum, and threatened to give him a hiding. Poddy picked up a mosquito peg, walked quietly over to Thomson and flattened him with a blow that nearly tore off one ear.

Later the Dane told the other fellows Poddy had tried to kill him. Next day one young bloke said: 'Poddy, I hear you had a row with Thomson last night?'

'I didn't have any row with him,' Murray replied. 'He tried to have a row with me.'

Poddy would never work in the homestead kitchen. He liked the open spaces and as a cook for the mustering camps he could get a job anywhere. He worked for me at Montejinnie during 1925.

In December, with the wet season about to set in, everybody was having a fairly easy time. We had laid in supplies of rum, wine, and beer for our Christmas jag which we planned to have at the Pigeon-Hole, an out-camp forty miles from the homestead.

But Poddy wanted a New Year's supply as well and he reckoned he would go in to the Victoria River Depot for more rum. I gave him the time off and away he went. He bought a few gallons of liquor but in Jasper Gorge, on the way home, he met some teamsters. They got to talking and of course the upshot was that they sat down and drank all the rum. So Poddy had to go back for more.

He was very sick after the party which had lasted for two days. But he reached the depot and loaded his packs with more rum. About five miles out, on the return journey, he became seriously ill. He rode back to the depot, climbed off his horse, lay down under a tree and died, without any fuss at all.

The police took his effects — including a case of rum — as evidence for the inquest. Two constables were stationed at the depot and one of them started on the liquor. In fact there was very little of it left by the day of the inquest.

The rum had been listed among Poddy's property. The policemen hated each other and the senior constable reported that his junior had drunk the evidence. Meanwhile the young chap had replaced the rum but he had bought the wrong brand and during the inquest the whole story came out.

The constable was sacked from the force. So Poddy had one joke at the last: he had been the cause of a policeman's dismissal.

Source: Keith Willey, *Boss Drover: Stories Related to the Author by Matt Savage*, Rigby, Adelaide, 1971, pp.36-42.

Buffalo shooting in Australia, 1890s

A.B. (Banjo) Paterson

Very few people in Australia know anything about the buffalo shooting to be had in that great tract of country to the north of South Australia known as the Northern Territory. Many people profess to know all about it and are very free with most extraordinary information on the subject. For instance, many will tell you that the buffaloes are not real buffaloes at all, but simply cattle gone wild; that they are Indian Brahmin cattle, very small and quiet; that there are no buffaloes at all, they were all shot out long ago; that the buffaloes are in myriads, but that they retreat to the dense jungles, where no one can follow them; that they are water buffalo, and never leave the water, and can only be captured by an expert swimmer; that they are land buffalo and are shot on foot, and are no sport at all, as one cannot well miss them, they being as big as haystacks; that they are always shot from horseback, the buffaloes preferring that method, and that the whole business is so rough and dangerous that no one but a lunatic would attempt it. Among these various statements one soon gets confused, and reference to the literature on the subject does not make matters much more cheerful. Rudyard Kipling describes the wild buffalo as 'the nastiest tempered animal in the jungle', while Lydekker's *Natural History* states that 'buffaloes are by far the boldest and most savage of the Indian Bovidae, and a bull not infrequently attacks without provocation. A wounded animal of either sex often charges, and has occasionally been known to knock an elephant down'; and the Badminton *Library of Sport* states that a buffalo would 'charge an elephant before or after being wounded'. Fortified and cheered by these assurances, I went to Port Darwin per s.s. *Guthrie* to make the closer acquaintance of these formidable animals, and to see what sport buffalo shooting could afford.

The Indian buffalo is the animal which is hunted in our Northern Territory. They were brought from the island of Timor to the settlement on Melville Island about 1829. This island is close to the northern shore of Australia. Later on, that settlement was abandoned and a fresh settlement made at Port Essington, on the mainland of Australia, and at this settlement also a few pairs of buffaloes were introduced from Timor. Both settlements were abandoned and the buffaloes were left to their own devices and they ran wild. The country must have suited them, as both on Melville Island and the mainland they increased at an amazing rate.

They are ungainly, savage-looking brutes, having a dull, bluish-coloured hide and enormous horns. They have little affinity to domestic cattle, and will not inter-breed with them. They are almost hairless, and the hide is enormously thick. The place where they are found is a tract of coast country on the extreme northern shore of Australia. Here are vast rolling plains, very little higher than sea level, covered with coarse jungle grass, reeds and bamboos. For three or four months of the year in the wet season the whole of the plains are under water, and in this swamp and quagmire the buffaloes make their home. They eat, and thrive on, any kind of green thing — grass, reeds, rushes, bamboos, water lilies, even mangrove leaves, all come alike to the buffaloes. The country is too sour and washy for cattle, but these animals are just suited by it. They are built very much like pigs, being tremendously deep in the body and broad in the back, with short powerful legs. They stand as high as a bullock and are much more solid. It was some years before anyone discovered that their hides were of any value, and during those years they throve and multiplied unmolested. The stockmen on the cattle camps used to see them walk right in among a mob of cattle, give a snort or two and a threatening shake of their huge horns and stroll out again unconcerned. They were then perfectly fearless of men or horses. Later on, the cattle stations were abandoned, and the country given up to the buffaloes, which then numbered thousands. It was ascertained that their skins had a market value of about fifteen shillings for large hides, and a few men began to shoot them for the hides. At first the shooting was done on foot, but this was found too slow, too unprofitable, and too dangerous, and soon some of the dashing cattlemen of the Territory took the matter up in earnest and started shooting from horseback, which is the plan that now prevails. It was found that the strength of the buffaloes was so great and their vitality so wonderful that half a dozen bullets would not stop them, but at last the shooters discovered that a bullet fired into the loins from above would paralyse the hindquarters, and cause the animal to drop in his tracks. This was the only method of shooting them that could be made to pay. If the beasts were shot anywhere else they would not fall at once, but would stop and charge, and, while the shooters were reloading to despatch a wounded animal, the rest of the herd would be making the best of their way to cover, and would ultimately escape. Even if mortally wounded, a buffalo will usually struggle on for half a mile or so before he drops, and in the long jungle grass the skinners could not find the carcase. So that it became evident, if the shooters wished to get a living at the business, they had to be prepared to race right alongside the buffalo and shoot downwards into the loins alongside the spine. This particular part of the animal can only be reached from above, as the high hips and croup protect the loins from any bullet fired from behind. Thus there was evolved the present method of buffalo shooting, where the shooter, holding the carbine in one hand like a pistol, races right alongside the buffalo and fires at full gallop, taking his chance of the animal wheeling and attacking him either before or after he fires. If the shot is properly placed, the buffalo drops as if struck by lightning, and the shooter races on after the flying herd, reloading as rapidly as he can for his next victim. An expert shooter will drop buffalo after buffalo at an average distance of two hundred yards apart, never needing more than one bullet to each, while a novice, not knowing the correct place to fire at, may shoot eight or nine bullets into a buffalo without bringing him down.

It is easy to understand that there is great danger in racing up alongside an animal that can 'knock over an elephant', and firing at him at such very close quarters. Still, if the men wish to get a living they have to do it, and it is marvellous how expert both men and horses become.

Having dealt so far with the buffaloes, it is only right to introduce the reader to the shooters and their horses. The shooters are, as a rule, men who have been stockmen — bold, fearless riders, with any amount of nerve; men who undertake the riding of unbroken horses, and the management of vindictive wild cattle, as a regular part of their lives. Usually a couple of men go into partnership as shooters, taking their buffalo horses and some twenty or thirty pack horses. They set out to the great coast plains and pitch their camp alongside the local blacks' camp, and enlist all the able-bodied blacks of the tribe in their service. Their stores consist of flour, tea, sugar, Worcester sauce, salt, and arsenic for the hides, and unlimited cartridges. For meat they eat buffalo beef, which is first-class, especially the tongues and tails. They use a small tent for their stores, but always sleep out in the open themselves, with no shelter except their mosquito nets. On these low-lying plains, amid the swamps and reed beds, the mosquitoes are something to shudder at. I have seen and felt mosquitoes at Port Hacking, the Hawkesbury, Hexham (where the famous Hexham greys come from), on the Castlereagh, in Gippsland, on the Diamantina and the Dawson River in Queensland, but all these places put together could not furnish enough mosquitoes to act as trumpeters for the vast mosquito army that every night spreads itself over the whole face of nature in the buffalo country. A stout cheese cloth mosquito net is the first and indispensable requisite of every man's outfit in this country. It never rains in the dry season, and, winter or summer alike, the temperature, day or night, is always blazing hot. The shooters make little or no pretence at camp, simply rigging their mosquito nets on a couple of sticks and spreading their blankets on the hard ground. The black gins do the cooking, such as it is.

One of the George Lambert sketches which accompanied Banjo Paterson's 'Buffalo shooting in Australia' (Sydney Mail, 7 January 1899). Note the rider is at close quarters in order to fire into the loins of the animal, thus killing it with only one shot. This common practice preserved ammunition, but decreased the life expectancy of the shooter.

From this it may be gathered that a buffalo shooter's life is not one of refinement and luxury. Hard and dangerous work and hard living make the men rough and ready, but they are genuinely good sportsmen and hospitable as Arabs. Their horses are a queer mixture. It is only one horse in a hundred that will make a buffalo horse. In addition to needing a lot of pace and determination, the horse has to be courageous enough to race right up alongside the formidable buffalo bulls and cool enough to dodge their onslaught if they wheel and charge without any warning, as they have a nasty way of doing. Added to this, the constant roar of the carbine close to their ears makes some horses timid and unmanageable. So that the shooters have to weed out the cowardly horses, the hot-headed, excitable ones, the lazy slow ones, and the timid gun-shy horses, and those that survive the ordeal are not selected for their style or quality, but simply because they have the requisite coolness and courage. These qualities are found to exist in most unlikely animals, and the crack buffalo horses of a camp comprise all sorts, shapes, and sizes, it being of course necessary that they are all fairly fast and up to weight. It is wonderful how clever they get. They watch every movement of the buffalo, being on the alert to swing off to one side at any moment if he wheels. If the ground is broken and cracked with great fissures, or crossed with water courses, they bide their time and rush up alongside the quarry with a great dash the moment they feel good ground under their feet again. And some of the older hands among the horses are cunning enough to tell at once a formidable old bull from a timid, frightened young cow, and they will race up alongside the cow boldly enough, but insist on running wide of the bull, causing the shooter to waste valuable cartridges and still more valuable time in his destruction.

Let us now give a description of a day's shooting from the point of view of a stranger. Let us suppose our stranger has arrived in the camp overnight, with no experience — with nothing but a hopeful mind and a well-oiled rifle. He finds that the camp consists of a small tent full of stores, while behind it are a few low rails that do duty as a catching place for the horses, and on which are deposited pack saddles, saddle cloths, bridles, riding saddles, hobbles and all manner of gear. Close round the tent are grouped the mosquito nets and blankets of the shooters, in close proximity to the nets and blankets of the black gins who do the cooking. A rough slab table with log seats occupies the foreground. A Chinaman, employed to skin buffalo, has his net and blankets a few yards away. Some pots, buckets, and cooking utensils are scattered around. A few yards off in a clear space are stretched dozens of buffalo hides, drying in the sun, and smelling villainously. And back of all, through the corkscrew palms and tree trunks, may be seen the small fires of the blacks' camp, where the sable chieftains and chieftainesses are sleeping off the effects of their daily gorge of buffalo meat. At bedtime the stranger crawls in under his mosquito net and tucks it well in under his blanket. His saddle does duty for a pillow. And so, on the hard ground, he lies awake and listens to the dull, booming roar of the mosquitoes as they hustle each other in myriads round his resting place, and the choking snores of the Chinese skinner who is sleeping in the next blankets. From away in the distance comes the howl of a dingo and the clink, clink of the horse bells; from a tree overhead a mopoke calls in wearisome iteration. And over all and above all is the steady, persistent stench of the drying buffalo hides. At dawn the camp is astir. The blacks are out after the horses, the gins are building the fire and frying buffalo steaks and boiling tea. The shooters emerge from their blankets yawning and stretching. Breakfast is soon despatched — buffalo beef, damper, and strong, black, well-stewed tea. The buffalo shooters, the Chinese skinner, and the stranger all feed together, each airing his views on any subject that occurs to him, while the gins sit silently by the fire and kill mosquitoes on their bare legs. By the time breakfast is over the horses are brought up by the blacks. The crack buffalo horses are usually given a nosebagful of much-cherished oats. The gins attend to this, and they are very solicitous that their pets get their full allowance and are not worked too many days consecutively. The Chinese skinner sharpens his knives to a razor-like keenness on an oilstone. The pack horses are first caught and saddled — some eight or nine of them. Then the black boys, or rather black men, catch their horses and mount, their clothing being limited to a very brief loincloth and a stick through their nose. The Chinese skinner climbs onto his quiet old nag. The shooters get their carbines out of the tent and strap on their belts filled with cartridges, and so they mount and away across the sunny plains at a slow jog, the pack horses, the blacks, and the Chinaman stringing slowly along in the rear. The sun is blazing down and the great plain dances and quivers in the heat as the procession straggles across it. In front the plain extends to the horizon, with never a tree to break the view — a vast, silent expanse of waving jungle grass, crossed here and there with watercourses and scarred with bare patches where fires have been. The procession moves along the edge of the plain, which is bordered by open paperbark forests, clumps of corkscrew palms, or dense jungles, where all sorts of tropical trees, creepers, and shrubs make a retreat impracticable to any animal except the thick-hided, heavy-horned buffalo. After riding perhaps a couple of hours one of the shooters says, 'There's buffalo!' The stranger sees far away on the plain some things that look like seven or eight large black mounds standing out solid against the background of jungle grass. A hurried consultation is held. The animals are rather near the edge of the plain, and it all depends on the start they get whether the shooters can get to them before they reach cover. Girths are tightened, hats firmly jammed on, and the novice, with beating heart, rides steadily off with two shooters towards the unsuspecting herd. The pack horses with their attendants pull up and watch the chase. Slowly and quietly the shooters approach the herd, the novice getting many whispered instructions on the way — to be sure and not fire till he can fire downwards into the loin, never to let his horse stand still when near a wounded buffalo lest the beast's sudden charge take him by surprise, not to pull his horse about in broken ground, and so on and so on. Steadily they draw nearer the herd, until, when they are about three hundred yards off, one of the mounds suddenly lifts up a huge, black-muzzled, bull-like head, decorated with immense sickle-shaped horns, reaching right back to the animal's shoulders. Instantly all the others throw up their heads, and stare for a few seconds with sullen fierce eyes at the intruders. Great ungainly brutes they look with their heavy shoulders and quarters. Suddenly they wheel and dash off at a lumbering canter towards the timber. 'Come on', yell the buffalo shooters, setting their horses at full speed, and the novice finds that his horse needs no urging once the game is afoot. Away they dash after the buffaloes, the horses making great springs through the long rank grass, exactly as if they were racing through a high and heavy crop of wheat. Under the crop of grass are all sorts of hidden dangers — great cracks in the ground made by the dry weather, huge circular holes where the buffaloes have wallowed, now overgrown and hidden with grass, patches of boggy ground where the water has lain. Over all these difficulties the horses go full speed with a cleverness really marvellous, every now and again 'pecking' almost on to their knees, but recovering themselves smartly and racing on, always with their eyes fixed on the flying mob. The buffaloes settle to a slogging, clumsy gallop, and the novice expects to run up to them easily, especially as the shooters are riding desperately, just as if finishing a race, urging the horses to their very utmost, as the cover is very close, and if once the mob reach the shelter of the corkscrew palms they will be lost. The novice finds his carbine a terrible weight on one hand while galloping, and the occasional stumbles of his horse almost jerk it out of his grasp, and for all their hard riding they do not seem to be gaining much on the buffaloes. Suddenly they reach a patch of short grass and firm ground, where the horses are better suited, and they draw up close to the mob. The buffaloes scatter slightly, and the novice, now thoroughly winded with his gallop, holds out the carbine out ready to fire and urges his horse after the nearest buffalo. Half-wild with excitement he tries to remember all the injunctions he got about firing, but the springing of the horse and the rolling gallop of the buffalo make it no easy matter to hold the carbine straight with one hand, more especially as the place to be fired at is not painted on the buffalo. His carbine points anywhere except the right place, and then, just as he intends to fire, the buffalo suddenly dodges to one side and makes for the timber at redoubled speed, while our hero pulls his horse round in pursuit. On they go, the novice having but one aim and object in life — to get the muzzle of the rifle up against that broad blue back. Suddenly, with sickening anxiety, he notices that the timber is very close, and without more ado he holds the carbine and fires at about a dozen yards' range. The quarry goes on with the same determined rolling gallop, giving no sign whether the shot has hit or missed, and the novice, with a dismal feeling of failure, clutches frantically at the lever of his carbine, ejects the cartridge, fumbles wildly in his belt for another, and jams it home just as the buffalo passes the first few outlying screw palms. Then there is a whiz and a rush of hoofs, and one of the professional shooters, sitting square in his saddle, dashes past the novice, shaves a palm tree or two by a hair's breadth, and swoops down on the buffalo like a hawk on a pigeon. He has no trouble in managing his rifle and his horse, recognising the urgency of the case, brings him alongside the quarry in three or four bounds. The buffalo swerves at once, but the trained horse follows his every movement. The shooter leans forward holding out his rifle, elbow up and muzzle down, exactly like a man going to spear pig.

Bang! goes the carbine, and through the jet of white smoke the novice sees the buffalo sink to the ground paralysed, shot through the loins, while the horse swings clear of his falling victim, and 'I'm sorry to rob you of him, mister,' says the shooter apologetically, 'but he would have got away in these palms.' The novice swallows his mortification, and asks how the two men got on. 'Shot every one of the mob,' is the answer. And, sure enough, outside the palms lie all the rest of the herd, still kicking in the agonies of death. The skinners come up and the hides are soon stripped off by the blacks and Chinaman and fastened on the pack saddles.

After a short rest to breathe the horses, another start is made out into the plain, and for an hour or two they jog on slowly, seeing no game until they have got right out into the solitude of the plain, and the nearest timber is a dim black line on the horizon. Suddenly, out of a mud hole, where he has been rolling, there rises a huge blue bull buffalo, a vast monster that glares fiercely at them and then turns to run. This is the novice's opportunity — there is no cover for the animal to get into, and jamming his hat down and sending the spurs home he starts off alone in pursuit of the monster. So they tear across the plain, pursuer and pursued. How the wind whistles past! The horse gains slowly — he will not go as confidently with a strange rider as with his own master — and the novice, as he draws near, has plenty of time to note the fierce backward glances of the buffalo and the ominous swing, swing of those terrific horns as the bull labours along in his swaying gallop. The novice fully intends to race right alongside, but somehow, each time that he draws near either the bull swerves and gains a little, or the horse loses ground on some rough going, and the result is that when he does fire he is not quite close enough, and instead of hitting the loin the bullet buries itself in the buffalo's massive hindquarters. Whoof! With a snort like a grizzly bear the bull wheels and charges his assailant, and all the rider's previous efforts are as nothing compared to the dash he puts into his riding while urging the horse out of harm's way. The bull follows for a hundred yards or so, and then, finding himself outpaced, wheels suddenly off and resumes his dogged canter. The novice canters after him, reloading as he goes, and then goes up for a second shot. The horse will not draw up close to a wounded bull; he knows too much for that. He swings off, and our hero gets a broadside shot, a red spurt of blood showing where the bullet has struck just behind the shoulders. Round comes the bull for another charge, and again the wary horse takes his rider out of harm's way. The bull stands for a while, then pretends to retreat, but wheels suddenly round and charges again, and this time the novice really thinks he is caught, so rapid is the onset. A slip or stumble would be fatal, but the horse draws away, and the bull 'bails up', charging everyone that comes near. Another bullet or two tell their tale, and soon the large creature sinks to the ground and expires without a sound. The novice receives the congratulations of the shooters on getting his first buffalo, but he feels in his heart that it was a case of buffalo assassination rather than legitimate shooting, and he resolves to do better in future. So the day wears on, small mobs being met with and shot right out, the patient skinners following up and getting the hides. Incidents there are in plenty. A buffalo swerves so suddenly that the man's boot brushes against the animal's forehead as the horse springs clear of the charge. A bull bails up in a patch of bamboo and makes sallies out of it and hurried retreats into it, trying to draw his foe in after him. Once he gets in, instead of running away he craftily hides behind a patch of thick bamboo and waits for someone to follow him. More and more hides are got, and the novice feels a glow of pride as he gets his first clean shot home in the loins, and sees his buffalo fall to one bullet. The pack horses are loaded until each has as much as he can stagger under. The sun sinks low, and a start is made for home, the shooters riding slowly on in front, the pack horses stringing after them, and the blacks silently smoking in the rear. The sun goes down and the moon rises, flooding the plain with a glorious golden light. A few wild buffaloes come sniffing up to the procession and bolt away again into the darkness. Far away is the glow of the campfire, and when the shooters reach it they have to unload the hides, eat their rough food in the smoke of the fire to protect themselves from mosquitoes, and so straight off to bed. There is no such thing as sitting about and talking in the camp where the mosquitoes make life outside the mosquito nets an absolute purgatory.

Such is life in a buffalo camp — about the last remaining relic of the old wild days. It is life as it was in the beginning of things. Risk and roughness there no doubt are. Sometimes the horses are killed by charging buffaloes and the riders seriously hurt. One of the Melville Island shooters was speared through the shoulder by a wild black, and the man who wants his sport combined with luxury had better leave buffalo shooting alone. But it is a rare experience to anyone who is not afraid of roughing it a little. Besides the buffalo shooting there is any amount of other game — alligators, dingoes, wild fowl and ducks, and pigeon and quail and snipe in thousands. But this sort of shooting is tame after the rushing gallop alongside the fierce buffalo bull. And it is satisfactory to know that the supply of buffaloes shows no signs of diminishing. In the visit that I have endeavoured to record here, which took place in September 1898, our camp shot 100 buffalo in a week. The two professional shooters had got 700 in three and a half months' shooting, and this sort of thing has been going on for years. Anyone intending to go up may be sure of getting plenty of game, and the shooters will be glad to take anybody into the camp who cares to go, but as the men are shooting for a living they would have to be paid for the use of their horses and their loss of time. A party going up could make quite a comfortable trip of it by going round by sea from Port Darwin, but the intending visitor must remember that the Northern Territory is a 'land of lots of time', and he cannot plan his trip (like the Americans planned their war) to get his buffalo and be back for lunch. All arrangements take time to make, and anyone desiring to go up should make enquiries long beforehand as to means of transport, etc., from the Eastern and Australian Steamship offices, on whose ships most of the hides come down.

(Since the above article was written news has reached Sydney of the murder of two buffalo shooters by the blacks. No details are to hand, but it will probably be found that drink had a good deal to do with it, as the blacks are quiet enough unless interfered with. Still, our black brother in the north is a child of impulse, and there is no saying how small a matter may have caused the attack. It was hard that, after finishing their season's shooting safely, these men should be killed by their own blacks. But it is all in the season's risk — the man who goes buffalo shooting has to reckon this chance in with his other risks. And it speaks well for the men and their management of the blacks that casualties are so few.)

Source: A. B. (Banjo) Paterson, *Singer of the Bush: Complete Works 1885-1900*, Angus & Robertson, Sydney, 1983, pp.309-15; appeared originally in the *Sydney Mail*, 7 January 1899.

Don't miss or you'll be a dead fella

Alex Jupurrurla Wilson

Tell me about your buffalo hunting days.

I went buffalo shooting. I got a job with a fella on Adelaide River called Fred Hardy. He asked me if I'd come out and have a go. He had a bit of a station, new one, just startin', down below Alligator River pub. He was battlin'. I went there, I done nearly twelve months, not quite. He was a bit too rough, I couldn't put up with him. I shot nearly 250 buffalo in that time from horseback and on foot with the 303 rifles with cut-off barrels made for buffalo. Skeleton rifles they used to call them. Two native boys were with me.

What was it like buffalo shooting — scary?

I was a bit scared when I started but I got too game in the end.

Too game? Why?

I used to stand right up close to them in the long grass, hardly any tree too, and I used to pump the bullets into them and they used to go down but there would be twenty more, layin' there, you can't see them in all that grass. I used to stand still then run up to that buffalo and lay along side of him.

The dead one?

Yes. I used to lay along side of the dead one and they would come and look — then bang! — sometimes two of us, one native boy too. He'd lay on one side and I'd lay on the other so he'd shoot that bugger that way, I'll shoot the one that side. I said: 'Don't miss or you'll be a dead blackfella.' He belonged to that country too.

Dead shot?

Oh yeah they used to just drop. Then one bloke stopped there and then the other run to the next dead one, course they used to go, they used to gallop away in the grass for a few hundred yards and come right round not far from where you shot these two. They wouldn't move out of the grass or anything, they'd just stand there like a dead tree. And one boy got killed there on the Mary River, right down low. We was crossin' a claypan, big swamp about two foot, three foot deep, not very deep. A few crocs there too them days — millions of them, every water had crocs in them and we wasn't takin' any chance and we walked across between two water holes one on the eastern side and one on the western side. Lookin' across the plain we didn't see that buffalo because that old buffalo was wounded before, someone had put a few bullets in him. And this boy he said: 'We'll walk along this track.' It was a deep one, made by buffalo — worn down and the water at the side. And he's walking along one side and I'm walking along the other and we're looking ahead. It was lignin country, big high lignin growin' ten feet high some of them and he's sleepin' behind that. He had a deep hole dug where he used to sleep from the buffalo flies. He must have been watching us, the wind was blowing that way, to him. And when we'd nearly got to him we seen him come out of this hole, we couldn't run either way — we were frightened of the crocs, man eaters. So the mistake we made was that we fired, both of us at the same time. We hit him in the shoulders all right and he went down but he got on his feet somehow and he come and he tore that lignin bush right through and time we load our gun up again he hit that bloke in the back with the point of his nose. He lifted him off and he lost his 303 rifle — it fell in the water, he went halfway in the air. While he was doing it I put one into his side, through the chest. And when the bloke come down, he put his head down and fell with him.

The buffalo fell with him!

Yeah. He stuck the horn through his back and the horn come out through the chest. I shot him a little bit too late. The other mob could all see him. The skinners were waiting about two hundred yards across the plain. They said: 'It's not your fault, you're alright.'

They all belonged to Alligator River. But I pulled out not long after that. I went back, reported it, Johnathon was there, we had an old T-model Ford truck. We went to the station, took the dead one. I give him a note made by another half-caste bloke there with me who could read and write telling how it had happened. I said: 'We'll wait for the policeman here.'

Two policeman come by motorcar from Darwin. They were frightened to go to where the bloke got killed, the bush was too thick there. They had a look at him and they took the horn of the dead buffalo, we had to go bloody court case after, two weeks after.

Then not long after that I pulled out, I got frightened see. But I got accident too with another boy again. I'm going along and I said: 'I'll go in this scrub to have a look.' This was not far from where the bloke got killed, jungle country, a big croc could be layin' alongside of you and you wouldn't see him. I come on out onto a big plain, four other blokes were with me. I looked across and told them in finger talk that there were two down there where they were going. He said 'Have a go.' They didn't gallop into the jungle, they were coming for where I was, they come straight.

Straight toward you?

Yeah. There was only one little tree, one of them white trees. They were coming for me and I went back and lay on the ground with the 303 ready because I had to get one of them, get the two of them for the skins. And they come past me and as soon as they went past I shot one and broke his front quarter and he dropped so I never loaded up me rifle, the other buffalo, he went straight on into the jungle. I was walking up to him. I could see his eye, his eye blinking. I got the rifle and was trying to put a bullet in it. He jumped straight on his feet, on three legs and I didn't have time to shoot him because my rifle wasn't really loaded so I made for this bloody little tree. I made one step there and another one on top! I didn't drop my rifle. When he come along he was flat out, really close. He had big horns and he smashed into the tree like bulldozer and the tree fell back with me as well.

You fell over!

With him! He went straight on before he could pull up, he had too much of a pace see. He pulled up and turned round, he looked around to see where I was dragging one leg. He only had three. He spotted me as I got out of the bush. I loaded up my rifle as I was laying on the ground. I said: 'I'll have to make sure of him this time, when he comes.' They were all runnin', all the native boys, they were coming to save me. But they was too far away from me. He come straight for me, flat out, on his three legs. He was a bullock. When he come as soon as he put his head down to get the horn into me he shut his eyes. I stepped back and put the barrel onto his head and dropped him. I said: 'This is my last buffalo!'

I pulled out and went up to Darwin.

Source: From the interview of Alex Jupurrurla Wilson by Peter Japaljarri Bartlett, in *Junga Yimi*, vol.4, no.4, 1981, pp.5-7.

Elegy on the reefs

Northern Territory Times, 1875

The following doggerel rhapsody was recited at a convivial meeting (not a tripe supper) held on the Union a short time ago. The composer ['A Local Loafer'] has not been heard of since.

Keep silence Bromley kites and crows,
Whilst I enumerate our woes ;
For well I wot 'tis all U.P.,
With prospects in the warm N.T.
Our speculators have been rash —
Our Companies have gone to smash ;
For gold would not turn out like ore,
And calls are listened to no more.
George Newman's gone, who did so much ;
Made roads and dams with magic touch ;
But could not touch the 'strike' of gold,
Nor Westcott's hidden wealth unfold.
So in despair he left the mill,
And seized the literary quill,
He gently let his Company down,
And now an author walks the town.
On Ford, Kapunda people pounce,
Because his stuff went just an ounce ;
The joke they could no longer see,
When they were told it would go three.
Poor Bowcher, too, is left alone
To pay his wages from the stone ;
And miners are not like to stay
When that's the only source of pay.
Old Nicholas says it serves him right,
For his was far the better site.
Now, Andy Forbes, chield of the North,
Let Caledonia stone come forth ;
And send it to the Standard mill ;
Don't see the Royal stampers still !
Pine Creek has left one slender staff ;
Her hopes rest on the Telegraph,
Where week by week the public learns
The stone is giving good returns.
What wonder if a mine wont't thrive,
When bank clerks manage, wash, and drive.
It must be something very strange,
If we get nothing from the change.

For men must hurry to their work,
With Wilson boss and Grierson clerk;
And Charley Levi must look smart
To clean amalgam and retort.
This management is better far,
Says noble Pat from Mullingar.

Dear Union — *dear* enough to some —
Thine hour of dissolution's come;
Thy reputation, once so great,
Has dwindled to a low estate;
And when thy brooks dry up this year,
Our hopes and prospects disappear!
Let not the blame lie at thy door,
Still rich in mines with golden store!
It rests with South Australian laws,
Thy deadly bane and direful cause
Of discontent within thy ranks;
In satire grimly bow your thanks
To statesmen and officials, who
Still aid monoply's vampire crew,
Who laid your limbs upon the rack,
And drove the working miner back.
McMinn and Brock first struck the blow
That brought thy gilded name so low.
Who raised a forest thick of pegs,
And then betook them to their legs,
Now others in their wake hold ground,
With no intent to spend a pound,
To raise a stone or strike a drill,
Or yield the claims to those who will.
By these and other wrongs, too soon
You're buried in oblivion's tomb.
Though well we know you'll rise again,
And yield your wealth for better men.

Dear Adam, our old pioneer,
We're heartily glad to see you here
Again; though we regret you find
Such poor returns from your old mine.
'Tween you and me 'twould better pay
If carried on another day.
No thank you, I decline to drink;
Our liquor is not quite the jink;
Consumption is reduced so small,
Glenlivet can't be found at all.
At one place, though you show the tin,
There's nothing in the bar but gin.
Another's only stock is rum,
Which may, indeed be drunk by some;
But fever on the creek must spread
When drink like this gets in the head.

Our spirits are descending fast,
We'll all be dead and gone at last.
We hear the dice-box ring no more
While passing by the shanty door ;
No more we count our points at whist,
And poker's clean struck off the list.
Our grand *elite* no more are seen
Around the royal cloth of green ;
And billiard champions are so few,
That Turner must put up his cue.
The conscious fact must o'er us steal
That every one is down at heel.
In fine, if truth doth stamp our story,
The Territory's gone to glory.
One chance remains — keep up you pluck,
And wait for one-eyed Charley's luck.

Source: *Northern Territory Times*, 29 May 1875.

The world's loneliest field

F. E. Baume

At the Granites, 30 October 1932

What, then, is this lonely place, the Granites? What manner of men live in it, 380 miles north-west of Alice Springs, and what is their daily life?

Away to the west as a traveller approaches , a low ridge of cruelly red stone rises a few feet from the open spinifex plain, for here no tree has being and the spear-point grass is monarch of a fiery domain. Look at the map of the Northern Territory. If it is fairly modern it will bear the words 'Granite H.' over near the borders of Western Australia. That low, red, stony patch, with streaks of gibbers radiating from it, is the beginning of 'The Granites'. Even in South Africa, where distances are great, the most remote field is but a stone's throw from civilisation compared with this horrible place in a horrible desert.

The first hill vanishes. A jagged ridge springs into being. As I type it is to the right of my tent, curiously low, serrated by the fires and the elements of ages, seemingly rock piled carefully on rock by a forgotten human agency, yet fashioned by primeval force and standing as a reminder of the old, old earth. Not a plant growth appears on it, not a streak of natural relief to its granite deadness. It is the second and biggest of the Granite Hills, from which the tiny mining settlement has taken its name.

To-day the sky is overcast and the Granite hill does not leer redly into the desert, its five lilliputian peaks, welcoming the scorching sun. But it dominates the settlement like some evil genius, and as the day goes on and men grow restless with desert nerve strain, it seems to live and jeer and laugh at those who seek gold in its very entrails.

To the west the plain stretches out toward Tanami and the Schist Hills, an almost treeless sweep of sinister olive green, broken by reddish patches, which mean red sand and gibbers of granite and of quartzite. So runs the desert to its sandy corridor east of Wyndham and the Kimberley ranges, where tropic trees grow lush on the West Australian Coast. To the right of the Granite hill is a tin shanty, as yet unoccupied. It is the property of the King, and it will house Trooper Anthony Lynch, of the Mounted Police. He is not yet in occupation, but is camped at the well, four miles out, with the Deputy-Administrator of the Northern Territory, who is inspecting his outpost. Soon Lynch's camels will arrive, with his two police trackers, and then woe betide the Myall native who presents himself with spear and his yam sticks within 10 miles of the Granites.

Looking out toward Lynch's hut and breathing too deeply, I have just swallowed a fly. I have been at the Granites for a day, but already I see no harm in swallowing a fly. The reason is this: Flies are the real owners of the Granites, and they get their way in any case, whether they want to give you barcoo rot dysentery or ptomaine. Because they mean business no one here takes any notice of them. Which is Australian, typically, and quite by the way.

To the left of the police hut camp Paddy O'Neill and Paddy Ryan — Black Paddy, whose claim at Bunker's Hill was bought by the Chapman syndicate at a good figure. They arrived back only yesterday from an extended holiday at Alice Springs, merely to peg out more claims 40 miles south-east. They are men of the Granites temperament — the temperament which holds money as dross and a whisper of gold as manna. 'We saw gold to the south a year ago,' they say. And, says another, 'The niggers showed me alluvial two years ago and promised to tell me where to get it next day. But they had a big talk at night and left camp before I woke up.' Thus men go out on camels to the dull sands southward. Sometimes they stagger back. Then when they can walk they leave again on the path to gold — and back to the camp fires at the Granites ...

Of the veterans whose lives have been bound up with The Granites, Jim Escreet is by far the strongest character. When I saw him at Alice Springs he was surveying the world in generally cynically, though he had received £1,666/3/4 for his share in the discovery of what was then regarded as the mother lode of a tremendous find. To a prospector such as Escreet, who had been digging and washing for gold in Australia and in New Guinea since 1902, one would imagine such a sum meant something to him. But it did not. Coatless, collarless, he used to sit in the shade outside the Stuart Arms Hotel and talk of his future. 'This money,' he said, 'may be all right or it may not. But I reckon I see myself back at the field — or at another field — very soon, keeping up the same fight for gold.' And then he would go into the old parlor and stand by the piano while Mrs. Hall or another identity of the Territory played and sang; and he would smoke innumerable cigarettes, with half-closed eyes, standing silently for half an hour on end. Not yet in his late forties, he is a remarkable character. His mate, old Jack Atherton, with whom he had found the Burdekin Duck, trusts him absolutely. 'Jim is my secretary,' he used to say to me. 'I don't know how I'll get on when he goes south.' Jim went south and old Jack cried on the station platform at the Alice; moreover, he could not be comforted for days. And Escreet, hard and shrewd though he was, never betrayed his trust with Atherton. The two of them had been at first broken hearted at The Granites. Then they came on an alluvial patch and what they thought and many mining companies were to think was the mother lode on a line estimated by the promoters in the early days of the boom to be seven miles long. For three weeks after that they lived on cornflour and kangaroo rats. Often before, in the Tanami area, men had run short of tucker, but not as badly as the two prospectors on this occasion. They had a terrible time. They had to wheel water three miles in a wheelbarrow; they boiled well water and cornflour until they hated the sight of the glutinous mess. To use Escreet's own words, 'We had rats all ways, boiled, baked or roasted. They taste alright when you're hungry and have plenty of rice or cornflour to eat with them.' For the benefit of the uninitiated, may I explain that the rats they ate were not the rats as they are known in the cities. They were the kangaroo rat, a species of bandicoot such as is found outside Cairns in North Queensland. At this time, Jackie Lewis — not of the same type as the other two men — came into the picture. He had a motor truck, and when he arrived at The Granites from Tanami, he was induced to join the two partners. He was sent into Alice Springs for supplies while the other men continued their kangaroo rat diet, and he appeared with them thereafter in The Granites picture. The last I heard of him was that he had married in Melbourne.

But even the imperturbable self confidence of Escreet faded when old Jack Atherton came into the picture. He was the doyen of The Granites veterans. Six feet or more, sixty-odd, with a light blue eye and a grey beard and snow-white hair, old Jack was a romanticist, a lover of poetry, of good beer, of talk and of his pipe. Only when he went to bed was his pipe ever removed from his mouth. He quoted Henry Lawson. Every day he threatened, at sunrise, to go out prospecting, though he had almost two thousand pounds in the bank, his share of the Burdekin Duck claim. He spent money like water; he gave five pound notes to little half-caste girls and boys because he thought they needed some sweets; he 'shouted' for fifty men at a time; he lavished money on all the dead-beats and loafers of Alice Springs; he refused to have meals in the first-class dining room, but sat always with the drovers and his old friends, and when a subscription was being taken up for someone or other (a common thing at Alice Springs, whether it happened to be for someone's tucker bag or someone else's wife's mother's broken leg), his amount headed it. Yet for more than a quarter of a century, old Jack Atherton had roughed it in almost unbelievable country without rest, without proper food. And when his time came for rest, he would not take it — although one of the earliest men from Queensland on the field after the discovery, told me that early in December old Jack left the hotel at the Alice and took a little shanty in the town, there to entertain his cronies and smoke his pipes. I have said previously that he cried when Escreet left for the south. He was a dear old sentimentalist and often when I was discussing persons or incidents with him, his eyes would fill with tears. This was the man who faced starvation nearly 400 miles from the nearest township!

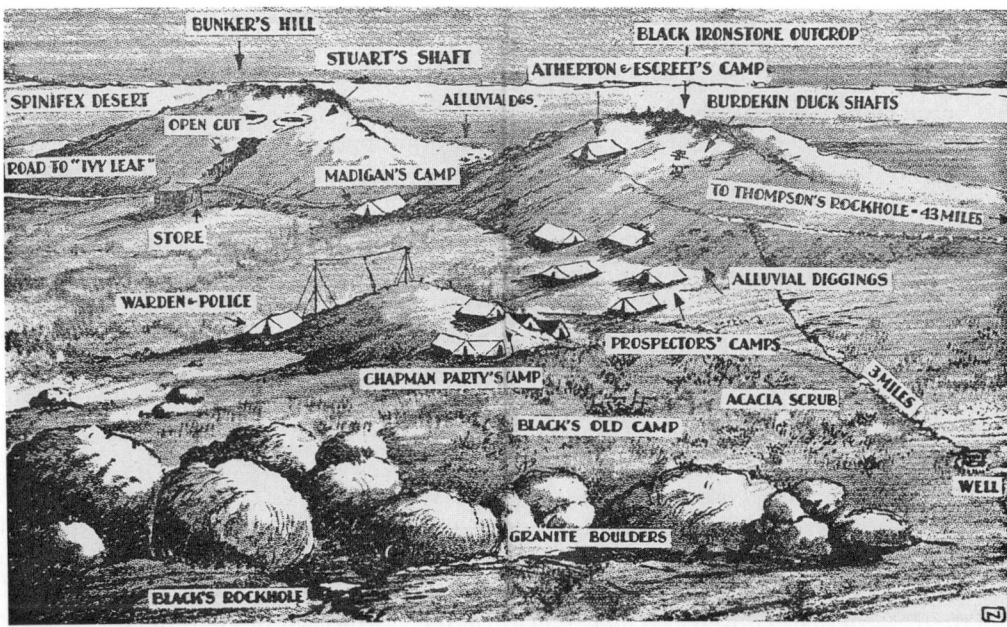

In 1932, journalist F.E. (Eric) Baume travelled to the Granites, Australia's most isolated diggings, 380 miles north-west of Alice Springs. Intimidated by the forbidding terrain and conscious of the scarcity of water (and gold!), Baume wrote Tragedy Track *(1933) to try and discourage foolhardy prospectors. This map appeared in the front of the book.*

One night at the Alice there was a party. The little bar-parlour was crowded. Someone suggested a sing-song; I was the unfortunate accompanist. There was an old song book in the room and the first piece I struck was, 'Won't you buy me pretty flowers.' Harry J —., a moderate tenor, sang the song. Old Jack was sitting behind me. From time to time I could hear snorts and grunts which I could not make out. Then a sob echoed through the room. Old Jack was weeping copiously — and not a soul laughed. No one, if he valued a sound hide, would have dared to laugh at Jack Atherton that night.

I was not so impressed by 'Deadsweet Joe' Stevenson, Ted Leahy or Frank Cooley, the other men, who, with 'Black Paddy' Ryan and Paddy O'Neill, have had their names before the public in The Granites blaze. Stevenson was a tall moustached prospector, hard-boiled and calculating. His talk on Cinesound's newsreel renewed the impression he had made on me at Alice Springs. But he was jovial and a good companion, and was the local humorist of Alice Springs. But he was not a veteran of the type of Escreet or of Atherton or Ted North, though he was good 'copy' while the boom lasted.

Two strange types were 'Black Paddy' Ryan and little Paddy O'Neill. They were Mutt and Jeff to the life, the discoverers of the claim known as Bunkers Hill, and later worked on option by the Chapman expedition. 'Black Paddy' was over six feet, thin as a rake, with a black drooping moustache, a typical 'Bulletin' Dave. Little Paddy was something under five feet, round faced as an orange, his little face crowned by a giant sombrero. When they breasted the bar, always together, they lifted a foot in quest of an imaginary rail, though both had been prospecting in the far North for years, and rails don't happen there. When they walked the dusty street they walked together. When they ate, they went together. When they spoke, it was something like this:

Black Paddy: 'We was thinkin' er goin' ter Schist Hills — '
Little Paddy: 'Fer to have a look, loike, at some quartzite —'
Black Paddy: 'We seen last May. An' I reckon — '
Little Paddy: 'If we get there afore the rains — '
Black Paddy: 'We'll strike some gold. Aint that right, Paddy?'
Little Paddy: 'Roight, Paddy.'
Black Paddy: 'That's jake, Paddy.'
Little Paddy: 'Yes, Paddy.'

And so on. When they got their option money they had a good time. They bought an old car and some new prospecting gear. They tripped out to The Granites just for the trip. To-day, even when things are bad up there, they will still drive out to the Gap in the ranges with a few kindred spirits in the township to drink a stray bottle of beer in the moonlight and sing 'Where the River Shannon's flowing' in seventeen parts and seventy keys.

Old Daniel O'Connell was another hoary veteran of the fields. Dan, in his cups, was a fiery old gentleman. I remember when little Beckett of Tanami, tired of being abused by old Dan'l, smote him hard and sure, and Dan measured his length on the ground. But he was back again, even though the well-sinker from the field, smaller than Beckett, smote him anew for a minor misdemeanour. Even the hop beer proprietor had words with Dan, who could make himself a greater pest than the plagues of Egypt.

Into the picture comes Ned Larkin, the veteran drover; Bert Croucher from Camooweal and a score of shirted dungareed men with elastic-sided boots and unquenchable thirsts. They were a happy, easy-going lot, for whom tomorrow was just the same as the week before last. May they strike it lucky somewhere, some time, and may Wallis Fogarty's give them perpetual grubstake. Which, you will agree, is a pious thought indeed.

Source: F. E. Baume, *Tragedy Track: The Story of the Granites,* Frank C. Johnson, Sydney, 1933, pp.98-102.

Daily work in the tin mine

Spider Brennan

SPIDER BRENNAN DESCRIBED HIS DAILY WORK IN MARANBOY (AS HE SURVEYED THE DECAYED SITE IN 1977 WITH PETER READ):

Somebody go down there first, and bucket him go down there, gottem winch, and I bin go down there longa ladder then, and gettem' all the drill, hammer, scraper, gettem about, you know, dirt. Inside, longa wall, like I bin gettem like that, gettem like that, puttem longa little tin, puttem longa this tin. That tin now bin bringem on top, and watchem, 'Oh yes, tin'.

    Keep going work, all the time. And that one there [pointing to a mine shaft] big one, right up there. I used to work like that, right up here. Bin plum tree here somewhere. Plum tree. I no more savvy now. But my wife he bin all day hanging up there, look look, while him bin young girl.

Is there a tunnel between all these holes?

Yes, tunnel, for me and ... And when I bin finish here, I bin, we bin tellem longa 'nother man, him bin name Jack Wilson, Jack Wilson. But I used to work longa Peter Lim[an Englishman for whom Brennan worked]. And we bin findem tin over there, we bin give it him, they bin work here, work longa old claim, all the way, behind. But I bin findem first. Tin, my boss belonga me-feller, bin work, and we bin findem proper really one that way longa ... what name ... no, Jack. Him bin what name, we two-feller, Jack, they bin callem Jack, but we bin callem, callem, blackfeller 'Goodboy'. Well, he bin all the day like that, 'Good boy!' Well, we bin callem 'Goodboy' And we bin havem two-feller work there now, altogether. [i.e., there were two white men, Lim and 'Goodboy', working in the same area].

How deep's this feller? We throw a stone down?

Chuck him ...

And what did you use for digging, like pick axe or something?

Got drill. No more this one [rotating drill]. But hand [hammered].

Oh, bang him. Puttem in ...

Bang, bang, bang, bang, bang. Puttem side, morning, I bin oughta makem three feller hole, you know, inside. And dinner time, makem five. That ... puttem dynamite then and cleanem, put 'nother ten hole for suppertime. And for morning, puttem straight away 'nother five and five. That make the hole. Like that [i.e. ten holes made to put the charges in].

Twenty altogether. You drill that big hole, get the dynamite. Where do they keep the dynamite? Munanga [white man's] house?

Yeah, munanga house. And bringem here, and puttem one dynamite, cuttem up, all right, and puttem in there inside. Cap and fuse. All right, cuttem up up like. No more this, really big long one, long one, up up. Makem go down, ten hole, ten fuse. Sometimes five fuse and five gelignite. One first one going, we lightem. One … two … three … four … five … six … seven … eight … nine … ten. Finish. I go up longa ladder, but lone one fuse, long one.

SPIDER BRENNAN WOULD SCRAMBLE UP THE LADDER, AND WAIT FOR THE EXPLOSIONS FROM A SAFE DISTANCE:

I run this way, sometime I run this way, behind, behind that house. Boom! We bin oughta countem. One … two … three … four … five … six … seven … eight … nine … ten. Finish. And go back now. Go back. We sit down little while, you now, smoke. Cap. Right, go down longa ladder. Look: 'Oh good tin, tin, yes!'

Gotta little hammer. Right, go down. Gotta little hammer. Look tin. Oh yeah, yeah, good tin all right. Oh, all about tin. Oh, look at that! All right. Bucket! Shovel! Pick! Righto.

Gotta men inside. And shovelem up now, shovelem up…

SPIDER BRENNAN THEN DESCRIBED THE RATE OF PAY, WHICH HE STATED WAS FIVE SHILLINGS (FIFTY CENTS) A WEEK:

Five shillings?

Five shillings, one week, five shilling 'nother week, next day [week] five shilling. That makem ten.

What about the tucker. What tucker you get?

Every week, you mean? Our tucker — half quart of flour, for weekend, and sugar and tea leaf, and tobacco, matches. Sometimes you know [Peter Lim] loanem shotgun, belonga kangaroo, go shootem again. And come back afternoon, on Sunday. Monday morning, work. Like that. Saturday morning longa big camp, police station [i.e., where the police station is now], where my mother, my daddy, where they bin gettem ration. Policeman bin look afterem. Give it ration.

They were too old to work?

Yeah, I bin work, and bringem tucker too there. Afternoon Sunday we leavem tucker, for daddy and mum. And we come back longa work. All day.

You went away for weekends sometimes? Go catching kangaroo?

That's right, back this way longa Elsey Station. Bamyili, creek high up. Fishing, come back. Or King River, walk King River, foot walk. Monday come, and come back here Sunday, and work. But really [long] weekend, one month time, camp out that, that way, rain time, but no more cold weather, all the munanga bin oughta say. 'No, can't work now. More better you holiday. When rain finish you come back.'

Where did you go in wet time?

I going bit river, [near] Bamyili, high up, this way. [We] used to camp there, longa spring, or longa creek. Go down this way longa King River.

When you went in the bush, did you live on bush tucker or take rations with you?

Yeah, yeah, whitefeller tucker and bush tucker. Kangaroo, no more bullock. Sometimes I bin oughta go back, gettem beef here longa my boss [i.e., sometimes he went back to get beef from Lim].

Source: From the interview of Spider Brennan in 1977 by Peter Read, in Jay Arthur & Peter Read (comps & eds), A view of the past: Aboriginal accounts of Northern Territory history (unpub.), MS pp.243-7.

15 Rock belong Jesus dreaming

It is a child's intellect, a fearfully neglected child's intellect, that meets the missionary. That intellect is not eager for being worked on — it is not responsive; it wants to be left alone. It has been pressed down to this brutal level by surrounding circumstances. The claims of human nature are very poorly satisfied here in the wilds of Australia. Hence the starved intellect, the starved spirit in a starved body.
— L. K. Kaibel, Lutheran missionary at Hermannsburg, n.d.

Virtue is a myth, and missionaries a decided failure.
— W. H. Willshire, *The Land of the Dawning*, 1896

First time, everything been come up out of the ground. Language, people, emu, kangaroo, grass, everything. That's Law. Missionaries just trying to bust everything up. They fuck em up right through. It's going to end up in a big war.
— Hobbles Danayarri, speaking to Debbie Rose, 1985

Although it is easy for anthropologists to take a negative attitude toward mission activity, the matter is not at all straightforward. Particularly during early periods of Aboriginal-European contact, mission stations were virtually the only refuge-places for Aborigines trying to escape from the depredations of the new settlers and their expanding townships. The writings of Salvado, Taplin, Threlkeld and many others make that quite clear. Without the protective authority of missionaries, the Aboriginal population would have been reduced even more savagely than it was.
— R. M. & C. H. Berndt, *Aboriginal Australians and Christian Missions*, 1988

Previous page: Sisters of the Order of Our Lady of the Sacred Heart, Darwin. The photograph appeared in Bishop Gsell's The Bishop With 150 Wives *(1956).*

Bring the heathen the true faith

F. X. Gsell

It must be remembered that in Australia, still with its vast Never-Never Land, one must always know how to give time its head.

Now, how does the missionary fit into this scheme? The aim of the missionary is obedience to a divine command: he must bring the heathen to the true faith. Even if this command were ignored today, which it could not be by a follower of Christ, no one, I think, would dare to deny that the true faith is the generating force of civilization. Thus it is in vain that some people say, 'Why not leave these people in peace? Why disturb their old customs if they make them happy?'

But we do not forget that these fine talkers, few of whom have given the subject any deep thought, themselves enjoy the benefits of Christian civilization: and they enjoy this security because, in day of old, missionaries brought these benefits to their forefathers. The heathens are men as we are men and, as such, they have the same right that we have to the benefits of Christianity.

'Go ye and teach all nations ...'

In Australia, particularly in those northern areas where the aborigines still maintain a foothold, the Christian has a double duty: of charity, in communicating his faith to his less fortunate brothers; of justice, in making what restitution can be made. The natives have largely lost their religious heritage with its beliefs and customs, and this heritage must be replaced. They have lost their lands.

The two compensations, moral and material, march together. Obviously the transformation of a nomadic native hunter into a husbandman and a producer without destroying,

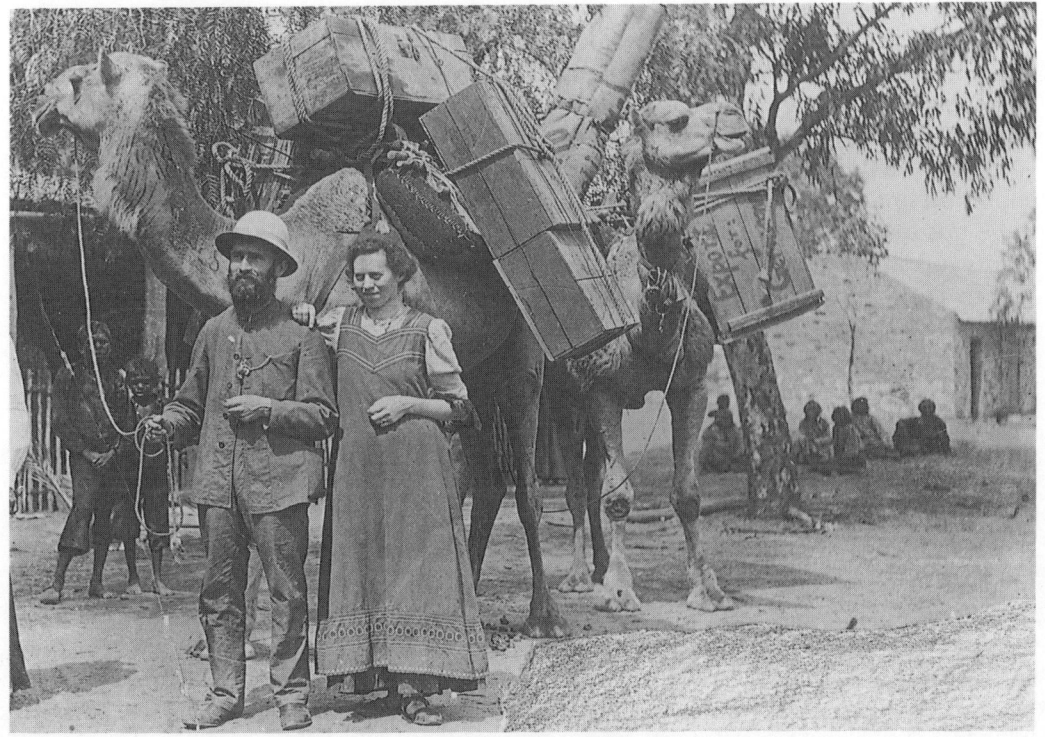

Missionary Liebler and Mrs Liebler, at Hermannsburg Lutheran Mission, 1910.

or at least upsetting, his tradition is a Utopian idea, as impossible as the making of a Christian from a nomadic pagan before converting him from his erring ways.

However, whatever may be said to the contrary, it is not impossible to reform the aboriginal attitude towards life so that he can become a planter and, indeed, a good Christian. Yes, the process must be long and inevitably obstructed by difficulties; but how many centuries did it take white men to emerge from barbarity? The main thing is to face up to the task and to stick to it, trusting in God ...

The popularity of Father Regis amongst the natives, something won effortlessly, was extraordinary; and he was never seen without being surrounded by a joyous band. This highly erudite theologian of brilliant intellect had a most inventive turn of mind, especially where hunting, fishing, gardening and other homely pursuits were concerned. Because the young on Bathurst Island differ little from the young everywhere else, whether black or white, the good Father's delightful way of finding new, better and more amusing ways of doing things won the adoration of our children. I have to admit that there was one thing which did not march nearly fast enough for him: and that was the conversion of the natives. I dare not try to imagine what he would have thought had he foreseen that even after thirty years of work we still could not claim one single adult convert.

Source: F. X. Gsell, *The Bishop with 150 Wives*, Angus & Robertson, Sydney, 1956, pp.38-9, 58-9.

We're going to take this little girl away

Topsy Naparrula Nelson

We had two missionaries, *yapa* [Aboriginal] ones here. We'd go in a big mob, with all the Warramunga kids. We was all coming into church at the Seven Mile ... The mission was there before. That was when I was a little kid. We used to bring in frogs you know. We was little bit silly ones. We caught them in the swamp, and we'd take them to the missionary. 'Ah, you kids, take them back, all those things, and put them back in the water. This is a really important one. There, take it back and kneel down and pray for that thing.' That is what those missionaries would say. We'd take them back, chuck them in the water, the little lizards and all. We'd put them back in their holes; and the crabs too.

Once, I was really crazy. I brought that crab over with me. It didn't have any legs on it. We was just bringing it in. 'Oh, I want some salt, please,' I was asking. We was really stupid ones. We didn't know. 'For what? Show me what is in your bag.' I was standing with my bag behind my back. 'I want salt, please.' 'For what?' that lady one was asking. 'Show me first.' I showed that thing for her. 'Na, take that thing back in the water and you come and pray for that thing.' And we did, with no legs on, we put it back into the water. No legs ... no claws ... we put it back. We got back, and the missionary said 'come inside'. We was just kneeling down and praying for that thing with no legs ...

In the morning, we would come and eat little bread, little scones. We would still be hungry. Drink. We only would have one little drink. Cordial, like that. We'd stand up, line up. All the Warramunga, Warlpiri and Kaititj — all mixed up. He used to ask us for a song. 'Come on you kids, what song are we going to sing?' I remember one. We would kneel down and sing that one.

We was hungry, and one day I was thinking, 'I'm going to keep that frog. I'm not taking it for Mrs Cameron.' I took it to the camp, to my father's place. I cooked it and ate it; and next morning I went to Mrs Cameron. She liked me very well. She tried to take me to her place in America. This day she was asking the boys and girls, 'Did you see little Topsy?' 'I don't know. We didn't see her ... We saw her in the creek ... She was swimming there.'

When I got the frog, I took it to camp and I ate it all. I didn't tell the story. I told me mum. I'm going for Mrs Cameron — she's looking for me. I did. I was walking along. I saw a lot of kids. 'Come on dear,' she was saying. 'Come into my place. Where you went yesterday?' She was patting my hair. 'No, I was swimming. I went straight home. I was a bit sick.' 'Don't you tell lies,' she said. I was thinking. She took me into a little room inside and she made me sit down on the bed. 'Now, tell me the truth. What happened to you yesterday, Topsy? I saw only the other mob of kids was here.' I told her straight: 'I took the frog.' 'What did you do with that frog?' 'I ate it all.' 'I see.' She put me in a little jail, in the home, a room with just her. She was telling me a story, about Jesus and Moses. 'Don't you eat anything. Don't hurt anything. It's not made to eat. It's made for your friend.'

The first missionaries was coming to help the people. The white fellas were trying to kill all the *yapa*, and the missionary was helping us. They gave us meat, only, that's all. Plenty of rations and clothes. After that they went away. Those two, Mr and Mrs Long came and stayed. That was when the Army was happening. I was little bit big then. He was good, that Mr Long — our cousin.

That other missionary, the *yapa* one ... he was talking to my mother and father. 'We're going to take this little girl away. She'll come back for you mob.' I had long hair then, you know. That missionary was telling my father he was going to take me away. Next time, next day, my father got away. We ran away at night into the bush. For good. We didn't return to go for that place again. We was just keep walking this way now to bush, because, you know, he was asking my mother and father for taking me away. He was going to try to make me a missionary to that America. In the night we came back to Greenwood, to the old station. We stayed there for good then. Mick [Topsy's half-brother] was a little baby then. We didn't go back to Tennant Creek. We stayed there until that Mr Long came to that old Telegraph Station. It took us about a week to walk. I was about ten, like Maureen [Topsy's mother's brother's daughter's daughter].

I remember that Army time. That Army mob was asking me, 'What's your name little boy?' I was only wearing shorts. All those Warramunga kids was saying, 'We got a new missionary.' We went back and they was telling me, 'We've got a new missionary now.' We stayed there for a long time. Mr Thomas was taking the place for Mr Long after he got away to Alice Springs.

Ted Egan [a popular Northern Territory Welfare Branch Officer during the 1960s, now (1985) a folk-singer], he used to run for us. 'You got lolly for we mob?' 'Yes, I got lolly.' He'd lift that big lid and get lollies in the tin. He was just Army bloke giving us lollies. (Now he comes and sings all around this country.) When he was really young, he was really good looking. Then he was coming back and he was saying, 'I know those greedy ones.' Everyone was really young then, and other mobs would visit us.

My father was cutting trees and making that airstrip. That white man, that Army mob, was really good. My father was just cutting trees. We used to stay at the Telegraph Station, and my father would go back into town and work for the week, from that hill the other side of the water hole.

Well, we was staying there. Mr Brown's father [an old Aboriginal man, now dead, known as 'Chicken Jack'], he was there too. In the morning one day, we was fighting for damper. The others was chasing us and saying, 'I'm going to hit you two.' And he [Chicken Jack] was throwing a stone at us. That Jungarrayi [Mr Brown] and me was up in a tree. I tried to jump over but it was little bit long way. I just let go and fell down. I broke my leg (it was a stony place). That was when we was only kids fighting for damper! They took me to the hospital in Tennant Creek and they rang up for that Mr Long. He came and prayed for us. The Army plane took me to Alice Springs. That was the first time I went in a plane. I was too sick to see anything. I stayed in Alice for a long time. I had family there. I was big when I came back. We went there, in the Army time, to the Bungalow [a government ration-depot near the Telegraph Station north of Alice Springs]. There was a big camp there. People from all different places. That *kuminjayi* [a term of respect used by Warlpiri to replace the name of a dead person] was there too, just working.

At the mission at Phillip Creek we used to stay in the dormitory. We was separate. Our parents stayed in the camp. They took the kids away from their parents.

Source: From the interview of Topsy Naparrula Nelson by Diane Bell, in Isobel White, Diane Barwick & Betty Meehan (eds), *Fighters and Singers: The Lives of Some Australian Aboriginal Women,* Allen & Unwin, Sydney, 1985, pp.9-12.

Mary

W. Hart-Smith

The bishop came, the bishop
Made a most uncomfortable journey
On foot, deplorably thirsty; also
By camel and by lugger

To visit his black
Congregation, all turned out in full
Muster because of a promise of
Tucker a'plenty ...

Seven hundred and twenty
Miles of withering, blistering
Heat, on foot, by camel,
And by lugger:

'Mary,' he said, 'do you pray to God?'
'Yes,' smirked she, 'Me talk-talk
Longa that cranky beggar!'

Source: W. Hart-Smith, *The Unceasing Ground: Poems,* Angus & Robertson, Sydney, 1946, p.3.

One 24 December 1882 four missionaries sailed into Darwin Harbour and landed at Palmerston. Their first settlement was a grant at Rapid Creek but after three years they decided to establish a station further inland. In 1886 they established the Holy Rosary Mission at Old Uniya on the south-west side of the Daly River. Standing *(left to right): Brothers Scharner, Haelbig, Melzer, Lange, Girschek and Pfalzer.* Seated *(left to right): Fathers Marschner, Milz, Conrath and Fleury. The Aboriginal children are in the standard Mission clothing. The photograph was taken in 1899.*

Daly River poem

George Lavater

The White Man boozed,
The Black Man snoozed,
The Brown was King.[1]
The river flowed,
The jungle growed,
Like anything.

Some came and went,
In such event
They had their reasons.
The wet and dry
Went rolling by
To mark the seasons.

A case of Rum
Would often come
To cheer the weary.
There came a tent,
Then some cement
And Father Leary.

Alas, no more
The settlers swore
In front of wowsers.
They even took
To reading books
And wearing trousers.

The farmers shaved,
The Brothers slaved
To build a Mission.
And made it rise
Before our eyes,
Like a magician.

But what is strange is
A sudden change is
Detectable.
The wicked Daly
Has gone gaily
Respectable.

1 'The Brown' is the King Brown, one of Australia's most deadly snakes.

Source: George Lavater, 'Daly River poem', in John Pye, *The Daly River Story*, Colemans Printing, Darwin, 1976, p.12.

God in the silver sea

Xavier Herbert

The Gospel Mission had been established many years, so long in fact and thoroughly that the island had been changed out of recognition. Not a stick of the old settlement remained. Even the ancient mango trees and skinny coconuts had been uprooted as though they were counted as original sins. A neat village of iron and asbestos buildings, including a steepled church and a double-story school, stood on the site of the humpies; and another village, this of white-washed iron, bark and hessian, scrupulously clean and neatly placed, stood where the native camp had stood. This second was the native quarter. It was drained and served by kitchens and latrines and shower-baths, and enclosed by a high barbed-wire fence. A grove of coconuts, comprising a thousand or more fine palms, lined the ocean-beach from end to end, these the virtues, as it were, supplanting the ousted sins. Above the palms from the sea could be seen the tip of the stack of the copra-mill and the sail of a great windmill that pumped water from the billabong. And the land between the billabong and the beach and creek, formerly overgrown with scrub and jungle, was laid out like a market-garden, fenced, and scored with irrigation streams. Birds and beasts had fled; so had the crocodiles; so no doubt had Krater's devil.

Building the station must have been difficult, but simple compared with the founding of the flock. Converts came of their own accord at first, thinking the station just an ordinary whiteman's business, and the religious practices in which they were invited to take part merely another kind of whiteman's incomprehensible amusement; they even offered their women to the male missionaries to secure their goodwill. But when the necessary discipline was brought to bear, most of the converts went bush, and warned their ignorant brethren against the Mission.

This did not surprise the Rev. Theodore Hollower, leader of the Mission, though he had not foreseen it. He knew that anything was to be expected of the Prince of Evil. So he went after the brands that had been snatched back, and with wiles equal to His Highness's, again plucked a fair number from the burning. And he took the schooner *Alice Carstairs* far away and combed the islands of the Silver Sea for converts. He even stole into the territory of the Catholic Mission near Port Zodiac and snatched a few more brands from there, considering the holy-water with which they had been baptised about as effective an extinguisher of Hell Fire as gasoline. And down the eastern coast he went as far as Cape Nordoster, gathering converts by simply blackbirding them. The *Alice Carstairs* made several quiet trips like this, so that within a year or two the islands and the coastlands were completely depopulated, though not with so much advantage to the Mission, since more than half of the natives had fled to avoid the *Alice Carstairs*. Naturally a number of converts turned out to be good Christians who could be relied upon to force their views on others. These kept order at the Mission and prevented the unwilling from escaping. No canoe was allowed on the island.

It was not Mr. Hollower's wish to keep a prison. He wished only to bring his victims into contact with Christianity and keep them there till they might grasp its significance, which was something in which he had such great faith himself that he was prepared to keep them in its neighbourhood till they died.

Better than those of natural Christian disposition to keep order in the Mission and prevent escapes were converts brought from lands so distant that they knew they could not find their way home if liberated. They were more robust than the natural Christians and harsh in their jealousy of those who knew their way home. Mr. Hollower would do anything to outwit His Highness.

But still that Spirit worked contrarily. The old order of things had changed in Yurracumbunga. Refugees from islands and distant coastlands joined the tribe, so that at length it became a mob with mixed philosophies, whose common tongue was Pidgin, whose purpose was to harass the Mission. This mob called itself the Cowboys, a name no doubt adopted by knowing fellows who had been to town many years before ... and had seen the pictures. They used to raid the Mission by night and slaughter pigs and poultry, beat the Christians who resisted them, debauch the large number of women who did not mind, and carry off as many as they could. Usually they raided only for raiding's sake, but sometimes it was for the purpose of stealing back their lubras. For the zealous Hollower, believing that no couple had right to conjugality unless joined according to his own particular formula, did not scruple to separate pagan husband and wife; in fact, he had found that an easy way to bring in converts was to catch stray lubras and keep them till their owners called for them and consented to be christened and to undergo a period of righteous living, in which event he married them to their wives and gave them freedom of the island. Consequently there was a preponderance of females at the Mission. But it was all great fun for everyone, including Mr. Hollower, who never would admit it. The Christian natives thanked their new-found god for Grace and Mr. Hollower, the Cowboys their ancient devils for the same good man and something for which to live.

The Missionaries did not mind the raiding as a rule, because that provided another easy means of making converts. Frequently the raiders fell into traps and were baptised, and frequently the Christians, mainly those robust ones unable to go home, assumed their right to counter-raid. Usually the violence in these affairs was limited to what was done with fists and sticks and stones, the opponent forces having no desire for bloodshed because for the most part they were brothers, but blood was spilt occasionally, as the result of which any raiders caught were sent up to town to jail.

Several times there was serious trouble when sentries at the Mission were clubbed to death and mutilated for the fat of their kidneys. Such outrages were usually dealt with by punitive expeditions brought from town. The fat-taking practice was introduced by refugees from the Jittabukka Country, who believed, in common with several other tribes, that if the bark of a certain tree were impregnated with the fat of an enemy's kidneys and burnt at billabongs or creeks or hunting-grounds, the devils responsible for the supply of fruit or fish or game would be more indulgent. It was a sort of religious rite, like the burning of blessed candles. The punitive expeditions brought out to punish these outrages did little more than scare the Cowboys away for a while. The Mission natives, who were of necessity the guides of the expeditions, having respect for their own kidneys and an un-Christian belief that the fat-takers were devils, were always too scared to follow tracks with certainty. Any natives caught on the mainland on these occasions, whether associated with the fat-takers or not, were taken to town and sent to the Calaboose for life.

The Reverend F. Greenwood and Mrs Greenwood reclining on the front verandah of the Methodist Parsonage in the 1890s.

This rather confused state of things was generally kept secret. However, occasionally it came to light, causing scoffers great amusement. But Mr. Hollower was never daunted, convinced that someday he or his successors would establish order and win the Aborigines to Him who had created and neglected them so long. And truly, year by year the confusion was being in a measure overcome. In reply to scoffers he would merely say, 'These people are human beings and children of the Lord. They must be found an honourable place among mankind and taught Salvation. Else how can we sleep of nights? Suggest a better plan to deal with them and I shall try it.' No one suggested anything but that he should mind his own business, leave the natives to go the way of old. To that he always gave the unanswerable reply, ' 'Tis not my business but the Lord's.'

At the time of the arrival of Tocky and Christobel, the Mission comprised some ninety persons, or Souls as Mr. Hollower called them, of whom all but eleven were Aborigines. There were six white people, Mr. Hollower and his wife, Brother Simon Bleeter and his, and two devoted spinsters, Sisters Wings and Harp. The assistants were five coloured missionaries, three Fijians and two Solomon Islanders and their wives, people of breeds that make most zealous Christians, in spite of, or perhaps on account of, the fact that they are by heritage head-hunters. These were assisted in turn by the best of the converts. And there were also eight Aboriginal halfcastes, five girls and three boys, not counting Tocky and Christobel, all of whom were nothing but pests just then, though Mr. Hollower hoped to make of them evangelists to deal with the natives in the bush, to which end he was patiently instructing them in the Yurracumbunga tongue.

Mr. Hollower himself brought Tocky and Christobel out. Thus in their opinion they met with the worst part of their exile first. His reward for doing everything conforming with his cult to win their regard was their whole-hearted detestation. Of all nicknames, they gave him the one of Lucifer, which they chose on account of his resemblance to their conception of the Prince of Evil as described to them in Compound sunday-school by the Rev. Finchley Randter. The name Lucifer was always used in teaching Aborigines about the Devil, lest they should confuse Him with the unauthentic devils of the bush. Mr. Hollower was tall and thin, gaunt of face and shaggy of eye, and swarthy. He gave the maids to understand that he expected much of them, and placed them in the care of the two white sisters, who controlled the department of young unmarried lubras and halfcaste girls.

On the second night after their arrival, at an hour when the humbler Souls were in bed, Mr. Hollower's attention was drawn from the subject of *God in the Silver Sea* as dealt with in a book he was writing, which he was discussing with all the white Souls on the high front veranda of his big white house, by the sound of music coming faintly from the building where the girls were housed. The sound was faint indeed, unheard by the others till Mr. Hollower drew attention to it. 'Listen!' he said, holding up a long index finger. 'What is that?'

Silence, while the tide lisped to the beach and the wind whispered to the coconuts.

'Music,' said Mr. Hollower. 'An harmonicon. It must be those new girls. It must be stopped.'

He rose, and with the sisters descended from the house and went into the brilliant moonlight and down a path of crushed white coral flowing like a stream of milk through the black and silver palms. His face and those of his companions were grave at first, but softened as their owners neared the dormitory and heard the music more distinctly. It was that old rollicking hymn *Roll the Chariot*, a great favourite with the Gospellers. Subdued voices were singing and feet lightly thumping. With one accord the feet of Hollower and the sisters trod less heavily. The refrain danced through their minds:

If the Devil's in the way we will roll it over him;
If the Devil's in the way we will roll it over him;
If the Devil's in the way we will roll it over him;
As we all go marching on.
Oh, roll the Old Chariot along!
Yes, roll the Old Chariot along —

Mr. Hollower chuckled, snapped his fingers, said, 'The young villains! But of course we must stop it.'

They reached the gate. Now their faces were grim. The tune was the same — but not the words! Mr. Hollower hissed, 'Open the gate — open the gate! Don't make a noise. We must see who's at the bottom of this. Give me your torch.'

The sister who had the key dropped it in long grass. All bent to search for it, while blasphemy and insult smote their ears. But oh, how the singers were enjoying it! The composition was the work of Christobel, who had a gift for such a thing.

> Oh, roll the Ol' Chariot along;
> Yes, roll the Ol' Chariot along;
> And fill the air with laughter and with song,
> As we all go down to Hell.
>
> If Ol' Hollower's in the way we will roll it over him;
> If Ol' Hollower's in the way we will roll it over him;
> And then we'll sin and sin and sin and sin,
> And we'll all go straight to Hell.
>
> But when Hollower meets Ol' Lucifer face to face;
> Yes, when Hollower meets Ol' Lucifer face to face;
> Oh, Ol' Lucifer's sure to offer him his place!
> So we won't stop long in Hell.
>
> Oh, roll the Ol' Chariot along;
> Yes, roll the Ol' Chariot along;
> Who cares a damn for what is right or wrong?
> Hurrah for good Ol' Hell!

The door burst open. The torch-light blazed. The voice of Mr. Hollower thundered, 'What is the meaning of —' The thunder fell flat. For the light revealed a group of yellow and black girls, most of them naked as usual in that stifling dormitory, the others in the long red nightgowns they were forbidden to remove, squatting on the floor between the rows of beds about Christobel and Tocky, the first half-clad, the other stark naked and holding to her mouth a mouth-organ.

'W-w-what —' gasped Mr. Hollower. He doused the light and hissed in the darkness, 'Heavens!'

For a second the place was in an uproar. Then silence fell, silence perfect but for the quiet breathing of a score of sleeping innocents.

Source: Xavier Herbert, *Capricornia*, Publicist Press, Sydney, 1938, excerpt from ch.19.

The night departs

W. E. (Bill) Harney

The night departs as day comes rolling in,
The day goes out and restful nights begin.
Shades of my fathers in their tribal land
Let they who think of me, but understand
That I am what I am, Yet first define
Whose God is right, my father's one or thine?

Our code was kinship, for we knew not Might,
Was yours the gun that made a white God, Right?
Right with that Might which bade stern killers ride
With fire and thunder through the countryside;
 So sheltered we beside the White man's God,
And thus were saved from Law's grim chain and rod.
Our ritual slowly changed to Bible law
Our culture-centre was the strange church floor.
We ate the white-men's food and thus became
— Lost in your world and mine — A tribe in name.
The mission people taught us how to pray,
They came as friends, but did they know the way?
For how can mortals know what fate portends,
That secret now is mine. Pass on my friends.

Source: W. E. (Bill) Harney, *To Ayers Rock and Beyond*, Robert Hale, London, 1963; Rigby, Adelaide, 1984, p.130.

Interview in a desert

Mark O'Connor

'We got nother-feller rock,
little-fella. Not much to see. Sometimes 'im
hide under other rock. Too soft for spear-point.
But 'im last, oh yes 'im last! Might be
two hundred piccaninny times. Dat yellow rock
go on, all same forever.'

'So you trade this yellow eternity rock?'
asked the anthropologist,
propping his notebook on freckled knee,
'You got big myth-cycle, big Dreaming, for him?
You make totem with him?'

'Nah, dat proper useless Whitefeller rock.
Only good for kids go play.
We got no story who put 'im dere.
But Whitefeller go hunt for dat yellow rock
to make 'im trade-bead. All day out in sun.
Poor bugga forget place where he born. Only look
for dat crazy rock. Dat Whitefeller totem;
we call dat *Rock belong Jesus Dreaming*.'

Source: Mark O'Connor, *Firestick Farming: Selected Poems, 1972-1990*, Hale & Iremonger, Sydney, 1990, p.167.

16 'Hang on like I done'

Previous page: Big Bill Neidjie (Bunitj clan), in his country (the Kakadu area).

Everywhere there is change

W. E. (Bill) Harney

So my tale is told, and as I write of these things which were, I ponder on that city in which I was living for a brief space of time. I have returned to the north again, but not by the steamer that used to carry us up in the days gone by. For me it was the open road, and the trees and hills, which at Alice Springs stand out in their rugged grandeur, brooding over the town below. What shades of colour are there: the blue hue of the distant hills; the high crag of Mount Gillien with a stone twig upon its crest, the marks of former days, placed there in memory of a man who lived here and understood the Arunta people who roamed this land. What legends abound in these hills? What tales of the dreamtime? Albert Namatjira, the painter, and member of this tribe, had set down in colours those changing scenes; and Strehlow, who lived at Jay Creek, has shown us the majesty of the Arunta myths.

Not far from the city in which I lived for a while were relics of the carvings by natives of those parts. Perhaps their shades or spirits look down upon that restless, teeming horde, which lives and dies between walls of stone. As I was hurried along in that human stream, darting here and there to escape the roaring motors and trams, watching the look on the faces in the street, I would think of the natives saying: 'All a same when you jump longa ant-nest.'

Yet, when I walked through the city parks, its museums and numerous places of art, I became deeply conscious of the debt we owe to these places; but the people of the bush and those of the city think and walk along different lines. Just as the aborigine thinks that the store at the station homestead produces the food, and therefore must be protected, so does the city dweller associate meat, vegetables and milk with shops and bottles and tins. He does not comprehend — and why should he? — those endless miles the cattle must travel before they reach the markets; or the patient tilling of soil and the anxious days when the rains refuse to come, and the hand of that master villain, drought, spreads over the land; or the milking of cows in the dead hour of the night, and the carting of milk on its dreary rounds, until presto! it arrives outside his door, sealed in a little bottle.

I am restless to-day, and my mind is in a turmoil; for I have discovered that when I was in the city, I pined for the bush, and now that I am in the bush, I think of the city. Perhaps it is the spirit within, which is ever seeking new fields to explore. Maybe the restless people of the city feel that way too.

One need not go out into the jungle or the bushland to be a pioneer; for I have seen the people in the cities scheming new ways to live: the scientist in his laboratory, the doctor in his healing, or the householder tilling his little plot to grow something, or tending to the flowers in his garden. They live their life, while we live ours.

I have met great people in the bush and great people in the city. The learned professors, I have found, are real, homely people, who think of flowers and trees, whereas their wives and children wonder about the bush, and its birds, and problems.

Dick, one of my great friends, sits patiently on his box to await a customer who may need a 'shoe shine.' What a grand philosophy is his, for here to-day in the twilight of his years, having given up a life of wandering over the face of the earth, he is still proud enough to offer his services in this social work.

I spent many comforting evenings with my bush pal, Gordon, the blacksmith, at a place kept by a widow, who has reared sons, now all fighting overseas[in World War II], while she and her daughter, Babs, stay at home to keep the home fires burning.

Memories come — Mick and his wife, their little shop and their grand philosophy of life, my Christmas Day at a family reunion, the father flying from New Zealand to be with them at this time of peace and goodwill, and I, a stranger, welcome in their midst; of Ruth, with tragedy behind and a future ahead, and little curly-headed Ian to carry on, let us hope, into a pleasant future.

Tragedy, despair, philosophy and happiness are in the bush and in the city. The bells tolled out that Christmas Day, 'Peace on earth, goodwill to men.'

I leave the Alice by convoy, heading north along a fine, well-made road, where once, not long ago, a camel pad pointed the way into the northland. The miles fly past and memories crowd in. Places, places, places: Ryan's Well, and I think of the Necker family; Eileron; Teatree Well, where, when I last saw it, the water was hauled up by a camel whose driver was a native woman. To-day it has an engine to do the work. Central Mount Stuart — what magic is here! Stuart, the explorer, and the central mountain in Australia. I gazed on it again, and thought of that day years ago when Linda [Harney's Aboriginal wife] and I had stopped on its crest and laughed as we viewed the scene beneath. The Barrow and its graves nearby of men who were 'killed' by the blacks.

Two of the most recognisable identities in the white community of the Northern Territory, authors Doug Lockwood and Bill Harney share a joke.

On we travelled; past Lydia's Well, which was called by the bushmen Bullocky Soak, a permanent waterhole in a dry land. At night there, when the stars shone brightly in the cold night air, the Parapa (lizard or worm, which?) would come out and whistle aloud in their thousands; perhaps a mating call, though the noise was queer, and made me wonder at it all.

So I returned, after many days, to the place where I work, looking after the native people of the Northern Territory. Vin is there to greet me, and I am pleased to see him, while Jack and his good friends, the natives, come over with a 'good-day, old man; how did you like the south?' I pass some remark; then Mollie, the native woman, calls out from the kitchen: 'cup of tea, cup of tea.'

I look around me at the trees and the native people of this settlement. Everywhere there is change. The war has brought new ideas, and the aborigine has been caught up in its hungry claw. The job lies in the future; — to save the blackman we must 'watch and wait.' Vin sits a little distance away. He is the boss of it all, and he is thinking, thinking.

From the camps come the drone of the didgeredoo; the natives dance; from the creek comes the bullroarer's cry. The old Mother goddess is calling the faithful to prayer, yet few heed, and the elders shake their heads in despair. The fires are lit, and crowding round them are groups of natives with eager, tense faces. I approach them and hear them mutter through clenched teeth 'Ace high, ace high.' They are at a game of cards.

The mook mook owl gives its cry; the bullroarers drone on. The Territory is in the process of change — its destiny and dreaming lie ahead.

Source: W.E. (Bill) Harney, *North of 23°*, Australasian Publishing Co., Sydney, 1946, pp.263-6.

We gotta be black and white in this country

Amy Laurie

Today you can't put any sense into people yet. Maybe they've got no mind or they're thinking about things like they were before, and not this year or next year or what's going to come. You go down and preach to them now, and they wouldn't understand what you mean and what you're trying to be. At the reserve, they say, 'You think you're *gadia*' — meaning white man. 'You think you're something bigger than everybody.' I said, 'Oh, I'm tellin'' you

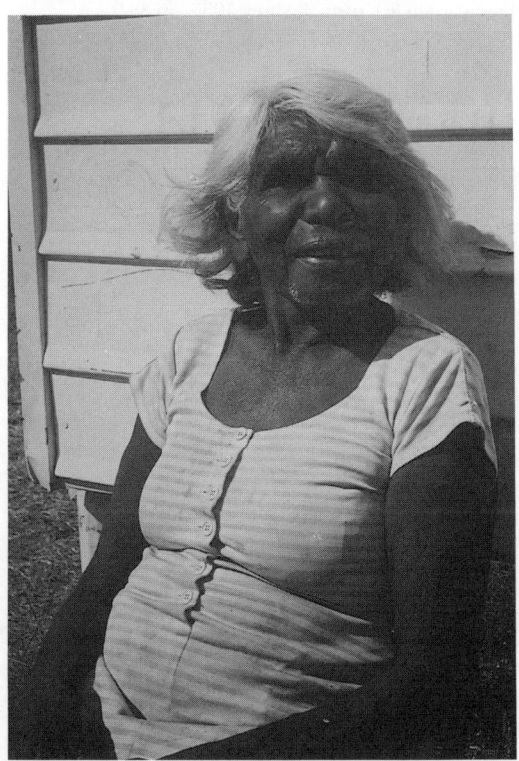

Amy Laurie.

for your own good. You wanta work your brains. One day you'll be like that puppy dog if you don't understand any English.' They say, 'What that for? We've got a government look after us.' See? All right, I just leave them alone.

That's why every time they want to go to a meeting now, like a land meeting, they all sit down and say, 'What this meeting is? What for?' I try to tell them, 'We've gotta help. We gotta be black and white in this country — *our* country — but we'll have more chance to fight back to keep our country because we have nothing like white man.' No, they can't understand that meeting — nothing. 'If you go to the meeting you'll see something what you gotta see, or you wanta be *myall* all your life?' I dunno. I go round to every house and tell them they've got to go tomorrow. Those girls don't go. I don't know why, maybe they're frightened, maybe ashamed. They don't have to talk; they can sit down there, sit around, and can ask you what you think about it.

Some white man is our relation now we're together. That's why they call them uncle, brother and so on, because they're living together. One time ago we walked from Wave Hill Station carrying our swags. A big man came up and took us back to Wattie Creek, and we were asked to sit down there. He gave us everything he had. He was like a father, uncle, all them country people. White man call them uncle, like old man black-fellers. They're all right; they understand them. Some people don't like colour, but better to be mixed like the birds and the flowers mixed. They look very nice all the colours mixed in the flowers.

I reckon they had a good mind these people round here, my countrymen; not like the cheeky mob — cheeky yet. I hear young people like my grandchildren say, 'We bin really silly bugger.' 'What for?' I ask them. 'Well, they never did anything to white man, who kicked him, knocked him out — everything. No nothing — no fight.' Old man black-fellers say, 'You know why we bin let 'em shoot we. Why? We frightened? No, we never gotim rifle.' And we didn't care, they reckon … 'We can die in our own country.'

Source: From the interview of Amy Laurie by Ann Magrath, in Isobel White, Diane Barwick & Betty Meehan (eds), *Fighters and Singers: The Lives of Some Australian Aboriginal Women*, Allen & Unwin, Sydney, 1985, pp.88-9.

if you stay too long in the third world

Lee Cataldi

if you stay too long in the third world
you learn
to hawk and spit like an old woman
you become
unfit for dinner parties
in the lands of the well fed

having dropped out of your original country
into this space from which
the coast with its oceans and gardens
the party on the terrace
the splash of green water over the bow of the yacht
are images projected on a screen
whose unreality you resent
the other side of the coin whose gain
is the loss you see all around

if you stay too long in the third world
death becomes a fact of life   the old
die quickly   the young
can't count on being old   this termite death
hollows out the roots of endeavour

as children leave toys you abandon
your previous explanations

if you stay too long in the third world
it will fill the space in your psyche
with a different discourse
you will begin to recognise
the unfamiliar in the unfamiliar
the outline of a landscape
in a pattern of dots
the faces of relations in the tragic and violent
repetitions of a song   the patterns of daily living
in the holy steps of a dance

if you stay too long in the third world
you will become
accustomed to silence and observation
leading to understanding
to abundance and malnutrition
immutably hand in hand

when that eager and rational voice
whose creature you are
whose instrument you had volunteered to become
grates like the radio on a bad day
you switch it off

if you stay too long in the third world
you will be unable to leave

Source: Lee Cataldi, *Women Who Live on the Ground: Poems 1978–1988*, Penguin, Ringwood, Vic., 1990, pp.54-5.

My people ... all dead

Big Bill Neidjie

My people ...
all dead.
We only got few left ...
that's all.
Not many.
We getting too old.
Young people ...
I don't know if they can hang onto this story.
But, now you know this story,
and you'll be coming to earth.
You'll be part of earth when you die.
You responsible now.
You got to go with us ...
to earth.
Might be you can hang on ...
hang onto this story ...
to this earth.

You got children ...
grandson.
Might be your grandson will get this story ...
keep going ...
hang on like I done.

Source: Big Bill Neidjie, 'My people ... all dead', in Big Bill Neidjie, Stephen Davis & Allan Fox, *Kakadu Man*, Resource Managers, Darwin, 1987, p.64.

Trying to hold this place

Riley Young Winpilin

We want to try to stick to this place, keep everything right, you know. Some of them might go longa nother place, knock something up, you might kill somebody. Or you can kill him even white man or dog, or bird, you can kill him. Or everybody. That's why got little bit of care, trying to hold this place, keep everything right. Some white men can go over this kind of thing. You know, some of this kind now we know. It's a bit cheaper, this one. Him cheaper, we don't worry about it much. But what got me worried, we don't want to dig it too much. That's another thing. We want to try and keep this one covered up. You a lot of them blokes got that worry. Even me I got worry, Daly got worry, even Snowy got worry, Wallaby.

Well this one here, look. This been put up by Dream time. Nobody put this. Even I never put him, even Daly or Snowy or nobody. Or old people from what they been here before. Before I born, before Daly born, or before Snowy born. That mob, they know this thing been here early days. This Dreaming, by Dreaming, by turtle.

That all the government trying to changing the law. He's never changing our law. This thing never changing his law. This thing been start from beginning. We follow that same rule. We never change him rule. We on the same road all the way, all the way, till we gonna die, this nother man gonna take same rule. No matter where. You go Western Australia, you go Wave Hill, Hooker Creek, Kununurra, all the same you get him same rule. That kind never break that law. He got him in the same rule. Government got that paper. He can change him that paper or map belong him, or any sort of thing he can put him on. That kind of rule, you can change him. That's his Dreaming. No more belong to blackfellow. Blackfellow can't change him that one. If I pull him out this one, I'll be die or somebody might sick. That can't happen. Belong to white man, you might have that bit of paper, that's what white man call that lease belong him. Him have him over there, bit wind come up, him blow him out, him gone. He got to get another one and write him down. That's his Dreaming, we can't change him that one, no. We'll be in the same rule. Why that government reckons he gonna change him everything. Change him round, how you going to change him round? You can't change him this one, you can't change him that big hill there, you can't change him this ground. How you going to change him? How you going to change that creek? How you going to change that creek? Put that creek this side, he'll come back to flood this side. You can't, no way. Blackfellow never change him. Why that government talking about him going to change him rule? He'll never change the rule. He's only liar. He want to trying to push people out of place, that's all. We been borning this country. We been grow up this country. We been walkabout this country. We been kill him everything this country. Kill him kangaroo, kill him goanna, we been eating longa bush tucker longa this country. We know all this country all over, no matter how far. Even that way, even this way, we know, we can go, how far we can go. But him, him driving gotem [in a] motorcar. He go la big shop, get him pie, get him sandwich, all that sort of thing, him. Not blackfellow. Blackfellow been grow la bush. He can eat sugarbag, he can eat goanna, or turtle, or any kind. That's all. He got bush tucker for him. That's what that government reckon he can change him rule. He can't change him rule belong to blackfellow. No way.

This ground is mother. This ground, he's my mother. He's mother for everybody. We born top of this ground. This our mother. That's why we worry about this ground. I know government say he can change him rule. But he'll never get out of this ground. This ground belong to blackfellow. Blackfellow been born top of that ground and blackfellow, blackfellow blood.

Source: Riley Young Winpilin made this statement in 1985, in *Lingara Speaking*, a ten-minute video prepared by Debbie Rose and Anne Pratten, and available from the Australian Institute of Aboriginal Studies. Transcript by D. Rose.

Speech at Daguragu (Wattie Creek)

Vincent Lingiari

This is the speech made by Vincent Lingiari, leader of the Gurindji people, on the occasion of the handover of a lease to 1250 sq. miles, formerly part of Wave Hill Station, by the (then) Prime Minister, Gough Whitlam, and the Minister of Aboriginal Affairs, Les Johnson, to the Mura mulla Gurindji Co. on 16 August 1975.

By 1977, the Gurindji were running over 5000 head of cattle on Daguragu Station, had put down several new bores and fenced new paddocks. Although they had won their long battle for their land, they still held only pastoral, not freehold lease, and were still engaged in helping other groups seeking land rights.

1 Jangkakaṇi-ma kaṭiya-ma nyawa ngu-ngala-ngkulu linkara-ma¹ jaying-ana, linkara-ma ngu-ngala-ngkulu jaying-ana yulu-ma.

2 Nyamu-ḷaa kari-nya kaṭiya-wu-ṇi yulu jalang ngaliwa-ngunyja ngumpit-ta wanyjiki-jak.

3 Marunyu ngali jimari² kar-u-ḷi-ngali jimari kar-u-ḷi, kula-li-nyunu-jiwaj pung-ku.

4 Ngu-lu yan-i jangkakaṇi-ma kaṭiya-ma muḷa-ngkura nyawa-ma ngura-ma ngu-ngala-ngkulu jaying-ana waṭ ngaliwa-ngunyjiri-waḷa.

5 Ngaṟin ngu-ngala-ngkulu jaying-ku, yawaṭa ngu-ngala-ngkulu jaying-ana marunyu ngu-ḷaa kar-u marunyu-waḷa ngu-ḷaa kar-u.

6 Ngu-ngala-ngkulu yikili yan-ana ngaliwa-ngunyjiri-waḷa lutju-kari lutju-kaṟi kula-ḷaa-yina pina-ngu ngala-ngkulu ngawuṭuṭu maṇ-ana.

Vincent Lingiari speaking at the ceremony to mark the handing back of Aboriginal land at Wattie Creek (near Wave Hill), 16 August 1975. Prime Minister E.G. Whitlam is an attentive listener.

7 Punyu-k ngu-ḷaa kar-u ngumpin kaṭiya punyu-k ngu-ḷaa kar-u ngali jimari kula kar-u-ḷaa kuliwarp nyampa-ka-ṇi ngali jimari.

8 Nyawa ngu-ngaliwa linkara jaying-ku ngaṟin yawaṭa, kula-ḷaa nya-nya, *bore*-ma nyampa-ma ngu-ngala-ngkulu jaying-ku mayingka nyampa-ma *wire*-ma *everything* ngu-ngala-ngkulu jaying-ku.

9 Nyawa jangkakaṇi kaṭiya-ma ngaliwa-nguny ngumpit-ku muḷa-ngkura pataṭi-yiri warik-kara ngu-lu yan-i nyampa-yala-ṇi kula nyampa-wu, kuya-wu-waḷa.

10 Ngu-laa ngali jimari kar-u katiya ngumpin nyawa karwa-lu langa-ngka-ma³ kula *welfare*-kari-wu kula *welfare*-kari-wu⁴.

11 Ngura ngu-ngala-ngkulu ka-nya, ngu-lu linkara ka-nya lurpu.

Translation

1 The important White men giving us this land ceremonially, ceremonially they are giving it to us.¹

2 It belonged to the Whites, but today it is in the hands of us Aboriginals all around here.

3 Let us live happily together as mates,² let us not make it hard for each other.

4 The important White men have come here, and they are giving our country back to us now.

5 They will give us cattle, they will give us horses, then we will be happy.

6 They came from different places away, we do not know them, but they are glad for us.

7 We want to live in a better way together, Aboriginals and White men, let us not fight over anything, let us be mates.

8 He (the Prime Minister) will give us cattle and horses ceremonially; we have not seen them yet; they will give us bores, axes, wire, all that sort of thing.

9 These important White men have come here to our ceremonial ground and they are welcome, because they have not come for any other reason, just for this (handover).

10 We will be mates, White and Black, you (Gurindji) must keep this land safe for yourselves,³ it does not belong to any different 'welfare' man.⁴

11 They took our country away from us, now they have brought it back ceremonially.

1 *Linkara*: this term refers specifically to the ceremony which takes place after boys have undergone the first stage of initiation, circumcision. Before they return to the secular world of the main camp from the initiation camp, they are re-introduced to normal activities in stages. These include hand-feeding the initiates with various meats which they have been prohibited from eating during seclusion, and 'teaching' them to climb trees, wield an axe, light a fire etc. A parallel is being drawn here and throughout the speech between the regaining of traditional land and the return or 'rebirth' into the world of everyday life from the liminal world of initiation.
2 *Ngali jimari*: literally 'you and I age-mates': this is a fixed idiom referring to a friendly relationship of equality. *Jimari* often refers to men who have undergone initiation at the same ceremony, but is also used more loosely to mean 'mate', in the colloquial sense.
3 *Karwalu langangka*: literally 'keep in your ear', an idiom meaning 'keep safe and don't neglect' and 'think seriously about and don't forget.'
4 *Welfare* refers both to the old Welfare Branch and the present Department of Aboriginal Affairs. Here the conviction is expressed that the hand-over is not merely a transfer of land from Vestey's to a government department, but that the Gurindji themselves should control the land.

Source: From the speech by Vincent Lingiari in August 1975, transcribed by Patrick McConvell, in Luise Hercus & Peter Sutton (eds), *This is What Happened: Historical Narratives by Aborigines*, Australian Institute of Aboriginal Studies, Canberra, 1986, pp.313-15.

Acknowledgments

The author and the publishers have made every effort to trace copyright holders, in some cases without success. We would be grateful to hear from any copyright holders not acknowledged.

1 Origins

Text
'Yiwarrakurlu/Milky Way' by permission of the Australian Institute of Aboriginal and Torres Strait Islander Studies. 'Ngapakurlu/Rain' by permission of the Australian Institute of Aboriginal and Torres Strait Islander Studies. 'The Milky Way' by permission of Ted Egan (another, illustrated version of this story by Narritjan Maymuru and told to Ted Egan, was published by Harcourt Brace Jovanovich, Sydney & Melbourne, 1978). 'The rainbow serpent' by permission of Roland Robinson. 'Dinosaur Dreamtime' by permission of Hale & Iremonger. 'The seasons of fire', from *Singing the Snake* © Billy Marshall-Stoneking, 1990, by permission of Collins/Angus & Robertson Publishers. 'The moon bone' by permission of the late Ronald M. Berndt. 'He's singing at Dhadutjmana' by permission of Alice Moyle. 'Form of taking possession of Port Essington and Melville and Bathurst Islands, September 1824' by courtesy of the Australian Government Publishing Service. 'Captain Cook' by permission of Debbie Rose. 'Too many Captain Cooks' © Paddy Wainburranga and Chips Mackinolty; by permission.

Illustrations
Paddy Wainburranga, 'Too many Captain Cooks', poster supplied courtesy Northern Territory Land Council and reproduced by permission. 'Yiwarrakurlu/Milky Way' by Paddy Japaljarri Sims, illustration from Warlukurlangu Artists, *Kuruwarri/Yuendumu Doors*, Australian Institute of Aboriginal Studies, Canberra, 1987, by permission of the Australian Institute of Aboriginal and Torres Strait Islander Studies. 'Ngapakurlu/Rain' by Paddy Japaljarri Sims, illustration from Warlukurlangu Artists, *Kuruwarri/Yuendumu Doors*, Australian Institute of Aboriginal Studies, Canberra, 1987, by permission of the Australian Institute of Aboriginal and Torres Strait Islander Studies. Illustration of Central Mount Stuart, from *Explorations in Australia: The Journals of John McDouall Stuart, During the Years 1858–62*, 2nd edn, William Hardman (ed.), Saunders, Otley & Co., London, 1865; Rex Nan Kivell Collection 3176, National Library of Australia.

2 'Bare-headed to the sun': Early white voyages and exploration

Text
'Bamboo creek' by permission of Mark O'Connor. 'The coming of the dingoes' by courtesy of Ms Robyn Pill c/- Curtis Brown (Aust) Pty Ltd, Sydney. 'Any act of cruelty or outrage against the natives' by courtesy of the Australian Government Publishing Service. 'Reconnaissance' by permission of the publisher, Georgian House.

Illustrations
Illustration of Fort Dundas and map of Port Cockburn from Phillip Parker King, *Narrative of a Survey of the Intertropical and Western Coasts of Australia, Performed Between the Years 1818 and 1822*, vol.II, John Murray, London, 1827; photograph: National Library of Australia. 'Interview with the natives of St Asaph's Bay, Melville Island', illustration from Phillip Parker King, *Narrative of a Survey of the Intertropical and Western Coasts of Australia, Performed Between the Years 1818 and 1822*, vol.I, John Murray, London, 1827; Ferguson Collection, National Library of Australia. 'Dance of the Aborigines of Raffles Bay', illustration from Thomas Braidwood Wilson, *Narrative of a Voyage Round the World*, Sherwood, Gilbert & Piper, London, 1835; photograph: National Library of Australia. 'Captain Stokes speared at Point Pearce', engraving by Conrad Martens, illustration from John Lort Stokes, *Discoveries in Australia, with an Account of the Coasts and Rivers Explored During the Voyage of the HMS Beagle in the Years 1837–43*, vol.II, T. & W. Boone, London, 1866; photograph: National Library of Australia.

3 'Bone-piled spots': The whites dig in

Text

'Camp at Barrow Creek', extract from *Gillen's Diary*, by permission of the Libraries Board of South Australia and Dr R.S. Gillen. 'The Daly River murders of 1884 and their aftermath', extract from Ernestine Hill, *The Territory* © R.D. Hill, 1951, by permission of Collins/Angus & Robertson Publishers. 'Bringin in a new wild gin', extract from the Diary of Emily Caroline Creaghe, by permission of the State Library of New South Wales. 'The Coniston "massacres" of August 1928' by courtesy of Mrs Downer. 'Coniston: Findings of Commonwealth Board of Enquiry', Commonwealth of Australia copyright, reproduced by permission.'On Women and wives', extract from *Boss Drover*, by permission of Mrs L. Willey. 'The combo's anthem' reproduced by permission of Mrs R. Lockwood.

Illustrations

'Native prisoners in chains', illustration from *The Lone Hand*, 1 March 1911, p.364; photograph: National Library of Australia. Barrow Creek Telegraph Station, June 1901; photograph: Museum of Victoria. 'The author and a boy native', illustration from W.H. Willshire, *The Land of the Dawning: Being Facts Gleaned from Cannibals in the Australian Stone Age*, W.K. Thomas & Co., Adelaide, 1896; photograph: National Library of Australia. Photograph of Matt Savage from Keith Willey, *Boss Drover: Stories Related to the Author by Matt Savage*, Rigby, Adelaide, 1971, by permission of Mrs Lee Willey and Ms Joanna Willey.

4 'Nobody knows what it means': White depiction of Aborigines

Text

'Moondeen' by permission of the publisher, Georgian House. 'goanna' by permission of Lee Cataldi. 'the honey tree' by permission of Lee Cataldi. 'In the bed of the River Todd' reprinted from *Aboriginal Voices*, published by the Curriculum Development Centre, copyright Commonwealth of Australia, 1978; reprinted by permission of the Curriculum Development Centre, Woden, ACT. 'Girls in a park' by permission of Jan Owen. 'Rain at Gunn Point' by courtesy of Tony Scanlon. 'Aborigines passing' by permission of Roland Robinson. 'Wash day', from *Singing the Snake* © Billy Marshall-Stoneking, 1990, by permission of Collins/Angus & Robertson Publishers. 'in th desert you remember' by permission of Eric Beach. 'A remote area' written with the assistance of the Literature Board of the Australia Council (New Writer's Grant 1977); Graeme Parsons has lived in the Territory since 1978; he lives and writes in Darwin; reprinted by permission of Graeme Parsons.

Illustrations

'Two Aranda women with a baby, Alice Springs', photograph by W. Baldwin Spencer, collection Museum of Victoria. Photograph of old Aranda man, by W. Baldwin Spencer, collection Museum of Victoria. Photograph of elderly Tiwi men, by W. Baldwin Spencer, collection Museum of Victoria. Nine illustrations from *Gillen's Diary: Camp Jottings of F.J. Gillen on the Spencer and Gillen Expedition Across Australia 1901–1902*, Libraries Board of South Australia, 1968, by permission of the Libraries Board of South Australia and Dr R.S. Gillen.

5 'Too much blackfeller': The black view

Text

'Wanderer's lament' by permission of Mrs R. Lockwood. 'The Malak Malak people lived here', extract from *Born in the Cattle*, by permission of Allen & Unwin, Sydney. 'An arrangement', extract from *Social History of the Northern Territory*, Commonwealth of Australia copyright, reproduced by permission. 'Coniston story' by permission of Jimmy Langdon. 'Wild ones, mate', extract from A View of the Past (MS), by permission of Peter Read. 'All children', extract from A View of the Past (MS), by permission of Peter Read and Michael J. Christie. 'All ashes', extract from A View of the Past (MS), by permission of Peter Read. 'Quiet country', extract from *Fighters and Singers*, by permission of Allen & Unwin, Sydney. 'This is our river, hill, trees, grass', from the interview of Pincher Numiari by Cheryl Buchanan, copyright © Cheryl Buchanan (editor, *Black News Service* 1975). 'In Darwin they call me Bobby Wilson', from the passage by Robert Tudawali, reproduced by courtesy of the nephew of the late Robert Tudawali. 'What's a whitefella?' reproduced by permission of Billy Marshall-Stoneking. 'First people come to us', extract from *Kakadu Man* © Resource Managers Pty Ltd, by permission of Collins/Angus & Robertson Publishers. 'Yirrkala Bark Petition' reproduced by courtesy of the Australian Government Publishing Service.

Illustrations

Striking Gurindji stockmen, illustration from Frank Hardy, *The Unlucky Australians*, Thomas Nelson,

Melbourne 1968, by permission of Frank Hardy; photograph: National Library of Australia. Photograph of Djawa by permission of his son Richard Barkal and family, and Peter Read. Charles Chauvel's 'Jedda' daybill from the National Film and Sound Archive, Canberra, and reproduced by permission of the copyright holder Susan Carlsson and the H.C. McIntyre Trust c/- Curtis Brown (Aust) Pty Ltd, Sydney. Robert Tudawali being interviewed, illustration from Frank Hardy, *The Unlucky Australians*, Thomas Nelson, Melbourne, 1968, by permission of Frank Hardy; photograph: National Library of Australia.

6 Pilgrims

Text
'I had no human speech' by permission of Roland Robinson. 'Down on the Daly River oh!' by permission of Mrs R. Lockwood. 'Mail oh!' extract from *We of the Never-Never*, by permission of the publisher, Century Hutchinson Australia. 'In the land of sweat and sandflies' by permission of Mrs. L. Willey. 'Talking history' reproduced by permission; *Land Rights News* published by the Northern Territory Land Council. 'The Afghans' by permission of Mrs Eileen Ingamells. 'Talking history', translated from Kriol and Rembarrnga by Chips Mackinolty, reproduced by permission of Paddy Fordham Wainburranga and Chips Mackinolty. 'Shark' by permission of Patrick McCauley. 'The pub owner's wife', extract from *Outback*, by permission of Thomas Keneally.

Illustrations
'Native camp, Port Essington, November 1877', by Paul Foelsche; from the Foelsche Collection, National Library of Australia. William Linklater, Jack McLeod and Tom Pearce, illustration from William Linklater & Lynda Tapp, *Gather No Moss*, Macmillan, South Melbourne, 1968; photograph: National Library of Australia. Photograph of Daisy Nawala Cusack and her brothers Peter and Spider Juluma, from *Land Rights News*, vol.2, no.5, courtesy of the Northern Territory Land Council and Mrs D.F. Ruddick. Drawing of Paddy Wainburranga by permission of Chips Mackinolty.

7 'My spirit, my country'

Text
'The land is the art', extract from *The Aborigines of Arnhem Land*, by permission of Dr Keith Cole. 'This earth', extract from *Kakadu Man* © Resource Managers Pty Ltd, by permission of Collins/Angus & Robertson Publishers. 'Yinungkwura/West wind' by permission of Alice Moyle. 'By the Grey Gulfwater' © Retusa Pty Ltd, by permission of Collins/Angus & Robertson Publishers.'Chugga-Kurri' by permission of Pergamon Press, Australia. 'High water' © John McInnes Auld, 1914, by permission of Collins/Angus & Robertson Publishers. 'Black cockatoos' by permission of Roland Robinson. 'White cockatoos' by permission of Tony Scanlon.'Flood plains on the coast facing Asia', from *The Daylight Moon* © Les A. Murray, 1987, by permission of Collins/Angus & Robertson Publishers. 'rain' by permission of Lee Cataldi. 'Instructions for honey ants', from *Singing the Snake* © Billy Marshall-Stoneking, 1990, by permission Collins/Angus & Robertson Publishers.

Illustrations
Collage of linocuts from Frederick T. Macartney's *Proof Against Failure*, Angus & Robertson, Sydney, 1967, by permission of Collins/Angus & Robertson Publishers. Photograph of Kakadu men and boys, by W. Baldwin Spencer, collection of Museum of Victoria.

8 'A bastard of a place'

Text
'Death of Voss', extract from *Voss* copyright Patrick White, by permission. 'The settler. Wet season, N.T.' by permission of Janet Dickinson, who has also published *Litchfield's Gold* (Darwin, 1988), about the life of Fred Litchfield, a member of the Finnis expedition to Escape Cliffs, NT, 1864–65. 'Jock Driver's funeral', extract from *Capricornia*, by courtesy of Ms Robyn Pill c/- Curtis Brown (Aust) Pty Ltd, Sydney. 'The paw paw tree' by permission of Margo Towie.

Illustrations
Alfred Searcy from his *In Australian Tropics*, 2nd edn, George Robertson, London & Sydney, 1909; photograph: National Library of Australia. Frontispiece from Ivan Archer Rosenblum, *Stella Sothern: A Story of Bohemia and the Bush*, NSW Bookstall, Sydney, 1911; photograph: National Library

of Australia. Photograph of Xavier Herbert by permission of Mrs Lee Willey and Ms Joanna Willey.

9 Sites and sightings

Text
'Five legends of Uluru' by permission of the Australian Institute for Aboriginal and Torres Strait Islander Studies. 'S.O.S., Ayers Rock, 1930' by permission of the Investigator Press and Mrs A. Coote. 'An apostrophe to Ayers Rock' by permission of Mrs Eileen Ingamells. 'Erecting forked sticks and rafters' reproduced by permission of the late Ronald M. Berndt. 'Yinuma/River' by permission of Alice Moyle. 'Borroloola, capital of the Gulf country', extract from *Gillen's Diary*, by permission of the Libraries Board of South Australia and Dr R.S. Gillen. 'The Roper River's flowing' by permission of Mrs R. Lockwood. 'Deep Well' by permission of Roland Robinson. 'Alice', extract from *Outback*, by permission of Thomas Keneally. 'Snapshots of Kakadu' by permission of Beverley Farmer.

Illustrations
MacDonnell ranges and the Pine Gap facility: Department of Defence photograph. Photograph of Kantju, illustration from *Uluru: An Aboriginal History of Ayers Rock*, Australian Institute of Aboriginal Studies, Canberra, 1986, by permission of the Australian Institute of Aboriginal and Torres Strait Islander Studies, the Mutitjulu Community and Robert Layton. Photograph of the members of the 1901–1902 Central Australian Expedition, collection Museum of Victoria.

10 Darwin, mad capital of the north

Text
'The cycloon, Paddy Cahill and the G.R.' © Retusa Pty Ltd, by permission of Collins/Angus & Robertson Publishers. 'Bloody, bloody Darwin' by courtesy of the compiler, Bill Wannan, c/o Curtus Brown (Aust.) Pty Ltd, Sydney. 'Mango juice' by permission of Graham Calley, Darwin. 'Louvres', from *The Daylight Moon* © Les A. Murray, 1987, by permission of Collins/Angus & Robertson Publishers. 'Jacques Tati at the Darwin Hotel' by permission of Fay Zwicky.

Illustrations
Cartoon by permission of Bruce Petty. View of Palmerston, photograph by Paul Foelsche; Foelsche Collection, National Library of Australia. Darwin, 19 December 1942; photograph: National Library of Australia. Darwin, 25 December 1974; photograph: Australian Information Service/National Library of Australia.

11 Adventures, incongruities, incredibilities

Text
'Tjukurrpa: Puli kulpi kutjarra/The two little round stones' by permission of the Alternative Publishing Co-op. 'Christmas, 1901', extract from *Gillen's Diary*, by permission of the Libraries Board of South Australia and Dr R.S. Gillen. 'Christmas, 1930', extract from *Grief, Gaiety and Aborigines*, by permission of Mrs R. Lockwood. 'Playing cricket, 1908', extract from *Hard Liberty* first published in England in 1938, copyright, all rights reserved, reproduced by permission of Harrap Publishing Group. 'On the value of blankets' by permission of Neil Murray. 'Tales not from the Dreamtime: Pukara (perishing)' by permission of Mark de Graaf.

Illustrations
Fred Blakely and two friends, illustration from Blakely's *Hard Liberty*, George G. Harrap & Co., London, 1938; photograph: National Library of Australia. H.S. Melville's illustration of Victoria Square, Port Essington, from J.B. Jukes, *Narrative of the Surveying Voyage of HMS Fly*, London, 1847; Rex Kivell Collection, National Library of Australia. Photograph of wooden cross, April 1963, by permission of Mark de Graaf.

12 Nature's stage

Text
'Drowning the cockroaches, Port Essington', extract from *The Journal of John Sweatman*, by permis-

sion of the University of Queensland Press. 'Mrs Englishwoman on the Daly River', extract from *Far-north Memories*, by permission of Collins/Angus & Robertson Publishers. 'White ants in Darwin', extract from *The Territory* © R.D. Hill, 1951, by permission of Collins/Angus & Robertson Publishers. 'Crocodile haiku' by permission of Hale & Iremonger. 'Frogday' by permission of Connie Gregory, Darwin. 'The gecko' © John McInnes Auld, 1941, by permission of Collins/Angus & Robertson Publishers. 'There were rats, rats' by permission of J. White. 'Auntie Annie and Monty' by permission of Graham Calley, Darwin.

Illustrations
'Alligator, Victoria River', watercolour (7.3 x 12.9 cm) by Thomas Baines (1822–75), by permission of the National Library of Australia. 'A little pleasantry in the tropics', photograph by H.W. Christie, from Alfred Searcy, *In Australian Tropics*, 2nd edn, George Robertson, London & Sydney, 1909; photograph: National Library of Australia. 'Ant hill, near Rum Jungle' 1887, photograph by Paul Foelsche; Foelsche Collection, National Library of Australia.

13 Sprees, drunks, and race meetings

Text
'Honey intoxication', extract from *The Journal of John Sweatman*, by permission of the University of Queensland Press. 'A 16th-century view of "Territory man"?' by courtesy of Don Campbell. 'White dog, the boozing hound', extract from *Eaters of the Lotus*, by permission of Mrs L. Willey. 'Alice Springs pub', extract from *Tracks*, by permission of Jonathan Cape Ltd, London.

Illustrations
Photograph of the Commercial Hotel, by Paul Foelsche; Foelsche Collection, National Library of Australia. Borroloola pub, illustration from Keith Willey, *Ghosts of the Big Country*, Robert Hale, London, 1975, facing p.48, by permission of Mrs Lee Willey and Ms Joanna Willey. Photograph of Fred Miners, illustration from Keith Willey, *Eaters of the Lotus*, Jacaranda Press, Brisbane, 1964, facing p.32, by permission of Mrs Lee Willey and Ms Joanna Willey.

14 Opening up the country: Drovers, buffalo hunters, and miners

Text
'Working in the stock camp', extract from *Fighters and Singers,* by permission of Allen & Unwin, Sydney. 'The drover's boy' by courtesy of Ted Egan. 'Black stockman' © W. Hart-Smith, 1946, by permission of Collins/Angus & Robertson publishers. 'Bush cooks', extract from *Boss Drover*, by permission of Mrs L. Willey. 'Buffalo shooting in Australia' © Retusa Pty Ltd, by permission of Collins/Angus & Robertson Publishers. 'Don't miss or you'll be a dead fella', extract from the interview in *Junga Yimi*, by permission of Alex Wilson. 'Daily work in the tin mine', extract from A View of the Past (MS), by permission of Peter Read.

Illustrations
Photograph of the late Spider Brennan by permission of Minnie Brennan. George Lambert's sketch from the *Sydney Mail*, 7 January 1899; photograph: General Reference Library, State Library of New South Wales. Map from the inside front cover of F.E. Baume, *Tragedy Track: The Story of the Granites*, Frank C. Johnson, Sydney, 1933; photograph: National Library of Australia.

15 Rock belong Jesus dreaming

Text
'Bring the heathen the true faith', extract from *The Bishop with 150 Wives*, by permission of Collins/Angus & Robertson Publishers. 'We're going to take this little girl away', extract from *Fighters and Singers*, by permission of Allen & Unwin, Sydney. 'Mary' © W. Hart-Smith, 1946, by permission of Collins/Angus & Robertson Publishers. 'Daly River poem' by permission of Br John Pye. 'God in the silver sea', extract from *Capricornia*, by courtesy of Ms Robyn Pill c/- Curtis Brown (Aust) Pty Ltd, Sydney. 'The night departs' by permission of Mrs R. Lockwood. 'Interview in a desert' by permission of Hale & Iremonger.

Illustrations
Sisters of the Order of Our Lady of the Sacred Heart, illustration from F.X. Gsell, *The Bishop with 150*

Wives, Angus & Robertson, Sydney, 1956, facing p.48; photograph: National Library of Australia. Photograph of Missionary Liebler and Mrs Liebler by permission of the Lutheran Church of Adelaide, Archives and Research Centre, North Adelaide. Photography of Jesuits and children at the Holy Rosary Mission, by courtesy of Mrs N.G. (Nancy) Eddy. Photograph of the Methodist Parsonage by permission of Darwin City Council (Mrs Turner (née Cox) Collection).

16 'Hang on like I done'

Text
'Everywhere there is change', extract from *North of 23°*, by permission of Mrs R. Lockwood. 'We gotta be black and white in this country', extract from *Fighters and Singers*, by permission of Allen & Unwin, Sydney. 'if you stay too long in the third world' by permission of Lee Cataldi. 'My people ... all dead', extract from *Kakadu Man* © Resource Managers Pty Ltd, by permission of Collins/Angus & Robertson Publishers. 'Trying to hold this place', extract from the transcript of *Lingarra Speaking*, by permission of Debbie Rose. 'Speech at Daguragu (Wattie Creek)' by permission of the Australian Institute of Aboriginal and Torres Strait Islander Studies.

Illustrations
Photograph of Big Bill Neidjie, by permission of A. Fox. Photograph of Bill Harney and Douglas Lockwood, illustration from Keith Willey, *Ghosts of the Big Country*, Robert Hale, London, 1975, facing p.49; by permission of Mrs Lee Willey and Ms Joanna Willey. Photograph of Amy Laurie by permission of Bruce Shaw. Vincent Lingiari and E.G. Whitlam; photograph: Australian Information Service/National Library of Australia.

Index of authors and storytellers

Adcock, W.E.   74
Australian soldier   218

Basedow, Herbert   244
Baume, F.E.   132, 307
Beach, Eric   88
Blakeley, Fred   242
Booth Minmienadgie, Fred   101
Bremer, J.J. Gordon   18
Brennan, Spider   311
Burgoyne, Jim   126

Calley, Graham   219, 266
Campbell, Don   281
Campbell, John   37
Cataldi, Lee   82, 83, 166, 334
Commonwealth Board of Enquiry (1929)   64
Coote, Errol   189
Creaghe, Emily Caroline   57
Croll, Robert Henderson   199
Cusack, Daisy Nawala   133

Daly, Mrs Dominic D.   196, 209, 235, 275
Daniyarri, Hobbles   21
Davidson, Robyn   283
de Graaf, Mark   249
Djauan legend   7
Djawa   101
Douglas, Pompy, Wanampi, Pompy, Uluru, Paddy, & Uluru, Albie   187
Downer, Sidney   62
Duncan   95

Egan, Ted   289
Elkin, A.P., & Harney, W.E.   95
Evans, George Essex   277

Farmer, Beverley   205
Favenc, Ernest   76, 177, 230
Flinders, Matthew   33
Flynn, Patrick (Paddy)   130
Fordham Wainburranga, Paddy   145

Galarrawuy Yunupingu, James   151
Gee, Lionel   137
Giles, Ernest   237
Gillen, F.J.   51, 196, 238
Goulburn Island song cycle   192
Graaf, Mark de   249
Gregory, Connie   263
Groote Eylandt song   155, 195
Gsell, F.X.   317

Gunn, Aeneas E.   178
Gunn, Mrs Aeneas   128

Harney, W.E. (Bill)   69, 201, 240, 326, 331
Harney, W.E., & Elkin, A.P.   95
Herbert, Xavier   29, 180, 322
Hart-Smith, William   47, 81, 291, 320
Hill, Ernestine   56, 217, 260

Ingamells, Rex   137, 190
Inginma, Little Mick   104

Jampijinpa, Martin   100
Jangala, Abie   139
Japaljarri Sims, Paddy   3, 4
Japangardi Langdon, Tim   97, 98
Jupurrurla Wilson, Alex   302

Keneally, Thomas   143, 202
King, Phillip Parker   35

Laiwonga, Joli, & Wainburranga, Paddy   24
Langdon, Tim Japangardi   97, 98
Laurie, Amy   105, 287, 333
Lavater, George   321
Leichhardt, Ludwig   46
Lingiari, Vincent   337
Linklater, William, & Tapp, Lynda   123, 278
Litchfield, Jessie   179, 258

Macartney, Frederick T.   161, 265
McCauley, Patrick   142
MacKay, David   127
Macleay, Alexander   40
Marlindi story   5
Marshall-Stoneking, Billy   11, 87, 167
Maymuru, Narritjan   5
Milingimbi song   18
Minmienadgie, Fred Booth   101
Mirritji, Jack   154
Murif, Jerome K.   73, 215
Murray, Les A.   163, 223
Murray, Neil   249

Naparrula Nelson, Topsy   318
Nawala Cusack, Daisy   133
Needham, J.S.   80
Neidjie, Big Bill   115, 151, 336
Nelson, Topsy Naparrula   318
Northern Territory Times (1874)   53, 210
Northern Territory Times (1875)   305

Northern Territory Times (1882) 273
Northern Territory Times (1884) 53, 74
Northern Territory Times (1885) 54
Northern Territory Times (1928) 66
Numiari, Pincher 108

O'Connor, Mark 10, 29, 263, 327
Owen, Jan 86
Oxford, G. 84

Papunya School 114
Parry, Bill 96
Parsons, Graeme 89
Paterson, A.B. (Banjo) 159, 212, 296

Raggett, Obed 229
Robinson, Roland 87, 121, 162, 202
Rosenblum, Ivan Archer 171

Savage, Matt 67, 291
Scanlon, Tony 86, 163
Searcy, Alfred 61, 121, 122, 276
Sims, Paddy Japaljarri 3, 4
Sowden, William J. 73
Stanton, Vi 106
Stokes, John Lort 19, 43, 234
Stuart, John McDouall 20
Sweatman, John 257, 273

Tapp, Lynda, & Linklater, William 123, 278
Tenison-Woods, J.E. 156
Terry, Michael 160
Tjapangarti, Tutama 246
Towie, Margo 182
Tudawali, Robert 110

Uluru, Albie, Douglas, Pompy, Wanampi, Pompy, & Uluru, Paddy 187
Uluru, Paddy, Uluru, Albie, Douglas, Pompy, & Wanampi, Pompy 187

Wainburranga, Paddy Fordham 145
Wainburranga, Paddy, & Laiwonga, Joli 24
Wanampi, Pompy, Uluru, Paddy, Uluru, Albie, & Douglas, Pompy 187
White, James 265
White, Patrick 173
Willey, Keith 282
Willshire, W.H. 58
Wilson, Alex Jupurrurla 302
Wilson, Thomas Braidwood 41
Winpilin, Riley Young 336
Wonguri–Manjikai song cycle 13

Yirrkala, Aboriginal people of 116
Young Winpilin, Riley 336
Yunupingu, James Galarrawuy 151

Zwicky, Fay 225